Take Three

TWO BOOKS IN ONE

Take Four

WHAT READERS ARE SAYING ABOUT KAREN KINGSBURY'S BOOKS

Karen's book *Oceans Apart* changed my life. She has an amazing gift of bringing a reader into her stories. I can only pray she never stops writing.

Susan L.

Everyone should have the opportunity to read or listen to a book by Karen Kingsbury. It should be in the *Bill of Rights*.

Rachel S.

I want to thank Karen Kingsbury for what she is doing with the power of her storytelling—touching hearts like mine and letting God use her to change the world for Him.

Brittney N.

Karen Kingsbury's books are filled with the unshakable, remarkable, miraculous fact that God's grace is greater than our suffering. There are no words for Ms. Kingsbury's writing.

Wendie K.

Because I loaned these books to my mother, she BECAME a Christian! Thank you for a richer life here and in heaven!

Jennifer E.

When I read my first Karen Kingsbury book, I couldn't stop.... I read thirteen more in one summer!

Jamie B.

I have never read anything so uplifting and entertaining. I'm shocked as I read each new release because it's always better than the last one.

Bonnie S.

I am unable to put your books down, and I plan to read many more of them. What a wonderful spiritual message I find in each one!

Rhonda T.

I love the way Karen Kingsbury writes, and the topics she chooses to write about! Thank you so much for sharing your talent with us, your readers!

Barbara S.

My husband is equally hooked on your books. It is a family affair for us now! Can't wait for the next one.

Angie

I can't even begin to tell you what your books mean to me.... Thank you for your wonderful books and the way they touch my life again and again.

Martje L.

Every time our school buys your next new book, everybody goes crazy trying to read it first!

Roxanne

Recently I made an effort to find GOOD Christian writers, and I've hit the jackpot with Karen Kingsbury!

Linda

When Karen Kingsbury calls her books "Life-Changing Fiction™," she's merely telling the unvarnished truth. I'm still sorting through the changes in my life that have come from reading just a few of her books!

Robert M.

I must admit that I wish I was a much slower reader ... or you were a much faster writer. Either way, I can't seem to get enough of Karen Kingsbury's books!

Jillian B.

I was offered $50 one time in the airport for the fourth book in the Redemption Series. The lady's husband just couldn't understand why I wasn't interested in selling it. Through sharing Karen's books with my friends, many have decided that contemporary Christian fiction is the next best thing to the Bible. Thank you so much, Karen. It is truly a God-thing that you write the way you do.

Sue Ellen H.

Karen Kingsbury's books have made me see things in ways that I had never thought about before. I have to force myself to put them down and come up for air!

Tabitha H.

I have read many of Karen's books and I cry with every one. I feel like I actually know the people in the story, and my heart goes out to all of them when something happens!

Kathy N.

Wow, what an amazing author Karen Kingsbury is! Her stories are so heart-wrenching ... I can't wait until the next book comes out.... Karen, please don't ever lay your pen down.

Nancy T.

Karen Kingsbury's words leap off the page.... I just finished a new series last night and once again she has touched me beyond compare!

Kendra S.

Other Life-Changing Fiction™ by Karen Kingsbury

9/11 Series
One Tuesday Morning
Beyond Tuesday Morning
Every Now and Then

Lost Love Series
Even Now
Ever After

Above the Line Series
Above the Line: Take One
Above the Line: Take Two
Above the Line: Take Three
Above the Line: Take Four

Stand-Alone Titles
Oceans Apart
Between Sundays
This Side of Heaven
When Joy Came to Stay
On Every Side
Divine
Like Dandelion Dust
Where Yesterday Lives
Shades of Blue
Unlocked (Fall 2010)

Redemption Series
Redemption
Remember
Return
Rejoice
Reunion

Firstborn Series
Fame
Forgiven
Found
Family
Forever

Sunrise Series
Sunrise
Summer
Someday
Sunset

Red Glove Series
Gideon's Gift
Maggie's Miracle
Sarah's Song
Hannah's Hope

Forever Faithful Series
Waiting for Morning
Moment of Weakness
Halfway to Forever

Women of Faith Fiction Series
A Time to Dance
A Time to Embrace

Cody Gunner Series
A Thousand Tomorrows
Just Beyond the Clouds

Children's Titles
Let Me Hold You Longer
Let's Go on a Mommy Date
We Believe in Christmas
Let's Have a Daddy Day

Miracle Collections
A Treasury of Christmas Miracles
A Treasury of Miracles for Women
A Treasury of Miracles for Teens
A Treasury of Miracles for Friends
A Treasury of Adoption Miracles

Gift Books
Stay Close Little Girl
Be Safe Little Boy
Forever Young: Ten Gifts of Faith
    for the Graduate

KAREN
#1 BESTSELLING AUTHOR
KINGSBURY

Take Three

TWO BOOKS IN ONE

Take Four

ZONDERVAN®

ZONDERVAN.com/
AUTHORTRACKER
follow your favorite authors

ZONDERVAN

Take Three / Take Four Compilation
Copyright © 2010 by Karen Kingsbury

Take Three
Copyright © 2010 by Karen Kingsbury

Take Four
Copyright © 2010 by Karen Kingsbury

This title is also available as a Zondervan ebook.
Visit www.zondervan.com/ebooks.

This title is also available in a Zondervan audio edition.
Visit www.zondervan.fm.

Requests for information should be addressed to:

Zondervan, *Grand Rapids, Michigan 49530*

Published in association with the literary agency of Alive Communications, Inc., 7680 Goddard Street, Suite 200, Colorado Springs, CO 80920. www.alivecommunications .com

ICover design: Ken Stewart, RM+D
Cover photography: Masterfile, Shutterstock, iStockphoto
Interior design: Michelle Espinoza

Printed in the United States of America

11 12 13 14 15 16 17 18 /DCI/ 20 19 18 17 16 15 14 13 12 11 10 9 8 7 6 5 4 3 2 1

DEDICATION

To Donald, my Prince Charming...

How I rejoice to see you coaching again, sharing your gift of teaching and your uncanny basketball ability with another generation of kids—and best yet, now our boys are part of the mix. Can you believe it? Josh, one of the leading rushers in our area in his freshman year? Sean catching everything thrown to him? And Tyler tearing up the basketball court? You and our boys, making memories together. Isn't this what we always dreamed of? I love sitting back this time and letting you and God figure it out. I'll always be here—cheering for you and the team from the bleachers. But God's taught me a thing or two about being a coach's wife. He's so good that way. It's fitting that you would find varsity coaching again now—after twenty years of marriage. Hard to believe that as you read this, our twentieth anniversary has come and gone. I look at you and I still see the blond, blue-eyed guy who would ride his bike to my house and read the Bible with me before a movie date. You stuck with me back then and you stand by me now—when I need you more than ever. I love you, my husband, my best friend, my Prince Charming. Stay with me, by my side, and let's watch our children take wing, savoring every memory and each day gone by. Always and always ... The ride is breathtakingly beautiful, my love. I pray it lasts far into our twilight years. Until then, I'll enjoy not always knowing where I end and you begin. I love you always and forever.

To Kelsey, my precious daughter...

You are twenty now, a young woman, and my heart soars with joy when I see all that you are, all you've become. I'll never forget your tears that last night when you were still nineteen. Not tears of sorrow or fear for the future. But quiet, pensive tears because your childhood is truly behind you. I remember what you said: "Mom, I've loved being your little girl, and I've loved being a part of this family. I can't imagine how leaving it all behind one day soon will be somehow better." My sweet, sweet girl. Remember that God walks with us every step of this life, and for those who love Him, the best is always yet to be. This year is a precious one for us because you're still home, attending junior college and spending nearly every day studying, preparing, readying for the future. When you're not dancing or singing, you're helping with the business and ministry of Life-Changing Fiction™—so we have many precious hours together. I know this time is short and won't last, but I'm enjoying it so much. I know that come some bright fall morning you'll be going to Los Angeles to finish college, and you will grow and become all that God desires of you. Meanwhile, you will always have a place here with us. Of course we pray you'll fall in love and find that special young man who will love God more than you, and who will treasure your innocence and integrity, your passion and purity. But even as you find him, you'll never really leave our family. Rather you will add to it, honey. You'll always be our little girl, Kelsey. And you'll always be part of this family. Forever and always. I'm so proud of the strength you're finding in this, your twenty-first year. You are beautiful inside and out, and I am more convinced than ever that God has great, wonderful plans for you. Take your talents and go find your platform for Him! In the meantime, we'll leave the porch light on. I love you, sweetheart.

To Tyler, my lasting song ...

What a tremendous year of growth for you, my precious son. You put aside the stage for now and focused on becoming the young man God wants you to be. In the process you have become convinced that you'd like to be a Christian artist—writing and singing songs for His glory. You'll never know how proud that makes me and your dad. We love our evenings when your homework is finished and you head into the piano room. The chords blend together as you create, and your golden voice fills our home. How blessed we are that your music is the soundtrack of our life. And yet I know that the song will only last so long. You are nearing the end of your junior year already. One more school year and you'll be off to college. One more trip for back-to-school supplies, one more homecoming, one more basketball season, one more prom. I'm holding onto every precious moment, with everything I have. These are the bittersweet years, when the end is all too clearly in sight. And yet, like Kelsey, you will always be a part of our lives here, Ty. You'll excel in the coming year, growing in your talents and convictions, I'm sure. And the deep and lasting relationships you've begun here in your childhood will remain. Thank you for the hours of joy you bring our family, and as you head into a year of lasts, I promise to stop and listen a little longer when I hear you singing. I'm proud of you, Ty. I'm proud of your talent and your compassion for people and your place in our family. However your dreams unfold, I'll be in the front row to watch them happen. Hold on to Jesus, son. I love you.

To Sean, my happy sunshine ...

What a thrill it was watching you take on varsity football, this, your freshman year of high school. You were concerned going in, and that's understandable. "What if I can't play as well as the older guys?" you asked me. "What if I can't tackle?" We prayed and believed and then, right before the season started, you did something I'll always remember. You came to me and asked if I could find custom wristbands for the team. "I want them to say Philippians 4:13," you told me. You'd seen the University of Florida's Timmy Tebow donning that verse on his eye black before each game, and now you wanted to have a similar show of faith. A week passed and another, and every few days you asked until finally I set everything aside and ordered them for the whole team. I'll never see that verse without seeing the sincerity in your eyes, the desperation, almost, that if you were going to play football, you needed to always remind yourself of the truth. You can do everything through Christ who gives you strength. And you can, Sean. You proved that this year by being the team's leading receiver. Oh, and one of the best tacklers on the team. You remain a bright sunbeam, bringing warmth to everyone around you. And now you are an example of faith as well. I'm proud of you, Sean. I love you so much. I pray God will use your dependence on Him to always make a difference in the lives around you. You're a precious gift, son. Keep smiling and keep seeking God's best for your life.

To Josh, my tenderhearted perfectionist ...

The weeks of this past school year have flown by, and you have grown right along with them, my precious son. So many memories will remind me of your first year of high school, but some will always stand out. The week, for instance, when you first appeared in the paper as one of the area's top leading rushers. The next game someone on the sidelines commented on your talents, and in your quiet, humble way, you simply pointed up and said, "It's all because of God." So young, and yet such a leader already. Another memory I'll hold tight to is the time you attended a youth rally at your Christian school. A few girls from the public middle school attended and spotted you. They walked up and made a face at you. "You go to this Christian school," they sneered. "Yes," you answered. "So what's that mean, you're a goody good?" Rather than be intimidated or feel the need to impress them, you smiled and nodded. "That's right. I want to be a goody good." More than all your touchdowns and more than your great grades, I'm proud of your character, son. Hold tight to that. With great talent comes great temptation, and I'm sure the years ahead will prove that. I have no doubt that someday we will see your name in headlines and that—if God allows it—you'll make it to the pros. You're that good, and everyone around you says so. Now flash back to that single moment in a broken-down Haitian orphanage. There I was meeting Sean and EJ for the first time when you walked up, reached up with your small fingers and brushed back my bangs, and said, "Hi, Mommy. I love you." It might've taken six months, but I knew as you said those words that you belonged with us. The picture becomes clearer all the time. Keep being a leader on the field and off. One day people will say, "Hmmm. Karen Kingsbury? Isn't she Josh's mom?" I can't wait for the day. You have an unlimited future ahead of you, Josh, and I'll forever be cheering on the sidelines. Keep God first in your life. I love you always.

To EJ, my chosen one ...

Here you are in the last few months of eighth grade, and I can barely recognize the social academic leader you've become. We worried that moving you to the Christian school with one year left in junior high might hurt you. Maybe you'd have trouble making new friends or adjusting. I think you worried too. But look at what you've become in this one short school year! You are one of our top students, and you're inviting a different set of friends over every weekend. I compare that to your utter silence back at the public schools and I can only celebrate and thank God that this was the best decision we've ever made for you. But even beyond your grades and your natural way of leading your peers in the right path, we are blessed to have you in our family for so many reasons. You are wonderful with our pets— always the first to feed them and pet them and look out for them—and you are a willing worker when it comes to chores. Besides all that, you make us laugh—oftentimes right out loud. I've always believed that getting through life's little difficulties and challenges requires a lot of laughter—and I thank you for bringing that to our home. You're a wonderful boy, son, a child with such potential. I'm amazed because you're so talented in so many ways, but all of them pale in comparison to your desire to truly live for the Lord. I'm praying you'll have a strong passion to use your gifts for God as you enter high school in the fall. Because EJ, God has great plans for you, and we want to be the first to congratulate you as you work to discover those. Thanks for your giving heart, EJ. I love you so.

To Austin, my miracle boy ...

Here it is, baseball season again—your very last in Little League. Funny how life goes so fast. We signed you up to play T-ball, and once in a while on hot summer days when you were playing, we'd gaze at the far end of the park, at the field where the big kids played. It was hard to picture you ever getting that big, because that seemed like forever away. So many stages and levels of baseball between T-Ball and the end of Little League. But now, precious son, you're there. One more season, one more All-Stars, and someday soon, one final at-bat in Little League. Your very last. You're an amazing athlete, Austin, defying the odds and proving again and again that you are our miracle boy. I'm sure you'll play baseball again in one of the older leagues or for your high school one day soon. But for now, I will gladly relinquish the role of author and speaker and simply sit in the stands and keep score for your team. Little League mom for one more season. I'm grateful you take your sports so seriously, but even more than that, I'm blessed that you take your role as a Christian so seriously. The other day we were driving somewhere and you said that your friend Karter made an observation. "Austin," he said, "I think you're going to grow up to be just exactly like your dad." You shared that story proudly and beamed at us from the backseat. And up in the front seat, your dad had tears in his eyes. Yes, Austin, you are growing up to be like your daddy. There could be no greater compliment, because your dad is the most amazing man. The bittersweet of knowing that every morning you stand a little taller is juxtaposed with the joy of knowing that Karter is right. You're a little more like your dad every day. I've said it before, and it's true. Heaven has windows, and I'm convinced Papa's still cheering for you, son. Especially this season. As you soar toward your teenage years, please don't forget that or him. You're my youngest, my last, Austin. I'm holding on to every moment, for sure. Thanks for giving me so many wonderful reasons to treasure today. I thank God for you, for the miracle of your life. I love you, Austin.

And to God Almighty, the Author of Life, who has — for now — blessed me with these.

ACKNOWLEDGMENTS

No BOOK COMES TOGETHER WITHOUT A great and talented team of people making it happen. For that reason, a special thanks to my friends at Zondervan who combined efforts to make *Take Three* all it could be. A special thanks to my dedicated editor, Sue Brower, and to my brilliant publicist Karen Campbell, and to Karwyn Bursma, whose creative marketing is unrivaled in the publishing business.

Also, thanks to my amazing agent, Rick Christian, president of Alive Communications. Rick, you've always believed only the best for me. When we talk about the highest possible goals, you see them as doable, reachable. You are a brilliant manager of my career, and I thank God for you. But even with all you do for my ministry of writing, I am doubly grateful for your encouragement and prayers. Every time I finish a book, you send me a letter that deserves to be framed, and when something big happens, yours is the first call I receive. Thank you for that. But even more, the fact that you and Debbie are praying for me and my family keeps me confident every morning that God will continue to breathe life into the stories in my heart. Thank you for being so much more than a brilliant agent.

A special thank-you to my husband, who puts up with me on deadline and doesn't mind driving through Taco Bell after a baseball game if I've been editing all day. This wild ride wouldn't be possible without you, Donald. Your love keeps me writing; your prayers keep me believing that God has a plan in this ministry of Life-Changing Fiction™. And thanks for the hours you put in working with the guestbook entries on my website. It's a full-time job, and I am grateful for your concern for my reader friends. I look forward to that time every day when you read through the entries, sharing them with me and releasing them to the public, lifting up the prayer requests. Thank you, honey, and thanks to all my kids, who pull together, bringing me iced green tea, and understanding my sometimes crazy schedule. I love that you know you're still first, before any deadline.

Thank you also to my mom, Anne Kingsbury, and to my sisters, Tricia, Sue, and Lynne. Mom, you are amazing as my assistant—working day and night sorting through the mail from my readers. I appreciate you more than you'll ever know.

Tricia, you are the best executive assistant I could ever hope to have. I treasure your loyalty and honesty, the way you include me in every decision and the daily exciting website changes. My site has been a different place since you stepped in, and the hits have grown tenfold. Along the way, the readers have so much more to help them in their faith, so much more than a story. Please know that I pray for God's blessings on you always, for your dedication to helping me in this season of writing, and for your wonderful son, Andrew. And aren't we having such a good time too? God works all things to the good!

Sue, I believe you should've been a counselor! From your home far from mine, you get batches of reader letters every day, and you diligently answer them using God's wisdom and His Word. When readers get a response from "Karen's sister Susan," I hope they know how carefully you've prayed for them and for the responses you give. Thank you for truly loving what you do, Sue. You're gifted with people, and I'm blessed to have you aboard.

A special thanks also to Will Montgomery, my manager. In the beginning, I was terrified to venture into the business of selling my books at events. First, I never wanted to profit from selling my books, and second, because I would never have the time to handle such details. More recently, I've been driven to alter my speaking events so that I can be home more often on the weekends. Through it all, you've been creative and hardworking, always ahead of me with ideas of how to continue marketing this ministry of fiction while still putting my family first. With a mission statement that reads, "To love and serve the readers," you have helped me supply books and free gifts to tens of thousands of readers at events across the country. More than that, you've become my friend, a very valuable part of this team. You are loyal and kind and fiercely protective of me, my family, and the work God has me doing. Thank you for everything you've done, and continue to do.

Thanks too, to Olga Kalachik, my office assistant, who helps organize my supplies and storage areas, and who prepares our home for the marketing events and research gatherings that take place here on a regular basis. I appreciate all you're doing to make sure I have time to write. You're wonderful, Olga, and I pray God continues to bless you and your precious family.

I also want to thank my friends at Extraordinary Women — Roy Morgan, Tim and Julie Clinton, Beth Cleveland, Charles Billingsley, Angela Thomas, Matthew West, Chonda Pierce, and so many others. How wonderful to be a part of what God is doing through all of you. Thank you for including me in your family.

Thanks also to my forever friends and family, the ones who have been there and continue to be there. Your love has been a tangible source of comfort, pulling us through the tough times and making us know how very blessed we are to have you in our lives.

And the greatest thanks to God. The gift is Yours. I pray I might use it for years to come in a way that will bring You honor and glory.

FOREVER IN FICTION™

WHENEVER I RECEIVE THE COMPLETED PAPERWORK for a Forever in Fiction™* winner, I read through the details of the life being honored in fiction — whether the person is alive or dead — and I am touched by the real-life stories that come my way.

That was especially true for seven-year-old Annalee Sullivan — or Annie, as her family and friends call her. Blonde, blue-eyed little Annie suffered a brain injury at three years old due to an undiagnosed case of Addison's Disease. The incident caused her to lose the ability to walk, talk, eat, and sing. Today she has a developmental age of just twelve months old. Even still, Annie is sweet and happy. She wears her pretty hair in a ponytail and always wants a colorful ribbon to hold it back. Despite her injury, Annie expresses a desire to go to heaven one day — a place where she will run and play and gaze at the stars the way she once did. Forever in Fiction was purchased by a number of people at the Annie Sullivan Auction in Bothel, Washington. Annie's friends and church family raised nearly ten thousand dollars for her continued medical care and support. In return, you will find Annie in the pages of this book. I chose to make Annie a famous child actress — one who can do all the things Annie loved doing before her injury. I pray that those who love little Annie will be honored by her placement in *Take Three*, where she will be Forever in Fiction.

A special thanks to those who helped place Annie Sullivan Forever in Fiction, including Jan Isakson, Annette Winter, Gerri Omli, Margo McPhail, Ralph and Donna Baggerly, Ed and Sharon Ferris, Shari Jaques, the Colon family, M and K, Becki

---

* Forever in Fiction™ is a registered trademark owned by Karen Kingsbury.

Hoyt, Connie Brockerman, Paul and Jackie Bonjean, Jackie Archambault, Sue Powell, the Kane family, Lynn and Nancy Hurley, Gretchen and Doug Hanna, Lori Lewis, ML McBride, Nancy Stiglets, the Palmaffy family, the Rickmans, the Kent Heyer family, and Karen Schroeder.

Also in *Take Three*, you will find the Kunzmann family. Felix Kunzmann, 44, and his family are citizens of Switzerland, where Felix is a banking executive and his active, young family loves and serves the Lord. Felix won Forever in Fiction on my annual ebay auction. The recipient of this year's ebay auction was our local Christian Youth Theater — the inspiration for my Christian Kids Theater that first appeared in the Firstborn Series.

Felix's winning bid was nearly $4,000. But he sent a check for $13,000 to CYT. His explanation? He told me that if I believed in a charitable cause, he could believe in it. He had one request. Could I please make his whole family Forever in Fiction, if possible? As it turned out, the fit was perfect for *Take Three*. The Kunzmann family plays a family visiting the United States for a year while the dad takes part in an American banking project. In Indianapolis they play a crucial counseling-type role in the life of Andi Ellison. Felix, thank you for your generosity and for helping me think outside the box when it comes to Forever in Fiction.

In addition to his banking expertise, Felix is known among his family and friends as a man very much in love with his wife. He met her at age ten at a Christian Scout camp, and he knew from the moment he saw her that one day he would marry her. But it took a little longer to convince Lucia. Seven years later he began to turn her head, and Felix still remembers their first kiss. Today Lucia remains a devoted follower of Jesus, and she oversees the lives of their three children. The Kunzmanns have a big house with lots of activities for kids, and an open door to the teens in their area who need to know someone cares for them. Lucia is taking counseling courses so she can better help teens and married couples. Their children are Marco, 17; Kenny, 15; and Nathalie, 13. Like their parents, the Kunzmann kids do Christian Scouts. They also love soccer, music, and being available to hang out with the kids who frequently visit their house. Felix, I hope you see yourself and your family in *Take Three*, and I hope you are honored to know that the five of you will now be Forever in Fiction.

For those of you who are not familiar with Forever in Fiction, it is my way of involving you, the readers, in my stories, while raising money for charities. To date, Forever in Fiction has raised more than $100,000 at charity auctions across the country. Obviously, I am only able to donate a limited number of these each year. For that reason, I have set a fairly high minimum bid on this package so that the maximum funds are raised for charities.

If you are interested in having a Forever in Fiction package donated to your auction, contact my assistant, Tricia Kingsbury, at Kingsburydesk@aol.com. Please write *Forever in Fiction* in the subject line.

Take Three

One

ANDI WAS SICK OF LYING TO herself.

After her first night with Taz, the two of them spent most of the next week in each other's arms. But then he began making strange excuses and standing her up. He was working on another film, he told her. Something that would take up most of his summer. It wasn't until one afternoon when she was walking from the library to the cafeteria that she saw Taz arm in arm with a petite brunette. Andi was almost certain she recognized the girl, and as they came closer, she knew where she'd seen her. The brunette had been part of the ensemble in *Scrooge*.

Which could only mean one thing. She was Taz's new actress, his new project. He was probably telling her that true beauty came from using her body as art, or something like that. Andi watched the way the girl gazed at him, how she laughed and giggled and walked close to his arm. The picture burned an image in her mind and tortured her late at night.

As the truth dawned on her, Andi could think only one thing: Bailey's warning had been right after all. Now Andi had no one but herself to blame. She was a fool, and her heart was broken in half. She couldn't eat or sleep, and she felt nauseous nearly every morning, drowning in the heartache of all she'd given up, all she'd lost to a guy who had played her for a fool.

Taz was a fraud. Everything he'd told her had been a lie, and once Andi admitted that much to herself, she knew she could move on. She was still devastated, but at least she wasn't waiting for his call while he was out sleeping with someone else.

The next lie was harder to handle, the one she'd been telling herself. The lie that the physical changes in her body could all be explained by a broken heart. The headaches and nausea, the vomiting some mornings. Her symptoms were too strong to be merely a physical manifestation of heartache. Finally, on the last day of May she drove to the local pharmacy and bought something she had never planned to need until well after she was married.

A pregnancy test.

She took it home, read the directions, and then drew a deep and steadying breath. In two minutes she'd have the results.

Results that—whatever they were—would change the rest of her life.

BAILEY GRABBED HER BROTHER'S DUFFEL BAG from the hall closet and raced back to her bedroom. Fifteen minutes until she had to be on the road, headed to Lake Monroe for the Campus Crusade retreat. She'd been waiting months for this weekend, but her history test for her summer course at Indiana University had run late and now she was scrambling. She felt frantic as she grabbed a pair of jeans, a few T-shirts, and a hooded sweatshirt. She looked around her room, and her eyes fell on a framed photo of her and Tim. For an instant she didn't move or breathe or remember what she was doing. Why did the picture bug her? It was taken on opening night of *Scrooge* last winter, she and Tim both dressed in their costumes. But something about his eyes weren't right, like she was any other fan, lucky to have her picture taken with him. He was her boyfriend, but his expression would've been the same if she wasn't in the picture at all.

"Focus." She turned her attention back to the bag and picked up where she left off. Socks, her Bible, the journal her mom gave her for the trip. Half a dozen other necessities and she zipped the top. Tim was attending the retreat for sure, which was good. They needed to talk. Bailey hoped time alone at the campsite would bring them closer to God and each other—something to help her remember why she was dating him when her heart couldn't stop thinking about Cody Coleman.

A sad sigh slipped through her lips as she slung the duffel bag over her shoulder. Cody wouldn't be there this weekend. He had plans with his mom, last Bailey heard. Just as well. Cody never seemed to want more than a friendship with her, but when Bailey was near him she could barely remember Tim's name. That had to mean something, right? She and Cody were closer now than they'd been for a while. They texted sometimes, and once in a while they even talked on the phone. Tim said he didn't mind this and was confident in who he was and with his place in Bailey's life.

Even if privately Bailey had doubts.

Bailey breathed deep and steadied her heart. Forget about the guys. This weekend was about time alone with God and her friends from Cru. Her ringtone went off just as she left her room. The caller ID told her it was Tim, and she smiled. He was a great guy, really. If it weren't for Cody, she'd probably be wondering whether Tim was maybe the one she could spend her life with. Her crush on Tim had lasted since she was a sophomore in high school, and now that they'd been dating for more than a year, she should've been the happiest girl on the Indiana campus.

She slid her phone open. "Hey!" She kept her tone upbeat. "Don't tell me you're already there!"

"Hey," his voice told her something was wrong. "I've got strep throat. A hundred and two fever. I'm a wreck."

"No." Disappointment came over her. She'd pictured taking walks with Tim during free time at the retreat, learning more about his dreams for the future. Maybe getting past her uncertainty and finding a stronger connection with him. "Did you go to the doctor?"

"We just got back. I'm in bed all weekend. Doc says no going out, no visitors, and to take all my antibiotics. I guess it's really contagious."

"That's terrible." Bailey flopped onto her bed. As sorry as she was about how this changed the feel of the retreat, she felt worse for him. "Okay. Well get some rest and take care of yourself. I'll call you Monday."

"Okay." He sounded defeated. "I'll pray for you."

"You too."

They hung up and Bailey slumped over her knees. Maybe she wouldn't go after all. There was a chance of rain, so how much fun would that be? Stuck in a cabin with a bunch of girls she didn't know that well, trying to stay dry all weekend. She sighed, but as she did she caught a glimpse of the sky. A sliver of blue between the clouds. The school year was wrapping up and classes this week had been tougher than she expected. She was worried about a couple upcoming finals. Between that and the New York audition she was hoping for in August, she needed this time. Needed to be close to God to prepare for whatever the next season in life held.

"Fine," she spoke the word out loud, as if God were standing there watching her. Which He was, in a way. "I'll go, Lord. And You go with me, okay?" She couldn't think of a single time when she'd gone to a church camp or retreat or listened to a sermon and not come home with something special, some way that the Lord had proved the time well spent.

This retreat would be no different. Maybe she'd get closer to the girls in her Bible study. They had plans to start up again in the fall, and next term maybe they would become closer friends outside Cru. She knew some of the girls had to be struggling the way Andi was—with the campus party life or guys who wanted more than they were willing to give. Their struggles were the same ones Bailey faced—uncertainty about life and their futures, and it helped to talk to each other. But so far the meetings had netted little more than a surface discussion about the weekly Bible passage. Maybe if she led the way and talked about her struggles, the tone of the meetings would change.

She gathered her bag, lifted it up onto her shoulder again, and tucked her sleeping bag and pillow under her other arm. When she reached the bottom of the stairs, her mom was sitting next to Ricky, helping him with his math.

"Okay, so if Susie has five horse stickers, Claire has three cat stickers, and Edward has four dog stickers, what is the average number of stickers they each have? That's the question."

Bailey smiled as she set her things down. She remembered those days, when the most difficult thing about life was figuring out how many stickers Edward had. She put her arm around Ricky's shoulders. "How's it going, bud?"

"Pretty good." He tapped his pencil on his paper and flashed her a crooked grin. "I hate word problems."

"I know." She shared a look with her mom. "I must've been the worst Flanigan kid at word problems, wouldn't you say?"

"You and Connor." Her mom laughed. "I had to use drawings and apples and oranges, sometimes full-on dramas just to get the problem to click in your head."

"Good news, bud," she kissed Ricky on the cheek. "If you don't major in math, you'll be finished with it after your first quarter in college." She pressed her fist in the air and did a little dance. "The way I'm finished with it."

"That's forever away." Ricky sighed and stared once more at the math paper.

Their mother's smile softened. "Not forever, buddy. I would slow life down if I could. You're my last little guy to go through Mrs. Ebner's word problems." She patted Ricky's hand. "We can take our time."

Ricky groaned and laughed at the same time. "As long as I finish before dinner. Me and Dad wanna play catch."

With Tim not going on the retreat, Bailey was no longer in a hurry. She would get there eventually, but she loved this—time around her family. The older she got, the more every weekend at home, every summer, felt precious. As if she could feel time pulling her toward a grown-up life. Whatever that might be.

"Where's Dad?"

"Meetings in the city. The team's excited about next season."

A smile lifted Bailey's spirits. That was the beauty of sports, the joy of having a coach for a father. Every season was full of hope and expectation. It kept life entertaining and full of possibility. "We'll have to take in a few days of summer camp."

"A few?" Ricky shook his head. "No, sir. I'm going as many days as I can. Dad says their new running back is the fastest guy he's ever seen." He puffed out his chest. "Other than me, of course."

They all laughed, and Bailey asked about the other boys.

"No homework." Jenny stood and got cups of water for herself and Ricky. "They're on a bike ride with Connor."

"Oh." Bailey took a seat at the kitchen bar. "I have that Campus Crusade retreat at Lake Monroe, but I'll wait till they come back. I haven't talked to Connor in two days. The other boys either."

"They're doing great. I can't believe how tall Connor's getting."

"Is he doing CKT's summer camp?"

"He said he'd like to focus more on football this summer." Jenny took a long sip of her water. "I'm proud of him. It isn't easy to switch gears."

"Definitely not." Bailey pictured her younger brother, her best friend. In the end, he was bound to be a better singer than a tackler, but he was willing to try new things. She loved that about him. Her mom returned to helping Ricky, and after five minutes, the other boys trudged through the back door.

"I can't believe it; I mean you could've been killed." Shawn was talking fast, his words running together. "That was the craziest thing I've ever seen."

Their mom was immediately on her feet. "Who could've been killed?"

"BJ." Shawn let out a long breath, as if he'd been holding it in the whole ride back. "It was a northern copperhead, Mom. I swear. I studied that snake this year, and it was exactly the same."

"Yep." BJ flexed his biceps. "I'm a hero. I saved all our lives."

"No, he was crazy, I swear." Shawn was adamant.

Jenny held up her hand. "Will someone start at the beginning? Please."

"We were riding off-road," Justin stepped forward, "through that field at the end of the street, just up from the stream. And all of a sudden, this snake crossed our path. Connor went around him, but BJ was next and he ran right over him, right across the middle of him."

BJ let his arms fall to his side. "I didn't really mean to, Mom. It just sort of happened."

"So we got off our bikes and looked at him, and sure enough," Shawn still looked stunned. "It was a northern copperhead. Same spade-shaped head, same puffy body. I'd know that snake anywhere."

Bailey walked up and listened to the conversation. In no time, their mom took control. "You should've gone around him, BJ. You need to respect snakes and keep your distance. Especially if it's poisonous."

"Yeah, you don't run right over them." Shawn waved at his brother and then flashed nervous eyes at their mom. "He could've been killed, Mom. I swear."

"And Connor, as for you … you rode around the snake, but maybe you should've stopped and told your brothers about the danger."

"I didn't know it was a copperhead."

"Still, you were the first to come across it. Next time, pull over and stop. Make sure your brothers follow your lead."

The whole drama was resolved in a matter of minutes, but Bailey shuddered at the way it might've played out. What if Connor had been bitten, or one of her other brothers? For that matter, what if there were copperhead snakes lurking near the cabins on the far side of Lake Monroe? She tried not to think about it as she said her good-byes. Certainly God would protect her from the wrath of the northern copperhead.

Her mom hugged her before she left. "I'm sorry about Tim. But God has a reason for you to be out there this weekend." She put her hand alongside Bailey's face. "You're my sweet girl, Bailey. I love you so much." She kissed her daughter's cheek. "I can't wait to hear about it when you get home."

Bailey hugged her mom for a long time, and as she walked to her car and started out, she kept thinking about her family, how much she loved them, and how a single snake encounter could've cost one of her brothers his life. She felt sick as she reached the main road. *Don't think about it*, she told herself. *Focus on what's ahead.*

The drive to the campground took longer than Bailey expected, and she found herself scanning the side of the road for snakes. Just in case. Maybe there was a copperhead infestation happening in the hills around Bloomington. If so, at the first possible chance, she would head back home. She could have a retreat in her own bedroom.

She pulled up at the camp as a few girls from her Bible study arrived. They checked in with Daniel — the retreat leader — and received their cabin assignments. Bailey felt her spirits lighten. Most of the girls from her small group were rooming with her. "Watch out for copperheads," Bailey allowed a half grin as they carried their sleeping bags and pillows to their cabin. Theirs was the one closest to the common area. "My brothers were nearly killed by one earlier."

They unpacked and were lying on their bunks talking about the weekend, when they heard the sound of a whistle, followed by a megaphone announcement. "Everyone report to the fire pit."

Not until they filed out and took their spots around a roaring campfire did Bailey look across the circle and see Cody. Her brow raised and she had to stop herself from getting up and going to him. Instead she locked eyes with him and showed her surprise with her expression. He wasn't supposed to be here, right? "You're here," she mouthed the words silently.

He smiled, his eyes lingering on hers. Whatever had happened, he'd explain later.

For now they needed to focus on Daniel. He explained that he hoped they would accomplish two goals while out in the woods that weekend. First, he had prayed they would all come away closer to Jesus, closer to the faith that bound them. And second, he hoped they would be closer with each other. He picked up a large stick and poked at the fire for a minute. As he did, he separated a few pieces of burning wood from the rest of the blaze.

"College life is a lot like this fire. Professors, class agendas, clubs, friends ... there's a bunch of things that will try to separate you from the fire of faith. And once you're separated," he poked at the lone pieces again and everyone watched, the realization clear. The flame around those pieces had already gone out. "Once you're separated, you can grow cold pretty fast. Especially on a college campus." Then, with one more push of his stick, he moved the once-burning pieces of wood back to the fire. Immediately the flames circled them and they began to burn once more. "We have to stay in the fire, friends. And what better way to do that than by building friendships through Cru."

Bailey thought of the cooling pieces of wood, at the way the glow from the fire faded entirely in a matter of seconds. Andi was like that. She'd come to Indiana University so strong—the daughter of missionaries, after all. But her doubts and curiosity had taken her in all the wrong directions. And toward Taz, which wasn't a wise direction at all. These days Andi was distant and gone most of the time. When Bailey tried to talk seriously with her, Andi always had a class or a study group to get to. Bailey's heart hurt for her friend. She should be here now, a part of the retreat.

She blinked and looked up, and without trying, her eyes found Cody's again. A memory came to mind, she and her family at Cedar Point in Ohio one summer vacation when she was in middle school. A new roller coaster had just opened, and Bailey and Connor couldn't wait to try it. They rode it four times that day, and every time they reached the long downhill, for a few thrilling seconds, her heart flew to her throat, and she felt dizzy and free and beyond wonderful.

The same way she felt now.

She turned her attention to Daniel again. The roller coaster feeling was gone, but her heart was pounding. *God, what's happening? Cody wasn't supposed to be here, and now ... why these feelings? Don't let me get distracted, please.* Daniel handed out a list of duties for the weekend. Each cabin would be responsible for cooking one meal and for cleaning up after another. Working as a team would be part of the fun, for sure. Daniel asked them to check the schedules, and with the girls gathered around her, Bailey pointed out that they were responsible for tonight's dinner. No matter how much she wanted to talk to Cody, the conversation would have to wait. Daniel went over the rest of the itinerary, and Bailey was glad to see that he'd included many hours of solitary time, chances when they could get to know each other or take time alone with God.

"The times with an asterisk are intended as silent times, moments when no one should be talking. Sometimes with God, it's important that we listen. Doesn't matter if you stay close by or find a bluff overlooking the water. Just don't talk." He grinned at Bailey and the girls on either side of her. "Of course, that might be harder for some Cru kids than others."

"Hey," Bailey was quick to tease him back, but then she immediately covered her mouth with her hands.

"See. Talking just comes easier for some of us."

Again Cody caught her eye and they shared a quiet laugh. If anyone knew about Bailey's ability to talk, it was Cody. He'd practically been another brother back when he lived with her family. The laughter faded, and a few guys threw more wood on the fire as Daniel dismissed them and gave out final directions for the night. "Bailey, your group should start dinner."

"We're on it," Bailey moved with the group toward a canopy covering a series of picnic tables and a camp stove setup. "Best burritos ever, coming up." She glanced over her shoulder and walked a little slower so Cody could catch up.

He wore jeans and a soft blue plaid button-down shirt layered over a white T-shirt. Bailey tried not to notice, but there was no denying the fact — he looked so handsome.

"Hey," he brushed his elbow against hers as he came alongside her, his voice low. "We'll talk later." He nodded toward the camp stove. "You're busy."

"Your mom?" Bailey let the other girls get ahead of them.

His smile faded. "It's a long story."

"Later." Again their eyes held. "I'm glad you're here."

"Me too." He glanced at the girls unloading coolers and pulling large pans from a box. Then he gave her a wary look. "Good luck on the burritos."

"Hey!" He was teasing her, but only because he knew her that well. "My cooking's gotten better. Seriously."

"Hmmm." He nodded, his expression one of mock doubt. "You mean you got over your fear of turning on the stove? Even for boiling water?"

"I wasn't that bad." She was laughing quietly now, because he was right. She used to have Connor cook Cream of Wheat for her because she was afraid of the stove. "I can even cook frozen lasagna now."

"Wow …" his eyes danced, but he backed further away, his eyes on the girls again. "Go work. We'll talk after dinner."

She waited a few seconds, then hurried to join her team. Already the girls had lit the stove and were warming up the pre-cooked ground beef in an oversized pan. They divided up the tasks, taking turns grating cheese and lettuce, and stirring the meat. Bailey put herself in charge of heating the tortillas.

While they worked, Bailey kept looking up and discretely finding Cody. He was working with the guys in his cabin, collecting wood from the campsite and stacking it near the fire. The muscles in his back flexed every time he bent down for another armful, and Bailey struggled to focus on the dinner.

"Don't know how much good the wood will do us," one of the girls sighed as she cut tomatoes and put them into a bowl. "If it rains, we'll be sitting around a bunch of soggy logs."

"Actually, the latest reports say the rain won't come till next week."

Another girl smiled big. "Which is why I'm here. I'm not a big fan of camping in the rain."

Bailey was glad to hear the updated weather report. They still would have had fun in the rain, but it would have limited the time they could spend outdoors. Either way, this weekend was bound to make Cody and her stronger friends. She could already feel that much. Even if they didn't quite find the sort of connection they'd shared all those yesterdays ago.

One of the girls came up beside her. "You're quiet." She glanced at the pan of warmed tortillas and used her hand to feel for heat. "What're you thinking about?"

"Life." She shifted the pan and turned down the heat. "And how glad I am that I didn't let a northern copperhead snake stop me from being here this weekend."

They both laughed, and Bailey promised to tell the story about the snake later, when they were all tucked in their sleeping bags, safe from whatever creepy crawly things might come out at night.

The meal took very little time to pull together, and the guys had two oversized piles of wood collected by the time Daniel called everyone to a double row of picnic tables. "Thank You for the food, God, and thanks for the dry weather. We really appreciate it." Daniel raised his fork. "Amen!"

Already Bailey could feel herself relax, feel the tension from the past week and her upcoming finals slipping away. She and Cody exchanged glances now and then, but Bailey sat with the girls around the fire and talked about the tests ahead and the grades they were expecting. A few of them, like Bailey, were taking classes, but the rest of them were going home in a few weeks or sticking around for summer jobs.

"You're lucky you live here," one of them told Bailey. "I'd be up at this lake all the time."

She thought about that, how living close to a place like Lake Monroe made it easier to take it for granted. Maybe after the retreat she could talk Andi into coming up here. Whatever it took to help her find the truth once more. She looked across the fire and watched Cody talking to a group of guys. With Daniel in charge, she and Cody might not have much time to talk alone. That was okay, really. She had a boyfriend, after all. This trip was about seeking God and finding direction for the days ahead.

And these days she needed that more than anything else.

Two

THE LOS ANGELES FILM FESTIVAL HAD been under way for three days, and Keith Ellison couldn't believe how well things were going. They'd put the Brandon Paul issue aside for now, but what they'd learned was encouraging. Despite a recent press release, the young heartthrob had never agreed to participate in an NTM original film with a storyline so much like *Unlocked*. The bestselling novel was the basis for the next movie Keith and his friend Chase Ryan were set to make, and Brandon Paul wanted to star in the picture. His agent and Luke Baxter—lawyer for Jeremiah Productions—were working behind the scenes putting big pressure on NTM to print a retraction.

Chase and Keith had both made up their minds, that no matter what stance NTM took when the discussions were complete, they wanted to work with a different studio. The buzz around town was that an announcement could come any day with NTM's retraction about the proposed film and Brandon Paul's decision to do the *Unlocked* picture with Jeremiah Productions.

Major studios were courting them like a high school prom queen, and now they were thirty minutes from the red carpet premiere of *The Last Letter*. Keith, Lisa, Chase, and Kendall were staying in hotel a mile away from the festival.

"Can you fix my bowtie?" Keith was in Chase's room. He stepped out of the bathroom. "It won't stay straight."

"Shouldn't Lisa do this?" Chase laughed. "No, seriously, come here. I'll fix it." He met his friend halfway and tweaked the back of the bowtie so that the front straightened out and stayed that way. "Where is she anyway?"

"Curling her hair. She won't make us late, but she'll be done with fifteen seconds to spare." Keith checked his look and visibly relaxed a little. He'd been praying for weeks about this event, and now it was here. "Can you believe this? Our first premiere just half an hour away?"

Chase smiled. "Makes me wonder how my feet are still on the ground." He slipped on his shoes and adjusted his pant legs. "I keep thinking back to all we've gone through, back when this day looked like it'd never come."

"Then God brought Ben Adams to the rescue." Keith grinned. "He'll be here, right?"

"He's in the lobby with Kendall. I stopped down to check on our ride and they were already there." He paused. "Kendall looks stunning. Made me remember what a big deal this is."

Keith studied his friend, and a hint of concern flashed across his heart. Chase and Kendall had gotten closer lately. Nothing overt, but Keith had seen a subtle joining of their hearts. Her tendency to stand next to Chase or the quiet way they had of sharing a quick conversation apart from the group. Keith hoped it was nothing to worry about, but he had to wonder. Chase's wife, Kelly, wasn't here, and the fact that Chase noticed how Kendall looked was a little unsettling. Keith made a mental note to watch his friends closely tonight. They had to stay above the line, or everything they'd prayed to accomplish would be nothing more than a mockery of their faith and their character.

"Five minutes til we need to leave for the red carpet!" Chase grinned. "This is the most amazing feeling."

Keith felt his heartbeat pick up. It was really about to happen, the first showing of their movie on a big screen. Two rows were reserved for cast—which had come in its entirety. The rest were for the public. After the showing, there would be a question-and-answer session with Keith and Chase and the cast.

The only one missing was Kelly.

Chase seemed to read his mind. "I called her."

"Kelly?"

"She feels fine, but Macy still has a fever. Doctor thinks it's the swine flu." He grimaced. "I should be there. Kelly's being strong, but she needs me."

"The timing's terrible."

"Even if Macy were fine, Molly had a doctor's appointment for her arm, and this is the last week of preschool." A sigh crossed his lips. "It just didn't work out."

Keith leaned against the hotel dresser and crossed his arms. "Lisa talked to Kelly this morning. Ever since the women's conference, she's like a new person. I've seen it too."

"She is." Chase smiled and it reached deep into his eyes. He was serious now, less flip. "She's happier and more at peace. It's like God worked some complete transformation in her soul all in one day. Or maybe He'd been working it all along and the conference was the final step." He smoothed his hands over his jacket. "I'll call her again. As soon as the premiere's over."

"Good." Keith felt himself relax. "I like knowing the two of you are okay. I can't imagine all this, gaining so much ground, and then losing ourselves. I can't imagine it for either of us."

Keith hoped Chase understood what he was getting at. It was possible to lose themselves and their marriages, their goals of serving God. It was possible because it had happened to other Christians in the public eye. Just because they loved the Lord and their wives, and even though they wanted to make movies with a message, they would always need to be on guard against a fall. They might as well have targets on their backs, and knowing so was half the battle. The bigger their names got in Hollywood, the more they needed to keep an eye on each other, to keep accountable to the highest standard.

"You ready?" Keith took a step toward the door and gave
Chase a hearty pat on the back.

"Ready."

Suddenly, Keith wasn't sure whether to laugh or cry. This was
a moment they had dreamed about since their days in the jungle.
He swallowed hard. "Let's find the rest of our team."

Down in the lobby they met up with Kendall and her father,
Ben. Luke was caught up in a conversation with one of the heads
from MGM studios, and he joined them a minute later. Ben had
arranged for a limo, and it was waiting to take them to the theater. Fitting for a red carpet affair.

"Our carriage awaits." Kendall's eyes sparkled. She wore a
long black dress accented with brilliant sequins.

Keith watched Chase, how he lingered a little longer at Kendall's side. He was wondering how to talk to Chase about his concerns when Lisa walked up. She also looked beautiful, so much
like their daughter, Andi. Lisa wore a navy pantsuit with flowing
sleeves—very Hollywood chic. The six of them headed for the
limo, and Chase was the last one to step inside, right after Kendall. Now that they were alone together, Keith wanted to pray.
"This is a big night. If God wants us to make an impact in this
city, it'll start here."

The others agreed, and in the little time they had on the short
trip, they held hands and asked for God's blessing on the night,
that the actors would feel God's presence in the work they'd accomplished, and that the audience would be changed by the film.
In addition, they asked the Lord for continued favor from the
media and for the *Unlocked* project, still being discussed behind
the scenes. They dedicated the night to God and uttered a round
of amens just as the limo pulled up in front of the red carpet.

Outside, a wall of paparazzi lined either side of the stretch of red. Keith had to put his hand on the cool metal of the limo door before he actually believed what he was seeing. The media had turned out in droves to celebrate their premiere, to see for themselves the film everyone was talking about.

As soon as he opened the door and stepped out, the cameras began clicking. Hundreds of them, thousands. So this was how it felt. The sensation was heady and intoxicating, but Keith stuffed it. *This isn't about us*, he told himself. *Ignore it.* But the cameras kept clicking, and Keith was conscious of every move he made. Every move his team made. He looked back at Chase just as he was helping Kendall from the limo. Keith winced, unwittingly. He wished he could freeze the moment and tell Chase to distance himself from Kendall before another camera caught their picture. But there was nothing he could do. Every camera was capturing Chase, his hand wrapped around Kendall's as she exited the limo.

Keith looked away, intent on smiling for the cameras and giving the accurate appearance that all was well. They moved along the red carpet as a group, and immediately someone yelled out from the sea of reporters. "Your wife's stunning, Chase. What's her name?"

"My wife's home with our girls," he yelled back. He took a step away from Kendall, but no matter where he turned, she was only inches away. Cameras were pointed at them from every angle.

Another photographer shouted, "Chase, Keith … pose with your wives!"

"Chase, Keith … over here!" The shouts continued at a frenzied pace.

"One more over here."

"Get together in a group! That's it, smile. Hold it … and another this way."

The voices blurred, the camera flashes so steady and constant that Keith wondered if his eyes would ever be the same. When the reporters asked them to form a group, there was no getting around the natural way of things. Keith and Lisa, Chase and Kendall. Luke and Ben off to the side, giving the team of producers their moment. Again the question flew at them. "Keith, your wife's Lisa, right?" a reporter yelled.

"And what about you, Chase? Introduce us to your wife."

There was no point trying to clear up the mess. As many times as Chase might yell that his wife was at home, his voice was drowned out by the paparazzi. They would simply have to make sure the mainstream reporters got it right later. Otherwise the pictures from the event would identify Kendall as Chase's wife. Something bound to hurt Kelly.

But once they were inside, Keith was distracted from thinking about Chase and Kendall as he stared at the scene playing out. Here was the entire cast of *The Last Letter*, a reunion Chase had longed for, and here the Lord was giving it to them. The faithfulness of God was beyond anything Keith could grasp.

The mingling time ended twenty minutes later as everyone took their seats in the theater and the lights dimmed. Keith noticed that Chase sat between him and Luke — almost as if he was unaware of Kendall or how things had looked earlier. Keith hoped the reporters took note. The theater went dark, and the movie came to life. From the opening scene, the audience was gripped. They laughed where they were supposed to laugh, and when Jake Olson read the last letter from his father, people around the dark theater weren't merely crying.

Some of them were quietly weeping.

Keith knew every line of the movie backwards and forwards. He'd helped create it and his work in the editing room had helped bring it to life. Now he watched the actors and the audience and checked for the reaction among the reporters who'd been invited to the premiere.

When it was over, he had the thrilling sense that once again the movie was better than anyone expected. The festival director was Liam Montgomery, a tuxedoed black man who was one of the top movie reviewers in Hollywood. His write-up of an independent film could make or break the picture's theatrical release. With audience members still wiping their eyes and blowing their noses, Liam moved to the front of the theater and summoned the actors and producers. As Keith and Chase arrived at the front, Liam held out his hand toward them. "The producers, ladies and gentlemen."

With that, the crowd spontaneously rose to their feet and the applause from earlier grew and built into a rousing ovation. Keith blinked back tears. He was torn between trying to believe this was happening and wishing Kelly was here to share the moment with Chase. Once the cast was lined up, the questions began. People wanted to know if the emotion they saw on the screen was evident on the set, and whether there had been any difficulties filming the movie.

"I can take that one," Keith reached for the microphone. He laughed as he exchanged a look with everyone up front. "The list of problems would last longer than the film. So we'll just say we had a lot of help from God in making this movie."

He watched to see the crowd's reaction at the mention of God, but no one bolted from their seat or stood up and chastised them. They were Christians. People seemed to understand that, and they liked them anyway.

A lady stood in the back row, and Liam called on her. "Go ahead. You'll have to yell so we can hear you."

The woman had no trouble raising her voice loud enough for the entire theater to hear her. "There was a powerful message of redemption in this film." She hesitated, choked by her own emotions. "I've been cut off from my father for ten years, and after seeing this film ... I'll call him as soon as I get home. Was that your intention when you made this film? That it would motivate people to make amends with those they love?"

Again Keith felt a lump in his throat. He reached for the microphone, and then changed his mind and passed it to Chase.

His friend cleared his throat, clearly struck by the same wave of emotion. "Well, actually, yes." He smiled back at Keith. "Our goal was that this movie might be life-changing. That people would find their way back to their families and lost loved ones, and even back to faith in God."

Keith took the microphone. "That was our intent from the beginning and it remains our intent now. We're shameless about it."

Throughout the audience people smiled and nodded, appreciating the fresh newness of watching a movie and being more than just entertained. Many of them were clearly changed in the process, and they apparently liked how that felt.

Before the question-and-answer time ended, Keith remembered the confusion about Kendall being Chase's wife. He took the microphone and smiled. "One more thing," he kept his tone casual. "I'd like to introduce the people who've helped make this movie possible." He gestured toward the audience. "Ben Adams, and his daughter, Kendall."

The two stood and offered a brief wave. Keith clapped, leading the audience in a polite applause for the father-daughter team.

"Also, our wives, Lisa Ellison," Keith waited until Lisa stood and received her applause, "and Kelly Ryan, who is home tonight with their two daughters."

Next, Liam made the announcement they'd been waiting for. The committee had made its decision. *The Last Letter* was indeed best film of the festival, and Jake Olson, best actor. In addition, Chase Ryan was awarded the top director award, meaning their film had raked up more honors than any other at the festival.

"I must say," Liam waved his hand toward Chase and Keith. "It's been a long time since we've been touched by a film this powerful. I think this is the beginning of a long and accomplished career in movie-making for both of you." He grinned. "My review will be in next week's paper."

Again the room burst into applause, and Keith shared a look with Chase. God was making it happen. Everything was panning out just like they'd prayed it might. *Thank You, Jesus ... thank You for this.* Keith said the silent prayer as he pointed upward, his eyes lifted to the ceiling. This was all because of God, nothing more. The experience was so great, the reality was overwhelming. God was winning, and if they continued to follow Him through film-making, He would win again and again and again. That's why he needed to talk to Chase later. Not only that, but he needed to talk to Andi, find out why she'd been so quiet, so withdrawn lately.

Only then could he be sure they were doing all they could to follow God now, the way they'd followed Him when they first began.

Three

By the time dinner was ready, more Cru kids had shown up and the camp bustled with conversation and activity. In one corner a few kids played the guitar, warming up for the worship time around the campfire later. While they ate, Bailey could feel Cody's presence like a physical touch. A couple times she glanced over her shoulder at him, and once she caught him looking too. He still hadn't explained what had happened with his mother.

One of the other guys' cabins had clean-up that night, so when they finished dinner, Bailey and her group of girls went to their cabin and made up their beds. They still had most of the hour before the worship time, and some of the girls wanted to make phone calls or write in their journals. Bailey made a quick call to her parents and then headed out to the fire pit. Cody was there, one of a group of guys gathering still more wood. He smiled at her and moved one more armful closer to the pit before taking the spot beside her.

She could feel his warmth even though their bodies weren't touching. "Okay, so talk to me." She kept her voice low. This wasn't the place for a deep conversation. That wouldn't happen until they were alone. But she still wondered why his plans had changed. "You were supposed to have dinner with your mom."

His expression cooled. "She forgot." He leaned over his knees and kept his eyes from hers. He wasn't angry, but there was no denying the hurt in his voice. "It's a long story. I'll tell you later." He stood and stretched. "I have to get my bunk made up."

She was on her feet too. Her heart felt like it had slipped down to her socks. "Umm ... okay."

He took a few steps toward his cabin, then stopped and turned. A long sigh rattled above the sound of the whisper of leaves overhead. "I'm sorry." He raked his fingers through his hair and stared off at the early evening sky for a moment. "It's not your fault." He looked at her, his eyes deep, more open to her. "If you have time ... meet me at my cabin. Ten minutes?"

She nodded and shrugged a little. What was going on? All of a sudden she was shy around him. *You're crazy*, she told herself. *You've known Cody forever.* She turned back to her cabin and found the other girls preoccupied. When she was sure none of them were looking to talk to her, she wandered back outside, down the path toward Cody's cabin. She saw him long before she reached his little log building. He was sitting on a tree stump, staring at the lake, his shoulders broad and muscled.

She stopped and watched him, the familiar way he held his head, the way the fading sunlight illuminated his profile. What was he thinking, sitting there like that? Was he worried about his mom, or a new girl in his life? Or maybe he was merely taking in God's beauty. She almost didn't want to disturb him, but then—as if he could read her mind—he looked her way and smiled. "Hey."

The path was smooth, but she watched her step anyway. Just in case some critter might cross in front of her. She was much more of a hotel girl, more comfortable at the Doubletree with samples of lotion and shampoo, than here in the woods. But she could appreciate both, and she was glad she'd come. Even with the threat of copperhead snakes.

She reached him and grinned. "I didn't want to interrupt."

For a second she thought he might tell her what he'd been thinking about, but then he set his jaw and his smile stayed guarded. "I'm glad you did." He pointed to a path that led closer to the lake. "Wanna take a walk?"

"Sure." They set out slowly side-by-side, and suddenly Bailey laughed out loud. "I just remembered something funny."

"Which thing?" He hooked his thumbs in his jean pockets and chuckled a little. The way he always did around her. "Something funny's always happening when you're around."

"Hey." She pretended to be hurt. "I'm not sure that's a compliment."

"It is." His eyes danced and he looked straight ahead again. "Believe me, it is."

"Well, okay ... remember when we were at the beach with my family, on the other side of the lake? We took a walk and you challenged me to a race."

"Me?" He stopped and pointed to himself. "That was you, Missy. You're the one who wanted to race."

"Anyway," she kept walking, undaunted. "I got about ten steps and I twisted my ankle. You had to practically carry me back to the picnic tables."

"The summer before I shipped out."

"Right." She allowed her laughter to fade softly, mingling with the evening summer breeze. They turned a corner and were out of view of the campsite. The lake spread out before them, but still they walked on. Up ahead, the lake side of the path was bordered by a rocky outcropping, and when they reached it, they climbed onto the top and sat together. Cody seemed careful to allow space between them. For a while they were quiet, watching the lake, taking in the beauty around them. Bailey could've spent the next half hour sitting there in silence. If Cody didn't want to talk, that was fine. It was enough simply to be with God, to be with him.

He broke the silence first. "My mom met some guy." He drew a slow breath and frowned. "I'm not sure about him. I was sort of hoping she'd meet someone at church, but she met him at the health club."

"They're out tonight?"

"Yeah. She said she forgot about our dinner. Then she said it didn't matter. She didn't want me to miss the retreat on her account."

"That was nice."

"I guess." He leaned back on both hands. "I worry about her."

"I know."

"It's like that with an addict. Relapse is always possible."

They were quiet for a while, and Bailey thought about Cody's world. She could always count on her parents. That wasn't true for him. She lifted her chin and filled her lungs with the sweet-smelling air. "I forget how great it feels to be out here."

"That's why I came." He looked intently at her. "To really pray about this coaching idea and what else lies ahead for me."

Bailey felt her heart warm, despite the cool stone beneath her. Even with his concerns for his mom, Cody's future seemed to be taking shape. He was finishing school soon and his desire was to coach at Clear Creek High. His life was a living miracle, every aspect. "I still pray for you all the time." Again she felt shy. "Every day, actually."

His eyes grew deeper, the connection between them as close as she shared with any of her brothers, but different. More intimate. "The way I still pray for you." He faced the water again. "Speaking of which, what happened to Tim? I thought he was going to be here."

"He got sick. Strep throat."

"Oooh." Cody frowned. "That's too bad."

"Yeah."

Cody was quiet for a long moment. In the distance there was the shrill haunting cry of an eagle, swooping low over the water. The sun had already gone down, and dusk was settling across the lake. "You and Tim," Cody said finally. "You're still serious, aren't you?"

She sighed. He never quite understood that she had loved him first, that if he'd come back from Iraq and declared his love for her, she would've moved on from Tim long ago.

"Sorry." Cody faced her. "You don't have to answer."

"No, it's fine." She folded her arms in front of her and pulled one foot up onto the rock. "Things are the same."

"Your dad said you and Tim are auditioning in New York this summer."

"In August." She shrugged. "It's something I've always wanted to do."

"They'll love you."

His compliment touched her, and she smiled despite the confusion clouding her soul. "I don't know. Last time I was there, the city didn't have the same appeal." She looked out at the water, at the way the breeze sent ripples across the width of the lake. "New York's crazy. Constant noise and strange smells, people living on top of each other. You have to look straight up to see the sky."

"Hmm." Cody gave a single shake of his head and narrowed his eyes. "Not my style."

"Definitely not." This time her smile felt sad. If she wound up in New York, that would be the end for her and Cody. Distance would have the final say. "My dad can't stand it either." The conversation was easy, without the walls she'd felt between the two of them for so much of the last school year. "When we go to New York, we shop, sightsee, go to the theater. We stay three days and then we're gone. But that's not how it would be if I lived there." She looked at him. "I'd be commuting in on a bridge or by subway, walking fast and afraid of getting accosted. I'd pay high rent for a small apartment and have almost no fresh air." The sky was nearly dark, but in the dim light that remained, a pair of eagles drifted up from the branches of a nearby pine. A breeze brushed against her face, and for a few seconds she closed her eyes. When she opened them, she smiled. "No moments like this."

"What about Tim?" Cody seemed guarded when he talked about Tim. "How does he feel about the city?"

"He loves it. I think he could live there for the next five years. Maybe forever. He really wants to perform."

"Are there churches in Manhattan?"

"A few." She uttered a sad laugh. "But Broadway's a long way from the Bible Belt." They talked for a few minutes about a church not far from Times Square. "If I lived there, I guess I'd go there."

Again Cody was quiet. Their hour was almost up, and they needed to get back soon. Besides, if it got too dark they could be in trouble. Neither of them had brought a flashlight. "So you really think it could happen, huh? You and Tim, performing on Broadway, living in New York City?" His smile was more guarded now.

"I guess." She'd longed for the chance to perform professionally since her early days with Christian Kids Theater. But here, with the crisp lake air around them, and Cody by her side, her dreams were no longer clear. "What about you?" She hadn't asked for a long time, and now she wanted to know. Even if she was afraid of his answer. "Any girls in your life?"

"Me?" A quiet laugh rattled around in his chest. "Definitely not. God's still making me into the guy I need to be. I want that before I want a girlfriend."

His answer left her starry-eyed.

"I'm saving my heart for her." His eyes shone as he looked at her. "Really."

"I'm impressed. Not many guys are willing to talk about something like that."

"Yeah, well. She'll be worth the wait." He looked out at the water again. "Whoever she is."

For the craziest moment, Bailey wondered if she might ever be that girl, the one Cody was saving his heart for. But she dismissed the idea as soon as it came. She had a boyfriend. She could hardly think about loving the friend beside her when she had just finished talking about possibly building a life with Tim in New York City.

"What are you thinking?" Again Cody seemed to read her mind.

"Nothing." Her smile faded. "Nothing I can tell *you* anyway." She stood, brushed the sand off her shorts, and kicked at his tennis shoe. She hopped off the rock and onto the path. "I'd say let's race back, but I can't afford another sprained ankle."

Again he laughed. He stepped on the path beside her. "That's just one of the things I love about you, Bailey. You make me laugh."

"Same with you."

"Can I tell you something?" They were facing each other, maybe a little too close. He took a slight step back, keeping distance between them.

"Sure." She tapped his foot again. "You can tell me anything, Cody Coleman."

"Okay, now don't weird out on me or think I'm trying to get between you and Tim or anything."

"Go on." She giggled. "At this rate you'll never spit it out."

He turned so they were both facing the lake, side by side. He crossed his arms and clenched his jaw, his eyes set straight ahead. Whatever he wanted to say, he was struggling. Finally he turned to her again and she watched his guard fall a little. "I'm glad we … I don't know, I'm glad we found this again." He hesitated. "I thank God every day for you. For your family and your friendship."

Bailey tilted her head and let her eyes get lost in his. The moon was making its way into the sky and it shone on his face. Whatever else the future held, she'd remember this moment as long as she lived. She didn't want it to end. Without wondering whether it was right or wrong, she put her arms around his neck and hugged him. "That means the world, Cody." The hug lasted longer than usual, and it took her breath. "I'm glad you told me." She pulled back and felt her eyes start to dance. "Okay, my turn."

He studied her, and there in the moonlight he almost looked like he had feelings for her. Feelings more than friendship. His voice was low and soft against her heart. "Go on."

She could feel her expression growing more serious, deeper. "I was so mad at you last fall, when you wouldn't talk to me." She gently touched her fingers to the side of his face. "I thought in all our lives we'd never have a day like this again."

"I was worried about it."

"But here we are." She eased her hands back to her sides, keeping her behavior appropriate. "That's why God's so amazing. He knows how to fix things, even after we make a mess of them."

"Exactly." He reached out his hand. "Come on; it'll be pitch dark in a few minutes."

She took his hand and felt the thrill of his touch all the way to her toes. Once they were on a steadier part of the path again she drew her fingers from his and kept the conversation light. But her heart was beating so hard she wondered if he would say something about the sound. Holding hands with Tim never made her feel like this, which was why she definitely couldn't hold hands with Cody now, here. She wasn't ready to analyze what that meant or what it said about her relationship with Tim. Better simply to keep her distance where Cody was concerned. Besides, he was holding out body and soul for the girl of his dreams. She didn't want to get in the way of that, even if a part of her desperately wished she were that girl.

On the way back, Cody told her about a bear sighting in the woods not far from the campsite.

"Great." She was about to tell him the story of her little brother BJ and the northern copperhead he rode his bike over, when her foot settled on something soft and slithery. She screamed and fell all at the same time, her ankle giving way beneath her as she dropped. She had no idea how Cody moved so fast or how in the dim light he was able to catch her, but the next thing she knew, she was in his arms, clinging to his neck. She pointed down at the ground. "There's a snake, Cody! Be careful."

He set her down a few feet away and went back to the spot where she'd felt the snake. Using the toe of his shoe, he pressed around and came up with something long and bendable. "This, you mean?"

He brought it closer and she stifled another scream. "Don't, Cody! It could be poisonous. Shawn says copperheads are all around this lake."

"Well," he held his hands out so she could see exactly what had frightened her. "This branch is definitely not part of the copperhead family. I promise."

Bailey straightened and stared at the thing Cody was holding. "A branch? You've gotta be kidding. I could feel it moving."

"It's a young branch. A little more flexible than some." He tossed it off the path and grinned at her. "You probably scared it to death."

She tested her ankle, but it was fine, and suddenly she pictured herself stepping on the branch and practically jumping into Cody's arms. She burst into laughter again and had to hold onto Cody's waist as they walked. Otherwise she would've fallen to the ground, unable to breathe.

The other campers already had flashlights out, and as they reached base camp, everyone wanted to know what was so funny. Bailey told her snake story, but when she reached the part about stepping on the branch, she cracked up again and Cody had to finish for her.

It was like that throughout the weekend. She had hours of solitude with the Lord, times when she could pray about the direction God had for her life, and whether New York City was something she really wanted. Other hours she and the girls talk-ed, and still others, when she and Cody sat alone, rebuilding their friendship. Always their time together ended in laughter, except for once—the last night of the retreat.

That night, with the moon a little more than a thumbnail of light overhead, they sat by the fire until everyone else had turned in. They talked about Cody's mother and Bailey's family and Cody's dream to help kids the way Bailey's parents had helped him. They sat close together, neither of them seeming to mind when their knees touched a time or two.

Before they turned in, Cody held out his hands to her. "Pray with me, Bailey. Will you?"

She didn't hesitate. She slipped her fingers into his and to-gether they bowed their heads. She started the prayer, the way she'd seen her mom and dad pray together so many times over the years. "Dear Lord, this time away has been so good for us, for the friendships that have grown stronger and for the way You feel closer than ever." She paused, working to focus. "Thank You for Cody and his friendship. Please, Lord, keep the two of us close to You, and let Cody know how much he means to me."

It was Cody's turn, and he gave her fingers a subtle squeeze as he started. "God, You know how I feel about Bailey," he hesitated for a moment, as if his feelings for her weren't something he was willing to actually put into words. "I begged You for a second chance at her friendship, and now here we are. Copperhead snake branches and all." They both shared a couple seconds of quiet laughter, the sound of the fire crackling a few feet away. When he had control again, he finished. "Lord, I ask that You protect what we've found on the far side of Lake Monroe this weekend. Life is too short to waste on half-hearted connections and meaningless run-throughs. Now I feel closer to Bailey than ever before, and I'm blessed for the fact.

"People could live all their lives and never have a friend like Bailey Flanigan. So thank You, Lord. And I pray for her audition coming up. If You want her to live in New York, to perform there and be part of maybe a revival taking place in that city, then throw open the doors for her this August. Let her stand out and let her get a role in a Broadway play." He paused, and there was no hiding the sadness that had crept into his voice. "But only if it's Your will, Father. Otherwise, shut the door. Then she'll know which way You're leading her. In Jesus' name, amen."

Bailey didn't want to let go of his hands, but slowly he let go first. She had lost her breath somewhere around the part about half-hearted connections and meaningless run-throughs, and when he asked God to let her go to New York only if it was His will, she felt her heart go into a rhythm she didn't recognize. She swallowed hard, trying to find a way to set her world back on its axis.

But as they stood and shared a long hug, and as he walked her to her cabin and they said good night, Bailey was breathing normally again. She was dating Tim, and until that changed, she couldn't let herself have feelings for Cody beyond the ones they'd found here at camp. She lay in her bed in her sleeping bag for a long time, looking out the window at a brilliant spread of stars.

God had met her in this place, in a number of ways. She felt ready to take her finals, ready to take on the challenges of the summer, ready for her audition. And she felt certain about one thing. She didn't want to settle for an existence of half-hearted connections and meaningless run-throughs. Not with Cody or Tim or God Himself.

And after this weekend, settling for anything less than God's best wasn't even an option.

Four

CHASE WAS GRATEFUL THE PREMIERE WAS almost over. The night seemed to last forever, and he could hardly wait to talk to Kelly, to see how she and the girls were doing. He'd been caught off guard earlier in the limo at the start of the night. He could barely focus on their prayer because of Kendall's hand in his. And so his prayer had been a personal one. *God, thank You for bringing Kendall and her father to us at a time when we were ready to close shop and quit. We're here at the top of a mountain that belongs only to You. Please ... don't let me forget our mission ...*

Keith was looking at him, which could only mean one thing. A question had come his way. He shot his friend a desperate look, one Keith must've read immediately.

"As a director," Keith spoke into the microphone, showing none of the concern he must've been feeling, "what was the most difficult part of making this movie?"

Chase nodded and took the mic. "The actors made it easy on me, really. The hardest part was making sure the intensity of their emotions came across in every scene."

"You pulled it off!" a person from the middle row shouted. "Great job, Chase!"

He nodded, humbled. How could this be happening, the audience so taken by a film they almost couldn't make? This moment, this realization that God was opening the floodgates was more than he could fully comprehend. He only wished Kelly were here to share it with him.

Finally the question-and-answer session ended, and as they filed out of the theater and into the lobby, as one person after another congratulated them, Chase's emotions shifted from exultation to something quite disturbing: Fear. Because the higher God took them, the more difficult the expectations. How were they going to top this moment? Chase swallowed hard and kept his attention on the moment at hand. *Don't be ridiculous*, he told himself.

He put his inner dialogue to rest and focused on the numerous executives in attendance from every major movie studio. Everyone wanted to talk to the up-and-coming producers from Jeremiah Productions—Chase or Keith, Luke or Ben. From across the room, Chase noticed that even Kendall was brought into a number of conversations by executives anxious for a chance. He admired her professionalism and ability to hold her own with Hollywood's movers and shakers.

"Where'd you get your experience?" a vice president from one of the top studios caught up with Chase at the food table. "Your work as a director ... it's amazing. Impeccable."

"We had training from some of the best college professors in LA before leaving the U.S. for mission work," Chase said. He tried to sound modest, but he couldn't fight an overwhelming desire to impress the man. He gave the guy an unassuming smile. "It's God's gift, but a highlight of this experience has been winning at the festival."

"You deserve it." The man nodded appreciatively. "It's uncanny, having the ability to produce and direct a film of this caliber, with virtually no experience." He shook his head, as if he couldn't quite get over Chase's talent. "Our team wants to work something out with you and Keith. For this film or the next. You're exactly the kind of team we want to work with."

They exchanged business cards and the conversation ended, but it was followed by another dozen like it. At the end of two hours, Chase felt the strangest sensation that he'd missed out. Not in making the movie, but because he hadn't really enjoyed what God had given them this night. He'd been tempted by Kendall, flattered by movie execs, and he'd spent much of the night regretting that he couldn't be with Kelly when she needed him back home.

Before the end of the night, Luke Baxter brought them a preliminary offer from American Pictures. The offer was beyond anything any of them had ever imagined: ten million dollars for *The Last Letter*. The figure was eight million more than any of them had hoped to get up front. In addition, the studio was still willing to front half the publicity and advertising money. Luke was giddy over the proposal. "They want a full theatrical release, a thousand screens across America."

Keith looked at him, and his eyes said everything he clearly couldn't put into words. He came to Chase and hugged him hard, the way two friends embrace after surviving a war together. As Keith released him, Chase looked across the room. Kendall and Ben were having what looked like a serious conversation in the opposite corner of the lobby.

Keith and Luke were going on about God's mercy and grace, His perfect timing, and how they would have the freedom to make more movies with the commitment from American Pictures. They were still celebrating, when Luke's cell phone rang. He checked the caller ID and his eyes lit up. "NTM." The last guests were gone by then, but Luke distanced himself from the group as he answered.

Kendall and her father must've finished their conversation, because they crossed the lobby and joined Chase and Keith. Kendall looked weary, her eyes darker than Chase had ever seen them. "What's all the excitement for?"

"We've got an offer!" Keith stepped up and hugged Ben Adams. "American Pictures wants to give us ten million for a theatrical release!"

Chase kept his attention on Keith and Ben. He could've been wrong, but Ben's enthusiasm seemed tempered, somehow. He would have to ask him about it later. Luke returned to them a few minutes later. As he reached them, a grin spread across his face. "It's happened!"

"What?" Chase couldn't imagine anything else tonight. Already he was dizzy from everything he was feeling.

Keith moved in close to Chase so they could hear, and Luke gave each of them a strong pat on their backs. "NTM is printing a retraction tomorrow. I guess they got pressure from Brandon's agent that he'd pull out of his existing contract Monday if they didn't run something taking back the story."

Chase wished he had something to hold onto, but since there was nothing, he put his hand on Keith's shoulder and grabbed tight. Wasn't this what they'd prayed for? Wasn't it what Keith had believed could happen, and what Kendall was absolutely convinced would take place? That NTM would back down and Hollywood's top young actor, Brandon Paul, could actually star in their next film?

Luke was going on about how NTM never does this, and how the news release would state that failed communication was to blame for their retraction. Chase wanted to be sure he understood. "What exactly does this mean for *Unlocked*?"

This time Luke leaned his head back and laughed out loud. "It means you and Brandon Paul can take this deal to whatever studio you'd like. Sounds like American Pictures might be your first stop. Either way, NTM is so worried about losing Brandon, they're even willing to let him film this movie before he fulfills his agreement with them. As long as he doesn't pull out of his contract."

When Ben and Kendall got up to speed about the latest developments, Ben directed everyone to hold hands one more time. "We've taken time to ask God for His blessing," Ben's voice was scratchy, thick with emotion. "Now it's time to thank Him."

Chase studied the older man. He seemed deeply emotional, maybe because of his earlier talk with Kendall. The conversation had been very private and seemed more intense than was fitting for a night like this. Chase wondered if Kendall's dad was warning her to keep her distance from Chase, reminding her that Chase was married. He hoped not. He'd be mortified if his errant thoughts were that obvious.

This time Keith was between him and Kendall as they linked hands and bowed their heads. This time the profound nature of the moment spilled into their prayer and they went on for ten minutes while each of them took turns praising God for His direction and wisdom, and thanking Him for the premiere and the way it was received, and the way it was already working to change lives for His glory, and finally for the deal with American Pictures and the breakthrough with Brandon Paul and their next film.

As they finally climbed into the waiting limo and drove across town to their hotel, Chase was positive he'd never felt like this before. He wasn't tired, and when Kendall asked him if he wanted to join her for a cup of coffee in the lobby, he agreed before he could remember a single reason why he shouldn't. Keith and Lisa went off to their room, and Luke to his—clearly assuming everyone was turning in, and Kendall's father set off for home.

And like that, Chase and Kendall were alone.

They chose a table tucked into the corner of the lobby, near a roaring fire and out of sight from the main traffic at the front desk. She put her elbows on the table and leaned in close, her eyes imploring him. "Before we talk, I need to apologize." She held his gaze. "That was awkward, on the red carpet. People thinking we were ... you know, married." She rushed ahead, her voice rich with regret. "I had no idea ... I mean, I would've walked five feet behind you if I'd known."

She seemed anxious for him to find her innocent in the situation, and Chase did so immediately. He clasped his hands around hers and squeezed gently before letting go. "Don't worry about it. You did nothing wrong."

Her remorse eased a bit, and something in her eyes made him feel uneasy. Did her expression hold a hint of desire, or were his own feelings shading the way she came across in a moment like this?

"Still." She blinked, and the desire—if there'd been desire—was gone completely. "It was awkward, and I apologize. Please tell Kelly it was one of those crazy moments. Neither of us meant anything by it."

Again Chase swallowed hard, and he moved his hands out onto the table again. For the next half hour he forgot about his promise to call Kelly. Instead, he and Kendall replayed every moment of the amazing night, the red carpet and the premiere, the reaction from the audience, and the telltale questions that followed. Through it all, their hands touched at times, and once their faces were so close Chase could imagine kissing her. He didn't want the moment to end. This was only the beginning, right? The start of all they would accomplish together as a team—Keith and him and Kendall and Ben. Luke working out the details.

Finally, she blinked twice, as if she was only just realizing how they might've looked together, how they'd been acting. She blinked twice and withdrew her hands to her lap. The color in her cheeks deepened. "Chase. I didn't only want to talk about the premiere ... or Brandon Paul." She looked away, as if the eye contact between them had become too much for her.

Only then did Chase notice that her fingers were trembling. She looked up and her eyes were deep with agony. Whatever was coming, it wasn't good. He felt his heart skip a beat and then pound into a faster rhythm.

Kendall lifted her eyes. "My dad asked me something tonight that shocked me. He wanted to know if I was falling for you."

"What?" Chase's heart slammed against his chest and he felt suddenly clammy. Had things between them become so obvious that Ben had picked up on it? When neither of them had even hinted at the possibility until tonight? "I can apologize to him if he thinks—"

"Chase." She peered at him through teary eyes, her heart clearly anguished. "I'm finished with Jeremiah Productions. I've loved every minute, but now … my dad made it clear tonight. I need to move on. There's too much at stake."

"You can't quit." He rose halfway out of his seat, shocked and angry, embarrassed at the implied accusation from Kendall's father. "We didn't do anything wrong. We were on the same team, Kendall. We were bound to get close. We were …"

His words trailed off and Kendall said nothing, only stared at him, deep into his eyes, and the message was beyond clear. He could lie to himself, but he couldn't lie to her. She must've known every time he'd been moved by her, every time he'd found her interesting or alluring. The proof was all over her face.

Chase studied her, unable to completely process the finality of what was happening. A few minutes ago they'd been celebrating, right? But the whole time Kendall had been harboring her father's warning, holding back about the fact that this wasn't only their greatest night as a team—it was their last.

Suddenly like a tsunami overtaking him, the truth hit. Never mind that he hadn't acted on his private wanderings. He had unwittingly given Kendall a piece of his heart. In doing so he had gone against God and Kelly and everything he believed in. Even if only in thought. This was God's answer to the half-hearted prayers he'd uttered off and on through the night. He couldn't possibly be a filmmaker looking to touch the world with God's message of hope and redemption if he was having feelings for someone other than his wife. And now the decision about how to handle himself around Kendall had been made for him. His hands suddenly felt uncomfortable on the table and he lowered them to his knees. "How soon?"

"Monday." Shame filled her eyes. "I'm sorry, Chase. It wasn't only you."

And like that, the second wave hit. He wasn't the only one entertaining wrong thoughts. This new truth was both flattering and horrifying at the same time. He couldn't possibly ask her to stay now. They'd avoided a disaster, but clearly the only option was to split ways. He didn't say anything, because there was nothing to say. Her admission had said it all.

She sat a little straighter, more composed than before. "Life is made up of seasons. My dad used to say that." No smile lifted the corners of her mouth. The sadness in her eyes was all-encompassing. "Maybe some other season I'll be back."

All Chase could think about was Kelly, and how badly he wanted to call her. "It's late."

They took the elevator up, and her floor was before his. As the door opened, she stepped out quickly without a hug or any physical contact. She waved. "Keep in touch."

"We will." He got out the words just as the door shut, and like that he was alone with his raging emotions. Guilt for his earlier thoughts, and shock over the news about Ben Adams. Relief because he no longer had to worry about Kendall.

But he still had to worry.

What flaw in his faith and commitment to Kelly had allowed him to take even a few steps down the path of infidelity? He was still buzzing from the shock when he reached his room and flipped on the TV. *Entertainment Tonight* was showing highlights from the premiere, but the thrill was overshadowed by the obvious impression the images gave off. He and Kendall looked like they were together, and Chase could only admit the obvious.

He had stood at the brink of disaster, toes over the edge of a cliff from which there would've been no return, nothing but certain destruction. The thought hit him like a freight train as he flipped off the television and stared at the darkened screen. There would be other women with every stage of filmmaking, actresses and casting agents and directors. People drawn to the success of

Jeremiah Productions. If he could so easily let his feelings get out of hand for Kendall, what about the next woman to come along? Or the one after that?

He lowered his head to his hands. *God, I need Your help. What's the answer? I don't care about the fame, but what if I can't handle the temptations? What if I mess up?* He squeezed his eyes shut and tried to picture his wife—his amazing wife—back home with their two daughters. Trusting him, believing in him. Needing him. And what about his little girls—Molly and Macy.

Marketing *The Last Letter*, planning and filming their next picture. All of it would take more time away from home. Already he'd missed much of the past year—time he wouldn't get back again. *Help me, God. Show me what You want me to do. Please, Lord.*

Suddenly he remembered the words Keith had said earlier, how easy it would be to win the world for Christ through film, and meanwhile lose themselves. Chase stood and walked to the bathroom, gripped the granite countertop, and stared at himself in the mirror. *I need an answer, God. Please show me how to survive this.*

Back in his bedroom he found the framed photo of Kelly and the girls, the one he took on road trips. His heart hurt as he picked it up and stared at the faces he loved. How close had he come tonight to falling? Slowly and with an ache in his chest, Chase dropped back to the bed, the picture still clutched in his hands. "No, God ... please no," his words were an anguished whisper. "I don't want to fail. I need Your protection." He couldn't have even a hint of impropriety. Not now or ever. "Show me the way, please."

When his desperate prayer was over, he struggled to his feet and realized how strange this night had been—the highest of highs and the lowest of lows. He was not going to make films for God only to lose his marriage along the way. He knew what he had to do, and he strode purposefully to his laptop, opened it, and set it on the small desk.

With a series of clicks he ordered a dozen long-stemmed roses sent to Kelly at their home address. On the note card he directed them to write only this: "We won big tonight, but it was not the same without you. I love you more than you know. Chase."

He scheduled the roses to be delivered the next day, and then he made the call he should've made an hour ago. Kelly had never sounded more glad to hear from him, more absolutely trusting. The girls were in bed, of course, and she'd been waiting for his call. Macy's fever was down, and Kelly thought she had turned the corner and was recovering from the flu. Chase savored every word that came across the line. Her voice was like an oasis, an embrace that brought a physical comfort, one that soothed every rough, jagged part of his heart.

"I prayed for you," she said. "Tell me everything."

Guilt sliced through his soul because he couldn't tell her everything. Not the part about his temptations and struggles or how the reporters thought Kendall was his wife or how even Ben Adams had been concerned that Chase and Kendall might have an attraction to each other. Kelly didn't deserve those details. Instead he told her everything else. About the paparazzi and the enormous crowd outside the theater, the packed house, and the representatives from every studio in Hollywood.

"Honey, that's amazing." She released a quiet squeal. "It's everything I asked God about."

He finished by telling her about the offer from American Pictures and the news that NTM had retracted their earlier announcement about Brandon Paul. "I keep thinking I'm going to wake up and the whole thing will be one wonderful dream." He closed his eyes and massaged his brow. He hated this, feeling like a phony. He didn't deserve any part of what was happening around him. Least of all, the loving woman waiting back home for him. He kept his tone appropriately upbeat. "It doesn't feel real."

"But it is. Because God's doing this, Chase." Her love, her support, warmed her words and touched him deeply. She paused, and passion filled her voice. "I only wish I were there with you."

They talked a while longer, and before their conversation ended, Kelly remembered one last thing. "Check your email. I forgot to tell you, but Pastor Hastings called. I guess he sent you something. Said it was time sensitive."

"About the movie?"

"He didn't say." Kelly didn't sound too concerned about the message. "I'm so proud of you, Chase. I love you so much."

Again Chase felt sick about what could've happened. He swallowed hard. "I love you too, baby. I can't wait to see you."

"This is just the beginning. "

"Exactly." *The beginning of what?* Chase wondered. A sick feeling wrapped its arms around him. "I miss you."

"You too. It's so good to hear your voice."

As the call ended, Chase set the phone down on the end table and stared at the plain beige wall across from him. If this was the beginning, then did that mean he'd face a life of temptation and terrible guilt? Years of being away from home and spending long days on the road? He felt weary and lifeless, and more than anything he wanted to be home with Kelly and the girls. He remembered the email, and he stood slowly, like a man twice his age.

Why would Pastor Hastings email him? The man was in his seventies, a respected teacher known throughout the area for his wisdom and Bible knowledge. Their church was made up of several leaders and thousands of members, but Chase doubted the main pastor had a clue about the movie industry or what Chase was working on. He opened his Mac, waited the few seconds while it sprang to life, and opened his mailbox. The email from the pastor was near the top. The subject line read "Opportunity."

Had the pastor come across local investors? Chase clicked the email open and saw that it was brief. Only a few lines. He narrowed his eyes, confused, and began reading.

Dear Chase,

I want to make you aware of a recent opportunity. Our youth pastor has unexpectedly moved back to New Jersey because of a family crisis. Our team met this morning and prayed about a replacement candidate, and your name quickly rose to the top of our list. We are aware of your previous experience and your education in ministry. I understand that your new ventures have taken you away much of the time. Therefore, this may not be something you're interested in pursuing. But then again, it might bring you closer to home and the role of raising your young daughters.

Please do not feel pressured to take the position. Either way our team would appreciate a response at your soonest convenience. Until then we are praying for your thoughtful consideration.

Because of Him,
Pastor Joseph Hastings

Chase stared at the email and then read it over again three times. If he thought he was dreaming before, this was the clincher. Pastor Hastings was asking him to be youth pastor at their church? A youth pastor, when already Chase had committed to making movies, to producing and directing? Did no one at the church know how much success they were having in Hollywood?

The email was still shouting at him, so Chase closed it and shut down his computer. Why in the world would his name rise to the top of the list of candidates capable of leading the church's youth? Sure he was trained in ministry, and he'd served as an ordained pastor on the mission fields. But still ... a youth pastor? He thought back, remembering a decade ago before filmmaking became a part of his life. For a brief season his dream had been youth ministry. But Pastor Hastings couldn't have known that.

Chase dismissed the thought and turned his heart once more to the Lord. *God, I have no idea why Pastor Hastings sent me that email, but help me turn him down gently. In the meantime, I need an answer about the future, God.* Chase rolled onto his back, restless. He sighed out loud, grabbed a pillow, and pulled it to his chest. He needed a way to handle times like tonight, a stronger spirit, a greater resolve. Whatever it took so he could survive this season of filmmaking and still come out the man he was before this crazy ride started. He stared at the ceiling, restless and unsure. God had given him a warning tonight. Now Chase could only believe that if God had helped him survive a night of temptation, He would show him how to survive a lifetime of it.

He wasn't going to let the devil tempt him with Kendall or anyone else. This was God's mission field, not a Hollywood playground. He wouldn't fail his wife or his faith or his family. Chase was surer about that than he was about his next breath. And with that certainty, he was finally able to drift off to sleep dreaming about the only woman he would ever love.

His precious wife, Kelly.

Five

ANDI HAD HER TEST RESULTS. MOST of the night she'd been staring at the white plastic stick, her pulse fast and irregular, her mouth dry, panic coursing through her. One minute she'd lie on her bed crying her eyes out, and the next she'd pace her room, frantic, desperate for a way out. There was none.

She was pregnant with Taz's child. There was no hiding from the fact any longer.

This new reality had been a part of her for several hours, but the shock was still decimating its way through her, tearing apart her soul and screaming at her for all the ways she'd failed. Andi looked at the clock and saw it was nearly two in the morning. She pulled herself out of bed, and in a rush, a wave of nausea dragged her down. As fast as she could move, she hurried to the bathroom and fell to her knees at the edge of the toilet. For the third time that night, she dry-heaved into the cold porcelain bowl, gasping for air between convulsions.

She hadn't eaten all night, so nothing came up. Nothing but the reality that her life was never going to be the same again. Her stomach twisted and turned until Andi wondered if she might collapse there on the bathroom floor. It was like her body was rebelling, the way she had rebelled against God and her family, against the wisdom of her roommate, Bailey, and her deceased friend, Rachel Baugher.

The wave passed, though her stomach still hurt desperately. She rocked back on her heels and hung her head. Maybe if she threw up enough times the pregnancy would go away. She clung to the toilet and tried to steady herself. But the room rocked and tilted and she didn't dare move.

Like she'd done countless times that night, she thought again about her lack of options. In the moments after she had her news she made a desperate call to Taz. *Stupid*, she told herself now. What good could he possibly do now that she was pregnant? Did she really expect him to take the news with kindness and compassion? Come to her and promise to stay by her side? Did she think he'd offer to marry her and make a life with her and their child?

Her attempt to reach him never even got that far. A girl answered his phone, and in the background she could hear Taz scolding her to hang up. "That's my phone," he hissed at her. Then the line went dead. Andi vowed it was the last time she would call him. Her next call had been to her parents, not that she was about to tell them her news. Rather, she wanted to hear their voices, to know that the safe world of hope and truth in Christ still existed somewhere.

But her father didn't answer his cell, and when her mom picked up, what sounded like a loud celebration in the background made it impossible for her to hear. "Andi," her mom shouted above the noise, "everyone loved the film! Your father and I are so happy, sweetheart. Wish you were here."

"Mom ... I don't feel good."

The noise on the other end grew louder. "What? Andi, can you speak up? Is everything okay?"

"Yes." She practically yelled her response, tears streaming down her face. "Go celebrate, Mama. I'm fine."

"Okay. Talk to you tomorrow. I love you, honey!"

And with that she was alone again, sitting in her room, the walls closing in around her. The room stopped spinning and Andi opened her eyes. She was weak and drenched in sweat and her stomachache spread through her whole body. She moved slowly to the bathroom and looked at herself in the mirror, but all she could see was Taz. She covered her face and shook her head. How could she have believed someone so opposed to God, someone so dangerous? What possessed her to agree with him, that nudity in film meant quality movie-making? The idea was disgusting. Or that sleeping with him was some sick form of art?

She shuddered and grabbed the toilet again. The memory of his sickly suggestive words choked her, made it hard for her to draw a breath. With everything in her she had known Taz was wrong for her, but she'd ignored every sound, godly thought that crossed her mind back then. How could she have let herself fall so fully, so thoroughly? She would give anything to be the old Andi again. To be Bailey Flanigan — sure of her convictions, confident in her faith. If only Bailey were here right now, maybe Andi could tell her the truth about being pregnant. But Bailey was at the Cru retreat — where Andi might've been if she hadn't chosen her own ways. And Rachel was with Jesus in heaven — where she couldn't do Andi a single bit of good.

What would it matter anyway? She could stand in the Indiana University commons and tell the whole student body she was pregnant. No amount of sympathy or understanding could change the fact. Taz's baby was growing inside her. She was no longer a virgin, no longer the sweet Andi Ellison, innocent daughter of missionaries, no longer a young girl with the world ahead of her. She had given up her innocence without a fight, and now she'd be better off dead.

For the first time in her life she understood why someone might want to die. If her heart stopped right now, her parents would never know the truth. She wouldn't have to go through life with the knowledge that she'd broken her promise to God and ruined her future. She swallowed hard and leaned closer to the cool white rim. In a violent rush, another series of dry heaves shook her body and made it almost impossible to breathe.

The room slowly stopped spinning and Andi opened her eyes tentatively. She was weak and drenched in sweat, but she needed to rest, even just a little. Her body shook as she planted her feet on the floor and dragged herself up.

Halfway to her bed she caught a glimpse of Rachel, smiling at her from the framed photo that still hung on the wall near the window. Andi had always felt sorry for Rachel, saving herself for the right guy, believing in God's plans for her life only to be snuffed out in a car accident far too soon. Rachel's death convinced Andi that God was unfair at best. If anyone deserved a rich, full life it was Rachel Baugher. But now, betrayed by her body and certain that her future was ruined, Rachel seemed like the lucky one. Safe in heaven, walking with Jesus, free of the confusion and hurt of this world. Rachel had hoped for an abundant life, and God had given her that, after all.

Just not the way any of them had expected.

She fell into bed and curled up on her side. Lying there, her heart raced, her lungs refused to work correctly, and Andi could only see two options, two ways out of her current nightmare. She could kill herself. First she'd have to find a way, and then she'd have to have the guts to pull it off. Pills maybe, or she could suffocate herself somehow. Her problems would be over, but what about her parents? What about Bailey? The people who knew her would suffer the aftereffects of her suicide for years. Maybe forever.

The idea made her feel more sick than before, and from the pit of her stomach a slow anger began to churn within her. Why should she kill herself? Why put her family through that sort of heartache and pain? This wasn't their fault, and it wasn't hers either. Taz was to blame for this mess she was in. He'd known about her faith and conviction, but he'd led her down the path of destruction anyway. He could've chosen any girl, but he chose her. This nightmare was his fault.

Which led her to her other conclusion: She would put Taz out of her mind and have the baby on her own, love the baby with every day of her life from this point on. She would be the sort of mother her own mom had been to her, even if she never had a man to help her.

Andi rolled onto her back and stared at the ceiling. She would move to California, live with her parents in San Jose. Her mom would help her know what to do, how to take care of the baby without the help of a husband. When to change the baby's diapers, when a cry meant the baby was hungry or tired or sick. And when the baby was a few months old, Andi would go back to school. When she had her degree she would make a great life for the two of them. She and her baby.

As soon as she had a plan, she put her hands protectively over her stomach and felt herself drifting off, dreaming about the days ahead and the life she would choose to live, not for herself. But for her baby. Andi felt fresh tears in her eyes. She had done everything wrong when it came to love, made every wrong choice and believed every wrong thing Taz had ever told her.

But this ... this she would do right.

Six

KEITH TOOK A SHAKY BREATH AS he parked deep in the cement garage beneath Delta Talent Agency's enormous Century City building. He looked at the clock on his dashboard. Nine-twenty. Ten minutes before the biggest meeting he'd ever taken — the one where Brandon Paul and his management team would sign a preliminary deal locking the young heartthrob as star of their film, *Unlocked.* Luke Baxter, their attorney, was joining Keith here with the paperwork, and by all indications the meeting was a matter of formality. Brandon wanted to make the picture, and his team wanted to keep Brandon happy. The deal shouldn't take more than half an hour to discuss and then they could celebrate the signatures. But Keith had never been more nervous in all his life for one reason.

Something was wrong with Chase.

It was Friday in a week that had been marked by some of the biggest meetings the team of Jeremiah Productions had ever taken part in. Three meetings with various brass at American Pictures, each of them fine-tuning the process of seeing *The Last Letter* released to the big screen. A key lunch with the author of *Unlocked* and her agent, and now this crucial session with Brandon Paul. And Chase had missed them all.

His phone call had come last weekend, hours before they were scheduled to fly out. "I need to be home," Chase had said. He was adamant, and unwilling to talk about the reasons. "Look, Keith, I'm sorry. It's not something I can talk about. Tell everyone I'll explain later. I can't be on the road this week. I just can't."

Of course Keith had pressed him, asked whether Macy's flu had gotten worse or whether something was wrong with Kelly. But Chase only sighed. "We can talk when you get back. Right now I need you to do one thing for me."

"What?" Keith was desperate. He wanted to shake Chase and bring him to his senses. Whatever the crisis at home, it could wait. These meetings were what they'd worked the past year to achieve. Keith hadn't felt this confused since he and Chase had dreamed up the idea of making movies back on the mission field. "What do you want me to do?"

"Pray for me. I've got a lot to think through."

Even now that the week of meetings had come and gone, Keith couldn't understand what his friend meant by that. A lot to think through? They were at the top of their game. What could Chase possibly have to think through now? It was one thing to doubt their direction back when the funds weren't available and everything about the production of *The Last Letter* seemed to be falling apart. But now? When they had a lucrative offer from American Pictures on the table and they were this close to a serious deal with Brandon Paul? Chase should've been thrilled to hit the road this week.

Keith glanced at the clock again. It was time. He climbed out of his car and felt the suffocating stillness of the underground garage. What was it about being in one of these parking structures? He shook off the strange feeling and made his way to the elevator. Three minutes later he met up with Luke Baxter in the lobby of DTA's lucrative firm. If a person didn't know the talent agency was top in the business, they would certainly figure it out by entering the firm's front doors. Granite and crystal, marble and plush carpet marked every inch of the place.

"This is it," Luke grinned. "We can make our own press announcement when we're finished here. Once Brandon is officially linked to the project, everything else will come together." Luke sorted through his paperwork. "Everything's very clear-cut at this point. We'll work out the finer details of the contract later."

Keith nodded, trying to feel enthusiastic. What if something really was wrong with Kelly? Or maybe one of the girls was sick with something worse than the flu and Chase wasn't ready to talk about it. What choices could he possibly need to make that would take a week of prayer and thought? He stared out the window, only dimly aware of Luke and his enthusiasm.

"Hey," Luke touched his shoulder. "You all right?"

"Huh?" Keith turned to his attorney. "Sorry." He allowed an uncomfortable pause. "Thinking about Chase."

Luke's expression showed his frustration. "He should be here. The two of you are a team."

"Exactly."

"Have you heard from him, why he missed this week?"

"Nothing." Keith shrugged. "I can only figure it's something with his family. Maybe he needed a week to regroup."

"Let's hope so. This is too big a project to handle alone. Besides, Chase is your director. I'm not sure where you'd be without him."

Keith didn't want to think about it, and at the moment he didn't have to. The receptionist invited them back to the meeting room, and they sat around a stunning burl wood table that looked like a piece of artwork. Luke and Keith had only just taken their seats when Brandon breezed in followed by five members of his management team and his agent from DTA.

"Hello, gentlemen." The lead DTA guy was Jacque Ruse, a Frenchman with a high-powered charisma that made Keith feel out of his league. But Luke was up for the challenge.

He stood and shook Ruse's hand. "Luke Baxter, attorney for Jeremiah Productions."

"Pleasure." Ruse moved quickly to Keith. "And the talk of the town—Keith Ellison, I presume."

Keith's heart felt like it would give out, but he hid the fact. He stood and shook hands with the man, and then moved down the table, greeting Brandon Paul. *God, what are we doing here? Can this really be us? Having a meeting like this and preparing to make a film with a star like Brandon Paul? Help me feel able, God. Please.*

Introductions and small talk lasted another five minutes, and during that time Keith snuck a few long looks at Brandon. His eyes looked a little bloodshot, and he had the hint of crow's feet around the corners of his eyes. Not a big deal if the guy was in his forties. But Brandon was only twenty-four. The physical signs were one more reason to worry. Lately, the paparazzi had talked about Brandon becoming a party boy. Once, a month ago, Keith had called Dayne Matthews — who had been at least as famous as Brandon Paul a few years ago — and asked about the young actor.

"You can't trust everything you read in the rags," Dayne had advised. "But if they're catching photos of Brandon partying, there's probably some truth to it."

Now Keith had to wonder, and again he wished Chase were here. They didn't need Brandon Paul, really. Yes, he was a huge actor, and yes he had gone to the author of *Unlocked* practically begging to play the lead. But if Brandon brought a tainted image to the film, or if he embarrassed them, the fallout could hurt Jeremiah Productions more than it might ever help.

As the meeting got under way, Ruse talked about the supporting cast. He pulled out a sheet of notes and grinned at the people around the table. "Great news just in from our children's division. The script calls for Brandon to have a younger sister, someone who is instrumental in helping bring the character out of his prison of autism." He passed out copies of a single headshot of a pretty young girl with shining blue eyes. "This is Annalee Sullivan. She's seven years old and by all accounts one of the fastest rising child stars in the business. Her agent says if Brandon's the lead, she definitely wants the part of his sister." He pointed to a few bullet points on the child's resume. "She goes by Annie Sullivan, and she loves to sing and dance. I imagine she might even sing a partial song in the movie." He winked at Brandon. "Talk about your heart-grabbers."

"Mmhmm." Brandon was texting, his entire focus on his phone.

"Right." Ruse chuckled. No one from DTA seemed bothered by Brandon's lack of focus. He was still something of a kid himself. At least that's what his team had called him a time or two.

Keith had a sense that whatever Brandon wanted, he got. Who was going to tell him what to do when he was the biggest box office draw around? Besides, Keith didn't have to be sold on Annie Sullivan. He knew who she was. The idea that she would co-star in *Unlocked* was only one more unbelievable development. He nodded at Luke and then at Ruse. "We'd love to work with Annie. She'd make a very believable sister for Brandon."

"Definitely." Brandon looked up from his phone. "Annie's great. I'll have to bring my A-game or the kid'll leave me in the dust."

The conversation shifted to other co-stars, and with each successive role Keith had to work to contain his excitement. He and Chase had talked about what it would mean to investors and creative types to have Brandon Paul. But he hadn't imagined they'd be able to round up such a star-studded cast. The film would easily be one of the most talked about of the year.

So why isn't Chase here, God? I need him. Keith hid his concern about his friend, and Chase's name came up just once toward the end of the meeting. Ruse handed a stack of documents to Brandon, and on the star's other side one of the team presented the actor with a pen. "Time to make it official." Ruse's face was a perpetual grin. "The lawyers can hammer out the rest later."

Brandon took the papers and read through none of it. His trust of his team was complete. "Where do I sign?"

The DTA executive on his right side pointed to a number of lines and Brandon easily signed everywhere he was told. While that was happening, Ruse focused an intense look at Keith. "I understand Chase has some family matter at home?"

Keith was caught off guard, but he rebounded quickly. "Uh ... yes, he's home this week. I expect to meet with him tomorrow and get him up to speed on all this."

"Good." Ruse tapped the table a few times. He was the antithesis of laid back. "Chase is a vital part of the team. We'll want to meet with both of you next week to set production dates, line up a director of photography, nail down a director. All the important pieces."

"Definitely." Keith figured Luke must've told Ruse about Chase's family issue. The explanation was honest and it bought Keith time. He would thank Luke later. He could hardly tell Ruse that he had no idea what was going on with Chase or that he could barely get him to talk on the phone.

The meeting was over, and Brandon stood first, reaching across the table and shaking both Keith's and Luke's hands. "This film is gonna rock! I'm already Twittering about it. Got a couple million followers. They can't wait to see it!" He flashed a sideways peace sign on his way toward the conference room door. "Got another meeting down the hall. Later, guys."

His team lingered a little longer, and Ruse was the last to leave. He set up specific meeting times with Luke, hours of discussion that would bring Keith back to LA for most of the next three weeks. Whatever Chase was working through at home, Keith hoped he had the details resolved. Things were picking up speed.

There was a chance they'd film *Unlocked* in Bloomington, Indiana, of all places. The state offered great tax incentives to filmmakers, and already Keith and Chase were connected with caterers and the technical staff needed to pull off a major motion picture. Either way, they wouldn't be home for a long time at this rate. Maybe this week at home would give Chase added energy and enthusiasm so he'd be ready for the race ahead.

Keith and Luke discussed a few more legalities in the lobby before Keith headed down the elevator three floors into the parking structure. He was halfway to his car when the ground began to move. It was an earthquake, Keith was certain. He'd lived through his share of temblors and now there was no denying the telltale signs — the way the lights swung above him and the noise of creaking cement and rebar.

He grabbed hold of the nearest cement post as the swaying strengthened. Was this only the beginning? Would the layers of rock and steel begin to collapse around him, crushing him? *God, be with me.* He braced himself, knowing there was nothing he could do if the intensity increased. But instead, gradually, the shaking stopped.

At that point he realized he wasn't alone. Half a dozen other business men and women sprang into action as the building stilled. All of them including Keith hurried into their cars and exited the structure as quickly as they could. Once out on the street, Keith turned on the radio in time to hear the announcement. A five-point-six earthquake had rocked the San Andreas Fault in an area ten miles east of San Bernardino. Aftershocks were expected.

Keith felt slightly sick to his stomach as he pulled onto the 101 and headed north toward home. If the earthquake had been worse, he and the others in the garage wouldn't have stood a chance. The weight of the building would've pancaked the garage structure, burying them so far beneath cement and steel, no one would've found their bodies.

He was still thanking God for sparing him when his cell phone rang. He glanced at it and saw it was Chase. The traffic was heavy, mostly stop and go. Typical for a Friday. He answered the phone with his bluetooth and kept both hands on the wheel. "Hello?"

"Did you feel it?" Chase sounded more relaxed than he had in months.

"Definitely." A chill passed over Keith's arms. "I was in the parking structure beneath DTA. Scary, man. Seriously."

"I bet." Chase's voice fell away, and for an uncomfortable moment there was silence between them. "Hey, what time are you home?"

"Depends on the traffic. Hopefully by six."

"Hmmm. Sort of late."

Keith wanted to scream at his friend. Whatever was going on, he wanted to know. Even if it meant talking at midnight. "What's on your mind?"

"I want to get together. Tonight, if you're up for it." Again Chase sounded easygoing, as if he didn't have a care in the world.

"Of course I'm up for it. Whatever time I get home." Keith worked to keep frustration from his voice. "Can you tell me what's happening here, Chase? You're killing me."

The pause on the other end was deafening. "It's not something I can discuss on the phone, Keith. Please understand. It's taken all week to work through this."

Keith held his breath and focused on the snarled traffic ahead. "Fine. I'll call you when I'm ten minutes from home. I'll tell Lisa to expect you."

"Great." Another awkward silence. "How did the meeting go?"

"Amazing. Jacque Ruse asked about you. He expects you to be at the next round of planning sessions. We're scheduled out for the next three weeks."

"Right. Okay, we'll talk about that." In the background there was the sound of little girl laughter. "Listen Keith, I gotta run. Call me."

The phone call ended and Keith ripped the bluetooth headset from his ear. He tossed it on the seat beside him and clenched his jaw. What was Chase doing? And why so cryptic about his past week? Keith gripped the wheel with an intensity that defined the moment, and then he slowly eased off. What was happening to their team? On the surface everything looked beyond amazing, like God was answering their prayers in ways they never could've imagined. But beneath the surface there were fault lines that rivaled the San Andreas.

Brandon Paul was certainly one of those. The kid was a huge box office draw, yes, but what about the red eyes and crow's feet? If he was partying, then anything could happen. They could sink millions into *Unlocked* only to have him turn up in the tabloids caught red-handed in a drug bust. Or overdosed on the streets of Hollywood like a number of other stars who'd gotten trapped by partying and wild living. He could get some girl pregnant or find himself in any number of uncompromising situations — all of which could bring the movie to its knees and impact Jeremiah Productions for all time.

Then there was the situation with Chase — whatever it was. Keith wanted to believe tonight's conversation would be nothing more than common courtesy, Chase's way of telling Keith how badly he'd needed time with his family. Now that his head was clear he was ready to move forward, fully committed. But he had the strange, sinking feeling Chase was coming over tonight not to apologize for a missed week of work, but to call it quits.

Now, in the middle of everything great and wonderful.

Keith could hardly stand the drive home, through hours of life-sucking LA traffic and long stretches of the 5 freeway toward San Jose. Even so, he made better time than he expected. It was only four thirty when he entered the city limits and called Chase. Again his friend sounded calm and deliberate, and again Keith was convinced something was very, very wrong. Never mind that they were on the brink of everything they'd ever dreamed, and forget the fact that God seemed to be opening doors faster than they could walk through them. As he pulled into his driveway, Keith had the feeling he was standing in the underground parking structure once again, the walls and ceiling beams shaking overhead.

Everything about his life as a producer about to collapse in around him.

Seven

CODY WAS FINISHED WITH HIS LAST final and hoping for a few hours with his mother. This new boyfriend she'd been seeing had Cody worried more than any time since her release from prison. Once an addict, there was always the temptation to fall again, and if this guy dabbled in any sort of drugs, his mother could lose everything because of him.

He drove across town and pulled up in front of her small house. A few weeks ago he'd convinced his mother to give him a key—though she'd been reluctant at first. "I'm fine, Cody. You don't need to check up on me."

His concerns about her relapsing couldn't be the reason for his wanting a way into her house, otherwise she would never agree to it. Instead he came at it from another angle. "You live alone. What if you fell and broke your leg and couldn't get up? Anyone who lives alone should have someone looking out for them. Whatever age they are."

His mother's expression had softened. "You really care, don't you?"

"Yes, Mom. You know I do." Since then Cody had kept her house key with him in anticipation of moments like this. He walked up her uneven sidewalk and knocked on the door. While he waited, he noticed that her front yard was littered with weeds, the edges uneven and the flowerbeds forgotten and untended. His mother waited tables at a diner near the campus. She probably had no time for gardening. He chided himself for not helping her with the work sooner.

"Mom," he knocked again, louder this time. When no one answered, he used the key. The house smelled the same—lavender with a hint of Marlboro. Cody suspected she still snuck a smoke now and then. The first thing he saw was an ashtray on the kitchen counter. Frustration shot through him, but he tried to temper it. Better cigarettes than pot. As long as she stayed sober. He raised his voice. "Mom?"

She worked the morning shift and normally she'd be home by four o'clock, watching *General Hospital*, which she recorded every day. She loved the new chief of staff on the show—a Christian guy who'd starred in soaps for years. The show was a good distraction for her. At least until she met her latest guy friend. Now, when she should've been home watching her soap, the house was empty. He thought about leaving, but curiosity got the better of him. She wouldn't want him snooping around, but how else could he be sure she was doing okay? He knew nothing about this new boyfriend of hers. And who else besides him would care if she were falling off the wagon?

He tiptoed into the kitchen and the sound of a cat's meow caught him off guard, made him lurch a little. "Shadow ... where's Mom?"

The black cat slinked around the corner and rubbed against Cody's left ankle. He couldn't feel it, since that was his prosthetic lower leg. Strange, he thought. How little he even thought about the fact that his left leg wasn't like his right one. He moved into the kitchen and peered into the fridge. No sign of alcohol or anything amiss. Still he had a strange feeling, like she was hiding something. Not telling him everything the way she had since her release.

He opened the cupboard beneath her kitchen sink and pulled out her white plastic trash bin. The top layer was rumpled paper towels and an empty cat food can. Cody almost pushed it back beneath the sink and assured himself everything was fine. He was only victim to his overactive imagination. But instead he dug past the paper towels and dirty can, and there near the bottom he saw something that made his heart stop cold.

Buried there were two Miller Lite bottles and a few half-pieces of plastic straws. His heart jolted back into action, pounding in double time. What was this? His mother was drinking again? She couldn't be drinking. She was an alcoholic, just like him. Every other time in her past when she started drinking, drugs weren't far off. And when she started doing drugs, she had no way of stopping.

He remembered something she'd told him when she got out of prison last time. "Don't ever let me start again, Cody. Please."

"I won't. Not ever."

"It'll kill me next time. If I start again they'll either take me out in a hearse or a squad car, and this time I won't be coming home."

She was right. Drugs had gotten her in trouble with the law too many times. She had a record as long as his arm, because whenever she used drugs she also dealt. Her way of supporting her habit. If she got caught dealing again they would lock her up and throw away the key for a decade. Fifteen years, maybe. It was that bad.

He could hear her now, if she walked in and saw him digging through her trash. *Come on, Cody, what's a couple beers? A girl needs to relax, right?*

But not when the girl was an addict. The Miller Lite bottles were a terrible sign, proof that she was indeed falling — maybe harder than it seemed. Shadow rubbed against his leg again and meowed loudly. Cody felt adrenaline rush through his veins as he peered at the other suspicious items sitting next to the beer bottles. The half-cut straws. He'd seen his mom when she was using, and the straws terrified him. Sure, some people cut straws in half and used them for coffee stirrers. But not his mother. The only time she'd ever used straws like that was when she was doing cocaine. The shorter straws worked as the preferred way to snort the cocaine. Less waste along the inside of the straw.

He straightened and braced himself against the kitchen counter. *Dear God, please, no. Don't let this be happening. Let there be some other explanation. Please.* He replaced the top layer of trash and had just situated the bin back beneath the sink when he heard his mother's laugh and the sound of the door opening. He took a few quick steps from the sink and swept Shadow into his arms.

His mother wasn't alone. The guy with her must've been the man she was seeing. He looked as shocked as Cody's mother to see him standing there in the kitchen. Cody smiled, desperate to cover up the guilt he felt for checking up on her. "Hi! Thought I'd stop in and see how your day was going."

The laughter on his mother's lips faded and she slowly set her purse down on a chair in the living room, her eyes never leaving his. "You came in — when I wasn't home?"

"This here's your mother's property, boy." The man looked like a biker. Sleeveless T-shirt, tattoos everywhere, a bushy dark beard. He glared at Cody as if he were an eight-year-old caught stealing quarters from his mother's coin box. "How long you been here?"

Cody wanted to tell the guy it was none of his business. But he didn't want the scene to turn ugly. Instead he focused his attention on his mother. "I thought you'd be home. I was worried about you."

"I didn't work today." She reached for the man's arm. "Benny and I spent the day at the lake." She smiled at him. "Fishing, right, Tiger?"

"All morning." The man winked at her.

Tiger? Cody resisted the impulse to ask his mother if she'd lost her mind. The last thing she needed was a guy like this character. For a long moment, the three of them stood staring at each other in what felt like a face-off. Finally Cody set the cat down and cleared his throat. "Mom, I'd like to talk to you." He shot a look at Benny. "Alone, if that's okay."

His mother looked nervous; there was no denying the fact. She uttered an anxious-sounding laugh and patted "Tiger" on his soft, oversized shoulder tattoo. "Go on into the TV room. I'll be right back."

Benny glared at Cody, but he did as he was told. Cody watched until the man was out of sight; then he grabbed his keys and walked out onto the front porch. His mother followed, and Cody was quick to shut the door behind her.

"Who's *he*?" Cody's tone hid none of his anger and concern. "Looks like you picked him up at some bar."

"He's a Harley guy." She sounded defensive, but her eyes still looked nervous. She kept glancing back toward the house. "Don't judge people by the way they look, Cody. You're a Christian. You should know better."

"I went through your trash." Cody had no reason to lie to her now. If she was falling, she should know he was on to her. "You're drinking beer, Mom? Is that the kind of influence he has on you?"

"Cody Coleman," she put her hands on her hips. "How dare you go through my things. I didn't give you a key so you could spy on me."

"I didn't plan on it. But you weren't home, so I came in. Figured I love you enough ... I had the right to look."

"You're worried about nothing." She blinked a few times, faster than usual, and her mouth sounded dry. "The beers were Benny's. I'm clean."

He wanted to ask about the straws, but he knew she'd have an answer. Also, if she were doing cocaine again he'd know soon enough. He'd rather come around unannounced over the next few weeks and try to catch her in the act. That way she'd have to agree to get help. "Mom, what's this guy got? I thought you were gonna find a church. Get into a Bible study."

"I tried that." Again she glanced back at the house. "Church people are ... I don't know, Cody. So different. Benny understands me."

"What about your new life?" He hated this, having to grill her about her personal decisions, but his heart hurt at the thought of her throwing away her sobriety. "How does Benny fit into that?"

"I'm not sure." She stared at her feet and began wringing her hands. "I have to go. Benny'll wonder what's happening."

"Benny should be working."

"He has a job." She lifted her chin, indignant. "He's a mechanic." She took a step back toward the door. "Things are a little slow right now, that's all. Gives us more time together."

Cody studied her for several seconds. "Okay. If that's what you want to believe." He hugged her. This close he was almost certain he could smell alcohol on her skin. It repulsed him, the way alcohol always did ever since the time he nearly died drinking, back when he was in high school. Again he saw no point in saying something about it to her. If she was drinking again, clearly she wasn't going to tell Cody. He drew back and searched her eyes. "I love you, Mom. I want you to make it this time." He was caught off guard by a wave of emotion too strong to fight. "I just ..." His voice cracked and he looked off at the place where the maple trees met with the blue sky overhead. He found her eyes again. "I want it so bad."

She put her hands on his shoulders and gave them a strong squeeze. "I want it too, son. I'm okay. Really." She glanced back once more. "I'd tell you."

He nodded, knowing she was only saying the words because they were what both of them wanted to believe. But as he walked away, as he reached his car where he'd parked down the street and drove off, tears blurred his vision. A block away from his mom's house, he pulled over and pressed his fists to his eyes. She wasn't okay; he could feel it. Benny was trouble, and his mom wouldn't tell him if she was struggling or falling. Not until she admitted it through the bars of a prison or a room in the ICU.

God, please show me how to help her. Get this guy out of her life, and let her desire be for You. Only with You will she beat this addiction, God. I know that, because ... because I'm the same way. I love her, God. I don't want to lose her. She's all I have.

You have me, son. Never forget that. Do not be afraid, for you are not alone. Not ever.

The voice echoed across his soul, and Cody wiped his eyes, regaining control. He heard the voice of God in his heart once in a while. But never this clearly. A verse flashed through his mind, one they'd focused on at the Cru retreat last weekend. *Be strong and courageous. Do not be terrified; do not be discouraged, for the Lord your God will be with you wherever you go.* It was from Joshua 1:8-9, and Cody felt it ring true alone in his car. His mother wasn't all he had. He had the Lord, certainly. And God had given him a second family long ago when he'd needed one most.

The Flanigan family.

Bailey might have a boyfriend, but that didn't mean he was any less welcome at the Flanigan home. He clenched his teeth, wrestling with his emotions. He hadn't been by in far too long. His classes had been tougher than usual, and now that finals were over, and in light of his concerns for his mother, he suddenly wanted to be with the Flanigans as badly as he wanted his next breath.

He flipped a U-turn, and ten minutes later he was pulling up the long driveway that marked the Flanigans' enormous house. Any time of the year the place was beautiful—beige with substantial white trim and a heavily defined black roof, wrapped halfway around with a covered porch that looked like something out of a storybook. He pulled his car up in the circle and stared at the front entrance. How many times had he walked through that door without giving his life here a second thought? As if he might be a part of this family forever.

Now he was grateful any time he found his way back. He still thought of Bailey's brothers like his own, and her father—her father was one of the most special people in Cody's whole life. No one would ever be a dad to him like Jim Flanigan. The man still coached the Indianapolis Colts, and they were in the middle of summer camp. But once in a while he was home on Friday for the weekend. That's what Bailey had told him.

He climbed out of his car and hoped this was one of those times.

Eight

BAILEY FLANIGAN PUSHED THE SHOPPING CART next to her mother through their local supermarket. They were out of practically everything, so they each pushed a cart. Her mom was slightly distracted, trying to remember what they needed. Even still she was able to catch up on Bailey's life the way they so easily did when they were together.

"Have you heard from Andi?"

"Not much." Bailey frowned as she reached for the produce display. "Four packs of blueberries?"

"Make it six. The boys go through them faster in the summer."

Bailey grabbed six and tossed them into her cart. "It's like she's avoiding me."

"The whole Taz thing?"

"Right. I mean, Mom, you know how hard I tried. The guy was so bad for her. Now he's broken her heart and she's more closed off than ever."

"Maybe she should move in with us. Skip the whole dorm scene."

"I'd love that." Bailey had thought about the possibility before. Andi had not turned out to be the friend she had hoped for, but here at her parents' house they might still become close.

They moved down the frozen food aisle to the produce section. "You think she'd be open to it?"

"Not really." Bailey wanted to be honest with her mom and herself. "She won't talk to me. I have no reason to think she'd want to live with us."

"That's too bad."

"It is. She needs a friend now, especially since she and Taz are broken up." Bailey grabbed three bunches of bananas and put them next to the blueberries. "Sometimes I wonder what she's thinking, why she's so distant."

"Guilt, maybe."

"Maybe."

"That's sad."

"It is. I can't find a way to get through to her."

Bailey's mom filled a plastic bag with vine-ripened tomatoes and another one with cilantro. Every summer she cut up fresh pico de gallo and kept it in a container in the fridge. They ate it on everything from fish to turkey sandwiches. "Tell me about your finals."

"I did okay." Bailey wrinkled her nose. "I'm a little worried about my statistics class. The questions she gave us weren't on the study sheet." They talked about the grades Bailey expected from the semester and the courses she would take in the fall. They were almost to the checkstand when her mom gave her a knowing look. "So … how's Tim?"

Bailey sighed, and she realized she was always doing that. Sighing when someone mentioned Tim. That had to be a problem, right? "I keep asking myself why I stay with him. I mean, he's nice and we have a lot of the same interests."

"He comes from a good family."

"Yes." Bailey pushed her cart more slowly. "But so do a lot of guys. That doesn't mean I should date them."

Her mom hesitated, her eyes more on Bailey than what was in front of her. She almost sideswiped a cart being pushed by a little gray-haired old lady. "Sorry." Jenny covered her mouth, embarrassed. Then she and Bailey swapped a quiet laugh. "I have to watch where I'm going."

"We both do."

This time her mom kept her eyes straight ahead. "Why, then, Bailey? Why date him?"

Bailey had thought about the question every night for what felt like months. "I guess because I spent so long crushing on him back when we were in CKT." Her heart sank a little as they reached the check stand. "He's easy to be with, likeable. He shares my faith. That, and because he's the only guy in my life. No one else is interested."

Jenny began unloading her cart, but she raised one eyebrow and flashed Bailey a kind look. "That isn't true."

"It is." She let the disappointment sound in her voice. She had no walls where her mother was concerned. The older she got, the more her mom was her best friend. "If Cody liked me, he'd say so. He's waiting for his dream girl. He told me so."

Jenny nodded slowly and didn't say more on the topic. They finished unloading the carts, and Bailey allowed herself to get lost in thought just a little. This was the sort of night when she would've loved nothing more than to ask Cody over to her parents' house. They were planning to watch a football movie — *Remember the Titans*. And before that, her mom was going to make the famous Baxter Enchilada Casserole — the recipe she got from Ashley Baxter Blake years ago. They'd probably even play a round of Pictionary before the night was over. Cody would love a night like that. Tim was still recovering from being sick, but even so, she couldn't call Cody and ask him over. So she did the only thing she could do.

She prayed that wherever Cody was, he'd know how much she cared. And that someday — if he really had feelings for her the way her mother believed — he would make his intentions clear.

Until then, nothing would ever change between them.

R<small>ICKY MET</small> C<small>ODY AT THE</small> F<small>LANIGAN</small> front door, a football in his hands. "Cody!"

"Wow, look at you." Cody jogged up the front steps and hugged the youngest Flanigan boy. "You must've grown a foot!"

Ricky beamed. "I think I did."

"You must be almost as tall as your brothers."

"Taller than Shawn and almost as tall as Justin." He stuck his chest out. "Dad thinks I'm gonna be six-five."

Cody stifled a quiet laugh. "Could be, buddy. You're the biggest twelve-year-old I've ever seen. That's for sure."

"Yeah, and guess what? I'm playing quarterback next year for the seventh grade team. Isn't that great?"

"Wow. That's great, Ricky. You'll be amazing."

Ricky led the way back into the house. "You have to come see my games."

They walked down an open hallway toward the kitchen. Every time he was back, Cody wished he never would've left. But joining the service was the best thing for him—no matter the personal cost. The army was paying for his college education, and he had done his part to defend his country. He didn't regret that for a single moment.

The kitchen was empty, but through a wall of windows Cody spotted Jim out back, an acre from the house tossing a football with Justin, Shawn, BJ, and Connor. All the Flanigan boys played football—though Connor, at seventeen, would rather spend an evening writing music at the family piano than watching a Monday Night game on ESPN.

"Come play with us," Ricky grinned as he tossed the ball to Cody. "Now we can go three-on-three!"

That's what he loved about the Flanigan boys. It didn't matter if he'd been gone for weeks or months. They treated him like family, like his presence here was as natural as if he'd never left. He wanted to ask Ricky how his heart was doing, and whether he'd had any more rhythm issues. But it didn't seem like the time. Plus, if he was planning on playing football next year for his middle school, he must be doing well. Cody was glad. He worried about the youngest Flanigan boy.

"Come on!" Ricky tried again as he was halfway out the back door. He cupped his hands around his mouth. "Cody's here," he shouted. "Game time!"

Cody looked around, listening for anyone else in the house. Bailey had moved home before summer classes started. He wondered if she was home now, but he didn't hear her. He hadn't come to play football, but now the idea sounded great. He still worked out every day, pushing himself on his prosthetic lower left leg so that now he could run and swim and bike better than before his war injury. Today he wore jeans and tennis shoes. As he jogged out to join Jim and the Flanigan boys, Cody was pleased that he didn't have even the slightest limp.

"Cody!" Jim held his hand high, his face taken up by a smile as genuine as the Bloomington sky. "Great to see you!"

"You're gonna play, right?" BJ ran up to him first, breathless. "We've needed a sixth guy all afternoon."

Cody laughed. "I'm in."

The game was wildly competitive for a backyard contest, but then that was always how the Flanigan kids played. Like the Super Bowl was on the line with every play. Ricky was the worst—calling fouls and arguing over yardage gained and whether a first down really was a first down. In the end, Cody won with a team of Justin and Connor. Ricky hung his head as they walked back to the house, but only for a minute. "I was terrible today."

"Hey," Jim roughed up his son's blond hair and gave him a somewhat stern look. "None of that. Someone has to lose. You all played well."

Ricky looked like he might disagree, but then he stopped short with a reluctant smile. "Okay."

They were almost to the house, when Jim stopped short. He put his hands on his waist, still catching his breath. "You boys go in and see if your mom and Bailey are home. See if they need help bringing in the groceries or getting dinner ready."

Not one of the kids argued. Instead they walked off as a group, already letting the intensity of the competition go. Justin slung his arm around Ricky's back. "You looked great today. We got lucky, that's all."

"A win's a win." They grinned at each other and a minute later they were all inside.

Cody watched, amazed. This family was exactly how he wanted his family to be one day. The kids truly were friends. Cody grabbed a full breath and exhaled slowly. The sun was in his eyes as he squinted at Jim. "How long did it take for them to get that close? After you adopted, I mean?"

"Adopting was a family decision." Jim held the football. He tossed it in the air and easily caught it, his eyes never leaving Cody's. "We all promised not to feel sorry for our new boys from Haiti. That way they would have the same love, the same expectations as our biological kids." He shrugged. "That and a lot of prayer. I can't remember a time when these kids weren't all as close as they are right now."

"I guess I never asked much about it when I lived here." Cody shaded his eyes. "Too caught up in myself."

"You had a lot going on."

Cody hadn't planned on having time alone with Jim, but now that they were here together, it only made sense to share what was on his mind. His breathing was back to normal, his body cooled off from the game. "You have a minute? To talk, I mean?"

"Sure." Jim didn't hesitate. Here was one of the most powerful pro football coaches in the country with a whole houseful of kids on one of his only days off. But there wasn't even a hesitation about whether he had time for Cody. That was Jim Flanigan. He threw a short spiral pass and the football landed near the back door. Then he nodded to Cody to follow him. "Let's walk. I want to see how the path through the woods is doing. Sometimes it gets overgrown during the spring."

Cody fell in beside him. "I've been thinking a lot about my future, what I want to do with my life."

"I'm glad." Jim grinned at him. "That's half the battle, putting a little thought into it. So many kids never even do that." Jim kept the pace slow, his focus entirely on Cody. In the distance a woodpecker's tap-tap-tap echoed through the woods, but otherwise there wasn't a sound. Not even a breeze to rustle the new summer leaves. "So ... what have you come up with?"

He narrowed his eyes, looking at the blue beyond the tree branches. "I keep remembering something you told me a long time ago when I still lived here. You said life isn't a dress rehearsal, and it's important to find joy in the short time you have."

"Yes." Jim nodded slowly. "I tell that to all my kids."

"You said joy comes first from knowing the Lord, from having a personal relationship with Jesus."

"Definitely."

The path ahead looked like it needed work, but there was room to pass. "Second, you said joy comes from your family. So it's more important who you marry than what you do for a living."

"True." His smile was easy. "Jobs come and go."

"Right." Cody could remember the conversation like it had just happened. Jim Flanigan had given him more direction in life than anyone he knew. "And you said joy came from having as little debt as possible. Living within your means."

"Very important."

"Finally, you told me that a joyful life was one where you loved your line of work."

"Absolutely." Jim breathed in deep and took in the beauty around them. "You'll never be sorry if you spend a lifetime doing what you love. No matter how much money you make."

"Exactly." Cody loved this, talking to Jim. "I've thought about being an EMT, and I've thought about going to law school. Being a big-shot prosecutor. Like the guys on TV." He chuckled, and Jim did the same. "Drive a nice car, live in a nice house. That sort of thing."

Jim tilted his head and raised his brow, his laughter giving way to a warning. "Stuff can be a trap. Jenny married me believing I'd be a penniless high school teacher. Both of us were okay with that."

"Right, which is what I've been thinking lately." He stopped and faced Jim. "I think I want to coach football. Make a living at it." He felt vulnerable sharing his feelings, not sure if Jim would think him crazy for even thinking he could coach. But before he could explain himself more fully, Jim was nodding in agreement.

"I've watched you around the game, around our kids. I think you'd be a natural, Cody. If you want to coach, then coach. Volunteer for Clear Creek High. If you hate it, move on to something else. But if you never try, you could miss a lifetime of doing something you might truly enjoy."

"Really?" With every word Jim uttered, Cody felt his heart soar. "Even for this coming season?"

"Of course. You're young. Younger than I was when I started coaching. There's no better time to try it than now. It could change your life."

Cody felt a thrill rush through him. Was it possible? Could he be coaching at Clear Creek as soon as fall? He stood a little straighter and suddenly he felt more excited about his future than he had all year. They walked a little further and Jim shifted the conversation. "How's your faith, Cody? You staying close to Jesus?"

"Definitely." He told Jim about the Cru retreat, how he'd enjoyed focused time to read his Bible and pray about God's direction for his life. "That's partly why I wanted to talk to you. The

Lord made it clear at the retreat that I needed to try coaching. It's something inside me."

"That's how it felt for me too." Jim grinned and patted Cody on the back. "I'm glad you stopped by." They turned around and headed back to the house. "Bailey was on the retreat."

"Yes." Cody never liked talking about Bailey with her family. He wasn't sure how they felt about Tim Reed, but he was her boyfriend. All of them knew that. "She and I talked. It was nice. Being together like that."

Jim slowed his pace, his attention more fully on Cody. "She cares a great deal for you." He looked like he might say something more, but he stopped himself. "Probably more than you know."

"I … I like hearing that." Cody wanted to say more too. He wanted to ask if Bailey cared so much, then why was she dating Tim. But that wasn't a conversation he could have with her father. And the last thing Cody wanted was any awkwardness between them. Instead he shifted the conversation again. "Pray for my mom, will you? She's acting funny. I'm worried about her."

Concern clouded Jim's eyes. "She's still clean?"

"I'm not sure. The guy she's dating, the way she seems nervous all the time. I think she's about to fall." He studied the ground for a few seconds. "There's nothing I can do to stop her, but I'd like to try."

Jim nodded, understanding. "I'll tell Jenny. We'll pray." He put his arm around Cody's shoulders. "Let us know if there's anything we can do."

"I will." Cody felt his emotions gather in his throat, a combination of the way Jim treated him like a son, and the certainty that his mother was about to suffer yet another crisis. He was so grateful for the Flanigans, for this time with Jim. As they reached the house, Cody hugged Jim hard. "Thanks. For letting me talk."

"Stay for dinner." Jim gathered the football and reached for the back door handle. "I'll call Ryan Taylor. See if he could use another assistant through summer league."

Cody could hardly believe it. "You don't have to do that."

"I want to. You're here all summer, right?" His smile was kind, compassionate.

"I am."

"Okay, then. You might as well be on a football field."

Cody grinned, again grateful. He hadn't imagined Jim would make a phone call this quickly. Ryan Taylor had been the assistant at Clear Creek High when Cody played there, back when Jim was the head coach. It was a position he'd taken after his first retirement from the NFL. But when the Colts hired Jim, Ryan took over at the high school. Cody followed Jim into the house.

The scene was happy chaos inside — typical Flanigan stuff. Bailey and Jenny were unloading grocery bags while a tag team of Flanigan boys carried in one armload after another. Jenny spotted him first. "Cody! The boys said you were here!" She blew at a wisp of hair in her eyes. "You'd think we were stocking up for a month."

Bailey exchanged a look with him then. She mouthed a quiet hi, her eyes sparkling in the sunlight streaming through the window. "The checker always gives us a funny look." She pulled five oversized packs of eggs from a single bag. "'You must run a day-care,' they say, or sometimes it's, 'What in the world are you doing with all these eggs!'" Bailey giggled and put her hand on her mother's shoulder. "What did we figure it was each week?"

"A hundred and eight eggs every seven days." Jenny laughed. "Unless we have extra kids on the weekend. Then it's more."

"It was more when I lived here." Cody moved into the kitchen and started unloading one of the bags lined across the counter. They worked together, while Jenny whipped up the great-smelling enchilada casserole and popped it into the oven. When the groceries were unloaded and the mess from two dozen plastic bags was cleaned up, when toilet paper had been taken to each of the Flanigans' nine bathrooms, and cleaning supplies had been distributed to the same, Cody motioned for Bailey to follow him into the piano room.

She did, and he was quick with his question. "I should've asked." He studied her, looking for signs that she might be upset he was here. "Is Tim coming by tonight? I mean ... it's Friday."

"No. He's going to bed early." Her eyes had a way of seeing to the very core of his being. "Still recovering."

"Oh." Cody nodded, hiding how happy that made him. "So ... I can hang out?"

"Of course." She hugged him quickly, impulsively. "I love when you're here. It's like ... I don't know." She drew back, searching his eyes. "Like old times."

He wanted to say that he felt the same way, that this was where he felt most at home and that she was the only girl he'd want to spend Friday night with as long as he lived. But he didn't say so then or while they were sharing stories around the dinner table or later when they played Pictionary. As usual, Bailey kept them laughing through the game.

The word was *cadaver* and Bailey was drawing for Cody and Ricky. She started with something that looked like a boot, then she carefully added the detail of a spiky thing near the ankle.

"What's that?" Ricky snapped his fingers, frustrated that he couldn't think of the word. He was as competitive around the game table as he was playing football.

Across from them, Bailey's brothers and her parents were snickering. None of them were drawing, so they all watched Bailey's attempt at the illustration. Cody knew where Ricky was headed with his guess so he quickly shouted out what had to be the answer. "Spur, cowboy spurs."

Bailey shook her head, but she motioned that they were close. This time she drew a very pointed arrow aimed directly at the spur-like thing. Her efforts lasted another ten seconds before time was up. She groaned out loud and threw her hands in the air. "I drew it perfectly."

The laughter from across the table was getting louder. Everyone but Bailey's team had already seen the card.

Bailey gave them a silly look as if she were offended, then she held up the picture so Cody and Ricky could see it better. She pointed to the object attached to the ankle of the boot. "It's right there. Cadaver. Clear as day."

Cody looked at Jim and Jenny, both of whom shrugged. At the same time Justin and BJ fell onto the floor laughing. "Seriously?" Cody shifted his attention to Bailey. "The word's cadaver?"

"Wow." Ricky smacked himself on the forehead. "Even I know what a cadaver is." He was half laughing, half frustrated. "Really, Dad? Can't she be on *your* team?"

"What?" Bailey studied her drawing. "That's not a cadaver?"

Jenny was the first one to have sympathy on her. "A cadaver's a dead body, honey. Not something you attach to your boot."

"Unless," Cody laughed out loud, "unless you're in the wild west, dragging a dead body out of town on your boot."

Bailey frowned at the photo. "A dead body? Seriously?"

"Cadaver!" Ricky had given up getting any points for the round. He patted his sister on the back as if he felt sorry for her. "Don't you ever see those police shows? They're always talking about some cadaver or another. No one ever says anything about boots."

Even Bailey laughed this time, and the night continued with all three teams close until the very end, when Jenny, BJ, and Connor won. "Just because Connor's the best drawer in the family." Ricky shrugged, careful not to get down because of the loss. "At least we get to watch the best movie ever."

They did that, too, celebrating with the Titans and wiping tears at the end when one of the star players was killed in a car accident. It was a night unlike any Cody had experienced for far too long. He wanted to say he'd be back every Friday, but that wasn't possible. Instead he savored the memories they'd made that night since he couldn't know when he'd have another chance like this one.

Before he left, Jim found him at the kitchen sink getting water. "I talked to Ryan before the movie. He said he'd love to have you. They'll be out on the field at three o'clock Monday if you can make it."

Cody remembered just a blink ago when he was one of the players suiting up for summer practices, dreaming of the fall ahead. Now he'd be dreaming up plays and play-breakers. He couldn't wipe the grin from his face if he wanted to. "He doesn't mind?"

"He's glad. He said he could use a quarterback coach." Jim patted Cody on the shoulder. "You were one of the best at Clear Creek High."

The compliment was the perfect ending to a perfect night. They talked a few more minutes about Ryan's coaching style and how Cody would be wise to watch a lot at first. When they were finished, Bailey walked him to the front door. He nudged his elbow against hers as they walked down the hallway. "Glad you're not going into forensics."

"Maybe I should." She cast teasing eyes at him. "At least now I know what to call a dead body."

"And what not to call a set of spurs."

"Right." She laughed out loud. "That too."

They reached the door, and Cody had to fight an overwhelming urge to kiss her. Was this what it would be like dating her? Being part of the Flanigan family night after night? He couldn't imagine anything better. But as soon as the thought crossed his mind, it was tempered by the greater reality. Bailey had made her choice—at least for now. And he wasn't that guy.

"I had fun tonight." He slipped his hands in his back pockets and took a step closer to the door.

"Me too." Bailey came closer. "You should come over more often."

He wanted to ask her about Tim. What would her boyfriend think of Cody hanging out with her family on a Friday night? But it was pointless. Nothing about Bailey and Tim made sense, so asking her about him would only confuse him more. Instead he smiled. "We'll see." He tried to back away without hugging her. The nearness of her was more than he could take—especially after being with her all night.

But she closed the distance and put her arms around his neck. Her hug lasted longer than any she'd given him since they'd found their friendship again. "Come back, Cody," she whispered near his ear. "I need you. We all do." She eased away, but only far enough so she could look into his eyes.

With her this close, he could feel her kiss on his lips, imagine what it would be like with her in his embrace. But before he lost all control, he gritted his teeth and slipped free of her grasp. "I'll try." He worked to keep his expression even. "I need you guys too." He stepped out onto the porch and gave her a single last wave. "See ya, Bailey."

She didn't answer him, not until he reached his car. As he opened the door, he heard her say, "You don't get it, do you?"

He stopped and turned toward her. "What?"

"Nothing." She crossed her arms in front of her and moved back into her house. "Bye, Cody."

He waved again, climbed into his car, and drove slowly down the driveway. What a great night. His game with the boys, and his great talk with Jim. The fact that Ryan Taylor wanted him on the field Monday afternoon. Laughing with Bailey. The apartment he shared with his three roommates would feel lonely indeed after so many hours with the Flanigans. The night was perfect. He pictured Tim Reed waiting at home for Bailey.

Okay, almost perfect.

The closer he got to home, the less he thought about the night and the more he thought about Bailey's last words. What could she possibly have meant? *You don't get it?* She was wrong if that's what she'd really said. Of course he got it. No matter how wonderful their time together, or how well he fit with her family, Bailey had a boyfriend. Period.

What else was there to understand?

Nine

CHASE STEADIED HIS NERVES AS HE drove the few miles from his house to the Ellisons'. He was dreading the next few hours and excited about them all the same. He'd never felt more right about anything in his life.

Once he got home after the premiere, once he walked through the door, the strangest thing happened. Kelly and the girls were in the backyard, so they didn't hear him come in. He set down his bags and walked to the back of the house. He stood at the kitchen sink and watched them through an open window, listened to their happy laughter, really studied them.

Kelly was taking turns pushing Molly and Macy on the swings, and all three of them giggled and talked as they played together. As Molly's swing slowed down, she reached back and took hold of Kelly's hand. "You're the best mommy in the whole world."

"And you're the best little Molly." Kelly kissed the top of their daughter's head.

"That means I'm the best Macy, right Mommy?" Their blonde little one leaned back, grinning at Kelly. She still looked pale, but clearly she was feeling better. "Right?"

"Of course." She kissed Macy's head next. "You're both the best daughters ever."

"And don't forget about Daddy." Molly looked from her mother to her sister. "He's the best daddy too."

Chase strained closer, wanting to hear every word.

"Yes." Kelly set one hand on each girl's shoulder. "Daddy loves you very much."

That's when it happened. Macy said something she might not have meant, but something Chase was convinced he was supposed to hear. Her smile fell away and she looked truly sad. Scared even. "Sometimes ... I forget what Daddy looks like."

The comment almost dropped Chase to his knees. His four-year-old daughter sometimes forgot what he looked like? Was that what making movies was doing to his family? He stood breathless, watching the scene play out.

"Honey," Kelly was quick to his defense. "You know what Daddy looks like. He's home almost every weekend."

"But he's busy when he's home." Molly's expression fell too. She reached out and took hold of her sister's hand. "On the 'puter." She looked at Macy. "Sometimes I forget his voice."

Chase felt a piercing shock, and sudden tears gathered in the corner of his eyes. Molly too? She was six this year. If she couldn't remember how he sounded, then he was doing something wrong. There was instantly no doubt in his mind. Kelly told the girls they could video chat with their daddy more often. "Then you won't forget so easily."

Chase had heard enough.

Standing there in the kitchen the answer was suddenly so loud it might as well have been blared through a loudspeaker right in his face. Pastor Hastings and his team had believed Chase to be at the top of a list of candidates to replace the youth pastor. Not because the team was unaware of his work in Hollywood. To the contrary. Because they were very well aware of his work, and the way it had taken him away from home week after week after week. Perhaps the email wasn't something to be dismissed as a crazy idea, but rather God throwing him a life rope.

Before his little girls didn't know him anymore.

Chase wiped at his eyes and moved to the back patio door. His heart was heavy, but a bright ray of light shone through the shadows that had gathered there. He opened the door just as his girls turned to see him.

"Daddy!" They cried out his name at the same time, flying off the swings and into his arms. Kelly walked up more slowly, her eyes warm and full of love. She wasn't angry with him or disappointed. She would defend his work in Hollywood even when their daughters were painfully honest about the cost.

But in that moment he knew something as clearly as he knew his name. His days of leaving his family were over. Someone else could help Keith change the world through the power of film. His mission field was here with his wife and daughters. As a youth pastor, he would be around them all the time. Kelly could teach Sunday school, maybe help out at the church office in future years when the girls were at school.

Most of all they could be a family again—something he hadn't realized he'd given up until now. That night in their bedroom he told Kelly what he'd seen when he came home, what he'd heard. And what he planned to do. "I'm not going back to Hollywood next week," he told her. "I want to be home, Kelly. I've been praying for an answer about how to handle the time away and God gave me one. It couldn't be any clearer."

She shook her head, not believing his words at first. Then a hesitant smile grew until it filled her face. "I never … never would've asked you to give this up," she told him. "But I've been praying too. I want you home so badly, Chase. Someone will make those movies. God will find the right person." She hugged him for a long time. "I remember when we first got married, how you wanted to teach kids about God."

"I figured the mission field was God's answer to that desire." He kissed her, a kiss that shared the promise of all that suddenly lay before them. "Until now." He would've thought he'd have more angst about the situation. That he'd feel at least a little torn. Instead he felt nothing but peace. He stroked Kelly's hair and he thought about what his daughters had said. "You know what's scary?"

She looked into his eyes, loving him. "What?"

"I had forgotten what they sounded like too. Their little voices, the way they laugh." A shiver ran down his arms, and the image of Kendall flashed in his mind. "I almost lost it all, Kelly." He pressed the side of his face to hers. "Thank God I came home when I did." He breathed in deep and laughed out loud. As he did he swung Kelly around. "You know how I feel?"

"How?" she laughed like she hadn't since he started working with Keith.

"Like life is just beginning for us." He let his smile drop off a bit. "I'm sorry, Kel. I didn't know how much time it would take and I … I hurt you in the process." He put his hand on her cheek. "Forgive me?"

"I have." She leaned in and tenderly kissed him, letting her lips linger as if to convince him. "I forgave you a long time ago. I knew if any change would come, it would have to come from God, not me." She smiled and her eyes lit up the way they'd done when she was a new bride. "And now it has."

He could hardly wait for morning to call Pastor Hastings. That call, too, had confirmed everything he now felt about his future. "I've prayed about your offer," he told the man. "I'd like to accept the position. I think it'll be good for me and my family."

"I expected your call." The pastor was a serious sort, and his tone now showed not a bit of surprise over Chase's acceptance. "God told me you needed this change."

Chase choked up, and he coughed to find his voice again. "The funny thing is, a long time ago it was my dream to be a youth pastor."

"Yes." There was a smile in the pastor's voice. "God told me that too." He paused. They talked about getting Chase's ordination papers in order, and Pastor Hastings grinned. "When would you like to start?"

Chase's mind raced. He could hardly start the job while Keith was taking meetings in LA, assuming Chase would be back at it come Monday. "Can I have a week?"

"Of course." Pastor Hastings was almost matter-of-fact about the news. "I'll share your acceptance with the team." His tone warmed. "We're excited to have you aboard, Chase."

"Yes, sir." Chase's mind raced. Was he really doing this? Changing directions so completely when everything in Hollywood was going so well? He blinked, clearing his mind. "I'm excited too." He thought about telling the news to Keith. He was excited and terrified at the same time. His friend would certainly struggle to understand any of this.

The next part was the best of all—telling the girls. Sunday before church, Chase helped Kelly make scrambled eggs and slice up fresh fruit. Over the meal, Chase set his napkin down and grinned at his precious daughters. "I have news for you."

"I know." Molly looked nervous. "You're leaving tomorrow, right?"

Chase swapped a long smile with Kelly, and under the table he reached for her hand. He turned his attention back to Molly. "No sweetheart, I'm not leaving."

Macy clapped her hands together. "You're staying home an extra day! Goody, Daddy. We can play hide-and-go-seek, okay?"

Chase and Kelly laughed. "Yes, sweetie. We can play hide-and-seek as much as you like." He reached across the table with his free hand and covered Macy's fingers with his own. "Daddy's not going away anymore, honey."

Molly's mouth fell open, and Macy tilted her head, clearly confused. Molly's question came first. "But … you have to be in Lollywood for the movies, right?"

He smiled, but he bit his lip. This was a serious moment, and he needed his girls to understand the change about to take place in their lives. "I'm not going to make movies anymore."

"So you can stay home and play with us?" Macy's eyes lit up.

"Sort of." Chase couldn't contain his excitement. As crazy and uncertain as the change might seem to anyone else, he had not one bit of regret over this decision. "Daddy's going to work at church. Teaching the kids."

Molly was on her feet now, her eyes so wide they could see the whites all the way around them. "If you work here, you can tuck me in at night!"

Peace and joy spread through him, assuring him he would look back on this time decades from now and know—absolutely know—it was a gift from God. "That's right, baby. Daddy's going to be here every night to tuck you in."

She danced in circles around the dining room. "Daddy's staying home ... Daddy's staying home ... my daddy's staying home!"

Macy joined her then, grabbing hold of her sister's hands and dancing with her. "Yay! Daddy's staying home!"

Kelly was laughing and crying at the same time, dabbing at her tears as she watched their girls celebrate. Chase stood and helped Kelly to her feet, holding her close, rocking her to the sound of their daughters' laughing and singing and dancing.

"It's the best thing I've ever done." He whispered to her. Then he kissed her softly. "My girls will never have to wonder what I look like again."

"There's just one thing left to do." Kelly framed his face with her hands, and a ripple of concern crossed her otherwise joyful face.

"What's that?" Chase was so happy, so sure this was the miraculous answer he'd prayed for; he couldn't imagine what might cause Kelly any concern at all.

She hesitated, studying him. "You have to tell Keith."

The memory faded, and a ripple of fear stirred the otherwise calm waters in his soul. Because now that's exactly what he was going to do. Kelly offered to come, but Chase asked her to stay home with the girls. He had joined forces with Keith in Jeremiah Productions. Now it would be his responsibility to tell Keith he was moving on. When he wasn't playing hide-and-seek or taking the girls to the park and the zoo, Chase had prayed all week that his friend would understand. That their friendship could survive his decision to leave.

Chase turned onto Keith's street, drove past four houses, and parked. His stomach was in his throat by the time he reached the front door. *God, give me Your peace. Help Keith understand I'm not crazy, that this is the best thing I can do for my family. Please, God ...*

My son, anyone who knows the good he ought to do and doesn't do it, sins. Go forward now and do what you know to do.

The answer that resonated through him came from something he'd heard from Pastor Hastings halfway through the week. They'd talked several times since Chase's acceptance. Chase had a feeling they were going to be close friends, that the older man would become an important mentor to him and his family.

He knocked and waited. Scripture was clear about the list of sins, choices people made that separated them from God. But something sometimes overlooked was the admonition from James, chapter four, where God reminded people that sin was also knowing the good one was supposed to do, and not doing it. Chase was convinced without a doubt of the good he was supposed to do. He was being called back to his family, to a life of leading the kids of their church. Back to his first calling, really. If he didn't respond, he would be in error. Certainly Keith would understand that.

His thoughts were still racing as Keith opened the door. He looked tired and worn down. "Come in."

Chase followed him and saw that Lisa was already sitting in the living room. She, too, looked concerned. Clearly the two of them were expecting bad news. The whole room felt weighted by a layer of awkward tension. "Lisa ..." He nodded at her.

"Hello, Chase." She stood briefly. "Can I get you water? Coffee?"

Keith took the seat next to his wife and crossed his arms. He didn't look angry. Just confused.

"No, thanks." Clearly Chase had let too much time go by without explaining himself. They couldn't go another moment with things feeling this strange between them. He felt sorry for the pain he was about to cause. With a heavy heart he sat opposite the two of them and leaned his forearms on his knees. "Let's start by praying. Would that be okay?"

"Sure." Keith looked at Lisa and then back at him. His tone was kind, despite his clear frustration. "We have no idea what's coming, buddy. You go ahead."

Chase closed his eyes and gripped his hands together. "Dear God, You've brought us here for an important meeting. We ask that Your Spirit of mercy and grace fall on this place, on each of us. That understanding would reign and love would prevail. Thank You for my great friends, Lord. Be with them and with me this night. In Your name, amen."

A quiet round of amens followed, and in the silence afterward, Chase grabbed onto God's strength. The time had come for him to explain himself. "A strange thing happened at the premiere." He decided to downplay the temptation from that night, and focus instead on his family. After all, that had been what caused him to make the change. He drew a long breath, steadying his voice. "There we were," he looked at Keith, "top of our game. But at the end of the night I felt like someone I didn't recognize. For a lot of reasons, I guess."

He told them about asking God for a way to reckon his family life with his life as a producer and director, and when he told them about seeing the footage of him and Kendall on the red carpet, an understanding filled Keith's eyes. As if from that point on he could see where Chase was headed. Chase continued, telling them about coming home and hearing his little girls talk about not remembering what he looked like, what he sounded like.

Lisa's eyes got teary during that part, and she looped her arm through Keith's. Chase wondered if she was thinking about their daughter, Andi. Sure she was in college, but how often were they able to talk to her or visit? The movie business took all their time.

"I guess that's when I knew," he sat straighter, his eyes on Keith's, imploring him to understand. He had to be very clear here. "I'm finished making movies, Keith. I've been offered a position at church." He shrugged, his eyes intent and unwavering. "I'm staying home with my family. It's what God's calling me to do."

Keith looked amazed and shocked and dizzy, like if he tried to stand he might topple over. But he didn't look angry. He was quiet for a long time before he raised his brow and allowed a soft chuckle. "I saw this coming, really I did." He looked at Lisa. "If I can be honest, I thought you and Kendall were getting a little too close."

His friend's admission brought with it another burst of shame, another confirmation that he was making the right move. "She's moving on. She told me so, but you're right. I was out of God's will in a lot of areas."

"We talked about you that night back in our room, how we were worried about you being away from Kelly and the girls." He breathed in deep, like he was trying to find his balance again. "But not for a minute did I expect this."

"I know." Chase couldn't help but offer a weak smile. The joy inside him was that great. "That's the best part. I didn't expect it either. But God did. He had this plan all along; I really have to believe that."

"I'm not sure where that leaves us—Jeremiah Productions, I mean." Keith looked at Lisa, and his eyes filled with a fear that was uncommon for him. For a moment it seemed he might recite all the company had going on—the great news about the theatrical release and American Pictures, the deal with Brandon Paul, and the potential success of that next film. "You and Kendall, both gone."

Chase waited, and for a few moments the silence became uncomfortable again.

Then Keith exhaled slowly and turned his eyes back to Chase. "God will show us what to do. Luke Baxter can draw up paperwork releasing you. But the bottom line is already clear. Whatever happens with Jeremiah Productions, it no longer concerns you."

Of all the things Keith could say, this touched Chase most of all. By acknowledging that Chase wasn't responsible for the trouble he'd caused or how Keith would move forward from here, he was releasing Chase. Releasing him with a full heart. For a long time none of them said anything. Keith folded his hands and looked at the floor for nearly a minute. When he lifted his face, there were tears in his eyes. "I've loved every minute of this journey. Even the scary times." His voice was strained. "I couldn't have done it without you, buddy."

For the first time since he'd made his decision, Chase fully registered that there was indeed a loss here, a loss that paled in comparison with the gift he was gaining. But a loss all the same. He stood and helped Keith to his feet, and the two of them hugged. Not the victory hug from the premiere night. But a hug that said no matter how difficult this moment was, the two of them would remain friends. "I'm sorry," Chase could barely speak the words. "God wants me to do this. I have no choice."

"I know." He sniffed hard and drew back, wiping the back of his hand beneath his eyes. Lisa was quietly crying on the couch, her hand to her mouth as she watched the two men. Keith nodded, still struggling. "I will pray for you and your new ministry every day. I promise you that."

Relief flooded Chase's heart. He put his hand on his friend's shoulder. "And I'll pray for you."

There were a thousand unanswered questions. How would Keith proceed alone, and how quickly could someone fill Chase's spot? But all that mattered here and now was that Keith understood, and he did so with a love and grace that didn't surprise Chase. It was one more answer to prayer, and Chase expected nothing less from their gracious God. The men hugged one more time and as Keith took his spot beside Lisa again, he laughed to break the sadness in the room.

"I don't have to ask this, but ... you know what you're walking away from, right?"

"I know." Chase chuckled a few times and shook his head. "Kelly's asked me more than once if I hit my head on the way home from LA last weekend. No one walks away from all you've got going on, Keith."

His friend seemed to note the way Chase distanced himself from the company, how he referred to the work of Jeremiah Productions as what Keith had going on, no longer the two of them. Keith nodded slowly. "I guess it's not about what you're walking away from." He smiled and put his arm around Lisa. "It's about what you're walking toward."

"Those sweet babies." Lisa's voice caught. "You're doing the right thing, Chase. I didn't see this coming. Not now with so much going on." She smiled and her sincerity rang with every word. "But you're doing the right thing."

"Thank you." Chase finally leaned back in his seat, able to relax. "I will always be here for the two of you. Anything I can do from my home, I'm happy to help out. And I believe God will bring someone along, someone who will be better for Jeremiah Productions than I ever could've been."

Keith raised one eyebrow. "Let's not get carried away."

They all laughed, and the conversation shifted away from work. As it did, there was nothing left to talk about. The two of them were no longer a team, no longer ready to take on the world of filmmaking in an attempt to change the culture. The dreams they'd believed in back on the mission fields of Indonesia had changed for Chase, and some sorrow colored the moment the way it was bound to.

Even so, Chase drove home with a smile in his heart, and when he walked through the front door, he found Kelly curled up on the sofa reading. "The girls are in bed," she whispered. "How did it go?"

"Perfectly. God met us there." He motioned that he'd tell her more later. First he needed to find his girls. He tiptoed down the hall and into the bedroom they shared, and he stood over them, watching the way their little bodies breathed so peacefully. He had almost lost this, the chance to watch them grow, to pray over them every night. But God had spared him, and now one thing was absolutely certain.

He wasn't going to miss another moment.

Ten

KEITH NO LONGER HAD TO WONDER what it would feel like to be trapped beneath thirty floors of rebar and cement. The moment his friend shut the door behind him, as soon as Keith and Lisa were alone in their silent living room, a weight like nothing he'd ever felt hit him square on the shoulders, dropping him to the edge of the sofa.

"Honey?" Lisa took the spot beside him. Her face was masked in worry, and she put one hand on his shoulder. "It's okay. God will show us a way out."

The pain of losing Chase now, when he needed him most, was so strong he struggled to breathe, struggled even to believe the events of the last hour had actually happened. Chase was gone. Their team was broken up, and now anything was possible. Every contract on the table was in jeopardy. "I … I'm not sure what to do." He stood and crossed the room. He wouldn't cry or raise his voice or fall apart. God would get him through this the way He'd gotten them through so many other situations.

If only Keith could figure out what to do next.

He crossed the room to the front window and stared out at the dark night. Not even the hint of a moon lit the ground outside, and Keith found that fitting. He was suddenly headed a hundred miles an hour into the thickest fog he'd ever seen. No idea what the next minute might hold, let alone tomorrow.

"Keith …" Lisa stood and came to him. "Talk to me." She put her hand gently on his shoulder. "What're you thinking?"

He looked back at her. "It might be over. Without Chase, every contract could be cancelled. That's how it works."

Lisa didn't look surprised. She nodded slowly. "Okay. So you walk away from Hollywood."

Her words had a strangely calming effect on him. His life in Hollywood had gotten so complicated that he rarely considered the obvious. He could walk away from it tomorrow—as long as his investors were taken care of. Because he could only do so much, and if American Pictures wanted to pull out, if Brandon Paul no longer wanted to work with him, then so be it.

He leaned his head against hers and remembered a sermon a year ago, something he'd forgotten until now. "Remember what Pastor Hastings said awhile back?" Keith's voice held a calm that he still didn't quite feel. "He said sometimes life gets too complicated to figure it out on your own. When that happens, God has to do the figuring."

"Mmm." Lisa eased her arm around his waist and pressed her body close to him. "I remember."

"And while God does the figuring, there's only one thing we can do."

He felt Lisa smile. "The next thing."

"Right. We just do the next thing and let God reveal the bigger answers." They were quiet, clinging to each other and to the certainty that God would see them through. Even if it was impossible to see the way out from here. Keith peered into the darkness. Chase had a right to follow God's plan for his life, even if that plan had seemingly come out of nowhere. It wasn't like Chase had a contract to fulfill. They were only now signing deals with American Pictures and DTA, with Brandon Paul and the author of *Unlocked*. They had yet to contact new investors about the publicity and advertising budget for their theatrical release of *The Last Letter*.

Legally, Chase was free and clear, and Keith could do nothing but release him with complete understanding. Keith sighed, feeling the heaviness around him again. Tomorrow he would need to call Luke Baxter and tell him. Luke would have ideas, someone in the industry who might be interested in filling Chase's position. But what about their vision? Making movies that could change the world? Would anyone else work as passionately to that end as Chase Ryan?

"Don't." Lisa whispered against his face.

He looked at her, loving her. "Don't what?"

"Don't borrow trouble from tomorrow." She kissed him on his cheek, her eyes never leaving his. "Do the next thing."

"Hmmm." His heart filled with gratitude for the strength of the woman beside him. She had been this way when he married her, and her resolve had helped him through their time in Indonesia. Now here she was again, her tender wisdom helping him believe that God hadn't abandoned them, that His plans were still good. He touched his fingers to her face, lost in her. "The next thing, huh?"

"Yes."

He shrugged, at a loss. "And what's that?"

"We call our daughter, read our Bibles, and go to sleep."

"Are you sure that's the next—" The phone rang before he could finish his sentence. He looked at the clock on the wall. It was just after seven, which meant it was ten o'clock in Bloomington. "Maybe that's her." The situation with Chase had distracted him much of the week, but now he was reminded about Andi. They'd talked to her just a few times since last weekend, and with each call she sounded more distant, distracted. Keith pointed toward the phone. "There it is ... the next thing."

Lisa smiled, and her unwavering joy relieved the pressure weighing on him. He moved to the phone and picked up the receiver. "Hello?"

"Keith, hey it's Dayne Matthews. I'm not calling too late, am I?"

"No, not at all." Keith wrinkled his brow, baffled. Dayne Matthews had never called him at home. The two hadn't talked since they were in Bloomington a year ago filming. He mouthed to Lisa that the caller was Dayne Matthews.

Her eyes grew wide, and she moved slowly to the nearest chair.

"Do you have a minute?" Dayne sounded excited, practically bursting with whatever he'd called about. "I mean, if this is a good time?"

"It's fine." Keith returned to his place by the window and leaned against the adjacent wall. "What's on your mind?"

"Well," he chuckled, as if he wasn't sure where to begin. "I've been following your work—you and Chase. I read earlier today about your premiere and the offer from American Pictures. The whole Brandon Paul deal that must be coming together based on the retraction from NTM." Dayne sounded impressed. "God's doing amazing work through you two, which got me thinking."

Dayne went on to say that he'd been away from movies for a long time—several years. "CKT is running itself. We have wonderful directors and people handling the office. The kids' theater group doesn't need Katy and me like it used to."

Keith felt his heart speed up. Where was Dayne going?

"What I'm saying is, Katy and I talked about it and we'd like to be a part of Jeremiah Productions. Sophie is old enough to travel, but too young for school. Katy and I could take her with us, spend time on the set. Help with the productions somehow or with the publicity and advertising."

Keith's head started to spin. He turned his back to the window and rested against it, his eyes closed. How was this happening? And was Dayne really proposing what it sounded like? Keith forced himself to concentrate.

"We'd like to invest as well. We and some friends of mine from Hollywood. We really believe in what you're doing." He paused but only for a second or two. "Of course, we wouldn't want you or Chase to feel like we were taking over. You might not have room for us, and that's fine. It's just … we talked about it all day, and I couldn't go to sleep without calling you and Chase to see if—"

"Dayne." Keith shot a disbelieving look at Lisa. Then he uttered a single awestruck laugh. "There is no Chase."

A long silence filled the line. "What?"

"There's no Chase. He resigned from Jeremiah Productions an hour ago."

Now it was Dayne's turn to be overcome with disbelief. "Because … because of some problem?"

"Yes. His family needs him. His girls are in preschool. They can't travel with him." Keith moved to the chair across from Lisa. He needed to sit down. "They need to be home and he needs to be on the road." He pictured Chase's young daughters. "They were forgetting what he looked like."

"This just happened?" Dayne was obviously confused. "Now? When you're on the verge of making history with Jeremiah Productions?"

"Yeah." Keith sucked in a long breath, but it didn't help. He was still dizzy, still too shocked to fully grasp what was happening. "But Chase had no doubts. Our church staff offered him a position as youth pastor, and he accepted." Another chuckle came from him. "Lisa and I were just reminding each other that God still had a plan for Jeremiah Productions. That everything wasn't really going to fall apart. We just couldn't see what was next."

Gradually Dayne must've understood. "Until now?"

"Yes." Keith reached for Lisa's hand, and he saw understanding dawn in her eyes. "Until now."

"Dear God, thank You." Lisa bowed her head, her whispered prayer little more than a breath. She must've heard some of Dayne's side of the conversation and pieced together what was happening.

"Well, then." Dayne's quiet laughter bridged the distance in the pause that followed. "I guess there's just one more question …"

"When can you start?"

They talked a few minutes more, and Keith promised to make a trip to Bloomington to talk about details. "But before that, how would you feel about taking meetings with me over the next few weeks? As my co-producer."

"This is crazy." Dayne's laugh was full now, his enthusiasm clear over the phone lines. "Just tell me when and where."

"Your brother Luke can rearrange things, fit the meetings into the next couple weeks, but we're needed out there pretty much all that time."

"Hmmm." Dayne thought for a moment. "I have an idea." He went on to explain that he still had friends in real estate outside Los Angeles. "They handle corporate rentals too." Dayne agreed to make a few phone calls and line up a house on the beach — something with enough room for both their wives and little Sophie. "That way they can have a vacation while we're taking care of business."

Keith's mind raced. Dayne would have to get up to speed very quickly. They would likely need another few hours on the phone tomorrow, but Dayne seemed certain he could have a place rented by Monday. They could fly in then and hit the ground full speed. What Dayne didn't know in background information and contract details he would learn. Until then, his name would raise the visibility and credibility of Jeremiah Productions to an even higher level.

The phone call finally ended and Keith stared at his wife, speechless.

"Am I understanding this right?" She came to him and knelt at his side, her hand alongside his face. "Dayne Matthews just called and asked if he could work with Jeremiah Productions?"

"Umm . . . Yes." A single laugh slipped from Keith and he lifted his hands, still stunned. "I think so." He looked around and then put both his hands on her shoulders. "I'm not dreaming, right?"

"No." They giggled, giddy over the unbelievable turn of

events. "You're walking in faith." She looped her arms around his neck and hugged him close.

As long as they lived they would remember this day. It was as if a sudden storm had come upon them and threatened to capsize their boat, threatened to destroy them and all they'd worked for. But then Jesus Himself had calmed the wind and the waves with a single phone call. Dayne Matthews, wanting to be a part of Jeremiah Productions. Minutes after Chase had stepped down. Only God could've done this, and Keith stood, helping Lisa to her feet as well.

The reality was sinking in and Keith let out a victory shout as he threw his arms around his wife. They weren't done making movies. God had a plan better than anything they could've come up with. Chase was going home to be with his family, and Keith would have the chance to work with one of the top names in Hollywood. A man who had seen the ugliest side of Hollywood, but who still believed that God could use the power of film.

"Keith!" Lisa pushed back and sucked in a quick gasp. "I have an idea!"

He laughed again. "I'm not sure I can take much more."

"No, this is perfect." She backed away and paced a few steps, her hand to her forehead. "Dayne lives in Bloomington."

"Yes." Keith wasn't sure where Lisa was headed with this, but he loved her enthusiasm.

"Andi will be there for another three years, right?"

"At least." He caught a glimpse of what she might be thinking. "You're saying we—"

"We move there! We can be closer to Andi, and you and Dayne will be better able to work together."

Keith nodded, letting the idea sink in. "Wouldn't it make more sense for everyone to move to LA?"

"Dayne won't want that." Lisa was adamant. "Neither would we. And LA would be the worst place for Andi. She's had trouble staying grounded in Indiana."

Her excitement was contagious. "We could rent a place in LA when we need to be there, and do most of our filming in Bloomington. Or somewhere close by."

"Exactly." Lisa raised her fist in the air and let out a joyous cry. "This just keeps getting better."

Keith realized then how much he'd missed his Andi. She wasn't young like Chase's daughters, but she was still their little girl. On the mission field they'd shared every day together for years. Never mind that she was an adult now. She was floundering —they all knew that much. And now they could be together again.

The receiver was still on the sofa where Keith had placed it after the call from Dayne. Now Lisa raced over and grabbed it. "Let's call her. She won't believe everything that's happened."

Keith thought about telling his wife that maybe they should wait. They shouldn't get Andi excited that her parents were moving closer unless they were sure. "Shouldn't we pray about it first?"

"Keith. God's the one who dropped this in our laps." Her smile lit the room, but she set the phone down on the arm of the sofa. "Okay, fine. Let's pray."

Again, laughter filled Keith's throat and he nodded at his wife. "You do it."

She took his hands and closed her eyes. "Dear Lord, thank You for making the answers so clear. Please let the pieces fall in place quickly. In Jesus' name, amen." She opened her eyes. "Let's call Andi."

Again they laughed together, reveling in God's goodness and the certainty of His plans for the next season of their lives. They called Andi twice that night, but both times the call went to her voicemail. Keith frowned. "I hope she's not out with that Taz guy. He's not good for her."

"She's not." Lisa stared at the phone and then at Keith. "They stopped seeing each other a month ago."

"Good."

"She's probably out with Bailey. She'll call us back when she gets in."

Keith was pensive for a moment, his mind lost on their only daughter. "She needs us." He looked at Lisa. "Maybe more than we know."

"Which leads us to the next thing." Lisa's smile was tender, her enthusiasm tempered some in light of their daughter.

Keith kissed her, this time slow and full on the lips. "What's the next thing, Mrs. Ellison?"

"That's easy." Her smile reached her eyes once more. "We need to list our house."

Eleven

LIFE HAD BECOME A SUDDEN AND complete whirlwind over-night, but Dayne couldn't have been happier. Katy was complete-ly on board with his idea—though the speed with which it was happening had taken them both by surprise. The next morning Dayne shared an early conversation with Keith, called his Califor-nia realtor to secure a beach house for Monday morning, and on Sunday he and Katy and Sophie headed to church.

The ten o'clock service was where all the Baxters met every Sunday morning. Dayne and Katy arrived early, and before the service began, Dayne found his father in the lobby. "Hey, Dad," he couldn't stop grinning. "We need to talk."

"I still love that." His father smiled. "Hearing you call me Dad."

Dayne slipped his arm around his father's shoulders. "I still love saying it." He took a step back and glanced toward the front door. He didn't want to get caught in a conversation with anyone else before he told his dad what was happening. "Can we do a Bax-ter dinner tonight? Katy and I need to talk to the whole family."

"Really?" John raised an eyebrow. "Is Sophie getting a baby brother?"

"No, no." Dayne laughed. "Nothing like that. But it's still big. We're flying out to Los Angeles in the morning."

"The three of you?"

"Yes. We have a lot to talk about." People were filing in, and Kari and Ryan and their kids were walking up, their kids chat-tering as they came. Dayne kept his eyes on his dad. "Dinner to-night?"

"Sure. I'll invite the rest." His dad looked happy to oblige. "Five o'clock?"

"Perfect." Dayne hugged his dad again and then hurried back into the sanctuary to join Katy. Sophie was asleep in her arms. Dayne leaned down and kissed his baby daughter's forehead. Then he did the same to Katy. "We're on for tonight."

"I can't believe how much we have to do." She giggled quietly. "You're a crazy man, Dayne. But what's life without an adventure?"

He took the seat beside her. "Think of it as a mission trip."

Pastor Mark spoke that morning on answering the call. Time and again, Jesus presented people with the chance to follow Him, and when people truly believed Him, they set down what they were doing that very moment and followed. Dayne listened intently, and beside him he felt Katy squeeze his hand.

"The point," Pastor Mark said, "is that we need to be listening. When God calls us, it's time to act—whatever He's asking us to do. We should have our yes on the table at all times."

Dayne smiled to himself throughout the hour. The sermon seemed written specifically for him. Clearly God was working in all this. The words from Scripture that morning were further proof. When church ended, the Baxters gathered in the foyer and John invited everyone for dinner. Brooke and Peter had to cancel plans with friends, but they didn't think it would be a problem. Everyone else was free.

"Looks like we'll all be there." John smiled at his kids and their families. Then he winked at Cole, Ashley's son. "I bet there are still tadpoles in the pond."

"Really?" Cole was eleven now, but he still loved spending time at the pond with his grandpa. He nudged his brother. "You hear that, Devin? We better get there first."

Landon gave his wife a questioning look. "What do you think, Ash? We can get there at four, maybe?"

"Yeah, because you're the biggest kid of all." Her eyes held an endless sort of love for him. "That's fine. I'll help Elaine with dinner. You and my dad and the boys can do your pond thing."

The plan was set and everyone headed out. Katy talked the whole way home about what to pack, but in the end she didn't put together much. Just enough clothes to get through a week. The house they were renting had a washer and dryer. And they could always shop if they needed something.

Time flew, and hours later when they pulled up at the Baxter house, Dayne was amazed at all they'd accomplished. "Who would've thought so much could change in a single weekend?" He cut the engine and let his head fall back against the seat.

"It's a little hard to believe, still. I mean, the idea of Chase stepping down now?" Katy reached back and took hold of Sophie's little hand. "Not that I blame him. Our kids are only little for so long."

"I wouldn't do this if you and Soph couldn't come with me." He looked back at his daughter. "I can't believe you're already two, right little one?"

"A'most two!" Sophie giggled and rocked forward in her car seat, pointing to the big farmhouse. "See Papa, Daddy?"

"Yes, baby. We're going to see Papa." Dayne opened his door, but he stayed seated. "No matter what happens, I don't want to move away." He looked at the Baxter house and a rush of memories flooded his heart. "This is where our family is; it's home."

Relief lifted Katy's expression. "We haven't talked about it, but I feel the same way. A few weeks in LA is one thing, but this ... the Baxter family? I couldn't walk away now."

"Not after all it took to find them."

"Exactly."

They climbed out, and Dayne unbuckled Sophie's car seat. She was running now, and Dayne watched her go as he set her down.

"Papa!" Her hair was as blonde as Katy's, as blonde as her big cousin, Cole. She had Katy's fine features, but her eyes were the same as most of the Baxter kids. Baxter blue, they called it.

As they walked in the side door, Cole and Devin came through the front with Landon and Dayne's dad in tow. "Papa was right!" Cole's enthusiasm never dimmed. "The best of the season!" He had a small fishbowl, and swimming inside were a number of tadpoles.

"Wonderful." Ashley stepped out of the kitchen, a spatula in her hand. She directed it at Cole. "They stay in the laundry room this time."

"Aw, Mom. They hate the laundry room." Cole peered in at them, and next to him, Devin did the same. "They like people. Tadpoles are social."

"They are." Dayne took a few steps toward Cole and squinted at the glass bowl. "I read that tadpoles are more social than dogs."

Laughter came from the kitchen. "Come on, Dayne." Katy was washing her hands at the sink. "No one's that good an actor!"

The conversation continued as first Kari and Ryan and their three kids, then Brooke and Peter and their two girls, and finally Erin and Sam and their four daughters all arrived. By then, Luke's wife Reagan and their two kids had been there most of the afternoon. With Luke doing business in LA more often, Reagan liked spending Sundays at the Baxter house.

Dayne found a kickball in the garage and set the cousins up outside. The three littlest girls were too small to play, so they sat on the porch steps and watched. Sophie, and Ashley's youngest — Janessa Faith, along with Kari's little one — three-year-old Annie.

But that still left twelve cousins suddenly engaged in a wild, rule-free game of kickball. "I'm captain," Cole announced. "Everyone line up and we'll pick teams."

"No! I'm captain." Tommy stuck out his chest. "I pick Maddie!"

Cole gave his younger cousin a patient look. "We can both be captains."

"And I'm on Tommy's team." Maddie high-fived Tommy. "We can beat Cole any day." She smiled sweetly at Cole. "You know it's true."

Cole surveyed the kids on the line and pointed at his strapping younger brother. "I pick Devin."

Dayne chuckled quietly from the porch steps. He loved times like this, and he sat by the little girls for a few minutes. He especially loved watching Hayley run with the other kids. Hayley was nine this summer, and her disabilities were almost too slight to notice. Dayne hadn't known his family back when Hayley had nearly died in a drowning in their family pool. But he'd heard stories from Brooke and Peter and the other Baxters. Hayley's doctors had given her only a slim chance at life back then, certain she'd never leave her bed if she survived. Every day was a miracle for Hayley, proof that God would forever have the final word.

Ashley stepped outside and took the spot beside him. Dayne was close to all his sisters, but he and Ashley would always have a special bond. She was the one who had pursued him the hardest, the sister who first figured out that Dayne was part of the Baxter family. "Hi, there."

"Hi." He had to talk loud to be heard above the kids.

"You coach?"

"Referee."

"Good luck." She laughed and hugged her knees to her chest. After a while she smiled at him. "It's hard to imagine heaven any better than this."

Dayne nodded, and he understood even more why Chase had to back out of Jeremiah Productions. He couldn't imagine a day when Sophie might forget what he looked like or no longer remember the sound of his voice. He thought about telling Ashley, but he decided to wait. The story was too long to tell twice. He smiled at his sister. "What's new?"

"We have tadpoles." Ashley grinned. "But that's not really new." She angled her face. "Landon's been promoted at the station, and I'm working on a new painting. The Baxter house with a bunch of blonde kids playing out front. Too many to count."

"Sounds perfect." He remembered the loss their family had suffered a few years ago when Ashley's baby, Sarah, had died hours after birth. She and Brooke had opened a crisis pregnancy center in honor of the infant. "How's Sarah's House?"

"Great." Ashley's eyes told him she was glad he'd asked, glad people still remembered little Sarah. "Every week girls are coming in. Only God knows how many babies have been saved because of the work taking place there."

Dayne was about to ask how Cole was doing in baseball. He'd made All-Stars, Dayne knew that much. But Elaine opened the door and called out, "Dinner! Everyone wash up!"

They filed in, and somehow through the craziness of so many kids and a dozen conversations, they wound up seated at two long tables in the Baxter dining room. Dayne was practically bursting with his and Katy's news, but he waited while the others talked. Sam's company was laying off, but he'd been told late last week that his position was safe. "We're grateful," Erin said. She looked beyond relieved. "Sam and I don't want to move again."

"I'd switch jobs first." He smiled at the faces around the table. "What we have here, it's too special to walk away from again."

Dayne knew their story, how they'd lived in Texas for several years. Now that they were here, Dayne had to agree. The family wouldn't be the same without them.

The conversation shifted to Brooke and Peter, and the way their medical practices were growing. "I think the recession must be lifting. Bloomington seems to be adding new families all the time."

"It's a great place to live!" Landon raised his glass of water and grinned at Ashley. "Right, honey?"

"As long as there are no fires." She gave him a wary smile. "I'm ready for you to run the department. Then you can keep your uniform clean."

They all murmured their agreement. The times when Landon had been injured in serious fires were before Dayne had come into the family. But the chance always remained. It reminded Dayne to pray for his brother-in-law every day. He needed absolute protection in his line of work.

The conversation was slowing when Reagan put down her fork and looked around the table. "I have some news. Luke asked for your prayers for us."

Concern showed on their father's face. "He's traveling a lot lately."

Dayne wondered if this was his segue. Maybe Luke wanted prayers because of the changes taking place with Jeremiah Productions. In addition to handling Dayne's business, Luke was now almost entirely working with Keith's production company. Dayne could barely contain his news.

"We're fine." Reagan's eyes warmed. "It's just ... we're thinking of adopting again. Maybe from the U.S. this time. I talked to Luke earlier today and he asked you to pray. He'll be home in a few weeks. We might start the process then."

"Reagan, that's great!" Ashley was sitting beside her. She reached out and took hold of her sister-in-law's hand. "We'll all pray."

"Can you make this one a boy, please?" Cole sat up straighter. "We need more boy cousins."

"They're talking about a baby." Landon put an arm around their oldest son. "I don't think cousin kickball will be a part of his or her life for quite a while."

"Ya," Cole looked disappointed. "I guess you're right."

They all laughed, and Reagan promised to keep them posted. The time had come, and Dayne couldn't keep the news a secret a moment longer. Besides, his father was watching him, waiting for whatever it was he'd called the dinner for. Dayne set his napkin down and grinned, first at Katy, then at the others. "Katy and I are taking Sophie to Los Angeles tomorrow."

"For Disneyland?" Tommy jumped out of his seat. "Daddy's taking me and Malin to Disneyland this summer, right Mommy?" He spun around and stared at Reagan, then spun back to the group again, eyes big. "Disneyland's the happiest place on earth."

Reagan helped Tommy back to his seat. Dayne waited for the commotion to die down. "No, not for Disneyland, not this time." He winked at his young nephew. "But maybe we'll join you later this summer!"

Cole whispered something to Ashley, but she held her finger to her lips and whispered, "Later." Then she turned to Dayne. "Is this business, then?"

"Yes." He grinned. "I'm joining Keith Ellison as the newest producer with Jeremiah Productions." His family leaned in closer, listening to every word while Dayne explained how Chase had stepped down, and how at the same time he and Katy had felt God calling them into moviemaking. "The timing is perfect. Katy and Sophie can travel with me when we need to be in LA. Otherwise we can work from here."

His father nodded thoughtfully. "Sounds fantastic."

"I talked to Keith this morning. He and Lisa are listing their house and moving here to Bloomington. We want to film as many movies in Indiana as possible." He held his hands out to the rest of the group. "That way we don't have to give up this."

"And Keith and Lisa can be closer to their daughter." Ashley sat back in her seat, beaming over Dayne's news. "That's wonderful. Congratulations!"

Peter asked if Dayne would consider acting in one of the Jeremiah Productions films. "Not yet." He remembered how crazy his life had been back when he was in two or three movies a year. He shared a knowing look with Katy. "God would have to make that very clear."

"When will the media know?" Elaine's question was a good one.

Dayne imagined the public attention just ahead of them. There would be major interest in him joining forces with one of the most talked about new producers in town. Especially since Jeremiah Productions was clearly a Christian-based company. "Luke's releasing a statement to the press tomorrow. I imagine we'll have interviews pretty quickly after that."

Reagan exhaled hard, as if she'd been holding her breath. "Luke told me before we came over." She smiled at Dayne. "If you didn't say something soon, I was going to tell them myself."

Their father expressed his gratitude that Luke and Dayne would once again be working closely together. "And it's great you and Katy and Sophie can do this together. When you have to be on the road," he patted Dayne's shoulder. "I'm very happy for you. For all of you."

By the time everyone left, the whole family was excited about the future of Jeremiah Productions, and Maddie had announced that she planned to star in one of the movies. Just as soon as she finished middle school. Dayne was still smiling when he and Katy and Sophie piled into their SUV and headed home. They were packed, but there was still one thing Dayne wanted to do before they turned in for the night.

Back at their lake house, they tucked Sophie into bed and Dayne took Katy's hand. "Come with me," he whispered.

She followed him down the hallway, through the dining room, and out onto the back porch. The stars were bright against the dark sky, and in the distance the soft cry of an owl carried across the lake. They stood beside each other against the porch railing, staring out across the sloped hillside toward the water.

"Everything's happened so fast." Dayne slipped his arm around Katy's shoulders and held her close. "I guess I didn't want to set off for Hollywood tomorrow without making a few things clear."

Katy smiled up at him. She didn't seem worried. Rather her eyes told him she completely trusted his lead in this new venture. She looked straight ahead again and rested her head on his chest. "Tell me."

"It's been awhile, and time ... well, time's healed a lot of the wounds from the past." He paused, choosing his words carefully. "But I want you to know I remember what making movies cost us when we first started out."

"Hmmm." She nodded. "You were nearly killed."

"Yes." He still had occasional aches and stiffness from the car accident that almost took his life. The paparazzi had been so intense that day, they'd run him off the road, straight into an oncoming truck. He spent weeks in a coma, and months of rehabilitation before he could come home to Bloomington to marry Katy. "The accident, and the lies the rags printed every week. Pretty tough times."

"They were."

A light breeze rolled up from the shore, brushing Katy's hair against Dayne's cheek. "I promise you, Katy, it won't be like that this time. We'll only be in LA on occasion. You and Sophie will be safe at our rented house, and the paparazzi will be more concerned with Brandon Paul than me."

She smiled again. "You can't promise that."

He lifted his eyes to the starry sky above. She was right, and that frustrated him. "I'm married with a baby now. I'm boring by the world's standards."

A light laugh slipped between her lips. "Hardly." She leaned up and kissed him softly. "You've never been more handsome."

"What I'm trying to say is—"

"Shhh." She held her finger to his lips. "I trust you, Dayne. That's all that matters. We won't be in LA any longer than we have to, and no matter what anyone says about you or me or our family, we know the truth." She paused, looking deep into his eyes. "We have God and we have each other. What you're doing by joining Jeremiah Productions is mission work. It's what God's calling you to do, and I'm in complete support." Her unwavering love lifted the corners of her lips again. "It'll be an adventure."

"And if it gets too crazy?" He wanted her to know he didn't have all the answers. "What then?"

"That's easy. If God releases us, we do what Chase did. We walk away. This time maybe forever."

He allowed himself to get lost in her eyes, in her smile. "I love you, Katy Matthews."

"I love you too. I always will."

Her words eased the question marks that had popped up in his heart throughout the day. He wanted her to know she came first, and that he'd never put her or Sophie in danger by taking his spot in the public eye again. But he should've known that this would be her response. She was his other half, his best friend. She had stood by him before, and she would stand by him now.

No matter how wild the adventure they were about to begin.

Twelve

BAILEY WAS PACKING UP THE LAST of her things she'd left in her dorm room, when she came across a program for *Scrooge*—the show she and Tim and Andi had starred in last winter. She opened it and looked closely at their photos. The show had been Andi's first, and yet she'd easily sung like an angel and won the lead female role. Bailey studied her roommate's eyes. She'd been full of joy and light back then, innocence shining from her face. Everything she was missing now, since she'd dated Taz.

Ever since the conversation with her mom in the market that day, Bailey had wondered about having Andi live with them. She was willing to make it work, if Andi would consider it. But Bailey guessed Andi wouldn't agree to move in. She was different now, and Bailey had a pretty good idea why. She hadn't said so, but Bailey's guess was that Andi had slept with Taz, that they'd gone too far, and that her compromise of her beliefs had something to do with why they'd broken up. Bailey would've loved the chance to show Andi she didn't judge her. But they hadn't shared a conversation in weeks.

She opened a desk drawer and pulled out a stack of old papers and notepads. Nothing much worth saving, but Bailey wanted to go through it all the same. Somewhere in this mess was a letter from Tim—and she had precious few of those. She pulled up a trash can and began sorting. Halfway through the stack, she heard someone at the door and turned to see Andi walk in. She was carrying an armload of boxes, and Bailey jumped to help her.

"Give me those." She took the stack, while Andi closed the door behind her.

"Thanks." She looked gaunt and withdrawn. "I thought I was going to drop them all on my way here."

Bailey waited until her friend caught her breath. "You … moving in with the girls from your humanities class?"

"No." Andi dropped to the edge of her bed. "A lot's happened since we last talked."

"Yeah." Bailey didn't mention that she'd tried to call half a dozen times. She didn't want to make Andi feel bad. As long as her friend knew she was here for her. "So what's new?"

"I'm staying here for another few weeks. After that I'm moving in with my parents."

Bailey was shocked. "You're moving to California?"

"No." She smiled, but it stopped short of her eyes. "They're moving here." Andi crossed her arms in front of her. "You remember Chase Ryan, the guy who worked with my dad?"

"Of course. Everyone says the movie's amazing. The one we were in." Their parts were small—featured extra roles, nothing more. But still, Bailey definitely remembered Chase.

"So anyway, Chase quit. He's staying home with his family. I guess the same day my dad got the news, Dayne Matthews called and said he'd like to work with Jeremiah Productions."

"Really?" Bailey was thrilled with this development, happy for Chase and certain that Dayne would be an asset for the production company. "So your parents are moving here?"

"Right. So they can work with Dayne and film in Bloomington. They already have a renter for their house. And a place to stay when they need to be in LA."

Bailey studied her roommate and wondered why she wasn't more enthused. "That's great. I mean, it'll be wonderful having your family here." She hesitated. "Right?"

Andi stood and slowly crossed the room to the photo of Rachel on the wall by the window. "I guess." She turned and crossed her arms again. "I'm different now. I've done some things I'm not so proud of."

"They still love you." Andi's answer stirred concern and sympathy in Bailey. "You know the truth. Even if you made a few bad choices this past year."

"How would you understand?" Andi cocked her head, defiant the way she'd been most of the time lately. "Your life's been perfect since the day you were born, Bailey Flanigan. It's easy for you to talk about being a Christian."

She wanted to argue, tell Andi that her life had not been easy. She'd been ignored by the girls in high school, and the guy she really loved had no interest in her. But she had a feeling her answer would sound laughable to Andi, so she kept quiet.

"Never mind." Andi returned to her bed and moved the stack of boxes to a corner of the room. "It's not your fault." She pulled her iPod from her purse and slipped her ear buds in. "I'm taking a nap."

Bailey's mouth hung open as Andi stretched out on her comforter and rolled onto her side facing the wall. She had to try one more time, no matter how Andi treated her. Something must be very wrong for her to act this way. She stood and moved to the edge of Andi's bed. Then she put her hand on her friend's shoulder. "Andi?"

She uttered a tired sigh, and slipped the ear buds loose. "What?"

"Don't be mad ... but is something wrong? I mean, really wrong?"

Andi rolled over just enough to meet Bailey's eyes. For a long moment it seemed she might say something, maybe share whatever was at the root of her obvious pain. But a darkness clouded her eyes and she gave a quick shake of her head. "I'm fine." She turned back toward the wall. "Don't worry about me."

Bailey stared at her for another few seconds before returning to her own bed and resuming her sorting. Something was definitely wrong, but whatever it was, her roommate didn't want to talk. Bailey had tried, but she couldn't force a conversation. A few minutes passed in awkward silence, when Bailey's cell phone rang. She glanced at the small window and saw it was Tim. The two of them hadn't talked much this past week. He was taking dance and voice at a local studio, getting ready for their August audition.

"Hello?"

"Hey. I'm on campus. What're you doing?" He sounded happy and interested in her — the way he hadn't sounded for a long time.

"Packing. Where are you?"

"The cafeteria. Come have coffee with me?"

Bailey stared at Andi's back and didn't hesitate. Maybe when she returned to their room, Andi would feel more like talking. This strange tension between them reminded Bailey of the way her friends in high school had turned against her — all because they could no longer relate to Bailey. Too pure, they'd tell her. Too much a goody-good. Was that how Andi saw her now? As she left the dorm, she prayed for her roommate, that God would break through the walls she'd built around her heart. And that whatever was wrong, Bailey might somehow be part of the solution.

Then, without looking back, she closed the door behind her.

ANDI WAITED UNTIL THE DOOR WAS shut before she let her tears come. She figured she was four weeks pregnant now — four weeks at least — and still she'd told no one. When Bailey asked her what was wrong, she almost broke down and explained everything. But she stopped herself for one reason.

Bailey would never understand.

And by now, Andi's plan to raise her baby with the help of her parents had crumbled like a sand castle at high tide. She had planned to move to California, but now her parents were moving here. Her father would be working with Dayne Matthews now, so everything about their lives would suddenly be very public. Bloomington was a small town, and if she moved home, alone and pregnant, everyone would blame her parents. People would think the Christian faith of the family at the helm of Jeremiah Productions was nothing more than a joke. The press had made a media circus out of other public figures whose conservative Christian kids had gotten pregnant. Her story would be no different.

She couldn't do that to her parents. No way.

So now she'd begun to entertain an entirely different plan, a terrible, gut-wrenching option. One that haunted her day and night, but one that sometimes seemed the only way out.

Either way, she needed to see a doctor. The trouble was money. The clinics she'd called wanted money up front for an appointment, more than she had. Finally Andi had scanned the local Yellow Pages until she found a small ad that said, "Sarah's House — Crisis Pregnancy Center. Free ultrasounds."

Andi didn't know the difference between a clinic and a crisis pregnancy center, but free was free. She had an appointment to be seen at the center tomorrow. After that she'd have her ultrasound and she'd know for sure how far along she was. And then she would face her options. If there were any.

But there was a problem.

She couldn't stop thinking about the baby. Abortions had been so foreign to her that after she found out she was pregnant, after she stopped freaking out and throwing up that first night, she looked up everything she could find on the internet. Some websites said very little about the process of the abortion except to reassure young women that the procedure was their choice, and that "only through an abortion could an unexpected pregnancy truly be resolved."

But other sites showed pictures of aborted babies, graphic pictures that turned Andi's stomach and made her feel like a monster for even considering such a thing. But what were her choices? She couldn't tell her parents now that they were moving here, and unless death mercifully claimed her in the next few weeks, abortion might be her only answer. And the longer she waited, the worse the situation would be.

She could hardly tell Bailey. Her roommate wouldn't consider sleeping with her boyfriend, let alone looking twice at a guy like Taz. Andi covered her stomach with her hands. How could she have gotten pregnant? Why would God have let a baby start to grow inside her? Andi felt the sting of still more tears, and she shut her eyes tight. If God loved her, he never would've let this happen.

Slowly she sat up and opened the drawer of the nightstand beside her bed. There on top was an old copy of the Bloomington paper, and on the front page was a photo of Katy and Dayne—taken back when they first met, when they worked on a movie together. They looked like they were in Arizona, or on some desert scene. Dayne was clearly caught up in the moment, and Katy was smiling at him.

Wasn't that all she ever wanted? Taz was supposed to be like Dayne Matthews, and she was supposed to be like Katy Hart—the way Katy had been back when this picture was taken. Andi stared at the photo, studying it.

Why couldn't that be her? Smiling and beautiful and sure that all of life would turn out okay? Back before she started dating Taz and hacked her hair off and dyed it dark, people would sometimes tell her she looked like Katy Hart Matthews. Her long blonde hair and tan skin, the way she lit up a room or brought a scene to life. But Taz ... Taz never was anything like Dayne. He'd made a mockery of God and her faith. Andi was at fault from the beginning for not seeing that he was the wrong guy for her.

Because of that, she would never be part of a scene like the one on the front page of the paper. What Katy and Dayne shared, she would never know. Whether she had an abortion or not. She tucked the newspaper back in the drawer and lay down on her side again. Bailey would come back soon enough, and she wanted to be asleep when that happened. Her friend meant well, but they no longer had anything in common. If anyone had a chance at living the storybook life of Katy and Dayne, it was Bailey Flanigan. She didn't want to talk to Bailey or her parents ever again. The three of them made her feel cheap and guilty and dirty.

Andi closed her eyes, and gradually an idea came to her, another way out. What if she moved away? She could board a bus and head for Indianapolis and start her own life. That way she could still have her baby, find a life for just the two of them. That way she wouldn't embarrass her parents and herself. She could move where no one knew her name or who her parents were. She could make a way for herself, and her parents would have to let her go. She was an adult, after all.

The longer she thought about the idea, the better it seemed. She needed out before her parents got here. She could tell them she was taking a few classes at the campus an hour away in Indianapolis, staying with students there. And in time that's just what she would do. Certainly she could find a room for rent, and once the baby was born, she could find a job. But then ... who would hire her? And who would watch her baby? How could she finish school if she was working full-time and raising a child? Her head hurt, and every option seemed unimaginable. She closed her eyes and let sleep catch her. The answers would come in time. Until then she only wanted two things: Sleep.

And distance from Bailey Flanigan.

BAILEY SPOTTED TIM WAITING FOR HER outside the cafeteria. He had two coffees and he'd found a table surrounded by shady trees. The afternoon was warm and blue and summer was bursting all around them. Tim stood and hugged her as she walked up. "You look beautiful."

"Really?" His comment caught her off guard. "That's sweet."

"It's true." They sat down opposite each other, and he pulled a piece of paper from his pocket and slid it across to her. "I found out more about New York. They're holding two separate auditions. Non-equity first, then equity."

"Hmmm." Bailey looked at the paper. It was a copy of two different *Back Stage* ads. "I'm not sure how that works."

"I wasn't either, so I called. Equity, well that's for Broadway people in the union. Anyone can go, but there's a good chance we won't get seen. We'd be last on the list after everyone in the union."

"And the non-equity?"

"Like it says, that audition is for newcomers, people trying to break in. The good news is they'll look at everyone." He hesitated and made a face. "Bad news? Only a few people will be picked for next year's shows. If that."

The odds sounded astronomically against them. But before she could say so, she remembered her father's words from a few weeks ago. *Bailey, believe in yourself. You're a beautiful singer and dancer. Someone has to be the next Broadway star—it might as well be you!*

She nodded at Tim. "So which should we go to?"

"I'm leaning toward the non-equity audition." He was holding another copy of the paper, and now he pursed his lips, concentrating on the information. "They'll be looking for someone to wow them. Also, that audition comes first. If it doesn't go well, we could always go back for the equity call."

Bailey wanted to feel more enthused, but something caught

her eye, and she turned in time to see Cody Coleman walk up. Her heart sank, and she felt her cheeks grow instantly hot. Tim followed her stare and saw who had caught her attention. He stayed seated and nodded in Cody's direction. "Cody." His enthusiasm fell off by half. "How are you?"

"Good." Cody acknowledged Tim, but he quickly turned his attention back to Bailey. "Did you see Katy and Dayne on the front page?"

"I did. Dayne's going to be great as a producer."

"And their plans for Bloomington?" Cody seemed to try to include Tim in the conversation, but Tim looked distracted. Cody again focused on Bailey. "They could make it the Hollywood of the Midwest."

Bailey's heart thudded in her throat. What was happening to her? Here she was sitting with a boy who cared deeply for her and still Cody took her breath away.

Cody looked at Tim and then back at Bailey. "What're you guys up to?"

"Talking about our New York audition." Tim had never been arrogant or condescending. But right now he sounded like he was both. "Privately, if you don't mind."

Cody hesitated, and Bailey watched a quick flash of anger burn in his eyes. It passed quickly. "Sure." The muscles in his jaw clenched a few times, but he nodded, taking a step back. "It's cool." He waved casually and began walking away. "See ya."

"Later." Tim sounded glad Cody was leaving.

"Bye." Bailey was too caught off guard to say anything else. She wanted to ask whether things were okay with Cody's mom. But clearly this wasn't the time. She would call him later. When Cody was out of earshot, Bailey turned frustrated eyes toward Tim. "That was rude."

"What?" He produced a blank expression. "We're busy here, Bailey. I have voice in ten minutes."

"So, you could've been cordial."

"I was." He rolled his eyes. "Come on, Bailey. The guy practically stalks you. He spends more time with you than I do."

There it was. Bailey had wondered, and now she knew. Tim had seemed a little frustrated that Cody had hung out with the Flanigans last weekend, but the incident had passed. Until now.

Tim's expression softened. He stretched his arm across the table and took hold of Bailey's fingers. "I'm sorry. Really. He shouldn't bug me."

Bailey resisted her desire to turn and watch Cody walk away. She couldn't do that, not now. She needed to focus on her boyfriend, needed to figure out why he even was her boyfriend. "You don't have to worry about Cody. He doesn't see me that way."

Tim watched her for a long time, studying her. "What about you? How do you see him?"

Bailey wished she could smile and come up with a confident answer, something about how Tim shouldn't be ridiculous because she could never see Cody as more than a good friend or a brother. But that would be a lie, so she studied the table instead.

"Bailey ... look at me." He waited, his tone patient this time.

She lifted her eyes, not sure what to say. Was this the conversation they needed to have, the one she'd been thinking about for months now? Was it finally time they break things off and figure out life on their own? At least for a while? "Tim ... I don't know."

"It's okay." He should've been hurt or angry, because her silence was admitting the obvious. She had feelings for Cody. There was no denying that now, not for either of them. But instead Tim only looked straight to her heart. "I understand you're feeling confused. I've been busy, focused on finals and New York, sick with strep throat. I haven't been the boyfriend you deserve. I'm sorry for that."

Bailey felt dizzy. Why was he saying this? Couldn't he see how torn she was?

"I want you to know something." His attention was completely on her, his eyes shining with feelings he rarely expressed. "I love you. I'll never love any girl like I love you. And whatever happens in New York, wherever the next few years take us, I'm going to marry you someday."

"Tim, I—"

"I understand." He gave her hand a tender squeeze. "Of course you have feelings for Cody. He's been part of your family longer than me." Tim seemed to gather his determination. "I need to treat you better. Then you'd have no doubts."

He stood and came to her, easing her to her feet. "We're perfect together. Our families and our passion for the stage." He grinned and he looked more striking than he had in a long time. "We grew up with the same values and standards, Bailey. A guy like Cody Coleman?" Tim was trying to explain himself, but he was coming off arrogant again. "He could never be your type." Tim brushed her cheek with his fingers. "Of course we'll marry someday. Until then, I'll be patient about Cody. I know he's a friend." Tim kissed her forehead softly.

Bailey wanted to feel swept off her feet. She swallowed, unable to swim in this sea of emotions. "I ... I don't know."

Tim looked at the time on his cell phone. "I gotta go." He touched her face, her hair. "Forgive me, okay? No one matters to me more than you."

"Okay." Bailey didn't know what else to say. Tim hugged her, and then in a blur of motion he gathered his things and hurried off toward the parking lot.

Bailey dropped back to the chair and stared at her coffee. What in the world had just happened? Tim had basically told her he wasn't threatened by Cody Coleman, and that he had every intention of marrying her. More than that, he'd dismissed any feelings she might have for Cody as little more than brotherly, because Tim—not Cody—had more in common with her. Their families and their pasts, their future interests.

It was a moment that should've swept Bailey off her feet, but it left her feeling swept under the table. Who but Tim Reed could say such romantic things and still come across unbearably self-righteous? As if she didn't have a say in the situation at all. She covered her face with her hands and sat there, unmoving. Tim was absolutely wrong. The two of them were not destined to get married or share a future or even go on another date together.

He talked about her as if she were a neglected pet. A little more interest on his part and he'd be back in her good graces, the object of her devotion once more. She took a sip of coffee and sat back in her chair. How dare he treat Cody like that? She grabbed her cell phone from her bag and called Cody. It rang three times before his voicemail picked up. Bailey didn't leave a message. She wanted to apologize for not being more vocal when Tim was rude to him, but she couldn't do that on a recording.

For a long time she sat there, sipping her coffee and replaying the conversation with Tim, the awkward scene with Cody. As much as she disliked Tim for the way he'd acted, she disliked herself more. She'd doubted her feelings for Tim, and now she needed to make herself clear on the matter. She could no longer be his girlfriend. Whatever that meant for her and Cody was irrelevant. Tim was becoming someone she no longer wanted to spend time with.

She would talk to her mom about her feelings tonight. After that it was time to let Tim know. Then he could move on and find a girl who would be right for him. She had no idea who that girl might be, but she suddenly and certainly knew one thing.

It wasn't her.

Thirteen

ASHLEY BAXTER HURRIED AROUND THE KITCHEN with Janessa on her hip. Brooke wasn't able to make her shift at Sarah's House, which meant Ashley needed to be there. An appointment was coming in, a girl Brooke was worried about. Apparently she'd already contacted an abortion clinic.

The day had already been planned. Janessa would nap in an hour and Ashley would work on her latest painting. But that was the thrill of life. Rarely did things go exactly according to a schedule. Landon had the day off, but he'd been lost beneath their family van for the past half hour, changing the oil, and he had a list of things to do around the house after that. Ashley didn't have the heart to tell him he needed to watch Janessa. Whatever Ashley did that day, Janessa could come along.

She rinsed the dishes in the sink with one hand and loaded them into the dishwasher.

"Down." Janessa stretched toward the floor, both hands outreached.

"Not yet." Ashley kissed her daughter's cheek. "The floor has to dry. Otherwise your sockies will get wet."

Janessa whimpered. "Down, Mama."

Ashley searched for a distraction and found one in the plastic spoon standing in the jar by the stove. She grabbed it and handed it to her daughter. "Here, Nessa, play with this."

Immediately, Janessa put the spoon into her mouth. She was almost two, and she was teething like crazy. Cutting her back molars. The spoon made her happy, and Ashley was able to go back to the dishes. She was still working over the sink when she felt someone come up behind her.

"Has anyone told you," Landon's voice was soft against her ear, "you have the most beautiful hair?"

Ashley stopped and leaned back against him, feeling the warmth of his body, the definition in his chest. "Not lately."

"Well, you do." He nuzzled her neck. "Someone should tell you more often." He grabbed a paper towel and wiped a few grease spots off his forehead. "One oil change completed."

"Thanks." She took the paper towel from him and tossed it in the trash. "You spoil me."

At the same time Janessa bopped Landon on the head with the plastic spoon. "Oops." Ashley laughed a little. "Sorry." She took the spoon from their little girl and set her down on the floor. "All dry. You can run around now."

Janessa giggled and hurried across the floor and back again, thrilled to be free.

"You're painting, right?" Landon poured a glass of water and leaned against the counter, clearly admiring her.

"Not anymore." She loaded the last of the dishes and gave him a lopsided grin. "Brooke needs me at the clinic. Something came up and she can't be there." Ashley had taken a night class and learned how to operate the ultrasound machine. That way they could meet the needs of more girls, and maybe play a part in saving more babies. "I guess someone's coming in. Brooke said she sounded really upset."

Landon stooped down and swept Janessa into his arms. The little girl's laughter sounded like silvery wind chimes. Ashley stopped what she was doing and watched the two of them together. She would never take for granted a minute of her time with Janessa Faith. After losing Sarah, Janessa was an unexpected gift. The daughter Ashley felt sure she'd never have. She was dot-

ed on by everyone in the family—her brothers and her daddy most of all.

Janessa's laughter rang through the kitchen again. "Daddy … down!"

"Okay, little wanderer." He kissed her head and set her back on the floor.

She ran into the living room and found her pacifier on the table. They'd been trying to break her of it, but this close to naptime neither of them was going to take it from her. She popped it in her mouth and sat down on the kitchen floor, her back against Landon's legs. He looked down at her and tousled her wispy brown hair. "She looks just like you, Ash."

"That's what my dad says."

"It's true." He met her eyes, and the moment took on a deeper feel to it. "You and your mother. Her expressions sometimes remind me of your mom."

Ashley dried her hands and hung the dish towel back on the stove. As she did, she studied their daughter. "I see it too. I think Mom must be very proud of her. From her window in heaven."

"She must be proud of all her grandkids. They're growing up so fast." He eased his leg free of Janessa and circled his arms around Ashley's waist. "I'll watch her. I can do the work around here later."

"That's okay. She can come with me. I might stop by Sunset Hills."

"They'd love her." His smile made him look boyish, the way he'd looked when she first met him. "Sounds like you have it figured out."

They talked for a few more minutes, and then Landon returned to the garage. Ashley cleaned up and found Janessa's shoes. A few minutes later they were headed for Sunset Hills. Halfway there, Ashley made an impulsive turn and took a side trip to the cemetery. It was a beautiful day, the sort where she liked to stop and place flowers on the two graves that mattered most to her.

She parked as close as she could and then helped Janessa out of her car seat. Holding her daughter's small hand, they crossed the quiet street to an empty field. Wild flowers grew there this time of year, and she gathered two small bundles.

"Pretty!" Janessa delicately touched the tips of the flowers. "Pretty flowers, Mama."

"Yes, baby. They are pretty."

They walked back to the cemetery, staying at Janessa's little-girl pace. When they reached the grave markers, Ashley bent down and put one handful of flowers on each. Then she dusted off the names. Elizabeth Baxter, and Sarah Blake. Her precious mother and firstborn daughter.

Ashley didn't come here often, and never had she come with Janessa. But between the warm sunshiny morning and the happy heart of her two-year-old, it was impossible to feel very sad. At least her mom and daughter were together, waiting for the rest of the family to join them.

She didn't linger, but rather lifted Janessa onto her hip and prayed out loud. "God, thank You for giving us time to remember." Then she lifted her eyes to the blue sky. "Tell my mom and little Sarah we miss them. We always will."

Janessa couldn't possibly understand what was happening, let alone where they were. But she rested her head on Ashley's shoulder and stuck her fingers in her mouth. As if she somehow knew there was something sacred about the moment. Ashley nuzzled her cheek against Janessa's and walked her back to the van. One day she would explain to Janessa about her grandmother and her sister—how their deaths had come too early. But how the number of days in their lives hadn't mattered nearly as much as the life in their days.

The rich, beautiful, unforgettable life.

KEITH AND LISA WERE DRIVING ACROSS country, stunned at the speed in which God had helped them wrap up details back in San Jose. They'd listed their house the day after Dayne Matthews had called, and the next day they heard from a couple at church about a family who needed a house to rent. They worked out all the details and would either sell their house later or continue to rent it out. Dayne had been kind enough to agree to take on a few of the meetings for Jeremiah Productions so Keith could drive out to Indiana with Lisa. When Keith and Lisa traveled back to LA, they would stay in the leased beach house with the Matthews family. God was helping them to work it all out.

Chase and Kelly and several families from church had helped them finish last-minute tasks, and now they were only a day's drive from Bloomington. Keith glanced at his wife, asleep beside him. He focused on the road and remembered the way Chase stayed around, helping until the very end.

Kelly was talking to Lisa in the house when Keith and his friend loaded the last few boxes. Chase dusted off his hands and stood back, looking at Keith. "I guess I still can't believe it. We dreamed about making movies together for so long."

It only figured that the reality was bound to hit Chase eventually. He'd made his decision based on God's leading, but the changes had happened so fast, there'd been almost no time to acknowledge all they were losing along the way. Keith came closer and patted his friend's shoulder. "We were good together."

"We were."

Keith wasn't sure what to say. This was a more final good-bye than they'd first expected. He'd be in Bloomington or in LA, but he and Lisa would have no reason to return to San Jose. It could be a very long time before their two families were together once more. Before Keith and Chase shared a moment like this again. "How's it going?" He grinned at Chase in the waning afternoon light. "The youth pastor job?"

"I think I'm going to love it." Chase shrugged. "I'm already learning so much about the kids."

"The church kids or yours?" Keith's question was pointed, filled with a depth of understanding. He wanted Chase to know just how fully his decision made sense to him.

"Both. I know Molly's favorite songs now, and how Macy likes her pancakes smothered in peanut butter." He chuckled. "No danger of them forgetting my voice now. We sing together every morning."

Keith nodded slowly. He would miss this friend. They'd been together through so much — the years of mission work, the season of dreaming about making movies, and their push through the maze of Hollywood. "You made the right choice. Really."

"I know." His voice caught in his throat. He hesitated, then he hugged Keith hard, holding him for a long time before letting go. "I'll miss you, buddy. As right as this choice is, I want you to know I'll miss you."

Now Keith stared at the road ahead. He was glad for that final scene, the chance to have closure with Chase. There was no undoing all they'd been through. The memories would last, even as they moved into this next season of life. As they did, Keith would pray for his friend, the same way he was sure Chase would pray for him.

Beside him, Lisa stirred and blinked her eyes open. "Mmmm. That was a good nap."

"For me too." He smiled at her.

"Want me to drive?" Her eyes were apologetic. "I haven't really done my share."

Keith laughed. "You haven't driven."

"That's what I mean."

"Don't worry about it." He patted her knee. "It's enough having you with me." The truck was a twenty-four-footer, and they were pulling their family sedan behind them. Lisa was nervous about driving the rig, and Keith didn't blame her. "Have you heard from Andi?"

"This morning. She knows we'll be there tomorrow." Worry creased Lisa's forehead. "I asked her how she was doing, like I always do. She says she's fine, but she's not. I think she's worried about something."

"Maybe it's her grades. Did you ask how she finished?"

"Mostly A's, a few B's—at least as far as she can tell." Lisa looked out the window, quiet for a while. "I keep wondering if she could be depressed." She turned back to Keith. "That happens to college kids sometimes."

"I don't know." He kept his eyes on the road. "Andi's always been one of the happiest kids I know. Her smile's the first thing people notice about her."

"Before." Lisa's voice was proof of her heavy heart for their daughter. "It's like she's a different person. This move is the best thing we could've done. I can't get there soon enough."

"Every time I pray for her, I feel an urgency. Like she's not telling us something."

"I feel it too."

Frustration welled up inside Keith. "It makes me wish we were closer. I feel so helpless out here on the road. Like maybe she needs us now. Today." He reached for Lisa's hand. "I want to help her, however I can."

They rode in silence for a minute or so. "There's one thing we can do."

Keith nodded. His wife was right. There was nothing small or limiting about praying for their daughter. It was the one thing they could most certainly do for her. Keith drew a long breath. "Dear Lord, You know our Andi. You know what she's going through and why she doesn't sound like herself lately. We ask that even this very minute You might be with her. Comfort her and remind her of the truth. Place people in her path who will point her back to You. In Your name, amen."

"Amen."

They stayed quiet after that. There wasn't much to say where Andi was concerned. Not until they saw her in person and figured out what was going on, why she sounded so different. In the meantime, they needed to keep praying.

The urgency in Keith's heart was constant proof.

Fourteen

ASHLEY STILL HAD AN HOUR BEFORE the appointment at Sarah's House.

This would be the perfect day to take Janessa by the Sunset Hills Adult Care Home. She hadn't been by the old place in far too long. Only Burt and Helen remained from among the Alzheimer's patients Ashley had once cared for at the four-bedroom assisted living home. Her favorite patient had been Irvel, a gentle woman who had cared very much for Ashley. It was Irvel who had commented so often about Ashley's hair, how beautiful it was. Ashley smiled at the memory. The kind woman's comments weren't so much because Ashley's hair was really all that beautiful. But because Irvel wanted something kind to say, and the comment about her hair always seemed to be the first thing that came to her mind. Five times an hour, most days.

The stop at Sunset Hills was just what Ashley needed. Burt was doing better than ever. He seemed to remember her, and Ashley introduced him to Janessa. She was shy around the older people, but she waved her fingers at Burt and he did the same in return, tears filling his eyes. Babies were a rarity at Sunset Hills.

Helen was awake too. She had a scowl on her face as Ashley entered the kitchen, and she was complaining about something swimming in her coffee. The girl working that morning gave Ashley a knowing look. Nothing was swimming in Helen's coffee.

Ashley introduced herself, and the girl did the same. "Helen has her good days," she told Ashley when they were in the next room. "She loves when her daughter stops by."

"Her daughter?" Ashley's heart leapt at the news. "She still remembers her?"

"Yes." The girl smiled. "Her name's Sue."

"I know. I ... I've met her several times." There was no point rehashing the story of how Sue had come to see her mother for years, and how always Helen would yell at her to leave, not believing she was really Sue, and demanding to know what the middle-aged woman had done with her real daughter.

Not until Ashley finally understood that Helen was expecting Sue to be a teenager still, were they able to gently, carefully bridge the gap between Helen's memory and the reality. Ashley had been there the day the breakthrough happened, when Helen finally understood that her daughter Sue was, in fact, a middle-aged woman now. That Helen still remembered Sue was enough to make Ashley's day. She stopped in the kitchen before she left and bid Helen good-bye. Janessa did the same.

Helen shook her head, her face a mask of disgust. "Your baby's pretty." She jerked her thumb toward her coffee. "But there's something swimming in my drink. No one will help me."

"I'll help you." The girl on duty walked up with a fresh cup of coffee. She replaced the perfectly fine one and smiled at Helen. "There you go. Nothing swimming."

Ashley was glad Cole wasn't with them. Her son would've inevitably launched into a talk about his tadpoles, and how they were swimming in their fishbowl. That would've really put Helen over the edge. Ashley thanked the girl for letting her and Janessa stop in. She said a final farewell to Burt and the two of them were on their way.

She reached Sarah's House well before the appointment. Janessa toddled around the waiting area while Ashley went over the notes in the schedule book. Brooke had written in the margins that she suspected an abortion was in order for the girl about to come in. She'd given her age as nineteen, and her name as Andi.

Whether that was her real name or not, Ashley couldn't be sure. Many girls facing a crisis pregnancy were reluctant to share their real identity.

In the time left, she and Janessa sat at a table and colored. Janessa was just starting to like drawing, and her pictures were still faint and unrecognizable. But Ashley wondered whether her daughter might follow in her footsteps, maybe become an artist creating memorable designs on canvas someday.

They were still sitting together coloring a picture of a rainbow and a flower when the front door opened. Ashley stood, but before she could welcome the young woman standing out front, she felt her breath catch in her throat. She knew this girl. She'd seen her before — on the set of the movie filmed in Bloomington last year. This was the producer's daughter, right?

"Andi?"

Fear iced the girl's expression and she shook her head, taking a single step back. "I'm ... I'm afraid I have the wrong ..."

"Andi." Ashley tried to still her pounding heart. The girl obviously recognized her too. "It's okay. Our work here is confidential."

Andi's face had lost color. She looked like she might be sick, but she took a slow step forward and clutched her purse to her stomach. "You ... you know Bailey Flanigan, right?"

"I do." Ashley wasn't sure how much to tell her. The less, the better. She racked her mind, trying to remember what she knew about the producer's daughter. Her parents had been missionaries in Indonesia. That much she remembered. If the girl was pregnant now, then no wonder she looked terrified. "I met you on the movie set last summer."

Andi nodded, and again she looked like she might pass out. Janessa jumped up from the table then and ran to the girl. The toddler stopped short and flashed her a grin, then she waved.

"Hi!"

"Hi." Andi sat down primly on the edge of a waiting room chair.

"Mama!" Janessa turned suddenly shy and ran, giggling, into Ashley's arms. Ashley lifted her up onto her hip. She pulled the pacifier from her diaper bag and handed it to Janessa. Her daughter stuck it in her mouth and instantly cradled her head against Ashley's shoulder. "It's almost naptime." Ashley smiled at Andi. "She'll be asleep in a few minutes."

Andi didn't look interested. She kept her eyes on her lap and nodded absently. "No one ..." she lifted her eyes to Ashley. "No one knows about this. I don't want anyone to know."

"I understand." She came slowly toward Andi and took the chair opposite her. Janessa stayed quiet, her head still on Ashley's shoulder. "This is a crisis pregnancy center, Andi. Do you know what that is?"

"I read the ad." She ran her tongue over her lower lip. Clearly she was scared to death. "You give free ultrasounds. I know that."

"We're a Christian center." Ashley wanted to be kind, but she also wanted to be very clear. "Our goal is to show you the truth, that your unborn baby is a very real little person, a life. From there we pray that every frightened girl like yourself who comes through the door might make a decision to go through with her pregnancy. Whether she gives up her baby for adoption or chooses to raise the baby herself."

Andi's shoulders tensed up. She covered her face with one hand and waited a long time before she looked up again. "I ... I'm not sure what to do." A number of emotions flickered across her face—frustration and anger, and most of all, desperation. "Do you know my parents?"

"I met them briefly, but I don't know them." She handed Andi a clipboard. "Here. We need you to fill this out before the ultrasound, okay?"

The girl still looked like she might bolt. But she took the paperwork and a pen and quietly filled out the form. There was so much Ashley wanted to say. She had her own story to share, her own personal understanding of the value of life. But right now Andi wouldn't hear her anyway. She was too caught up in the nightmare happening to her. Ashley tried another tactic instead.

Andi handed the paperwork back, and Ashley looked it over. "Are you ready for the ultrasound?"

"Yes, please." She looked like she might run out of the center at any moment. "I need to know how ... how far along I am."

Ashley knew what that might mean. Abortion clinics would want that information, and testing at other clinics wouldn't be free. If Andi hadn't planned on getting pregnant, she probably had no idea how many weeks pregnant she was. She stood and smiled at Andi, willing the girl to feel safe and protected. "Follow me. We'll get started, okay?"

Ashley led her to a changing room and told her she could leave on her jeans as long as she unzipped them. "Put the gown on open in the front, and tie it loosely. I'll meet you in the examination room."

Andi was shaking, so scared she seemed barely able to move, let alone respond. Ashley was still holding Janessa, who had fallen asleep. There was a crib in the exam room, so she laid her daughter there and turned on the ultrasound machine. The whole time her heart broke for Andi and the decisions she was facing. *Dear God, this is why we opened the center. For girls like Andi. Please, Father, let Your Spirit fill this room. Let her feel Your supernatural peace so that she can truly grasp the reality of the life inside her, so she can hear the words You give me to say. I can't do this, Lord. This is beyond me. Please spare this little one. Both the baby and the precious young mother.*

You will not have to fight this battle, my daughter. Stand firm and see the deliverance I will give you.

Ashley felt the response soothe the wrinkles in her soul.

Thank You, God. I will stand firm. Help me stand firm. She loved the picture the Lord had given her. Ashley was a fighter—she always had been. But in a time like this, the battle wasn't hers. It was God's alone. The reality eased her anxiety and helped her know that the Lord was in control.

Andi knocked on the door, and Ashley opened it. The machine was warmed up and ready. "Lie down on the table. Try to get comfortable." Ashley remembered the music. A donor had given them a portable stereo system with six CDs of calming Christian songs, music by Jeremy Camp and Matthew West, Britt Nicole and Mandisa and NewSong. Music about life and peace and hope and grace. While Andi eased herself up onto the table, Ashley hit the Play button and adjusted the volume.

The gentle refrains of Mandisa's song "Voice of a Savior" quietly filled the room.

Andi sniffed, and a single tear slid down the side of her face. "I love this song."

"Me too." Ashley smiled. She checked once more on Janessa asleep in the crib across the room. Then she returned to Andi's side. Already the girl had pushed her jeans down and exposed her stomach. Ashley took a bottle of warm gel and dispensed enough across Andi's belly for the machine to work. "This won't take long."

In the lobby, she heard the sound of the door opening again. A retired nurse worked the day shift at the front desk. The door to the examination room was still open. "Is that you, Betty?"

"It is. You're working with the first appointment?"

Ashley turned compassionate eyes to the college girl on the table. "Yes. We're just getting started."

Betty appeared at the door with a clipboard. She wasn't trained in ultrasounds, but she would register the results. She stood a few feet away and waited.

Ashley took the wand of the machine and began working

it slowly across Andi's stomach. The machine made a series of sounds, and in no time she settled the probe over an area just beneath Andi's belly button. At the same time, a rhythmic wooshing sound filled the room, pulsing in an unmistakable pattern.

Andi drew a soft gasp. "That's ..."

"The baby's heartbeat." Ashley never tired of this, catching the first sounds of new life. Tears gathered in her eyes, but she blinked them away, smiling. "Your baby's heart sounds very healthy, Andi."

The girl craned her neck forward, peering at the screen. "Can I see it?"

Ashley adjusted the probe a little more until a tiny pulsating picture could be seen at the center of the screen. "There it is." She pointed to the image. "That's your baby's heart." She moved her finger along a curved area adjacent to the baby's beating heart. "That's the spine. Can you see that?"

"Yes. I ... I didn't think it would be so clear."

"It is. Your baby's a little miracle. Already growing and becoming." Ashley kept her tone kind and tender. The music added to the emotion of the moment and she thanked God again for the wonder of the ultrasound machine. Anyone could tell a pregnant woman her body contained nothing more than a mass of tissues. But ultrasounds were different. The pictures, the sounds ... the images didn't lie. A baby was growing inside Andi, no question.

"How far along am I?"

"Let's see." Ashley was new at this, but she captured a few pictures of the unborn baby and clicked a few buttons. The machine computed the age of the fetus. "Looks like you're ten weeks. Maybe ten and a half."

"Ten weeks?" Andi looked shocked at the news. Her face grew ashen again and she turned away from the images. "Can ... I be done now?"

"Of course."

Betty made a few notations on the clipboard, and she handed Andi a clean towel.

Ashley turned off the machine and wiped down the wand. "Go ahead and dry off, then you can get dressed in the changing room. Let's meet back here in a few minutes."

"Thank you." Andi's voice was almost inaudible. She pulled the gown tight around herself as she took the towel and left for the changing room.

When she was gone, Betty exchanged a sad look with Ashley. "She's so scared."

"I know." They were whispering. "Pray, Betty."

"I am." Her eyes softened. "I have been the whole time."

Betty caught the printout from the ultrasound and finished filling in the chart. She was back at her desk by the time Andi returned to the examination area. There was a sofa in the far corner, next to the crib where Janessa was sleeping. Ashley led Andi there, and they sat on opposite ends. Andi kept her eyes focused intently on her hands.

Give me the words, please God. "I've been in your seat, Andi. People make mistakes."

Andi kept her face downturned, but she lifted her eyes to Ashley's. "You were pregnant before … when you weren't married?"

"Yes." Ashley felt a surge of joy. Andi was willing to listen. "I was in France, about your age. I'd left home and I wanted to make my own way. Live by my own rules." Ashley didn't know anything about Andi's story, how she'd gotten into this situation or who the guy might be. But she could sense Andi listening a little more intently. "I began dating a famous painter, and after a few months I wound up pregnant." She paused, still ashamed of the details. "He was a married man. He told me he wasn't about to leave his wife, and he gave me the address of an abortion clinic in Paris."

"You … had an abortion?" Andi crossed her arms tight across

her stomach. She looked small and frail, completely overwhelmed by her situation.

"I didn't." Ashley would forever be grateful for her answer. She pictured her precious Cole. "I got as far as the waiting room, and I couldn't do it. I didn't know what to do, but I was sure of one thing. My baby wasn't to blame for my actions."

Quiet tears slipped from Andi's eyes and trickled down her face. Ashley handed her a tissue and continued. "Do you know my family?"

Andi sniffed. "The ... the Baxters?"

"Yes." Ashley felt the heaviness of those long ago days. "I came home alone and pregnant. No one in my family had ever done anything like that. I felt like the worst person in the world."

"What did your parents say?"

"They were disappointed." It was important to keep the details real. "But they welcomed me home, and when Cole was born, they loved him with all the love they had to give." Ashley pictured her mother, caring for little Cole, teaching Ashley how to be a mommy. "There are lots of grandkids in our family today. But I think my mom always loved Cole the best. Because he didn't have the easiest start."

Andi sniffed again. "I don't know how my parents will react. They're busy. A baby would ... it would make life hard for them. In their line of work." She shook her head, fear gathering around her again.

"There are options." Again Ashley didn't want to be pushy. But it was important Andi have all the information before she left. Ashley reached for a folder on the table next to the couch. Then she stood and collected a few photos from the printer. She tucked them into the folder and handed it to Andi. "Take this. Pictures of your baby, and other information about adoption—both closed and open. Ways you can connect with a private Christian agency and even choose your baby's adoptive parents."

Andi looked terrified at the thought. She took the folder and struggled to her feet. "Thank you. For your time." For a quick moment she looked at Janessa sleeping in the crib. Then she took a few steps toward the door. "I ... I have to go."

Ashley walked her to the door, praying that Andi would stop, that she'd stay and talk a little longer. But nothing would stop her this time. She thanked Ashley once more and practically ran from the clinic. Ashley felt the disappointment settle in around her heart.

Be with her, God. Save her baby's life. Please, Lord.

"I have a feeling about this one." Betty smiled sadly from her place behind the desk. "That God has a very special plan for both of them. The mother and the baby."

"Me too." Ashley sighed. "I just wish she would've stayed."

Only then did she look more closely at Andi's paperwork. She'd put her name as Andi Smith, and the address and phone number were clearly made up. Ashley could reach her if she needed to. She could get the girl's information from Jenny and Bailey Flanigan. Without giving away anything, of course.

But she hoped she wouldn't need to do that. Andi had the material she needed to choose life. Now Ashley could only stand firm and pray.

And let God Himself fight the battle for the life of Andi's baby.

Fifteen

CODY STOOD NEXT TO RYAN TAYLOR and listened as the head coach shouted orders to the lineman.

"Get low," Coach Taylor strode closer and leaned down, eye level to the lineman. "That's not low enough. You have to get lower, men." He put himself on the line and got down so low he looked like he was sitting in an invisible chair. "This is low. Can you see this?" He straightened. "Now get low." He walked the line, analyzing their efforts. "I know this is summer, but that doesn't mean we give half an effort. What we do in June will determine who we'll be in October."

Cody soaked in every word, every piece of advice. He loved everything about being at Clear Creek High this week. He'd been given a playbook, and already he had memorized most of it. Coaching was a whole new world to him, and the lessons he was learning were enough to convince him he was right about his suspicions. He loved being out here. Already he was sure that he wanted nothing more than to be a coach. Like Ryan Taylor.

Like Jim Flanigan.

This week of practice had been good for him in another way too. It had taken his mind off Bailey and the strange incident with her and Tim at the school cafeteria the other day. Cody crossed his arms and kept his feet shoulder-width apart—the way he'd seen the other coaches stand for as far back as he could remember playing. It felt amazing to be on this side of the game, but this week he was supposed to spend his time watching.

"There," Ryan yelled—mostly so he could be heard across

the field. Coach Taylor was not one of those coaches who ruled by fear. "That's getting low. Everyone look at McCoy. See that? Get low like that. All your power comes from the explosion off the line, and that only happens if you're low."

Cody blinked, and the action before him blurred. Instead he was back on campus, spotting Bailey and Tim and deciding to stop by for a quick hello. Cody couldn't lie to himself. It hurt, seeing her with him. Especially when Cody and Bailey had been together so often lately. Almost like Tim was some imaginary boyfriend who didn't really exist in Bailey's world. But seeing them that afternoon was painful proof.

You told her you'd be her friend, he reminded himself. *Now's your chance to prove it.* With that he'd altered his course across the mall so he'd walk past their table. Bailey seemed surprised to see him. She blushed as soon as he walked up—whatever that meant. But before she could say anything, Tim's attitude kicked in. It wasn't just that he seemed bothered by Cody's interruption. He seemed condescending. Like he thought he was better than Cody. Or that maybe Cody was wasting their time. Cody was already getting the point when Tim made his blunt comment, about how he and Bailey wanted to talk about their auditions alone.

In his younger football-playing, high school partying days, Cody would've solved the problem with a single blow to Tim Reed's face. And he was sorely tempted in that moment. But in the same instant, he realized there was no point. If Tim wanted to be a jerk, if that was the kind of guy he was becoming, then so be it. He was the guy Bailey had chosen, after all. If she wanted to be with a guy like that, then fine.

Bailey had tried to call him three times since then, but each time he let the call go. What could she possibly want to say? That she was sorry for sitting by while Tim treated him like some lower class citizen? That she still wasn't sure she wanted to be serious with Tim? He was sick of her explanations, no matter how much fun he had with her. She had chosen Tim. Now let her spend her time with him.

A whistle blew. "Take five, men. Get some water and get back here." Ryan Taylor jogged easily over to the other coaches and motioned for Cody to join them. "During the season we'll have a line coach working with the guys. But they need to understand their importance on the line. Everything fails or succeeds based on that, absolutely everything."

The other coaches agreed, and Ryan dismissed them for the five minutes. Only Cody stayed. "I love this. I'm soaking it all in, Coach. Thanks so much for having me."

"I'm watching you. The times I have you working with our quarterbacks. You're a natural, Cody." Ryan grinned at him. "I've already thanked Jim for sending you out here." They walked together toward the water cooler. "Seems like yesterday you were out there yourself."

"It's been three years. Amazing how time goes."

"Gets worse as you get older." Ryan squinted at the empty field. "A blink ago I was out there playing pro ball." He patted his still flat stomach. "Now I couldn't run a series of forty-yard dashes to save my life."

"I think you could." Cody laughed. He loved the camaraderie he was finding with Coach Taylor. "You're in better shape than most of the kids out there."

"Now you sound like Kari."

Cody grinned and helped himself to a few quick gulps of water. He knew a little of Coach Taylor's story. Pretty sensational stuff. He and Kari Baxter had dated when they were in high school, but then Ryan had gone off to a big college to play football and she had gone on to work as a fashion model. On one fateful college football Saturday, Ryan suffered an injury that nearly paralyzed him. Kari and her dad, John Baxter, rushed to his side, but somehow Kari came away from the hospital believing Ryan had fallen in love with someone else. A year later she married someone else, but the guy had an affair and wound up getting shot and killed by some lunatic stalker guy on the IU campus.

After that, Ryan and Kari found each other again, and a few years later the two of them married. Ryan left pro football five or six years ago and moved to Bloomington so Kari could be near her family. That's how he wound up coaching at Clear Creek High.

Coach Taylor's story had resonated with Cody since Bailey had shared it with him. Maybe because he could relate to Ryan's patience, the way he'd kept his love for Kari all those years. The way he was willing to be her friend after she lost her husband. Even if that's all he ever was to her. It made him think of his friendship with Bailey.

But there was a difference.

Kari Baxter had been convinced Ryan loved someone else. Bailey knew better. How much clearer could Cody possibly be? He had sat on that rock overlooking the lake at the Cru retreat and told her he wasn't dating because he was waiting for that one special girl. She couldn't possibly think he meant anyone but her, right?

He finished his paper cup of water, crumpled it, and threw it in the trash. They had another hour before practice was over. Action was about to start up again when Connor came up to him. Connor was playing tight end and backup quarterback for Clear Creek next year. Already he was impressing the coaches with his speed and agility. He had his father's build, and even if football wasn't his first love, he was bound to start next fall.

Connor grinned at him. "Think Coach wants us to stay low?"

Cody laughed so hard he spit his water on the grass. "Way to listen, Flanigan."

"I try." He chuckled hard as he walked off. His younger brothers

—Justin and Shawn—were both freshmen with a shot at making varsity. They were fast and strong, and they could jump a mile in the air, hanging there until the football landed in their hands.

On the next set of plays, Coach Taylor placed Shawn at wide receiver and ran three plays at him. Each time Shawn soared off the ground, snatched the ball from the sky, and scored a touchdown. No one could touch him. Cody was on the sidelines with Connor and the rest of the team, and all of them whooped and hollered at Shawn Flanigan's impressive showing.

"Yep," Connor raised his fist in the air. "That's my brother. We might as well be twins. Two peas in a pod."

Everyone laughed and hit Connor on the back. The Flanigan boys always had fun talking as if they were blood related. Once when Cody lived with them, Connor brought a girl to the house. As they walked into the kitchen, Cody was sitting on one side of the bar, Shawn and Justin on the other. Connor introduced Cody as an adopted member of the family, but with Shawn and Justin he said simply, "These are my brothers."

The girl hesitated, then she gave Connor a skeptical look. "Your brothers?"

Connor didn't skip a beat. He wrinkled his brow, walked up to Shawn, and held his white arm next to his brother's black one. "What, you think he's not my brother 'cause he's a little tanner than me?"

It was the same thing here. Connor's Haitian brothers might out-perform him on the football field, but that only gave Connor another reason to claim them as his brothers. The Flanigan family had a love that could laugh through anything, a love that knew no color barriers or resentment.

When practice was over, Connor rounded up Cody and his younger brothers. "Bailey called. Her roommate Andi needs our help." Connor checked his cell phone. "I guess Andi's parents pulled into town this morning with their moving van." Connor flexed his arms. "At least she knew who to call."

They all laughed, and Cody agreed to join them. The only thing he needed to do tonight was check on his mother. She was still hanging out with Benny the Tiger, much to Cody's dismay. He liked to stop by unexpectedly, in case he might find her at a time when she needed him.

He drove the boys in his car, and they pulled up at the address Bailey had given them in time to see her park across the street. For a long few seconds, Cody's eyes met hers and neither of them made a move to get out of their cars.

"Uh ... it's okay if we get out, right?" Connor tapped Cody's shoulder. He and Shawn were in the back seat. "You and Bailey can look at each other later."

"Hey ... be nice." Cody leaned back and playfully punched the oldest Flanigan boy. But as he got out, he avoided looking at Bailey again. He hadn't thought much about what he would feel seeing her here. This was the first time they'd been together since the Tim incident.

Jim Flanigan must've been off this afternoon, because he was already there, along with John Baxter and Ashley and Landon Blake. Ryan Taylor was pulling up too. The Flanigan boys ran to be with their dad, and Cody took his time locking his car. As he did, Bailey approached him, her voice softer than usual. "Hey."

"Hey." Cody turned to face her, but he kept his guard up, leaning against his car, his hands in his shorts pockets. He never felt self-conscious about his prosthetic leg, but for some reason here, he did. He wasn't sure Bailey had seen him in shorts since his injury. He thought about glancing down, trying to imagine how it might've looked to someone who hadn't seen it before. He wore a knee brace to bridge the look of his real leg and the artificial lower limb, and with the socks and his shoes matching, most people would have to look hard to tell the difference.

Maybe it was the way Tim had treated him. Whatever it was, the leg or Bailey's boyfriend, Cody felt inadequate standing there. Awkward, like he didn't belong in her life—even as her friend. She was looking hard at him, searching his eyes. "You haven't answered my calls."

He shrugged one shoulder. "I've been busy."

"No." Bailey knew him better. "That's not true. You're mad about the Tim thing." She released a frustrated breath and paced a few steps away, then back again. "He was a jerk that day. I called so I could apologize for him."

Cody stayed chill, determined that she wouldn't see the hurt he'd felt then or now. "No big deal." He tried a smile, but it fell short. "Don't worry about it, Bailey. If there's an apology made, it should come from him." He pointed his thumb over his right shoulder. "There's work to do. Talk to you later." And with that, he side-stepped her and headed for the guys clustered at the back of the moving van.

After the first few loads, he was setting a box down in the back bedroom when Bailey showed up at the doorway. He smiled politely at her and tried to walk around her, but she wouldn't move. "Don't do this. Please."

He felt his shoulders sink, and a sigh died on his lips. "Do what?"

"Punish me for the way he acted." Bailey's voice was quiet, so none of the others would hear her. But the passion in her tone was loud and clear. "He was rude and I told him so."

Cody stared at her, disbelieving what he was hearing. "You told him he was rude?"

"Yes." She sounded indignant. "He was rude, and I wanted him to know it."

Normally Cody kept his comments about Tim and Bailey to himself. The last thing he wanted was to push her away from a guy she still clearly wanted to date. And she was still seeing him.

She had to be. How else could he read that? But here, he felt a desperate need to comment. "You're in love with the guy, right?" He refused to get angry. Instead he used his softest voice so she wouldn't feel cornered.

She hesitated, her lips parted. "I need to talk to him ... I think it's over between us."

"You think?" He dropped his tone to a more passionate hiss. "You just told me yourself, he was rude. And for the record, you were right. He was rude and condescending and arrogant." A laugh came from him, but it held not even a little humor. "And this is the guy you've been dating?" He stared at her, unable to stop himself. "Can I tell you something, Bailey?"

She didn't seem to have any way to fight back. Instead she hung her head. When she looked up, tears pooled in her eyes.

"You don't look happy when you're with him."

"I told you, I'm going to talk to him. Our schedules haven't worked out."

"That's it." Cody held up his hands and let them fall to his sides again. "I have to get back to work." He tried to walk past her, hoping she would step aside so he could pass.

Instead, she put her hands on his shoulders. "Please, Cody," her voice was strained, her eyes pleading with him. "Don't do this. My relationship with Tim has nothing to do with you and me. Don't be mad."

"Why?" He hated his tone, but he was too hurt to sound any softer. Carefully he moved her hands from his shoulders and slid past her. "You have Tim if you need someone to talk to." And with that he walked fast down the hall and back outside to the moving truck. He wasn't sure where Bailey went, or whether she stayed to help Mrs. Ellison inside the house. Either way, he didn't see her again.

No matter how many times he tried to convince himself, he knew he was wrong. He had no right getting mad at Bailey, just because of his own hurt. The way he saw it, she should've known how he was feeling about Tim. But that didn't mean he wanted to fight with her. It certainly didn't mean he wanted distance between them. But that's exactly what he'd created by being so harsh back in the house.

He was trying to decide whether to find her and apologize, when his cell phone sounded from his pocket. His ringtone was the hit song by Matthew West — "The Motions." Every time his phone rang it reminded him of the truth — he didn't want to live his life going through the motions. He wanted to live every moment for Christ. Whatever the cost. He wished he would've heard his ringtone before his earlier exchange with Bailey.

The call was from his mother's house, so he moved a few yards away from the others and answered it. "Hello? Mom?"

"Cody?" Her voice sounded slurred. "Can y'come over? I don't feel so good."

"I'm on my way." He was halfway to his car by the time the call ended. He yelled to Coach Taylor, who was just coming out for another load. "Something's come up. Gotta run."

"See you tomorrow." Coach waved. "Keep memorizing the playbook."

Cody slid into his car, started the engine, and sped off. Whatever was going on between him and Bailey, it would have to wait. Right now he needed to get to his mother's house, and the whole way he could only thank God for the obvious. No matter what his mother had done, she wasn't where she thought she'd be when she fell off the wagon. She wasn't in a hearse or in the back of a squad car.

Not yet anyway.

BAILEY COULDN'T BELIEVE CODY WOULD LEAVE without saying good-bye. He must've been much more upset than she knew, but she couldn't give the matter much attention because almost as soon as Cody left, Andi walked into the house. Bailey went to her, happy to be part of the moving crew. But from the moment she saw Andi's face, Bailey felt the mood in the house change. Andi looked distant and lost, nothing like the girl she'd been when they first met.

"Hi." Bailey kept her tone tempered. Her friend's mood didn't call for anything too upbeat. "You okay?"

"Fine." Andi's voice was as lifeless as her eyes. She set a bag of cleaning supplies on the kitchen counter and turned to Bailey. "Thanks for being here. Your family too."

Mrs. Ellison walked into the room then, but she stopped short when she saw Andi. "Sweetheart ... what's wrong?"

Andi tried to smile. "I don't feel good." She clutched her stomach, and anyone could see the dark circles beneath her eyes.

Andi's mother came to her, worry lining her face. "Do you have a fever?" She kissed her daughter's forehead. "Hmmm. No." She stood back and assessed Andi. "What are your symptoms?"

Bailey felt awkward, like she should go back to helping with the move. But she wasn't sure if it might be more rude to leave, so she stayed still, quietly watching.

"I'm just tired." Andi shivered a little. "Maybe if I take a nap."

"I don't like this." Her mom's concern seemed stronger than before. "You were in bed by six last night, and you slept in this morning." She ran her hand along Andi's arm. "Maybe it's mono. That happens to lots of college kids. Especially their first year."

The idea seemed possible. Bailey had heard of others in their dorm battling mono.

"I'm fine. Just run down."

"I don't know." Mrs. Ellison circled her arms around Andi and swayed with her. "I hate seeing you like this."

Andi pulled back and tried another smile. "I'm fine. I'll feel better tomorrow."

Her mom hesitated, searching Andi's eyes. But then she smiled with the sort of deep compassion only a mother could muster. "Go sleep. We'll see how you feel in a few hours."

Andi hugged her mom and then turned toward the hallway. She was almost out of sight when she must've remembered Bailey, because she stopped and looked back. "Sorry. I guess I'm out of it."

"That's okay." As much as the idea of mono seemed plausible, Bailey had the feeling once more that something else was responsible for the change in Andi. She smiled at her friend anyway. "Hope you feel better."

"Thanks." Then without another word or even a slight hesitation, she was gone.

Mrs. Ellison waited until she heard Andi shut her new bedroom door before she released a desperate-sounding sigh. She braced herself against the kitchen counter and hung her head for a long moment. When she looked up, she focused grief-stricken eyes at Bailey. "Do you see it? How different she is?"

Bailey wasn't sure how much she should say, but she could certainly agree about the change in Andi. "Definitely." She kept her voice low. "I see it, for sure."

"We were worried about her before we arrived. But seeing her this morning ... she's thin and withdrawn, her dark hair and the dark circles under her eyes. It's like she's an entirely different girl." She massaged her temples. "I've been praying constantly, but I have no answers, no idea what to do." Andi's mom looked intently at Bailey, a pleading sort of look. "Please, tell me what you know. Is she drinking again? Taking drugs?"

"Well ..." Again Bailey wasn't sure it was her place to say much. But then she thought about the friendship she shared with her mother. The best thing for Andi would be a closer relationship with her mom. If she could tell the woman anything that might help, then she would be doing Andi a favor. She gathered her thoughts and hoped Andi wouldn't feel betrayed by anything she might say. She wanted to be a friend more than anything.

"Please, Bailey ... whatever you know."

"Okay, well ..." Bailey looked once back toward the hallway. Andi couldn't hear them, she was sure of that. She moved closer to Andi's mom and leaned on the opposite side of the counter. "I don't think she's drinking. I mean, she might be. But I never smell alcohol around her or see it in the dorm." She hesitated. "She changed a lot when she started seeing Taz. But this depression she's in, that started after they broke up."

"He was bad for her. We knew that, but there was nothing we could do to stop her from seeing him."

"Yes, ma'am."

"So this Taz ..." Mrs. Ellison seemed to dread whatever she was about to ask. But she pushed ahead anyway. "Do you think he and Andi were physical?"

Bailey bit her lip. She wanted to stick to the facts, but she thought maybe Andi's mom should know her suspicions. "I don't know. He's seeing someone else now. But when they were dating, Taz did a film with her and ... I think there might have been some nudity. He told Andi to think of the film as art, and the body as the paint."

"Dear, God ... no." The woman seemed to age ten years in as many seconds. Her hands trembled as she held them to her mouth. "What has she done?"

"I asked her what was wrong. I've tried lots of times. She always tells me she's fine." Bailey pictured the last time, when Andi wouldn't even look at her. "Can you take her to a doctor?"

"I've brought it up three times since we pulled in. She doesn't want to go."

Bailey's heart hurt for her friend. "If there's anything I can do, please ... let me know."

"My sweet Andi." She groaned. "How could this happen?"

"I'm sorry. I wish … I wish I had more to tell you. I've been at home more often this last semester. I missed my family, and … well … Andi didn't seem to want me around. She stopped going to Campus Crusade, and she didn't want to talk about her faith. She just seemed, I don't know, different."

"She is." Mrs. Ellison reached across the counter and patted Bailey's hand. "You go on with the others, Bailey. But pray for her, will you? She's our only child, and I won't stand by while she slips away."

"I'll pray, yes ma'am. Again, I'm sorry." Bailey bid the woman good-bye and joined the others outside. The minute she was back out in the sunshine, she felt like she could breathe again. The tension inside the house was that thick. Even then the sadness of the situation remained. Bailey remembered Andi once saying she needed to experience life. Real life. But now her choices had darkened everything about her world and her existence. Her eyes no longer shone with life. That was the saddest, scariest part about this new Andi.

The life she had tried to find looked a whole lot more like death.

Sixteen

LISA WAS FINISHED BEING PASSIVE. IT was their third day in Bloomington, and Andi's behavior was terrifying her. When Andi wasn't sleeping, she was slipping out of the house and taking off for hours at a time without a word to either her or Keith. When she'd return, she'd act despondent and nonplussed, as if it were perfectly normal to come and go without checking in.

This morning Lisa had woken to a quiet house, tiptoed back to Andi's room, and peeked in to find her gone again. Fear and sorrow twisted around her heart as she leaned on Andi's bedroom door frame. *What's happening, Lord ... what's going on with her? And why can't we reach her? I know You're here, and I know You care ... so why is this happening?*

Faith without works is dead, my daughter ... you must take action ...

The answer was quick and clear, and it seemed to come straight from God. Faith without works was dead ... that was a Bible verse from James. But what action was she supposed to take?

She walked back down the hallway, collected her well-worn Bible from the desk in their new office, and sat at the dining room table. As she thumbed through the book, sunlight streamed through the window and splashed rays of hope across the pages. She knew exactly where she was headed—the same place she turned as a missionary when she'd reached the end of herself, when the walls were closing in and defeat seemed certain.

1 Chronicles 28:20. She reached it quickly and ran her thumb

over the oft-read section. *Be strong and courageous, and do the work. Do not be afraid or discouraged, for the Lord God, my God, is with you. He will not fail you or forsake you …*

God was with her. That's what she needed to remember. The Lord knew the battle they were fighting for Andi, and He knew what needed to happen next. She and Keith needed to stay in the fight, they needed to take action somehow and stay courageous. Even when fear over the changes in Andi threatened to consume them. Lisa picked up the phone and made an appointment with a Christian counselor she'd read about in the local Yellow Pages. Then she waited for Keith to wake up.

A few minutes later she heard him in the kitchen making coffee. "Morning, honey."

"Morning."

"I'm in here."

He crossed the kitchen and leaned into the dining room. "Hi." His half smile warmed the chilly space between them. "Where's Andi?"

"Gone again."

He exhaled long and slowly and rubbed the back of his neck. "We need to talk to her."

"Bring the coffee in here when it's ready." Lisa could feel the fight building inside her, the one for her daughter's life. "I booked her an appointment with the Christian counselor I told you about."

Keith held her eyes for a long few seconds. "We'll get through this."

"We will."

As Keith returned to the coffee, Lisa leaned back in her seat and stared out the window at the small fenced yard. Had they really left their house and moved across country in a matter of days? And what about the other changes they'd gone through? Chase done with making movies … Dayne Matthews jumping in as Keith's new co-producer and ministry partner ... everything was happening so fast Lisa could barely see for the dizziness she sometimes felt.

She closed her eyes and breathed in slowly. God was in this; even when life felt crazy, God was in the details for those who loved Him. Dayne was proof. He was a perfect fit for Keith, savvy to the industry and with a name that brought instant respect and open doors. Thankfully, Dayne and Katy had been able to stay on in LA for the last few business meetings pertaining to the release of *The Last Letter* and the pre-production for *Unlocked*. Keith had been there for most of the appointments, but then they'd found renters for their San Jose house so quickly. Since then life had been a crazy race. Professional movers packed up their house, and they were on the road to Bloomington.

So Dayne Matthews was definitely proof God was still providing. Even so Keith needed a week to help catch Dayne up to speed on the history of Jeremiah Productions and all that went on during the filming of *The Last Letter*, all that was at stake with *Unlocked*. Dayne and his family were flying home from LA this weekend, and early next week Brandon Paul was coming here to meet them. Brandon was happy for the trip. Something about needing a break from Hollywood and wanting to clear his head.

As great as Bloomington was, Lisa couldn't imagine staying here very long. They were renting — a one-year lease. A good call, really. It would allow Keith to work closely with Dayne Matthews and film *Unlocked*. Most of all it had brought them to Andi. But she and Keith had a feeling this wasn't home. Not for any of them. They were missionaries, and the fields God had given them were the ripe ones of Hollywood. It was fine for Dayne to live here and commute, but Lisa had a feeling she and Keith would wind up in Los Angeles.

When that happened, she wanted Andi with them.

From the moment they saw their daughter, Lisa and Keith

knew something was terribly wrong. Lisa guessed Andi was on drugs, and maybe she was. But she'd looked through her daughter's things when Andi was out and found nothing to support the notion. Whatever the reason, the changes were drastic. A year ago Andi was the happiest teenage girl Lisa and Keith knew. Now she seemed trapped in a full-blown case of depression with all the accompanying symptoms. Exhaustion, a lack of interest in life, no appetite, despondency. Lisa stared at her open Bible. Of course there was the other unthinkable possibility, the one Lisa hated to consider.

Andi might be pregnant with Taz's baby.

Whatever was wrong, when Andi came home this time— from wherever she'd gone that morning—she and Keith would sit her down and explain as kindly as they could what they were about to do.

Keith joined her with two cups of coffee. He gave her the one with cream and took the seat opposite her. "I've been praying all morning. I hope she'll at least agree to the appointment."

"She will." Lisa had to believe her daughter wasn't so far gone that she'd defy them to their faces. "The woman's a Christian counselor. That shouldn't feel threatening."

Keith held his coffee up to his face and closed his eyes. He looked weary and worn out. "Tell me more about what Bailey said." He blinked and stared at her, as if he were hoping for a different answer this time.

"Just that the change happened when she started dating this Taz character. But she got worse after they broke up."

"How could a complete stranger convince her to take off her clothes?" Anger simmered in Keith's tone. "That's not how we raised her."

"Honey," Lisa felt compassion for her daughter, even if she didn't understand her decisions. "I think that was the point. She wanted to be different."

"Is this because of the movies? Because we chose Bailey and not her for that extra role?"

"Keith, don't." She took hold of his hand across the table. "We could both blame ourselves. That isn't the point. We have to deal with where she's at now."

"What about ..." his voice broke and he looked at the ceiling for a few seconds. A quick shake of his head and he struggled to find control again. "What if she's pregnant? We have to help her, Lisa. We can't just ... you know, take her to some shrink and hope for the best." He waved his hand toward the front door. "She could be out there having an abortion right now."

Lisa had thought about that. Last night she'd gone into Andi's room and found her curled up beneath the covers before it was dark out. She'd sat on the bed beside her daughter and smoothed her hand over her newly dark short hair. "Baby, tell me ... whatever it is, just tell me."

But Andi only reached out her hand and took hold of Lisa's.

"Really, honey," Lisa kept her voice as kind and non-judgmental as possible. She prayed her daughter would hear the love of God with every word. "You can tell me anything. Trust me, Andi, please, sweetheart."

"I'm sorry." She muttered without once even turning to look at Lisa. "I'm just tired."

Keith set his coffee down. "Have you seen her eat since we've been home?"

"A bowl of oatmeal yesterday. That's about it."

"Maybe that's where she is now—having breakfast with the guy. Maybe she's running off with him."

"No." Lisa was convinced that wasn't the case. Andi wouldn't have come home at all if Taz still had that kind of control over her. "Bailey says he's seeing someone else."

Keith pursed his lips, seething with anger toward the guy and whatever he'd done to exact such a change in their daughter. But before he could say anything else, they heard the front door open. "Andi?" Keith was on his feet.

"Careful," Lisa whispered. Her look warned him to go easy. She wasn't a minor; she could leave anytime and never come back. It happened with grown kids all the time.

With a quick nod, Keith mouthed that it would be okay. Then he stepped into the entryway. "Andi ..."

"Hi." She walked into the dining room with Keith at her side. As soon as she saw Lisa, she stopped and looked from one of them to the other. "Am I in trouble?"

"We're worried about you." Lisa felt like she was walking a tightrope. She couldn't sound like a martyr or a victim, but she had to get her point across. "As long as you're living with us, you need to tell us where you're going. When you'll be home."

"Okay." Andi set her backpack down. "I wasn't sure you were awake. I went to school and talked to a counselor. I'm thinking about moving to Indianapolis for the summer. So I can take classes at IU's Indianapolis campus."

Nothing Andi said lately added up, and this was no exception. Lisa tried to keep her expression even. "Honey ... don't they offer summer classes here?"

Andi looked nervously from Keith back to Lisa. "Yes, but ... three of my friends from theater are spending the summer in the city. They already have an apartment there, and they said I can live with them." She paused, but when neither Lisa nor Keith said anything, she rushed on. "Plus there's an acting coach there; she's offering us discounted classes, and Mom, you said so yourself, I can't expect to walk into an audition and get a part just because my dad's a producer. Not without training." Andi grabbed a quick breath. "Oh, and the Indianapolis campus has a stronger art department—that's what the counselor told me this morning. I need three art courses to complete my general ed and the pre-reqs for my major."

Andi went on about exactly which art classes she wanted to take, and Lisa listened, skeptical. Her daughter's explanation reminded her of an incident in Indonesia when Andi brought a painted vase home from the village women's craft table. Lisa had a feeling her daughter didn't have permission to take the item, but when she asked about it Andi rattled off a long explanation. It was the first time Lisa had caught her in a lie, and now Andi's tone, the look in her eyes, was the very same. Struggling to create an explanation where in all honesty there was none.

When she finished, Keith looked at Andi for a long time. His eyes told her that clearly he was concerned. "Sounds like your mind's made up."

"It is." Andi was practically breathless from the monologue, but she seemed about to slip back into her new, more sedate personality. She was still standing near the dining room table, but she slouched back against the wall. "I'm driving there Friday to get things settled."

It was already Thursday, so the idea of Andi leaving so soon stirred instant anxiety in Lisa's heart. If they were going to help her, they didn't have much time. "Can I ask, honey, how you're planning to pay for a summer in Indianapolis?"

Andi's hesitation was just long enough for Lisa to be sure. Her daughter clearly hadn't thought about this part of her plan. "I can get a job. I might do some acting too. The coach might have some leads. I was hoping you would help out like you do during the regular school year."

Lisa figured this wasn't the time to explain that expenses would begin the minute she arrived. No one would let her share an apartment without paying rent. Then there would be meals and gas and a number of other costs. She looked at Keith, and his eyes told her it was time to move on, get to the point.

Keith took the lead. He sucked in a long, steadying breath. "Sit down, sweetheart. Your mother and I need to talk to you."

Again Andi looked from him to Lisa and back again. "About what?"

"Just sit down." Keith was struggling to stay patient. "Please, Andi."

She slowly pulled out the seat at the head of the table, putting her between the two of them. Lisa closed her eyes for a few seconds. *Give us the words, Lord. We don't want to turn her away. Please.*

"In the few days since we've been here, your mom and I have seen a drastic change in you, honey." Keith kept his words slow and measured. He sat back and folded his hands on the table. "Something's clearly wrong and we've made you an appointment with—"

"Dad! I told you, I'm fine!" Panic pierced Andi's eyes. She made a sound that was part frustration, part fearful defiance. "Just because I'm tired? Do you know how many college students are tired after finals?" With a quick, jerky motion, she ran her fingers through her bangs, struggling. "I don't need a doctor; I need to catch my breath."

Keith waited a long moment after Andi's interruption before trying again. "What I was saying," his voice was calmer than before, "is that we've made an appointment for you to see a Christian counselor." He looked at Lisa. "It's at one this afternoon, right?"

"Right." Lisa felt tears in her eyes. She was sitting close enough that she put her hand on Andi's shoulder. "Honey, you need to talk to someone. We think maybe you're dealing with some depression."

Lisa expected Andi to fight back about this, too, but she didn't. She slumped in her chair and laid her arms on the table, defeated. "So like, an hour with a counselor? That's what you want me to do?"

"Yes." Keith's tone said that the matter wasn't open to

debate. "If there's something going on, maybe she can help you talk through it." His expression softened. "Sweetheart, we love you, but you're scaring us."

"You were always so happy, Andi." Lisa hoped her daughter could see the concern in her eyes. "You lit up every room you ever entered. And now ... now we don't know how to find that in you again."

"You've only been home three days." Her words were practically mumbled, and she wouldn't make eye contact with them.

"This has been going on longer than that." Keith put his hand on Andi's other shoulder. "We want you to get help, baby. That's all."

For most of the brief talk, Lisa had been praying and now she begged God that Andi would understand. She watched her daughter, wondering how they could possibly feel so distant from each other. For a moment she thought Andi might argue, or worse — refuse to go. Instead she looked long at both of them and slowly nodded. "Fine." She stood and again fear tinged her voice. "I don't think it'll help, but I'll go." She started toward the hallway. "I'll be in my room until then."

When she was gone, Lisa looked at Keith. "What do you think?"

"You want to know?" Keith's shoulders hunched forward a little. He looked like he might break down. "I feel like I'm losing my little girl." He looked out the window, clearly struggling with his composure. "Like someone took my daughter and replaced her with a stranger ... someone I don't even know."

Tears blurred Lisa's vision. "Maybe ... we've been too busy."

"Of course we've been too busy." Keith raised his voice, but then shook his head, clearly frustrated with himself. "I'm sorry. It's not your fault." He shaded his eyes with his hand, and when he looked up, the desperation in his eyes was evident. "What am I doing, Lisa? Spending my days making *movies*?" He seemed to almost spit out the last word. "I have this big dream to change the world with film, but at what cost?" He waved his hand toward the hallway. "At the cost of losing Andi? Because if that's the cost, I'll be like Chase and quit. I can't do it."

Lisa wanted to say something wise and compassionate, a Scripture or bit of advice that would calm her husband and give him hope that he didn't need to quit making movies in order to reach their daughter. But the words wouldn't come. "Maybe we'll know more after today."

Keith nodded. "I'll go with you to the appointment." He stood and pulled Lisa into his arms. "But I mean it. I'll turn the whole thing over to Dayne if that's what it takes. I can't stand by and watch her slip away."

They held onto each other for several minutes, both in silence and in prayer for their daughter. As they got ready for the appointment, Lisa thought about what her husband had said, and she agreed. If they had to leave moviemaking, so be it. They needed to do whatever they could to reach their daughter, to help her become the young woman she'd been before this year at school.

Now Lisa could only pray it wasn't too late.

Seventeen

ANDI SAT RIGIDLY, SILENTLY BETWEEN HER parents in a non-descript chair in the stuffy lobby of the Bloomington Christian Counseling Center and tried to imagine how she'd let herself get into this situation. Had she really gotten into a car with her parents and willingly come here? When she'd lied to her parents every few hours since they'd arrived in Bloomington?

Nausea welled inside her and made her wonder if she'd survive the hour. This visit was a waste of their time and money, and Andi felt terrible for agreeing to it. But maybe if she gave the right answers and got through the hour, her parents would stop worrying about her. She needed an abortion clinic, not a counseling center. She'd made up her mind. And until then she couldn't begin to figure out who she'd been back in the fall or whether she even wanted to find her way back to that girl. But none of that was her parents' fault, so that's why she was here.

A kind-faced older woman stepped into the lobby and smiled at them. "Andi Ellison?"

A moment of disbelief consumed her as she rose to her feet. Was this really happening? Her mother squeezed her hand and whispered, "We love you."

Andi nodded absently and then followed the woman to a room halfway down a carpeted hallway. "Caroline will be right with you," the kind woman smiled, and then she was gone.

This would be the perfect time to run. Andi looked around the room, but there was no door. Just the one that led back to the hallway, and there would be no way past the woman at the front desk. She reminded herself to breathe as she looked around the room. It was inviting, with a small fireplace and two comfortable leather chairs facing each other. A framed water feature hung on one wall, and on the other was an enormous aquarium situated on a table that seemed custom-built for it. A painting hung over the fireplace with the Scripture, "Cast your cares on Him, for He cares for you." The entire room exuded a peace Andi had forgotten about.

She sat in one of the leather chairs and a minute later another woman entered the room, this one trim and neatly dressed, maybe in her mid-thirties. "Andi, hello." She held out her hand. "I'm Caroline. I'm a counselor."

Andi nodded and shook the woman's hand. "Hello." *You're a fraud, Andi Ellison,* she told herself. *Stop wasting everyone's time. This woman can't help you.* She forced the voices in her head to cease so she could carry on a conversation.

The woman was calm and in no hurry to get to the reasons behind Andi's supposed depression. She asked about Andi's year at Indiana University and what sort of things she'd been involved in. Against her will, Andi found the woman easy to talk to. Because she was a stranger, not someone emotionally invested in Andi's right or wrong choices, the answers came easily.

"What about guys?" Caroline's smile didn't hold a hint of judgment. "Did you date anyone special this year?"

The question caught her heart off guard. Anyone special? Someone like Cody Coleman or Tim Reed? Sure, Andi had met guys like that, but she hadn't dated them. "I ... uh ... I haven't met a lot of special guys. Not really special."

"But you met some?"

"I guess. My roommate has a couple special guys in her life." Andi hadn't cried since the days after she learned she was pregnant. But here when she hadn't expected to feel anything, she was realizing something she hadn't before. Her voice fell. "I think I forgot what special really meant."

"Hmmm. Yes, that happens sometimes."

"I did date someone, to answer your question." She looked down at her knees. "He was a film major."

"I see." Caroline still maintained an absolutely kind tone. "Did you think he was a special guy at first?"

Did she? Andi blinked and a few tears dropped to her lap. No, she hadn't thought Taz was special, not if she was honest with herself. Dangerous and charismatic, bold and daring. Risky, certainly. She shook her head, working to find her voice. "No ... not special. He was ... he was different from the guys I was supposed to date. He complimented me and told me he'd never met anyone so beautiful."

"I see." Caroline paused. "Do you remember, Andi ... what you were hoping to get out of dating this guy?"

Hoping to get? She stared at her knees again. "My friend Rachel was killed in a car accident."

Caroline sat back, her eyes tender and patient, waiting for Andi to explain herself.

"What I mean is," Andi sniffed. "Rachel was waiting for a special guy, someone ... strong in his faith. The kind of guy you marry. But ... she died before ..." A swell of tears caught Andi off guard.

A box of tissues sat on a small coffee table between the two leather chairs. Caroline slid it closer to Andi. "It's okay. We have time."

Andi nodded and took a few tissues. What was she doing, spilling everything to this woman? And how come she'd agreed to an appointment with a counselor before she'd thought through this stuff? "I think ... I dated Taz because he was different. He was dangerous." She dabbed her nose and held the tissues tight in her hand. "I wanted to live like everyone else. Not have to wait for someone special."

"The way Rachel waited."

"Right." Andi hadn't hurt this much over losing Rachel in a very long time. But the pain was as real and raw now as it had been the day she got the news. "Rachel lived for God." She gave a sad shrug. "Where did it get her?"

"Where do you think it got her?"

Andi thought for a moment. The answer was obvious, but she hadn't really voiced it. "I think she's in heaven, if that's what you mean." Andi looked at Caroline through bleary eyes. "You're saying she's in heaven because she lived right?"

"No." Caroline smiled, her patience and understanding limitless. "She's in heaven because Jesus died on the cross for her salvation, and she trusted Him for eternal life." Caroline paused. "So why did Rachel live right when she was here on earth?"

"Because ..." Andi hadn't worked through this part before. "Because she loved God, and she wanted to. Rachel wanted to live right."

"So tell me, Andi ... was Rachel an unhappy girl?"

New tears sprang to Andi's eyes and she pictured Rachel Baugher, the bigger-than-life kindness she had for everyone she met, the way her eyes and her smile could warm a person on the coldest day of the year. She took another tissue and pressed it to her eyes as she shook her head again. "Rachel loved her family and her friends. She loved school and helping people. She loved me." A small sob came from her and she hesitated until she had more control. "Rachel was one of the happiest people I ever knew. Just like my roommate this year."

Caroline nodded slowly, her sad smile filled with a wisdom that made it easy to believe she cared. "Your roommate?"

"Bailey." Andi stood and crossed the room, dropping the damp tissues in a trash can near the door. When she returned, she sat down and met Caroline's gaze again. "Bailey's the same way. She wants to live right."

"And she's happy?"

"Very happy." There was no need for the counselor to draw conclusions. Andi was drawing them for herself. Rachel and Bailey stayed away from parties and wild guys. They didn't drink or pose nude for some stupid student picture, and they certainly would never trade their virginity for a month of craziness. Yet they were happy, their lives filled with love and peace and laughter — the way Andi's had once been. Meanwhile, Andi was unable to get out of bed, practically drugged with the desire to sleep, and unable to remember even how it felt to smile. She was pregnant and afraid and unwilling to tell her parents the truth.

"Are you happy now?" Caroline kept all sarcasm from her voice, as if she truly wasn't sure what Andi's answer would be even after all she'd said.

It wasn't a question Andi had given much thought to, but the answer was ludicrously simply. "No." She made a sound that was more cry than laugh. "I'm not happy."

They talked a little longer about Taz and the way he'd treated her. Every sentence was excruciating for Andi, since she knew now that he had only used her. He'd gotten what he wanted from her and dumped her like moldy remains of yesterday's roses. Caroline never quite asked her if she was pregnant, but she did ask how Andi was feeling now. "Are you able to move on? Or do you feel somehow trapped by your time with Taz?"

Andi hesitated. This was the line she wasn't willing to cross. "I'm working on it."

"Okay, that's a start." Caroline leaned over her knees, her voice slightly more intense than before. "Who's helping you?"

"Helping me?"

"Yes. Andi, when you have something to work through, it's important to have guidelines or rules. Time-tested wisdom that will help you make healthy choices as you go." Caroline reached for a worn leather Bible next to her chair. "A starting place, of course, is Scripture. When you're not happy, one great way to help yourself is to line up your actions with the truth of the Bible."

"Yes." *After my abortion*, Andi told herself.

"Is there someone you trust ... someone you could share your thoughts with, someone you could present your plan to, so that together you could see if that plan measures up with God's Word?"

Her parents, of course. And Bailey. Maybe Bailey's mother. But if she told any of them the truth—that she was pregnant and planning to have an abortion—the truth in God's Word would prevent her from getting the only sort of help she needed right now. And she couldn't embarrass her parents now, not with all of Bloomington excited about their arrival, their plans for making movies in the city. She'd heard her father talking the other night to Dayne Matthews. They were worried that Brandon Paul's partying could hurt the film and Jeremiah Productions. She could only imagine what her pregnancy would do to them.

Andi looked at her watch. She needed to get out of here. They would only talk in circles on this issue. She cleared her throat. "Yes. I have people I can talk to."

"Good." Caroline was quiet for a moment. "Andi, your mother's concerned that you might be pregnant. Is that something you're concerned about?"

What? Her mother suspected that? Andi swallowed hard and shook her head, recovering as quickly as she could. "No. No, I'm not concerned about that." Andi felt the slightest bit of relief. She'd told the truth, right? She wasn't concerned about being pregnant. She already *knew* she was pregnant. After her abortion next week, she wouldn't be concerned about that either.

Caroline wasn't about to call her a liar or ask her a second time. Instead she slid to the edge of her seat, her eyes shining with an even deeper compassion than before. "I'm here, Andi. Your parents know how to reach me. You can come back next week or more often, if you'd like. The important thing is that you have a chance to process how you're feeling." She kept her pace unrushed. "I want you to go home and think about the things you told me. About Rachel and Bailey and the guys they like to date. About how happy they are, and about why they're happy." Caroline smiled. "You have wonderful parents who love you. They've raised you with the truth, is that right?"

"Yes, ma'am." Andi's heart was beating harder than before. She couldn't wait to leave.

"That's right. You know the answers, Andi. I'm just here to help you remember them."

Andi thanked the counselor. "Am I done?"

"For today." Caroline hesitated. "Would you mind if I talked to your parents to fill them in on a little of our conversation? They just want to make sure you're okay. I don't have to talk to them if you'd rather I didn't."

"Um ... sure, you can talk to them." Andi figured that if the counselor talked to her parents, they might stop worrying about her. She signed a form stating that Caroline could discuss their session, thanked the counselor again, and headed down the hall to the lobby. But with every step, her heart beat faster. What was this about talking to her parents? Did Caroline know Andi was lying, that she really was pregnant? Or would she tell her parents to take Andi immediately to a doctor's office for a pregnancy test? Andi wouldn't do it. She couldn't. She tried to stand a little taller, look a little more composed. That way her mom and dad would think they'd spent their money wisely and that Andi was on her way back to being the girl they remembered her being.

Her parents were on their feet as soon as she walked through the door. They didn't rush toward her, but their eyes were filled with questions and hope. Her mom spoke first. "How did it go?"

"Good." Andi remembered to smile, at least a little. "Her name's Caroline. She wants to talk to you before we go."

"I'm proud of you, honey." Her dad kissed her cheek. "I know it wasn't easy for you to come here. But sometimes we need a little help."

Andi's heart raced, but she forced herself to look happier than before. "Thanks, Daddy. That means a lot." She watched her parents walk down the hall and she took her same seat in the lobby. This time her knees were shaking. What sort of person was she, lying to her parents, pretending a session with a Christian counselor had cured her problems? She was the worst possible daughter. If she could walk across the street and have the abortion now, she would. Because then she could start figuring out who she was going to be from that point forward. She could hardly be the old Andi, the untainted, innocent Andi. That girl was gone forever. Now she was a used-up coward, a person unfit to be a mother or a daughter. She had walked away from God and her parents and her upbringing, and every time she opened her mouth she spoke nothing but lies. But at least she wasn't going to shame her parents. Not by having a baby.

Andi thought about her time with Caroline. There was one thing she'd learned from her time with the counselor, a truth that would stay with her forever. Rachel and Bailey had special guys in their lives, of course that much she already knew. But today she finally figured out why no special guys had sought after her. The answer was simple, and it brought with it a sting of tears.

Special guys wanted special girls.

Eighteen

BAILEY HAD BEEN LOOKING FORWARD TO this night since summer began. It was the third week of June, and the Clear Creek High School football team was having its annual Cross-Town Scrimmage, against their rivals from Bloomington. The contest was a tradition in the community, and today it would also be the first time Bailey could watch her younger brothers Shawn and Justin play alongside Connor. The first time she could watch Cody on the sidelines, coaching.

Coach Taylor had worked out the timing of the scrimmage so that Bailey's dad could be there, and now he and her mom were in the front seat of the family Suburban, and Bailey, BJ, and Ricky were in the back as they headed to the field. She and Tim still hadn't gotten together — Tim's schedule had been full as he prepared for their upcoming audition. Bailey hated the thought of breaking up with him, so she didn't care if it took a little longer to make it happen.

But when they had talked, Tim had been kind again. The arrogance from a few weeks ago was gone. His thoughtfulness when they talked the last few times made her wonder if she was supposed to break up with him, after all. Especially when she and Cody were still not back to what they'd been at the Cru retreat. Maybe she could talk to Cody today after the scrimmage. Even if they only had a few minutes.

"Dad, you think Cody's gonna be a good coach?" Ricky sat in the middle. He leaned forward, his eyes big. "Connor said he's helping a lot."

Bailey's dad grinned in the rearview mirror. "Coach Taylor says he's a natural."

"Yeah, because all that time he's spent around you." BJ patted their dad's shoulder. "Every time you watched films, Cody would sit next to you. Remember, Dad?"

"He did do that a lot." Bailey's mom shifted so she could see the rest of the family.

Bailey remembered dozens of times like that, Saturday mornings when Cody lived with them and she'd wake up to find him sitting next to her dad, the two of them watching game film on the family computer. Sometimes Bailey would stop and take in the scene, completely unnoticed because the guys were so caught up in watching and re-watching the images on the screen. She didn't say so now, but she always figured more than the football talk, Cody enjoyed sitting next to her dad, because for a few minutes he could feel what it was like to have a father.

"I miss Cody living with us." Ricky settled back in his seat. "He should move in again."

The heat in Bailey's cheeks told her she was better off staying quiet about that possibility. The feelings in her heart stirred up a familiar guilt and confusion that she still hadn't found a way to deal with.

"You think he could, Dad? Huh?" Ricky was relentless once he hit on an idea. "That'd be perfect. He could work with Connor and Shawn and Justin all the time, and just think how good Clear Creek would be then!"

"He's always welcome." Bailey's mom smiled back at Ricky.

"But he's doing well on his own." Their dad's voice told them he wasn't opposed to the idea, but he wanted what was truly best for Cody. "He's a successful young man, and part of that is being self-sufficient."

Self-sufficient. Bailey liked the way that sounded when it came to Cody. She liked thinking of him more man than boy, moving into his future a different guy because of the time her parents had invested in him. And she loved that he was coaching football.

"Tim's coming to the game, right?" BJ looked at her.

"Who?" Bailey blinked and her thoughts cleared quickly. "Oh, Tim. Um ... I don't think so."

BJ was thirteen this summer, not a kid anymore. He looked at Bailey for a long time, as if to say her response was more than a little strange. Tim was her boyfriend, after all.

"I like Tim for you," Ricky grinned at her. "I just like Cody better."

A grin spread across BJ's face and he winked at their younger brother. "I think Bailey feels the same way."

"Okay, okay." Their mom turned around, her expression part smile, part warning. "Enough. Cody's a friend to all of us."

"Exactly." Bailey worked to muster up a lighthearted look for BJ. She couldn't let anyone see how the remark had hit her heart dead center. "Cody's our friend, buddy. Don't let your imagination get ahead of you."

"It wasn't my idea." BJ reached over and gave Ricky's knee a friendly squeeze. "Ricky brought it up."

"I think he likes Bailey." Ricky shrugged. "I'm just saying."

Bailey worked to slow her racing heart. What if he did have feelings for her? What if he were only waiting for her to figure out how to break things off with Tim, and then he would declare that she had been the girl for him all along? She stared out the window as Clear Creek High School came into view. But all she could see was Cody standing on her porch the day he came home from Iraq, telling her she should date Tim Reed, that he was the right sort of guy for her. How was she supposed to take that except the way she had ever since then? Cody didn't have feelings for her that way.

They parked and spilled out, grabbing blankets and water

bottles from the back of the Suburban. The Friday afternoon was warm and clear and blue, perfect for a summer scrimmage. Bailey's mom came up alongside her as they crossed the field. "Ricky didn't mean anything."

Bailey loved this, how her mom knew what she was thinking and feeling before they shared a word about it. "I know."

"I thought Cody would be around more now that he's coaching the boys."

"He's mad at me." Bailey slowed her pace, her eyes on the coaches lined up along the sidelines half a field away. "Over the whole Tim thing at the cafeteria a few weeks ago."

"Still?"

"I don't know what else it could be."

Her mom was quiet, keeping pace with her. "Maybe it's hard for him to be your friend."

"Because of Tim?" Bailey couldn't understand that. "I really don't see Tim that much. I mean, he's busy with voice lessons and acting classes, getting ready for the New York audition."

Bailey's mom slowed and breathed in deeply, her eyes on the distant blue sky. "Not because of Tim." She paused and looked straight to Bailey's heart. "Because he's in love with you."

Over the years Bailey's mom had thought this about Cody before — though she didn't always like the idea — and often Bailey agreed with her. Even if thinking so was a secret the two of them alone shared. But now Bailey shook her head. "He's not, Mom. Maybe before, but not since he's been home."

She raised an eyebrow and angled her head, as if she couldn't quite agree with Bailey. "I watched you that day when he came home from the war, the way he looked at you." She smiled and her expression said she wasn't going to push the subject. "I know what I saw."

Bailey sighed. They were almost to the bleachers, and she could see Cody standing next to Coach Taylor. He looked tall and

KAREN KINGSBURY

confident. A couple players ran up and asked him something, and Cody put a hand on one of their shoulders. Whatever advice he was giving, he looked intense. Like this was more than a summer scrimmage with the cross-town rival. She glanced at her mother. "I need to end things with Tim, right? Don't you think?"

"It's more about what you think." Her mom's tone was genuine. "Tim's a great guy."

"He is."

They reached the bleachers and spread out a couple blankets on a bench near the top. Bailey's mom was quiet while she waited for Bailey to continue.

Bailey took the spot beside her mom and opened her water bottle. "I go back and forth about whether Tim and I should be together. You know? I mean nothing's really bad between us."

Her mom narrowed her eyes and looked out at the players on the field. "I hope, honey, that if you stay with Tim, one day you'll be able to say more than, 'nothing's bad.'"

Bailey allowed a feeble laugh. "I didn't mean it like that."

Her mom looked over her shoulder. "Oh," she stood and smiled. "Hi Tim."

Bailey felt her heart skip a beat as she whipped around and saw Tim make his way up the bleachers toward them. He hadn't heard what she'd said, right? The guilt inside her swelled and she quickly patted the spot beside her. "You came!"

He wore khaki shorts and a nice T-shirt, a little too dressed for an afternoon summer football game. He gave Bailey a quick hug and nodded his hello to Bailey's mom. "I had my headshots taken this morning. My mom found a photographer from Indianapolis. She drove in today for the shoot."

"Oh." Bailey wasn't sure what to say. "I guess I need a headshot too. Before August anyway."

"Yeah, sorry. On the way here I thought I should've told you. We could've split the cost and done the shoot together."

"Don't worry about it." Bailey squinted at the field. She reached into her purse, pulled out her sunglasses, and slipped them into place. "Looks like it's about to start." Bailey kept a few inches between her and Tim. Why did she feel so frustrated with him? He needed a headshot, right? That was part of the audition, bringing an eight-by-ten glossy. Bailey hadn't thought much about the picture or the audition, but she figured she could get it done by their neighbor—a woman who did photography from her house. Tim just seemed a little over the top. Way more involved in the audition than she was.

So why did that frustrate her?

Bailey stared at the guys on the field. Maybe because this was the most passion she'd seen in Tim Reed since he won the part of Scrooge last fall. It was an enthusiasm Bailey hadn't seen him express about anything else. Not about his faith or his relationship with her or his education. Which was fine. Bailey sniffed in a gulp of fresh air and sat straighter, with more of an attitude. Maybe Tim just bugged her. She didn't like how she felt, but she couldn't stop herself.

Just as the game was getting started, Coach Taylor's wife, Kari, and their three kids arrived with Ashley and Landon Blake and their three. Landon was in his firefighting uniform, and Bailey glanced back and saw his fire truck in the parking lot. His partner looked like he was sitting in the rig, on the phone. They must've been on call—a slow fire day in Bloomington. As the group walked up, Bailey saw that they were happy and relaxed. Their laughter added to the sounds of the afternoon. Bailey was grateful for the distraction. "Hey guys ..." She waved at them. "Sit by us!"

Ashley hurried up the bleachers and hugged Bailey and then Tim. "We sure miss you guys at CKT. I'm still painting sets, but the new kids aren't the same." She sat with her family in front of Bailey and Tim. "Well, here we are. It wouldn't be summer without the Cross-Town Scrimmage!"

Jenny leaned forward and gave Ashley a quick hug. "I'm glad you're all here."

"Wouldn't miss it." Kari shaded her eyes and stared at the field. "My husband thinks this is the Super Bowl. It might as well be for how much preparation went into it."

They all laughed, and after a few minutes the game began. Like every year, it was a close contest, with four lead changes. The sort of game that kept their attention to the end. Bailey was grateful. The close game meant she didn't have to think about Tim or talk to him or wonder about her frustrations toward him.

Clear Creek pulled out a seven-point win in the last quarter with Bailey and her family and the other fans on their feet. The whole time Cody was completely engaged in the action. He was either consulting urgently with Coach Taylor or intently talking to one of the players, motioning toward the field and giving constant instruction. Bailey tried not to stare. She couldn't help but see the similarities between Cody and her father. She'd spent her whole life watching her daddy coach, and now—watching Cody help guide Clear Creek to a victory was as wonderful as summer itself.

At the end, only Tim wasn't cheering with them. He'd gotten a phone call and he was standing off to the side on his cell. Bailey tried to pretend he wasn't here. He didn't care about football, anyway, so she wasn't sure why he'd come.

The phone call turned out to be the photographer who had taken Tim's headshots. Everyone was going to Bortolomi's Pizza after the game, but Tim begged off. "I guess she loves what she got, but she wants to do a few shots over. She's only in town today." His hands were in his pockets and he looked anxious to leave. He chuckled nervously and his eyes sparkled, not quite arrogant but clearly proud of himself. "She said I could model if the Broadway thing doesn't work out."

"That's great." Bailey tried to feel something, but the only pressing emotion stirring inside her was the urgency to congratulate her brothers and Cody. She gave him a happy shrug that said their time was clearly up. "I guess you better go."

He hugged her, but she pulled away quickly. Before he left he grinned. "I had fun with you today."

"Thanks." She took another step back. "Me too." She moved to walk away, but Tim caught her hand.

"Hey, tell me about Andi ... what've you heard?"

Everyone was headed toward the field and Bailey wanted to join them. "Uh ... I talked to her mom the other day. She's worried about her. I think we all agree Taz wasn't good for her."

"Definitely not." Tim frowned. "I was reading my Bible this morning and Andi came to mind. This whole change in her, the way she's been so down ... it just shows that God's Word is true. There are consequences for sin—and Andi's living proof."

Bailey felt her shoulders sink. "We're all living proof."

"Right." Tim seemed taken aback. "That's what I mean. Hey, meet me for lunch tomorrow. At the Campus Café? One o'clock?"

"Sure," Bailey backed up. "Hey, I gotta go." She started toward the field, waving back at him. "Call me." She couldn't run off fast enough, and once she left she didn't look back to see if he was leaving or still standing there. She didn't care. If she stayed around Tim another five minutes she would say something she might regret. She tried to shake off the conversation with him as she caught up to her mom and brothers.

"Where's Tim?" Her mom kept her voice low, as if the others might not notice he wasn't with them any longer.

"Places to go." She smiled, more because they were approaching the field than because of anything about Tim. Bailey gave her mom a side glance. "I'll tell you more later." Ahead, the players and coaches milled about with the fans, accepting congratulations and celebrating the game. Her dad was already out there, standing next to Coach Taylor and Cody.

Bailey made a point of finding her brothers first, hugging them and posing for a phone picture with them. "Three Flanigan boys on one team!" she beamed at them. Shawn and Justin had each scored a touchdown, and Connor's interception set up the winning drive. "I can't wait for the season."

Her mom agreed. "We've looked forward to this for so long." She hugged each of the boys too. "You three were wonderful."

Finally Bailey looked around and spotted Cody, still standing with Bailey's dad and Coach Taylor. She walked up and looped her arm around her father's waist while they were mid-conversation about the Clear Creek pass defense. Bailey listened for a few minutes, understanding most of what they talked about as only a coach's daughter could.

"We can't run the prevent," Coach Taylor was saying. "The quarterbacks in our league will nickel and dime us to death."

"Exactly." Her dad was still passionate about seeing Clear Creek play well. "We need man coverage, and we need to watch the tight ends. If they shoot straight through, it's a pass every time."

Cody wasn't adding much, so Bailey tried to catch his attention—something that usually was as natural as breathing. But not today. She might as well have been invisible for how little he seemed to notice her.

Bailey's dad kissed the top of her head. "The fans liked it, right?"

"It was great." She grinned at Coach Taylor and then at Cody. Again Cody only looked at her long enough to not seem rude. "Best Cross-Town Scrimmage ever."

The guys talked another few minutes, and then Cody gathered his gear bag from the ground a few feet away. "Gotta go, guys." He waved at Coach Taylor. "Thanks for letting me be out here."

"You added a lot today." Coach pointed at him. "We need you, Coleman. See you at practice."

Bailey drew back from her dad and followed Cody as he waved and turned toward the parking lot.

"Hey," she kept her tone light. The other guys were still in earshot, and she didn't want to make a scene. She caught up with Cody and walked alongside him. "You're leaving?"

"Yeah." He kept up his pace, and shot her a quick glance as he looked briefly back to the bleachers. "Where's Tim?"

Bailey wanted to scream. "Cody." She fought to keep her tone even. "Can you stop? Please."

He was more than halfway to the parking lot now, and they were by themselves, the rest of her family and the others still back on the field talking to the players. Cody took another few steps and stopped. He didn't act put out, but his body language made the implication anyway. He cocked his head, his eyes never really making contact with hers. "What?"

"You're mad at me." She took a step closer but kept her distance. She had a feeling if she came too close he'd back up. "I know you are."

"We've been over this." He sucked in a frustrated breath and released it in a hurry, his eyes searching the air between them as if the answers might be written in the summer breeze. "You've got Tim. The way he treated me the other day ... I don't know. I didn't feel like I mattered that much to you." He smiled, clearly working to keep things light. "No big deal. You've got your life, and I've got mine." He gave her the lightest pat on her shoulder. "See you, Bailey."

"Cody ... wait. I can explain." She wanted to run after him, but that would create more drama than either of them needed. Especially here with sixty football players who respected him as a coach.

"Nothing to explain." He waved once, the smile still firmly in place. "Don't worry about it."

And with that he was gone, jogging toward his car, every bit the athlete he'd been back when he'd worn the Clear Creek Uniform. Bailey stood in place and watched as he reached his car, climbed in, and drove off.

Angry tears burned her eyes and she blinked them back. Nothing was turning out like she wanted it to. Wherever Cody was going, he seemed in a hurry to get there. She turned and walked slowly back to her family, but along the way she kept replaying Tim's actions, his words. Why was she still dating him? She was going to break up with him a month ago, right? She slowed, still bitterly disappointed at the way the afternoon had turned out. *What am I doing, God?*

No loud and clear answer came to her, but she suddenly could hear her dad's voice talking to Coach Taylor above the others ten yards away. "Never be passive. Victories happen when you take charge of a game. You can't win by playing not to lose."

Her dad had told that to his players as long as Bailey could remember, but here—with Cody driving off to who knew where and Tim lost in his own world, it was like she was hearing his words for the first time. How self-centered she'd been, staying with Tim because of convenience, because it was easier than breaking up with him. Of course she was frustrated. She'd been as mean and thoughtless to Tim as Tim had been to Cody. She should've ended it with Tim when the thought first hit her. That would've been the fair thing—maybe for all of them.

So what if Cody didn't want to date her? She didn't need a boyfriend. She needed time with God, time praying about the plans He had for her. She thought about Tim's comment earlier, about the consequences of sin. By being passive, she was getting what she deserved. She was ashamed of herself because she'd been wrong in how she'd acted toward Tim, how she'd been playing not to lose. Certainly God wanted more from her than that. With His help, it was time to recognize her faults and take action.

The way she should have a month ago.

Nineteen

CODY DIDN'T SPEED. THE LAST THING he needed was a ticket on his way to see his mother. She had left a strange message on his cell phone, half crying, half talking and asking him to come as soon as he could. Between that and the scene with Bailey, the day hadn't exactly turned out the way he'd hoped it would.

The game was the single bright light. On the sidelines, helping the guys read the defense and run the offense, Cody felt vibrantly alive. Like he'd been born to do this. The only time he lost focus was once when he scanned the bleachers looking for Bailey. He expected to see her sitting with her mom and brothers, but for some crazy reason he hadn't expected to see Tim beside her. Tim dressed for success in his preppy shorts and Buckle T-shirt, already looking like a part of the Flanigan family. Or at least the way anyone would expect Bailey Flanigan's boyfriend to look.

Cody wanted to be Bailey's friend, really he did. But lately the idea felt like a colossal exercise in futility, because every time they were together, all he could think was that he didn't want to be her friend. He wanted to hold her hand and run along the shores of Lake Monroe with her. He wanted to take walks in the summer moonlight and sit on her porch swing poring over the truths in Scripture, dreaming about their future together. He wanted to take a wild and dangerous jump and fall madly and marvelously in love with her, and the fact was this: He was tired of pretending otherwise.

He wasn't jealous of Tim Reed. Every time Bailey talked about him—every single time—her tone was lukewarm. She liked him, yes. He was kind and they shared common interests, but she wasn't sure if he was the guy ... wasn't sure if this was forever. The story was as repetitive as Mondays, but still Bailey stayed. And now that Tim had taken to talking down to him, Cody couldn't think of a reason why he should make an effort to be Bailey's friend. She was young and immature at love. They could be distant friends, yes. Acquaintances, of course. But he had to help his heart move on; otherwise he wouldn't know the right girl when she walked through the door.

His mother's message flashed in his mind again and he felt a rush of nervous energy work through his veins. What was she doing, calling him like that, her words sounding all slurred? Was this about Benny? Or had she jumped off the wagon on her own? He clenched his teeth and gripped the steering wheel harder than before. *God, help me get through this next hour.* He relaxed his grip and sank back against the seat. The last time she called, she hadn't been drunk or drugged. Just sick with a fever. Maybe that was all it was this time too. But he'd found more beer bottles at her house, and he worried about her constantly. *I'm not mad at her, God. I want her to succeed. If she falls again I could lose her.*

It was a familiar prayer where his mother was concerned. That was the problem, really. All of his life felt like a series of familiar prayers. Praying about Bailey, praying about his mother, praying about God's direction for his life. Cody wondered how long a person could feel stuck at the starting line.

He pulled into his mother's driveway, and even before he reached her front door he had a feeling something was very wrong. A stillness in the air, or the lack of sounds from inside the house. Something about the moment made his skin crawl, and by the time he'd knocked on the door twice, he pulled out his key and hurried inside.

"Mom!" The living room was empty, but there were sofa pillows on the floor and the bookcase was half empty, the contents of its shelves scattered about in hurried disarray. A quick look toward the kitchen and Cody saw a dozen broken plates shattered across the linoleum. His heart thudded against the walls of his chest as he rushed toward the hallway. "Mom! Where are you?"

No answer. He pushed his way past a chair that was smashed against the bathroom door. If Benny had done this, he might still be here. Cody hoped so. He'd love the chance to level the guy, chuck him out onto the street. Still, he had to be careful. Benny could easily be armed, hiding around any wall, behind any door. Cody tore around a corner and into his mother's room. She was there, passed out on the bed. Passed out or —

"Mom!" He raced to her side, grabbed her wrist, and felt for a pulse. It was slow and weak, but she was still alive. He surveyed her, the black eye and ripped shirt, the scratches on her arms. A few smears of blood on the bedspread told him her head was bleeding from somewhere. He gave her a firm shake. "Mom, wake up!"

A low moan came from her and she turned her head slightly, before going still again. Cody glanced frantically around the room. Was she knocked out from being hit, or had she taken something? He moved to her nightstand, and there in the top drawer was all he needed to see. A pipe and an amber-colored vile, a small mirror, a half straw, and a razor blade. He stepped on something and looked down to see an empty Jack Daniels bottle.

"Mom, why?" He shouted the words, furious and terrified all at the same time. He went to her again and took hold of her shoulder. "Wake up!"

He waited, trembling, and that's when he heard it. The rattle in her chest, the strange uneven breathing. Whatever she was suffering from, she wasn't okay. She wouldn't want him to call an ambulance, but he had no choice. He wasn't going to stand here and watch her die. Cody grabbed the phone by her bed and dialed 9-1-1. His heart was racing so hard and fast he could barely think.

"Nine-one-one, what's your emergency?"

"My mom's unconscious. She's not breathing right." His words spilled out one on top of the other. "Please hurry ... she's in a lot of trouble. Someone broke into her house. Everything's a mess."

"You're with her, is that right?"

"Yes, ma'am." Cody sat on the bed, his hand on his mother's head. *Please, God ... don't let her die like this. Please.*

"Are the perpetrators still in the house or are you alone with her?"

"I'm ... I'm not sure."

"Fine, we'll send police as well." The operator talked quickly and efficiently. "She's breathing, and she has a pulse?"

"Yes, but it's not good. Not strong."

"Okay, someone's on the way." The operator asked Cody's name and the address, to make sure it matched with their records. "Are you able to perform CPR if the need arises?"

"Yes, ma'am." He felt suddenly dizzy, fear and anger dancing at a frenzied pace across his heart. "I'll stay with her."

The call ended and Cody stared at his mother. Her skin looked gray; it was cooler than usual and clammy. What had happened to her? Had she and Benny gotten in a fight or had someone broken in and robbed her? And what about the drugs? Was she high when the assault happened, or the other way around? He pulled his cell phone from his pocket and checked the time on her voicemail. Guilt hit him like a bullet, shattering what remained of his composure. Her call had come almost an hour ago. What if he'd found a quiet place and taken her message right when it came in? Would he have caught the jerk who'd torn up her house and beat her up? And would she have avoided the drug bash—whatever she'd taken?

"Mom?" His voice was softer now, and he leaned in close to her face. "Mom, can you hear me?"

There was no response. Just her raspy, shallow breathing—which sounded worse now than it had a couple minutes ago. He was taking her pulse again when he heard squealing tires outside. He'd expected sirens, but sometimes they didn't use them when they reached a residential location like this.

He heard the door fly open and he stood, one hand still on his mother's shoulder. "We're in here!"

"Baby!" A string of cuss words rang through the house. "Baby ... I'm coming!" The voice was hardly the professional one of a paramedic or emergency worker.

Cody felt his anger explode into rage as Benny barreled into the room. "What the—"

"Oh, you're back?" Cody was on his feet, grabbing Benny by the shoulders and shoving him against the wall. The biker was heavier than Cody, but that didn't stop him. His military training kicked in and Cody could only see red. Blood red. He shoved the guy again. "What? Did you come back to finish her off?"

"Back up!" Benny jerked Cody, and he bounced against the edge of his mother's bed. "I didn't do this! I was out riding when she—"

Heavy footsteps sounded in the hall, and in a matter of seconds two officers burst through the doorway. "Police. Freeze!"

Cody and Benny slowly raised their hands, and Cody gulped. *This was crazy. How had everything gotten so out of hand? God, help me ... help my mom. Please.* "Officer, I made the 9-1-1 call." He still had his hands up. "My mom needs help."

Sirens pulled up outside as the police officer and his partner turned to Benny. "Who are you?"

"Benjamin Roth." He blinked, clearly petrified. "I'm her boyfriend, but I ..." he gestured toward Cody's mother and the disarray on the floor. "I didn't do this." He ran his tongue across his lip, his eyes wide. "But I might ... I might know who did."

"Keep your hands up." The police officer patted Benny down

and directed the other officer to do the same to Cody. When they were satisfied that neither of them were armed, the officers tried to lead them into the living room.

"I need to stay!" Cody couldn't believe what was happening. The police were treating him like a criminal when his mom was lying there dying on the bed. "Please ... let me stay with her."

The officers exchanged a look and the second one nodded. "We'll need to talk to you once they take her."

"Yes, sir." Cody nodded, barely breathing. As the police led Benny out of the room, the paramedics rushed in.

One of them was Landon Blake—who had just been at the football game. He was at Cody's mother's side immediately, checking her pulse, her breathing. "Cody ... what's going on here?"

"I'm not sure." Cody felt a burst of panic again. "She left me a message and I came to check on her. The house is a mess and she's been beaten up pretty bad."

Landon nodded. "What about the other guy?"

"Her boyfriend." Rage flooded him again. "The guy's not good for her. I'm not sure if he did this." Cody tried to think clearly. "He just showed up ... before the police."

Another two paramedics were working on his mom now, and Cody stepped back against the wall, watching. *Please, God ... not like this.* To think his mom would spend most of his childhood in prison for drugs, and then die like this—just when she was starting to live ... the idea was devastating, and it consumed him. *Please, God ... help her.*

Landon and the other guys were moving quickly, starting an IV and getting her on a gurney.

"I think she's on something." Cody pointed to the open drawer on the nightstand. "I found that."

"Is she a user?"

Was she a user? The question felt like a dagger, slashing every dream and hope he'd ever held out for his mother. There was only one answer, no matter how long she'd been clean. Before she was a woman, before she was his mother, before she was anything else she might've been or become, she was definitely a user.

Landon was collecting the drugs and drug paraphernalia, putting them in a large Ziploc bag. He looked back at Cody, still waiting for an answer. "She's done this before?"

"Yes," Cody's vision blurred with angry tears. Because his mother had done this to him since he was a little boy, and because unless something drastic changed, she was going to do this to him as long as she lived. Choosing drugs over a healthy life, over living for God or loving her son. Real life, real love, was never enough for her, and the truth hurt like crazy. "She's been clean for a while, but she's fallen before."

Landon must've caught the pain in his tone, because he reached back and took firm hold of Cody's shoulder. "We're gonna get her help, Cody. We are."

He nodded, biting his lip, his eyes locked on his mother's face. He wanted her to wake up and tell them all it was a joke, a trick. She would never in a million years go back to the drugs that had cost her the chance to raise her son, drugs that had kept her in prison through Cody's high school years and stopped her from seeing him play even a single football game. But she didn't move or speak, and in a blur of motion the paramedics wheeled her from the room.

Landon trailed the gurney, and he looked back at Cody as they left. "We're taking her to Bloomington Community Hospital. Meet us there when you're finished with the police."

The police. Cody nodded, his mind racing. What were they learning from Benny, and how would they figure out who had torn apart his mother's house. He moved down the hall behind Landon. "Is she ... is she going to be okay?"

"We have to figure out what she took." The compassion in

his eyes brought the first peace to the moment. "Her vitals aren't great, but they're steady." He hesitated briefly, still moving with the gurney. "Still, I'd get to the hospital."

"I will." He watched them go, and he moved to the corner of the living room where the police were still talking to Benny.

The first officer looked at Cody. All accusation from earlier was gone from his eyes. "Benny says he wasn't here earlier, but he knows who was."

His mother's boyfriend shot him an indignant look. "I would never hurt her." He crossed his meaty arms. His tattoos twisted around his biceps. "She's been getting back into drugs. Sometimes when I'm here, sometimes not." He seemed to measure his words, especially since the officer to his right was taking notes. "I told her she was getting in too deep, but she wouldn't listen."

That much rang true, but there was something about the guy that made Cody doubt his story. Something in his eyes.

The second officer looked up from his notes. "And you say she told you she was having a drug dealer over to the house?"

"Yes. She wanted crack, and she'd made a few phone calls."

Cody felt his heart split in half. How could she do this? When she knew where it would lead? She'd told him so herself, that if she used again she'd leave in an ambulance, a hearse, or a squad car. And she'd been right.

"So you knew she'd invited a crack dealer here?"

"Just for a quick purchase." He waved his hand at the torn-up room. "Something must've gone wrong, because this ... this is how I found the place."

"Something definitely went wrong." Cody glared at him.

"What're you, the doting son? Why don't you shut the—" Benny cussed and the police officer closest to him grabbed his arm.

"Quit it." The officer released Benny with a slight shove. He glanced back at Cody. "Work out your differences later."

They asked Benny a few more questions and then released him. Before he left he looked back once at Cody, and this time he didn't glare or cuss or make a single threat. But the look in his eyes was chilling, a sneer almost. As if he'd just gotten away with murder and he was happy about the fact.

When he was gone, Cody had another couple minutes with the officers. "I'm still worried about that guy. He could be the dealer for all we know."

"We're on it." The first officer looked grim. "We have no reason to detain him, but his record has us suspicious." They stood and the other officer slipped his notepad into his pocket. "We'll be in touch. You can go ahead to the hospital."

The three of them left at the same time. It wasn't until Cody reached his car and started off to the hospital that his tears came in earnest. Angry, defeated tears because this was his life—the son of a single mom who was engaged in a lifelong battle with drugs. She'd missed whole sections of his life—his grade school years when he lived with his grandparents because she was in prison, and his middle school days when she was in and out of rehab. By the time he graduated from eighth grade, she'd been arrested again for dealing and using, and her prison sentence kept her locked away while he had his first day of high school and his first homecoming game, his first prom and his final summers of being a kid.

By then his grandparents had both died, Cody was caught up in his own alcoholism, and the Flanigans were his only hope.

He took rough swipes at his wet cheeks and forced himself to gain control. But the thought of the Flanigans only made him more aware of his reality. Whether Bailey stayed with Tim Reed forever didn't really matter. Cody wasn't the right guy for her. Look at him. He was a recovering alcoholic with a prosthetic lower left leg, no family support, and none of the easy money people like Bailey and Tim took for granted. He was the son of a drug addict. No matter how he felt when he was with Bailey or how he sometimes wanted to believe she had feelings for him, the answer was painfully obvious.

Bailey deserved better.

Twenty

THE COUNSELING APPOINTMENT TURNED OUT TO be the best thing Andi could've done, even though she felt terrible pretending the session had helped. Still, Andi was grateful for the reprieve from her parents. They were convinced she was on the road to becoming her old self, able to think a little more clearly and committed to finding her way back to God again.

Once the counseling session was behind them, her parents made it very clear that Andi simply couldn't spend the summer in Indianapolis—even if she found a job and paid for the experience herself. She needed help, counseling, and time with her family. Andi didn't fight them ... She had no idea what the future held, but there was no point arguing with her mom and dad now. Otherwise they wouldn't want her going to the city for even a few days. And she desperately needed to go.

"Maybe you can take classes in Indianapolis next summer," her mom had told her last night. "When you're feeling better."

Andi listened politely, nodding and smiling at the appropriate times. She had no intention of taking art classes in Indianapolis this summer or next. If she stayed with her friends, it would only be for her abortion, and to clear her head so she could figure out what to do next.

But for now she couldn't think about her future past this afternoon at four o'clock.

She'd found an abortion clinic in Indianapolis, and a week ago she'd made an appointment for the last appointment today. The abortion wouldn't take more than an hour, they'd told her.

Once she had the appointment in hand, Andi had called her friend Sherry who had already moved to the city for the summer. She asked if she could come on Friday for a visit.

"Definitely. Stay with us." The girl was very open-minded, and now she didn't hesitate. "We have room on the couch. You need a week or what?"

"Just through the weekend." Andi had planned it this way. Have the abortion on a Friday, stay with Sherry and the girls through the weekend, and head home Monday. Her parents would never suspect a thing that way. Her stomach hurt from the planning, from the fact that she refused to think about what she was about to do. "Oh, and Sherry ... I have another favor to ask."

Andi explained that she was pregnant and that she'd scheduled an abortion for that afternoon. "I need someone to drive me there and back. They said it won't take long."

"Oh, honey. I'm sorry." Sherry was immediately sympathetic and glad to help. Andi had met Sherry on the mall during rush week last fall. She stood for everything contrary to Andi's beliefs and upbringing, but Andi found her funny and refreshing. Then Sherry turned up in two of Andi's classes and they became friends, studying for tests a few times and having coffee together once in a while. Sherry liked Taz—at least at first—and thought the experience was good for Andi. Even the heartbreak at the end.

"We learn the most through pain," she'd told Andi back then, and she reiterated the mantra on the recent phone call.

Andi wasn't sure she agreed, but this time the pain was inevitable. Because she wouldn't embarrass her parents, wouldn't do anything to ruin all the good they'd accomplished. The last thing they needed now was a scandal—especially a public one. People would think Jeremiah Productions was a joke.

Now, with the plan set, Andi packed a small roller suitcase and tried to keep from panicking. Was she really doing this, heading out to Indianapolis for an abortion? What about her baby? It wasn't his or her fault, right? She glanced at the piece of paper on her bookcase. She'd jotted down the name of the abortion clinic and her appointment time, as well as the clinic phone number. All the details she needed. Next she pulled out her cell phone and copied the information into her phone's address book.

Tossing the paper in the trash, Andi stuffed her thoughts back to the basement of her soul and pulled her suitcase down the hallway. She found her parents at the computer in their new office. They were reading a review on *The Last Letter* — Andi could see that much on the screen. Her dad turned and grinned at her. "The critics love it! The whole world's going to know about this movie!"

Andi tried to look enthusiastic, but she didn't have even the slightest interest in what the review said. "I'm leaving. The girls are expecting me in the city."

"Honey, I don't know." Her mom stood and came to her, pressing the back of her hand to Andi's forehead. "Are you feeling up to it? I mean, it was just a week ago that you were sleeping all day."

"I'm fine." She was touched by her mom's concern, but she struggled to make eye contact. *Mom, if you only knew . . .* Again she pushed back her fear and found a quick smile. "It's a short drive. Just an hour and hardly any heavy traffic until the end."

Her mom hesitated, and her dad turned and looked at her from his computer chair. His eyes clouded with doubt. "Are you sure, honey?"

"Yes." She ignored the strange rhythm of her heart. "I really need this."

Her dad stood and gave her a tender hug. "Please be careful."

"Oh, I don't think we told you." Her mom's expression suddenly changed. "Brandon Paul's coming Sunday. He'll be here for a few nights."

Andi was glad she was still holding onto her suitcase handle.

Otherwise she might've fallen flat onto the floor. Brandon Paul? "*The* Brandon Paul?"

"Right." Her dad chuckled. "He's meeting with Dayne and me, so most of the day will be business." He hesitated. "Brandon's an interesting kid. He's not much older than you. A few years, maybe. I think he wants to know the Lord, wants to do right. Maybe that's why he's drawn to work with us in *Unlocked*. But he still has a wild side ... I'm not sure he understands the scope of the battle he's in."

Andi was sure her father was right. Even she hadn't understood the scope of the battle until she imagined what her pregnancy might do to her father's reputation. A megastar like Brandon Paul? Of course he didn't understand it. "He's staying here?"

"Actually at Dayne's house. We're meeting there." Her dad angled his head, as if he was processing the possibilities. "Anyway, maybe you can come by. Take him around campus and give him a breather that afternoon. It might be fun ..."

"And good for him." Her mom nodded. "Not because he's Brandon Paul ... but because we want him to have good, solid people around him."

"If he gives his life to God during the filming of *Unlocked*, think of our country — the millions of kids that could be affected."

And if she moved home unwed and pregnant, imagine what that would do? She doubled her determination to make it to her appointment this afternoon.

"Anyway, just think about it." Her dad hugged her one last time. "Drive safely, honey."

Her mom hugged her, too, and after another round of promises that she'd be safe and that she'd call later that night, Andi was behind the wheel of her four-door, headed to Indianapolis. Her mind stayed ten miles ahead of her the whole ride. Brandon Paul was coming to Bloomington? How different might this weekend be if she hadn't gone with Taz? If she hadn't let him have his way with her? Her parents clearly still thought she'd be a good influence on the nation's top celebrity. The idea was ludicrous, and now the last thing Andi wanted was to spend time with Brandon. She would still be aching from an abortion. Her world had no room for frivolous afternoons with movie stars—not anymore.

She would stay in Indianapolis a few days longer and miss his visit altogether. He wouldn't be interested in her anyway. She looked ragged and worn out, and her stomach would be swollen from the procedure. No, there would be no meeting with Brandon Paul.

As that thought lifted, the more pressing one filled her mind. After a lifetime of believing God's Word, of holding tight to the value of life, she was only hours away from killing her baby. It wasn't a thought she allowed very often. Ever since she'd made up her mind, she'd acknowledged it only as a procedure or an abortion—the way the woman at the Indianapolis clinic called it. But here—driving into the city—she couldn't stop the truth from consuming her.

The closer she got to the city, the more she became convinced she was making a mistake. If she went through with the abortion she would carry the secret to her grave. But she would also carry the guilt. She allowed her mind to race, imagining other options. She couldn't tell her parents or ask for their support. Not without ruining her dad's reputation, his credibility with the public. She could hardly call Taz and ask him to step up and help raise their child. Every option seemed wrought with terrible implications.

As she passed the city limits sign, tears began to choke her. They streamed down her face and compromised her ability to see the road. She needed to call Taz. She hadn't gotten through to him last time she tried, and now he needed to know. The baby was his, too, and he deserved the chance to give her advice or offer his help. He wasn't a terrible person, really; he had simply moved on to another love. But back when the two of them were an item he had always been kind, his words flattering, his actions gentle.

She pulled off the freeway at the next exit and turned into a gas station parking lot. Her hands shook as she snagged her cell phone from the seat beside her and found his number in her address book. She hit Send and waited while it rang. Just when it seemed his voicemail might come on, she heard him. He sounded groggy and distracted. "Hey ..."

Andi felt another wave of panic, as she searched in a hurry for the right words. "Taz ... it's me. Andi."

"What?" He made a sound like he was yawning. "Sorry, I didn't hear you. Who?"

"Andi." Frustration raised the level of her voice. "Andi Ellison, Taz. Remember me?"

"Oh, Andi." He laughed lightly. "Sorry sweetheart, I was half asleep. Long night."

"It's three in the afternoon."

"I know." Most of the humor faded from his tone. "It's summer, okay?"

This was a terrible start. Andi covered her face with her free hand and pressed the phone to her ear. There was no easy way to say this. "Taz ... I'm pregnant."

For a long time he said nothing, and she wondered if he'd hung up. "You're ... pregnant? Do you ... do you know who the father is?"

If he'd been sitting across from her she would've gladly slapped his face. "I've never been with anyone but you."

Another silence. "I see." He exhaled loudly, slowly. As if the truth were finally hitting him. "What're you gonna do?"

"I scheduled an abortion for today. But," her voice broke, "I'm struggling. It isn't fair to the baby."

"There is no baby." His voice took on an authoritative voice, the one that mixed passion and charisma with absolute power.

The voice he'd used when he was directing her in his film. "You know better than that, Andi. You're what—three months along?"

"Not yet."

"Then it's not a baby." His easy laughter was back. "You had me worried there. I don't want to be a father. No way."

She felt sick, and she couldn't tell if the ache was in her heart or her stomach. She clutched her middle. "God says it's a baby, Taz. I don't care what you think. If I have the abortion, I kill our baby."

He cussed under his breath. "God says you shouldn't have slept with me, isn't that right?" His voice had become a menacing hiss. "Do what you have to do to get rid of it. No one's forcing me to be a father."

Andi was still thinking what to say in response when she realized he'd hung up on her. How dare he talk to her that way? Throwing it in her face that she'd slept with him, when he was the one who had talked her into it. She began to shiver, disgusted with herself for losing her virginity to someone so manipulative, so hateful. She pounded on the steering wheel and hung her head. What had she done? How could she be trapped in this nightmare? For five minutes she sat there, weeping and occasionally hitting her fist against the wheel or her own leg.

What about Rachel? Her friend wouldn't recognize her now. No one who had known her back in high school would see anything in this Andi that was familiar to the one they'd known. She was a terrible person, cheap and used and without a hope in the world. If she drove her car off a cliff, everyone would be better off. Her parents would be sad, of course, but they would get over the loss. That way they'd never have to know that she'd slept with Taz, or that she'd had an abortion.

But gradually a thought began to dawn on her. Maybe when the baby was conceived under such horrific conditions, abortion was the only answer. Certainly she didn't want to be linked to Taz the rest of her life. And what were her other options? For a split instant she could hear Ashley Baxter Blake at the crisis pregnancy clinic telling her about adoption — how beautiful it could be to give her child the gift of life with a family praying for a baby.

Pregnant with Taz's baby for nine months? Facing her parents and their circle of Hollywood friends and investors? Having the whole entertainment world know that Keith Ellison — Christian producer — had a daughter dealing with an unwanted pregnancy? The picture was too horrific to imagine. She needed to get into the city, call Sherry, and find her way to her friend's house. By tonight it would be over, the agonizing behind her. Andi wiped her tears and pulled her car back onto the road, back up the on-ramp onto the freeway. Traffic had built up and she inched her way into the slow lane.

She had forty minutes before her appointment, and she couldn't be late.

LISA ELLISON FELT UNEASY FROM THE moment her daughter drove away earlier that afternoon. Something wasn't right. Yes, in the year that Andi had been living on her own at Indiana University she was bound to have gotten used to a certain sense of freedom, and of course she had made friends that Lisa and Keith knew nothing about.

But the two of them had just landed in Bloomington. They weren't even unpacked, and with the meetings and busyness ahead, Andi might not get another chance to spend this sort of time with them. So why the sudden rush to head to the city? Keith was caught up in phone calls back to LA, and discussions with Dayne about the theatrical release for *The Last Letter*, so Lisa was forced to keep her fears to herself.

Her daughter might have changed considerably. She might be suffering from depression and unsure of her faith. But Lisa still knew her, and something about this trip to Indianapolis simply didn't add up. By three that afternoon, Lisa wandered back to Andi's bedroom and sat on the corner of her mattress. *Dear God, my daughter's in trouble. I can feel it. But there's nothing I can do to reach her, Lord.* Lisa put her hand on the familiar bedspread and ran her fingers over the soft cotton. None of this would've happened if Rachel hadn't died. The girl's death had rocked Andi's world and opened possibilities she hadn't considered before. Doubts about God she hadn't dared imagine.

Lisa stood and wandered slowly around the room. Andi had moved her things from the dorm and already she'd unpacked her belongings. The photo of Rachel that Andi loved so dearly stood on her small bookcase in the corner of her room. Lisa went to it and picked up the picture. Sweet Rachel. Such a good influence on Andi after they'd returned from Indonesia. Andi had come back to the States looking for life, for adventures she hadn't experienced on the mission field. But Rachel had kept her grounded, convincing her that the best adventures were those taken with the Lord.

Sunlight streamed through the window revealing a layer of dust along the top of the bookcase. Lisa absently used the arm of her sweatshirt to remove the dust. The layer came off easily, the way she wished it would with Andi's heart.

She glanced around and her eyes fell on a few pieces of notebook paper in the nearby trash can. She recognized Andi's handwriting on them, and she bent down, lifting them from the container. A few scribblings, dates and addresses. Nothing important. She stacked the notes on Andi's bedside table and returned to the window again. With every breath she could feel it. *Something's wrong with her, God, something very bad.* The ache in her soul was absolute proof, a heaviness that wouldn't be relieved until she bathed her daughter in prayer.

Slowly, and with all the love she could muster, she dropped to her knees and covered her face with her hands. Then, for the next thirty minutes, she prayed for Andi as if both their lives depended on it. She begged God to protect Andi and guard her, to grant her peace and clarity and to remind her of the truth. "Put your angels around her, Father. Whatever's taking her to the city, meet her there." She begged God over and over again, barely aware of her tears. "If she's pregnant, convince her to tell us." Lisa wasn't sure what else she could do on that topic. The counselor had asked Andi point-blank—and Andi had denied being pregnant.

So what was this terrible hurt in Lisa's heart, the awful certainty that something terrible was about to happen to Andi even at this very moment? She kept praying, committing Andi to the Lord, and beseeching Him for His protection over her daughter. When she was finally finished, when she pulled herself wearily to her feet and looked out the window again at some far-off place in the clear summer sky, Lisa was no closer to knowing what her daughter was doing in Indianapolis, or what sort of trouble she might be in. But she was sure of this much: No matter how much she and Keith loved Andi, God loved her more. So much more. And this afternoon—whatever Andi was doing—God would be with her.

For now, that would have to be enough.

Twenty-One

TRAFFIC GREW WORSE AS ANDI NEARED the city, and she chided herself for not being more mindful of the possible delays. Of course there'd be traffic on a Friday afternoon. Andi had just hoped most of the traffic would be heading out of the city, not into it. Twenty minutes passed, and finally Andi was at the turn-off for Sherry's rented house and the IU Indianapolis campus. According to the directions from Google, the clinic was only a few miles away. She drove off the freeway at the next exit and pulled into the parking lot of a place called Megan's Diner. It looked fairly upscale, the neighborhood one of the nicer ones on the outer edges of the city. But time was ticking away, and she silently willed Sherry to answer as she called her friend's cell number.

Instead, there was no answer, so Andi tried again. *Come on, Sherry ... don't let me down.* The phone rang and rang, but again the call went to her friend's voicemail. Thick walls of anxiety closed in around Andi. She hadn't counted on this. In her wallet was a debit card with access to barely enough money to pay for the abortion, and a ten-dollar bill. She didn't have money for a cab or a hotel room. Frantically, she hit Redial four more times, but Sherry never answered her phone.

Andi locked her car doors and leaned her head against her steering wheel. She had no address for Sherry, no land line, and none of the other girls' cell numbers. No way to reach her except the way she'd been trying—and that wasn't working. Something must've come up, but that wouldn't help Andi now. She checked the time on her phone. A quarter till four. Fifteen minutes and she was supposed to be walking through the doors of the clinic. Even if she reached Sherry this moment she wouldn't have time to get to the clinic by four. And she couldn't go by herself.

Her heartbeat jumped around, from slow and erratic to speeding fast. What was she supposed to do now? Turn around and go home? And if so, what would she tell her parents? They would be completely suspicious if she tried to explain how her friends didn't answer, and how they must not have been expecting her. They'd definitely be wary if she explained she was going again next Friday.

For as terrible as the past hour had been, Andi realized she was hungry. She hadn't eaten since breakfast, and then only a couple scrambled eggs. She had no choice but to go into the diner and find something cheap on the menu—a salad, maybe. Then she could keep trying Sherry, and eventually her friend would answer. They would laugh about the miscommunication, and Andi could stay the night with her and the girls. When the weekend was over, she would reschedule the abortion for Monday afternoon. Yes, that's what she'd have to do. Besides, she wanted to stay in Indianapolis to avoid the Brandon Paul visit anyway.

She climbed out, locked her car, and headed into the restaurant. Inside, she was seated at a table near the back—adjacent to a pretty woman and her three children. All of them were very attractive, and Andi noticed they spoke with a strong accent. Something European, maybe.

Andi checked the menu. She had enough money for an order of cheese sticks, a side salad, and water. Nothing more. If the bill was too high, she'd have to use her debit card and then she wouldn't have enough money for the abortion. She'd earned the money working part-time jobs for a photo shop near campus in Bloomington. Between that and the hundred dollars a month her parents gave her, she had saved up enough for the clinic.

Her cell phone was still in her hand. *Come on. Answer the*

phone. She hit Redial again, but still Sherry didn't pick up. Three more times she tried before the waitress walked up. The girl wasn't much older than she was, and after Andi placed her order the waitress hesitated. "Hey ... are you okay?"

Her tears came despite the fact that she tried everything in her power to stop them. "Y-y-yes." She dabbed at her cheeks with her fingertips. "Just a long day."

The waitress looked uncomfortable, like she wanted to help but she had no idea what to do. Finally she backed up some. "Okay, well ... if you need anything, let me know."

Andi nodded, refusing to look up. If she needed anything? She didn't know where to begin. With shaking fingers she lifted her cell phone once more and tried three final times to reach Sherry. The last time she left a message. "Hey, Sherry," her voice gave away the fact that she was crying. "I missed my appointment. If you could ... if you could call me back ... that'd be great."

Her tears kept coming, even though she wasn't sobbing or making any noise. It was like her heart had sprung a leak and nothing was going to stop it from breaking right there in Megan's Diner. She forced herself to stay quiet, praying that no one besides the waitress would see her meltdown. What was she supposed to do now? Drive home and find a clinic in Bloomington? Tell her parents the truth? Every possibility only made the walls close in a little tighter around her, until she was sure she would suffocate before her dinner arrived.

But even with tears falling onto her lap, Andi couldn't help but hear the conversation at the table beside her.

"We're starting a band, did I tell you?" The voice belonged to a boy in his mid teens, maybe.

Andi blinked back her tears and dabbed her eyes with her napkin. As she did she stole a look at the family. The boy talking was tall and blond, maybe sixteen or seventeen. "Nathalie's going to sing and Kenny'll play the piano."

"Really?" Their mother was a pretty dark-haired woman, her

eyes full of life and something Andi inherently knew was a strong faith in Christ. The same eyes her parents had. The eyes she'd had before this year at college. Their mom's expression brightened. "What about you, Mr. Marco?"

The oldest teenage boy stuck out his chest. "I'm bass guitar and drums."

"Both?" Their mom was teasing now. "People will pay to see that."

"Not at the same time." The middle boy's eyes were wide with possibility. "Some songs I'll do the guitar and he'll do the drums."

"Actually, I might have to do the drums most of the time." Marco swapped a look with his brother and sister. "Kenny, you'll play guitar or piano. Depending on the song."

"Right. That's a better plan." Kenny grinned at Marco and then at their mother. "What? You don't think we can do it?"

"Oh, yes. With your faith and determination, you can do anything you want. Just like your father."

"He's meeting us, right?" The little girl was darling, beautiful and blonde, with striking blue eyes. The family clearly wasn't from the United States.

"Yes, honey. But he can't stay long. He has a meeting tonight."

The girl put her elbows on the table and frowned. "Another meeting."

"We knew it would be like this when we agreed to a year abroad." She smiled at the kids, and then without warning she turned her eyes to Andi. With a slight nod of her head, she seemed to express a sympathy and caring that Andi desperately needed.

Andi could only imagine how she must've looked. Tear-streaked and swollen-eyed. But something told her she didn't have to worry about this woman judging her, so she found the slightest smile and returned the nod. Then she looked immediately back at her lap. The woman's children didn't seem to notice Andi, or the silent greeting from their mother in her direction.

They chattered on about their pending band, and how they were going to sing at churches all over America, and how they couldn't book any dates during soccer season.

"I might be a pro soccer player." The middle boy, Kenny, sounded happy and confident. "When the band's not playing."

Andi recognized young Kenny's tone, because once a lifetime ago that had been her—ready to take on the world, certain that success would find her wherever she turned, trusting on God's grace and goodness to take her into a life of happiness and joy. She was still listening to the family's happy banter when the children's father hurried up and hugged and kissed each of them.

Again Andi couldn't help but discretely watch.

"Felix, you smell wonderful." His wife looked totally in love as she snuggled up next to her handsome husband. "Hard to believe you've put in a day at the office."

"It's all so new and amazing. So much to take back to Switzerland."

So that was it. The family was here for a year from Switzerland. Andi couldn't help but feel jealous of the joy they had together. This was how she'd pictured her life, right? Successful and faith-filled, like Katy and Dayne Matthews. Happy and adventurous like the family a few feet away. She dabbed at her eyes again and willed herself to be invisible.

The waitress brought food for the family, and then for her, and like the woman had warned, her husband didn't stay long. When he left it was with promises of watching a movie together when he got home. "Friday's movie night," he grinned at them. Then he was off and running. Once he was gone, the kids finished picking at their plates, still talking about their band and the songs they'd write together. They paid their bill, and Andi did the same.

She was trying to decide what to do next, whether she should sit in her car waiting for Sherry to call back, or drive home and hope for some sane-sounding explanation for her parents. As she sorted through the fragmented thoughts clouding her mind, Andi looked up. The woman at the next table was looking straight at her, sympathy marking her expression. Andi wanted to wave off the attention, explain that she wasn't worth the woman interrupting her meal and her joyous time with her family. But just then, the woman whispered something to her kids. She stood and approached Andi. "Can I talk to you?"

There was no way Andi could reject the woman's offer. To do so would've caused more of a scene than she'd clearly already made. Andi nodded and turned her back slightly to the woman's children. She waited, not wanting to let the woman see her eyes.

"I've been watching you." Her voice was soft, rich with understanding and a willingness to help. "You're very upset."

"Yes." What could she say? The woman was a stranger ... she wouldn't want to get involved in Andi's messy life. "I'm ... sorry. You were having a nice time together."

"You didn't bother us." She leaned in a little closer. "Are you hurt? Is someone threatening you?"

"No." Andi looked up, and she realized how desperately she needed help. Even from a stranger. "I ... I live in Bloomington, but ... I had a doctor's appointment today. My friend was supposed to meet me here, but she didn't answer her phone and I missed the appointment, and now I'm not sure what to do. I was supposed to stay with my friend, but now I don't know where to stay." Andi couldn't believe she was spilling her entire story. Something about the woman's patient way of listening encouraged her to continue. "I can't afford a hotel, but now my appointment will have to be Monday, so I really need to stay. If only I could get hold of my friend."

"My name's Lucia Kunzmann." She held out her hand and patted Andi's fingers. "What's your name, dear?"

"Andi. Andi Ellison." She wanted to add that she came from a great family, and she wasn't a crazy person. But maybe the woman could already tell that somehow.

"My husband, Felix, and I are in the US for a year because of his work. He's an international banker. But in our hearts we're missionaries." She smiled and it warmed the space between them. "We pray for God to bring people into our lives who need help." She paused, her smile never wavering. "You can stay with us tonight, if you'd like. We live just a few blocks from here."

Andi could hardly believe what she was hearing. Was the woman serious? Would she really take in a stranger like this? She studied the woman, her trusting eyes. "You're a Christian, aren't you?"

"I am. We've been involved in youth ministry and counseling all our lives. We love Jesus very much." Lucia gave Andi's hand a quick, tender squeeze. "You too?"

"Yes." She thought about the choices she'd made the last year, the ways she'd compromised her faith and taken on viewpoints contrary to God's Word. She thought about the abortion she should've already had by now. She looked down at her hands. "At least ... I was."

"I thought so." Lucia ignored Andi's doubt. "God told me you were a believer." She stood and waited for Andi to look up again. "So you'll come? Be our guest tonight?"

The woman seemed sent straight from the Lord, exactly what she needed at this moment. She gathered her purse and stood, feeling desperately awkward. "It would just be for one night. If you really don't mind."

"We'd love it." Lucia put her arm around Andi's shoulders and walked her the few steps to her own table. "Kids, this is Andi. She's staying with us tonight." She introduced Marco, Kenny, and Nathalie. The kids seemed completely at ease with the idea that their mother had just invited a complete stranger to spend the night with them. The only explanation was the one Lucia had already given. The family lived out their days looking for people to help, looking for opportunities to be missionaries where God had placed them. In the year away from her parents, it was a concept Andi had almost forgotten. And as she and the Kunzmann family walked out to the parking lot, Andi had a sudden and certain thought.

Somewhere in Bloomington her parents must be praying for her.

IN A PERFECT WORLD, NO ONE would ever have to know that Cody's mother had been taken by ambulance to Bloomington Hospital, or that after they ran tests the truth was painfully clear. Yes, she'd been beat up, but that wasn't why she nearly died that day. The reason was the drugs. If Cody could've hidden the fact from all of Bloomington, he would've. But Landon Blake was one of the paramedics, and John Baxter was a doctor in the area. People would see Cody here—the families of football players, teachers at Clear Creek High visiting a relative. Bloomington was a small town. People were bound to find out.

After pumping her stomach and giving her medication to offset the way her organs were starting to fail, his mother was alive. But Cody could barely bring himself to talk to her. He was sitting by her bedside now, and she was sleeping, stable after hours of critical care. Bailey would be out tonight with Tim, no doubt, or home with her family—doing everything Cody would've loved to have been doing right now. Anything but wrestling with the blaring realization that his mother was using again.

He wasn't sure how long he sat there, but eventually his thoughts took him back to Iraq—when he'd been a prisoner of war. No matter how bad things got back then he believed he'd find a way out. He prayed and trusted God and determined that one day he would be free—and when the day came, he was ready.

But drugs? Watching his mother slowly kill herself? There was no escaping this prison, no way around the fact that he was the only one who could care for her. And even then, any day, at any minute she could take a fatal dose or wind up crossing paths with the wrong drug dealer. She could be arrested or killed or die in a scene like the one he'd found earlier today.

It was a life of guilt and shame and regret, and Cody couldn't free himself from it no matter what. He loved his mom, so he would stay. He would see her through the ups and downs to the end—whenever that came. He would pray and he would believe she could be set free if she chose Jesus over her addiction. The way he had done so many years ago. He would never give up, but he would never be free either. And that realization made him miss Bailey and her family until his body physically hurt from the pain.

Finally when he couldn't take another minute watching his mom sleep off the effects of the drugs, when he wasn't sure he could draw a breath without hearing Bailey's voice, Cody stepped out of the room and called her number. It was late by then, almost ten o'clock, and he was pretty sure he'd be interrupting some sort of date night she'd be having with Tim. But he didn't care. He wouldn't take up much of her time.

She answered on the fourth ring, just when he was about to hang up.

"Hello?" Her voice was soft, and she sounded sleepy. "Cody?"

"Hi." Tears scratched at his eyes and made his throat too tight to talk. He coughed quietly. He didn't want to wake up his mother. Not now. "Am I ... are you with Tim?"

"No." She yawned. "I'm in bed. The boys are going fishing early with my dad. We turned in early."

He wanted to ask if she'd seen Tim that night, but he had no right. His jealousy over the guy was getting out of hand. He massaged his brow and closed his eyes. "Bailey, I ... I was wrong earlier. How I treated you." He pictured the way she'd looked—at the football field—begging him to stay and talk to her. Her long brown hair blowing softly alongside her beautiful face, her blue eyes piercing his. Her long dancer legs and slight frame—no longer the kid she'd been when he had lived with them. She was so irresistible he'd had no choice but to leave. Otherwise she would've seen what had to be obvious to anyone.

He was in love with her.

"It's okay." She sounded more awake now, and a depth filled her tone. "I wanted you to know I'm done struggling. With Tim … with being his girlfriend." She sighed, long and slow. "I hate how he treated you at the cafeteria, and I don't know. Everything. I was gonna ask you to pray for me."

"I will." He savored her voice, the goodness of her. He held on as if by doing so he could will her here beside him. "I always pray for you. I told you that."

"But today … you didn't want to talk to me." Her tone told him how hurt she'd been by his actions. "You've never been like that before."

"I know. I'm sorry." How could he explain that he could feel her slipping away? That a chasm lay between the reality of her life and the reality of his, and it was growing all the time? *God … if You'd only give me a chance with her … I'd love her with every breath, the rest of my days.* But even as he uttered the silent prayer, he knew it could never happen. Their worlds were simply too different. He clutched the phone more tightly, pressed it to his ear. "I'll let you get back to sleep." He wanted to say it, tell her how much he loved her. But it wouldn't be fair to either of them. No matter what troubles she was having with Tim, he was better for her. Cody had known that since the day he returned from Iraq.

"Okay, well …" Bailey paused, as if she didn't want to get off the phone. "Maybe you should get some sleep too."

"Yeah." He looked back at the hospital bed, at his mother still passed out from the effects of her drug binge. He turned away. "Sleep would be good." He wanted to tell Bailey, wanted to pour out his heart and beg her to come down to the hospital with him. Just so he could hold her hand and believe somehow everything was going to get better. But he could never tell her what had happened that afternoon. The truth would only put more distance between them. No, hearing her voice, feeling her against his heart this way, would have to be enough.

"Hey, you were amazing today." Her words were a caress against his wounded soul. "My dad talked about you all the way home. He says you're very talented."

"Thanks." The compliment opened a window to a future that must have still existed outside the prison of the hospital room, the prison of his mother's addiction. "I thought I'd love it, but it's more than that. Really, Bailey. Like I was born to do this."

"I'm not surprised." She laughed lightly, keeping their conversation quiet since everyone else was asleep. "I mean, think about it, Cody. All those boring film sessions with my dad? Sitting there all those hours? We all should've known you'd be a coach one day. It was God's destiny for you." A softness filled her voice. "And look how good you are."

"Hmm." This was the best he'd felt all day. "That means a lot. Thanks."

Again he had the sense Bailey wanted to talk longer, but there was nothing to say. He had no right to let the conversation go longer, and she must've sensed his desire to keep the call brief. "I'm glad you called."

"Me too." He held onto these final seconds, the way her words felt as close as breath against his skin. "I needed to hear your voice." As soon as he said that, he wondered if he'd gone too far, let her see too much of how he was feeling.

But she didn't act upset or taken aback. "Same here. Because now I know you're not mad at me anymore."

"I never was." Again he longed to tell her everything he was feeling. But it was time to go. "Good night, Bailey."

"Good night."

He clicked the End button on his phone and slipped it back into his jeans pocket. Then he stepped into his mother's room and fell back against the first wall he came to. He closed his eyes and willed himself to remember Bailey's voice, her words. The nearness of her. If there was a way, he would run from the hospital room, from everything about his past and his mother's past, and he wouldn't stop until he had Bailey Flanigan in his arms.

But that could never happen. It was wrong to think of Bailey breaking up with Tim, no matter what she said. Wrong to think about her dating a recovering alcoholic whose mother was in the throes of drug addiction. Bailey wasn't the girl for him, though she would forever set the standard for everything good about love. But that was just it — Bailey was too good. He'd known it for a long time, and the sooner he acknowledged that to his heart the better.

Somewhere out there, Cody had to believe God had a girl for him — a young woman who would love him despite his past, and who together with him would raise the sort of family he still believed in. A family who laughed and prayed together, cried and played together. The sort of family he believed in because once — for a short season — he'd been a part of a family like that. A family he would love forever.

The Flanigan family.

Twenty-Two

IN ABOUT TWELVE HOURS, BRANDON PAUL would be in Bloomington, Indiana, meeting with the producers of *Unlocked*. Which meant tonight was the absolute last night he could party this hard for a long time. A week at least.

"Around back!" The music in the custom Escalade was loud, the way Brandon liked it. Beyoncé singing about her halo. Brandon crooned along with her. "Baby I can see your halo ..."

His driver whipped the SUV to the back door of Club 21 — the hottest new spot in Los Angeles. The paparazzi were waiting, but Brandon didn't care. It wasn't going in that got him in trouble. It was coming out. For that he'd have to be a little more careful.

Brandon gave the cameras a quick grin and ducked inside. Part of his entourage was already waiting—a couple guys he'd known back in his middle school football-playing days, and a new round of girls. Always a new round. The club was dark and loud and packed, the music pulsing.

"You're finally here!" TJ, one of his friends, slapped him on the back. "We got a whole cheerleading team in the private room."

"Really?" Brandon felt the thrill of all that lay ahead.

"Nah." TJ laughed a little too hard, too loud. He was probably already on something—cocaine, maybe. "But a couple of the girls are hot. Come on ... they got a sick spread back there."

Brandon followed his friend toward the private room, and he realized he should've done something to disguise himself. A hat or dark glasses. Something. His arrival was causing too much commotion. People were pressing in, shoving paper at him, shouting for an autograph. Screaming his name.

"Let us through!" TJ held up his hand and pushed back, creating space.

For a moment, panic rose in Brandon's heart. He had no bodyguards here, no one to stop the crowd. If they didn't back off, Brandon and TJ could be crushed. That was the reality. TJ shouted again, and another minute of finagling and they were through to the private room.

Brandon looked around. TJ had greatly exaggerated. The room held a few of their buddies and a handful of girls. The night would be calmer than he expected. He stretched, still shaking off the sensation of being suffocated. As he did, a girl walked up — a brunette he'd never seen before. Her eyes were red and puffy, and she couldn't walk straight.

Higher than a kite, he thought. *Just the way I like 'em.* "Hey, sweetheart, what's your name?" Brandon met her partway across the room, leaving almost no space between them. The music wasn't as loud in here, but the lights were dim. Brandon squinted at her, trying to make out her face. "Tell me your name."

The girl did, but Brandon forgot it almost instantly. Names didn't matter. He downed a couple of whiskey shots and felt himself loosen up. The girl was telling him about her modeling career, something about a runway job she had next weekend, when her friend walked up.

"Brandon Paul . . . what's this I hear about you doing a Christian film?"

Heat filled his face and he chuckled, buying time. "You must have the wrong guy."

"No. I read it in the paper." She eyed him, obviously doubting that he would be aligned with anything Christian. "'Brandon Paul to star in *Unlocked.*' That's what it said."

He laughed again, like this was the funniest thing he'd heard in a long time. "*Unlocked* was a national bestseller." He grabbed another shot from a passing tray and downed it. "The author's a Christian, but don't worry, baby." He walked up to the new girl and kissed her full on the mouth. Really kissed her. It lasted half a minute before he pulled back. "There. That ease your doubts?" He grinned at the girl and her friend, and he took a few steps toward a table where people were doing coke. "Don't think I'm turning Christian any time soon."

He laughed then and he laughed as he set about doing blow with the guys. No one mentioned anything Christian the rest of the night, so he'd done what he wanted to do. He'd stopped anyone talking about him like that. Craziest thing, right? Brandon Paul doing a Christian film. He laughed at the idea the rest of the night. Never happen, not in a million years.

But no matter how often Brandon laughed about the comment, the scene haunted him. His words stayed with him while he was doing lines and later when he and some of the guys downed a few more shots. He skipped the girls. Couldn't concentrate long enough to care. By the time TJ helped him back to his ride, he was wasted and even then the sound of his own voice screamed at him.

Don't think I'm turning Christian any time soon ... any time soon ... any time soon.

Was that really how he felt? Could he make jokes about a faith he'd run from all his life? He collapsed in the backseat of the empty SUV and closed his eyes. Dimly he could hear the sound of cameras outside the vehicle, but he didn't care. TJ wouldn't let them get a clear shot of him like this, and with the tinted windows, he was safe from the paparazzi.

But was he safe from God?

Fear whispered in his ear and blew hot breath in his face. He thought about *Unlocked* and everything it stood for. Why was he compelled to do a picture like that when everything the girl had said was true? The book *was* written by a Christian novelist, and the producers were definitely Christians. Even Dayne Matthews — whose reputation was once bigger than Brandon's. He put his hands over his ears and tried to block out the noise in his head.

This was crazy. He was Brandon Paul. Top star of NTM Studios. Heartthrob for teenage girls across the country. Every producer wanted him in one of their movies, right? So why choose a film like *Unlocked*? He felt sick to his stomach, scared about his flippant words. What had his mother told him once? The voices from a dozen conversations that night ran through his head, but he could hear his mother's above the rest. *Being a big star doesn't mean anything to God, Brandon ... one day you'll have to stop running. I only hope it's not too late.*

Not too late ... not too late...

"Stop it!" His words slurred together.

"'Sup, man?" The driver looked over his shoulder. "You chill, B?"

"Chill. Way chill." He slumped back against the seat. "Get me home."

But even that didn't help, because once he was alone in his palatial hillside house, the voices only got louder. His own most of all. *Don't think I'm turning Christian any time soon ...*

The last thing he thought about before he crashed was his little co-star. Sweetheart Annie Sullivan. Innocent and wide-eyed. When they met for the first time, Annie peered up at him with those pretty blue eyes and said, "Do you love Jesus, Brandon? Because you should."

He hadn't even answered her. Just playfully flicked one of her braids and grinned. "You ask a lot of questions, little Annie."

And that was that.

But now he couldn't get the child's face out of his mind. Annie Sullivan. So untainted by everything Hollywood, everything fame and fortune could someday do to her. Brandon put the pillow over his head and breathed through the crack. But that didn't stop the voices. He had all the money in the world, but he couldn't buy the one thing he wanted. The thing Annie Sullivan still had. The thing that eluded him every night, whether he was home alone or out getting wasted.

Peace of mind.

Especially tonight, with his own words keeping him awake, preventing sleep from getting a word in edgewise. Had he really said that about not being a Christian? Who was he like? Some Bible guy, some jerk who announced to the crowd something about not knowing Jesus, right? Brandon tried to remember the story from his childhood Sunday school days. Was it Paul ... He rolled onto his other side, hating the dizziness, wanting the drugs and drink gone from his body now. No, it wasn't Paul. He thought back, picturing himself as he'd once been. Just like Annie Sullivan.

But now he was just like ... like ...

He opened his eyes wide, the pillow still smashed to his head. "Peter!" he muttered. That was it; he was like Peter. Denying Jesus. He thought about the scene back at the club and he knew—for absolute certain—that if the girl asked the same question again, he'd answer it exactly the same. *Don't think I'm turning Christian any time soon ...* The words smothered him and spat at him, strangled him and mocked him. When he finally fell asleep he was sure of one thing. Fear was watching him, and it would be there waiting for him in the morning. Because he had lied to the girl at the club. The truth was something the world didn't know about Brandon Paul.

He had given his life to Jesus a long time ago.

KEITH PULLED INTO DAYNE'S LONG DRIVEWAY and parked his car near the front door. He hadn't been to Dayne and Katy's lake house, and though the place was bound to be nice any time of the year, here in June it was breathtaking. The views stretched out across the entire lake and the foliage around the house looked like something from a movie.

Appropriate, Keith told himself as he walked up to the door. He stopped before he knocked and he looked out, savoring the view. *God ... I've been looking forward to this meeting for a year. Please be with us today ... let us see whether Brandon's a right fit for this film.* He paused, his heart and mind torn. As much as he wanted to be here, he agreed with Lisa. Something was wrong with Andi, and if he had his way, he'd be driving to Indianapolis, finding her and bringing her home where she belonged. Since she'd been gone, she'd sent only a few text messages. Every time they tried to call her, she didn't answer her phone. Both he and Lisa were frustrated at themselves for not getting more information about the place where she was staying. They didn't know the girls' names or where they lived in the city.

In her last text, Andi had said she was fine, and she'd be home Tuesday. *Sorry I haven't been around when you call. God's with me here. Please don't worry.* And that was that. Lisa texted back right away, telling Andi they were going to call, asking her to answer her phone this time. But Andi neither replied with another text nor picked up her phone. Andi wasn't missing; she wasn't in danger —at least as far as they could tell. They could drive around Indianapolis all day and night and still not be any closer to finding her.

Which meant there was nothing Keith and Lisa could do but wait.

Keith knocked on the door and heard Dayne's voice inviting him in. He made his way to the back den where the meeting was set to take place, and there they were—two of America's most recognizable faces. Dayne Matthews and Brandon Paul. The table was round and solid mahogany. Dayne and Brandon sat opposite each other, and after a round of greetings, Keith took the seat between them.

Dayne's demeanor was easygoing, light-hearted. If anyone in the world could relate to Brandon Paul, it was Dayne. Keith decided to take a more passive role in the conversation, observe Brandon's actions and personality, analyze his motives for wanting to star in *Unlocked*.

"So how's the party scene?" Dayne leaned back, his pose casually confident, like something a magazine would run on the cover page.

Keith watched Dayne, amazed. This wasn't anything like Dayne had acted any other time the two of them had been together. Dayne was humble and funny, a family man through and through. But clearly he still knew how to play the Hollywood role. Not only that, but his acting was still top-notch. Only by coming across as relatable to Brandon Paul would either of them catch a glimpse of the young star with his guard down. Already his method seemed to be working.

Brandon linked his hands behind his head and grinned at Dayne. "You remember the days."

"Things were crazy." Dayne stopped short of giving off any sense of approval. But he raised his brow and let out a low whistle. "I mean so crazy."

"It's worse now. All the private rooms at the clubs." He laughed, and then just as quickly he seemed to remember where he was and who he was talking to. He eased himself into a straighter, more business-like position. "But we're here to talk about *Unlocked*, right?"

"It's a great story."

"Love it." Brandon looked more serious now. No question he truly liked the story. "Read it three times. Really, man." He looked at Keith. "You've read it, obviously."

"I have. It's phenomenal." Keith leaned his forearms on the

table and looked straight at Brandon in a way that was just short of intimidating. "The fact that it was inspired by the author's sister makes it even more amazing. It's a great responsibility to develop a film on a project this special."

Brandon nodded, but his attention seemed to have slipped. He reached for the can of Coke sitting in front of him, popped the top, and took a long sip. "Which reminds me. I haven't read the latest version of the script, but there's gotta be a love scene, right?"

Dayne glanced at Keith, deferring the answer. As much as Dayne had done to get up to speed, he hadn't read *Unlocked* yet. The screenplay, yes. But not the novel. Keith cleared his throat and tried not to sound too intense. "For your character?"

The surprise on Brandon's face told them he was surprised by the question. "Yeah, of course." He looked from Keith to Dayne. "My audience will expect that, don't you think?"

A warning light flashed in Keith's mind. "The guy's autistic. He has friendships and tender moments." Keith hesitated. He couldn't believe they were having this conversation. "But a love scene?"

"It's not a deal breaker." Brandon shrugged, as if to say he wasn't going to make any demands on the topic. "Just think it'd help at the box office if I get a make-out scene or two." He flashed his famous grin. "The girls love that sort of thing."

Enough time had been spent on the issue. Keith shook his head. "No love scenes. No kissing, no sex. It's not that sort of picture." He didn't let his frustration show but kept his tone matter-of-fact. "It's great we're talking about this. That way we won't have any surprises later."

The conversation shifted to the supporting cast and Brandon's favorite choices for his co-star, the peer who introduces him to the arts. "I want someone fresh, someone new." Brandon

KAREN KINGSBURY

pulled a sheet of paper from his bag. "Here's a few ideas from my agent, but the girl can't be all Hollywood weird, you know?"

Something in Dayne's eyes softened, and Keith figured he was thinking about his own past, how he'd come to know his wife, Katy. He'd seen her once at a Bloomington Christian Kids Theater performance, and he'd been struck by the fact that the girls in Hollywood lacked her small-town charm, her innocence. He'd done everything in his power to cast Katy in his next film—the impact she'd made on him in a single evening was that powerful.

Now here was Brandon feeling the same way, that only a girl with true innocence could play opposite him in a film as powerful as *Unlocked*. Keith jotted down Brandon's preference. "We'll take a look at your agent's suggestions."

"I mean, seriously, you probably have girls around here who would do a better job with the part than the girls lining up around the block at LA casting calls."

"She's out there," Dayne grinned at Brandon. "Keith and I are asking God to put together the perfect cast for this film. It'll happen; I can feel it."

Keith wasn't sure, but he thought Brandon reacted negatively to the mention of God. Nothing overt, just a downward glance and a slight change in his mood. Again he couldn't let the moment pass. "What are your thoughts on God, Brandon?" Keith didn't want to come across pushy, but they had to discuss this. "You understand this film will have a strong faith message, right?"

Seconds passed while Brandon struggled with the question. He leaned back in his seat and squirmed in a way that showed he was beyond uncomfortable. "Well," he raised his hands and let them fall back down to the table. "It's not a Christian film. I mean, there won't be a lot of preaching in it or anything. That's my understanding."

"The faith message will be authentic, integrated into the story the way it is in the book," Keith wanted to tackle this part of the discussion, because he was the producer with the reputation for bringing faith to Hollywood. "But the message will be there." Keith looked at his notes and then back at Brandon. "Some things to think about ... you'll be asked about why you chose this film. People will want to know your stance on Christianity and faith. Are you ready for that?"

Again Brandon seemed troubled by the question. He shifted his body, clearly antsy. "I'm an actor." He let loose a nervous laugh. "I'd like to avoid the topic of faith and defer to the character. The character's faith experience, the character's view on Jesus, that sort of thing." He raised an eyebrow toward Dayne. "That'll work, right?"

"Probably." Dayne was still playing the role of fellow actor, and not so much the businessman probing Brandon Paul for proof of his commitment. But his eyes told them he took this part of the meeting very seriously. "It's less important what you say than how you live. A film like this, people will be watching. More closely than ever."

Brandon laughed again, more in disbelief. "So, you're saying I have to be perfect? Clean up my image?"

"Your image is actually pretty clean." Dayne wasn't laughing. "I think it's important to keep it that way. Stay low on the paparazzi radar. Do your best to honor the faith of the character — even if you can't relate to him on a personal level."

In some ways this was nothing new. Producers often met with their key actors to lay out what was expected of them based on the character. A male lead in a story about the devastating effects of alcoholism could hardly be caught drunk in the clubs during the filming of the movie without damage to the project. "It's like any picture." Keith searched Brandon's eyes for even a hint of rebellion. "The off-camera choices of the actors always affect the film."

Brandon nodded slowly, and the professionalism that had

been wavering for the last couple minutes returned. "I understand that." He glanced at Dayne and then Keith. "I'll lay low,
guys. I won't let you down. This is a big movie for me. My agent
thinks it's a chance to win a couple awards, even." He grinned. "A
year from now we could be talking Oscars."

Keith wanted to say that first they needed to talk about committing to the current script. But he chose his words carefully.
"Okay, then ... I'm sure we'll have ongoing talks about the faith
element in the movie. And as for the script, I've got a copy of the
latest draft. You can get into it tonight and we can talk about it
tomorrow."

The meeting went another hour before they broke for dinner. Lisa and Dayne's wife, Katy, were back at the Ellison house
unpacking, so Keith offered to drive the fifteen minutes back
into town for sandwiches. Even if their wives had been available
to bring in a meal, Keith would've jumped at the chance to be
alone for a while, sort through the implications of the first couple
hours with Brandon Paul.

He flipped on his radio—a Christian talk station—and
stared at the pretty drive ahead. A pastor was talking about living
for God. His voice was passionate. "That means you take a hard
look at what drives you. If it's your wife and kids, you're out of
alignment with God ... if it's your promotion at the office, you're
off base. If it's the climb to get ahead of the pack, your priorities
are askew." He paused. "Folks, hear me on this. Living for God
means waking every day with the same question in mind: How
can I get through the next twelve hours in God's power, accom-
plishing His purposes, and concerned only about pleasing Him?"

Keith agreed with every word, but he turned down the volume. The reminder troubled his usually calm soul. Brandon Paul
wasn't sold out to God. By the sounds of it, he wasn't willing to
admit to having even the slightest faith. He definitely didn't want
to be aligned with Christianity.

So why were they having the meeting with the kid at all? Was it that important that Brandon Paul star in their movie? Even Brandon wanted an innocent, untainted girl as his co-star. Isn't that what the world would want in Brandon if he took the leading role, if he played an autistic teenager whose world was unlocked by the power of God through the arts?

They had two days with the young actor, but it wasn't like they could change their minds. Contracts had already been signed. This was the only chance they had to discern any threat Brandon might be to the message of the film, the power of it to change lives for Christ. The only chance to coach him on how to act and what to say during the process. And what they'd heard so far was beyond troubling. Brandon had alluded to his partying ways, joking that he kept things in control. He'd expressed a desire for a make out scene in a film where one would absolutely not be appropriate, and he'd flinched when they brought up faith. There were enough notes of concern on Keith's pad of paper that he was going to run out of space before the day was through.

For one thing, if Brandon wanted a make-out scene or a full-on sex scene, once they got into production, once a studio had agreed to fund half the picture, Keith and Dayne would struggle to keep it from happening. Brandon could add it on the spot, and if the cameras caught it and the studio liked it—the scene would appear in the film. He thought hard. It was a problem they could solve if they tackled it up front. They'd have to get with Luke Baxter quickly to make sure the final contracts were very clear about what would and wouldn't be allowed in the last edit.

But even then, Brandon was a wild card, a loose cannon who could destroy the reputation of the film and Jeremiah Productions in a single night on the town. Yes, having him in the film meant more people would see it. But was the risk worth the reward? Keith heard a text come into his phone. He picked it up and glanced at the message. It was from Andi.

KAREN KINGSBURY

Tell Mom I'm fine. Just didn't want you to worry. I'll call soon.

Keith tossed the phone back on the console. He didn't believe a word she said at this point. The old Andi would've called a few times a day, shared details of her time in Indianapolis, and talked about when she'd be home. Something was clearly wrong, and Keith felt sick that he couldn't do anything to help her. He remembered Brandon's request—that they find someone new and innocent to play his co-star. A year ago he would've thought of Andi before anyone else. She could've at least read for the part. But now she'd changed her looks and her love for God. She was distant and moody with brooding eyes where once she had shone brighter than the sun.

Andi could hardly play the part now. But if she wasn't suitable as the music student who helps unlock the world of Brandon's autistic character, then how was Brandon suitable? The only answer, the one Keith hated to admit, was that Brandon was a bigger box office draw. Period. By having him star in the film, Jeremiah Productions would become one of the most powerful moviemakers in the business.

Keith sighed and focused again on the beauty around him. *God ... give us the answers. As sunny as the day is, my heart has nothing but clouds and rain ... please guide us.*

He turned up the radio again. The preacher was just finishing, reciting a verse from Matthew 16. "Remember, friends. What good will it be for a man if he—gains the whole world, yet forfeits his soul. Live for God. Start today."

Keith couldn't have said it any better. Maybe if he'd been more involved in Andi's life this past year she wouldn't be fighting whatever she was fighting. Which meant just one question remained. If they didn't control Brandon Paul, if they gained the whole world's attention, the whole world's box office receipts, the whole world's praise and cheers ...

What exactly might they lose in the process?

Twenty-Three

ACTING LESSONS HADN'T BEEN BAILEY'S IDEA.

But after the Cross-Town Scrimmage, she talked with her mom about what the summer would hold. She had pictured lazy days by their backyard pool, swimming with her brothers, and having game nights as often as they were all together. Helping out with CKT summer camps and heading off to New York at summer's end for the audition.

Bailey's mom was always sympathetic to whatever was on her heart. But she was honest too. It was what kept them so close. That afternoon she took her time responding, but when she did, her opinion surprised Bailey. "Maybe Tim's approach to the audition is right, honey. This audition is one of the biggest breaks either of you have ever had." She gave a slight shrug. "I think it's okay that he's consumed. Passion is important when it comes to using the talents God gives us. We've always taught you kids that, right?"

Her answer was right on, and the rest of the morning Bailey wrestled with her feelings. In the end she realized it wasn't that she had a problem with Tim's passion. She had a problem with Tim. The one God had clearly pointed out earlier that day. When Katy Hart Matthews called that morning, the timing couldn't have been more perfect.

"I have an idea." Katy's voice was as cheerful as it was familiar. She went on to explain how Dayne had signed on as co-producer of Jeremiah Productions, working with Andi's dad. CKT was thriving with several directors running the shows so Katy could spend most of her time with little Sophie. "But I miss teaching." Her smile rang through in her voice. "Or maybe I just miss the Flanigans."

Katy's idea was perfect. She would bring Sophie over a few times a week. If Bailey's mom was willing to watch her, Katy would give Bailey acting lessons. And Katy was willing to start right away. It was midday Saturday and they'd already had their first lesson. Bailey was practically buzzing with excitement. They rejoined Bailey's mom and Sophie in the kitchen, and Bailey couldn't stop talking about the past hour. "Katy's so good." Bailey poured water for all of them. "It takes me back to when I was in CKT." She grinned at Katy. "We all knew you were talented, but I mean, you're so gifted. Everything you told me today ... I feel like after just one lesson I'm way more ready for the audition."

"You're a joy to work with." Katy took Sophie in her arms and cooed at her daughter. "You're a joy, too, isn't that right, Soph?" The blonde little girl giggled at Katy and tried to reach for her earring. Katy laughed and settled Sophie on her hip. "Everything in the mouth ... I know how you teethers are." She turned her attention to Bailey again. "You, you're very good, Bailey. I always saw that in you, but after today ..." Her eyes lit up a little more. "It'll be interesting to see how the audition goes. God's given you a gift, Bailey. No question about that."

They talked a while longer about Tim and his preparations for August, but Katy seemed to sense that Bailey didn't want to linger on the topic. The conversation moved around to Katy's help that morning over at the Ellison house and how Lisa Ellison was deeply worried about Andi.

"She won't return my calls," Bailey said. She took a long drink of water, picturing her roommate. "Something's very wrong with her. I've been asking God to show me how I can help."

Katy agreed that for now prayer was what Andi needed most. She shifted the talk to Jeremiah Productions and Brandon Paul's part in it. "He's in town, you know. They're meeting at our house today."

"Brandon Paul?" Bailey gasped. "Brandon Paul's at your house?" She jumped to her feet. "We should've had today's lesson in your living room."

Katy laughed. "The guys need this time." She looked at Jenny, then Bailey. "Just to make sure he's clear on what they expect."

The thought was sobering, and Bailey let her initial exuberance fade a little. "He isn't a Christian, is he?"

"Not that I know of. He doesn't have to be, but his off-screen actions will affect the film. The guys are aware of that. You can pray for them to have wisdom."

"On the other hand," Jenny raised an eyebrow, "imagine if Brandon Paul works with Dayne and Keith, and in the process he gives his life to Jesus."

"Yeah," Bailey tried to imagine the impact. "That would be something."

"Exactly." Katy didn't look in a hurry to leave. "That's why they need this time."

They caught up on the Baxter family next, how John and Elaine were coming up on their anniversary—both of them in great health and enjoying their respective families. "The biggest news is Luke and Reagan. They're looking to adopt again, so we're all praying for them. Asking that God bring about the right baby in His time. They're thinking they want a boy."

"The new little guy better be tough." Bailey gave a mock look of exhaustion. "That Tommy's a little terror."

Katy laughed. "He's getting better. Becoming a little more like Ashley's Cole. But his imagination is still stronger than all the other grandkids put together."

Next Jenny talked about summer football and how great Cody was working out as a coach for Clear Creek. At the mention of his name, a curiosity tugged at Bailey's heart. Why had he really called her last night? He'd sounded so sincere, so much more like the Cody she'd known when he lived here. All day she'd thought about texting or calling him and asking what had triggered the call.

A half hour passed quickly, and Katy and Sophie needed to leave — too soon for Bailey. She loved this, the chance to catch up with Katy again. They saw each other once in a while of course, but not like when she had lived with them, back when she and Dayne first met. It was one more reason Bailey was grateful Katy had come up with the idea. They made a plan to meet every Saturday, Monday, and Wednesday until the audition in August, and then Katy and Sophie headed home.

Bailey checked the time on the microwave and her breath caught in her throat. "Oh, no." She raced her glass to the dishwasher and hurried toward the stairs.

Her mom was pulling cans of tuna from the cupboard. Football practice was earlier today, and she had promised the boys a platter of tuna salad sandwiches after practice. She watched Bailey run past. "What's the rush?"

"Tim. I forgot about him." She groaned as she reached the stairs. "I'm so bad. We were supposed to meet for lunch at one."

Bailey flew to her room, fixed her hair, and grabbed her purse and was pulling out of the driveway in five minutes. Even then she pulled up at the restaurant fifteen minutes late. She grumbled at herself. "So rude ... he's probably gone by now."

She ran across the parking lot and burst through the back door of the diner, breathless. Tim was still there, sitting by himself in a booth by the windows. He was on his cell phone, and he looked relaxed. Bailey smoothed out her pale pink T-shirt and caught her breath. Then she calmly crossed the restaurant and took her place opposite him. She'd texted Tim earlier about the lesson with Katy, so he probably figured she was late because the lesson ran over.

"Hi," he mouthed. He pointed at the phone and held up his finger, letting her know he was almost finished. Then he turned his attention back to the call. "Well, hey … I'm glad I got hold of you. We've been worried, Andi."

Bailey sat back against the vinyl booth and stared at him. Andi Ellison? He'd called Andi and she'd actually answered? Bailey was torn between feeling grateful someone had gotten hold of her and wondering why she had taken Tim's call but not hers.

The call ended and Tim made a point of looking long and hard at the time on his phone before setting it on the table beside him. "Lose track of the day?" His smile told her he wasn't too mad. "I mean, I figured the lesson would get intense. Katy's a great teacher."

He figured the lesson would get intense? Bailey wrinkled her brow. What was that supposed to mean? She thought about asking but changed her mind. If she became angry every time they were together, there wouldn't be any point. "So … that was Andi?"

"I called her." He winked. "Figured it would give me something to do while I waited."

Bailey nodded, anxious to get past the issue of her lateness. "How is she? Her mom and dad are worried sick about her."

"She sounded okay, a little confused maybe. She's hanging out with friends in Indianapolis for a few days. She told me she wants to get back into acting." Tim picked up the menu and absently looked at it. "I told her she definitely should." His eyes met Bailey's over the top of the menu. "She's a natural."

His words settled in Bailey's gut like a mouthful of thistle weeds. Again, she refused to react. "Definitely. Andi's amazing."

"What I didn't tell her," he set the menu down again, "was that God could hardly bless her now. Not without a complete change of heart."

Bailey was losing her appetite. "Because of Taz, you mean."

"Of course. You give yourself to a guy like that and what do

you expect? Taz is the Cody Coleman of Indiana University—
leaving a trail of used girls in his path."

A seething anger bubbled quickly and completely to the surface of Bailey's heart. "Cody's not like that."

"He was in high school." Tim acted like he had every right to
defend the comparison. "That's what I meant. Guys like that, I
mean, what do girls expect?"

Beneath the table, Bailey started tapping her foot. Her heart
seemed to shout at her to leave the restaurant, find any other way
to spend her afternoon. She exhaled, gathering what remained of
her control. "Actually," she lifted her napkin from her lap and set
it on the table in front of her, "I have housework to catch up on
back home." She inched toward the edge of the seat. "Sorry I was
late. I just … I don't have time for this."

If Tim had been trying to push her, trying to punish her for
being late, in that moment the instant remorse in his eyes told
her he was sorry. Clearly he'd gone too far. "Hey, Bailey … I was
wrong. I shouldn't have said that."

"No, it's fine." She studied him, searching her heart for any
sort of feelings. Anything that would keep her here another hour.
She remembered the conviction she'd felt the other day, that
she'd let God down by not acting on how she truly felt about
Tim. "You're right." She couldn't defend Cody's past. It was what
it was. "Cody wasn't a great guy back then."

"Yeah, but I shouldn't have said anything." Here, in his apology, was a little of the guy he'd once been, the one Bailey had
fallen for so long ago. "I'm sorry, really."

Bailey forced herself to calm down, not to bolt from the restaurant and never talk to Tim again. She was still his girlfriend,
after all. He deserved to know how she was feeling. She exhaled,
knowing there was only one thing to do. "Tim … I think we need
a break."

Tim's expression went completely blank. "A break?" He blinked twice. "What sort of a break?"

"You know ... a break. Time apart." Her eyes were dry, and she realized how wrong she'd been not to have this talk with Tim a long time ago. A modicum of compassion eased her anger. Tim clearly hadn't seen this coming. "We both have a lot going on this summer. Maybe time apart would give us ... I don't know, a better sense of direction."

"So, you mean like break up?" He set down his menu and leaned back, dazed. "That's what you want?"

"I guess." She'd never done this before, and it was harder than she thought. "It doesn't have to be like some awful thing where we never talk. And maybe things will work out between us later. When we're older."

Tim slouched forward and shaded his eyes with his hand. When he looked at her again, his eyes weren't damp, but they were hurting. "So you're serious? You want to break up?"

"Yes." She bit her lip, trying to feel appropriately broken-hearted. But even as she did, a hint of brilliant joy splashed light across the awkward moment. Suddenly Bailey knew this was what she desperately wanted. She needed a closer walk with the Lord, not with Tim Reed. "I think it's best. For both of us."

"Is that why you agreed to meet today? To break up with me?" He allowed a weak laugh, as if he were dizzy and trying to remember which way was up. "Without even talking about it first?"

There was nothing to talk about, but Bailey couldn't say so. She didn't want to come across heartless. *Make my words kind, God ... I don't want to hurt him.* She breathed the silent prayer and drew a steadying breath. "I wanted to be your girlfriend for a long time." She smiled, hoping he could see that she truly cared for him. "Way before you ever saw me that way."

"But I do see you that way." He let his hands fall to the table. "I still do. We have so much ahead."

"Maybe." She was anxious to leave. "Right now I need to think about my life, the future. I want my faith to be stronger so I can tell where God's leading me. Staying together now would only hurt our chances of a future. Don't you see that?"

The realization of what had just happened was hitting Tim harder, and the shock was wearing off. He was sad now, more sad than he'd ever looked before. "What about the audition? We're supposed to go to New York together."

"We'll still go." She thought about reaching across the table and taking hold of his hand, just to show she still cared. But she didn't want to confuse him. "We were friends before we dated … there's no reason we can't have fun in New York City."

He stared out the window, quiet for a long time. Finally he turned to her and shrugged one shoulder. "I guess this is it, then."

"No." She gave him a sad smile. "Don't say that, Cody, not when—" her hand flew to her mouth and she felt the color leave her face.

"*Cody?*" The sorrow in Tim's eyes was instantly replaced by a deeper hurt.

"Tim, it was an accident … I'm nervous, that's all." Her mouth was acting on its own, because her heart was still too horrified to believe she'd just done the unthinkable. She'd actually called him Cody.

"That's what this is really about, right? The undying love you have for Cody Coleman." He glared at her, but after a few seconds, his anger faded. In its place was a forced indifference. He stood and dropped his napkin on the table near hers. "You and Cody have a good summer. I'll find my own way to New York."

"Tim …" she stood and grabbed her purse, working to keep up with him. They walked out the back door together and in the parking lot she took gentle hold of his arm. "Stop … don't do this."

"Do what?" He groaned and crossed his arms, staring at her. "You're not the only one who's felt it, Bailey. Something's been missing between us for a while. I know that. But I figured we just needed more time together, more chances to laugh and play at the lake. See a movie together."

"That would've helped."

"No." He shook his head. His tone took on a deeper understanding. "You've never given me your heart. You've kept me at a distance. Even in the best times."

Bailey could hardly argue. She deserved some of the blame for why they weren't closer, more connected. God had shown her that. But she wasn't willing to argue with Tim. He deserved a better ending. "Can I say something?"

He stared at the ground for a long while, and when he looked up the fight was gone for him too. "What?"

"Thank you." She put her hand on his shoulder. "You respected me, you treated me with honor." It was partly why she'd stayed with him so long. "I'll always love that about you."

The compliment hit him square in the heart, Bailey could tell. It softened the tension in the moment. "I care about you." He wrapped her in a long hug, and when he released her his eyes were damp for the first time. "I'll always care."

"See?" She smiled at him, remembering a hundred good times. "That's why we have to stay close. We both care too much to walk away forever."

He searched her eyes a final time. "I'll be in touch then? Before New York?"

"Yes." She gave him one last quick hug. "And you're coming with us. We already have your ticket."

There was no need for him to respond, no need to do anything but slowly step back and go their own ways. As they did, they both waved, and then in a blur Bailey was back in her car headed home. Her emotions scattered wildly across the surface of her heart. She ached for Tim and the loss he was feeling. Clearly he hadn't been expecting a break-up. But the truth was, Tim would be fine. He would have more time for his family and his lessons, more time to focus on his audition.

But as sad as she felt for Tim, as final as it felt to be broken up after two years, Bailey couldn't deny the greater joy bursting through her. Because this was a freedom unlike anything she'd ever felt. Her mom had asked if she felt tied down, and she'd said no. Just a week ago she'd said that. But she must've felt that way, and she must've been missing God's leading in her life, because now she felt free and amazing! She didn't have to think about Tim or worry about their relationship or wonder why she didn't want to spend time with him. She was free! Free to be herself and free to be open to whatever future God had for her.

She sang along to the radio as she drove, Five for Fighting's song "100 Years," about how short life was, with only a hundred years to live. Such a finite number of days. She couldn't spend one more moment in mediocrity, not in love or life or any part of her future. She would never settle again, the way she'd settled these last months with Tim. Yes, he was a great guy, a strong Christian. And yes, he'd respected her. She would always be grateful to him for that. But he didn't love her — no matter when he'd toyed with the word before. Even today he couldn't quite say it. Just that he cared for her, nothing more.

And that was fine. She cared for him too. But that didn't mean they should be dating. Bailey felt lighter than she had in a year. Sure, she would have days when she would feel lonely, when the reality of what she'd just done would hit her hard. But it was the right choice — Bailey had no doubt. As she pulled into the driveway, she remembered her horrible slip-up. How could she have called him Cody? And at a time like that? The question hung in the early afternoon breeze as Bailey parked her car, and suddenly the answer was obvious.

She pictured dozens of times when she and her brothers had said something they shouldn't have said. A criticism or unkind word. And other times when the opposite was true, and one of them would compliment someone in the family, saying something that made the other person walk away smiling, his head higher. Always their parents would remind them of a Bible verse from Matthew 12—"Out of the overflow of the heart the mouth speaks." With that truth in mind, Bailey wasn't surprised she'd called her first boyfriend Cody. Bailey knew what was in her heart, the feelings for Cody she'd carried for so long. Based on that, it wasn't a question of why she'd slipped and said his name. It was a question of how she'd kept from saying it sooner.

As she walked into the house, she felt the finality of the break-up with Tim. She couldn't imagine getting back together with him, though only time would tell. For now it felt like a chapter in her life had ended—and for that reason she was more subdued as she found her mom in the kitchen, as she told her what happened, and as the two of them hugged.

"God knows the plans He has for you, sweetheart." Her mom still held her hand. "I've told you that since you were a little girl."

"I believe that." Bailey frowned. "I'm not sad the way I thought I'd be. But I feel bad. God wanted me to do this sooner, and I didn't listen." She hesitated. "I feel bad about that."

"Well, you did the right thing now."

"Yes." She gave her mom a crooked smile. "I'll miss him."

"Mmm." Her mom nodded, keeping the moment unrushed. "I'm sorry."

Bailey made a face. "I didn't tell you the worst part."

"Worse than breaking up?" Her mom waited, listening with her whole heart.

Bailey told her about calling Tim the wrong name. "I wanted to take it back as soon as it was out of my mouth ... but it was too late."

"Ooooh." Her mom bit her lip. "That must've been awkward."

"It was awful."

Again her mom waited, studying Bailey. "You know what I think?"

"What?" Bailey still felt terrible. She hoped Tim wasn't home reliving the moment the way she was.

"I have a feeling next time around," her mom pulled her close again, "if you find yourself calling your boyfriend by that same name—it won't be awkward at all."

Bailey took a few seconds to realize what her mom was saying. Then, despite her conflicting emotions, she laughed just a little and hugged her mom tight. Her heart felt lighter than it had all day. Because one thing she'd learned and come to count on being close to her mom all these years.

Her mom was usually right.

Twenty-Four

ANDI'S WEEKEND HAD BEEN LIKE SOMETHING from a dream. That first night she'd gone home with the Kunzmanns, and since then they'd insisted that she stay. Lucia knew about Andi's doctor appointment, and the fact that Sherry had let her down, never called her back. Of course, Andi hadn't explained exactly what type of doctor appointment she'd missed.

"You were planning to stay in the city for the weekend," Lucia told her at breakfast that morning. "Now you'll stay with us."

"Yeah, and we're better!" Young Nathalie beamed a bright smile in her direction. The girl was so sweet and full of life—so much like Andi had been at that age.

Everything about the Kunzmann family felt like Andi had stepped into another world, like the nightmare of her own life didn't even exist. She loved the way the Kunzmanns did everything as a family, the meals and clean-up, their homework and reading time. And even though they didn't know her, they included her like she'd been a part of them forever.

Andi appreciated their welcome hearts, but she kept her distance, watching them, studying them. This was the sort of life she'd always wanted, and there were times with the Kunzmanns when she actually thought it was possible. She would go home and find her faith again, put God first and make her way back to innocence. But that's when the reality of her situation would hit.

She was pregnant, about to have an abortion Monday morning. She could never find her way back to innocence.

A couple times since she'd come home with them, Lucia

271

would find a private moment with her and try to learn more about her situation. Once she even asked about her doctor's appointment. "You aren't sick, are you?"

"No." Andi's answer was quick. "Nothing like that."

"What about your parents? Where are they?"

Andi explained that they were in Bloomington, and that they knew she was okay. She had a feeling Lucia could see house-size holes in her story, but not once did Lucia push for details. Andi knew her parents were worrying, so she tried to text them more often. But she couldn't talk to them, otherwise she'd break down. She'd made up her mind — now she had to follow through.

On Saturday night they ate roasted chicken, and after dinner, Felix — Lucia's husband — poured himself a second towering glass of milk. "Best drink ever," he raised his glass. He nodded to the jug of milk. "You want some?"

It'd be good for the baby, she thought. Then she dismissed the thought in horror. What did it matter? Her baby would be dead in a few days. "No," she looked down, certain he could see the guilt in her eyes. "No thank you."

Felix and Lucia talked to her about school, her major, and her interests. Watching them was a lot like watching her parents. The two of them were clearly in love, sharing a chemistry and private sort of love that time had only made stronger. Later, Andi watched the way Felix related to his kids, getting down on the floor to wrestle with them, or hovering over his oldest son's algebra homework. The sort of dad Taz never would've been. It was another reason to go through with the abortion. Why should her baby have anything less than what the Kunzmann kids had?

Andi learned quickly that the Kunzmanns loved playing board games — more than any family Andi had ever known. It was Apples to Apples Friday night when their movie ended, and Pictionary on Saturday night. Sunday they played Catch Phrase, and everyone was glad for Andi because her presence meant the teams were even. "Finally," Lucia announced as they settled in to play, "Felix has no excuse if he loses!"

The family laughed, and Nathalie giggled so hard she spilled her milk. The ordeal sent everyone into action, helping clean the mess. The whole time Andi could only watch them and long for what they shared. Long for it and mourn it at the same time. She'd made her choice. She'd walked away from the chance at having what the Kunzmanns had. She resolved to enjoy the time there while she could.

Monday was coming soon enough.

LISA FELT LIKE SHE WAS GOING crazy. Andi wouldn't answer her phone, and her text messages were so brief they felt cryptic. She and Keith had been praying all weekend, and now that it was Sunday, Keith could barely focus on the meetings with Brandon Paul. This morning they'd all gone to church, and Brandon had stayed at the Matthews' house — reading the newest script.

"I might have you hang out with him the rest of the day." Keith told him as they left the service.

Dayne nodded. He had Sophie in his arms, and he reached for Katy's hand. "He might open up more to me if you weren't there right now."

"Exactly." Keith put his arm around Lisa. "I couldn't concentrate anyway. We're worried sick about Andi."

Lisa worked to keep from crying. "We both feel the situation's dire — but we can't do anything to help until she comes home." Lisa shared a look with Katy. Her new friend already knew how grave Lisa's concern was for Andi. "I'm afraid if we wait till she comes home it'll be too late."

She didn't have to explain that she was worried Andi was pregnant. But after days of praying for their daughter, that's what she and Keith had come to believe. If she was pregnant, then she might be in Indianapolis for an abortion, or worse ... because she no longer believed she had a reason to live. The idea made Lisa sick to her stomach, and she'd begged God all day for a sign, a clue. A way to reach her before it was too late.

With Brandon taken care of, Keith talked the whole way home about what they might do to find her. They could talk to her other friends — starting with Bailey — and find phone numbers of Andi's classmates. Anyone. Eventually they might come across someone who would know the names and whereabouts of the girls Andi was staying with. Another plan was to call the phone company and see if her phone had a GPS finder built into it. Maybe then they could pinpoint exactly where she was and be at her side in an hour.

They decided on that plan, and Lisa had the phone company on the line minutes after they walked through the door.

"We need to find our daughter. She has her phone, but we don't know where she is."

"Yes, ma'am. How old is your daughter?" His tone suggested he'd been through this before.

"She's nineteen."

"She's an adult, ma'am. We can't give out the whereabouts of the cell phone of an adult unless there's reason to suspect foul play. When's the last time you heard from her?"

Lisa wanted to lie, but she couldn't. "She's been texting us off and on." She pushed her fingers through her hair and stared helplessly at Keith. God was aware of their problem. If doing things His way meant missing out on this information, then He would have another plan.

"Ma'am, if you're hearing from her and she's an adult, I'm afraid there's nothing I can do. She has a right to her privacy."

Lisa tried once more. "She isn't acting like herself. If you could just tell us —"

"I'm sorry, ma'am." And with that the man hung up.

She dropped the phone on the kitchen counter and moved into Keith's arms. "What are we supposed to do?"

For a long time neither of them said anything, but then Keith stepped free and studied her. "What about her room? You sure there was nothing? No sign, nothing she might've written down?"

Lisa sucked in a quick breath. "Yes!" How could she not have thought about this sooner? She hurried down the hallway to Andi's room, with Keith behind her.

"What is it?"

"Notes. Papers I found in the trash." She rushed through the doorway and grabbed the stack of papers, the ones she herself had collected from the can and set there on Friday afternoon. Why hadn't she thought to look at them sooner? If something happened to Andi, if she did something she would regret, Lisa could never forgive herself. She sat on the edge of Andi's bed, and Keith sat beside her.

"What are these?"

"I'm not sure. They have to be recent. She hasn't been home long enough to have anything old in the trash." Her hands shook as she sorted through the papers, scrutinizing the scribble marks and bits of writing. Suddenly one of them practically screamed at her. "Look at this." She held it out for Keith to see. In Andi's printing was this notation: Indianapolis Family Planning Center. The words were followed by an address and a phone number.

Lisa felt the floor give way. She lowered the paper and looked at Keith. No matter how often they'd mentioned the possibility, Lisa had never really believed it until now. There could be only one reason Andi had written down the name and address of a family planning center.

"You think ..." Keith's face was ashen.

"She must be." Lisa hung her head as the reality shot shrapnel across her heart. Their precious daughter — the one who had taught countless village women about Jesus and His plan for their lives—was pregnant. Worse, she was clearly considering an abortion. That's what family planning centers did.

Lisa sat up straighter. She couldn't afford to break down now, not when Andi clearly needed her. There were other notations, scribbles on the pieces of paper, and after a few seconds she made sense of something else. Written at the bottom of one page were the words, *Sarah's House—Crisis Pregnancy Center. Bloomington.* Surrounding it were a dozen question marks, each of them heavily doodled over. Not far from that were the words *free ultrasound* and more question marks.

Suddenly Lisa's heart leaped with hope. "Sarah's House is here in town, remember?"

A dawning came across Keith's expression. "Dayne's talked about it. His sisters run it."

Lisa couldn't move fast enough. "Come on, we have to hurry." She and Keith ran back to the kitchen and Lisa handed him the phone. "Call Dayne."

As fast as his fingers could move, Keith did as she asked. Three minutes later he had Ashley Baxter Blake's phone number. "Dayne told me she might not be able to talk about it. Confidentiality rules."

"I'll call her." Lisa felt like a mother bear, ready to tear doors off walls if it meant getting to her daughter. She dialed the number and waited until Ashley picked up.

"Hello?"

"Hi, Ashley. This is Lisa Ellison. Keith's wife." She worked to keep her tears from taking over. It was important that she sound calm and clear-minded. "We have reason to believe our daughter Andi is pregnant. She's in Indianapolis and she won't answer our calls. Did she come to your clinic?"

There was a long pause on the other end. "Mrs. Ellison … Lisa … our clients trust us with their confidentiality. I'm not sure how much I can—"

"Your center, it's there to save lives — isn't that right?"

Another long beat. "Of course."

"I have the name of a family planning center in Indianapolis, and if I'm right about this, I think Andi might be planning to have an abortion. "Please ... tell me if she's been to see you."

Another long pause across the line. "I've seen her. Yes." Ashley hesitated. "Andi's in trouble, Mrs. Ellison. I'm sorry ... I can't say much more. She only came in once."

"So she's ... she's pregnant?"

Ashley's silence clearly conveyed the truth.

Lisa closed her eyes and grabbed for Keith's arm. "Dear God ... why didn't she tell us?"

"We give all of our clients information about raising their babies or releasing them for adoption." Ashley sounded broken by the situation.

For a split moment, Lisa wanted to be angry with Ashley. If she'd known about Andi, why hadn't she come to them? Told them about their daughter's pregnancy before this weekend? Then they wouldn't be in this situation.

Ashley seemed to read her mind, because she explained again that the reason pregnant girls came in for a pregnancy test was because they believed the results would be private. "Have you talked to Bailey? She might know something, a way you could reach her."

"We'll try that next." Lisa's anger dissolved, and all that remained was gratitude. "Thank you, Ashley. If we have to go camp outside the abortion clinic Andi wrote about, we will. At least we know what she's up against." Lisa thanked her again and the call ended.

Keith looked despondent. The news was overwhelming, and Lisa felt practically paralyzed by it. First, their daughter was definitely pregnant. And second, she clearly planned to end the life of her baby. At least that. There was no telling what else was going through her mind while she was in Indianapolis this weekend.

"What next?" Keith took the phone from Lisa and set it back on the base.

There was only one answer, one way to get another step closer to Andi so they could help her. Lisa grabbed her purse from the kitchen counter. "We need to go see Bailey."

They reached the Flanigan house in ten minutes. Much to Lisa's relief, Bailey answered the front door and invited them in. They must've both looked crazy with worry, because Bailey froze in place. "Is this … about Andi?"

"Yes." Again Lisa fought to keep control. "She's in a lot of trouble. We'd like to talk, if you have a minute."

Bailey called her parents to join them, and the group went into the Flanigans' living room. It was the first day in a week that hadn't been brilliantly sunny, and Lisa found it fitting. The clouds cast dark shadows through the wall of windows, and even though it was late June, Lisa began to shiver as she sat down. Keith took the spot beside her, the two of them opposite Jim and Jenny Flanigan. Bailey sat in the closest chair.

"You've heard something from Andi?" Jenny started the conversation.

"Not really." The mere fact that this kind woman knew even that much—that Andi was out of town and not communicating much—was proof that Bailey told her everything. The way Andi used to tell Lisa everything. She focused her thoughts, as she squeezed her husband's hand. "We found out today. Andi's pregnant."

Bailey groaned and gripped the arms of the chair, her eyes downcast. "I was afraid of this."

"Us too." Keith sat rigid beside her. His posture told Lisa he wasn't willing to give up. "She's in the city, and she's texted us now and then. But she won't answer our calls. We think she's scheduled an abortion there. We found the name of an Indianapolis clinic."

They were quiet for a few seconds, each of them grasping what Andi might've already done, what she might be going through this very moment. And how they could possibly reach her.

"Wait!" Bailey looked up. "Tim talked to her yesterday afternoon. He called her around noon. She told him she was staying with friends, thinking of taking classes there."

"Same thing she told us." Lisa frowned. "We're here because we hoped you might know these girls, the friends she's staying with."

"No." Bailey frowned. "I have an idea who they are. One's a girl named Sherry. She's involved in theater."

"Do you know her last name?"

"No."

Lisa's mind raced. "There has to be someone who would know. Maybe if we talk to Tim."

"Absolutely. He might not have told me everything." Bailey rattled off Tim's number and Lisa dialed it.

But after a brief conversation, the call ended. "He doesn't know anything. Just that she sounded upbeat."

"Which maybe does tell us something," Jim had been thinking. He put his arm around Jenny and looked from her to the others. "If she just had an abortion, I doubt she'd be taking a call from Tim Reed."

"True." This was helping. Even if no one had any exact answers, they were getting somewhere.

"You're pretty sure you know which clinic she's been in contact with?" Jenny's tone was grave.

"We found the name and an address written on a piece of paper in her room." Had the expectations they'd placed on her really been so hard to live up to? So much that she couldn't face them in her greatest hour of need?

Please God ... we need an answer, some sort of direction. We're getting nowhere, and Andi needs us. "Maybe ... maybe if we pray for her."

They all agreed, and for the next several minutes they took turns asking God to protect Andi, to prompt her to call home. And they asked Him for a sign, some sort of direction so that if Andi was resistant to their help, they could find her.

The prayer ended and Lisa was about to thank the Flanigans for their time when her phone vibrated. It was still in her hand from the call to Tim, and Lisa saw that a text message had come in from Andi. "It's her!" She tapped a few buttons and there it was, Andi's latest message.

She took a quick breath and read it out loud. "It says, '*Hi Mom ... I know you're mad at me, and I'm sorry. I'm really okay. But it looks like I won't be coming home until Tuesday evening.*'" Lisa paused, distraught at this latest news. "'*The girls and I are having fun, and we want a few days to look around the campus here. Thanks for understanding.*'" She shrugged. "That's all she said." In the old days, she never would've texted Lisa without saying she loved her. But now ... she must've been so racked with guilt and shame she couldn't even think clearly.

"You know what that means ..." Jenny looked at Lisa.

"Her appointment—if she has an appointment—must be Monday morning."

"Exactly." Bailey hadn't said much. She still looked pale and shocked—worried sick about her friend. "Someone has to be there."

Jim clasped his hands hard, his knuckles white. "If she were my daughter, I'd be waiting at the clinic for her tomorrow morning."

"Absolutely." The idea was the most natural answer of all. Lisa's heart lifted for the first time since they'd heard the news about Andi's pregnancy. "We can see if the clinic has a website. Find out their hours and be there first thing in the morning."

"We could wait in the parking lot and pray for her." Keith

looked relieved. "Just in case. I mean, the text coming when it did. We have to believe that's a sign, that God's leading us to her."

They talked for a few more minutes, and the Flanigans promised to keep praying. Before they left, Bailey hugged Lisa. "When you see her, tell her I love her. I'm here for her."

"I will." Lisa couldn't express how much Bailey's comment meant.

With that, Lisa and Keith hurried home again. On the way, Lisa texted Andi, asking if she'd please call. But there was no response. They tried several more attempts at reaching her, but she didn't answer, and no more text messages came the rest of the evening. They found a website for the Indianapolis Family Planning Center, and they learned that the clinic opened at nine the next day. After that there was nothing to do but pray and wait.

They'd be on the road to Indianapolis first thing in the morning.

Twenty-Five

LUKE BAXTER HAD BEEN ON THE road far more often than usual, and he was grateful for a weekend at home. Even still he'd be back in Los Angeles by tomorrow night for one more round of meetings. He'd talked to Dayne, and for now at least it looked like Jeremiah Productions was ready to finalize the deal with Brandon Paul.

"We have our reservations, but that's where you come in," Dayne told him. "The contract has to be a steel trap. No loopholes, brother." Dayne laughed. "Of course, that's why we have you. You're the best."

Already Luke was hammering out a first draft of the contract. Money wouldn't be an issue. Any studio in town would take on the movie and pay Brandon's considerable salary for a chance to have a picture with him. It was the other details that concerned Dayne and Keith—the morality clauses, that if broken, could destroy the movie.

Luke loved the challenge as much as he loved the personnel changes at Jeremiah Productions. Chase would be missed, of course. But he needed to be home with his family, and now Luke could work more closely with Dayne, his brother. After a lifetime of missing out on having a brother, these days were golden—getting to work with Dayne, being close to him.

The only downside lately was the time he'd spent away from home. Now it was Sunday night and he'd tucked Tommy in four times already. Tommy was still telling people he was a Tommy-saurus Rex—the meanest dinosaur of all. If his behavior at bedtime was any indication, Luke could only believe him. But on the last round of good nights, Luke had used a more serious voice. "This is it, buddy. Don't get up again."

A repentant look came over Tommy and he settled down on his pillow. "Okay, Daddy." He waved his fingers, meek-like. "Sorry."

"It's fine. Just don't get up."

"Okay." One more quick wave. "Wuv you."

"Love you too." Luke stifled a grin as he left his son's room. Malin was already asleep down the hall, so finally he could go find Reagan. He'd told her to take the night off, curl up with a book while he managed the bedtime routine. It was the least he could do since he'd been gone so much lately. He tiptoed down the stairs, past the place where Tommy had gotten his head stuck in the spindles when they first moved into the house. He found Reagan in a T-shirt and comfy-looking sweats, reading *Unlocked* next to an open window.

She smiled up at him. "The breeze is amazing. I can smell the jasmine you planted last summer."

He sat beside her and breathed in. "It's great."

"See?" She leaned close and kissed him. "I knew you'd like it."

"I believed you." He nuzzled up against her. "I always believe you."

"Mmm." Reagan looked straight at him, past the lighthearted banter between them. "Like about the adoption?"

"Exactly." He grinned and crooked his finger beneath her chin, kissing her more slowly this time. "But that one didn't take any convincing. I'd love another baby."

"You don't care—girl or boy?"

"Nope. Whatever baby God brings us is fine with me." He felt relaxed and content. Being with Reagan filled his senses, and the smell of jasmine only heightened the moment. Like the peacefulness of the night would go on forever. He leaned back, watching her. "Our paperwork's in, right?"

"Everything's done. The agency called last week. It's just a matter of a birth mother choosing us, finding the right match."

It was the first time they'd done a domestic adoption, and Luke was a little nervous about the fact. International adoptions like Malin's carried virtually no risk of a birth mother showing up after so many years with a lawyer in tow. But this time around they were willing to consider a more open adoption. Children were on loan anyway. That's what his mother had always said. "God's probably picking a baby for us right now."

"I've been thinking about her lately." Reagan pressed her head into the sofa cushion, a dreamy look on her face.

"So now it's a girl?" Luke was teasing her, enjoying the easy way they had with each other. Their marriage had only gotten stronger this last year, and now that they were dreaming about a third child, Luke felt like God was blessing them beyond anything he could've imagined.

"Not the baby, silly." Reagan's expression deepened. "The girl, the birth mother. She's out there somewhere. Maybe already pregnant. Trying to decide what to do with a pregnancy she didn't plan for."

"Hmm." Luke angled his head, imagining the same thing. "I haven't thought about that."

"I think God put the idea on my heart. We pray for the baby all the time, of course."

"For years." Luke was serious. They'd known from the beginning that Reagan couldn't have more biological children after Tommy. Which meant whenever they prayed about their family, they prayed for the children yet to come, the boys or girls only God knew about.

"So maybe it's time we pray for the girl, our baby's birth mother."

"What if she's in her forties—and this baby just doesn't fit in her plans?"

Reagan giggled. "Girl, woman. Whatever." Her laughter faded. "I'm serious. We should pray for her, don't you think?"

Luke was quiet, thinking about the troubled mother somewhere out there in the city of Indianapolis, maybe just getting news of an unwanted pregnancy or worse—thinking about whether to release the baby for adoption or abort. A shudder ran through him and he sat up straighter. "You're right. Let's pray for her."

"Right now?" Reagan leaned forward too. Her face close to Luke's.

A sense of urgency filled Luke's heart, robbing him of some of the serenity from just a few minutes ago. He pictured this woman—young or old—one more time. The woman who might even this moment be carrying their next child. "Yeah, baby. I think so. Right now." Then he took Reagan's hands in his and prayed with an intensity that surprised him—that God would know exactly who the birth mother of their baby was, and that even this very night he would surround her with his angels and protect her and the baby. That God would grant her peace in her decision, and finally one last thing.

That he'd grant her baby life.

Andi wanted to get there early.

Her appointment was for nine that morning, but the woman she'd talked to said they opened the doors half an hour early. So their clients could avoid the protestors who sometimes gathered near the front of the clinic during business hours. The last thing Andi wanted was to run into a protestor—someone who would scream threats in her face and call her names for killing her baby.

She wanted to slip in unnoticed, and slip back into life the same way. The problem gone, no one the wiser for what she'd done. No one but her and God. Of course, she hadn't planned on thinking much about God this day, but all that changed at the Kunzmann house. Their family lived and breathed God's presence. His Word and truth, His ways and peace were a part of everything the Kunzmann family said and did. There was no getting around it.

Before she left this morning, Lucia pulled her aside. "Your appointment is this morning, right?"

"Yes." Andi couldn't make eye contact with the woman. She didn't deserve the woman's kindness, and she felt ashamed for what she was about to do. As if by looking into Lucia's eyes, the woman would know exactly where she was headed.

"Before you go, let's pray. Whatever's wrong with you, Andi, God knows. He will meet you there."

Praying before an abortion? Andi's heart pounded in her throat, but she couldn't escape. Before she knew what was happening, Lucia had hold of her hands and she was praying, asking the Holy Spirit to be Andi's constant companion in the coming hours, and asking that Andi hear His voice whatever lay ahead. It was like Lucia already knew her plans. Like God Himself had told her.

Andi pulled into a bank parking lot across the street from the clinic and slumped behind the steering wheel. *What're you worried about?* she asked herself. *No one knows you're here.* For a full minute she surveyed the clinic across the street, making sure there were no protestors, no one to interfere with her quick and certain entrance. She placed her hand on her stomach and wondered if her baby would feel what was about to happen. As soon as the question hit her, she banished it. The woman at the clinic had promised her there was no baby. The only thing her body contained right now was tissue. Tissue that would become a baby.

Ashley Baxter's face came to mind, telling her that people at abortion clinics would lie to her. The ultrasound told the real story. Growing inside her was a very tiny baby and a very tiny heart.

She felt sick to her stomach, and finally she'd had enough. She jolted from the car and ran lightly across the street. But just as she was about to cross into the clinic parking lot, a man stepped in front of her.

"Hello." He was older, white hair and a neatly trimmed white beard. His eyes were so piercing blue, they almost looked other-worldly. "I'm Clarence." He checked his watch. "I thought you'd be early, Andi."

A slice of terror cut at Andi and she took a few frantic steps back. How did he know her name? "Don't … please don't hurt me."

The man stepped aside, but even though her path to the clinic was wide open, Andi had the sense she couldn't get by the gentleman, no matter what she tried. His voice was soft as he tried again. "I'm not here to harm you. I bring you truth. Please …" he held a pamphlet to her. "Take this. Your appointment's not until nine o'clock."

"How do you … I don't have an appointment. I'm just … I'm looking into it."

He watched her, kind and gentle. "I've prayed for you and your baby … I've prayed all morning." He was still holding out the brochure. "Please take this. Go back to your car and read it." What was it about his eyes? He smiled at her, and his tenderness touched her much the way she felt when she was around her father. She made a quick grab of the pamphlet and looked around, hoping no one else could see them.

"You'll read it? For your baby?"

"There's no ba—"

He held up one hand and nodded at her. "Read it. I'll be praying."

She still had the sensation she couldn't get past the older gentleman, even if she made a run for it. So instead she turned around and ran the other way. Halfway to her car she turned back to see which way the man went, where he'd come from. But he was gone. Her heart thudded in her neck, making it hard to breathe. Where was he? Clarence, right? Wasn't that his name? He was too old to race off, and there was no other car or doorway in sight. Could he be hiding in the bushes? Was that how he handed his material to unsuspecting girls like her? And how had he known her name?

Shaking from fear and the adrenaline coursing through her, Andi ran as fast as she could back to her car. She didn't want to stay here. What if the man turned up by her car somehow? She set the pamphlet down on her passenger seat, started her engine, and pulled out of the bank parking lot as fast as she could. Halfway down the block she saw a public library, and she turned her car quickly into the parking lot. It was empty, so she could be alone—without wondering whether the man with the strange eyes was watching her.

Her forehead was damp with sweat, and her heart still sped along at double speed inside her chest. What sort of crazy thing had just happened to her? She'd scanned the parking lot and made sure no one—absolutely no one—was lurking anywhere near the clinic. She'd been walking toward the parking lot, her eyes fixed on the clinic door, and he was suddenly there. From out of nowhere.

She made sure her doors were locked, and she leaned her head against the seat rest. *Breathe*, she told herself. *This is insane. Go back, and get inside before more protestors show up.* But the man's words filled her mind, consumed her soul. He thought she'd be early? Like he knew her? Another series of shivers ran down her arms. Then without wanting to, she reached for the brochure and looked at the cover. It was a picture of an unborn baby, very little. Probably about the age of her own baby. The title read, "Give Life a Chance."

Her heart pounded harder in response. She couldn't give life a chance. If she did, she'd have to tell her parents and have the baby and then what? Embarrass her father … mar his chances at making movies with a Christian message? Or spend a lifetime raising Taz's child alone? Or somehow find a way to put the baby into the arms of another family? None of the answers felt even remotely possible. But as if some supernatural force was compelling her, she opened the pamphlet and read the entire thing, every word. The minutes ticked away, and still Andi sat there.

One of the lines from inside the brochure jumped out at her. For every abortion, two lives are destroyed. Most women will spend a lifetime seeking healing and forgiveness from this one single choice.

Could that be true? Was the brochure right, that she'd spend a lifetime regretting this? Her mind was so full of conflicting thoughts she could barely think or see straight. Even so she started her car again and pulled back onto the busy street. She drove without thinking, first toward the clinic and then after a quick U-turn she drove away. Suddenly, without knowing how or why, she pulled into another parking lot and looked at the building near the back. The blood drained from her face as she read the sign.

Bethany Christian Services — an Adoption Agency.

This couldn't be happening. She couldn't have driven aimlessly into the parking lot of an adoption agency. Maybe she was dreaming. The whole strange situation with the man and his unforgettable eyes, the way he'd come from nowhere and disappeared as soon as she turned around. Now this. She shut her eyes as tightly as she could. Yes, she was dreaming. That had to be it. But then why was her heart pounding, and how come she couldn't catch her breath? She opened her eyes slowly, hoping she would find herself in the guestroom of the Kunzmann house, the morning not yet begun.

But she was exactly where she'd been a minute ago. A Christian adoption agency staring her straight in the face.

Suddenly ... like scales from her eyes, the truth began to dawn on her. Nothing that morning had been strange or coincidental. God was reaching down from heaven to spare her life and the life of her baby. First the Kunzmann family—and Lucia's prayer that the Holy Spirit stay with her over the next few hours ... then the strange, kind-eyed man.

Andi thought about her family's time in Indonesia. The supernatural was more accepted there, and believers regularly experienced encounters with beings they believed to be angels. She thought about the man, pictured his unusual blue eyes and his way of speaking straight to her. Maybe he was an angel. It was possible. How else could he possibly have known her name? Hebrews 13 talked about being careful to entertain strangers, for in doing so some had entertained angels without knowing it, right?

Another set of shivers ran through her. The man had been aware that she'd be early, and he'd known private details about her appointment, her name. Even what it would take to change her mind. There could be no other answer. She covered her stomach tenderly with her hands. "Little one, I'm sorry ... I'm so sorry."

Her tears came like they hadn't since she first found out she was pregnant. How had she lied to herself these past few weeks, refusing to think of her baby, but only of the abortion? The brochure was right. She would've hated herself forever if she'd gone through with it. She stepped out of her car and walked slowly to the front door of the adoption agency. Stuck to the window was a list of hours, same as those of the abortion clinic down the street. Fitting, Andi thought. Life or death, a few blocks apart.

She tapped the agency's number into her phone's address book and walked slowly back to her car. A new sense of hope filled her heart. Her baby was going to live! She wasn't going through the doors of the abortion clinic, not today and not ever. It had been her choice to sleep with Taz, to believe him that in some twisted way, breaking her vow to God would be art. The lie was flat-out diabolical. Breaking a promise to God, going against what Scripture taught, could only be called one thing.

Sin.

Yes, Andi had sinned against God and her parents. Even against herself and the plans God had for her life. But Andi hadn't lost all her Bible knowledge in one year. She remembered a verse her parents had referenced often. Romans 8:28 — all things work to the good for those who love the Lord.

And she did love Him. She'd put Him off and walked away, but the truth was now as clear as the sky overhead. She loved God and she wanted to live for Him again — the way she hadn't lived for Him since she'd set foot on the IU campus. Andi started her car one more time to head back to the Kunzmann house. Lucia would be the first person she would tell about this decision. But before she drove very far, she realized something. She had to go back to the clinic and look for Clarence. She wanted to hug him and thank him and tell him what a difference he'd made. Let him know his prayers had been answered. She was choosing life.

One last time she turned her car around, and as she drove she suddenly pictured her sweet friend, Rachel. Something dawned on her, the way it hadn't for an entire year. Rachel would finally recognize her. And somewhere in heaven she had a feeling Rachel was celebrating with the angels.

Maybe even a blue-eyed old gentleman named Clarence.

Twenty-Six

KEITH AND LISA SAT IN SILENCE, their car parked in a lot across the street from the clinic. They'd been here since 8:35, but still they hadn't seen Andi. A few protestors were gathered outside the clinic, talking amongst themselves. Keith watched as three of them circled on the sidewalk and bowed their heads, clearly praying for the work ahead of them.

"Interesting." Lisa was as nervous as him, but she seemed struck by the protestors. "I've always seen them portrayed as violent, screaming and waving signs."

"A few extreme people probably are like that." Keith narrowed his eyes, watching the group as they continued to pray. "But this doesn't surprise me. There's a mission field here — if it's handled right, anyway."

Lisa sighed and glanced around. "You think she's coming."

"I do." Keith felt a peace in his heart, a certainty. "I can't explain it. I just think she'll be here."

They had prayed together for almost an hour that morning — most of the drive here. The goal, of course, was to tell Andi they'd help her, to change her mind about the abortion. But beyond that they'd talked about what might come next. Whether Andi would raise her child, or give the baby up for adoption. They both agreed that they would welcome Andi home, and help her parent the child if that's what she wanted to do. No matter what circumstances led to this life — the life mattered. This was their first grandchild, after all.

Also, early this morning Keith had called Chase. They might've parted ways, but no one knew him better. No one besides Lisa would hurt for his Andi more than Chase and Kelly. The friends who had watched her grow up, the two who knew how great Andi's love for the Lord had once been, and how drastic the changes in her this past year.

Chase promised to tell Kelly, and even now Keith knew his friends were praying. God was hearing from the people who loved their Andi, and Keith believed this was where they'd find her. God had led them here, after all. He took hold of Lisa's hand. "She'll be here."

He'd no sooner said the words, when a car pulled up a few spots away and parked facing the clinic.

"Andi!" Lisa practically shrieked her name. "Dear God, it's her ..."

"Thank You, Lord ... thank you." Keith's eyes blurred with tears, and he held his wife's hand more tightly. "Don't rush. There's no hurry now."

They stepped out at the same time, and as they did, Andi spotted them. From the moment Keith saw his daughter's eyes, he knew something had changed. They shone almost as if she'd seen a vision. She jumped out of her little sedan and rushed into their arms, the three of them hugging and rocking and not ever wanting to let go.

"Mom ... Dad ... I'm sorry." She spoke the words against Keith's chest, and he clung to her. His precious daughter. His baby girl. As he did, he realized that this was how the father in *Unlocked* must've felt. Holding his child and knowing that in this moment a miracle had happened.

Because here and now he had his Andi back.

"You know," she looked up at them, tears spilling from her eyes. "You must know, right?"

"We do." Lisa pulled a piece of paper from her pocket. "We found this in your trash can. When we didn't hear from you we figured we'd come here and wait."

"I made the worst mistake of my life." The guilt that seemed to consume her was almost a physical presence. "I knew better, but I wanted to do things my way. I'm so sorry."

Lisa pulled a tissue from her pocket and handed it to Andi. "It's okay now, baby. Everything's going to be okay."

"I know." The guilt lifted, and the newfound light shone in her eyes once again. She told them a rambling story about some family named Kunzmann who took her in over the weekend and how they lived out their faith, and that the woman prayed with her this very morning, and how an older man named Clarence stopped her from going into the clinic, and how God—only God—could've led her to the adoption agency down the street.

"Wait!" Keith searched his daughter's eyes. "You drove down the street and randomly came across an adoption agency?"

"Yes!" Unbridled laughter came from Andi, and she tipped her head back for a moment. "Isn't God so good? He led me there, Dad. I'll show you."

Keith felt a slight sadness, one that he had to acknowledge. Andi had apparently made up her mind—she was giving the baby up for adoption. It was the best decision by far, and Keith would spend the next months applauding his daughter for having the courage and compassion to give her baby to a Christian family, parents ready for a child.

But in this single moment, he marked the loss—Andi's firstborn, their grandchild. A little boy or girl none of them would ever know.

Andi linked arms with her parents and walked across the street. Boldly and with great joy she talked to the protestors and thanked them for the work they were doing. Then she asked about Clarence.

A woman in her forties shook her head, glancing at the others. "I've been coming here every day for two years. For a few hours each morning." She looked back at Andi. "I've never met a Clarence."

The others agreed. There was no one named Clarence working this clinic, helping girls know the mistake they were about to make, trying to compassionately lead them to choose life. Andi nodded, and thanked them again. Keith had never been more proud of her in all his life.

"You get it, right, Dad?" The shine in her eyes made her look alive again. "He must've been an angel. What other explanation is there?"

Keith could only agree. God was answering every prayer they'd breathed this past weekend. Why wouldn't He send an angel for Andi? They caravanned together to the adoption agency a few blocks down — Lisa riding with Andi. Once there, they went inside and Andi took the lead.

"My name's Andi. I'm pregnant, but I'm not ready to be a mother," she told the woman at the desk. "And God led me here." She looked at her parents on either side. "I'd like to give my baby up for adoption to a Christian family."

The woman must've dealt with scenes like this one every day, but listening to Andi — her joy and certainty — brought tears to the woman's eyes. She blinked a few times and handed Andi a packet. "Why don't you have a seat in the lobby. Look this over. Someone will be out to talk to you in a few minutes."

Keith could hardly believe the morning was playing out this way. They'd jumped major hurdles all in less than an hour — and now Andi — her childlike faith once more a driving force in her life — was ready to tackle what would inevitably be the hardest decision of her life. They looked through a book of families ready to adopt, but the counselor told Andi she didn't need to make a decision yet. That could come in time. She'd have several more counseling appointments — one a month, tied in with her checkups. The agency worked with a doctor a few minutes away. All medical expenses were covered by the agency.

Throughout the hour, Andi never wavered in her decision.

She was happy and talkative, and when she looked at the pictures of families she dabbed quietly at her eyes. With Lisa's help, Andi filled out the paperwork while Keith mostly took in the scene. A life had been saved today. He was too awestruck to do more than think on that single fact. Besides, between the Kunzmann family and Clarence and the time here at the adoption agency, Keith didn't need to say much, really.

They were all three on hallowed ground.

ANDI COULDN'T BELIEVE HOW GREAT SHE felt. How had she gotten through the last year without her faith? God had never given up on her, that much she knew for sure. But she'd chosen to walk through her days without His constant presence, His perfect friendship. And she'd made a mess of things as a result.

But God had opened her eyes, and in the light of His mercy and grace she could breathe again. She wouldn't ever again turn her back on the truths she'd been raised with, never again listen to the lies of the enemy. There was no truth but God's alone, no other way to eternity. The miracles of this morning were more proof than she deserved. She would live with her parents until the baby was born, and then she'd say good-bye to her firstborn. Maybe if the adoptive family was willing, she'd stay in touch here and there. Send letters and pictures. That way her baby would know how she felt right now. That she loved this child with a love she'd forgotten existed. A love that was God's alone. Yes, she had mixed feelings about the adoption, but definitely no doubts.

As they left the adoption agency, she stopped and looked intently into her father's eyes. "I'm sorry, Daddy. If this embarrasses you. If it hurts Jeremiah Productions."

Her father looked shocked by her apology. "Is that what you thought? That this would embarrass me?"

She nodded, ashamed again. "It'll look terrible."

"I don't care about any of that. If the media wants to write about this, I'll defend you to anyone, sweetheart." He hugged her, caring for her. "You're doing the right thing."

Andi's heart soared, lifted by his love and acceptance. Why hadn't she believed they'd respond this way? She could've avoided the heartache of the weekend, but then she might not have heard God calling her back to Him. Now she had a plan, and after the baby, she couldn't wait to get back on campus and start up once more with Cru. If they'd let her, she wanted to be a group leader. No one could help the girls on campus avoid the lies that surrounded them more than she could. She couldn't wait to build her relationship with her parents and get back to church. And she couldn't wait to talk to Bailey.

Before they left Indianapolis, Andi wanted them to make one more stop—to the Kunzmann home. Again her mom rode with her, and Andi tried to explain how God had placed her in their home for His purposes. "It was a miracle, Mom. I'm serious."

Her mom could only smile and listen. Andi was grateful she didn't lecture her about not calling or about making them worry. She'd been blinded just hours ago. Now that she could see, she only wanted her parents to love her and forgive her. The way they were doing.

They pulled up in front of a large home, and Andi led her parents up the walk. Lucia answered, and Andi made the introductions. Then without another moment's hesitation, she flew into Lucia's arms and hugged her close. "How did you know? You prayed like you knew."

Lucia laughed, her eyes filled with joy. As she stepped back she looked at the trio on her porch. "About the baby?"

Andi felt the chills across her arms again. "Yes. See ... how did you know?"

"Honestly? God told me. I knew from the moment I saw you crying at Megan's Diner." She smiled at Andi's parents. "I figured if she were my daughter, I'd want someone to step in. Sometimes mission work happens when you least expect it."

Lucia invited them in and they stayed half an hour, eating lunch with her and the kids—all of whom were homeschooled. When they left, Andi promised to stay in touch. And her mother hugged Lucia for a long time. "You were my answer to prayer."

"That's our job as believers," Lucia smiled at Andi's mother. "To be an answer to someone's prayer—every day ... as long as we live."

The whole day was one miracle after another, and on the way home Andi let her mom drive. She was exhausted, certain she would be asleep before they hit the open road. But even as she nodded off, she acknowledged one more miracle—something she hadn't shared with her parents. She'd found the adoptive family for her baby. The counselor had been clear, she didn't need to decide yet.

But as she looked through the book, one family stood out.

Andi wasn't sure exactly what struck her about the family. Maybe because the dad looked a lot like a young Dayne Matthews, and his wife—with her blonde hair—looked a little like Dayne's wife Katy. Andi had memorized the page, the way the family looked, the description of them. They lived in Indianapolis, and the mom stayed at home with the kids. They loved Jesus and each other, and they were praying for a special birth mother—that she would choose to bring their baby into the world. The book didn't give last names, but Andi had memorized their first names. She was that certain about her choice.

Luke, Reagan, Tommy, and Malin.

Her baby's family.

Twenty-Seven

THE REST OF JUNE SLIPPED THROUGH Bailey's fingers, in a blur of long talks with her mom and Andi and acting lessons with Katy. Andi had apologized for the way she'd treated Bailey, and the girls had found the beginning of a friendship that had escaped them all last year. Bailey apologized too. For not trying harder, for in some ways writing Andi off once she started dating Taz.

Somehow July had snuck in unannounced and now suddenly it was the Fourth already. Andi and her parents had flown to Los Angeles for the holiday—time to be alone together, just the three of them. But Bailey and her family were joining the Baxters in their annual barbecue. It was a nice break from the usual all-day backyard party her parents threw most years.

Humidity filled the air, and the sun was already warming the fields surrounding Bloomington. Bailey had wanted to do something different with her hair, something so she'd look as young and free as she felt. So that morning she'd asked her mom to braid it. Two braids framing her face, from beneath a red American Eagle baseball cap. It matched her red T-shirt and navy capris. They were minutes from leaving so she darted back upstairs to her closet and picked out a pair of shoes she hadn't worn all winter—her white Jack Purcells. While she was slipping them on, her eye caught the same framed picture of her and Tim from last winter—the one when they were in *Scrooge*.

They'd been broken up for more than a week, so that was long enough, right? She sprang across the room, took the picture, and slipped it into one of her desk drawers. *Never liked the photo anyway*, she told herself. She plopped down on the edge of her mattress and finished tying her shoes. She hadn't heard from Tim, and she figured that was best. They both needed time to sort through their feelings about the breakup. Besides, by the time Tim gave the situation any real thought, he was bound to see it the way she did. They hadn't been more than friends for a long time anyway.

Somewhere some girl would meet Tim and fall in love with him, and Tim would look back and thank her for setting him free.

Wherever Tim's future took him, Bailey would never settle for a passive life again. Never play not to lose, but only to win. Seizing every day, the way God wanted her to live. Love needed to be so much more. She wanted someone who felt alive beside her, a guy who dreamed about her when she was away and hung on her every word when they were together. Someone who in time would make it difficult to know where she ended and he began. A love so bright and beautiful a hundred years would never be enough time together.

Bailey bounced down the stairs to the kitchen and found her mom finishing up a bowl of homemade potato salad. "Grab the pepper, will you, Bailey?"

"What about paper towels?" Bailey grinned as she reached for the pepper and handed it to her mom. "Look at you. You've got potatoes halfway to your elbows."

"That's what makes it so amazing." She was using two spoons, digging them deep in the salad and tossing the pieces of potatoes. "You can't get this kind of touch from a supermarket carton." Her mom peered at her and blew her hair off her face. "You look adorable, Bailey. Very all-American."

"Thanks." She leaned in and helped her mom tuck a strand of hair off her face and behind her ear. "I feel that way. Glad to be alive, grateful to be an American, happy that we can still worship

God and that most everyone I know still loves Him. Happy to have a reason to celebrate." She leaned against the kitchen counter and watched as her dad and brothers filed into the kitchen. Their conversations were loud, their laughter contagious. Bailey helped her mom get to the sink without dropping blobs of potato salad on the floor. They laughed while Bailey handed her a dishrag and her mom pumped a handful of soap into her hands.

While they were wrapping the bowl with tinfoil, Bailey reminded herself again to soak in these precious moments—all of them still at home, her brothers excited about a day at the lake. An Independence Day to celebrate. These were the times of their lives—moments they would always remember.

"You're so happy today." Her mom gave her a knowing look. "I don't remember you being this excited last Fourth."

"Mom ... I'm hurt." Bailey could feel her eyes begin to dance. "I love all holidays."

"But this time ... maybe a little more." She dried her hands and arms on a dish towel. "What time will Cody be there anyway?"

Bailey felt her cheeks grow hot. Her mom knew her so well— there was no hiding that Cody was one of the main reasons she was so happy, the reason she'd been singing all morning. "Three o'clock. Same as us."

Her mom held her gaze for a special few seconds, time where they needed no words to know what the other was thinking. "I'm praying for you. Don't get ahead of yourself."

"I won't. Cody doesn't even know about Tim and me." She took hold of the potato salad and grinned. "It's just a great day, that's all."

Her dad caught the fact that the women were ready. He raised his hand and made a sweeping motion toward the garage. "Okay, guys, everyone into the Suburban! The Baxter family barbecue can't start without us!"

Bailey had done everything in her power not to dwell on the

fact that Cody was coming to the barbecue. They'd talked last night—the first time since that strange call the night of the football scrimmage. When he'd seemed like he had so much more to tell her than he was actually saying. When he didn't call for a week, Bailey finally decided she could call him. Her brothers had said he'd been quieter lately—and that worried Bailey. Had something happened to his mom, or had he met someone who had turned his head?

Either way, it felt wonderful talking to him last night. She asked him about his plans for the Fourth, and he had nothing. He wanted to drop by the cemetery and put flowers on the graves of a couple fallen soldiers he knew. But he was doing that in the morning.

"Meet us at Lake Monroe!" Bailey couldn't hide her enthusiasm. "Remember when you went that one time with us?"

"The famous ankle-twisting." Cody chuckled, but the sound dropped off. "I don't know ... Tim doesn't like me being around your family."

"Tim isn't coming." She wanted to tell him about the break-up face-to-face, so she kept her tone even. "Meet us there, please Cody. Come on—we need a day of fun, you and me."

In the end he agreed, and promised to bring a bag of hotdog buns for the barbecue. Bailey conveyed the information to Elaine Baxter, and everything was set. Now, though, she could hardly wait to see him. She wondered a dozen times if she'd dressed too young or if he'd think she was being too forward for inviting him. She tried to remember her mother's advice—take it slowly. She'd known Cody since she was in middle school, and he'd made it clear he only wanted to be her friend—both then and now. There was nothing to rush, so her mom didn't need to worry. Even still the time couldn't go fast enough.

They reached the lake and hauled their coolers and picnic baskets down the hill to the place where the Baxters were set up.

Bailey was struck by how much the crowd had grown over the years. Everyone was there—most of them having arrived hours earlier to set up. A quick scan of the sandy beach and she saw all the Baxter kids and their spouses, their children. Too many to count, anymore. She spotted Dayne and Luke playing with their kids near the water's edge. Every one of the kids wore matching life jackets, and as Bailey came closer she could make out the words stitched in white across the back of each one. "Baxter Baby," they read.

Bailey had a feeling they were Dayne's doing. It was at the annual Fourth of July picnic that he'd first found his family, after all. The event held more meaning for the Baxters than anyone outside the circle could ever know.

"Flanigans!" John Baxter raised his hand and motioned to a table adjacent to the trees and not far from the water. "We saved that one for you. So glad you could join us!"

They were setting up their table, she and Connor spreading out the checkered plastic tablecloth when she felt someone behind her. Before she could turn around, Ricky and Justin came running up from the water. "Cody!" They shouted his name at the same time.

Bailey turned and saw that he was only a few feet from her, his eyes on hers. He didn't make the moment awkward, or let his eyes linger on hers. Nothing that could be construed as anything out of the ordinary for a couple of old friends. He hugged her quickly and turned to the boys. "Hey, guys! I brought a football!"

He and the boys helped get the rest of the things down the hill from the Flanigans' SUV, and then, with a quick look back at her, Cody followed the boys to the water. They played football for a long time, splashing through the water and knocking each other into the gentle waves lapping at the water's edge.

Bailey met up with Katy and the two of them talked about the progress with Jeremiah Productions—how the guys felt good about Luke Baxter's contract. "Brandon Paul can't change the movie," Katy seemed satisfied. "Now we're all praying the movie changes him."

With everything in her, Bailey tried to stay focused. She believed in Jeremiah Productions, and she most certainly would pray for Dayne and Keith. But she was grateful for her dark sunglasses, because she kept being distracted by Cody. At times, she couldn't take her eyes off him. He was tan from being outdoors every day with football, and his white tank top only emphasized the fact. He was tall and muscled and supremely athletic. His hair was cut short, the way Bailey loved it—accenting the handsome ruggedness of his face.

She had to remind herself again and again not to stare.

Finally, when she'd been social enough and helped all she could help, Bailey kicked off her Jack Purcells and joined the boys near the water.

"She's on your team!" The announcement came from Ricky.

Bailey put her hands on her hips and made a face at him. "You'll be sorry."

"You will." Connor grinned at her. "She can throw the ball, little brother."

"So whose team am I on?"

Cody ran close for a pass and caught it inches from her. He stopped, his chest heaving, his breath minty against her face. "Mine." He took a few steps and flung the ball back to BJ, then he glanced back at her. "Okay? Just follow my lead."

Her knees felt weak, and she silently yelled at herself. *Get a grip, Bailey Flanigan. This is Cody who you've known forever. Cody who only wants to be your friend.* Even so she wanted to tell him that wouldn't be a problem. She'd follow him anywhere.

He was going on about the rules. "It's a passing game. Sort of football and volleyball mixed. Main thing is don't drop the ball."

"Okay." She was ready. She really could throw the ball and she wouldn't mind getting splashed a little. It was easily the hottest day so far that summer.

"Better take off the hat." Connor backed up, his feet in the sand, body in position.

"It's fine. I won't be getting that crazy."

But just at that moment Ricky winged the ball in their direction. Bailey ran forward to catch it just as Cody shuffled sideways, neither of them more than a little aware of the other. In a rush the two of them collided and fell together into the knee-deep water.

As hot as the day was, the cool lake water made Bailey catch her breath. She was soaked as she wiped sand from her eyes and propped herself up on her knees. Her cute hat was still somewhere in the water. "It's freezing."

"Yep." Cody was drenched too. He started laughing, and the sound of it was contagious. He held up his hand for Bailey to help him up. "I'm stuck in the sand. Seriously."

She was laughing too, now, and she helped him to his knees. Side by side, he put his arm around her waist and the two of them struggled to their feet. Cody snatched her hat from just beneath the surface and handed it to her—drenched and covered with slimy pieces of lake grass. "I forgot to tell you … the most important part."

"What's that?" Gradually they tried to trudge toward the shore, but Bailey tripped on something. She fell against Cody and knocked them both back into the water. Now Bailey was laughing so hard she wasn't sure she could do anything but sit back and let the moment have its way with her.

"The most important part is …" Cody was barely able to catch his breath, laughing at least as hard as she was, "you have to call it."

"Call it?" Bailey was sitting in waist deep water, alongside Cody, and as soon as she could talk through her laughter she looked at him, at a piece of lake grass strung across his face. She picked it off, falling into another wave of laughter too strong to fight. When she could finally talk, she put her sorry-looking hat back on her head and looked right at him, her eyes bleary. "Call it?"

"Yes." He splashed her a little. "You have to call it."

"Okay, fine." She laughed again. "Call it what? It's a football."

That was all Cody needed to hear. Now he let himself fall completely back into the water. As he did, he intentionally pulled her with him, splashing her and teasing her. "You told me you could play!"

A crowd of Baxters and Flanigans had gathered along the near shore, laughing and enjoying the moment. "Way to go, honey," her dad called out. "Way to use everything I taught you."

They were on their feet now, more careful to watch their steps so they would actually make it to shore. Somehow, Bailey still had her hat, though she could only imagine how they looked together. The moment they reached the shore, Connor stepped up and snapped their picture, arms around each other's waists, lake grass hanging from their clothes and hair. And smiles wider than the lake behind them.

Bailey had a feeling it was a picture they'd remember forever.

Once the commotion died down, she found her sunglasses, and she and Cody took their towels down the beach a stretch and spread them out next to each other. Bailey was glad she'd worn her hair in braids. Once she'd brushed herself off, and after she dried, she'd be good as new. A little rumpled, but that didn't matter. Rumpled worked for a Fourth of July picnic.

"I thought you were one of the boys trying to tackle me," Cody said as he settled onto his towel. He sat up and leaned back on his hands. "It was a pretty good bit of contact."

"I know." Bailey rubbed her shoulder. She, too, leaned back on her hands. Their shoulders were close, though nowhere near touching, but still Bailey felt like she was dreaming. She and Cody so close together, laughing and sharing a day like this. Bailey reminded herself to breathe. She laughed lightly, and turned her face to the sun. "I remember thinking, 'Wait ... you're supposed to be on my team.'"

He chuckled a few times and shook his head. "See what I mean ... I'm always laughing around you."

She made a funny face and peered at him warily. "I don't give you much choice."

"Ah, that's okay." He nudged his elbow against hers. "I love laughing, Bailey. You should know that."

Neither of them needed to talk, and still Bailey felt close to him. It was that way now as they let the sun dry them, their faces turned upward. Cody broke the silence first. "Tim had something with his family? That why he didn't come?"

Funny how long she'd waited to tell him her news. When she first broke up with Tim, she'd thought about calling Cody constantly. But the timing had never seemed right.

Until now.

She turned slightly, studying him, still unable to believe that he was here beside her and that she was free to enjoy the fact. She drew a steady breath. "I wanted to tell you in person."

He looked at her, and she could see his eyes through his sunglasses, the way they locked on hers. "Tell me what?" Cody knew her so well, he must've sensed the subtle change in her tone.

"Tim and I ... we broke up."

Slowly Cody turned to face her, searching her eyes and her face. He wasn't smiling or rejoicing, just wanting to hear every detail. "Like ... a serious breakup?"

"Yes." It would be inappropriate for her to smile, so she bit her lip and looked down at the sand between them. "Ten days ago. But I told you, Cody ..." she lifted her eyes to his. "It was coming for a long time."

"So you're ..." he looked like he wasn't sure if he should hug her or offer words of comfort. "You're okay?"

This time she couldn't help but smile just a little. "It was my idea." She winced, sensing the laughter in her voice again. "The whole breakup scene didn't go that well."

"It didn't?" He was still maintaining his respect toward Bailey's two years with Tim, but even then she watched the corners of his lips lift a little. "What happened? You didn't push him in a lake, did you?"

She covered her mouth, trying to stop from losing herself to a laughing attack when she was supposed to be upset over her break-up. "No." She returned the elbow nudge and shook her head. "I didn't push him in a lake." Again she made a nervous face. "Worse than that."

"Worse?" Cody raised his brow, as he fanned his still soaking wet tank top. "What could be worse?"

"I called him the wrong name."

"What?" Cody sat up straight, his eyes wide. "You did not."

"I did." She had a feeling Cody was trying not to laugh, same as her. "I felt terrible. Seriously."

Cody started to laugh, and he quickly lost control. He let himself fall back on his towel and Bailey did the same on hers. They lay there on the sand, their bodies a foot apart, laughing until they had to stop to catch their breath. "Sorry … it's really not funny."

"I know." Bailey dabbed at her eyes. "I guess it's just … I keep seeing Tim the way he talked to you that day."

"I wasn't going to say so." Cody chuckled again, little bursts that threatened to consume him once more. "But the wrong name? During a breakup?"

They fell silent then, needing a moment to regroup from the laughter and the lake water and this new reality between them. The reality that Bailey no longer had a boyfriend. Every minute or so one of them would start to laugh again, and for the next hour and even after they were dry and back with the group eating dinner, Bailey caught Cody's shoulders shaking a few times, silent laughter racking his body. He sat across from her, and when she had taken a full drink of iced tea, he mouthed the words, "The wrong name?"

Her tea came spewing out on her plate, soaking her burger. But she didn't care. A hamburger had never tasted better. Not until after the picnic, after Landon and John Baxter had staged their annual fishing derby and again John had won, did Cody find her and pull her aside. This time his eyes lingered, and she loved the feeling. "Wanna take a walk?"

"Sure." She checked in with her mom and the two of them set off for the path that led through the woods and around the perimeter of the lake. It was already dusk, so Bailey was sure the walk wouldn't take long. There would be fireworks over the lake tonight, and all of them wanted to get lined up on blankets, shoulder-to-shoulder, so they could take in the display.

They walked slowly, closer together than they'd been since their lake fiasco. Bailey's clothes were dry, but the air had cooled considerably. That or Bailey couldn't fight the constant chill she felt in his presence. Either way, she was grateful for Cody's warmth beside her.

"Seriously," he grinned at her, but he was in control now. No bursts of laughter threatening his composure. "You're doing okay? About Tim?"

"I should've done it sooner." Her eyes locked on his, and gradually they slowed to a stop. "He never had my heart." She leaned against a tree at the edge of the path, and he faced her.

"No?" He looked mesmerized, lost in the moment. The same way she felt.

"No." Bailey wanted to capture this, slow it down and freeze it. But already everything seemed to be happening in slow motion. What was happening to them? The feeling consuming her was too great to fight.

"I have a question." He ran his finger along the side of her face, his voice deep with emotions neither of them were ready to admit. Not yet, anyway. In the distance they could hear the laughter and voices from the picnic, but they had walked far enough that they were alone.

They were definitely alone.

"Ask it." She lowered her chin, a new shyness coming over her. Could he finally see how she felt about him? How long she'd wanted to be lost in a moment like this? "Go ahead," her tone fell to a whisper. "You can ask me anything."

Cody came a step closer. They wore no sunglasses, so the raw emotion in their eyes was there for both of them, capturing them, intoxicating them. He searched her face, and for a brief second fear tried to edge in on the moment. Like he was afraid of asking the question, even if he couldn't help himself. "When you and Tim broke up … when you called him the wrong name …"

She knew where he was going, knew exactly what he wanted to know, but she waited for him to say it anyway.

Cody took her hand, eased his fingers between hers, his eyes never once looking away. "What name did you call him?"

As long as she lived, Bailey would remember this moment with Cody, the anticipation of her answer, the answer she knew he wanted to hear. He didn't want to be her friend; he was in love with her. Finally she knew for sure. His eyes told her that without saying a single word. Their faces were only a breath apart now, and Bailey knew … she just knew what was about to happen. Night was falling, and the waning moon shone light off the water and onto the pathway.

"Tell me." He was still waiting, motionless, the rest of the world lost to the incredible beauty of all they were feeling. "What name?"

As naturally as the beat of her heart, she reached up and put her hand alongside his face. "Yours, Cody. Who else?"

In a dance as old as time, he came to her and took her face tenderly in his hands. "Bailey ..." Then, like she'd wanted him to do for so very long, he touched his lips to hers and kissed her—slow and with years of love that had never been expressed until now. The sort of kiss a princess would wait a lifetime for. The way Bailey had waited.

Cody was careful—the kiss was over before it had time to become something more. And that was a very real possibility. Bailey had never felt this way in all her life. She didn't know feelings this intense even existed. A ripple of laughter tugged at her, and this time she kissed him. Slowly and with so much love and meaning she thought her heart would burst. "Why," she said as she eased back, "Why did we wait so long for this?"

His expression grew more serious, his smile fading. "Because you deserve better than—"

"Shhh." She put her finger to his lips. "Not today. Don't talk like that. Please, Cody."

He hesitated, then he kissed her one last time, and he grinned at her. That slow, lazy grin that had turned her head so many years ago. He stepped back, the private moment over for now. "If I'm not mistaken ... someone has a footrace to finish."

"What?" She was still dizzy from his kiss, from the newness of feelings she'd never felt with anyone but Cody Coleman. "That was years ago."

"We never finished it." He put his hands in his pockets and let his eyes melt into hers again.

"You're crazy." Bailey laughed again, and the sensation felt wonderful.

"Come on." He pretended to strike a racing pose. "And ... set, go!"

"Fine." Bailey set off, light on her feet, careful of the path ahead of her as she ran. "Try and catch me."

He let her have the lead, and she could feel him just behind her, hear him laughing like she was laughing. Just before they reached the open beach, he gently caught her hand and pulled her into another hug, one that felt more desperate than before. "You win," he whispered into her hair. Then he drew back far enough to look to the places in her heart that had long been reserved only for him. "This is really happening." His voice was still a whisper, his breath warm against her face. "Tell me it's really happening."

They wouldn't have the freedom later, so she allowed herself one more kiss, savoring the sensation. "It's really happening!" She stepped back and then impulsively hugged him again.

His hands found hers, his fingers melting between hers. His eyes sparkled, teasing her. "Can I say something?"

"Go ahead." She was already giggling.

"Finally!" They both laughed and headed down the last section of the path toward the others. Bailey had never felt anything as wonderful as his fingers wrapped around hers. They were almost to the clearing when they heard a whistling sound and through the trees they saw a distant explosion of light.

"Fireworks." She smiled up at him.

Again he held her eyes. "Not like the ones back there."

Bailey was glad he couldn't see the heat in her cheeks. She wasn't sure anyone would notice they were holding hands as they joined the group, but she didn't care. They found an open spot and Cody wrapped his blanket around their shoulders as they took a spot near her parents. The display across the sky over Lake Monroe was beautiful, each firework more stunning than the last. Bailey rested her head on Cody's shoulder, and tried to believe this was really happening. She and Cody, together the way she'd dreamed about practically forever. She smiled, dizzy from the feel of him beside her, from the way she felt protected with his arm around her.

She wasn't sure what would come next. There remained a

hundred unanswered questions, and neither of them could possibly have those answers. Not yet. One thing was sure. After tonight they could no longer lie to themselves about how they felt, about the crazy intensity of their feelings for each other. But Bailey was confident of one thing—they would take this slowly, because they had to. God would come first, or they would have nothing. Because she could see in Cody's eyes that neither of them would do anything to risk what they'd found here tonight. On Lake Monroe, in each other's arms ... on a Fourth of July they would remember as long as they lived. She thought about what Cody had said about all this. The one word that truly summed it all up:

Finally.

CODY LOOKED AT HER, AND HE could feel his eyes shining in the light of the fireworks. The intensity of emotions filling him was more than he was willing to share right now. She still didn't know about his mother, how she was taking part in an intense rehab, and how Cody still worried every day that she might relapse again.

Logic still told him Bailey was out of his league. But here, now, there was only this moment together. He relaxed a little and a quiet laugh hit him. "You know what?" he whispered.

"What?" Her eyes danced, and he felt himself getting lost in them.

He held her eyes, memorizing the way he felt. "It's just like football on the beach." He didn't look away, and neither did she. Both of them lost in the way it felt to be together like this.

"Like football on the beach?" she whispered. She looked like she, too, wanted this time to last forever. "The two of us ... finally finding this ... that's like football?"

"Yes." He smiled at her. "Someone has to call it."

A NOTE FROM KAREN

Dear Reader Friends,

Thanks again for traveling with me through the pages of *Take Three*. This time, telling the story felt like a sprint — a flat-out run. I always outline my books, and *Take Three* was no exception. But this time the characters kept getting ahead of me. I know, I know. For people who never live in imaginary worlds, the idea of the characters taking charge sounds a little crazy. Like maybe I need more time with people who breathe. But that's seriously what happened this time. Major events happened in *Take Three* that simply weren't on my outline. I'd get to the next chapter, and the characters would basically refuse to cooperate. Which, of course, was fine for me because it was fun. It was a full-out, fast-paced run through a story I came to love deeply — as differently as it turned out.

Here's the most exciting part — now that we've gotten to this point, *Take Four* will be a blast to write. New events and crazy changes are definitely going to happen because some of what happened here was supposed to happen there. One example? Bailey's breakup with Tim. That girl was supposed to take a break, only. Find a little space away from Tim. But I was sitting with her at that restaurant table, listening to Tim trash talk Cody Coleman, and that girl absolutely demanded a complete breakup. I could only agree, and so it was.

Another surprise move — bringing Dayne in as one of the producers. It made sense that Chase would go home with his family, because he missed his girls, and he wasn't sure if he could take another year away from them. But Dayne was a huge surprise. It just happened that as Chase wanted to be home again, Dayne was missing movies. This time around, he wanted to see a different side of Hollywood—the side that believes a faith-based film is exactly what the market wants. And he wanted to work with his brother, Luke Baxter. Anyway, the whole process was a thrill ride. I hope you thought so too. Of course, it was hard going through Andi's part of the journey, but I loved how God met her at every turn in the road. She still has a lot to walk through, but it was wonderful to see her come back to her family and make the first step in turning back to Jesus.

By the end of *Take Three*, I could hardly wait to get the book into your hands, and I was struck by an exciting realization: There would now be much more to write about in *Take Four*! In the final book of the Above the Line Series, Bailey will take part in an adventure that I never imagined until I finished *Take Three*. That's what happens when the characters take over the storytelling!

And guess what my next stand-alone book is? That's right— *Unlocked*! The story has pressed in and around my heart for a few years, and I believe it will be one of my strongest ever. God gave me the complete outline on a recent cross-country flight from Dulles Airport to Portland. Twenty-four pages of handwritten notes in a spiral-bound notebook. When I was finished, I was quietly crying—the story that real and rich in my heart. I could only thank God because the outline, the story, felt like such a complete gift. And maybe one day a real-life Dayne Matthews will want to turn it into a movie. Only God knows!

Also, I have a big surprise for you at the end of this series. My next series is already coming to life, and it will involve many of your favorite characters! Stay tuned, and know that I pray for God to continue to lead me as these stories fill my heart. As always, I look forward to hearing your feedback on *Take Three*. Take a minute and visit my website at www.KarenKingsbury.com, where you can find my contact information and my guestbook.

Feel free to write me a private letter or post a public guestbook entry about how God is using these books in your life.

On my website you can check out my upcoming events page in case I'll be speaking somewhere near you. At my events we'll have the chance to meet and share a hug and a picture together. Also on my website, you can get to know other readers and become part of a community that agrees there is life-changing power in something as simple as a story. You can post prayer requests or read those already posted and pray for those in need. You can send in a photo of your loved one serving our country, or let us know of a fallen soldier we can honor on our Fallen Heroes page.

My website also tells you about my ongoing contests including "Shared a Book," which encourages you to tell me when you've shared one of my books with someone. Each time you email me about this, you're entered for the chance to spend a summer weekend with my family. In addition, everyone signed up for my monthly newsletter is automatically entered into an ongoing once-a-month drawing for a free, signed copy of my latest novel.

There are links on my website that will help you with matters that are important to you — faith and family, adoption, and ways to reach out to others. Of course, on my site you can also find out a little more about me and my family, my Facebook and YouTube channel, and my Karen's Movie Monday — where I release occasional Monday YouTube clips dealing with some aspect of my family and faith, and the wonderful world of Life-Changing Fiction™.

Another way to stay in touch is to follow me on Twitter. I will be giving a free cruise passage to two of my Twitter friends this fall — so join up. It's free and fun, and much less time-consuming than Facebook.

Finally, if you gave your life over to God during the reading of this book, or if you found your way back to a faith you'd let grow cold, send me a letter at Office@KarenKingsbury.com and write "New Life" in the subject line. I would encourage you to connect with a Bible-believing church in your area and get hold of a Bible. But if you can't get hold of one, can't afford one, or don't already have one, write "Bible" in the subject line. Tell me how God used this book to change your life, and then include your address in your email. My wonderful publisher Zondervan has supplied me with free copies of the New Testament, so that if you are unable to find a Bible any other way, I can send you one. I'll pay for shipping.

One more thing. I've started a program where I will donate a book to any high school or middle school librarian who makes a request. Check out my website for details. Again, thanks for journeying with me through the pages of this book. I can't wait to see you next time for *Take Four*, the final installment in the Above the Line Series. *Take Four* will answer a lot of questions you might have about Bailey and Cody and the future for the producers.

Until then, my friends, keep your eyes on the cross, and don't forget to look for angels.

In His light and love,
Karen Kingsbury

www.KarenKingsbury.com

READER STUDY GUIDE

1. In the early part of *Take Three*, Chase Ryan feels concerned about his ability to handle the pressures of producing. Have you or someone you know ever been in a job or a season of life when these feelings were an issue? Explain.

2. Chase's pastor asked him to consider becoming the church's new youth pastor at a time when the idea seemed crazy to Chase. The pastor's explanation was an easy one—he had prayed about the position, and Chase's name came to the top of the list. Have you or someone you know ever had God present a change in careers or locations that at the time seemed crazy, but that turned out to be God working in mysterious ways? Describe.

3. How did Chase come to see that the change in careers was God's plan for his life? How did that scene with Chase's wife and daughters in the backyard of their home make you feel?

4. How did Keith feel when he realized he might be losing his co-producer? Give an example of a time when you felt as if God had forgotten you. How did that situation turn out?

5. What was Dayne Matthews' last experience with Hollywood? Why do you think he'd choose to come back to the entertainment field at this time?

6. Describe your thoughts on the recent increase of faith-based films. What do you think this area of filmmaking should strive for, and how do you see it affecting today's culture?

7. The book mentions that Andi Ellison cut her hair and dyed it dark. Why do you think she did this? Have you or someone you love ever attempted to change something on the outside when the real change needed to come from within? Describe.

8. Through most of the book, Andi is determined to have an abortion. What do you think led to this decision?

9. How could Keith and Lisa have done a better job with Andi through her freshman year at Indiana University? What is a mistake some parents make in raising Christian kids toward adulthood, and how can this mistake be avoided?

10. Tim and Bailey are in their second year of dating through most of this book. What did you like about their relationship? How was it lacking?

11. Who do you like better for Bailey—Tim or Cody? Explain why.

12. When Bailey and Cody go on the retreat to Lake Monroe, what in their conversation shows that Cody has matured from the guy he once was? Do you think it's possible for single young women to have friendships with single young guys? Why or why not?

13. Bailey's family often spends time together—like the time they all went to the summer scrimmage football game. Why is this important for the Flanigan family? Tell about a time when you or someone you know made an effort at creating family together times.

14. Keith and Lisa make an attempt to help Andi by taking her to a Christian counselor. How have you seen Christian counseling be beneficial in your life or in the life of someone you know? Explain.

15. Andi makes a decision to lie to her parents about her pregnancy, and about her trip to Indianapolis. The Bible calls the devil "the father of lies." How is this evident in the lies Andi tells? How does lying about her situation nearly destroy Andi?

16. Tell about a time when lying nearly destroyed you or someone you know. How did you or that person finally come around to the truth? What was the outcome?

17. Andi runs into the Kunzmann family, and their intervention makes a dramatic impact on her. Describe a time when you or someone you know was affected by a stranger who came along just at the right moment.

18. Andi plans to arrive at the abortion clinic earlier than it opens to avoid protestors. What do you know of people who protest outside abortion clinics? What do you think about them and their mission to save lives of unborn babies? Which of their methods are effective? Why or why not?

19. On her way into the clinic, Andi is approached by Clarence. What is his role in her life? Explain whether you think he might've been an angel. The Bible says in Hebrews, chapter 13, "Do not forget to entertain strangers, for by doing so some people have entertained angels without knowing it." What does this verse mean to you?

20. Tell about a time when you or someone you know experienced what might've been an angel encounter.

Take Four

Take Four

One

BAILEY FLANIGAN'S LEGS SHOOK and her arms felt like limp noodles. Outside, the heat in the heart of New York City sweltered, the humidity some of the worst of the summer. If the dance studio had air conditioning, it wasn't working. The mix of sweaty bodies and thick air made it almost impossible for Bailey or any of the dancers to catch their breath.

"And again!" Sebastian, the casting director from *West Side Story* shouted at them. "Five, six, seven, eight ..."

The music kicked in and Bailey grabbed a quick breath. *Keep moving*, she told herself. *Don't stop!* She couldn't quit no matter how hard the director pushed them. This was her dream; an actual Broadway audition in a New York studio. She would give it everything she had, until she dropped to the floor trying.

She'd worked with Katy Hart Matthews on her acting and stage presence, and that would help if she got past this stage. But the intensity of the audition was crazy. If she'd known how many hours of dancing they'd do and how they'd be expected to sing without any sign of exertion she would've practiced more. She wasn't sure if her old boyfriend Tim Reed felt the same way. He spent most of the summer working with a private dance and vocal coach, and from what Bailey could see, his efforts were paying off.

One thing was certain. Sebastian was right about the numbers. At the beginning of the audition he had told them there would be hundreds of talented dancers trying for a handful of ensemble spots. Bailey remembered the scene from earlier that day. There had to be a thousand dancers lined up around the block looking for a shot. The only flicker of hope was that the audition had grown into a combined talent search for not just the *West Side Story*, but also *Wicked* and *Mary Poppins*. Each show had at least two ensemble spots to fill.

Bailey's feet had blisters and she could barely lift her arms as she ran through the dance routine one more time. But she didn't care. She would've been thrilled with a part in any of those shows.

"Okay, take five minutes," the director waved his hand. "We'll pick up again after that."

Bailey moved to the side of the room and wiped her forehead with a towel from her bag. Every Christian Kids Theater performance, every dance or voice lesson, the hours of practicing and praying and dreaming — all of it came together for this moment in time. Her lungs burned as she pulled a water bottle from her backpack and downed it in three long swigs. Her mom had flown with her and Tim to New York the day before, and this morning she'd given each of them several water bottles, which was a good thing. Already the audition had gone on for five hours, and cuts were made every hour. So far, she and Tim were still in the running.

Throughout the studio the dancers clustered in groups of two or three while they drank water and caught their breath. Bailey wanted to talk to Tim, but she needed to get word to her mom about what was happening. She turned her cell phone on and moved into the hallway. Her mom answered almost instantly. "Honey, I'm dying ... are you in?"

"It's still going on." She tried to keep the weariness from her voice, but it was impossible. She could barely hold her phone to her ear. "It'll be at least another hour."

"How's it going?"

"The directors are tough. But they like us ... at least I think so. But the competition is so intense. It's overwhelming."

Her mom had hired a car for the day, and after dropping Bailey and Tim off early that morning, she was shopping along Fifth Avenue, killing time until the audition was over. "Okay." Her mom sounded upbeat, her enthusiasm contagious. "Give it your best, sweetheart. I'll be praying."

Bailey's heart melted at her mother's words. In the last few years her mom had admitted only a couple times that she wasn't looking forward to the possibility of Bailey moving to New York City. She and Cody had talked about it too. He made her promise she wouldn't think about the two of them or their future. Not this weekend, with her dreams on the line. Even so, Cody filled her mind constantly. If she won a part, they'd only see each other on visits. And would her stint here last six months or a year? Or maybe longer? There were too many questions and not enough answers, so Bailey doubled her determination. She had to win the part first. The answers would come after that.

The break ended much too quickly, before Bailey could connect with Tim. The next set started off with just the guys. There were maybe a hundred dancers left, and Sebastian placed Tim in the front row. "Follow me and pay attention. I won't repeat myself. Once we're up to speed, I'll walk the aisles. If I tap you, you're finished for the day. Thank you for coming out. If you remain untapped, stay here. You've made it to the next round."

Sebastian launched into a difficult series of eight-counts, all set to a ridiculously fast beat. Bailey wasn't sure what show the dance came from, but she doubted the ensemble would perform it at this speed. Probably just one more way the director could make cuts. Dancers who couldn't keep up would be eliminated. End of story.

The teaching session lasted only ten minutes, and then the guys were on their own, running over the series of eight-counts again and again while Sebastian and three of his assistants walked between the rows and tapped the shoulder of one guy after another. When they'd passed by every guy in the room, only eight dancers remained.

Tim was one of them.

Bailey wanted to stand up and applaud, but it wasn't the time. She hoped he could feel how proud she was. His dreams were coming true right here before her eyes. Enough time had passed since their breakup that they really had found their friendship again. A casual friendship, void of deep conversations or text messages — or any desire for something more. Best of all, there seemed to be no hard feelings between them.

Sebastian gave the guys a ten-minute break and ordered them back in the room to watch the girls. Then he barked orders to the female dancers, arranging them in rows similar to the guys. "Same thing, ladies. I'll teach you the dance and you'll perform it over and over until I've walked past every one of you. Same drill as the guys. If I tap you, thank you for coming out. If not, please stay for the next round."

Bailey walked out to her place on the floor. *Here goes,* she thought. *Please, God ... give me the energy ... help me shine for You. I want this so badly, Lord ... please.* Her legs shook as she found her spot in a middle row. Maybe she should've pushed her way to the front, or tried for an end position. So the directors could see her better. *Please, God ... You made me for this, I know You did.* She stretched her legs one at a time and again wished she'd done more to prepare. She was so tired she wasn't sure she could learn a single eight-count, let alone dance a series of them.

Sebastian clapped his hands, fast and intense. "This is the beat, girls. Stay with me."

He launched into a dance harder than anything Bailey had ever done. All her life she had figured she'd be ready for an audition like this, ready to leap and twirl and soar across a Broadway stage. After all, she'd done this for CKT for years, and she'd performed on the Indiana University stage only months ago. But it took all her physical and mental energy to grasp the dance in the brief time they'd been given, and in a blur Sebastian was finished teaching. "Ready, ladies?" he shouted, "Five, six, seven, eight . . . ."

With that, the pulsing music began and the rows of dancers burst into action, performing as if their lives depended on their next moves. Bailey fought past the pain and exhaustion, and found another level — an ability she didn't know she possessed. *Thank you, God ... I'm doing it ... I'm dancing better than any time in all my life! I can do this, I know I can. Thank you ...*

Sebastian seemed to know exactly what he was looking for. He walked the rows, tapping the shoulder of nearly every girl he passed. She could imagine him passing her by, letting her stay. This was the best she'd ever danced, so she had to win a part, right? Bailey wanted to pray again, but all she could do was dance.

Finally it was her turn, and again she could picture the victory, feel him walking past her, avoiding her shoulder, giving her the privilege of making it to the next round. They sort of knew each other, really. They'd met last year when her mom brought a group of CKT kids to New York City. So maybe he'd have pity on her and...

She kept dancing, pushing herself, but just then Sebastian hesitated near her. He gave her a sad look and a quick raise of his brow, as if to say she should've worked harder. Then without giving her another few seconds to prove herself, he tapped her shoulder.

And that was that.

When the music stopped, Bailey did everything she could not to cry. Her limbs ached, and every step hurt. She felt the blisters on her feet as she made her way to her backpack. Her lungs gasped for enough air to meet the demands of her worn out body. What had just happened? Had she really lasted all day only to get cut at the very end? She walked as if in a trance and found her things along the wall. *God ... why?* The prayer came instantly, silently. *Is this really your will for me, the plans you have for me? I gave it everything I had, and I thought ... I thought You were going to let me shine for You here in the city. I thought this was Your will, Father ... so why? Why ...*

But even as her wounded prayer overflowed from her hurting heart, she had a realization. This wasn't the last time she would try out for a Broadway show. She would go home and work harder, practice more often. Next time she wouldn't leave a doubt in the minds of the directors. But even as the plan formed in her mind, her disappointment caused her to slump against the wall. She sank to the ground and for a few seconds she covered her face with her hands. How would she tell her mom, her dad and her brothers? And what about Cody? He'd been so sure she'd get a part. He believed in her, and now ... now she'd have to tell them what happened. She'd let them all down — herself and God, and everyone who loved her.

She had told Cody at their Lake Monroe Campus Crusade retreat that she wasn't sure she wanted to live in New York City. But she did — she was ready for this, the next step in her future. But now ... now she'd have to go home and find a way to become better. She would return home to Bloomington, Indiana, for the rest of the summer and see Cody Coleman as often as she wanted. Rather than living nearly a thousand miles away, she would be home for college for another year and in the Clear Creek High School stands for every fall football game. But all of that did nothing to ease her defeat in this moment. The longer she thought about how God had opened this door, and how sure she'd been that she'd win a part, the more determined she became.

Next time the outcome would be different.

Tim was taking his place for the last and final stage of his audition. Bailey pulled her last water bottle from her backpack and twisted off the lid, her eyes on Tim. The other girls were gone, and she wasn't sure if she was allowed to stay. But until someone

asked her to leave, she figured she could watch. She was too tired
to stand, anyway. And she wanted to be there, because what if
… what if Tim was chosen? How weird would that be, him living here and performing without her? Her heart pounded in her
chest, because Tim's future was being decided in the coming few
minutes by strangers in an oversized New York City dance studio.
She dragged her towel over her forehead and sipped her water.
Your will, God … let Tim receive your will …

Sebastian paired up the eight remaining girls with the eight
remaining guys. This time Bailey had no doubt where the dance
came from. It was the ensemble number "Dancing through Life,"
one of the biggest in the musical *Wicked*. The dance was one any
musical theater kid would've loved to learn.

Again Sebastian wasted no time. He taught them half the
dance and then counted down as the music began. Tim was
paired up with a small Asian girl, a beautiful dancer whose stage
presence made up for what she lacked in height. Bailey watched
them, and she couldn't blink, couldn't look away. When had Tim
gotten so strong, so good at commanding the stage?

The decision was made quickly that four pairs would remain.
"If I call your number, you may sit down. If not, please get your
things and leave. Again, thank you for your time." He read from
a list without fanfare or buildup. A minute later, half the dancers
were leaving and the other half — including Tim — were sitting
down on the floor, their eyes on Sebastian.

"Congratulations. We saw more than twelve-hundred dancers today, and you eight have won the jobs. You'll each be given a
minimum six-month contract and … "

The director was going on, giving them final instructions
about connecting with a housing director and their weekly pay.
Bailey couldn't concentrate on what he was saying after that. This
was really happening for Tim, and it was all a little hard to believe. Tim Reed? Her first crush … her longtime CKT friend …

now a professional Broadway actor and dancer? And he was taking on the role she'd always dreamed about. *Dear God, how come I couldn't be here with him? It would've been great knowing someone, having a friend to connect with ... it would've been perfect ...*

Tim didn't dare turn around until Sebastian released them, but then he dashed across the floor to Bailey. "I did it!" He helped her to her feet and picked her up, then swung her around in two full circles. "I can't believe it, Bailey. I'm in a real Broadway show!"

"I know!" She smiled as he set her down, and she tried to find a lighthearted laugh, but it wouldn't come. *Quit feeling sorry for yourself, Bailey. This is ridiculous ... Help me be happy for him, Lord.* She felt like an awful friend, unable to delight fully in his victory.

"Wow," he was breathing hard, dazed, clearly trying to grasp what had just happened, the reality of his success. Then he blinked twice and suddenly he seemed to remember that she didn't have anything to celebrate. She hadn't made it. He faced her, his hands on her shoulders, and his smile fell off a little. "They should've picked you, Bailey. You were amazing."

She blinked back tears, her smile firmly in place. "I'll try again." She leaned close and kissed his cheek. "But, hey, congratulations. I'm so proud of you. When will you know what show you're in?"

"Didn't you hear him? At the end there he pointed to each of us and told us where we'd be working." His face lit up again. "I'm in *Wicked.* I can't even believe this is happening."

Bailey couldn't draw a breath for a moment. *Wicked?* The top show on Broadway? "That's perfect!" She found a thrill of joy for Tim, her own disappointment pushed back for the moment. If he could win a role in the ensemble for that show, this first six-month contract would only be the beginning. She was grateful they'd broken up nearly two months ago. Otherwise they might've been confused by this goodbye — since the separation here was out of their hands. But Bailey had long since let Tim go, long before their breakup. Now she was truly happy for him and his future here in New York City.

"You'll be here one day, I know it." He hugged her loosely, their bodies both drenched in sweat. "Keep trying, Bailey. Don't ever settle."

She felt a tenderness work its way into her smile. She hadn't settled in love — that's why she was dating Cody Coleman. And she wouldn't settle when it came to her dreams of performing, either. "Thanks for that. I won't settle."

"Promise?"

"Promise." Bailey took out her cell phone. "I need to call my mom." She dreaded this conversation, but she had to have it. She kept her tone upbeat and simply asked her mom to pick them up out front. No details yet. Five minutes later the car pulled up. Her mom jumped out and gave each of them a quick hug. "So ... what happened?"

Bailey waited until they were in the car, then she took the lead. "They passed on me." She smiled, even as another layer of tears built in her eyes. She wasn't shaking as badly as before, but she was weary, worn out from the physical and emotional drain. She didn't make eye contact with her mom, because if she did, she'd break down. And she didn't want to do that until later, when she and her mom were alone. "But guess what?" Her voice trembled a little, but she fought for control. "Tim got a job with *Wicked*! Can you believe it? He was one of four guys chosen. You should've seen him. He was easily the best out there."

Her mom's immediate response was to congratulate Tim, but at the same time she reached out and took hold of Bailey's knee, squeezing it as if to say her heart was breaking. Her mom loved her so much, and clearly she hadn't missed the obvious. Bailey hadn't been chosen. But her mom also knew her well enough to know this wasn't the time or place for sadness. It was Tim's shining moment, and he deserved their excitement.

Not until later in their hotel room, when the door was finally shut and they were alone, did Bailey fall into her mother's arms and let her tears come. "I wanted it so badly, Mom. I've never tried so hard for anything in all my life." The sobs came in waves, and for a long time her mom simply held her.

"Oh honey, it's okay to cry. I know you're disappointed."

After a minute or so, Bailey pulled back and met her mom's eyes. Her heartbreak sounded in every word. "I thought it was God's will. I mean ... I prayed about this for months, and ... and I thought I was ready. I'd have Tim here to help keep an eye on me and ... and it would've been perfect." A few more sobs shook her body and she pressed her fingers beneath her eyes.

"You can try again."

"I know." Bailey sniffed and nodded. But the tears came once more and she brushed them away. She paced to the window of their hotel room and stared out at the city. "I will." She looked over her shoulder at her mother. "And next time I'll work harder. God would want that from me."

"I agree." Her mom's expression showed how badly she hurt for Bailey.

They ate pizza in their room that night, and Tim turned in early. Bailey and her mother watched an ESPN special on the Indianapolis Colts, and how Bailey's father — the Colts' offensive coordinator — was one of the top coaches in the NFL. When the special was over, they called Bailey's dad and congratulated him. "Every team in pro football will want you after that," Bailey settled into the sofa closest to their hotel window. "I'm proud of you, Daddy."

By now he knew about her audition. "I'm proud of you, too, sweetheart. And next time you'll be first one picked." His voice was tender. "I know you. This will only make you stronger."

While they were talking, her mom took a call on her cell. She slipped into the hotel bedroom for the conversation and when she joined Bailey in the sitting area, her eyes were dancing and a smile tugged at her lips. "That was Katy Matthews." She uttered a disbelieving laugh. "God's timing is amazing, as always."

"Why?" Bailey sat up a little straighter. "What'd she say?"

"I guess the casting director for *Unlocked* saw your footage from *The Last Letter*. She loves you, Bailey." Her mom sat down across from her. "She said Dayne might contact you about an audition." She brushed aside a section of Bailey's long brown hair. "God has a plan in this, honey. Even if we can't see it now."

"I know. I believe that." Bailey thought about the possibility of being an extra in *Unlocked*. It was bound to be a big movie — the book was a major *New York Times* runaway bestseller. Everyone had read it, and everyone loved it. Now the film was being produced by Jeremiah Productions — Dayne Matthews and Keith Ellison, the father of Bailey's friend, Andi. "Being an extra in a movie like that would be nice. It would look good on my resume, I guess."

"Hmmm." Her mom tilted her head. "Maybe they want you to read for a bigger part. It's possible, right?"

Bailey smiled. "I don't have experience for anything more." She shrugged, trying to stay light-hearted. "It'll be fun. I'll definitely meet with them if they're interested."

"That's my girl." Her mom's eyes showed a support some kids only dream of having. "Let's get some sleep, okay?"

They turned in, and Bailey realized how exhausted she still was. She could sleep ten hours easily. But before she drifted off, she thought about Cody and Bloomington and the season ahead. She would enjoy every minute, hold onto the time with the people she loved. But she would also work harder than ever before. Because with God's help and her own determination, this time next year she wouldn't be heading back home after an audition in New York City.

She'd be looking for an apartment.

Two

KEITH ELLISON STILL WASN'T USED TO the attention Dayne received wherever they went. After Dayne replaced Chase Ryan as the other lead producer for Jeremiah Productions, Keith quickly forgot Dayne Matthews had once been a big-time Hollywood star. He had instead become a friend, a confidante, and a very talented part of their production company. When they were on the road, however, the reality of Dayne's past was constantly an issue.

That was the case now on this late Friday afternoon as they boarded a United Airlines flight from Los Angeles International Airport to Indianapolis. Never mind that LAX was used to seeing celebrities frequent the ticket counters. Even after a few years of virtual seclusion, Dayne Matthews was enough to cause the sort of disruption that required extra security.

"Here goes," Dayne grinned as they pulled up at the United outdoor baggage counter. He kept his head low as he stepped out of the black Navigator that had shuttled them about all week for various meetings regarding the first two Jeremiah Productions films, *The Last Letter* and *Unlocked*.

Keith signed for the ride, thanked the driver, and stepped out beside Dayne. The driver set their luggage on the sidewalk beside them and they headed for the line at the United counter.

"Shorter out here," Dayne continued to keep his face downcast, as if he'd developed a sudden and intense interest in the zipper on his rollerboard suitcase. "Less chance of getting recognized."

They'd traveled together enough times in the last month that Keith knew the drill. He'd keep Dayne engaged in what seemed like an intense conversation until they had boarding passes and were headed for security. Dayne had more than a million air miles built up from his days of acting, so they upgraded to first class every time they flew. That also added to some sense of privacy.

Even so, as they reached the baggage counter, a young woman in her twenties ran up and touched Dayne's arm. "Dayne Matthews!" She screamed and looked around, as if she needed someone to appreciate what had just happened. "I can't believe this! Everyone look! It's Dayne Matthews!"

Keith felt his adrenaline kick into gear. They had a plan for moments like this. "Ma'am, here you go." Keith pulled an autographed mini-picture of Dayne from his bag and handed it to her.

"I wondered what happened to you after that terrible car accident." The woman stood as close as she could to Dayne, babbling so fast it was difficult to understand her. "I mean, you were in the hospital for a really long time and a lot of us wondered if you'd ever walk again. But then didn't you fall in love with someone from the Midwest? I read about it in one of the magazines and —"

"Ooops, sorry." Dayne smiled and held up his forefinger, just as he pulled his phone from his back pocket and pushed his wife Katy's number — all in a quick rush of motion. "Got a phone call," Dayne whispered. "It's important!"

On the other end, Katy must've answered because Dayne lowered his head and covered the phone as he began to talk.

Keith stood between Dayne and the woman. "He's busy, ma'am. Thanks for your interest." He motioned toward the distant door. "If you could move on that'd be great."

The woman seemed bewildered by the turn of events, but she did as she was asked, grateful for the autographed picture. As soon as she was gone, Dayne wrapped up what was a very quick call to his wife, then he put his phone back in his pocket and winked at Keith. "Worked again."

"Like a charm." Keith was amazed at how practiced Dayne was at diffusing moments like that one. "How's Katy?"

"She's great. Sophie was saying, 'Da-da,' in the background." Dayne's eyes shone. "Can't wait to get home."

They got through the baggage counter, and at the security line the man checking IDs looked hard at Dayne. "You look a lot like another Dayne Matthews — used to be an actor a while back."

"Hmmm." Dayne grinned. "I hear that now and then."

The man moved on to Keith's ID and let the matter pass. When they were through security, Keith laughed about the incident. "It's not like you grew a long beard and let yourself go." He grabbed his roller computer bag and hurried alongside Dayne to the concourse.

"Hey, it works for me. The last thing you want is to sign an autograph for the guy checking security." He chuckled. "The whole line figures something's up."

They had only a little time at the gate before they boarded, and only after the plane was in the air did an older flight attendant bring him a piece of paper and a discreet smile. "Please, Mr. Matthews, could I get an autograph for my daughter? She's a huge fan."

Dayne was sitting near the window and seemed happy to oblige. He kept the matter quiet, the paper low to his lap, so no one would see what was happening. After the interruption things settled down and Dayne turned to Keith. "What a week."

"It was." Keith's head was still spinning from everything that had fallen into place in the meetings these past few days. "We finally have a release date."

"I'm glad they let us have input on that. Some dates can kill a movie." Dayne recalled an incident to Keith from a few years back, where a major studio released a Christmas movie in early November, thinking there'd be more holiday weekends for people to see the film. Instead, moviegoers disregarded the picture as something not to see until the Christmas season. People weren't ready for a Christmas story just days after Halloween. Dayne turned, his shoulder pressed into the seat, his attention on Keith. "The movie needed a Thanksgiving Day release, of course. But by Thanksgiving it was already doing so poorly it was on its way out of theaters."

"I agree. The release date is huge. I was glad for your input. Your experience is priceless, Dayne. Really."

They'd agreed on a December 26 release for *The Last Letter* — meaning the film would go head-to-head with some of the top pictures of the holiday season. Generally, Christmas films would release around Thanksgiving, and the day after Christmas a slew of family-friendly movies would hit theaters, giving people on Christmas break another reason to line up at box offices.

"A year ago if you'd told me we'd have a release date the day after Christmas I would've thought I was dreaming." Keith pulled a folder of notes from his travel bag and looked over a summary of their various meetings. "I think they respect us more with you on the team." He paused. "You feel good about it, right?"

"It's perfect." Dayne didn't look even the slightest bit concerned. "*The Last Letter* is a great picture, and with the buzz from film festivals it'll be huge. Might as well put it on a weekend when everyone can see it."

Keith tried to believe that was true. The stakes were high, because if viewers chose to support a different film that weekend, there might not be much of a second weekend for *The Last Letter*. And if that happened, the movie wouldn't only bomb at the box offices, it would lose money and fail to repay investors — a death knell to Jeremiah Productions and everything it hoped to accomplish.

"I know what you're thinking." Dayne's eyes danced, his confidence like a physical presence around him. "It won't bomb. It'll be the top box office draw, for sure."

Keith didn't quite share Dayne's certainty, but he liked the optimism of his new co-producer and he liked the deals they'd worked out that week. God was moving in a big way ... he needed to believe that the way Dayne did. They had their release date, and American Pictures had made good on its promise — a ten-million-dollar advance toward publicity and marketing. With Dayne's connections, they'd raised the other ten million dollars — unthinkable amounts when Keith and Chase first started out. But with a twenty-million-dollar budget, people everywhere would see the trailer, and maybe Dayne was right. Maybe *The Last Letter* would be the picture everyone would flock to see once Christmas was behind them.

Keith would pray about it every day until then.

The flight attendant brought them rolled up warm washcloths to clean their hands prior to the meal. Keith laughed softly as he took his. "Just as well the people in coach don't see this. It's a little ridiculous."

"Completely." Dayne wiped his hands just as the woman came back around collecting the used cloths. "But you have to admire their efforts at customer service."

"True." Keith pulled down his tray table as the flight attendant came again and spread linen cloths for each of them. No matter how many times they traded Dayne's miles for first class, the experience would never seem normal to Keith. He checked his notes again. "And the filming dates for *Unlocked*, you're happy about them too?"

"I am. It's soon, but I think it'll work out."

"What about the cold weather and the snow?"

"I think we can avoid it. But if not, it works." Dayne angled his head. "There's something symbolic about a boy struggling with autism through winter, and finding his way out of that internal prison come spring and summer. We can do the later scenes first, before there's a chance of snow."

Keith nodded, pensive. "That should work."

"It will." Dayne looked content with the plan. "Last year we didn't have snow until well into November."

"Is that right?" Keith was surprised. "I always pictured Indiana colder than that."

"Oh, it gets cold." Dayne rolled his eyes. "You should see me drive in the snow."

"Not pretty?"

"Definitely not. I get snow tires each year on the first of November. But usually I'm the only one driving around with them until the end of the month."

They start filming October 25, and hope for a six-week schedule. That way they'd wrap up two weeks before Christmas, which was just enough time for a brief break before the public premiere of *The Last Letter*. Depending on the editing process, *Unlocked* could be in theaters the day after Christmas a year from now — twelve months later.

A man across the aisle from them reached over and tapped on Keith's shoulder. Keith was on the aisle, with Dayne on the window — the way Dayne always flew. "Excuse me," the man motioned past Keith to Dayne. "Your friend, can you get his attention for me?"

As soon as the man leaned over, Dayne instantly appeared lost in some tremendous sight beyond his window. Keith had no choice but to tap Dayne's shoulder. "Hey, quick question."

"What?" Dayne turned, surprised, and looked from Keith to the man. He smiled. "Sorry ... what?"

"I hate to bug you." The man scrutinized Dayne. "My wife wants me to say ... you look a lot like Dayne Matthews, the actor."

Dayne shook his head, like this might be one of the few times in his life he'd heard such a thing. "I used to hear that all the time. Not so much anymore."

"Yeah." The guy nodded and settled back into his seat. "Just thought I'd tell you."

Dayne gave the man a friendly wave and did the same for the guy's wife. It was all Keith could do to keep a straight face. He'd seen Dayne handle attention this way enough times that now it seemed like an art form. Dayne didn't deny the resemblance, but he didn't confirm it either. Almost no one went on to the next question, asking Dayne if he really was the actor. Most assumed by his response the resemblance was only that.

Once more Dayne resumed looking out the window, and only a few minutes later after the flight attendants brought lunch did he stare at his meal and mutter under his breath, "You know what's really wild? How come no one ever tells you how much you look like Keith Ellison?"

This time, Keith couldn't stop a single laugh from slipping through his lips. He, too, kept his attention on his meal, and they let the matter pass. They spent the rest of the flight talking about their families and all that laid ahead for them in the coming year. Dayne's little girl, Sophie, was walking and saying her first words, and his wife, Katy, was excited to be alongside the two of them through the moviemaking process.

Hearing about Dayne's young family made Keith miss the early days with his own daughter, Andi, back when she was still an innocent child and life on the mission field was wrought with very different dangers than the one they faced here in the States — before the heartache and challenges of the past year.

"How's she doing?" Dayne's expression deepened. He knew about Andi's pregnancy and her decision to give her baby up for adoption.

"We're getting close again, so that's what matters." Keith pressed his lips together, still struggling to believe his precious Andi was four months pregnant. She was only nineteen, and not married. The guy had ditched her long before Andi found out she was pregnant. It was the sort of situation Keith would never have imagined for his only daughter. He sighed. "She's due at the end of January."

"She still wants to give the baby up?"

"That's what she says." Keith hadn't allowed himself to think about the adoption much. It was the right decision, he and his wife, Lisa, were sure. But this was their first grandchild, Andi's firstborn. Giving up the baby would bring pain for all of them — no matter how the next several months played out. "She's been talking lately about a family she saw in the listing at the adoption agency. It's a little early, but she's pretty sure they're the ones she wants to have her baby."

"Wow." Dayne let his head fall slowly back against the headrest. "It's a lot for a girl her age."

"I'm just glad she's home. She's a different person than she was last spring. Closer to us and to God. If it took this to bring her back, then I guess we'll always be grateful to some extent."

"It's Romans 8:28 proving itself true again."

"Exactly." Keith let the verse run through his mind. *"In everything, God works for the good of those who love Him."* It was a Scripture he'd thought about often in the days since learning about Andi's pregnancy. No matter what consequences came as a result of bad choices, no matter how a father's dreams for his daughter might seem lost, God was still at work. He still had plans for Andi and for all of them. That was the great reality of following Jesus.

The rest of the flight was uneventful, and Keith finally walked through the garage door into his newly rented Bloomington house at nearly midnight. The lights were off, and he figured everyone was sleeping. He tiptoed inside, left his bag by the kitchen entryway, and used the light from his cell phone to make his way back to Andi's bedroom.

He stood at her door and watched her, sleeping beneath the

patchwork quilt Lisa made for her tenth birthday. The blanket had been Andi's favorite since then, and here in the darkly lit room it was easy to pretend they were back in that time ... Andi a fourth-grader and the quilt her only gift that birthday — a gift Lisa had spent weeks secretly making.

Had they known then what they knew now, maybe they never would've returned from the mission field to work in movies. The cost had been so much higher than Keith ever imagined back then, back when he and Chase dreamed about making films with a Christian message and changing the world through popular culture.

Keith leaned against the doorframe and turned his attention to the dark shadows outside Andi's bedroom window. Yes, the cost had been great, and they were still only halfway to seeing their dreams realized. Chase was no longer a part of Jeremiah Productions, and was working now at his home church back in San Jose, California. They didn't talk nearly as much as Keith had figured they would. Chase had moved on. He loved being the church's youth pastor, and he and his wife, Kelly, were closer than ever. Her issues of inferiority and insecurity were resolved in her new commitment to God and in having Chase home again.

A recent conversation with Chase came to mind, and Keith marveled again at how his longtime friend barely sounded like the same person. He talked at length about the programs at church, new families moving into the area, and getting their children involved. If Keith hadn't offered details about the movies, he wasn't sure Chase would've even asked. He remembered a conversation with Chase in the first few months of their time together as missionaries in Indonesia.

"It's like all of life before this never even happened," he had told Keith. And now that's how Chase must've been viewing his time in Hollywood with Keith — like it had never happened.

Of course, Chase's departure had been an answer to both his

own prayers and Keith's, because it opened the door for Dayne Matthews — and Dayne's presence had changed everything. But still, losing Chase's constant friendship hurt. It was another sacrifice along the way to making movies that glorified God. Another cost was Ben Adams and Kendall — the father/daughter team Keith expected would be part of their production company for years. But Ben was fighting for his life, the cancer in his liver now, and Kendall was caring for him, barely having time for her work as his office manager.

Making movies hadn't caused Ben to get sick, of course, but his and Kendall's absence was a loss all the same. Keith looked down again at Andi. His daughter's innocence was the greatest cost of all. He and Lisa had trusted Andi's upbringing would be enough to keep her strong at Indiana University. For some kids, of course, it was enough. But not for Andi. They'd sent her off and basically put all their time and attention into making movies. Lisa ran things at home — the email and phone correspondences, the updates to investors, the scheduling details. And Keith had been busy dealing with every other aspect of filmmaking.

Meanwhile, they had been losing their daughter, and they hadn't known it.

He walked quietly to her side and sat on the edge of her bed. Softly he brushed her bangs aside, and then he leaned down and kissed her forehead. His sweet girl ... his Andi. If he and Lisa had known then what they knew now, they would've moved to Bloomington a year ago, let Andi live with them, and do whatever they could to keep her grounded. Maybe then he and Dayne would be talking about having Andi — not her friend Bailey Flanigan — read for the lead role opposite Brandon Paul. Bailey would be wonderful, he and Dayne were sure. The role would stretch her, but they wanted someone wide-eyed and untouched by the world. Bailey would only have to play herself, and she'd be marvelous. Andi didn't know they were about to ask Bailey to read for the female lead. Even Bailey didn't know how big a part they were considering her for. But still ...

A sad sigh came from him, interrupting the silence of the room. *God, you still have a plan for my girl ... I know you do. Please be with her in the coming months. Help her hear your voice. Help her believe the best is yet to be, that she hasn't lost her future because of her mistakes this year.*

There was no answer. Not one that spoke loudly in his mind or rattled the windows in his soul. But Keith's eyes fell on a small framed print on Andi's bookcase. It was her favorite verse, the one she had believed in when she was a little girl: "*'For I know the plans I have for you,' declares the Lord. 'Plans to prosper you and not harm you, plans to give you hope and a future.'*"

Tears stung at Keith's eyes and he blinked them back. They were going to be okay, all of them. They would get their movies out to the people, and the culture would be changed because they would pray believing, absolutely believing, God wouldn't have led them this far without giving them the strength and blessings to see the mission through to completion. Sitting there beside his pregnant daughter, Keith prayed like he hadn't in weeks, months maybe. He prayed God would part the waters of Hollywood and their mission would be wildly successful. If it was going to happen, the change would need to occur in the coming year — and so Keith prayed.

As he finished, as he took a final look at his daughter and tenderly touched her cheek, his heart broke for the hard road she had ahead. In time people would notice her growing belly. They would stare and whisper and use her as an example of what not to do, how not to be. His precious Andi. And there was the emotional cost, as well ... going through the second half of her pregnancy when she'd feel her baby moving, when she would feel an undeniable connection to a baby she would never know, never hold or teach or read to. A baby who would never know her.

Only one truth gave him hope Andi would get through this, that they all would: the fact that Andi still clung to God's Word. This had to be true, because otherwise she would've taken down the framed verse from her bookcase. But it remained. Telling the world and anyone who looked that Andi Ellison still believed in God's plans for her future. And because of that, Keith would believe too.

Even if it took everything he had.

Three

FOOTBALL SEASON WAS RIGHT AROUND THE CORNER and Cody could hardly wait for the first game. But that wasn't why this late August was better than any Cody Coleman could remember. The reason was Bailey Flanigan.

Now, with twenty minutes left in practice on the third Saturday in August, Cody couldn't stop thinking about her. Six weeks had passed since the Fourth of July when everything had changed. Only then did Cody learn Bailey and Tim Reed had broken up, and only then did he finally understand what he had never known until that day: Bailey had feelings for him, the same way he had feelings for her.

Since then they'd taken things slowly. Bailey had dated Tim for two years, so neither of them wanted to rush into a relationship. But still, Cody spent much of his free time at the Flanigan house, and every day felt more unbelievable than the last. Being with Bailey, letting himself imagine this might be the beginning of a long-term relationship, made even the troubles with his mother pale in comparison. She was spending hours each day dancing, working out, and training for her next Broadway audition — and Cody encouraged every minute of it. If they'd survived everything up to this point, a little distance couldn't keep them apart. Not for long, anyway.

Cody was working with the quarterbacks, lining them up on the ten-yard line. Bailey's younger brother Connor Flanigan hadn't come out thinking he'd be a backup quarterback, but his arm strength had surprised the entire coaching staff. They were training Conner as the primary go-to guy if anything happened to their starter. Cody lined his quarterbacks up on the ten-yard line and shouted, "Footwork!"

The guys responded instantly, dropping into a squat for their ready position.

"Left," Cody kept his eye on Connor and pointed where he wanted the quarterbacks to move. "Left again! Right ... left."

Connor looked almost better than their starter. By next year the job would be his, and by then Cody and Bailey might be ... might be what? More serious, for sure, even if she was living in New York. She wasn't a city girl at heart. If she took a job, she wouldn't live there indefinitely. At least he didn't think so. And if she did, then he'd follow her. She was his world, his reason for believing in God and hope and life and dreams. He loved her more every day.

He roped his thoughts back to the moment. He couldn't think too long about Bailey, because when he did he wanted too badly to be three years down the road, with rings on their fingers and all the answers behind him.

Sunshine beat down on the field and humidity added to the late afternoon heat. The guys were given one more water break and another series of drills before practice was over. The Flanigan boys walked out of the locker room together and found Cody waiting for them. The plan was to head home and swim for an hour or so. Connor grinned and wiped the sweat off his forehead. "I can already feel that pool."

"Me too." Justin had his gear bag on his shoulder. "That was a long one." He elbowed Connor. "You looked great today. Maybe you'll get the nod to start."

Cody thought the same thing, but he couldn't talk about it. The decision belonged to Coach Ryan Taylor. They piled into the car and Shawn waited until they were out of the parking lot before he leaned forward and put his hand on Cody's shoulder. "So, what's the deal with you and Bailey? You gonna ask her to be your girlfriend?"

"Hey," Justin was sitting in the backseat next to Shawn. He gave his brother a friendly punch in the arm. "You can't ask that."

In the front seat, Connor stayed quiet. He was closer to Bailey than any of the Flanigan boys. Instead of joining the conversation he only turned a half-smile in Cody's direction, as if to say, "Yeah, what are your intentions for her?"

Cody laughed under his breath. "Well, guys, sorry to disappoint you." He kept his eyes on the road. "I don't have any answers yet. It's not smart to rush things with girls."

"But you like her, right? I mean more than a friend?" Shawn was relentless.

Again Justin gave him a shove. "He said he didn't know."

By then they were all laughing. Cody glanced at the rear view mirror and raised his brow at Shawn. "If things get serious with me and Bailey, I'm sure you'll be one of the first to find out."

"Probably not." Shawn slumped back against the seat, teasing. "She tells Connor and Mom everything first."

"Okay, you'll be second."

"Probably third."

Cody enjoyed the banter. The Flanigan boys had been like brothers to him for years — ever since he lived with their family. Cody had watched the boys grow up, and he loved the easy way they had with each other. He turned up the music, and in five minutes they pulled into the Flanigan driveway.

The boys emptied out with their gear, and Cody went inside with his own bag. The family's downstairs guest bedroom was still always open for his use if he needed it, especially now that he was back from Iraq and in their lives on a regular basis again. He didn't see Bailey, so he went to the guestroom and took a shower. He fitted his leg with his waterproof prosthetic, the one he used for swimming. Again he was grateful his doctors had been able to save so much of his left leg. He had his knee and several inches below that. It was why his prosthetic looked so real and why he was still so competitive in sports. Most people never noticed his injury.

He headed to the backyard and stretched out on one of the Flanigans' chaise lounges. Since the Fourth of July, Cody had thought constantly about how to handle this new connection with Bailey. Yes, they'd kissed — but only once. Since then he remembered once more how precious she was, how he'd looked after her and protected her when he was nothing more than her big brother, back when he lived here.

She was a precious girl, a gift from God. He didn't plan to kiss her randomly, and maybe not at all until they had an understanding between them. Cody felt butterflies in his stomach, and he looked up at a single puffy white cloud making its way across the sky. He wanted to ask her soon, make it official so he could call her his girlfriend. But he didn't want her to feel rushed. A two-year relationship, like the one she'd had with Tim Reed, needed a little time to heal — no matter who initiated the breakup.

Also, in the days since the Fourth, they'd spent their time with her family, and not alone. Cody liked this because being with her family helped him keep his focus, helped him think with his head and not his heart. Bailey was a forever sort of girl; there was no need to hurry things.

He heard the screen door and he sat up a little higher. Bailey and Ricky led the way, with her other brothers a few feet behind. They were talking about practice, Shawn and Justin bragging that Connor was proving to be the best quarterback on the Clear Creek field.

"Seriously?" Bailey wore shorts and a T-shirt. She had a towel draped over her arm and a smile Cody could feel across the patio. Bailey looped her arm around Connor's waist. "Way to go, buddy. I knew you'd love playing this year."

"I miss CKT," Connor grinned and put his arm easily around her shoulders. "But I have to admit, I'm loving me some football."

The boys had already rinsed off, and all of them were in their swim trunks. They lined up and did a group cannonball into the pool. At the same time, Bailey looked at Cody across the deck. Their eyes met as she walked toward him, and Cody felt his heart slam against his chest. He couldn't look away, could barely remember his name. That's the affect she had on him.

She took the chair beside him, sitting on the edge, her feet on the ground. "Hi." Her eyes turned softer, a little shy — not because she wasn't able to open up to him, but because they both felt so deeply for each other. And because those feelings were out in the open now. It was all a little more than either of them could believe. She angled her head, her pretty blue eyes shining in the sunlight, her chestnut hair hanging in long layers around her face. "How was practice?"

"Your brothers were right," he laughed and nodded toward Connor in the pool. "He's about to beat out the starter." He put his finger to his lips. "But shhh, don't say anything. Coach Taylor has to make that call."

Bailey laughed. "Hey, after we swim, wanna take a bike ride?" It was already almost five o'clock. "My dad's barbecuing ribs for dinner. But after that, maybe?"

She could've asked him to walk on coals, and he would've said yes. Even on a day as hot as this one. He reached out and took her fingers in his for a few seconds. "Like a race, you mean?" He was teasing her, because that's what he did. It was how they'd related to each other since she was a very young girl.

"Yeah, a race." She flexed her arms. "You know me. Miss Triathlete." She laughed again. "Then after you beat me, let's take a slow bike ride. The kind where we can actually talk for a few minutes." She looked over her shoulder. "Without every one of my brothers trying to figure out ..." again her expression turned shy. "You know."

"I do know." Cody told her about the ride home, how Shawn wanted to know what was happening. "Justin stuck up for us though. He said it was no one's business."

The conversation between them stayed easy and intimate. There was none of the getting-to-know-each-other awkwardness most couples had to go through. Through the swim and later after dinner when they took a couple bikes from the Flanigan garage and set out through Bailey's neighborhood, Cody kept feeling the same way. He might be able to ask her soon. She wasn't grieving the loss of her relationship with Tim. They'd basically been broken up for months before the actual ending. That's what Bailey had said.

"What're you thinking?" Bailey was riding beside him, the warm breeze on their faces.

"About you." Cody smiled at her. The sun was setting, and the sky was streaked with pinks and pale blues.

They turned right out of her parents' driveway, down a hill toward a dead-end cul-de-sac.

"Oh, yeah?" Bailey's eyes danced. "What about me?"

"How you really should become a triathlete. I mean, the power in your pedaling is impressive."

"Stop." She laughed, her head back. Then with a burst of speed she took the lead, lowering her body over the handlebars and flying down the hill. At the bottom, she skidded to a stop and pointed at him, her face taken up by her smile. "See, I can ride a bike."

"I know." He was out of breath, but more from the thrill of being with her than any exertion from the ride. "Maybe you could train me."

They were at the bottom of the hill at the end of the road, where a gravel path took off through a section of woods surrounding the Flanigans' neighborhood. She was still laughing when she climbed off her bike and shaded her eyes. "The sunset's so pretty."

"It's one more reason I love living here." Cody stepped off his bike, too. He had a feeling Bailey wanted to walk the path. Either way he enjoyed this, being alone with her. A short walk through the woods would be nice. There was a stream a quarter mile in where a family of box turtles had created a home, probably preparing to hibernate for the coming winter. "Let's go find the turtles."

"The ones Ricky says are in there somewhere?" She took a few steps toward the gravel path. "As long as we stay away from snakes."

Earlier in the summer Bailey's brothers had come across a copperhead snake, and Bailey hadn't forgotten it. Cody laughed. "They're in for the night by now."

"I'm not sure." She waited for him to start out on the path, and she walked alongside him.

This was the sort of moment they hadn't shared much of this summer. Cody could've pushed for it, but again he wanted to make sure Bailey was comfortable with things between them first. He reached for her hand and gently eased his fingers between hers.

"I still can't believe it." She walked close enough to him that their arms brushed against each other.

Cody didn't have to ask. He knew very well what she was talking about. "Me either."

"Tell me something." She lifted her eyes to him, their pace slow. The trees were still a ways off, so for now the sunlight still danced on her face.

"Anything." He didn't look away, didn't want to be anywhere but lost in her eyes.

"Why did you tell me to stay with Tim when you came home

from Iraq?" The slightest shadow fell over the moment. "I figured you didn't see me ..." she lifted their joined hands, "... like this. You know?"

How could he answer her? It was too soon to put his feelings for her into words — the intensity of how he felt might scare her off, even now that they'd found this connection. He swallowed hard and looked straight ahead. "I told you why."

"You said he was better for me."

"I thought he was." Cody slowed his pace and looked at her. "His background isn't complicated like mine ... he doesn't have a past. I felt old, like I'd seen too much. I guess I wanted to keep you away from all that."

"I care about your past." Her voice was kind, but still a little hurt. "It's not your fault ... what happened in Iraq."

"Not just Iraq." He thought about his drinking problem, and the trouble with his mother. "I come with baggage, Bailey. You know that."

"None of that matters." She smiled, but there was sorrow in her eyes. "You know what I wanted you to say that day? The day you came home from Iraq?"

"What?" He ached to take her in his arms, but he resisted. He focused on her eyes, her heart.

"I wanted you to tell me to leave Tim. I wanted you to say you'd been thinking about me the whole time you were at war."

Again Cody wasn't sure how much to tell her. They kept walking, heading into a thicket at the entrance to the woods. They could hear the creek somewhere up ahead. "I wouldn't have told you to break up with him." He kept his tone soft, tender. "That had to be your idea."

"You could've said that." She wasn't trying to fight with him, that much was obvious in her expression. "Instead I spent every day from then until this last Fourth of July thinking you weren't interested."

At that, a single laugh rattled in Cody's throat. "Yeah, Bailey … I was interested. I was always interested."

He could feel her smile. "Really?" She gave his hand a slight squeeze. "Always?"

Cody stopped and touched her cheek as gently as he could. "Always, Bailey." They hadn't talked about this, even since the Fourth of July. Almost as if it had been enough that they'd found something special together. Like they didn't need to define it or analyze it or wonder about why it hadn't happened sooner. Not until now. "Every moment … every day."

She smiled, and for a moment it seemed like they would kiss again. The electricity between them, the connection was enough to stop his breathing. The air was cooling, and the deeper they got into the woods the less the fading sun cast light on the path. He wanted to talk more about this, but not here, with darkness falling around them. What if there really were snakes out here? They didn't bother him, but he'd never forgive himself if something happened to her. "I think the turtles are a few yards up."

The stream was on their right, and Cody led her off the path toward the water. He slipped his arm around her waist, the two of them standing shoulder-to-shoulder. "Keep quiet. We might hear them moving."

Bailey snuggled against him, waiting — the air around them silent except for a subtle rustle of leaves overhead. Suddenly, further on a little, came the sound of something splashing into the water. Bailey gasped. "Was that a turtle or a snake?"

"Snakes aren't that loud." He kept from laughing, since she was serious. "It's gotta be the turtles. Maybe a couple of them." They kept walking, slowly, softly, and there in the last remaining rays of sunlight were two turtles swimming in the stream.

"Oh," Bailey whispered. "They're so cute."

"They are. That's why there aren't lots of them left in the countryside. People take them home for pets."

"They like it out here." Bailey rested her head on Cody's shoulder. "They look happy."

He smiled. "Sort of like they're smiling."

"Exactly." She giggled softly.

For a few minutes they stayed, watching the turtles swim together, and then exit onto a bank at the other side of the creek. When the turtles were out of sight, Cody led her back to the path. He wanted to kiss her so badly, here in the woods amidst the wonder of the turtles and the seclusion of the trees. But something about making that sort of move didn't feel right. Especially with the questions Bailey had. She deserved his conversation first.

They were on the edge of the woods, with the clearing and their bikes in sight, when Cody spotted a fallen log. He pointed to it. "Let's sit a minute."

Side by side they sat, hands joined, their bodies close. The humidity had let up, and the slightest damp chill filled the air — a first hint of the impending fall. Cody enjoyed the warmth of her there next to him. He took a full breath and looked at her, straight into her heart. "You mentioned Iraq ... how you hoped I'd been thinking about you when I was there."

"Yeah. It was a fantasy, I guess." Despite the shadows that fell across her face, her eyes shone with a depth that was unmistakable. "Before you left ... I don't know, I thought you and I found something special."

"We did." Cody wasn't ready to tell her he silently cried into his pillow all the way to the airport when he shipped out, but it was time she knew a few of the details of that time in his life. "I thought about you constantly. Back when we were writing to each other."

"I remember that." Her eyes took on a faraway look. "I was so worried. I prayed for you every day." She shivered a little. "I'll never forget hearing that you were missing. After a while I thought ..." she looked down and for a long time she said nothing. When she lifted her eyes to his, they were flooded with unshed tears. "I thought I'd never see you again."

She didn't have to say it, but the truth remained. It was after that time — after he escaped life as a prisoner of war — that Cody's letters grew further apart, his tone more distant. Eventually Bailey started spending more time with Tim. By the time Cody returned to Bloomington, Bailey had a boyfriend. None of that mattered now, because here they were. But still Cody struggled to explain why he'd distanced himself. The truth was, he didn't think Bailey deserved him battered and broken. His baggage was too great.

He sighed. "When they captured me, I believed every single day I'd find a way out." An intensity filled his voice, passion and pain over the memory of that time. "I couldn't stand up in my cell, couldn't straighten my legs or raise my arms. They beat us every day. Gave us some sort of watered down cereal and crusts of moldy bread."

Bailey slid her hand up his arm and held on, clinging to him. "I hate that. I can't picture you trapped that way."

"At night there were rats." He looked straight ahead, seeing life the way it had been those lonely weeks. "You could hear them in the dark, scurrying on the floor. Some of the guys wanted to give up, so that was the other part. Keeping them strong, making them believe." He spared her the graphic details, because that time was behind him. He would tell her someday, if the two of them stayed together. But for now she needed to know only one thing. He shifted so he could see her better. Then he brought his hand to her cheek. "God was with me, that was my constant hope."

Her expression told him she had no idea what was coming.

"Every day, every long night — not for a single moment did I think I'd die there. I prayed and I always believed I'd get out." He lifted her chin with the crook of his finger. Their eyes met, and after a few seconds he watched her fears ease some. "You know why?"

She shook her head.

"Because of you." He hadn't intended the conversation to get so intense, but she needed to know. She was right; he'd kept his feelings from her for a very long time. He was finished believing he wasn't good enough for Bailey Flanigan. God had brought them together, and now nothing could make him leave. He would fight for her, stand by her, and here ... here he would tell her how he felt because he loved her that much.

"Me?" Her voice was barely a whisper. She searched his face, not believing him. "You thought about me?"

"I wasn't sure we'd ever have this." He brought her hand to his lips and kissed her fingers. "But if I could see you again, spend an afternoon with you again, I was going to find my way out."

"Cody ..." Tears filled her voice. "Why didn't you tell me?" The sky was dusk now, the pinks and blues faded to charcoal gray. The early evening shadows created an intimacy they hadn't shared together since the Fourth. "You came home and I thought ... I thought you'd changed. That you didn't care about me the way you did before. I wasn't sure you ever cared in the first place."

"I cared." He wasn't sure if he should kiss her, but the timing seemed right, one of the only ways he could let her know how he felt then, how he felt now. He drew closer to her until his lips found hers. The kiss was marked with a passion and longing, a desperation ... because what if he hadn't made it home? He drew back and let himself get lost in her eyes again. "I always cared."

"Mmm." She returned his kiss, bringing her hand up alongside his face and pushing her fingers into his hair. The kiss was slow and filled with emotion, the years of wondering answered in this single moment. She drew back and her eyes were so blue, so full of love. "All that time?" She kissed him again, briefly and the moment was interrupted by a ripple of her sweet laughter. "Really?"

"Really." He resisted the desire to kiss her again, longer this time. Her touch reminded him he still had to be careful. No matter how much control he thought he had, he couldn't let his desire get ahead of him. He kissed her one last time, letting his fingers linger alongside her pretty face. For a long time he looked at her. "Sometimes I can't believe this is really happening."

"Me, either." Her tears from earlier were gone, and her eyes danced.

Cody could feel his resistance fading, so before he could find a reason to stay he stood and helped her to her feet. "We have to get back."

"Okay." But instead of heading toward the bikes, she turned to him and hugged him, laying her head on his chest. "Thank you." Her eyes found his once more. "For telling me."

"There's more." He could feel himself regaining control as they walked slowly down the gravel path. He smiled at her. "But we have time."

"We do, don't we?" She grinned at him. Then after a brief hesitation, she turned and raced ahead. "First one home's a triathlete."

Cody laughed and it cost him a few seconds. By the time he reached his bike, Bailey was already pedaling up the hill, lowered over the handlebars once more, pushing herself toward home. Cody let her keep the lead, because he wanted to savor everything that had just happened, the conversation, the closeness they shared. Their kiss. They had found something rare and special these past few months. They had laughter and longing — and a faith that could get them through whatever tomorrow held. And they had something that made every day better than the last.

They had time.

Four

NOT ONCE SINCE SHE'D FIRST STEPPED FOOT in the adoption agency had Andi Ellison wavered about her decision to give up her baby, but today was bound to be difficult. There was no way around it. Today she and her mom would walk into the doctor's office where she would have her second ultrasound. The first had shown her the baby's heartbeat.

This one would tell her if she were carrying a boy or a girl.

"How're you feeling?" Her mom was driving and already they were halfway to Indianapolis.

"It's weird." Andi put her hand on her stomach. "The baby's moving more today." She looked at her mom. "I guess it's making me think." She was five months along, and her belly was growing, pushing against her dance pants and making jeans no longer an option.

"You're still sure?" It was the question her mom and dad never asked, the one they all walked around and didn't mention. But here ... on the way to this very key appointment, it was time. If her mom didn't ask the question, no one would.

Not even Andi.

"I think so." She spread her fingers across her middle and thought about the little life growing inside her. Yes, the child was Taz's baby, and in that sense she could let go. He had kept his distance since the day he walked out of her life and even now — when he knew about the baby — he didn't care enough to even ask how she was doing. She could give up Taz's baby, for sure. She'd already picked the adoptive family — the husband and wife who had looked so much like Katy and Dayne Matthews — Luke and Reagan and their kids, Tommy and Malin. Andi still didn't know their last names, and she hadn't yet showed their photopage to her parents. But they were the family she was sure would take her baby.

At least that's how she thought she felt.

"Honey," Lisa Ellison's voice was soft, not wanting to push her daughter too far on the topic. "Are you doubting this? The adoption?"

"I don't know." Andi sighed. The part she hadn't acknowledged until the past few weeks, when she began feeling the baby move inside her, was the obvious: the baby was hers too. Her firstborn child. She ran her thumbs over her firm stomach. Her mom was still waiting for an answer, and she shifted in her seat so she could see her better. "It's harder. Feeling the baby move makes me realize ... my daughter or son is growing inside me."

"It's an amazing feeling." Her mom reached over and took hold of her hand. "I remember when you were that small, the fluttering ... realizing I was finally going to be a mother."

"Do you think about the babies you lost?" Andi had thought often lately about her lost siblings — the babies her mom had lost through miscarriage.

"Of course." Her mom kept her eyes on the road, but she could see a shine that hadn't been there before. "We wanted four kids or five. But after three miscarriages ... all of them so late in the pregnancies ... It was time." She looked sad, like she still carried the loss with her. "The doctor told us we were done." Her chin trembled a little and she shrugged one shoulder. "That was that."

Andi had never talked about it. She didn't know about the miscarriages at all until their last year in Indonesia. Andi was fifteen and even then her parents hadn't talked about the details. "They were all boys, right?"

"They were." Lisa smiled, but her eyes still showed her sorrow. "I like knowing that one day you'll meet them. Your little brothers."

For a while they were quiet, and she wondered about the boys — the three that were lost. Maybe if they'd lived, Andi never would've gone to Indiana University. She might've stayed home so she could be part of their lives, and she never would've met Taz. Never would've been in this situation. It was a loss she hadn't truly felt until now. She gave her mom's hand a squeeze that told her without words how sorry she was for her heartache. For the loss their family had spent a lifetime living with.

"I remember when you told me about losing the babies, how they were all boys," Andi looked at the highway ahead, but all she could see was herself, the way she was back then, so sure she could solve any problem. "I figured one day I'd have a whole houseful of boys. All the boys you never got to raise, all the brothers I never got to have. And somehow that would make up for it."

"You can't make up for my pain," her mom kept her eyes on the road, but she softly squeezed Andi's hand.

"I guess." She smiled at the memory of her innocent, all-believing self at that age. "You know what?"

"What, sweetheart?" Her mom put both hands on the wheel again.

"I'd still like a houseful of boys." She looked down, suddenly aware that whether she was carrying a girl or boy, this baby would not be part of her future picture. "When the time's right, I mean."

Her mom's smile was still laced with sadness, because she clearly understood. "And your dad and I will live right next door."

They spent the rest of the drive talking about her dad's movies. The upcoming filming of *Unlocked* and the theatrical release for *The Last Letter*. Her dad was meeting with Dayne Matthews this afternoon, working out movie details and waiting to hear news about Andi's appointment. The conversation made the time fly and in no time they were at the clinic.

An arrangement between the adoption agency and a top-notch medical clinic a few miles away meant that Andi's care was paid for. It was why they made this trek for her appointments. So far the staff had been very compassionate and sensitive to what Andi was going through. They regularly talked about her decision to give her baby up for adoption, assuring her that she could still keep her baby if she chose.

"Andi," a young technician named Oksana stepped into the waiting room only seconds after they arrived. She'd taken part in Andi's visits before, and her smile was pleasant and understanding. "You and your mom can follow me."

Andi nodded. *I'm doing the right thing ... isn't that so, God? You alone could've reached down from heaven and stopped me from ending this baby's life. So this is what I'm supposed to do, right? Give the baby away ... ? But then why do I feel this way?*

Daughter, I am with you ... always.

I have to believe that ... God's with me. He's with me right here, right now. She breathed deeply as she stood. And when she had gathered her strength, she followed the woman. This was the right choice ... it had to be. The knowledge gave every appointment here purpose and meaning, but this one especially.

As she prepared for the ultrasound, as she switched into a gown and laid down on the table, Andi remembered the time three months ago when she went to the crisis pregnancy center in Bloomington for her first ultrasound. How wonderful, this technology that could inform a woman of the truth about the baby inside her. She had talked to her friend Ashley Baxter several times since she'd come home to live with her parents, and she'd thanked Ashley for talking to her parents about her pregnancy. She and Ashley had even thought up ways Andi could help teenage girls better understand the importance of abstinence.

Andi stretched out on the table and noticed again how tight her stomach felt, the strange way it rose to a firm bump near her belly button. In this position, she could easily feel the flutterings her mother had talked about in the car, the way the baby seemed to be gradually exploring his or her surroundings.

The ultrasound wouldn't take long. Oksana entered the room and prepared the machine, tapping a number of buttons and switches. "How've you been feeling?"

"Good." Andi's answer was quick, but honest. "I'm not nauseous anymore."

"The second trimester is usually the easiest." Oksana looked to be in her mid-twenties. She grinned at Andi and then at her mother, sitting a few feet away. "That, and we've all been praying for you."

Andi smiled. Like most people at this doctor's office, Oksana seemed to have a strong faith in God and an easy way of sharing it. "Wait till you see what this ultrasound machine can do." Oksana worked another few switches. "In a minute or so you'll be looking right into the face of your baby."

"Technology has improved." Andi's mother focused on the moniter. "When I was pregnant with Andi, we could barely tell her head from her feet."

"Well, let's take a look." Oksana positioned a wand over Andi's stomach.

The anticipation made Andi's heart race, and she had to remember to breathe. Gradually and then more quickly images began to appear on the screen. Fully shaped little arms and shoulders, feet and legs. And then Oksana turned to Andi. "Do you want to know what you're having?"

Andi held her breath. In some ways she wanted to stop the information from ever reaching her heart. Because once she knew, the baby's existence would feel so much more real ... the loss she was facing in choosing adoption, so much more real. Andi's throat felt dry as she nodded. "Yes, please. I'd like to know."

"It used to be we couldn't always tell, but the way your baby's positioned, this one's easy." Her smile was tender, mixed with the understanding that this news was bittersweet. "You're having a boy, Andi."

A boy.

Andi had expected this day to be tougher than any since she'd decided to give her baby up. But she hadn't expected the rush of emotions washing over her now. She was having a boy, the way she'd dreamed of having her firstborn be a boy since that long ago conversation with her mother. Without realizing she was crying, two tears slid down the sides of her face. "Are ... are you sure?"

"These ultrasounds are much more dependable than they used to be." Oksana adjusted the wand and a better view came into focus. "This little one is a boy."

Andi looked at her mother, at the tears on her cheeks. The news seemed to be hitting her the same way, with an emotional impact neither of them had expected. Andi stretched out her arm and took hold of her mother's hand. She turned her attention again to the monitor as Oksana moved the wand and suddenly there he was, the face of her little boy. His eyes were closed, and he had one small fist pressed peacefully to his cheek. Andi heard herself utter the softest gasp, because the image was remarkably clear, as if her little son were looking at her through a window.

"He's beautiful," she whispered. Another set of tears fell hot and wet along the sides of her face. "Mom, isn't he so beautiful?"

Her mom pressed her free hand to her lips and stifled what seemed like a sudden, soft couple of sobs. She couldn't talk, so she only nodded, her eyes never leaving the baby's face.

Andi looked again at the image of the little boy, and she saw him move his hand, almost as if he were stretching. It couldn't be, but his face seemed to smile at her, telling her thank you for letting him live, and that he couldn't wait to get out and see her face to face. The notion was ridiculous, of course. But looking into his face, that's how Andi felt. She blinked back her tears so she could see better. He didn't look anything like Taz, at least not at this point. He had her cheekbones and nose, and his fingers looked chunky and strong, not slender like Taz's. Like maybe he'd be tall and athletic the way her father was.

Oksana was giving them this time, allowing the wand to linger so Andi and her mother could stare at the baby as long as they wanted. She didn't speak, since clearly the moment was personal.

"He ... he looks like me," Andi glanced at her mom again. "Don't you think?"

"He does." She pressed her fingers to her eyes and coughed a few times, until she seemed to have her voice again. "He looks like your little brothers. They all ... when they were stillborn, they all had that same nose."

Andi was so sure about giving her baby up for adoption that she hadn't allowed herself to feel maternal. She wasn't an expectant mother so much as she was a college girl who'd made a terrible mistake. She'd given up her virginity, and now she would pay for that choice all the days of her life. Especially now, when people tended to stare at her when they were out around town. Up until now, her body was merely carrying this baby to term so that someone else could take him as their own.

But here, watching her baby move and reposition himself inside her, looking at the softness of his cheeks and the definition of his face, Andi ached to hold him. The feeling was stronger than anything she'd ever known, a longing and a love that wasn't learned and couldn't be reasoned away. It simply was.

Oksana pushed another button on the machine to take several photos of the baby, his face and his spine, his toes and his midsection. She printed them, placed them in a folder, and told Andi the doctor would be in to see her in a few minutes. Before she left, she came to Andi's side, handed her a tissue, and looked into her eyes, her compassion tangible. "Have you chosen a family?"

"I have." Andi sniffed and wiped her nose. "The agency is informing them this week."

"I'd encourage you at this point to talk to your parents, really pray about your decision." She looked at Andi's mother and then back at Andi. "Seeing your baby this way makes the idea of giving birth much more real." She hesitated, and when she spoke again there was a catch in her voice. "I was adopted. My birth mom was a teenage girl ... too young to be a mom. I'll be forever grateful to her for having the courage to let me live. And the courage to give me up." She sniffed, finding control again. "But it's a very difficult decision ... it's not for everyone, and once you make the choice, once you sign over your rights, there's no going back."

Andi squeezed her eyes shut and tried to keep her building tears from overtaking her. She wasn't ready to be a mother, not for years. When that time came, she wanted to be married to a man like her daddy or a man like Dayne Matthews. She wanted to feel as certain about her decision now as she had when she first walked into the adoption agency three months ago.

But all she could see was the face of her baby.

She nodded and breathed in a few quick times from her nose, struggling for composure. "Th-thank you."

Oksana patted Andi's hand and then left the room. Andi turned her attention to her mom, who was still wiping at her eyes, the impact of the images still fresh for both of them. Her mom released her hand, stood, and found fresh tissues. She handed a few to Andi, and helped her to a sitting position. "He's perfect. Absolutely perfect."

"I know." Confusion racked Andi's heart, and questions assaulted her. What did this mean, these feelings inside her? Was she supposed to raise her baby after all? Did her parents want her to keep him? She had no time to ask a single one, because there was a knock at the door and Dr. Wilmington walked in.

"Andi ..." he smiled. "How are you?"

She started to answer, but then a sound which was more a cry than a laugh came from her. She must've looked like a wreck, her eyes red and swollen. "I'm fine." She dabbed the tissue at her eyes and nose again. "I wasn't ready for that ... how clearly I could see him."

"It's amazing." He was a young doctor, mid-thirties, maybe. "This is the stage when a lot of young pregnant women rethink their decision to give a baby up for adoption."

"Do a lot of them change their minds?" Andi's mom still had red cheeks and bleary eyes, but she was more composed now. "I think the reality of the little guy, how clearly we could see him ... it caught us both off guard."

"Yes." Dr. Wilmington leaned back against a nearby wall, unrushed in his response. "Lots of moms change their mind at this point. We believe the ultrasound is a helpful tool in guiding a woman to make the right choice. The decision best for her and her family, best for the baby."

"Do women ... do the ones who give their babies up, do they regret it later?" Andi had never even wondered before. "From what you've seen?"

"I'll be honest, Andi. It's a tough decision either way. It'll stay with you all your life no matter what you do." He crossed his arms, his expression thoughtful. "The young women with family support and a stronger faith handle their decision better — whichever way it goes."

Andi appreciated his answer, but she wanted more than that. "But do you think it's possible to give ... to give up a baby and feel at peace? Like it was the right decision?"

"Absolutely." The doctor smiled. "We've seen many beautiful adoptions happen over the years. Truly, it's one of the bravest decisions a young woman can make. That is, if she's not ready to be a mother."

Suddenly Andi's head was spinning, because maybe she was ready to be a mom. She was almost twenty, so she was old enough, right? And just because she wasn't married and the timing wasn't convenient, didn't mean she shouldn't step up to the responsibility. "It's … a lot to think about."

"It is." He reached for her chart. "That's why we encourage our clients not to inform the adoptive family until a little later in the pregnancy. When the decision has been made and it's one the birthmother has lived with for a while."

Andi let that idea sink in while Dr. Wilmington performed her checkup and looked over the ultrasound. Maybe she should call the adoption agency and ask them to wait before telling Luke and Reagan. At least a few weeks. The doctor finished his exam and crossed his arms, his eyes kind. "You and the baby are very healthy. Everything's on schedule."

"Good." Andi smiled, but all she could think was that something had changed in the past hour. The peace of mind she had about giving up her baby was no longer an assumed emotion. The images of her baby son had rocked her world off its axis, and Andi wasn't sure how to right it again.

On the way home Andi had planned to have her mother stop by the adoption agency. She wanted to show her the picture of the family, the one she'd chosen back on her first visit. But as her mom neared the driveway of the agency, she raised her brow in Andi's direction. "Still want to stop?"

Andi put her hand over her stomach. The baby was moving again, touching the underside part of her belly with those now familiar hands of his. "No … not today." She couldn't make eye contact with her mother. If she did, her mom would see right through her, at just how difficult the decision had become. Again her mom didn't push, didn't ask if Andi was sure or probe her about why she'd changed her mind. The only answer needed was the one Andi held in her hand the rest of the way back home to Bloomington.

The ultrasound photos of her son.

Five

BAILEY COULD BARELY CONCENTRATE ON HER CLASSES that September morning, because this was the day. Her screen test for Jeremiah Productions was set for later that afternoon. She still hurt from the failed Broadway audition, but in the last few weeks she'd allowed herself to get excited about this opportunity. Her mom planned to go with her, and both of them agreed the audition would probably be for little more than a featured extra role. But that didn't matter. The audition would take her one step closer to doing what she loved: performing. If she kept moving ahead, kept dancing and singing and finding small acting roles, then one day she'd make it on Broadway. She had to believe that.

Sunshine streamed through the trees as Bailey pulled out of the Indiana University parking lot and headed a block west to Starbucks. Tuesdays were often the days she visited Andi, since they both finished class by noon that day. Lately she'd fallen into a routine, picking up a couple decaf lattes and bringing them to Andi's house. It was one way she could let Andi know how much she cared.

Andi had talked to her last night about how she was no longer sure she wanted to give her baby up for adoption. So especially today, Bailey wanted to make herself available. That way Andi had someone other than her parents who could listen and offer input. Not that Bailey had a strong opinion one way or another. If she'd made the same mistakes and gotten pregnant, she was pretty sure she couldn't give her baby up. But then she knew lots of people whose lives were forever changed for the better because a brave young woman was able to give up her baby. Recently Bailey had even heard a well-known Christian singer include, as part of his life story, a thank you to his birthmother for giving him up.

So Bailey didn't have the answers, but she loved Andi and she could at least listen. Hopefully today that would be enough. She dashed into Starbucks and bought a latte for herself and at the last minute, she changed Andi's order to a decaf green tea frappuccino. Andi didn't have the sweet drink often, but it was her favorite. Three miles down the road, Bailey pulled into the driveway of the ranch house where Andi lived with her parents.

As Bailey parked, she remembered the first time she reconnected with her friend after Andi's mom called and told Bailey what had happened — that Andi was indeed pregnant and had been about to have an abortion when God intervened. The story was absolute proof the Lord had worked a miracle to stop Andi from doing something she would regret all her life. The day after Andi came home from Indianapolis with her parents, Bailey drove over and the two of them took a walk around Andi's new neighborhood.

"It's my fault," Andi told her then. "I should've listened to you about Taz ... about the parties I was going to ... all of it." Andi's eyes clouded with shame. "I feel so stupid."

"We all do stupid things once in a while." Bailey thought about her decision to date Tim, the months she'd gone in a relationship she should've ended long ago. "That's why we need a Savior."

"I know." Andi's expression looked pained. "I've missed Jesus so much this past year. It was like ... I don't know, like I wanted to do things my own way. I didn't want anyone telling me what to do — not even God."

Bailey had let that sit for a few seconds as they kept walking, their pace slow. "And now?"

"Now?" Andi stood straighter, her expression determined.

"Now I want to follow His plan every day, for the rest of my life." She crossed her arms tight across her stomach. "I sure made a mess of things on my own."

"You aren't the only one, Andi. Jesus forgives us."

Andi smiled. "I'm holding onto that."

They talked some then, about the experience at the abortion clinic, how maybe God sent an angel to stop Andi from having an abortion. Then they talked about how strained their friendship had been last semester. "Taz didn't like you." Andi winced a little. She had never admitted that before.

"I'm not surprised." Bailey pictured the young student producer, the way he wouldn't make eye contact with her, and his way of having somewhere to go if Bailey walked up. "He didn't like what I stood for."

"Exactly." Andi looked down for a long moment. "Bailey, I'm sorry. You were a friend to me, and I … I took you for granted. I rebelled against everything good and right and true. Even Rachel and you."

Rachel Baugher had been Andi's best friend from high school, a girl who had been killed in a tragic car accident just after graduating. Bailey figured losing Rachel was part of why Andi had rebelled in the first place, but that hadn't been the time to talk about it, and Andi hadn't brought Rachel up again in their past several Tuesdays together.

She took the drinks from her front console, shut her car door behind her, and hurried up Andi's walkway. Her friend's mother answered the door, her eyes deep with gratitude. "Hello, Bailey."

"Hi, Mrs. Ellison." Bailey stepped inside. The early afternoon temperature was in the high sixties, too warm for a coat. But still, there was a chill in the air that made Bailey grateful for her hot drink.

"Thank you for coming by. Andi looks so forward to this."

She pointed to the back bedroom. "She's home from class, in her room."

This was the usual routine. Andi was determined to finish the semester with strong grades in each of her five classes, but sometimes when she got home she was more tired than usual. She'd stretch out on her bed and nap for half an hour until Bailey got there.

She tiptoed down the hall, a drink in each hand, and peeked her head into Andi's room. Sunshine flooded the room, but Andi's eyes were closed. "You awake, or should I go?"

"Don't go." Andi stretched and slowly sat up. "I can sleep later." She smiled at Bailey and patted the spot next to her on the bed.

"Here." Bailey handed her friend the cold drink.

"You don't have to do that, buy me a drink all the time." Andi took the green tea frappuccino. "But thanks. It means a lot."

"It's no big deal." She held out her paper cup and tapped it against the plastic one in Andi's hands. "Here's to another Tuesday."

"Because God keeps getting me through."

"Exactly." Bailey kicked off her shoes and sat at the end of the bed.

For a moment, they sipped their drinks and neither of them said anything. Something about Andi's attitude felt a little off. She studied Bailey for half a second. "Cute jeans." Andi's compliment sounded laced with something less than sincere. Not that she was bitter, or even resentful. Just a little jealous, maybe, like Andi was realizing her situation more now. Maybe because she was showing. Even still, she smiled, maybe trying to lighten the moment again, but it fell short of her eyes. "Are they new?"

Bailey nodded. "Anthropologie. Bought them yesterday." She tried to find the right smile in response. "After January you have to get some. They're super comfortable." Again, the silence

KAREN KINGSBURY

between them was more awkward than usual. Bailey shifted, restless. "Right?"

"I don't know." Andi's eyes looked distant. She was quiet for awhile again. "Do you ever think about it? You and I are in such different places now." She lowered her drink. "I'm not thinking about jeans."

The comment stung, and Bailey considered defending herself. She wasn't trying to be flip. After all, it was Andi who had brought up the jeans. "Sorry." Bailey sipped her coffee. Sometimes it was hard being with Andi. She was right ... they were in different places now. "I didn't mean to frustrate you."

Andi looked out the window and shrugged one shoulder. "I know." She sighed. "It's not you. I have a lot on my mind." She looked at Bailey, and again there was something sad in her eyes. "I have the ultrasound pictures."

Bailey felt guilty for taking Andi's attitude personally. Of course she wasn't thinking about jeans. "Can I see them?"

Andi reached for a folder on her bedside table. "You won't believe how clear they are." Her voice sounded lighter. "It's like there was a window into my stomach or something."

When they had talked last night, Andi mentioned that the ultrasound made her pregnancy so much more real. From what Bailey could tell, her friend was doubting her decision to give the baby up. Bailey took the folder, opened it, and felt her eyes grow wide. "Wow ..." She looked at Andi. "It's like a photograph. I was eight when Ricky was born, and I remember seeing my mom's ultrasound pictures." She looked at the first photo again, a picture of the baby's face. "But they weren't like this." Even with a quick glance there was no denying that the baby was Andi's. "He looks just like you."

"My mom says he looks like my baby pictures." Her tone was soft, more maternal than before. "And like my three brothers who died before they were born."

Bailey stared at the photo, at the clarity of the lines and definition of his face, and she understood why Andi would be struggling now. The baby had to feel so much more real with pictures like this. Then knowing the child you were carrying looked so much like you — how would that feel? Bailey sorted through the other photos and handed the folder back to Andi. "So you're thinking about keeping him?"

"I'm not sure." Andi set the folder down and pulled one knee up to her chest. "I guess it's not *that*, so much as I can't imagine giving him away. One day soon he'll be born and instead of a picture there he'll be. A tiny little boy who looks just like me. They'll place him in my arms, and I'll feel this crazy connection." Her voice faded but she didn't look away. "How am I supposed to let him go after that?"

Bailey had no answers. The waters Andi was navigating were far too unknown for her to offer any real opinion. "Do your parents know how you feel?"

"I think they'd like me to keep him." Andi tilted her head, pensive. "They haven't said that exactly, but you know ... my mom was with me at the ultrasound. We were both crying." Andi put her hand on her stomach. "Just thinking about having to say goodbye to him."

"What about the adoptive family?" Bailey kept her questions kind and unrushed. She didn't want to push Andi, especially when she was clearly hurting. "Do they know about you yet?"

"I've told the agency about my choice, but we haven't arranged a meeting yet. I haven't signed anything. The family's supposed to find out soon."

"Hmmm." Bailey's heart ached for her friend. She took a few swallows of her latte. "There are no easy answers."

They talked awhile about the physical changes Andi was going through, how wild it was to feel a baby moving inside her and what it was like to know God was knitting him together a little more every day. And they talked about the classes they were taking. Andi wanted to go into social work or public speaking, so she could use her story to help girls realize the value of staying abstinent.

"I have a feeling I'll finish up in Los Angeles somewhere." Andi hadn't mentioned that before now. She took a long sip from her drink. "My parents talk about moving there after this movie. I think it'd be good. A change of scenery. Whether I give up the baby or not."

Their conversation lasted another half hour, and it was time for Bailey to go.

"You have that screen test today, right?" Andi stood and hugged Bailey, but the struggle was back in her voice. "My dad mentioned it this morning."

"I do." They shared a look, one tinged by the regret that on a day like this Andi should've been going to the screen test too. "It's probably an extra part, but still . . ."

"I got the feeling it might be more." Andi bit her lip, and for a long moment she seemed to wrestle with herself, fighting the jealousy or regret. Whatever she was dealing with. But finally she grinned, and the look in her eyes lightened for the first time that morning. She hugged Bailey once more. "You go get 'em, Bailey Flanigan. I'll pray for you."

"Thanks." Bailey still felt the bittersweet reality of this time between them, the different directions their lives were headed. She made a silly face as she stepped toward the bedroom door. "And I'll pray for you. About your decision."

"Thanks." Andi's smile faded. "If only God would text me what He wants me to do."

"Yeah," Bailey angled her head, trying to imagine being in Andi's situation. "I wish it were that easy."

On her way out, Bailey thanked Andi's mom and drove home to drop off her books, change clothes, and grab something to eat.

She was in her room getting ready when Cody called. "I finished class early, so I had to call." His voice still made her knees weak. "I'm praying for you."

"Thanks." She sat slowly on the edge of her mattress and for a minute she told him about Andi. "It was weird, like we were strangers, almost."

"She has a lot on her mind."

"That's what I told myself." She still felt a little guilty about the earlier conversation, even if she couldn't figure out exactly why. "I guess it's bound to be awkward once in a while."

They talked a few more minutes about his classes and how he was excited about graduating. He'd increased his class-load the last few semesters and now he was slated to finish his degree in education a year from January. After that he would go for his teaching credential so he could coach and teach like her dad had always done. Cody was about to start his first full season as assistant coach for Clear Creek High, and he loved every minute. Already he had confided that he could see himself coaching football forever.

"I miss you," Bailey wished she could see him, but they were both too busy today. "Have a great practice. I'll be thinking of you."

"Miss you, too. Call me when you know anything." His tone was warm, and she could hear the smile in his voice.

A quick fifteen minutes passed, and Bailey was sitting breathless in the passenger seat of her mother's Suburban, headed to the production office where Andi's dad and Dayne Matthews would be waiting for her.

"Are you nervous?" Her mom was planning to stay with her if possible.

"So much." Bailey laughed. She thought about the audition in New York and how great the disappointment had been. But then she sat straighter in the car and shook off the memory. This was a new day, a different moment. She would shine for God, no matter what the outcome. But just as quickly the doubts crept back. "What if God doesn't want me to perform?" She turned to her mom. "Maybe He wants me to do something else. Be a nurse or something."

Her mom smiled and touched Bailey's arm. "Sweetheart, rejection is part of this business. You might try a hundred times before the door opens." She paused. "That doesn't mean it's not God's will."

"True." Bailey knew that, of course. She'd heard it from her professors and from Katy Hart Matthews and so many others. But she didn't see herself knocking a hundred times. At some point she would want to get married and raise a family, and performing would only be a dream she'd had as a younger girl.

But today the dream was very much alive, the possibility still very real. She kept that in mind as they reached the office for Jeremiah Productions and her mom parked the car. Before they went in, her mom held her hand and prayed for her, that God would shine through her acting and she would rely on His strength to do her best in the coming hour.

They entered the building, and found a woman sitting at a desk. "You're here to read for Dayne and Keith?"

Bailey summoned her courage. "Yes, ma'am. My name's Bailey Flanigan." She turned to her mom. "Is it okay if my mom waits for me?"

"Definitely." She nodded to a row of chairs against the wall. "It shouldn't take too long. Half an hour, maybe." The woman looked over a list, and when she found Bailey's name she smiled and checked it off. Then she handed Bailey a clipboard with a few sheets of paperwork to fill out. "We'll need your agent's information as well. On the last page."

"Agent?" Bailey took hold of the clipboard and blinked. She

looked at her mom and then back at the woman behind the desk. "I don't have an agent."

"Really?" The woman frowned at the list of names in front of her. "You're reading for a lead. Most of you have agents at this level."

A lead? Bailey's heart fluttered wildly in her chest. "There must be a mistake ..." She stared at the woman's clipboard, trying to see if her name could possibly be there. "No one said anything about a lead."

"Hmmm ... Bailey Flanigan?" The woman found her name again. "That's you, right?"

"Yes, ma'am." Bailey felt dizzy. She didn't dare look at her mother or she might scream from the thrill working its way through her. A lead? Could this really be happening?

The woman smiled again. "According to the producers, you're here to read for a lead."

Bailey almost dropped the clipboard. Instead she remembered to smile and give a quick nod. "Okay, thank you. I'll fill out the form, but yeah, no agent. Is that okay?"

"I'm pretty sure." The woman shrugged. "I guess you can talk to the producers about it. They'll be ready for you in a few minutes." She directed them to the chairs.

Once they were there, and when the woman left her desk and disappeared down a hallway, Bailey grabbed hold of her mother's arm. "Did you hear that?"

"A lead part!" Her mom kept her voice to a whisper. "No one told us."

"I know. Now I'm freaking out." She stood, walked to the door and back again, shaking out her arms and exhaling in short bursts. "A lead part? Seriously, Mom? That has to be a mistake, right?"

"Bailey," her mom laughed quietly. "Get a grip, sweetheart. Sit down and fill out the paperwork."

"Okay, okay." Bailey squealed, but she did as she was told. But she could barely draw a full breath, barely remember her address. She was reading for a lead part? Was this really happening? And was this why God had shut the door on her Broadway dreams the first time around? Another thought hit her. What if the woman at the desk was wrong, what if she had Bailey confused with someone else?

Dear God, if this is real, give me the ability. I can't do something this big, not without your help ... please, God, be with me.

I am with you always, Daughter ... Do not be afraid or terrified, for I will go with you.

The truth echoed through her and brought a sense of peace and certainty. God wouldn't take her into a situation where He wouldn't also provide. He'd walked with her through the Broadway audition, but clearly that hadn't been His plan for her. At least not then. So maybe this was where He wanted her to be. She filled out the forms, handed them back to the woman, and in a blur of confusion and quiet prayer, Dayne Matthews stepped into the waiting area and grinned at them. "Hey, guys ... come on back."

"Me, too?" Her mom looked surprised.

"Sure." Dayne's smile lit the room. It was easy to see how he'd been America's top leading man for so many years. "You won't get in the way."

Both Bailey and her mother stood, and Dayne led them down a hallway to a boxy room. Andi's father and a middle-aged woman were sitting at a long table, with photos and notes spread out before them. They stood when they saw Bailey and her mom enter the room. "Hi ... thanks for coming."

"Thanks for having me." Bailey wasn't sure where to go or what to do. She shook Keith Ellison's hand and did the same with Dayne.

Mr. Ellison explained the woman with them was Eleanor

Ainsworth, casting director for *Unlocked*. He went on to list a few of Ms. Ainsworth's recent films — all of them huge box office hits. "We're glad you're here," she told Bailey, with a polite nod.

Bailey thanked her and then she turned to Mr. Ellison again. "I saw Andi today. She's doing well."

"She is. Thanks, Bailey." Mr. Ellison's smile was genuine. "Your friendship is an answer to all our prayers. Especially now."

Bailey wondered if the casting director was a Christian. If she wasn't, she didn't seem bothered by Mr. Ellison's mention of prayer. Bailey's mom discreetly took a chair in the corner of the room, out of the way. Bailey noticed a camera set up and aimed toward the empty half of the room. She gulped, fighting off her anxiety.

Dayne handed her a script. "Turn to page forty-five, will you, Bailey?"

"Sure." She did as she was asked. With a quick glance, she could easily see a lengthy monologue from a character named Ella. Bailey had read the book *Unlocked* and loved it. She knew immediately Ella was the music student who helps Holden Harris, a boy locked in his own world of autism since he was three years old. The role was indeed a lead and one of the most pivotal in the story.

"Take a minute and read Ella's monologue to yourself." Dayne sat on the edge of the long table. "Then we'd like to film you reading it. I'll play the drama instructor, so you'll have someone to focus on."

Bailey felt her head start to spin. She lowered the script and looked from Dayne to Mr. Ellison. "I ... I thought I was reading for an extra role."

Andi's dad laughed and rubbed his temples. Then he exchanged a look with Dayne. "You didn't tell her?"

"I thought you did." Dayne shot a funny look toward Bailey. "Sorry about that." He shrugged. "I guess you know now. We're looking at about a hundred newer faces, fresher girls who could pull off the role of Ella. We're auditioning ten girls from the university drama department, and Keith and I both wanted to include you in this round."

"Oh." Again her head hurt from the craziness of it all. A hundred girls? All with acting experience? She had no right being nervous then. Nothing could possibly come from those odds. "So … how many have you seen?"

"We've already seen ninety or so girls, screened them in LA." Ms. Ainsworth kept matter-of-fact about this part, not letting on whether they felt they'd found their Ella or not. "Since we're filming here, we wanted to look at local girls too. We're doing that today and tomorrow."

"Okay." Bailey felt faint. Suddenly something occurred to her. Andi would be reading for the part if she wasn't pregnant. No wonder she hadn't been herself today. She stared at the script. *Focus, Bailey … you have to focus.*

Dayne motioned in her direction. "Take your time. We'll give you a couple minutes."

She nodded and focused on the script again. As she did, she realized the enormous odds. Other girls would have agents and resumes, years of experience, sometimes dating back to when they were babies. What experience did Bailey have? A number of stage productions? She didn't even belong here. She'd probably only been given the chance because she was Andi's friend, or because she'd had a small one-line part in *The Last Letter*.

Still, a peace came over her as she began to read the monologue.

How she'd gotten here and why they were screen-testing her was irrelevant. God had placed her here, and she would do her best with the audition. At least then she'd have no regrets, even if she wasn't anywhere near ready for a part this size.

The monologue was touching, and Bailey resonated with it

immediately. Again, because she'd read the book and loved it, she knew which part of the story Ella's monologue came from. Ella was a high school senior making a passionate plea to her drama instructor to let Holden try out for the school musical. It was a section of the novel where Ella explained how the private prison of autism might actually become unlocked through the power of song.

In the few minutes she had to read through the part, Bailey forgot everyone else in the room. When she looked up, Dayne stood and came to her. "You ready?"

"Yes, sir."

Dayne smiled and gave her a private wink, as if to say the *sir* was a little formal for the two of them. Still, with Eleanor Ainsworth here, this was definitely a moment to be as professional as possible. Dayne moved toward the camera. "I'll sit here, off to the side a little with my back to the camera." He took his spot on a barstool, off-center. Like he'd said earlier, his presence here was only meant to give her a point of focus, somewhere to direct her passion. "Roll the cameras."

Ms. Ainsworth stood, went to the camera, and pressed a button. "Rolling."

Dayne looked at Bailey, his eyes offering her a kind of warmth she needed. He made her feel like she was reading for family, which was practically the case anyway. "Okay, say your name and age and the part you're reading for."

Bailey nodded. Then she set the script down on the floor near Dayne and returned to her place in front of the camera. A taped *X* on the floor made it obvious where she was supposed to stand. She looked straight into the camera — the only time it would be appropriate to do so — and she did as she was asked. When she finished, Ms. Ainsworth pointed with her finger, clearly cuing Bailey to begin.

For a quick moment, Bailey couldn't remember anything

she'd just read or what character she was supposed to play or even why she was here. But the flash of terror disappeared as quickly as it hit, and suddenly she was no longer in a small boxy room auditioning before a cold camera, her best friend's father, and two of Hollywood's most powerful people. Instead, everything Katy Hart Matthews had ever taught her about acting came rushing back. And in the time it took to inhale, she was no longer Bailey Flanigan. She was a high school girl, passionate that if the teacher in front of her would only see it her way, Holden might find a way free of his autism.

Bailey paced a few steps away and then back again, allowing her frustration, her passion to become palpable. "Maybe you don't really understand the power of music, Mr. Hawkins." She stopped and made a frustrated sound. "Music like that isn't something out here, something people are merely entertained by." She pressed her fingers to her chest, her eyes locked on Dayne's. "It's in here, where love lives and life begins. Music is to the soul like … like air to the lungs. Holden feels it, I know he does."

Bailey turned, as if she could see Holden standing beside her, rocking slightly, locked in his own world. "I've seen him respond, no matter what his therapists say. He feels it, and now you have to give him a chance. I believe … I really believe that music can reach him where nothing else has. No one else. Not since he was three years old."

The monologue continued, but Bailey couldn't feel anything but the character. The passing of time, the looks from Dayne and Mr. Ellison and the casting director, every possible distraction faded in the fervor of her plea, the realness of her argument. It actually startled her when Ms. Ainsworth finally lifted her hand.

"That's all, Bailey. Thank you."

Bailey exhaled and looked around, suddenly self-conscious. The casting director and Mr. Ellison had their heads together, penciling notes and talking in whispered tones.

Dayne stood and walked to her. "Wow." His eyes told her he was sincerely moved. "Where'd that come from?"

Again she felt slightly embarrassed. She hadn't once stopped to consider how she looked or sounded. Rather she only allowed herself to become the part. "I don't know." She moved her toe in small circles on the floor, adrenaline still racing through her. "I love the book. It's one of the best I've ever read."

"You can tell." He took the script from the floor and walked slowly with her to the table. Once there, the three of them thanked her and told her they'd be in touch. Bailey's mom waited until they were outside the building before she let out a high-pitched muted scream. "Bailey! I couldn't believe that was really you!"

"Seriously?" The thrill coursing through her was so great she thought she could run all the way home and still have the energy to run back again. "I don't know if it was *that* good. I don't have experience for a part like this." She looped her arm around her mom's waist as they walked to the car. "So I let my heart convey the character. I tried not to get in the way. That's how Katy's taught me."

The whole way home her mom marveled at how genuine she'd come across, how sincere and how natural she looked on camera. "You're perfect for Ella. Who would've ever thought?"

"I'm glad you think so." Bailey laughed, not letting her hopes get too high. "Too bad you're not making the decision."

Her mom's enthusiasm settled down a little, and as they stepped into the house she took hold of both Bailey's hands. "Honey, what I saw in there … you have such a gift. I mean, I've seen it before with CKT, and of course you've been training with Katy. But still … that was amazing, sweetheart."

The compliment stayed with her long into the afternoon and, deep inside her, Bailey realized something she hadn't known before the screening. Even as badly as she'd wanted the Broadway part, she had underestimated her passion for performing, for bringing a character to life — whether on stage or in front of a camera. Now she knew better. Whether it took a hundred tries or a thousand ... whether she auditioned in New York or Los Angeles or right here in Bloomington. She would keep trying, keep auditioning. And as her resolve grew, she felt God assuring her in a way that made her soul sing.

Because maybe her dreams of performing were about to come true.

Six

KEITH ELLISON BARELY WAITED UNTIL BAILEY was out the door before he let out a victory whoop and grinned at the rest of his team. "Did you see that?"

"I couldn't catch my breath." Dayne wiped his hand across his damp forehead. "The girl has the most natural talent I've seen in years. Maybe ever." He grabbed her paperwork from the desk and glanced over it. "I mean, my wife's been working with her, but I had no idea. She's had one speaking part in one film and she can bring *that*? On a cold screen test?"

Eleanor was an understated woman. After working with her for the past few weeks, Keith knew she wasn't often effusive about her opinions of actors. She'd rather assess quietly from the back of the room and wait until she'd seen all possible talent before carefully weighing her options and making a decision. But here, for the first time, Eleanor looked visibly rocked. She took off her glasses, set them on the table, and chuckled with a shake of her head. "How much experience did you say she had?"

"Virtually none." Keith stared at Bailey's paperwork. "She doesn't even have a formal resume. Told me earlier she could put one together if I need it."

"If it weren't for Katy, I'm not sure I would've taken a look at her." Dayne went to the camera and hit the rewind button. Attached by a cable was a full-sized monitor; and as he reached the end of Bailey's section, he hit play.

Keith moved closer, anxious to see if the screen would reveal the same level of purity they'd seen in person with Bailey. Her scene began and, sure enough, from the opening few seconds she grabbed the attention of everyone in the room. After a minute, Keith was pretty sure everyone must've felt the way he did — like they'd just found the perfect Ella.

The reel ended and Dayne hit the power switch on the camera. "Well?" His expression asked Keith and Eleanor what they thought.

"I've never seen anyone like her." Eleanor leaned forward, her hands folded on the table in front of her. "She's as authentic as the farmlands in Bloomington ... as charming as a school girl. And there's an innocence about her ..." Eleanor let her voice die off. "You don't see that anymore."

Keith thought about Andi, sitting home with her ultrasound pictures. Eleanor was right. Real innocence was beautiful and refreshing and impossible to imitate. But still the comment stung because of Andi. His little girl would never again be innocent the way Bailey was. He pushed the pain aside and nodded slowly. "Ella needs to be innocent. Her passion needs to be almost child-like."

Keith remembered how they'd seen this with Bailey when she had the featured extra part in *The Last Letter*. "What Bailey has is very special." He leaned against the wall and folded his arms in front of him. "It can't be faked."

"We've seen girls try the whole last week." Eleanor looked from Keith to Dayne. "We can still see the other actresses scheduled for today and tomorrow. And of course we'll need to test Bailey with Brandon Paul." She nodded at Dayne. "Let's check his availability to fly out and have a screen test with her." She looked at her notepad and then at the guys again. "I can't imagine someone more likeable, more genuine walking through those doors. The girl is amazing."

Eleanor stepped out for a lunch run, which gave Keith and Dayne a chance to talk about the next most pressing matter: Brandon Paul's recent spike in tabloid mentions.

Dayne cleared the resumes and headshots for a moment and spread a dozen Hollywood gossip rags across the table. "Look at those headlines."

Keith gripped the edge of the table and studied the pictures and headlines. On one, Brandon was stepping into a black Escalade, his eyes barely opened. He seemed to struggle to keep his balance. The headline read: *'Brandon Takes a Tumble — Star Caught Partying at All Hours.'* Another one had Brandon sitting on a sofa between two voluptuous blondes, both of whom were kissing his cheeks. The picture seemed to imply Brandon was about to have a night that went beyond wild. Over that picture, the headline said: *'Brandon Doubles His Pleasure — Spends the Night with Two Girls Gone Wild.'*

"Great," Keith muttered, sifting through the magazines. Another one of them simply asked: *'Brandon Paul Caught with Cocaine?'* And still another: *'When Will the Partying End?'*

Anger rose in Keith and he straightened, his eyes blazing. "This has to stop."

"I've been telling you." Dayne leaned against the wall, his expression as disgusted as Keith's. "I see the tabs more than you do. I guess with my background, you never stop looking, feeling sorry for the next guy they set their mark on."

"But Brandon isn't a victim. This is his doing."

"That's certainly how it looks." Dayne sifted through the magazines, turning a few of the pages and looking at the photos of Brandon caught in one compromising situation after another. "We used to say back in my acting days, this much smoke and there's bound to be a fire somewhere."

"Or a whole series of them." Keith was still grasping the gravity of the situation. They were a month away from filming, and Brandon was being this crazy in his free time? "Doesn't he get it? *Unlocked* is a Christian film."

"Not in his mind." Dayne frowned. "I talked to his agent

yesterday. They both acknowledge that *Unlocked* was a Christian novel, but the guy told me Brandon's taking the job because the novel was a *New York Times* runaway bestseller, because of the strength of the story. He wanted to be very clear Brandon wouldn't do interviews endorsing the faith views of the author or Jeremiah Productions. He was only taking the part because it stretched him as an actor and because he believed in the book."

Keith remembered back to a feeling he had during the summer when Brandon came out to discuss taking the role. He'd had his doubts about Brandon back then, but he hadn't spoken up. Every time the issue arose, he told himself he was being too critical of the kid. And, while the movie would certainly benefit from a name like Brandon Paul's, certainly Brandon Paul would also benefit from the movie. Brandon could change his ways. If a miracle happened, the young star could even find a genuine faith in God, being surrounded by people with such strong faith. But there was a line between believing they could help Brandon and the very real possibility that his participation could hurt the film's message. With the latest tabloid stories, they were headed to a place where Brandon would make it impossible for Keith — with a clear conscience — to cast him. The way it stood now, people would have to wonder if the Christian producers at Jeremiah Productions had sold out by giving the lead to Brandon.

Keith and Dayne talked about what had gone wrong, how the star's image had changed. They both agreed, today Brandon was perceived far differently from the way people saw him just a year ago — when his role as a teen star for NTM Studios had made him the guy with the fresh face and the squeaky clean image. NTM had made him into a mega-star, no question. He was the heartthrob for every young teenage girl in America, and now he wanted to take on more serious roles. Keith looked at the magazines again. "What did his agent say about all this? The partying and girls?"

"He said it's under control." Dayne looked baffled. "Seriously. He told me his star client could party once in a while, otherwise he wouldn't be seen as a competitive adult actor."

"Mission accomplished." Keith's heart felt like it had settled around his waist. "We need to get word to him that we're hesitating, that we'll cast someone else if the craziness doesn't stop."

"You wanna have that talk with him, or you want me to do it?"

"He'll hear it better from you."

Dayne agreed. He still had Brandon's cell number. He pulled his phone from his back jeans pocket and tapped a few times. In seconds he held the phone to his ear and waited. "Hey, Brandon. Yeah, man, it's Dayne Matthews. Wondered if you had a minute?"

Keith could only hear Dayne's side of the conversation, but his new co-producer seemed very adept at getting to the point. They talked about the film and the schedule, and the idea that Brandon needed to make time for a screen test in Bloomington. Then Dayne lowered the boom. "By the way, Keith and I have a dozen magazines spread across the table. Gotta be honest, buddy. We don't like what we're seeing."

Brandon's answers didn't take long, and from the sounds of Dayne's responses, the young star was contrite. "Okay, so it's pretty serious. You understand, right?" Dayne was wrapping up the call. "Good. We still have a few weeks. If the tabs keep making you their star player, we might need a different Holden Harris."

Dayne paused, pacing the floor a few feet from Keith.

"Good." He went on, "This is very serious. Absolutely. This kinda' film we need you on your game, buddy. Really."

After another few minutes the call ended, and Dayne slipped his phone back in his pocket. "He's worried. I could hear it in his voice."

"Should we call his agent, let him know his role's in jeopardy?"

"I think so. I'll let you handle that one."

Keith was more than happy to make the call. They answered

to God for their actions as producers. If that meant cutting a star as big as Brandon Paul, they would do it and let God show them who was supposed to play the part instead. Keith immediately called Brandon's agent and explained the contract had included a character clause.

"The tabloids, right?" Brandon's agent didn't sound surprised.

"Exactly." Keith kept his tone even. "The way it is now, if we were filming, Brandon would be breaking that part of the contract. Which means we'd no longer be obligated to keep him in the film. And we wouldn't be obligated to pay him, either."

The agent ranted for a while, explaining Brandon was an angel compared to so many Hollywood stars. But by the end of the conversation, Keith was sure that they had gotten the attention of the agent. He expected the man's next call would be to Brandon, ordering him to clean up his act immediately.

"I keep thinking about that verse in the Bible, about what good is it for a man to gain the whole world and lose his soul." Keith sat back down at the table and felt the heaviness of the past hour hit him square on his shoulders. "It applies to all of us." He smiled, weary from the thought of Brandon's antics. "I'm glad we made those calls."

"Me too." Dayne took the seat beside him. "I could've done movies full of compromise all day long. That's all that was available when I walked away from Hollywood. But this ... what we've got with Jeremiah Productions. This is special. We have to be the gatekeepers."

Yes, that was it. Keith nodded. *Gatekeepers.* God had assigned them a small kingdom in the land of moviemaking, and now they needed to guard the gates with every breath, every action they took. "Let's pray for a minute. I feel like the enemy is pushing in on us. We need the Lord's Spirit so we can tell when someone's rushing the gate."

Dayne nodded, his face pensive, serious. "Absolutely." He folded his hands and hung his head.

Keith did the same, and he prayed as intensely as he had back when they were filming *The Last Letter* and the union tried to shut them down. This wasn't as overt, but it was even more a threat to the work they wanted to accomplish for Christ. Keith asked God to give them wisdom and discernment in the decisions that lie ahead. "And most of all, Lord, please give us courage. Make us brave enough to walk away from something the world would never walk away from. Give us ears to hear your voice above the noise of Hollywood, so that *Unlocked* becomes a film that turns the hearts of the people back to you. In Jesus' name, amen."

As they finished, Dayne's eyes lit up. "Hey, I didn't tell you. On our break, my brother called. He and his wife just got news — their adoption agency has a baby for them. A boy."

"A baby! That's fantastic." Keith thought how different life must be right now in Luke Baxter's house. He and his wife would be celebrating, thanking God for the new life headed their way. None of the heartbreak he and Lisa were experiencing with Andi. It was a tremendous coincidence, really. That Dayne's brother would be preparing their home for a baby, while he and Lisa and Andi were preparing to say goodbye to Andi's son, their first grandchild. "Have they met the birthmother?"

"I think so. I guess she just signed the paperwork." He hesitated. "I think that's what he said. He kept cutting out." Dayne grinned. "Reception here still isn't what it is in LA. Besides, I guess it's pretty early."

Suddenly Keith realized this was no coincidence. If God wanted Andi to give up her baby, then maybe He planned this timing just perfectly. In the coming weeks, Andi could meet with Luke and his wife and see what a gift adoption was for a family like theirs. In fact, maybe he and Lisa could join Andi in that conversation. So that all their hearts could better understand what

God was calling Andi to do. He sat back in his chair. "Let's pray for Luke, okay. We should do that right now."

"Definitely." Dayne's eyes danced. "My brother sounded giddy, so yeah ... he would appreciate our prayers for sure."

Keith took the lead. "Lord, You have this precious baby boy set apart for Luke and Reagan and their family, and now ... we ask You to protect the birthmother, protect the baby, and let the situation work out the way You intend. Adoption is a miracle, but it's never easy ... so use this situation for all of us. In Jesus' name, amen."

Eleanor had returned as they finished the prayer. She was situating herself back at the table, a look on her face of mild amusement. "Praying again, boys?"

"Always." Keith smiled at her. Eleanor claimed a nominal faith, but the intensity of Keith's and Dayne's beliefs didn't bother her. She smiled at them, as if to say she thought it quaint they were praying between screen tests. As she took her seat she patted Keith on the back. "I could already tell you and Dayne had been praying."

"That right?"

"Absolutely." She pointed up, her eyes shining. "Who else could've brought us Miss Bailey Flanigan?"

Keith smiled at Eleanor's observation, and silently he prayed that the process of making *Unlocked* would bring the casting director closer to God and create in her a hunger for His truth, the same way he prayed it for everyone involved in the film — especially Brandon Paul.

Over the next few hours they welcomed four more young actresses, all of whom read for the role of Ella. But each performance fell flat compared with Bailey's. By the end of the afternoon, Eleanor pulled the resumes, paperwork, and headshots together into a file marked *Ella*. "If you ask me, after seeing Bailey we could tell tomorrow's crop to stay home. Now we need

Brandon Paul out here to read with her. See if the two have the chemistry to pull it off."

Keith was pretty sure that wouldn't be a problem. Brandon might've been messing up in his off time, but he was a professional. Anyone who had watched him grow up in his NTM teen series could tell that one day the kid would be a very strong actor. Directors had only begun to draw out of him what he was capable of.

"Chemistry won't be a problem for Brandon." Keith was still worried about all the issues that would be a problem.

"You don't think so?" Eleanor was more skeptical. "He's very young."

"Only one guy has more natural charm and charisma on screen than Brandon Paul." Keith elbowed his co-producer. "But Dayne here's a little too old to play a high school boy."

They all laughed and after a few minutes, Keith bid the others goodbye. He and Andi had planned to spend an hour together late this afternoon. She needed to turn in an essay to her English professor, and he'd offered to go with her. Even with all that was happening with the movies, Keith thought about his daughter constantly. He'd seen the pictures from her ultrasound; and he knew how badly she was struggling, how she was no longer sure about giving the baby up.

Keith wasn't sure either — regardless of his revelation moments ago. Adoption wasn't for everyone, right? Even if Luke and his wife were celebrating the decision of a different birthmother somewhere in the state of Indiana. The baby looked so much like Andi and her younger brothers — the ones who had never had the chance to live. She could keep her baby, right? They could help her and everything would be okay for all of them. But then, maybe that was only his selfish heart thinking that way. Because he could hardly imagine holding the baby in the pictures, cradling him close to his chest, and realizing he was a grandfather.

Only to let the baby go.

Seven

ANDI WAS WAITING FOR KEITH when he got home. She'd taken to wearing sweats and baggy sweaters lately — her way of covering up her expanding middle. Even so, as she hurried down the sidewalk to his car, she looked thin and young and so much like the high school girl with the bold ideals and strong convictions, the girl everyone thought would never stumble.

She climbed into the car and buckled her belt. "Hi." Her hair was still short and dark, the way she'd dyed it at the beginning of summer. But it had grown out some and her blonde roots were starting to show.

"Hi, honey." He leaned over and hugged her. "You've got your essay?"

"Right here." She pulled a folder from her oversized bag and held it on her lap. There was a heaviness in her voice. "How was Bailey's audition?"

Again Keith's heart sank. If things had been different, if Andi had remained the innocent girl she'd been during her senior year of high school, the scene today might've involved her and not Bailey. It was one more consequence to her choices, and it weighed on him heavily in light of her question. He gripped the steering wheel, taking them out of the neighborhood and closer to the university. "Bailey was amazing." He smiled at his daughter, hoping she could see in his eyes how much he loved her, how much he still believed in her. "I think she might get the part of Ella."

"Really?" Andi sat back, breathless. "That's amazing. Does she know?"

"Not yet. We have to wait a while. Lots to work through first."

"Wow." Andi's tone was proof that she was stunned. "I won't tell her, but I can't believe it." She glanced at him again. "I mean I can, because Bailey's a good actress. But this is huge for her. What made them audition her for such a big part?"

"The casting director wanted someone new. A fresh face."

"That's how Katy Matthews got discovered." Andi's shoulders seemed to slump a little, as if maybe she was realizing again all she'd loss by compromising her purity with Taz.

"Yes. Since then directors are more likely to look at an unknown." He kept his eyes on the road. "We looked at more than a hundred girls. Dayne's wife actually suggested we take a look at Bailey. She's been coaching her privately for awhile now."

"Right." Andi looked out the window and she was quiet. When she turned back to him, her eyes were damp. "I wish ..." she sniffed and the words didn't seem to come easily. "I wish I could've read for the part."

Keith felt a wave of sorrow hit his heart. "Yes, sweetheart." He reached for her hand. "I wish that, too."

They were quiet for a long time. Then Andi said it again. "So Bailey Flanigan as Ella. Working with Brandon Paul. Crazy stuff." Andi's tone was softer than before. "She must be so happy."

Keith felt the weight of Andi's disappointment. But he was proud of her attitude. "Like I said, honey, we still have a lot ahead before we can hire her. We're more concerned with Brandon Paul." Keith squinted against the sun streaming through the windshield. "He's been getting in trouble almost every day. The tabs are loving it."

"Hmmm." Andi looked concerned. "I didn't know."

"We talked to him and his agent today." Keith kept his eyes on the traffic ahead. "We can't be afraid to walk away from him."

"I don't know." Andi found her sunglasses in her purse and

slipped them on. "I mean, Dad, what if he needs this movie? To teach him about God?"

"I've thought about that." Keith understood the struggle Andi was feeling. They were all missionaries at heart — it would be that way forever after their time in Indonesia. His daughter's comment reminded him that she was truly back — her focus was in place again. "The problem is, I can't sacrifice the reputation of Jeremiah Productions or the integrity and message of the film in the hopes of reaching Brandon."

They rode in silence for a while, and when they reached the university, Keith walked with Andi to the English building and up a flight of stairs to the professor's office. He waited while she dropped off the essay. As he waited, three other students — two guys and a girl — entered the office, and a few minutes later Andi returned and as they left the room Keith heard the girl whisper to her friends, "Look ... she's pregnant!"

They were halfway down the stairs when Andi stopped and looked at her dad. "It's okay. It's happened before."

Keith didn't know what to say. He opened his mouth and then changed his mind. How could this be his daughter people were talking about? He met her eyes and hoped she could see how badly he hurt for her. "Honey ..." he hugged her. "I'm sorry. I'm so sorry."

The idea of Andi being the brunt of people's gossip or pity made him feel defeated and sad. She was his little girl, and he should've been able to save her from this situation. He would've done anything to help her if he could, but now ... now it was too late. She pulled away first, her face set, resolve in place. This was her lot, and she looked ready to face it. Even so her smile was tinged with sadness and regret. "Ready?"

"Yes." He kept his pace slow this time, because he wanted to talk to her. There were things he hadn't said since they'd found out about her pregnancy, things that didn't come up easily around the dinner table or before turning in each night. Thoughts swimming close to the surface of his heart. If he didn't say them now, there might not be another chance. He waited until they were outside on a wide pathway that cut through the campus. Hardly anyone was around at this hour, so they had the moment to themselves.

"You're quiet," she smiled at him. "What're you thinking about?"

It had always been this way with them, this uncanny way they had of reading each other. That was another reason why he needed to tell her how he felt. Otherwise this pregnancy could come between them, render them the sort of father-daughter team that only shared information on a surface level. He slowed a little, catching her eye. "You always know me."

"I try." She pushed a section of her hair behind her ear and studied him. "So tell me."

"I guess I feel like I owe you an apology. It's my fault this happened."

"What?" Surprise filled her eyes, but she seemed to know what he was talking about. "None of this was your fault. You raised me to know better."

"I raised you right, but …" This was the place in his heart he hadn't allowed himself to visit since he got word his daughter was pregnant. He swallowed hard, fighting to keep his voice steady. "We never should've let you come here by yourself. You were … you were too young." He felt his chin quiver, and he breathed in hard through his nose. "I let you down, baby. I want you to know I'm sorry for that."

Andi stopped walking and faced him. "That's not true." She hugged him and held on the way she used to when she was a little girl. When she let go, she searched his face, his eyes. "It was my fault. I wanted to see what life was like. Without restrictions.

Outside my faith." There was a bench nearby and she motioned to her dad to sit beside her.

Anger welled up in Keith. Anger at Taz for taking advantage of his daughter. Even anger at Andi — because here she was admitting that she'd intentionally gone against God and everything she knew to be true, everything they'd taught her. He stood and paced a few feet away, his back to her. "Why would you ever … ever want to live outside your faith?" The intensity in his tone caught him off guard. He turned and faced her. "Is this what you wanted? To have people talk about you behind your back? To miss out on the chance to read for a lead role in one of my movies?" His anger took hold and he couldn't stop himself. "To embarrass yourself and us? Is that what you wanted?"

A couple football players walked by on a path not far from them, and both of them turned to see the commotion. Anger flashed in Andi's eyes, too. She stood and pressed her hand to her stomach. "Of course I didn't want this!" Her eyes welled up. "I thought I was missing out on something." She crossed her arms, her voice louder than before. "And I kept thinking about Rachel Baugher. Lot of good it did her, living for God!" She backed up a few steps. "And if I'm an embarrassment to you, fine. I can do this without you!"

"Andi …" He was seized with sudden remorse. What was he doing, yelling at her? Blaming her for his own fear and pride. Keith felt the fight leave him. "Andi, come here."

Tears slid down her cheeks, and the hurt in her eyes was more than he could take. "Daddy …" her voice broke. "I never meant to hurt you and mom." She spread her fingers over her heart. "I'm sorry." She hung her head, trembling despite the afternoon sun. "You'll never know how sorry I am."

Keith felt like the world's worst father. He sighed and felt it rattle all the way down to his ankles. "Honey … I didn't mean it that way." He went to her, and when she fell into his arms he silently thanked God. She didn't hate him. Even after the unkind things he'd just said, she was still here. "Of course you're sorry."

"I c-c-can't," quiet sobs shook her small body. "I can't change things now. I'm s-s-sorry I embarrassed you."

Keith wanted to crawl in a hole. How could he make her believe that he hadn't meant it that way. "It's my fault, baby. My own pride. Please ..." he leaned back and lifted her chin so their eyes met. "I'm not embarrassed of you. I'm embarrassed at myself — because I wasn't here to help you." He gritted his teeth, fighting an overwhelming sadness. "I wasn't here to keep that ... that jerk away from you."

She nodded, but fresh tears slid down her cheeks.

"Forgive me, Andi. I'm sorry. Your mom and I, we're here for you." He kissed her forehead, again begging God that they could move past this. "You're brave and kind and you want your baby to live. Your mom and I," his voice caught, and he waited a moment until he could talk. "Your mom and I are very, very proud of you, sweetheart." He hugged her again and stroked her back. "We'll get through this. We will."

He felt her nod against his chest.

"Do you forgive me?" He looked into her eyes again, his only daughter.

"Yes." She managed a weak smile, but her eyes told him what he desperately needed to know. This was a moment both of them regretted. But they would survive it. They would move on from here. She pulled away and walked back to her purse. She pulled a tissue from inside and used it to blow her nose. Then she sat on the bench again and patted the spot beside her. "I still want to explain. Okay?"

Keith wasn't sure he was ready for this. After his outburst, he still felt terrible. It was enough that she was sorry, that she'd found her love for God again, right? She didn't need to explain what had led her to make her decisions. It was like listening to someone else talk, and it only reinforced his guilt — that if he'd been here she wouldn't have allowed herself to forget who she was.

"It was me, Daddy." Andi looked off at the sky above a row of trees that lined the path. "I wasn't trying to get pregnant." She sniffed and pressed the tissue beneath her eyes again. "I wanted to know how other people lived." She breathed in slowly and looked at him again. "I looked at Rachel and saw how her good life hadn't gotten her anywhere, and I wanted to find out for myself. I wanted to experience life without any restrictions." Shame darkened her features. "So that's what I did."

He shook his head and narrowed his eyes, struggling with his emotions, unable to look at her, at the little-girl eyes that reminded him of her growing-up years. "We should've been here ... or you should've been there. In San Jose. You could've gone to college there, baby. If you would've brought this ... this Taz character home I would've seen right through him. You never would've dated him."

"Daddy, don't ..."

"It's true." He hung his head, and the tears came against his will. He'd fought these feelings all summer, but now he had to be honest with her. His pent-up anger wasn't at her, it was at himself. "I'm your father." His voice broke. "I'm supposed to protect you, keep you safe." He felt his face twist in sorrow, and he brought his hand to his eyes. When he had a little more composure, he looked at her and put his hand on her shoulder. "When you were a baby, I stood by your crib listening to you breathe, making sure nothing ever harmed you, and when ... when you learned to walk I held your hand so you wouldn't fall."

"Daddy ..." Andi put her hand over his.

"I ran beside you when you learned to ride your bike, because I couldn't stand the thought of you hitting the ground."

Andi had tears in her eyes too, but she laughed at the picture he painted. "I remember that."

He blinked so he could see her better. "When we had the chance to move to Indonesia, the only thing that made me hesitate was you, Andi. Not knowing whether I could keep you safe. But I did. I let everyone in that village know that nothing — nothing could ever happen to you." He could feel his heart breaking inside him. "I would've laid down my life for you anytime along the way."

"I felt safe the whole time we were there."

"You were." He found her eyes again and wished with everything inside him they could go back, that her freshman year had only just begun and that he and Lisa had moved here a year ago. "You were safe because that was my job. Protecting you, my baby girl. My princess."

She dabbed the tissue at a few errant tears on her cheeks and listened.

"But this year, when you needed me, I wasn't around. I was out," he gestured toward an unseen public, "out making movies so I could save the world, when ..." he took hold of her hand, "when my daughter needed me more than any of them."

"You did what you thought was right, Daddy. I told you, it was my fault."

Keith brushed the back of his hand across his face and sniffed hard. "We can't go back, I know that. But if I could ..." He put his hand alongside Andi's cheek. "If I could, I'd be here a year ago, and you would bring your questions to me and your mother. We would help you keep your faith and your foundation, and you wouldn't ... you wouldn't be in this situation." He hugged her once more. "I just want you to know I'm sorry."

For a long time Andi only looked at him, and he watched a number of emotions slide across her face. Shame and regret and sorrow ... and finally forgiveness. "I have a question." She waited until she saw he was listening intently. "Can I still be your princess, Daddy? Even now that I messed up?"

Fresh tears blurred his eyes and he hugged her tight again. He couldn't protect her from the consequences of her actions, but maybe he could protect her from the pain. When he drew back, he helped her to her feet, and he willed her to hear him all the way to her soul. "You will always be my princess, Andi. Nothing could ever change that."

As they walked back to the car, Keith felt certain they'd reached a breakthrough. Though he hadn't been there to protect her, and though she would suffer for the choices she'd made during the past year, and even though he'd gotten angry at her, one thing was clear again: how much he loved her and desired to protect her. He'd told her the truth. She was still his little girl, his princess.

Nothing could ever change that.

Eight

CODY HAD KNOWN ALL SUMMER DURING WORKOUTS that this moment would come and now it was here. Clear Creek's starting quarterback had gone down in the first quarter with a knee injury in the game against their cross-town rival, Bloomington High. Which meant one thing for the team: Connor Flanigan was the new starter. Already Connor had thrown two touchdown passes, and now Clear Creek had the ball, down by just six points with three minutes to go. Bloomington's head coach had called a time out, so Connor jogged off the field and headed straight for Cody. "What do I do?" His eyes were wide, his confidence not nearly as strong as his abilty.

"Breathe." Cody put his hands on Connor's shoulders. The kid was six-foot-three now, an inch taller than Cody. "You can do this. We wouldn't have you out there if it wasn't a game you could win for us."

"But they're blitzing every play. They know we're gonna throw."

That's another thing Cody loved about coaching Connor. He was one of the smartest players Cody had ever worked with. "We'll contain the blitz. Let the line coach worry about that. Everyone knows their roles."

"So we're throwing?"

"On first and ten." The spread offense was another thing Cody couldn't get enough of. As the quarterback coach, it gave him a reason to work hard, presenting Connor with a number of options on every play. The receivers' coach came up and the three of them conferred. They'd go with the spread. "This is your game, Connor. You've worked for this."

Connor's eyes were still big, still wide with fear, but he nodded and took a few steps toward the field. "Pray for me."

"I am." Cody watched the kid go, and he kept his word, silently asking God to give Connor protection and vision as he commandeered this last drive. The second he finished praying, he cupped his hands around his mouth. "Okay, guys! Hit someone!"

Over the next minute and a half, Connor made the drive look easy. He connected on first and ten for twenty-three yards, and again on the next play for another thirty. He missed on just two passes over the next eight throws, and with fifteen seconds to go, Clear Creek had notched another victory — making four straight for the season.

While the team celebrated, as the players jumped on Connor's back and patted his helmet, Cody did what he'd been dying to do all night. He stole a glance up at the packed stands and found Bailey. She had her eyes shaded against the glare of the stadium lights, and when she saw him look at her, she jumped a few times, waving furiously. He waved back and then turned his attention to the team. But even while the head coach congratulated the guys and singled out Connor as the game's most valuable player, Cody couldn't keep his mind off the bigger picture.

Tomorrow after the team met to watch game film on tonight's contest, Cody and Bailey were taking her brothers to see a new football movie, one that figured to be a classic. Then on Sunday they were going to Indianapolis to watch Bailey's dad coach the Colts. Mr. Flanigan had invited him to walk the sidelines as a stat guy, a temporary assistant of sorts. The idea that he'd be on the sidelines of an NFL game, helping the coaching staff, was more than Cody could fully grasp. He hadn't been able to think of much else all week.

He could still hardly believe this was his life, coaching Bailey's brothers, and spending most of his free time at her house. He hadn't asked her to be his girlfriend yet, but that would come this weekend. He wanted the timing to be right, and then he would ask her. And he would believe, as he wanted to believe here in this magical moment under the Friday night lights of Clear Creek High School, that this wasn't only some crazy wonderful season when God was finally allowing everything to go right.

Rather it was a glimpse of his future — the future he'd only dreamed about before this fall.

BAILEY WISHED SHE HAD A CAMERA, but even that wouldn't capture exactly how she was feeling right now — with Cody on the field helping coach Clear Creek to another victory and Connor playing quarterback. She remembered before this season how Connor had doubted his ability to even play football. He could've stayed with CKT, doing shows on a stage where he was more comfortable. But instead he'd taken this challenge head on, and now ... now Bailey couldn't be happier for him.

They were sitting in the stands with most of the Baxter family, all of whom loved coming out to support the head coach, Ryan Taylor, Kari Baxter Taylor's husband. Kari and Ashley sat in front of Bailey with their kids, and down the bench a little ways were Peter and Brooke and their girls. The patriarch of the Baxter family — John Baxter — was here with his wife, Elaine, along with Dayne Matthews — the Baxter family's eldest son — and his wife Katy, and their little Sophie. The last Baxter daughter, Erin, wasn't here because her family was sick with the flu.

Dayne had said hello when they first arrived, and Bailey was dying to sit by him, ask him about whether they were interested in having her come back for a second audition. But Dayne's attention was on his wife and baby, and Bailey didn't want to bother him. It had only been four days, but still, if they were filming in a month she figured she'd have heard by now.

During halftime, her mom had leaned close and whispered, "It's out of your control." She smiled. "So stop thinking about it, sweetheart."

"You're right." Bailey had determined again to focus on the football game.

"Dayne couldn't tell you now, even if there was something to say."

After that she kept her eyes on the game, but that didn't stop her from thinking about it. At least if they would tell her they weren't interested, she could move on. But the way it stood, there were moments when the audition was all she could think about. That and Cody. She was so proud of him, out there calling plays and acting like he'd been coaching for years.

Later, when they were back at her house, Cody couldn't stop smiling. "Did you seem him? Your brother was incredible!"

Bailey's dad — who never would've forced Connor to play football and who was just as proud of Connor when he had the lead in a CKT play — gathered the family around the computer screen so they could all watch highlights of the game. "Look at that!" Bailey's dad elbowed Connor. "I wish I could get my million-dollar quarterback to sit in the pocket like that." He puffed out his chest, beaming and playing up the moment. "Yessirree, that's my boy. Making everyone else look silly."

They all laughed, and the good times lasted for hours. It was a Friday night Bailey would always remember, marked by the smell of hot butter and salt coming from the kitchen as her mom made one cheese crisp after another for the hungry group. All the guys Bailey loved in her life were in one house, celebrating each other's strengths and the lingering feeling of victory.

Only one thing could've made the night any better. Bailey watched Cody, the way he hung on every word her father said as they analyzed game film and how he fit right in as part of their family — the way he had from the beginning. But why hadn't he asked her to be his girlfriend? Ever since the Fourth of July he had to know how she felt about him, so why the wait?

They'd kissed twice, both times were when they were alone. But Cody seemed to prefer being with her entire family around. Bailey chided herself for not being more patient. Clearly Cody respected her. He cherished her and now he wanted his actions to reflect the way he felt. That had to be it. Besides, she'd only been broken up with Tim for a few months. It made sense that Cody would want to wait a little while. She just wished they'd take more walks or hang out more often on her front porch. That way they could talk about how he was feeling, where this might be leading, and whether now was the time for them to be more serious.

Bailey hung back in the kitchen, sitting on one of the barstools and watching the boys. As she did, she caught herself silently praying for this new relationship with Cody, that God would bless it and make it grow and that all things would happen in His timing.

Her mom walked up, her sleeves rolled back, her forehead damp. "I think I've cooked a hundred cheese crisps."

"The boys each ate about twenty." Bailey laughed. This was part of their Friday night tradition. They'd come back to the Flanigan house — sometimes with half the team — and Bailey's mom would grab a Costco-sized package of tortillas, an enormous bag of grated cheese, and a couple sticks of butter. Then she'd set about making cheese crisps for the group until every last person was stuffed.

"You sure you're not tired of it?" Bailey planted her elbows on the granite countertop. "All that cooking on Friday nights?"

"It's better than eating out." Her mom leaned against the counter and watched the boys, still hovering around the computer. "When we bought this house, your father and I promised

God we'd use it. We'd fill it with people and feed everyone who came in, and put reminders of His Word on the walls." Her eyes found Bailey's again. "No, sweetie, I'm not tired of it."

"Good. Because I love it too." She breathed in deeply of the smell and sounds around her. "Don't be surprised if I show up here with my family every Friday night in fall. I can't imagine being anywhere else."

Her mom was quiet for a moment, and her gaze shifted to Cody — at the center of the cluster of guys. "He hasn't asked you yet."

It wasn't a question. Her mom knew Bailey would tell her if anything that dramatic happened. Tonight her comment was more of an observation.

"I think he's waiting," Bailey wasn't frustrated, just antsy. Like a six-year-old anxious for Christmas morning. "Like the timing has to be perfect or something."

"You don't need a title to tell you the obvious."

Bailey grinned, dizzy over her feelings for Cody. "Meaning what?"

"That boy's plum crazy about you. He's loved you for years." Her mom's eyes danced. "Of course, I believe I told you that a while ago, yes?"

"Yes." Bailey felt her cheeks grow hot. "I saw it … I just couldn't believe he cared when he never said so."

"That's because Cody won't settle for being your boyfriend." Her mom's look held a fondness for Cody. "He's looking long-term." She raised a single brow. "And whether that happens or not, only God knows."

It used to scare Bailey, thinking that far into the future about who she might marry and when that would happen — and how she would ever leave her family and start her own. But when it came to Cody, she never felt afraid at all. Just impatient. The same way she felt all of Saturday, the next day, when she and Cody took her brothers to the movies, and on Sunday when they went to her father's game. The Colts won, and everyone was talking about how the team might actually become the first team since the Miami Dolphins to finish a season undefeated. They were that good.

But the day wasn't going to be perfect until she and Cody had time to talk.

Her parents had both driven to the game, since her dad had to be there so much sooner. So the ride home had Bailey and Connor and Justin and BJ in the car with Bailey's mom, and the rest of the boys and Cody driving back with her dad. The arrangement made sense. Cody had been on the field all day with her father. Bailey's mom brought binoculars to the game, and the few times Bailey used them she looked down at Cody. Every time she saw that he was completely absorbed in whatever her father was saying or doing.

When they finally reached the Flanigan house again it was after nine o'clock, and Bailey could hardly wait to be alone with him. The boys began heating up leftover cheese crisps, and before Cody could get caught up in game film or ESPN highlights, she tugged on his sleeve. "Can we go outside ... sit on the swing?"

As distracted as he'd been all weekend, suddenly his eyes were lost in hers. He reached for her hand and nodded. "I've been looking forward to that all day."

"Me too." They walked outside, and once they were seated together on the swing, Bailey noticed how cool it was.

"Are you cold? I can get you a blanket."

She pictured that, the two of them snuggled under a blanket, gazing at the stars and catching up on the last few days. "That'd be perfect."

He hurried back inside, and in a minute he returned with the softest, warmest blanket they had — a deep brown plush throw perfect for this chilly September night. "Wow," Cody put the blanket over them, his arm around her shoulders. "I feel like we haven't talked all weekend."

"We haven't." She giggled, savoring the way she felt small and protected next to him. "So what was it like?" She craned her neck a little so she could see his eyes. "You were helping coach an NFL team today. Has that hit you yet?"

"Not really." He looked a little dazed. "I mean it was surreal, Bailey. Standing down there next to your dad, gathering stats from the upstairs team of stat guys and passing them on to your father. I felt absolutely sure that someday that's where I want to be. Walking the sidelines of an NFL game, making the calls or assisting some way."

"That's how I felt about my audition. Like I was born to do this."

"Exactly." He breathed in and leaned his head on hers. "Any idea when you'll hear?"

"No." Bailey had let the issue go a little since Friday night. "It could be a few weeks, or I might not hear at all. I've put the matter in God's hands. Otherwise it'll drive me crazy."

"I know." He took his arm from her shoulders and angled himself so he could see her better. As he did, he reached for her hand, weaving his fingers between hers. "The whole weekend, whether I was on the Clear Creek field or today out there with the Colts, I couldn't stop thinking about you."

"Come on ... you were thinking about football." She was teasing him, loving that they finally were having this time together.

"No, really." He brought her hand to his lips and kissed it. "I don't deserve to be here. I don't deserve any of this."

Bailey cringed a little, because she hated when he talked like that. It was the same reason he hadn't thought about telling her his feelings sooner. Because he thought she deserved someone better. "No one deserves anything good we have in life. Because all good things are gifts from God."

"True." He touched the fingers of his free hand to her cheek. "And you're the best gift of all." The look in his eyes changed, and his expression deepened with a mix of passion and love — a love that knew no limits, because it had waited so long for this moment.

Bailey could feel what was coming, she could feel it and she wanted to hold onto every beautiful breath they drew together. He was going to ask her to be his girlfriend, because what night could be more perfect than this one?

He drew a slow breath, and she could hear his nervousness in the way his voice sounded a little shakier than usual. "Bailey ... I wanted to wait until — "

Before he could finish his sentence, his text message alert sounded. He reached for his phone, but before he could silence it, his ringtone went off. He looked like he might ignore the call or throw the phone into the yard, but as he pulled it from his pocket, his eye caught the caller ID window. Though he didn't take the call, his face clouded. "Great," he mumbled.

"Who is it?" Bailey rarely saw Cody with this sort of expression. He looked almost distraught.

A hard sigh came from him and he slid forward, staring at the text message. "It's my mom. Her text says she's in trouble. She needs me to come over."

Bailey felt her heartbeat quicken. "Is ... is she sick?" He hadn't talked much about his mom lately, and now she felt bad for not asking.

"Maybe." He looked at her and regret filled his eyes. "I better go. I'll try to make it fast and get back here in an hour." He stood and helped her to her feet. "You'll still be up?"

"Definitely." She tried to read him, read whether he was truly worried or more annoyed with his mother's message. "Want me to come?"

"No." He put his hand to the side of her face and let himself stay there in her eyes for a long while. "Thanks for being willing."

"I care about her, Cody." Back when Cassie Coleman was in prison through much of Cody's high school years, Bailey's mother had been one of her only friends. "Let me know that everything's okay."

"I will." He kissed her softly on her lips. Not the kiss of desire and passion and longing for all their future might hold, but a kiss that apologized because the moment they'd been caught up in was lost now. At least until later that night. "See you in a while."

He jogged down her porch steps toward his car and wasted no time heading out toward his mother's house. Bailey watched him go, and she hoped his mother was okay, that maybe she had a problem with her house or the bug going around. Something simple. As long as everything was okay with his mother, Cody might still ask her to be his girlfriend later tonight. The way she hoped he would.

She was headed inside when her own cell phone went off. Probably Cody telling her he'd talked to his mom and she would only need him for a few minutes. Then he would be headed back to her. But as Bailey went to answer it, she saw the name Ellison on her caller ID. At this hour, she couldn't imagine why anyone from Andi's house would be calling. Unless something was wrong with her, too —

"Hello?" Bailey tried to keep the panic from her voice.

"Bailey, it's Keith Ellison. Sorry for calling so late."

"Is everything okay with Andi?" She stopped just short of her front door and put her hand to her head.

"Yes, of course." His tone told her he was sorry for making her worry. "This is about your screen test. Dayne and I have been here going over the next round of auditions, trying to put the cast together." He paused. "Bailey, we were very impressed with your test. We think you'd make a terrific Ella, if you're interested in another round of auditions."

If she was interested? She started to scream, but caught herself and made the sound only a quiet shriek. "Are you serious? Yes, I'm interested. Of course!"

Keith Ellison laughed lightly on the other end. "I thought you might be." He went on to explain that Brandon Paul was flying in early next week. "We'd like you back in our office for a screen test with Brandon this Wednesday. Does that work?"

Bailey gripped her hair at the roots and paced down the length of her porch and back again. "Yes, yes it works just fine. Mr. Ellison, thank you so much. I can't tell you what this means, just having the chance is … it's a gift from God, truly."

"The fact that you think so is the reason you're perfect for the part. Your faith shone through in your screen test. Eleanor didn't know what to make of it. Said she'd never seen anyone like you before."

If she didn't hold onto the porch rail Bailey was sure she'd float off and never be found again. She thanked Mr. Ellison a number of times and the conversation ended. She raced into the house, her hair flying behind her. "Mom! Dad! You won't believe this!"

Through the foyer and down the hallway she went, as fast as her feet would carry her, until she ran smack into her father — who was clearly coming after her to see what the commotion was. "Oh." She dusted herself off and adjusted her dad's sweatshirt. "Sorry about that."

Her mom walked up, eyes wide with concern. "Bailey you can't yell like that. The whole neighborhood must've heard you."

"I might have the part!" She screamed again, quieter this time. As she did, her brothers gathered around, each of them confused and laughing softly at the crazy way she sounded. "That was Mr. Ellison on the phone. He asked me to come in and read with Brandon Paul on Wednesday." Her words ran together, and she had to remind herself to slow down so they could understand her.

"No way!" Connor brought both hands to his head, his face slightly pale. "That's huge!"

"I knew it!" Her mom hugged her and stepped back to hug her dad too. "I just knew they'd call her back. She was unbelievable. You all would've been so proud of her."

"I can't believe it." Connor was still looking dazed. "Do you know what this means?"

Shawn high-fived Justin and BJ and Ricky. "It means everyone at school will want Bailey to get them an autograph," Shawn grinned big. "Every girl will be talking to us. We'll be the most popular kids on campus." He put his hand on Bailey's shoulder. "Let's make it an even dozen autographs. We'll figure out who gets 'em."

Her dad put his arm around her. "Honey, we're not surprised. God's given you a very great gift. This is only the beginning."

"Wait ... where's Cody?" Shawn looked behind Bailey, down the hallway. "Wasn't he here?"

"He had to go." Bailey felt the slightest disappointment. "His mom called. She needed his help with something."

"I hope she's okay." Her mom frowned, her eyes suddenly dark with worry. "She's been on my heart a lot lately."

"Cody didn't seem too worried." Bailey tried to shake off her concern about the situation. "I think it's something small. I hope so, anyway."

She was proud of Cody for being the type of son who would jump when his mother needed him. And she didn't need him often, not like this. Whatever it was, Bailey hoped it didn't take long. Cody should be here to celebrate this news with her. But when he didn't return right away, as things settled down at the Flanigan house, Bailey decided to call him. That way she could find out what the trouble was and maybe tell him about the call from Mr. Ellison.

Over the next thirty minutes she tried three times, but always the call went to his voice mail. Only then did Bailey really start to feel worried for Cody's mother. Whatever was wrong, it must've been significant. Otherwise Cody would've answered his phone. The more time passed, the more Bailey prayed and the less she even remembered her good news or the fact that she had an audition in three days with Brandon Paul.

The only thing consuming her heart was Cody and whatever he might be going through at this very moment with his mother.

Nine

THE WORDS IN HER TEXT MESSAGE were spelled wrong. That was the first sign. His mother had still been dating Benny the biker, which was why Cody didn't spend more time with her. He'd told her several times that the guy was trouble, but she wouldn't listen. Lately he could only pray she'd stay sober. Especially after her overdose and the trip to the hospital a few months ago. Since then, she was supposed to be in drug rehab three times a week, having blood tests to make sure she was staying clean. It was a condition of her parole, and now that she'd nearly died of an overdose, the police had informed her they'd be watching more closely.

Every time he called lately he asked the same thing: "Have you been to rehab? Are you getting your blood tests? Are you staying clean?"

She would always only laugh — this strange, high-pitched, nervous-sounding laugh. "Cody, you worry too much. I'm a grown woman. Go live your own life and let me live mine."

But that didn't sound like the mother he was starting to know. She'd missed so much of his childhood and teenage years, and when she came out of prison last time she was determined to be a better mother, spend time with him, talk about his past and his dreams for the future. For a while, when Bailey was so busy with Tim Reed, Cody hung out with his mom a lot. They'd see plays and go to dinner, and Cody allowed himself to believe she'd actually escaped, that the trap of drugs no longer had a hold on her.

But as he pulled out of the Flanigans' driveway, he listened to the message from his mother and that's when he knew for sure. The trouble she was in had to do with drugs, absolutely for sure. Her words were slurred, and she was crying, her tone filled with hysteria. "Cody ... Cody, get here fas'. I'm in big trouble, baby. I need you. Please get here. Don't be ma' at me, 'kay? Don't be ma.'"

The words ran together and the message rambled until the voice mail cut her off. He clicked his phone off and tossed it on the seat beside him. Why would she do this? Didn't she know where it would go, how her life would wind up if she went back to using? He was too angry to cry, too afraid to do anything but get to her house as fast as he could. *Dear God, be with me ... I don't know what to do ... I'm not sure how to help her. She's my mom, Father. She's supposed to have the answers, not me.* He released an angry breath. *Give me the strength ... Let her be okay. Please.*

I am with you, my son. I am your Father, and I will go ahead of you. Do not be anxious ... my perfect peace will be with you.

The quiet response soothed his soul, but still the drive seemed to take forever. Finally he turned onto her street and his heart slammed against his chest. Parked in front of the house were two police cars. A third was just pulling up. Cody's heartbeat flipped into overdrive as he parked a few houses down and tore out of his car. Not the police, not again. How could she let this happen? He stopped himself from racing onto the scene, since the police didn't know him or why he was approaching.

"Excuse me?" He shouted the words in the direction of a pair of officers standing near his mother's car. "I'm her son. Can I help you?"

One of the officers stepped forward, his face a mask of anger tinged only slightly by pity for Cody. "Your mother's in big trouble." The guy was older, one of the senior officers for sure. He had a black and gray mustache and serious eyes. "She's on parole for dealing. I'm sure you know that."

"Yes, sir." He glanced at the house and saw that other officers were inside talking to his mother. "Why are you ... I guess I don't know what happened?"

"Are you familiar with a guy named Benny Dirk? Apparently he and your mother have been dating."

"Yes." Disgust rose up in Cody, but it didn't stop his racing heart. His throat was dry and his knees felt weak. This was so much worse than he thought. "I've met him."

"He's a bad, bad guy." The officer crossed his arms, his lips pursed. "We've been working a sting operation in the area, and from what we've learned he's the chief supplier. Your mom was working for him. Dealing to people in the neighborhood and down the street at the park. Lots of places." He looked at the house. "He threatened her, and she told him she was calling the police. She's agreed to turn him in for a lighter sentence. But he's dangerous. He's ready to hurt someone."

Cody wanted to fall to the ground or scream or run into the house and shout at the top of his lungs. She was dealing on this very street? And at the park? He forced himself to breathe. "So ... so you're arresting her? Even if she's willing to turn in Benny?"

"We have to. We found drugs in her car and lists of clients." He made a face and nodded toward the house. "We'll work out the lighter sentence later. But right now we're taking her in." He sighed. "She isn't in good shape ... she's definitely been using."

Cody had a million questions. Had his mom provided enough information so they could arrest Benny Dirk? And if he was dangerous, did that mean her life was in jeopardy? But more than that he needed to see her. Now, before another minute went by. "Can I go in? She ... she called. She's expecting me."

"I'll take you up. The house is a crime scene at this point. Our officers will be going through everything." As he talked, still another pair of policemen pulled up. Cody felt his heart sink. How could this be happening? He was furious with his mother and terrified for her all at the same time. Of course Benny was trouble. Wasn't that what Cody had told his mother? And now she'd been dealing? Was that even possible? That meant she'd been lying to him all along, not just about the drugs and drinking. About everything.

His whole body shook as he walked with the officer toward the house and through the front door. His mom was barely standing, and then only with the help of an officer. The other policeman was about to handcuff her.

"Mom!" He couldn't lurch forward or run to her. Like the officer had told him, this was a crime scene.

"It's okay." The mustached policeman who had walked him up stood a few feet back now. "This is her son."

"Cody!" His mom turned and nearly fell over. Her eyes were only half open, her breathing raspy the way it had been when she went to the hospital that time. She reached out and again almost lost her balance. "Cody, I'm so sorry. I'm sorry, baby. I'm so sorry."

Her words blurred with her tears, and the picture she made was horrific. A skinny, strung-out blonde, dirty clothes hanging off her, lunging for her son and trying to apologize for a lifetime of mistakes. A nightmare of drugs and addiction.

Cody didn't want to cry in front of the officers, but seeing her this way, he couldn't stop the tears from building in his eyes. Angry, frustrated tears — proof that the truth was sinking in. His mother had actually been caught dealing again. She would go back to prison, for sure, and this time it could be many years before she got out. Even if they did cut her a deal. And what about Benny Dirk? Exactly how dangerous was he?

"Can I go to her?" Cody looked back at the older officer.

"That's fine. We'll cuff her after you have a minute." He motioned for the other two to give Cody a moment.

She was too drugged to stand by herself, so they waited until Cody was at her side. When he had support of her, they stepped away and suddenly Cody was thirteen again, watching TV and hearing a knock at the door, answering it to find police officers standing on the porch steps. He was panicking because this was his mother, and they couldn't just take her away from him. Wasn't that scene just like this one? Only back then he hadn't understood what it meant to deal or why his mom had to go to jail.

He blinked and he could see the way he looked back then, screaming as the police took his mom, as they slapped handcuffs on her wrists, begging them to let her go and watching as they jerked her from the house and pulled her down the steps to a waiting police car. He was so young and he was falling to the floor, shouting for her to come back and pushing away the policeman who stayed and tried to help him. It had been the last time he saw her outside a prison until after he graduated from high school.

And now it was happening all over again.

He grasped her shoulders and looked down at her, into her wasted eyes. She was so small, not a hundred pounds if Cody had to guess. Clearly she hadn't been eating these past few weeks, because she was emaciated — the way she always looked when the drugs took control of her. "Mom," he whispered the word straight to her face. "Why? Why'd you do it?"

"I ... needed money, Cody. I couldn' ask you all the time." Her words were still very slurred and tears poured from her eyes. But she was sober enough to at least try to explain herself.

But the explanation made Cody more angry.

"I would've given you anything. I would've sold whatever I had for you." He hissed the words, because he couldn't believe he was losing her again. She was the only family he had. And now this? "You could've lived with me."

"I can't." She shook her head so hard she almost toppled to the ground. "Benny would hurt you, Cody."

"Forget Benny." He seethed at the mention of the guy.

"No," she shook her head, frantic. "He's a ba' guy and ..." she could barely focus, every word an effort. "I tol' the cops on him, because he was gonna kill me tonight. And I don't wanna die, Cody!" Tears splashed onto her cheeks and she sobbed out loud a few times. "I wanna be a momma to you." She wailed, and the sound echoed loud and pathetic. "I'm so sorry! Be careful a' Benny! He's gonna kill us!"

She started to fall, and Cody worked to right her again. "Mom, you need help." She wasn't making sense. She'd agreed to testify against Benny, so she could be out of prison sooner. But now she was worried her testimony might get them killed? He kept his voice steady. "You can't live like this."

"Don't let them take me, Cody. I wanna be a good mom. I need another chance," her voice grew louder, until she was shrieking. "One more chance, Cody. Tell them I need one more chance!"

He hung his head, still holding onto her, still keeping her from falling. "It's too late." The words were a cry, the only thing he could say. He shook his head and looked at the officers. "Thank you."

They stepped in and Cody watched, his arms crossed tightly in front of him.

"Ma'am, we'll need you to place your hands behind your back. We have to take you in."

His mother writhed and jerked from the officers, the whole time her eyes fixed as best they could on Cody's. "Please, Cody ... don't let them take me! I'll do better. I'll make it right. Please, Cody!"

He squeezed his eyes shut. *God, I can't take this.* He remembered a Scripture from a sermon he'd heard a few weeks ago. The pastor told them God would never give them more than they could handle; He'd never lead them where He himself hadn't first gone ahead. Cody gripped the corner of the wall, willing the sound of his mother's screams to stop. *I can't take this, God ... it's more than I can bear. Please, be with me. Be with my mom. Get us through this, God ... I need You. Please...*

There was no audible answer, but then Cody wouldn't have been able to hear it even if there were. He opened his eyes and saw that his mother was no longer struggling with the officers. She'd given in, and her wrists were now cuffed behind her back. But still her eyes were locked on his, and still she wept his name over and over again. "Cody ... look out for Benny!" She glanced about, as if he might be coming through the front door any second. "Don't let 'em take me. Please!"

But he had to let her go. The officers took her down the steps of the house, and the whole time — even though she could barely stand — she turned back, looking at him. "Cody ..."

He and the other officer followed, moving down the steps, watching the horrific scene. Neighbors were outside their houses, lined up along the sidewalk catching all the drama. It was Sunday night, and even though it was ten o'clock, most of them must've heard the commotion, seen the flashing lights.

Cody ignored the gawking stares and forced himself to think, to figure out what was supposed to happen next. When he was thirteen and his mother had been arrested, child protective services stepped in and handled everything — including helping him find a foster home only hours later. In high school he wound up living with the Flanigan family, and then after graduation he joined the Army.

But here ... now ... he was a man, even if he was only a twenty-two-year-old college student. The police would expect him to handle his mother's court dates, her legal matters, and whatever else laid ahead. He turned to the mustached officer, the one beside him. "What happens next?"

"We're taking her to the Bloomington jail. You can post bail, if you'd like. They'll have all the information down there." He checked his watch. "You can follow us down to the station."

"Okay." Cody could barely focus on all the details. "What about the courts? And her parole?" His head was spinning. He had a history exam first thing in the morning, and he wasn't sure he had enough money in the bank to cover her bail.

"She'll have an arraignment in the next few days, and a judge will look at the evidence. Because of her past record, the decision will be made without a jury trial. She'll probably be sentenced pretty quickly." He paused and raised an eyebrow. "Your mother's right about Benny Dirk. He threatened to kill her and her family."

His blood ran cold. He watched the car pull away with his mother in the backseat. Then he turned back to the officer. "You know that for sure?"

"He left a phone message." The officer checked his notepad. "Dirk's a very bad guy. He's vindictive. If he could get back at your mother by killing you, he'd do it. We think he's killed before in Indianapolis and Columbus, Ohio." The officer scowled. "He doesn't get caught. But when your mom told him she was calling us, he went ballistic. Left a death threat on her voicemail. With that and her testimony, we might have enough to put him away." He shook his head. "But we have to catch him first."

Cody felt like he was back on the battlefield of Iraq. Death threats? He pictured the enemy firing at him and his guys ... near an abandoned building in the Iraqi desert. He could feel the heat of the desert, see the sand stretched out in every direction. But this time he wasn't armed, he didn't have a platoon of guys around him. Just him against a crazy drug dealer. The futility of the moment sucked the wind from his lungs. Was this really happening? And what about Bailey and the Flanigans? How could he call her and tell her his mother had been arrested for dealing drugs? The Flanigan family would help him once he found a way to tell them. But first the police had to catch Benny Dirk.

Again he could practically feel his Army uniform hot against his skin, feel the sweaty helmet and taste the desert dust in his mouth. Suddenly another thought hit him. If he was in danger, that meant ...

"Bailey ..." he whispered her name, and then glanced at the officer.

The guy didn't hear him. He was radioing something to the car that now held his mother in the back seat.

Cody couldn't make out anything the officer was saying, because suddenly he couldn't shake the horrific thought. If there was a risk ... if there was even a possibility that his presence in Bailey's life could put her in danger, then —

"They're ready to pull out." The officer motioned for Cody to follow.

"Yes, sir." Scenes flashed in Cody's mind ... getting orders from his sergeant ... heading out to the mission that went awry ... getting captured by the enemy ... Cody blinked, shaking off the images. He walked slowly back to the car, avoiding the stares and whispers from the neighbors. But even so he had to admit the obvious: he was messy. His life was messy. Because the only family he had was cuffed and drugged and crying and on her way to the police station. And now both their lives were in danger. He was a former alcoholic, with a war injury that would last a lifetime, and a mother who would spend the rest of her days in and out of prison using drugs, dealing, and exposing Cody and whoever he might be dating to the sort of tawdry, dangerous lifestyle that went along with the drug culture. And now danger would follow him until Benny Dirk was arrested.

What business did he have even thinking about Bailey Flanigan?

As he climbed in his car, he looked at his mother in the back of the police car. She was no longer crying out, as far as he could tell. Her head was hung so far forward her neck looked broken. As they pulled away, she didn't look up or motion to him or make any connection at all. She didn't need to.

The lights on the police car said all there was to say.

Ten

BRANDON PAUL WAS PRETTY SURE HE'D made a mistake by agreeing to the lead role in *Unlocked*. The closer they got to filming, the more people came up to him on the street or in clubs, just about anywhere he was. They'd act surprised he'd taken a part in a Christian film, and they'd joke about how he was hardly a Christian role model.

Now that the movie was supposed to shoot in just a few weeks, he was already sick of the pressure. He never promised to be a choir boy, so why was everyone expecting that? The comments only made him want to prove everyone wrong. He wasn't a sissy Christian, no sir. And in the last few months he'd gone out of his way to silence anyone who thought differently.

One problem: his partying was getting a little too crazy. He had tried, but he hadn't found a way to slow himself down. Between the late nights and the drinking and drugs and girls, he could barely remember one day to the next. He'd been with more ladies than he could count, and taken more drugs and combinations of drugs than he wanted to admit. Now it was Monday morning, and he could hardly get out of bed.

His stomach hurt, and even the sliver of light from beneath his blinds was making his head pound. He groaned and grabbed a pillow from the other side of his bed. Only then did he realize he wasn't alone. There was a girl beside him. He leaned up on his elbow and squinted at her. Who was she, and how did she get there? He had a standing agreement with his driver that he was never — no way, ever — allowed to bring a girl back to his house.

It was one thing to hang with them at the club, fool around in the private rooms the club owners provided for him. But this?

"Hey ..." He nudged her once. Then again. "Hey!" he leaned closer to her, and the rancid smell of alcohol mixed with puke filled his nostrils. "Sick," he whispered. He fought his own urge to throw up right there beside her. Instead he kicked the covers off and stumbled through the darkness to his dresser. His phone had to be somewhere. He groped around the tabletop, not wanting to turn on the lights. He had no idea what he'd find in his bed, but he didn't want to see it. Finally he grasped his phone, and as the screen lit up his eyes narrowed in self-defense. His head was killing him now, and he realized he was still drugged or drunk. One of the two. The way his body felt, this was worse than a hangover. His driver lived in the back house, and he was always on call. Whatever Brandon needed.

This was one of those times.

He hit the button and waited while the phone rang. "Hey Brandon. What you need, man?"

"Trace ..." he whispered only loud enough for his driver to hear him. "There's a girl in my bed."

"I know. You insisted." Trace sounded frustrated. "I told you to leave her, man. Don't you remember what you told me?"

"How would I remember?" He winced at the pain in his head. "I barely remember my name."

"You told me you'd fire me, man. Told me I had to bring the girl back here or that was it. I could find a new job."

Brandon slumped against his bedroom wall. He rattled off a string of obscenities. "Look, man, I'm sorry. That wasn't me."

"I told you that last night." Trace sounded a little relieved. "You wouldn't have it any other way."

"Okay, okay." He rubbed his temples, trying to focus. "I don't know who she is or where she lives." Every word took effort. "But I need her out of here. She's ... she's made a mess in my bed."

"How romantic."

"Shut up." Brandon needed Trace. The guy was the most loyal member of his staff. But he didn't need sarcasm. Not feeling the way he did. "Just get the help in here, will you? Send one of the women. Someone to get her sobered up and dressed. Someone to clean the bed."

Again Brandon fought a wave of nausea. How had he let himself sink this low? What if the girl had diseases? He couldn't remember what she looked like or where he'd met her or anything about what they might've done together.

"I'm on it, boss. Don't worry." Trace hung up and Brandon set his phone down.

What was he supposed to do now? He realized he was naked, and he pulled open his second dresser drawer to find a pair of shorts. He slipped them on and slunk out of his room, down the hall and into one of the guestrooms. There, he hit a button on the wall and the blinds shut out the glaring morning sunlight.

The effort of getting here had taken all his energy, so as soon as the room was pitch black, he peeled back the covers and fell into bed. What was happening to him? If the paparazzi got wind that he'd brought a girl home — a total stranger, no less — they'd run it on the front pages the way they'd been running everything about him lately.

All of which took him back to the first thought he'd had as he came to this morning. Why had he agreed to star in *Unlocked*? The producers were angry with him already. That's the message his agent gave him yesterday. Brock Baker was the top agent in town, and he expected a high degree of professionalism from his clients. As soon as Brandon heard Brock's tone he knew he was in trouble.

"Look, buddy, I've talked to you about the partying. You have to keep it under wraps." Brock sounded more frustrated than ever before. "The producers from Jeremiah Productions called. They tell me you're in violation of your contract, the character clause."

"I don't like that clause."

"Well, I do. It'll keep you healthy and working."

"I'm perfectly healthy and I've got too many offers to work in a lifetime." Brandon didn't care if he sounded flip. He didn't like anyone telling him what to do. Especially in light of the whole Christian thing.

"I'm going to say this once, so listen hard." Brock's voice held a new sort of edge, one Brandon had never heard from him before. "You're not invincible. Lots of guys as big as you go down in flames. They overdose, and a maid finds them face down, dead in their pillow. They drop cold on a sidewalk outside some club, or they get in a car wreck before their thirtieth birthday. The way you're going, that'll be you, Brandon. In our world, the brightest flames burn out the fastest." He paused, and his intensity could be felt through the phone lines. "Tone it down. Before it's too late."

The conversation stayed with Brandon through the night, but he didn't heed it. Didn't feel like heeding it. Why couldn't he party and hang with a bunch of different girls? He'd earned this, right? The chance to do what he wanted when he was off the clock.

Brandon rolled over in his guest bed, and through the walls he heard the sound of female voices. He had a staff of four workers who kept the house clean and cooked for him. The four workers and Trace were always available for anything he might need. Right now he didn't envy them. The cleanup in the next room had to be horrific.

He grimaced and tried to will their voices to quiet down. He remembered getting his agent's call, and he remembered disregarding it. But he couldn't remember anything after that, which could only mean one thing.

His agent was right.

He needed to tone it down. He wanted to have fun, sure, but

he wanted to go the distance in his career. The thought of waking up next to a stranger again scared him. He could've just as easily not woken up at all. He was that unaware of his actions.

Images of headlines from days and years gone by flashed in his mind — like Brock said, the brightest stars, burned out too soon. For the first time his fear wasn't a fleeting feeling. It was real and alive, as if the girl in his bed had been replaced with a living fear twice his size. And now the fear breathed its hot breath in his face and laughed at him, mocking him because there wasn't a thing Brandon could do to make it go away. No phone call or staff member who would cart it off.

Fear this strong could work its way under his skin and stay there for an hour or a day. Maybe even forever. He tried to take a deep breath, but his lungs wouldn't cooperate. What was wrong with them? Had he taken something last night that made them stop working? Maybe that's why he still wasn't feeling right, hours after his wild night.

Suddenly he remembered one other time he'd felt this afraid. It was the time some girl first mentioned her surprise he was starring in a Christian film. She had teased him, insinuating he must be a believer now and maybe he was changing his image. But he had kissed her square on the lips and told her he wouldn't be turning Christian any time soon. That statement had stayed close to him, and with it this same sort of heart-stopping fear. He tried another breath. And another. And finally, since he couldn't fill his lungs, he pushed the air out, exhaled as hard as he could.

Come on? What was this? Why was he feeling like he wouldn't live to see noon? Sweat broke out across his forehead, and he kicked off the covers once more. He couldn't lie here, not another minute. He needed water. Water and a warm shower. That would help him feel better. But over the next hour, through a few glasses of cool water and after he'd taken a long hot shower, Brandon still felt a strange, strangling sort of anxiety. He dressed and checked his bedroom. The girl — whoever she was — had been taken away. Trace must've figured out where she lived. His bed was clean and freshly made, and a candle burned on the dresser — the staff's way of ridding the room of the stench.

He shuddered. How could he have let things get so out of control? The answer was obvious. It was because this was what he'd wanted, what he'd demanded. Life on his terms, no one telling him what to do. But here he was, having done what he wanted, and he felt terrible. He felt sick over whatever must've happened last night.

Breathe, he ordered himself. *Stop shaking and breathe.*

His body barely cooperated, so he powered up the blinds and let the sunlight hit him square in his face. It was a beautiful day outside — nothing but sunshine and great weather across Los Angeles. He was more sober now than before, so everything was okay, right? He didn't need to be afraid of the impending night and all it held. No matter where he went or how he made it home, the morning always came.

Brandon blinked, and realized his thoughts were rambling. As if maybe he weren't okay. Maybe his brain had been messed up permanently by the drugs and drinking. He gulped another drink of air, and slowly he crossed his room and sat down. His parents wouldn't recognize him now. They were back in Missouri, back in their slow lifestyle, living in the fear of the Lord — everything Brandon had rejected when he left home.

His mother's voice rang through his mind, the way it did more often these days. *What good is it for a man to gain the whole world and yet forfeit his soul . . . ?* That's what she'd reminded him when they had finally talked again for the first time after too many years of silence. *Be careful, Brandon,* she'd told him. *God wants His people to forgive.*

Was that why these things were happening to him now? Was God finding him out? Was that this strange fear that wouldn't leave his side, even now when he should've been well into his day? And was it because he was doing *Unlocked* that God was hunting him down? Because he had agreed to a Christian film? Did he really think he could avoid the wrath of God forever? Or that because he'd stopped believing in God that meant God ceased to be real?

Another shiver ran over him, and he checked his email on his phone. Maybe he should write the producers a note and pull out. Better to stay clear of the whole Christianity thing. If the paparazzi looked too closely, they'd find a story that would make them run for photos and details. He could see the headlines now: 'Brandon Paul, *Former Sunday School Kid ...*'

He'd worked so hard. He'd created a persona that left the past entirely behind, back in a place he never would've thought about visiting again.

Until now.

His hands trembled as he looked through his mail, and there near the top of his inbox was something from Keith Ellison. Keith made him nervous. The guy had a way of looking straight through him. Dayne was easier. Dayne might be a believer now, all sold out to his faith or whatever, but not long ago he'd been exactly like Brandon. At least the two of them could relate to each other. Dayne was one of the reasons Brandon hadn't pulled out of the picture already.

He opened the email and read it. Apparently he was being flown back to Bloomington, Indiana, for a screen test with a fresh face, a new talent. A girl named Bailey Flanigan. Just to be sure they'd have chemistry together. The email included a video link to her first test and a short bio on her. A picture was also attached, and—as his interest piqued—Brandon suddenly forgot the fear he'd been running from all morning.

In a few seconds, the photo downloaded and filled up the screen on his iPhone. A low whistle came from him and he stared at her, at those beautiful blue eyes. She was gorgeous, and not like the girls he knew in Hollywood. This girl would never be seen in a club — her shining eyes told him that much. Whoever she was, he could tell by looking at her that flying out for the screen test would be a waste of time. He would have chemistry with her wherever they filmed, whatever roles the two of them played.

She looked like a doe-eyed starlet from a bygone era ... when innocence was real and films — like life — were watched in black and white. Her cameo face and long shiny brown hair that hung in different lengths of layers around her cheekbones. Brandon sat up straighter in his seat. Maybe he'd stay with the movie after all. He clicked the video link and hovered over his phone, breathless as he waited for her reel to come to life. As it did, his admiration for her doubled. She might not have a lengthy bio, and this might be her first lead in a feature film, but she was a natural. She had passion and energy and a sincerity Brandon hadn't seen in far too long.

She would bring an authenticity to the role of Ella another actress would've had to fake. Ella was the most Christian character in the story. It was her belief that Holden Harris could be helped by the power of prayer and music, and in the end it was her determination that allowed his character to become unlocked — to step out of his prison of autism.

He had asked the producers from the beginning if they would find a wholesome new face for the role of Ella — someone he could play off of easily, someone that would make his job of playing Holden Harris that much more believable.

This Bailey Flanigan — whoever she was — couldn't have been more perfect.

Brandon watched her reel five times through, until he was so mesmerized by her eyes, he felt like a new person. Invigorated. The fear that had suffocated him all morning was gone completely. *Bailey Flanigan,* he said her name over and over again in his mind. He needed more information about her, more details.

He stood, slipped his phone into his pocket, and padded through the house to his office. Two of the women on his cleaning staff smiled at him as he walked past. Not the sort of smile that approved of him or asked for more time and attention from him. The sort of smile that reminded him they were paid by him, and they would do their jobs. Even if they hated them.

As he walked into the office and shut the door behind him, for the first time since becoming a star, Brandon felt embarrassed. The staff shouldn't have to deal with random women in his bed or the sort of mess they'd cleaned up today. He gritted his teeth and gave a single shake of his head. It wouldn't happen again. He needed to turn over a new leaf. His agent was right.

He moved his mouse, and the screen on his Mac came to life. Maybe she was on Facebook. Maybe she had a Twitter account. He had to have a way to learn more about her. He started with a simple search of her name on YouTube and, sure enough, there was a two-minute clip of her and some guy singing a duet. Brandon scrutinized the wording that accompanied the clip. The guy was her brother? Good. Maybe she was single. He watched her perform, listened to her voice and again he felt his insides turn to mush. She was breathtaking, in every possible way. Maybe the screenwriter could work a musical number into *Unlocked*. That way everyone could hear her sing.

When he'd exhausted his search on YouTube, he moved to Facebook. After a few searches, he felt his heart skip a beat. There she was, staring straight at him. Her blue eyes calling to him from somewhere inside the computer screen. He quickly pulled up her profile and immediately noticed something that made his heart soar. First, she didn't have her Facebook set to private — because everything was visible for him to see. And second, she wasn't in a relationship. At the same time, the photos just below her status showed her on a football field surrounded by what looked like high school players — some black, some white — and a young-looking guy who seemed to be a coach. He had his arm around her, which irked Brandon a little.

Not that it mattered. Whoever the guy was, Brandon wasn't worried. Bailey Flanigan simply hadn't met *him* yet. When she did, she wouldn't know what hit her. Because he could be charming if he wanted. He scanned her profile, reading her updates and checking out her other pictures. What he learned in the next hour told him Bailey was the real deal. A girl strong in her faith, with a great family. Something else caught Brandon's eye, and he ran a quick Google search.

Sure enough. Bailey Flanigan's father was Jim Flanigan, offensive coordinator for the Indianapolis Colts. So little Miss Bailey was a rich girl, no doubt. Used to the finer things in life. Maybe they weren't that different, after all. He made a quick call to Keith Ellison and gave the go-ahead for the flight. He'd fly into Indianapolis early Tuesday night and be ready for Wednesday's screen test.

"Did you watch her reel?"

"I did." He tried to keep his enthusiasm from sounding too loudly in his voice. "She's impressive."

"I think you'll love her."

Brandon chuckled quietly because after spending an hour studying Bailey on Facebook, he already loved her. The fear and disgust from last night were little more than a distant memory after spending time with Bailey. He could hardly wait to meet her and test with her. After that, maybe they could hit the town, see what Bloomington was really all about. "She's ... she's the daughter of a pro coach, right?"

"She is." Keith sounded skeptical, like he wondered why Brandon was asking.

"So is she really, you know ... all that innocent? The way she comes across?"

A long silence met him in response, and when Keith started

talking again there was a critical sound to his voice. "She's definitely very innocent, Brandon. That's why we're thinking about offering her a contract." He paused. "Based on your recent escapades in the tabloids lately, the two of you won't have much in common. That's why we need a screen test. If you have no chemistry, we want to find out now."

This time Brandon's laugh sounded over the phone lines. "Oh, don't worry." He tried to sound nonthreatening. "We'll have chemistry. Even if she is a little church girl."

Again there was a loud silence from Keith. "Brock talked to you, right? About the contract — the character clause?"

"He did." Brandon forced himself to be more serious. If he wasn't careful, Keith really might fire him. And then he'd never get the chance to meet Bailey in person. And suddenly he wanted that more than he'd wanted anything in a long time. He cleared his voice. "Look, I'm sorry about the last few months. I ... well, I let things get out of hand."

"Yeah, I'd say." Sarcasm painted broad strokes over the producer's words. "Completely out of hand."

"It won't happen again." He thought about the plans he had for that night. The guys were counting on him, but he'd have to turn them down. He needed a few nights at home if he was going to have his mind straight for the trip to Bloomington. "I mean it, Keith. I'm staying home tonight."

"Good." Keith sounded relieved. "I'll have my assistant book the flight and get the confirmation to you."

"First class, okay?" He laughed. "My private jet's in the shop. Otherwise I'd find my own way out there."

"Of course." Keith hesitated. He sounded far less friendly than the last time they spoke. "Just make sure you're sober."

Brandon promised, and the call ended. He stared out the window at the hazy blue sky and thought about what laid ahead. He'd been telling the truth. His private jet really was in the shop — even though Keith probably thought he was trying to be smart. He shared the jet with a well-known pop star, and they took turns using it to get to location shoots or appearances, concerts, those types of things. He thought about Bailey Flanigan again. He pulled her image back up on Facebook and stared into her eyes. What would it take to get her attention, to make it so she was as excited to meet him as he was to meet her? Maybe he could convince her to take a trip with him when the jet was fixed. They could fly to New York ... catch a Broadway show. That would turn her head, right?

Of course, his name would be enough for most girls. But she wasn't most girls. With a quick catch of his breath, an idea came to him. In a series of hurried taps on his phone he friend-requested her. A smile crept up his face as he pictured Bailey at home with her family, getting an email notice that Brandon Paul wanted to be her Facebook friend.

Again he stared at her, at the innocence in her eyes and the passion in her expression. "You're not like the rest, are you Bailey? I can see that," he voiced the question out loud. "So what will it take?" He thought about how he'd dress and what he'd say to her, how he'd let her know he wasn't ignorant to her faith or her values. They were something he could play off if he needed to. That's why he had to stay away from the partying between now and then. Otherwise she'd see right through him. Whatever it took, he'd find a way to get her attention. Because one way or another he was going to make Bailey Flanigan fall in love with him.

The job was as good as done.

BAILEY WAS HELPING RICKY WITH HIS MATH HOMEWORK, sitting at the game table in the corner of the family room, when the alert sounded on her phone, telling her a new email had come in. She ignored it at first, since Ricky was right in the middle of a word problem.

"You get it right, buddy? If Susie walks two miles an hour and Bobby walks three miles an hour, and the walk from their house to school is four miles, then you see the formula, right? So you can figure out how long it takes each of them to get there?"

"I think so." Ricky squinted and tapped his pencil. Then, the way it sometimes happened with math, his expression changed and he grinned big. "Oh, I get it. I have to multiply."

"Right." Bailey was happy to help her little brother. She'd struggled with math most of her life, so now it felt good to give back a little, use some of what her schooling had taught her so Ricky might understand math a little sooner than she did. All around her the boys were caught up in some form of homework. Shawn and Justin were on the kitchen floor, using glue sticks to attach photos and blocks of text on a poster board for a health project due tomorrow. BJ was reading on the couch, and Connor was playing the piano in the next room. After a full day of school-work and football, Connor usually spent an hour or so writing songs and singing. His music was the soundtrack of their home.

Bailey smiled, because this was what she'd remember. The life and love and music in her home. When she left here — however that happened, whenever that was — she would always remember nights like this. Her dad was still at practice, but he'd be home anytime, usually before Monday night football. It was a family tradition to watch the game together, no matter who was playing. Tonight's contest between the Green Bay Packers and the Minnesota Vikings was particularly important since both teams would inevitably have a shot at winning their division. The Flanigan kids knew those sorts of details.

The only thing missing tonight was Cody. Normally he brought the boys home after practice and stayed around for the Monday night game. But Bailey hadn't been able to reach him since yesterday, when he left so suddenly. They'd texted, but only briefly. Bailey finally got word from him around noon that day, but his texts were brief and without any of his usual sweet words or emotion. He told her his mother was going to be okay, and that he'd explain more later.

But that afternoon Coach Taylor brought the boys home, and Justin came right up to her, his expression baffled. "What's up with Cody?"

"What do you mean?" Bailey felt a nervousness run through her. Everything had been going so well. If something was wrong, why hadn't he told her?

Shawn joined them. "He was like a different person today. Barely talked to anyone, barking out orders. He left right after practice."

Connor had gone straight for a glass of water, but he shrugged as he entered the conversation. "He seemed fine. Just a little distant, maybe."

That had been an hour ago, and since then Bailey had texted Cody three times — but he hadn't answered any of them. She even tried calling, but like last night he didn't pick up. If this was about his mother, why was he ignoring her? She was on his side. Whatever was wrong, he could tell her. Besides, she hadn't told him about the audition yet. She didn't want to tell him in a text, but she was practically bursting with the news.

Ricky began working out the problem, and as he did Bailey remembered the email alert. She checked her inbox, and what she saw made her push back from the table. "What?" She let out a half scream. "I can't believe this! Oh my goodness, this is unreal!" She held up her phone as she stood and did a little dance around the table. "Mom, listen!"

Her mom had been in the kids' computer room, just off the kitchen, working on a magazine piece about being a coach's wife. The area was adjacent to the family room, so her mom slid her chair back so she could see Bailey. Her look was baffled. "Did Cody get ahold of you?"

"No." She ignored the momentary disappointment as she raised her phone in the air. "Brandon Paul friend-requested me!" She squealed again. "Can you believe it? Brandon Paul wants to be my Facebook friend!"

"No way!" Ricky put his pencil down. "Wait'll the kids at school hear about this!" He stood and pumped his fist in the air. "I think this calls for a math break."

"No math break." Their mom smiled, one eyebrow raised. "Get a drink, and back to work." She shook her head, more amused than bothered. "Brandon Paul is just a person like anyone else."

"I know, but still ..." Bailey settled back down, still amazed. Was this really happening? Was she actually being considered for a lead role in a major motion picture opposite Brandon Paul? What would Cody think? The answer came immediately. He'd be thrilled for her, the way he always celebrated anything good that happened in her life. The way she rejoiced at his success as a football coach. She could hardly wait to tell him, and once more she tried calling. But again he didn't pick up, and she tried to remind herself it was still a school night. She had homework, and so did Cody, most likely. Maybe his mom was sick and he was doing his homework at her house. But the fact remained, her whole world was about to change. Maybe she and Brandon could become friends ... maybe he'd get to know her whole family and if she won the part, he might come to share the Flanigan family's faith in Christ. The same way Cody did years ago.

How great would that be?

Bailey tried to sit still, tried not to bounce around the house bubbling over with excitement for all that laid ahead. As she worked through another half hour of math with Ricky, she prayed between problems that God would use her to make a difference in Brandon's life. That she would be a very bright light and God would keep her steady and strong. Because she had a feeling the ride ahead would be the wildest one she'd ever experienced.

For her and for Brandon Paul.

Eleven

THE SCENE AT THE JAIL HAD gone from bad to worse. His mother threw up, and then she passed out in her cell and bruised her head in the fall. The jailer told Cody he would have to wait until late Monday before he could post bail. She had to be sober before they would release her. Cody stayed with her, sitting in the jail waiting room most of the night, and barely dragging himself to class Monday morning. After football practice, he hurried back to the jail, ready to bail her out. In the end, Cody could only afford it one way: his coaching money. Her bail cost more than he would make in ten seasons coaching at Clear Creek High, but the bail bondsman wanted only a small percentage to spring her. So Cody paid it.

The drive back to her house was marked with silence and tension, and halfway there Cody decided they should go to his off-campus apartment instead. Benny wouldn't look for them there —at least he hoped not. The Iraq flashbacks had continued, and he hated the feeling—like he was entering a war without a weapon. Avoiding her house was at least one way to protect the two of them. As they crossed Bloomington, Cody wanted to ask his mom every question slamming around in his head. But he knew if he did, the questions would become a verbal attack, so he kept quiet. As he pulled up out front of his apartment complex, he scanned the street for Benny's red Honda. Just in case.

"They haven't caught him, have they?" His mom must've known what Cody was looking for, why he was acting so cautious.

"No." Cody stole a glance at her. Dark circles cut into her face beneath her eyes and her voice trembled. She looked like she'd been run over and left in the gutter overnight. She didn't smell great, either. He clenched his jaw. "They didn't catch him."

"He knows. I'm sure he knows." She shuddered a little as they parked outside his apartment complex. "He'll figure out where I am, and then he'll kill me." She turned to him, her eyes full of terror. "He would do it, Cody. He said he would. He would kill you, too." She covered her face, clearly distraught at the possibility.

He wanted to scream at her, but he restrained himself. "Why?" It took all his effort to keep his voice controlled. "Why would you date a guy like that?"

Slowly she lowered her hands, and shame deepened the lines on her face. She stared at her hands and then finally at him again. "Free dope ..." she looked like she hated herself. "That's it. Free dope."

He stuffed his anger as far down as he could. "Let's go in."

He cooked scrambled eggs and toast, piling on the butter because she needed meat on her bones. Especially if she were headed back to prison, and she was. No matter what she testified about Benny Dirk. The officer and the bail bondsman had told him that much.

Not until late that night did his mom open up about her slide back into drugs. "He told me I was pretty." She was huddled in the corner of his sofa, her elbows and shoulders jutting out, her body more frail than Cody had first thought. "We partied together, and I told myself ... I promised it would happen just one time. One night with a guy who thought I was pretty."

Cody didn't say anything. He kept thinking about Bailey and how in the world he could ever tell her what had happened. He wished he were back on her parents' porch swing, cuddled beside her and ready to ask her to be his girlfriend. Instead he was here, and the problem with his mother, the danger of Benny Dirk wasn't going away.

"Cody, say something." She lifted weary eyes to him. "You're mad at me, right?"

"Mom..." He uttered a futile groan. "What sort of question is that?" He stood and walked to the window and back. He was angry and hurt and he felt like she'd betrayed him just when she was starting to live. He was afraid for her life, and for his ... maybe even for the people he loved. People like Bailey and her family —or the kids at Clear Creek. There was no telling how crazy Benny Dirk might be. He exhaled, defeated. Telling his mom all that would destroy her. Instead, he walked closer and sat on the sofa beside her. "We'll get through this." He hugged her, and it occurred to him that soon enough he wouldn't even be able to hug her. Not whenever he wanted to, anyway. "We'll get through it."

"When's the hearing?" His mom trembled as she asked the question.

"Wednesday. Two days from now." Cody's voice sounded flat, unemotional. He still couldn't believe this was happening, that his mother was about to be locked away for three or four years. Maybe longer.

"You don't think they'll put me back in prison, do you? If I testify against Benny?" She sounded like a little girl, helpless and scared. "Promise me ... Please. Don't let them lock me up."

"Mom." Cody stood and paced to the kitchen. From there he turned and looked straight at her. "You knew the terms of your parole. Another offense, and you'd go back to prison. There's nothing I can do to stop it from happening. You'll get a lighter sentence, maybe. But you'll still serve time."

For a moment it looked like his mother might argue the fact. But then the reality seemed to come over her. The truth brought tears to her eyes, and the picture she made sitting there hurt Cody to the center of his heart. He wanted to run from here, jump in his car and go to Bailey's house. Take her with him and drive until he couldn't drive another mile. As if maybe then he could escape the reality of the upcoming hearing, and the danger of Benny Dirk, and all that would come with it.

But there was no escape.

Not then, and not two days later when he drove his mother to the county courthouse and took a seat beside her in the middle row. She'd been assigned free counsel, but so far they hadn't met her lawyer. Cody could only hope he would show up before his mother's case came up.

"I'm scared," she whispered in Cody's ear. "I can't believe this is happening."

Cody wanted to say he couldn't believe it either. Instead, he leaned close to her. "Pray, Mom. That's what you need to do. Pray to Jesus."

He reminded himself to do the same thing as he watched the sad and broken dregs of humanity flow in and out of the courtroom. *God ... what will happen after this? How can I let her go off to Indianapolis? No one will care about her there. And what about Benny?* They were the sorts of questions he hadn't asked himself back when he was thirteen and she'd gone to prison. But now he was older. He had a responsibility to his mother, no matter what happened here today. He thought about Bailey, about the quick conversation they'd had earlier. He still hadn't told her about his mother — because how could he? Especially when she had been full of such great news. All he could do was celebrate with her over the phone and hope he sounded sincere. Her big screen test was today — and if it went well she'd star opposite Brandon Paul in *Unlocked.* She was having the biggest day of her life.

While he sat in a courtroom with his mother.

The judge had a full docket, but he moved through each item quickly. After an hour he looked up and called her name. "Cassie Coleman. You're present, I assume."

His mother stood. "Yes, your honor."

"And counsel?" Just as the judge asked, a heavy set man with an overstuffed briefcase burst into the room. The judge looked amazed at the man, as if this sort of unprofessional behavior would certainly not be tolerated. "Are you counsel for Ms. Cassie Coleman?"

"I am, your honor. I just got the case an hour ago."

Wonderful, Cody thought to himself. *She might as well not have an attorney.* The guy couldn't help her now, no matter how timely or talented he was. The evidence combined with his mother's past record would weigh heavier than anything a lawyer could say. The man held up one finger. "Your honor, I'd like five minutes with my client, if you please."

The judge glared at the disheveled attorney. Then he looked at Cody's mother, and his expression eased a little. "Very well." He rapped his gavel on the desk in front of him. "We'll take a five-minute recess and convene after that." The judge hurried from his chair to his chambers behind the courtroom.

Cody's mom reached down and squeezed his hand. "Pray for me."

"I am." Cody wished he could take her far from here and will away the past few months and every mistake his mother had made. But he couldn't. He watched her walk timidly toward the attorney, whose nose was stuck in a file. The man seemed surprised by her presence, and he led her to a few chairs at the front of the courtroom. The place where defendants sat.

Cody watched, praying for her, begging God for some way out. *Save her, Lord. Please ... I don't know if either of us can take another prison sentence. And please help the police find Benny Dirk. Let us find a way out of this nightmare ... please. We can't do this without You.* There was no answer, but Cody felt God's presence. He wasn't alone — that much was sure. Cody stared at the quiet meeting between his mom and the attorney. Five minutes. What could possibly be discussed in that little time?

The recess flew by, and the judge reappeared with a flourish of his robes. He sat down and rapped his gavel again. "Court is in session. We'll address the matter of the state of Indiana versus Cassie Coleman." He gave an exaggerated look at the still breathless attorney. "Is counsel ready?"

A nervous look passed over the man's face. He gave Cody's mom an awkward lopsided smile and then nodded at the judge. "Yes, your honor. We're ready."

Cody hadn't watched a proceeding like this before, but he was sure of one thing: If it hadn't been for the Flanigan family, if God hadn't reached in and saved him from alcoholism back when Cody was a senior in high school, this would've been a familiar scene in his own life. Because he certainly would've wound up on drugs and in and out of prison, just like his mother. He was headed that way when he nearly died — when God spared his life.

Thinking of the Flanigans made him think of Bailey. If his mother had handled things differently, today he'd be making plans to celebrate with her. He could feel her in his arms, see her eyes the way they felt when they were lost in his. How long until it would be safe to spend time with her? He hurt at the thought, and he forced himself not to think about her.

The judge read from a piece of paper stating the evidence against Cody's mom. "Ms. Coleman you're on parole for dealing drugs, are you aware of that?"

His mom looked at her attorney, but the man was lost in his file again. She nodded. "Yes, your honor."

"And you're aware that another offense brings with it a mandatory five years in state prison and a maximum sentence of twenty years?"

This time his mom looked like she might pass out. "Yes, your honor." Her voice was weak, her face pale.

Cody pushed himself to the edge of his seat, ready to spring into action if she fainted. *Mom, hang in there ... God, please save her. Help us.*

The judge scanned the evidence. "I'd like to state for the record that Ms. Coleman was arrested by police Sunday night as part of a drug bust involving a major drug dealer — Benny Dirk." He looked further down the piece of paper. "It looks like police confiscated seven ounces of cocaine from Ms. Coleman's car and nearly half a pound of marijuana."

Cody closed his eyes and hung his head. It was over. He had no idea the police had found those amounts. A trace of drugs, a small baggie — that was one thing. But seven ounces of coke? Half a pound of marijuana? The judge would lock his mother up and throw away the key. He could already feel the sentence coming.

"I also understand you're willing to testify against Mr. Dirk — who remains at large. But at this time, I can only go with the evidence." He paused, his brow raised. "By the authority of the previous parole agreement, Ms. Coleman, I'm afraid I have to mandate you to five years in state prison. This could possibly be adjusted by a year or so if you actually turn state's evidence against Mr. Dirk. But that would require his arrest, obviously."

Five years? Cody felt like he'd been sucker-punched. Five years until his mother would be out? He'd be pushing thirty by then. The news was worse than he had ever imagined. He was still trying to get his mind around their new reality when his mother's attorney stood.

"Your honor," his mother's lawyer raised his hand. "I'd like to add that Ms. Coleman had gone nearly three years without an incident prior to this." He had a piece of paper in his hand. "If the court pleases, I'd like to present a hospital chart for the record."

"What's the point of this, counsel?" The judge looked bothered again. He had other cases ahead, more people to lock up. Clearly he didn't like the delay.

"The point is, this woman was making a serious attempt at living a normal, law-abiding, contributing lifestyle. The problem, as you'll see here," he handed the piece of paper over, "is that Ms. Coleman is a drug addict. She needs help, not a prison sentence. Certainly, your honor, five years is a very aggressive punishment for this defendant given her history."

Cody held his breath. This was more than he had expected from the man. *Please, God ... be with us.*

The judge took the paper and studied it for less than a minute. "You make a good point, counsel." He looked surprised anything good could come from the attorney. "It's within my power to lessen the sentence for Ms. Coleman based on her past three years and her ongoing battle with drug addiction. That said, it is still very important to keep in mind what's at stake here." He looked at Cody's mom. "Ms. Coleman, if you had merely been caught using drugs, I might allow a different outcome. But as it stands, you not only returned to using but to dealing. This court will not tolerate dealing from any citizen, at any time. Do you understand that, Ms. Coleman?"

"Yes." His mom was visibly shaking, barely able to speak. "Yes, your honor, I do."

"Very well, then." He took a long breath and looked from the lawyer back to Cody's mother again. "This court will allow a reduced sentence of four years and I will reserve the right to reduce that further based on future testimony against Mr. Dirk. As previously stated. Until that time, the defendant will serve her punishment at the Indiana Women's Prison. The defendant is to be remanded into custody immediately ..."

Four years ... Cody could breathe again — even if it took effort. With a simple argument, the judge had shaved off a year, so maybe he'd cut her remaining sentence in half if she testified. Of course, by doing so his mother would remain in danger — maybe for the rest of her life. The possibility was daunting, more than Cody could think about.

He closed his eyes and suddenly he was in the cage again, a

prisoner of war in the middle of Iraq, and a militant soldier was blindfolding him and spinning him around, jabbing the butt of a gun into his stomach. And his captor was shouting something Cody couldn't understand. He gasped and opened his eyes, and the scene from Iraq disappeared. What was happening to him? Why the flashbacks now, when he'd been home for two years?

He grabbed the back of the bench in front of him and steadied himself. The judge was going on. "Ms. Coleman, while at Indiana Women's Prison you will be assigned work duty in the laundry facility. I'm also making a note that you should receive ongoing drug counseling while in residence at the prison. Perhaps when you are released next time you'll be more successful at life on the outside." He rapped his gavel. "The court will take a fifteen-minute recess."

Cody watched the judge leave, as if the woman standing before him were no one special, just another lowdown drug dealer headed back to prison. The people in the audience stood and talked in quiet tones to their attorneys or family members. Cody couldn't hear any of it. The only voice he could hear was the pitiful whimpering coming from his mother. "Cody ..."

His eyes met hers, and she shook her head in small frantic movements. Her face was grayish white, and again she looked ready to faint. "Cody ... help me." Her voice wasn't so much audible as it was a quiet muttering. But he could read her lips, and he knew deep in his heart every word she was saying. "Please, Cody ... don't let them take me. Please ..."

He had no idea what to do. It was one thing to fight a war and survive capture by a foreign army. But this? How was he supposed to handle this? Was he supposed to ask for a second chance or tell the attorney to push for a still shorter sentence? He clenched his jaw and released the hold he had on the bench. He reached her just as the bailiff was approaching with handcuffs.

"Don't we ... don't we get some time?"

The bailiff gave him a puzzled look, but after a few seconds a slight bit of pity filled the guy's eyes. "It doesn't work that way."

"Yeah, but ..." Cody looked at his mother's attorney. "We need time. I have to tell her goodbye."

"The sentence is already in effect." The attorney held his worn briefcase at his side. "I'm sorry. I did the best I could."

Cody thanked the man, but he didn't want to talk to the attorney. These were his final moments with his mom. She was shivering harder now, and Cody wished he would've brought her a coat or a sweater — something to put over her shoulders, so she didn't have to go away so freezing cold.

The lawyer left without another word, and now just Cody and the bailiff remained with her. "Couldn't I bring her back tomorrow? After we pack her things?"

"She violated parole." The bailiff seemed confused. "You should've known she'd be sent away today."

"It's o-o-okay, Cody." His mother was no longer crying out for help, begging Cody to save her from being hauled away. Like the bailiff said, her sentence was already in effect. In a few hours, she'd be signed in at the women's prison, issued her orange jumpsuit, and given a bunk like the other inmates.

There was nothing Cody could do about it. "Mom ..." The bailiff handcuffed her while people in the courtroom watched. Cody felt his heart breaking, felt his lungs bursting from the sadness of it. He wanted to scream at everyone in the room to look away. This was his mother. She deserved some respect, after all. But instead he only reached out and put his hand on her shoulder.

"I need to take her." The bailiff clearly had a job to do. He shook his head, indicating Cody didn't have the right to touch his prisoner or stop him in any way.

Cody withdrew his hand. "I'll bring you your things. I'll come see you, Mom. I will."

"I'm sorry." She started crying, quietly but with an intensity that shook her soul. "I'm so sorry, Cody ... you don't de-de-de-serve this." Alarm filled her eyes. "And watch out for Benny ... please, Cody ... stay away from him."

"I will."

The bailiff began to lead her from the room. "We have to go."

"Mom ... pray." This time he spoke louder than before. "Pray to Jesus!" He didn't care who was listening or what sort of scene they were making. If this was his last time to talk to his mother before they locked her away, he had to tell her the only thing that mattered.

She craned her neck, using every bit of strength to look over her shoulder one last time at him. She didn't cry out or scream or weep or say any actual words. But she did the only thing that mattered in light of what he'd asked her to do.

She nodded.

Twelve

BAILEY WAS QUIET ON THE WAY to the screen test, even though her nerves were rattling wildly inside her. She wanted to be thrilled about the audition, thanking God for the opportunity. But her mind was preoccupied by something that had been troubling her since Sunday. What in the world was wrong with Cody?

"You okay?" Her mom was driving. Again Bailey was grateful her mom had time like this, time to take her to the audition and stay by her side making sure Bailey had a confidante if she needed one.

"I'm fine." She looked out the window at the maple trees that lined Main Street. "Just thinking about Cody."

"You still haven't heard from him?"

"We talked for a few minutes today." Bailey turned toward her mother. "I told him about the audition." She paused. "He seemed happy for me, I guess. He said he was tired, something about getting off the phone so he could study for a test tomorrow."

"Well." Her mom's expression said she didn't feel Cody's explanation was far-fetched. "He's taking a full load of classes. Maybe the test had him distracted."

"Maybe." Bailey leaned her head back against the seat. "But I know him better than that. He isn't himself. Something's wrong."

"Whatever it is, I'm sure he'll talk to you about it later." Her mom patted her knee. "He wouldn't want you worrying about it now. Right?"

"Right." Bailey was quiet again. Maybe that was it ... maybe Cody was worried about her audition, thinking she was going to get the part and fall for Brandon Paul. He'd done this before ... thinking she deserved someone better, a different life, a different sort of guy than him. She pictured the way he'd looked sitting on the porch with her Sunday night before the call from his mother. The depth and love in his eyes. No, it wasn't possible. He wasn't going to walk away again. Not after all they'd found together this past summer. They pulled into the parking lot and Bailey let her worries about Cody go. "Pray for me, will you?"

Her mom took her hand and spoke a brief but powerful prayer, asking the Lord to shine through Bailey and make this performance her best ever. They left the car, and as they neared the front door Bailey reminded herself what was happening. She was about to do a screen test with Brandon Paul! She could feel a smile light up her face, and she turned dancing eyes at her mom. "Can you believe this?"

Her mom's eyes lit up and she did a stationary little dance while Bailey opened the front door. Once inside it was only a minute before Keith Ellison entered from the other room and welcomed them. He explained that the screen test would last about an hour, and that Bailey's mom was welcome to stay — same as before. Then he ushered them in.

Bailey exhaled in small, short bursts, forcing herself to stay in the moment and not drop from disbelief. She was about to meet Brandon Paul. *The* Brandon Paul. She steadied herself and walked behind Mr. Ellison, and suddenly there he was — America's favorite new actor — the star of NTM's hottest teen series.

He was talking to Dayne and Eleanor Ainsworth at one end of the room. Another man was with them — someone Bailey didn't recognize. But before she could think about who he might be, Brandon turned toward them and his eyes met hers. His grin was immediate and genuine. "Bailey?"

"Yes." Her mouth was dry, and she had no idea how she'd screen test with him. But then, just when she wasn't sure how she'd survive another second, she remembered her mother's advice. He was just a person, like anyone else. She exhaled through pursed lips and held out her hand as he approached. "Hi." She smiled. "Nice to meet you."

"Pleasure's mine." His eyes were flirty and there was a power about him, a charisma that filled the room. Brandon held her gaze for a long moment before turning to Bailey's mom. "You must be Mrs. Flanigan."

"Yes." She shook Brandon's hand, nowhere near as bowled over as Bailey. But still, she seemed affected by his charm. "Thanks for flying out."

Brandon looked straight into Bailey's eyes. "I wouldn't have missed it."

Heat filled Bailey's cheeks, and she wondered if a screen test was really necessary. She was in love with Cody, but clearly she and Brandon had chemistry. Her mom excused herself to a chair in the far corner again, and Keith explained what was about to happen. The man at the table was the director: Channing O'Neal, a veteran with two Academy Awards in recent years.

Only after meeting Mr. O'Neal did Bailey truly understand the breadth and scope of this movie, how huge it could be, and how many people might be affected by it. The message of *Unlocked* was so powerful — strong enough to change a generation. *Get a grip*, she told herself. This was a mission field. She was here because God had granted her a place in their midst. And He'd only done that because He wanted her to make a difference, to be a bright light for Him. Enough being star-struck — even if Brandon was so very, very good looking. And taller than she had expected. *Focus*, she ordered herself. He wasn't Cody. And he wasn't the reason she was here. God's plan for her life — that was the reason.

The group of them sat in an informal circle, and Andi's dad

went over what they were looking for, why they were gathered. "Holden Harris is a very special teenage boy."

Brandon winked at her, and again Bailey felt her cheeks grow hot. "Very special," he mouthed.

"Brandon." Mr. Ellison wasn't amused. "If I could have your attention for a solid five minutes, I'd appreciate it."

"Sorry." He grew serious. "Just looking for chemistry."

"Chemistry will take care of itself." Dayne raised an eyebrow at Brandon. "We need you to be on your game here."

Brandon nodded, the silliness from a moment ago gone completely. Bailey ordered herself to not look at him again until it was time for the screen test. Mr. Ellison went on about how only the pure love of Ella Reynolds and the miracle of a song could finally reach through Holden's prison of autism.

"In this scene, Ella and Holden are in the musical theater room, on stage and alone for the first time."

Bailey knew the scene well. Ella was practicing, singing a solo by herself, when Holden walked in. He was drawn to her voice, to the song, and in the process he walked on stage. Instead of rocking or withdrawing to a corner of the room, he took his place alongside her and began to sing along. It was the first time anything like that had ever happened for Holden. The scene was a breakthrough, and it reinforced in Ella's mind that it was possible for Holden to find a way out, possible for him to be unlocked.

"We've talked about whether we'll have you sing or not, and after reviewing some of your other work we've decided to let you do it. If we cast you, that is." Andi's dad took his place at the table alongside Mr. O'Neal, Ms. Ainsworth, and Dayne. "Since the music for the movie will be an original piece, today you'll sing something you're familiar with. You've played Belle on stage in *Beauty and the Beast* before, right?"

"Yes, sir." Bailey tried not to gulp. "For CKT, but it was a while ago." She could feel Brandon's eyes on her, but she wouldn't look at him, wouldn't do anything to further upset Keith Ellison.

"We have the music for the song 'Home.'" Andi's dad smiled. "If you could start the screen test by singing along with the music." He looked at Brandon. "Then you'll come in. Obviously we don't have a stage or stairs here, but you get the idea."

He handed both of them copies of the script and asked them to step into the next room. "Take five minutes together. Work on blocking and look over your lines. Then we'd like you to come back and give it a shot."

Brandon nodded, his expression no longer even the slightest bit humorous. He nodded at Mr. Ellison and the others. "Thank you."

Bailey followed his lead, thanking the professionals before following Brandon into the adjacent room. As soon as they were alone, he turned to her and grinned. "Talk about uptight."

She wanted to find common ground with him, but not this way. A smile tugged at her lips and she allowed the slightest shrug. "He's doing his job."

"Right." Brandon gave her a mock serious look and a salute. "I guess we better do ours."

"Okay." She looked at the script. "Let's read our parts, then we can block it."

"Listen to you." His tone told her he was impressed. He elbowed her lightly. "Like a pro." He studied her. "There's something special about you, Miss Bailey Flanigan. I have a feeling we're about to become very good friends."

"First," she held up the script so he wouldn't see her heart pounding inside her chest, "we'd better read our parts. Otherwise they'll find someone else."

He chuckled as if the idea wasn't even remotely possible. For a minute they read their lines, though Bailey could hardly concentrate, his nearness a constant distraction, his cologne filling her senses. It took everything to focus on the pages of the script.

Again Bailey was grateful she loved the book. She'd read it several times, and with just a quick read of the scene she knew the part. Mr. Ellison was right — the scene was emotional and pivotal. They'd have to pull this off if they were going to convince an audience that here — in these lines — laid the keys to unlocking Holden's isolation.

"Okay," Brandon put his hand on her shoulder. He hesitated and laughed, a light-hearted almost embarrassed laugh. "Sorry. You have the most amazing eyes. They make me forget what I'm doing."

"Thanks." Bailey felt herself buzzing. Was this part of his usual approach with a possible costar? Or was he really attracted to her? She thought about how she'd describe this to Cody later. *He's just a person . . .* she told herself. *Keep your focus.*

He gave a slight shake of his head, as if he had to try something to make him come to his senses since they were running out of time. "Let's try again." He put his hand on her shoulder once more. "I'll see you singing and I'll walk up to you like this."

Bailey giggled. "I don't think Holden touches her."

"He should." Brandon held her eyes again. "If he had any sense."

"Brandon . . ." She made an attempt at a stern look. He had a way of making everything else fade away. No wonder he'd won the hearts of American teenage girls. She would tell Cody everything later, how Brandon could turn on the charm at will. She concentrated on the script once more. "Let's have you walk up and look at me."

"That'll be easy."

She gave him another look, and just like that Mr. Ellison opened the door and motioned for them to return. "You're ready, I assume?"

"Definitely." Again Brandon's voice was serious, the consummate professional.

Bailey had no idea how they'd pull off a screen test with so little practice. Her character was in charge for this scene, so all she could do was hope he could follow. She took her place in front of the camera. Again an X marked the spot where she was clearly supposed to stand, and so she went to it.

The director, Mr. O'Neal, stood and moved to the iPod and speakers on a small table near the sidewall. "The song's cued up." He nodded to Dayne. "Go ahead and run the camera."

Dayne clicked a button on the camera and Keith Ellison nodded. "Camera's rolling."

Eleanor stood. "Why don't you both introduce yourself for the reel, please."

Bailey didn't wait to be asked twice. She said her name the way she'd said it last time, and then she glanced at Brandon. He, too, gave his name and age — although she sensed a slight bit of humorous sarcasm in his tone, as if Brandon Paul needed no introduction. His attitude rubbed her the wrong way — but she didn't let the fact show.

"Ready?" Eleanor asked them. She didn't wait for an answer, but pointed to the director, who clicked the play button on the stereo.

The music began, and gradually Bailey felt every distraction fall away. "Home" was the perfect piece for this moment because it fit the mood and because Holden couldn't connect with people even at home, where he was loved. Since he'd succumbed to autism fifteen years earlier, he'd lived inside his mind, non-communicative even where he was most comfortable.

Bailey looked off camera, to the right. Brandon positioned himself off to her left, where she wasn't supposed to notice him until he was almost beside her. The opening lines swept her away, and she sang them with all the emotion she could muster. Suddenly she was truly caught off guard by a presence beside her, a presence bigger than life.

She glanced to the left, and there was Brandon. Only he was no longer the young, brash actor who had done everything in his power to flirt with her, tease her, and come on to her in the past half hour.

He was Holden Harris.

The way he walked and held his head was different, and his eyes looked vacant, his glances only furtively reaching her face. She kept singing, and right on cue the director cut the music.

"Holden ..." Bailey believed she was Ella. "I didn't see you come in."

He swayed a little and looked back toward the imaginary door he would've entered through. "The music ..." he met her eyes, and this time there was more there, as if he truly wanted to connect. "You sing very ... very pretty."

"Thank you." Bailey turned to him, careful not to touch him or startle him in any way. Then she launched into a brief monologue about the song, and why it spoke to her heart.

"Here." Brandon touched his heart, his eyes childlike. "It talks to me here."

The scene went another minute, and then Eleanor stood. "Cut. That's all." She looked at the men in the room, all of whom were back at the table, clearly gripped by what they'd just seen play out before them.

"Wow." Mr. O'Neal wiped his brow. "I liked it."

"Very much." Eleanor grinned at Brandon. "You've studied."

"Yes, ma'am."

"I'm impressed."

Bailey had almost forgotten about her mom sitting in the corner, and now she caught a glance from her, a look that said what had just happened in this room went beyond anyone's greatest hope for *Unlocked*.

"Would it be okay if Bailey and I get a Starbucks?" Brandon turned innocent eyes to the director and then to Mr. Ellison. "Just fifteen minutes or so?"

"Actually, that would be good. We need to look over the reel." Andi's dad stood and came around the table to Bailey. "You were perfect today. Thank you, Bailey."

"I'm just ... I'm honored to be here, Mr. Ellison."

"Okay." He stepped back toward the group. "Go get some coffee." He looked at Bailey's mom. "If you could stay, that would help. We'd like to talk about Bailey's schedule. How much you could be around if we cast her."

Bailey wasn't sure it was a smart idea for her and Brandon to head off to Starbucks alone. But then she reminded herself it was just a fifteen-minute break. Her mom handed her the keys to the Suburban, and Brandon walked alongside her, opening doors along the way.

When they were in her mother's SUV, he released a long breath. "Did you feel that?"

"What?" She smiled at him. "Your crazy acting? I mean where in the world did you pull that from? You were totally scattered in the other room, and then all the sudden you were Holden Harris. I mean, as if Holden had come to life and walked right up to me."

"You made it easy. I could imagine what it might be like, locked away from the world for so many years, and then having the door crack open the slightest bit. All because your music spoke straight to my soul." His smile was intended to melt her heart.

But even after their brief time together, she could see through his attempts to win her over. Besides, she was in love with Cody Coleman. That simple fact helped her stay levelheaded, both then and as they headed into Starbucks together. Brandon had done nothing to disguise himself, not a hat or glasses. Nothing.

He placed his arm around her shoulders. "I like this, being

here with you in your town." He didn't seem to notice the way people were already staring at them.

Bailey eased out of his grasp and pointed to the menu. "You know what you want?"

"Always." Again he didn't take his eyes from her. He grinned, and looked at the drink board above the counter. "Oh ... you mean the coffee?"

She shook her head, moved by his charm even when she didn't want to be. Instead of waiting for him to be serious, she stepped up. "A grande latte, please. Extra hot, extra foam."

The girl's mouth hung open, and she blinked three times fast. Then she stepped back from the counter and grabbed the sleeve of her coworker. Without saying a word she pointed at Brandon and let out a stifled scream. "I can't believe it." She rushed back to the counter. "You're Brandon Paul!"

At the sound of her cry, the coffeehouse came alive with commotion. All five workers gathered at the counter, oohing and aahing at him, and asking for his autograph. He was patient and accommodating, signing everything handed to him, and posing for several cell-phone pictures with various Starbucks staff and random customers who happened to come in.

The whole time, Brandon included Bailey in what was happening. He kept an ongoing dialogue with her, and — when he wasn't signing or posing — he had his arm around her shoulders. Bailey was less affected by him with every passing minute. He was handsome and charming, but he had nothing on Cody. She believed that with all her heart. She could picture Cody coming by her house tonight, the two of them laughing as Bailey described her time with Brandon. His blatant flirting. But even with that knowledge, there was no way around the heady feeling she had being with him, knowing she was suddenly and certainly important to him.

As they walked out of the building back toward the Suburban,

Bailey heard the click of cameras. Two photographers had been waiting outside the building. Brandon put his arm around her and whispered close to her face. "Ignore them. If you act surprised they'll make some story up about how we already hate each other and how the movie is doomed to failure."

She didn't know any better; so she nodded, intent on keeping things as cool and comfortable as they'd been all afternoon. Still it was unnerving. By the time they climbed into her mom's SUV, the photographers probably had a hundred or more shots.

"How do you stand that?" She was breathless, like she'd just escaped someone who'd been chasing after her.

"You get used to it." He grinned. "And you will. Once the public gets a load of you, Miss Bailey, you'll have cameramen documenting your every outing."

Bailey felt suddenly claustrophobic. She pushed the possibility from her mind as she got into the car. She wasn't a movie star. She was a simple girl from Bloomington, Indiana. No one would want her picture — even after the movie came out.

But then she remembered Katy Hart Matthews, and how she'd become a focus of the paparazzi for a season. Bailey felt suddenly sick, because she hadn't thought about that. She didn't want to give up her privacy or have someone snap her picture everywhere she went. If she won a part on a Broadway show in New York, there would be none of that. She thought about Katy again. The paparazzi had been more interested in her because she was dating Dayne — otherwise they would've left her alone. So all Bailey had to do was keep clear of Brandon and the paparazzi wouldn't care less about her. The realization brought with it a sense of relief. Brandon would have an entourage during the filming, no doubt. A girlfriend or two, bodyguards, and hordes of fans. She wouldn't have any trouble keeping her distance.

"You're quiet." Brandon watched her as they drove. "Everything okay?"

"Just thinking. About the shoot, what it'll be like. If I get the part, of course." She smiled at him. He was a nice guy, just not the sort of guy she would ever fall for.

"First ... you'll get the part. I have no doubt. And, about the shoot, I can tell you how it'll be." He turned in his seat so he was facing her. "It'll be me and you falling head over heels for each other." He tapped the side of his head. "I know these things."

"Oh, really?" He was crazy and way too over-the-top, but still he made Bailey laugh.

"Yes." His confidence was as much a part of him as his smile. "I see us falling madly in love, probably on the first day of filming."

"Is that what usually happens with you and your leading ladies?" She gave him a wary look, returning his teasing tone and refusing to take him seriously.

"I'm hurt." His expression was familiar. The one she'd seen on the cover of magazines for the past year. "Leading ladies have never turned my head until now."

"Mmhmm." She flashed him a wary look. "You really are quite the actor, Brandon Paul." They both laughed, and when they returned to the production office Bailey's mom was beaming. She bit her lip as if to tell Bailey she couldn't say anything yet. But the news came almost immediately anyhow.

Eleanor shook Bailey's hand, then Brandon's. "Congratulations. We'd like to cast the two of you as Holden and Ella in *Unlocked*."

Brandon nodded politely and smiled at Eleanor and the guys, who had come out from behind the table to exchange congratulations with him. This wasn't the moment to dance around and shout for joy, so Bailey followed Brandon's lead, shaking hands and thanking the team for giving her this chance. "I won't let you down," she told them. "I'll work very, very hard. I know I have a lot to learn."

When it was okay for them to leave, Brandon walked Bailey

and her mom to the Suburban. There, he shook her mother's hand and told her again how great it was to meet her. When her mom was in the driver's seat, her door shut, Brandon turned to Bailey. "I forgot to ask you the most important question."

"What's that?" She could feel her eyes sparkling, feel herself drawn in. Not in a romantic way, but in a way that felt like she'd known him all his life. Nothing had prepared her for the charm of Brandon Paul.

"Your Facebook page says you're single." He cocked his head, a confident grin—the one she'd seen on TV a hundred times— spread across his face. "Is that true?"

Bailey felt her own grin fade a little and she quickly shook her head. "Not really. I mean ... we haven't exactly defined our relationship. But we will."

"It's the coach, right? The young guy in the pictures with you and the team?"

Bailey laughed. "That's not the team, it's my family. Three of my brothers are adopted from Haiti." She lowered her chin, wanting him to see that in this matter she wasn't teasing. "And yes, it's the young coach. His name is Cody. We've ... cared about each other for a long time."

His expression didn't change, but Brandon gave a couple slow nods of his head. "Well, then ... looks like I've got a little competition." He stepped close and—with practiced skill that took Bailey's breath away—he pulled her into a lingering hug. "Looking forward to working with you, Miss Bailey."

She gently pushed back, putting distance between them again. This wasn't the time to chastise him or stand up for Cody. He was probably only teasing anyway. "Yes, Brandon." She braced herself against the Suburban door. "I'm sure it'll be quite an experience."

On the way home, Bailey told her mother everything, about how Brandon had acted when they were alone before the screen test and how he'd been relentlessly flirty the whole time at Starbucks. "I know he doesn't really have a thing for me, but wow ... I've never been around someone like him."

Her mom didn't say anything, only gave her a side glance that said she wasn't so sure Bailey was right about Brandon.

"Seriously, Mom, he was just playing around." She pulled her phone from her purse. "Besides, I told him about Cody. Speaking of which ..." she checked if there were any messages from him, but again there were none. "I thought he'd call. He knew I'd be done by now."

Her mother was quiet again. She waited until the next stoplight before turning to Bailey. "Maybe Cody doesn't know what to make of all this. I mean the idea that you were auditioning with Brandon Paul. It's a lot to deal with."

"Not for Cody." It was easier to think clearly now that Brandon wasn't with them. "Nothing could change how I feel about him."

"I wonder if he knows that."

Bailey felt frustrated by her mom's doubts. Cody should certainly know by now how she felt. But then ... he hadn't asked her to be his girlfriend. So she hadn't really had the chance to share exactly how she felt. She called him, but again his phone went to voicemail.

"Cody, it's me ... the audition was so great." She tried to sound as excited as she'd felt ten minutes ago, but her tone fell flat. "They asked me to take the part of Ella, so ... yeah, looks like I'll be doing the movie." She paused, not sure what to say. "Remember what you said about God having a plan after the Broadway audition?" She hesitated. "You were right. Call me back, okay?"

The rest of the night passed in a blur. Her dad brought home pizza and her brothers kept asking her to repeat the details of the audition. But through it all, Bailey was aware of one very strange fact. Cody didn't call, didn't text. If she didn't know better, she would've thought he'd been in an accident or fallen into a coma.

Because the Cody she knew would never have ignored a moment this big in her life. He would've been here. Which told her more than his words had told her all week. Something was wrong, and it was up to her to find out what. Even if it meant putting aside her own celebration to do so. So that night as she fell asleep she didn't relive her audition or any aspect of her time with Brandon Paul. She did the only thing she could possibly do.

She slipped out of bed, fell softly onto her knees, and she prayed for Cody Coleman.

Thirteen

THE DRIVE TO INDIANAPOLIS GAVE CODY time to think.

He couldn't ignore Bailey's calls forever, but maybe he could put off talking with her about his mother. Especially now that she'd won the lead in *Unlocked*. The movie was bound to make her busier than ever, her attention split between her classes and filming and time with her family. She would hardly have time to notice how he'd eased back, slipped out of her life again the way he always did. The way he always had to do.

The distance was only temporary, after all. Until the police caught up with Benny Dirk. Twice yesterday, Cody could've sworn he was being followed by a red Honda. But both times the car was gone before he could catch a license plate number or call the police. Either way, sooner or later the guy would make a wrong move and he'd be arrested. Then Cody would be at Bailey's side in the time it took to get to her house. Maybe faster.

He checked his rearview mirror. No red cars. He exhaled and focused on the freeway ahead. He was halfway to the prison now, a bag of his mother's belongings and special books in the backseat of his truck. This Saturday morning the rain was coming down in sheets, but Cody found the storm strangely comforting. It fit his mood. Because he missed Bailey so much, he could barely function. He narrowed his eyes, trying to see the road through the downpour. But instead of the pavement, all he could see was the scene from last night: the football game at Clear Creek High.

It was the team's second home contest, and after soundly beating the visitors, Clear Creek was undefeated in six straight games. Coach Taylor pulled him aside after the clock ran out and patted his shoulder. "You're good, kid. This is your gift. Don't ever stop coaching."

"Yes, sir." He found a smile. "I'm learning from the best, sir."

Cody blinked, and the freeway came into view again. He had pictured himself becoming a head coach one day, maybe working with a college team or the pros like Bailey's father. But now, with his mother in prison ... nothing felt certain anymore. He wasn't even sure he should be here with the kids of Clear Creek. What if Benny Dirk was in the bleachers somewhere, waiting for a chance to pick him off? It was possible, right? No, nothing felt certain. Not even his relationship with Bailey.

Yesterday things had felt strained with her. Of course, he was more worried about whether Benny was lurking somewhere outside the stadium. He refused to put her in danger, but he wasn't ready to tell her about his mother. Not yet — and certainly not at the Clear Creek football stadium. They needed privacy, and so as long as Benny was at large, he had to keep his distance and hope that someday she'd understand.

Rain pounded his truck, and he remembered how it felt seeing her last night, how good it felt to hold her in his arms even for a few seconds. The stadium had been loud and chaotic. In the stands the band was still playing the Clear Creek fight song. Definitely not the place to tell Bailey what had happened since the last time they were together .

"Cody ... were you leaving?"

"I didn't see you." It wasn't a lie. He hadn't looked. It was enough that she stayed with him in his mind and soul, without searching the bleachers for her throughout the game. He ached to take her hand and head back to the Flanigan house, but he couldn't ... would never dream of putting her in danger. Instead he wished there was a way to turn back the clock and forbid his mother to even spend a single moment with a guy like Benny.

But no amount of wishing could undo what had happened. He hugged her, because he couldn't look into her eyes another moment. "I'm sorry ..." he held on, struggling with his emotions.

If things were different, if he weren't in love with her, he would've told Bailey everything. Because as much as she had stolen his heart, she was also his best friend. And he would tell her, someday. The police were bound to catch the drug dealer soon, right?

She pushed back first. Not rudely, but with a frustration he rarely saw in her. "Something's wrong ... why won't you tell me?"

"I've been busy, that's all." He remembered to smile. "You, too." It took effort to make her hear him above the noise around them. "We won. Your brothers played great."

"Stop." This time anger flashed in her eyes. "I've been calling and texting and praying for you constantly, and you haven't tried once — not once — to reach me." She was talking loud, above the noise, and Cody had a feeling that would've been the case even if they were standing in complete silence. "So what's wrong? Is it me?" She slipped her hands into the pockets of her sweatshirt jacket. "Did I do something?"

"Of course not." The last thing he wanted was for her to feel that his distance was her fault. How could he make her understand he was only acting out of love for her — that he would go to his grave loving her, but he couldn't possibly get her mixed up in his life now. Not when she might be in danger just being with him. He put his hand on her shoulder. "It isn't you, it's me. My mom's ... she's sick. I've been spending time with her. That and school ... it's a crazy time, that's all."

She twisted her face, as if he were speaking a foreign language. "She's sick? I mean, Cody, what is this?" She tossed her hands, frustrated tears in her eyes. "Is she using ... is that the problem?"

"She's not using, no." It was the truth. In prison she had no other option but to stay clean. He took Bailey's hands in his, and it took everything not to run with her, fast and far away from Bloomington and Benny Dirk and the new reality that was his life. "We'll talk more later. I promise." He allowed himself to look deep into her eyes just this once. "Please understand. This isn't about you."

"I miss you." She looked hurt. "I think about you all the time."

"Me, too." If she only knew how much. "Listen ..." he ran his thumbs over her hands, wishing they had more time. "Let's get through the next six weeks. Classes and your movie ... we'll see each other when we can." He hugged her once more. "This crazy time won't last ... I promise."

"Then come over. It's Friday night." She looked up at him, and the frustration in her eyes was replaced by a belief in him. "Can't you do that?"

If she asked again, he'd find a way to say yes. Benny Dirk hadn't been around, anyway, so why was he so worried? But as soon as the thought came to him, he could hear the officer's voice. *The guy's trouble ... he's tried to kill before ...* He steeled himself against every desire of his heart. "Not tonight." He kissed her forehead. "Soon, okay?"

Her eyes clouded and she stepped back. "Call me, then? When you get home?"

"I will." He wanted to hug her one more time, but she held his eyes for only a few seconds longer and then turned away. She hurried over to her brothers and this time she didn't look back. *I hate this, God ... help me find a way to tell her ... to include her in my life without putting her at risk.* He'd do anything for her, even if she couldn't see that right now. He reminded himself of that as he drove home from the game alone, and later that night when they talked for half an hour on the phone. The conversation was wonderful, the closest he'd felt to her since his mother's arrest. She told him about Brandon Paul's relentless flirting, and how Katy and Dayne had advised her not to be seen with him in public.

"Have you seen the tabloids?"

"No." Cody never looked at them, but he made a mental note to check out the magazines in the next day or so. "Bunch of lies, huh?"

"It's terrible." Righteous anger filled her voice. "They already have us in some steamy affair."

Cody felt a twinge of jealousy, but he let it pass. "They don't know you, Bailey. That's all."

She talked a little more about Brandon, how hard the guy worked to keep up a happy front. "He's hurting inside. That's what I think," her voice was soft again, the Bailey he knew and loved. "I keep praying I'll have a chance to tell him about God."

Every minute, every word they shared over the phone reminded him how much he missed her, how he needed a solution to the madness that had become his life. And now, as he pulled into the Indiana Women's Prison, he felt his anger building over the situation. The police better catch Benny Dirk soon, because Cody couldn't keep up this charade for long. The dreams of war came more often now, the daytime flashbacks a frequent reminder that maybe he hadn't resolved the trauma from his time in Iraq. Maybe his love for Bailey had allowed him to ignore the post-traumatic stress disorder other soldiers struggled with. Or maybe not.

Maybe he simply missed Bailey so much he was losing his mind.

ANDI HAD BEEN WRESTLING WITH HER FEELINGS ever since the ultrasound. Every day she'd head out for class, and when she came home — instead of lying down for a nap the way she'd done in the earlier weeks of her pregnancy — she'd lie on her bed and stare at her baby's pictures.

Her very own baby boy.

Each day that passed she could feel herself becoming more attached. She came to know his sleep cycles; when he would rest peacefully within her and when he wanted to play. He would take little jabs at her ribs, and if she put her hand on her stomach, he would respond by pushing against her. Now, as she got ready for a movie night with her parents, she couldn't go another minute without telling them what she was thinking.

She found them in the kitchen, making spaghetti for dinner. "Hey." She sat on one of the wobbly kitchen barstools and leaned on the counter. "Do you guys have a minute?"

Her dad was browning beef in a skillet, but at the sound of her voice he turned down the heat and faced her. "Sounds serious."

"It is." Andi could barely concentrate. And even though it was impossible, she could hear her baby's heartbeat inside her, filling her senses, confirming the decision that had finally come to light in her heart today.

Her mom came closer and spread her hands on the counter between them. "You're not sick?"

"No." Andi smiled. Below the counter where her parents couldn't see, she kept her hand on her stomach, feeling the way her baby was moving around, cheering her on with this decision. "I'm fine. At least, I feel fine."

Her parents waited, watching her.

Andi drew a long breath. "I've been thinking about the baby, about my decision to give him up."

Something in her mom's expression changed when Andi used the word *him*. She had a feeling her mother knew what was coming. Now that she had found her way back to God and she was living with them, Andi and her mom were close the way they once were. She and her dad too. Especially since their talk on the Indiana University campus that day.

"What I'm trying to say is ... I don't think I can do it."

Her dad took a step closer. His eyes were filled with love and understanding. "The adoption?"

"Right." She felt so scared, so unsure of knowing the right thing. "I mean, after I saw the pictures, I felt like I knew him."

Her mom's eyes filled with tears. "So you're saying ..."

"I'd like to keep him. I really would." She needed her parents' complete support, so the next few minutes were crucial. If they were opposed to the idea, she'd have to rethink whether this was really the way God was leading her. She bit her lip. "I've been praying about it every day."

Her dad came around the counter and hugged her. "Your mother and I have talked about this, how we would respond if you changed your mind." He ran his hand along her back. "If that's how you feel, we'll do everything we can to support you— to be here for you and the baby."

Her mom joined them, forming a cluster of love and pain and uncertainty. "He looks so much like you, honey." There were tears in her mother's voice. "I can't imagine finding the strength to give him away."

"So, then ..." She leaned back enough to see her parents' faces. "You're okay with this? You don't think I have to go through with the adoption?"

"Giving a baby up is something you have to be absolutely sure about." Her dad, too, seemed on the verge of tears. But his face held no sorrow. "We'll love this baby alongside you, and together we'll all get through it. If God wants you to keep him, then He'll work out the plans He has for both of you."

Andi nodded, and for the first time since she'd found out she was pregnant, she allowed herself to accept the possibility that she could keep the baby. She was about to be a mother! She was carrying a beautiful little boy, and come January she would give birth and start the lifelong job of raising him and loving him and giving him a wonderful home.

She thanked her parents and hugged them, and they shared a happy night of dinner and watching one of their favorite Kate Hudson movies, *Raising Helen*. Andi wiped away tears at the end, when the two sisters find common ground and are able to reach an understanding. When the movie was over, she kissed her parents goodnight and returned to her bedroom where — like she did every night — she pulled out the pictures of her unborn son and studied them, staring for a long time into his perfect face.

She'd made up her mind, and she had the full support of her parents. She was keeping her baby! She set the photos back in their folder and put the folder on her nightstand once again. Everything had gone exactly how she'd hoped it would go, and now she could let the agency know she'd changed her mind. Then she could get on with figuring out how to be a single mom.

Single mom.

The term felt like gravel in her mouth. This wasn't how she wanted to start out, and it wouldn't be the perfect beginning for her son. But it was where her prayers had led her and so it had to be the right decision. It had to be. She tossed onto one side and turned onto the other, wrestling with her pillow and trying to feel sleepy enough to drift off. But she kept thinking about the words she'd only just now thought about for the first time. *Single mom* ... Would she be strong enough? Would she be good at it? Could she ever make a living for her son without her parents' help?

One question after another hit her, and with each she found a quick and easy answer. Of course she was strong enough; and she would definitely be good at it, because she would learn. Just like any other mother. But there was one question that plagued her long after she turned her light on again and read her Bible, and even after she finally felt tired enough to try to sleep once more.

The question was this: If she was making the right decision, why all the anxiety?

Especially on a night when she should be feeling nothing but perfect, unsurpassed peace.

Fourteen

THAT WEEKEND TURNED OUT TO BE the warmest in October, so Bailey's family took up the offer when Coach Taylor called and invited them out for a day of boating on Lake Monroe. Bailey wasn't sure if she'd stay all day, so she and Connor drove in her car behind her parents. The whole way she and Connor blared music from the Broadway musical, "Last Five Years". Anything for a diversion from real life, at least for Bailey.

By now everyone had seen the tabloids.

She and Brandon in Starbucks, his arm around her. The two of them leaving the coffee shop and getting into her mother's Suburban. *Brandon Paul Falls for His Costar before* Unlocked *Starts Filming,* the headlines screamed. Bailey was stunned. She and her parents met with Katy and Dayne hours after the magazines appeared in the grocery store. She was angry and afraid and unsure about whether she should pull out of doing *Unlocked.* Only after Katy and Dayne talked to her did she feel a little better. At least she had a game plan.

"If they don't catch you two together, they won't run stories about you." Dayne's voice was sympathetic. "Sometimes it can't be avoided, I realize that. Especially when you're starring in a film together."

"We could talk for hours about that." Katy had Sophie on her lap, and she and Dayne shared weary smiles. "The thing is," Katy was more intense, not wanting Bailey to give up. "You have to stay away from him. Don't give them even a little something to run in their rags."

It was good advice, and now that Bailey knew, she would act differently tomorrow when filming began. Already Brandon was in town — staying with Katy and Dayne. Apparently part of his contract stated he had to stay in their guestroom during the shoot. They didn't want him getting in any more trouble than he'd already been in over the last few months.

The crazy thing was, Bailey didn't read tabloids. She didn't have a clue about Brandon's wild summer or the compromising situations photographers had captured him in for one magazine cover after another. If she'd known, she wouldn't have acted so silly when they did their screen test. Never mind his charm. The only reason she would hang out with Brandon over the next six weeks, other than when they were working, was to tell him about Jesus — since she doubted anyone else ever had.

She turned the music up and rolled down her window. Already it was seventy degrees according to her car's temperature gauge. The forecasters had said today's heat could be record-breaking. It was a day when Cody should've been with them, the two of them taking this last day before the filming began to walk around the lake and pray and remember the magic of July Fourth.

But whatever was wrong with Cody, the situation between them was better than it had been. They were talking more, sharing their hearts over the phone even if they rarely saw each other. Bailey had asked about his mother, since it was her call that seemed to change everything. But though Cody easily talked about every other area of his life, when it came to his mother his answers were short and matter-of-fact. "She's fine," or "She's in a Bible study," or "She's figuring things out." Bailey leaned her head back against her seat and tried to imagine what was going on in Cody's head. Was it her role in the movie? Because if that was it, then she'd pull out. She wouldn't take the part if it meant losing

Cody. The thought rumbled through her mind like a truck with a flat tire.

Acting was her dream, right? Her failure in New York had been redeemed by this opportunity. The movie wasn't the problem ... it couldn't be. Cody cared about her. He loved her and he wouldn't do anything to stop her from taking this part. Especially not when the film had such a great message and her role was so pivotal, so driven by faith. Cody would never ask her to choose between him or playing Ella in *Unlocked*. No, there had to be something else. Or maybe he really was completely absorbed with schoolwork. He was taking six classes this term, so maybe that was it. This was a busy season, and by Christmas, it would pass.

Bailey sighed, but the sound was absorbed by the refrains of the music. The trouble was, they missed each other like crazy. The way they were going, he felt a thousand miles away, like she was in love with a guy who lived halfway across the country.

They reached the lake minutes after the Taylor family, and Bailey determined to put Cody out of her mind. At least for today. She parked next to her parents' car, and in no time the two families had unloaded their cars and were headed down the path to the boat docks.

Kari and Ryan Taylor were beautiful together, Bailey had almost forgotten how much so. They held hands, taking the lead as the group walked toward their boat. Trailing behind them were eleven-year-old Jessie — a little girl who was Kari's miniature; eight-year-old RJ, who had a fishing pole slung over his shoulder; and on Ryan's hip was their youngest, three-year-old Annie. Kari was the second oldest of John Baxter's daughters. Later today, most of the Baxter family would meet here at the lake. Bailey loved times like these, when her family was included in the Baxter get-togethers.

Bailey's parents walked close behind their friends and, as they boarded the Taylors' boat and donned life jackets, Bailey listened to the latest Baxter family news. Apparently Dayne and Katy were thrilled to be making movies again, and though the paparazzi had already landed in Bloomington, this time they didn't mind people taking their pictures.

"They've never been happier," Kari laughed and held up her hands. "Like Dayne said, let them take pictures."

Easy for Dayne to say, Bailey thought. But she kept her thoughts to herself and continued to listen.

"One sad bit of news," Ryan wore his Clear Creek High baseball cap. He adjusted it as he set little Annie on the seat next to Kari. As he looked up, his expression was troubled. "We all had dinner at Ashley and Landon's house last night." He pursed his lips. "Luke and Reagan got a call from the adoption agency. Apparently the birthmother changed her mind. So the baby they thought was coming in a few months won't be theirs, after all."

"That's so sad." Bailey's mom groaned. "They must be devastated."

"They are." Kari made sure Annie's tiny life jacket was buckled securely. "They'd already told the kids and everything. Last night Tommy kept asking why everyone was so sad. He insists that his brother is coming in January, no matter what."

Ryan started the boat's engine and took the captain's seat. "Of course next thing we know, Ashley's Cole runs to a drawer in the kitchen and pulls out a rubber bracelet for Tommy. The one Cole wore every day for a year."

"It says P.U.S.H." Kari's smile was marked by sadness. "Pray Until Something Happens. He told Tommy to keep praying, and God would make sure he got his brother."

Bailey's mom tilted her head, her face full of understanding. "Kids make it all sound so easy."

Bailey's mom and dad took the seats nearest Kari and Ryan. Once the engine was warmed up, Ryan checked his passengers.

The boat was an Air Nautique, with room for fifteen passengers. Everyone was snug around the perimeter of the boat, and Bailey's four younger brothers were seated up at the bow. "Everyone ready?" Ryan called out, grinning at the boys up front.

"Ready!" The kids shouted their response, and Bailey's dad helped push the boat away from the dock. Ten minutes later they were flying across the center of the lake, the sun glistening off the water, the wind in their faces.

Bailey was glad she'd heard about Luke and Reagan's troubles. Their story was a reminder for her to pray for them, and also that her troubles weren't nearly that bad. If Cody needed time away from her, she would do her best to understand. She would work hard in her classes and do her absolute best when filming started tomorrow. She would pray for Brandon to give his life to God, and she would let Katy and Dayne coach her through the maze of quasi-celebrity. By Thanksgiving the craziness would be over, and she and Cody could figure things out.

Until then she could only be thankful for times like this.

CODY SPOTTED THE RED HONDA as soon as he stepped out of his apartment on his way to the women's prison. His heart jolted and he leaned back out of sight. It was him ... Cody would've recognized his car anywhere. He breathed hard, his back pressed against the brick wall. Had Benny seen him? And if not, why was he here now? So much time had passed without seeing the guy, Cody had begun to wonder if maybe he had left town. He'd be crazy to stay in Bloomington, right? He was wanted, after all. Police had even reported that a car like his with similar license plates had been spotted in Illinois, so Cody had almost stopped looking.

He positioned himself so he could see a hint of the red car, but his heart was pounding so loud he could barely focus. In Iraq he would've known what to do, he would've been ready. But not here. He lifted his cell phone, but as he started pushing 9-1-1, the red Honda pulled back onto the road and headed his way. Cody had only a second or two, but he pushed back through the apartment door and slammed it shut just as the Honda drove slowly past.

The guy must be out of his mind, hunting him down, stalking him like this. Cody's breaths came in raspy gasps and he leaned against the wall of his apartment. Suddenly he could see Iraqi soldiers coming at him from his kitchen, from the hallway that led to his room, from the corner of the living room. "Go!" he shouted. "Get out of here!" He blinked and the images disappeared. Sweat beaded up on his forehead and he doubled over, catching his breath. What was happening to him? Had he really seen Benny Dirk, or was the red Honda only an aberration like the soldiers in his apartment?

His hands shook, but he dialed the number the detective on the case had given him. "I saw him," he kept his voice steady. His tone held none of the paranoia flirting with the boundaries of his sanity. "Benny Dirk was parked outside."

"We had another report of him earlier today. Someone called in a man with his description casing the sidewalk outside your mother's house." The detective cursed under his breath. "We're on it, Cody. We'll get him." The man paused. "Stay away from him. We think he gunned down a gas station attendant last night. He's crazy mad. He doesn't care what happens to him."

Cody hung up the phone and steadied himself against the door frame of his apartment. He wasn't going crazy, not completely. Benny Dirk really had been parked outside his apartment. So that meant he was doing the right thing, staying away from Bailey. Even if the distance was killing him. He cracked the door and peered out. The Honda was gone. Cody hurried down the steps and into his car.

His mother was waiting for him.

Cody watched his rearview mirror the whole drive to Indianapolis. When he reached the prison, he parked and walked toward the front gate. The pain of missing Bailey hurt so much he could barely walk upright. Maybe he needed a gun to protect himself. If the police didn't catch Benny soon, that's what he'd have to do. And what about the kids at Clear Creek High? Was he putting them in danger too? He didn't think so. Benny Dirk hadn't followed him to work — Cody had made sure of that.

He focused on the matter at hand. This was his third straight Saturday visiting his mom, making the commute to Indianapolis, and Cody knew the routine. He made his way past the first several guards, leaving his belongings with the last one, so that all he took into the waiting room were the clothes on his back. He glanced at a table full of tabloids and financial magazines.

He was about to look away when something caught his eye and he jerked forward, unable to believe what he was seeing. It couldn't be her … he picked up the magazine and stared at the picture. She'd warned him about this, right? And sure enough, there she was taking up half the cover. His Bailey. Walking beside her, with his arm around her shoulders, was Brandon Paul. His face close to hers, the two of them grinning and sharing some secret moment.

The headline read: *Brandon Paul Crushes on New Leading Lady — Get the Inside Scoop on Bailey Flanigan.* Cody sat back slowly in the hard plastic chair and stared at the picture for a long time, reading the title over and over again. How could this be happening already? And what was he supposed to make of the picture? Brandon and Bailey had only been together for a few hours at the screen test, from what Bailey told him. How had the paparazzi caught them in a moment like this?

When he couldn't stand it any longer, he opened the front cover and thumbed his way to the story. The layout was mostly pictures and a screaming headline — the same one from the cover. A brief story was tucked between three other photos of Bailey and Brandon. Clearly they'd gone to Starbucks together. The photographer must've caught them coming out of the coffee shop, and then done a little research on Bailey.

Cody read the story, his heart pounding. This wasn't some small-town girl who'd made it big. She was his best friend, the girl he would love as long as he lived. But here was this magazine telling the world all about her — details only people close to her should know. The article opened with the announcement that the search was over — a leading lady had been found to star opposite Brandon Paul in the highly anticipated movie, *Unlocked*. "Bailey Flanigan is exactly the type of girl to play Ella Reynolds," the story explained. "Because for all intents and purposes, she is Ella."

A few sentences down, the article went into Bailey's past, how she was the only daughter of the respected Indianapolis Colts offensive coordinator, Jim Flanigan, and how she lived in a family with six kids, including three brothers adopted from Haiti. She attended church and, up until this film, had only had a brief speaking role, which happened to be in the other Jeremiah Productions film, *The Last Letter*, along with several performances in something called Christian Kids Theater.

"This girl is pure as they come. But not for long with Brandon Paul around."

Cody felt sick to his stomach as he kept reading. "Bailey had her first taste of love with high school sweetheart Tim Reed — now an ensemble dancer in the Broadway cast of *Wicked*. But sources say she's ripe for a love affair with America's favorite movie star."

Bailey hadn't mentioned this part, and for a split second Cody thought about calling her, telling her to run as far and as fast as she could from Brandon Paul. But then, she was already aware of his reputation. Already she planned to never be caught in the same viewfinder as the guy. At least she had Katy Hart Matthews to help her through this craziness. Katy and Dayne.

He read through the story once more, and he realized something that hadn't hit him the first time. Nowhere in the story did the reporter mention Cody. Of course not. He was some troubled kid who'd lived with Bailey's family, a guy whose only family member was serving time for dealing drugs, and who was being hunted down by a deadly drug dealer. A guy whose only accomplishment to date was a stint in the Army. Even that hadn't gone so well. He absently rubbed his hand over his prosthetic lower left leg.

"Cody Coleman?" A guard poked his head into the waiting room. "She can see you now."

Cody's legs felt heavy as he stood and crossed the room. A month ago he never could've seen this happening, the way his life was playing out now. He forced himself down the hallway and into the small room where his mother sat at a cafeteria-style round table. The room had one window and little else.

"You came." She always started their visits this way. Her face shadowed with shame and remorse, her hand on the Bible he'd given her his first time here. It was a special edition with notes for addicts.

He took the seat opposite her, reached across the table, and folded his hands around hers. "I told you I would."

"But this has to be hard." Her lips trembled, and her stringy blonde hair was pulled back away from her face. The skin on her hands was dry and wrinkled, and her shoulders seemed permanently slumped, her chest concave. She looked like someone the world had run over and forgotten.

"It isn't hard, Mama."

She shook her head, her attention on the place where their hands were joined. "You've got football and Bailey, the Flanigan family." Her eyes found his again. "You don't need this, son. Really." A thought seemed to occur to her. "What about Benny? Have they caught him?"

Cody pictured the red Honda parked outside his apartment. "They're close." He took the Bible and opened it to John. "How far are you in your reading?"

"Well . . ." a hint of hope sounded in her voice. "I like the Bible study, the one you found out about. For users."

"Good." This was one of the reasons he kept coming, to help her find a reason to believe in God, to believe in the plans He still had for her. "What'd you learn?"

"I learned," she swallowed hard, and her fingers tightened around his. "I learned that I'm here because of my choices, and that . . . that I'm not a victim. I'm an addict."

Once she started talking, she kept on for the next ten minutes, telling him about the other women in the study and how much life they, too, had traded for their addictions. "I used to think the world was against me, that I was someone to be pitied because everything bad always happened in my life. But now . . . I'm starting to see it differently. The right choices are always hard."

"That's why you need Jesus." Cody felt tired, worn out from the emotions of the day. But every word was filled with passion. Because only God had saved him from the same sort of addiction. "He's the only one who can help you choose life."

"Yes." She smiled for the first time since he'd walked into the room. "Something else, Cody." Her eyes sparkled the way he'd rarely seen them before. "I gave my life to Jesus. I pictured putting myself in His big Father God hands, and I asked Him to come into my heart."

Cody thought about all he'd lost in the last month, all the ways his life had changed. But, in that moment, every torturous loss was worth it just to hear his mom say those words: *She'd given her life to Jesus.* He wanted to get up and circle around the table, hug her tight, and cry with her over what this change could mean in her life — now and in the future. But the guards didn't like sudden movements, and hugs were generally saved for the end of visits. So he squeezed her fingers instead. "It's a beginning, Mama. It is."

"I know. I feel that way." Her smile dropped off again. "I just wish . . . I wish you didn't have to see me like this. It isn't right. You taking care of me."

It wasn't right, Cody agreed. But it had been this way since she'd gotten out of prison three years ago, and their relationship would probably stay this way for a long time. Maybe always. He wouldn't coddle or carry her — and he would constantly point her to the cross — but he would not walk away from her. She was his mother, and he would treat her with respect and love as long as he lived.

They read the Bible together, Philippians chapter four, about finding peace in God and knowing His strength was enough for any task, and then they prayed. Cody hugged her at the end of their visit, and she clung to him. Her eyes held a slight panic, as if each time he said goodbye the reality hit her again that she couldn't leave. Her freedom was a thing of the past. She whispered close to his face, still holding onto him. "I love you, son."

"I love you, too." He kissed her cheek. "Keep reading the Bible."

"I will." She held onto him until he gently pulled back. One last wave, and then he headed with the guard back down the hallway through the waiting room. As he passed by the table full of magazines, he picked up the one with Bailey on the cover and looked back at the guard. "You mind if I take this one?"

The guy shrugged. "Don't matter to me."

"Thanks." Cody tucked it under his arm and followed the hallway past several stations on the way out. Back in his truck he stared at Bailey's picture once more before putting the magazine on the seat behind him.

He was five minutes into the drive home when his cell phone rang. He hoped it was Bailey. Now that they were talking more, he could hardly wait to hear her voice again. But as he checked the caller ID he saw it was Dave, an Army buddy he'd served with in Iraq.

"Hello?"

"Coleman! Is that really you?"

"Dave . . ." Cody smiled, his heart warmed by the sound of his buddy's voice. "I thought you fell off the edge of the earth."

"Practically." He chuckled. "You don't know what it does to me, hearing your voice like that. It's been too long, man, how you been doing?"

"Good . . . good." That was the only answer, of course. No one wanted the truth with a question like that. "How 'bout you, man? You been hunting and fishing or what?"

The conversation felt good, even if it was shallow. Cody needed this right now, and God must've known it. Someone to talk to, someone to help him remember he had a life outside football and school, missing Bailey, running from Benny and driving to Indiana Women's Prison. At the end of the conversation, Dave invited him to a dinner at the house of another of their Army buddies. One who didn't make it home from Iraq.

"His mom lives in Indianapolis. She wants us to come for dinner next weekend — to celebrate an early Veteran's Day." Dave's tone was more somber now. "I guess on the actual day she wants to be alone. But next week a bunch of his family will be there and the girl he was gonna marry."

It sounded like a sad occasion, and Cody said so. But Dave assured him that wasn't what their friend's mother planned. "She wants everyone to play games and tell funny stories. She said she wants her house to feel alive again."

How could Cody say no? He asked about the location and time of the dinner, and he gave his word he'd be there. He tried to picture gathering around their dead friend's house, playing games and telling jokes like everything was okay, like it was possible to find life again after such a loss. This was the theme of his life these days — something God must want him to learn: helping people find life where there was none. And if that was the case, he was up for the challenge. After all, this was God's calling for humanity, really. He could do this, even while his heart was breaking from missing Bailey, even when all he wanted to do was drive to the Flanigan house, join their family in whatever happy thing they were doing today, and never, ever leave again. The visits to his mom, the dinner with the family of his dead Army buddy. It was possible because the Scripture from Philippians chapter four rang in his heart the whole ride back to Bloomington. No matter how difficult the road ahead seemed, the truth was this: *he could do all things through Christ who gave him strength.*

Even this.

Fifteen

KEITH HAD WORKED AROUND THE CLOCK finding the right Bloomington locations and hiring electricians, tech guys, cameramen and grips. Dayne and Luke Baxter took care of the contracts, and finally it was the first day of filming. Most of the shots would be filmed in the new, unopened wing of a local Christian high school — complete with a state-of-the-art theater and auditorium. Behind the campus was a quaint football field, and beyond that endless scenic woods. The perfect setting for the story's outdoor shots.

The sun wasn't up yet, but Keith and Dayne had long since planned to meet here at the school's bleachers to pray. Keith arrived first, the crunching of his feet through the fallen leaves the only sound. He stared out across the blackened field. A hundred memories filled his mind. The times when he and Chase had met with the author of *Unlocked*, and the times when it looked like NTM Studios would keep them from making this picture. The time not long ago when Chase pulled out, and Keith was left wondering whether God wanted him to do the same.

But he'd taken every enormous roadblock to God, and he'd done the only thing he could: he'd waited. Waited and prayed and believed the Lord wouldn't have moved him back from Indonesia to make movies unless something very big and very life-changing were at stake. The day figured to be unseasonably warm, same as yesterday, but for now the morning was cool with a gentle breeze that sifted across the fresh-cut grass. Keith breathed in deep and he was filled with a supernatural peace.

God had cleared the way as only He could do, and now here he was. About to film the biggest movie of his career, the biggest movie of the year by any standard, for any producer. Based on the runaway *New York Times* bestseller, *Unlocked* was a movie the whole country was talking about. Even now, a year before it would show up in theaters.

Yes, there were great elements of newsworthiness. Brandon Paul — coming off a run of bad decisions and now aligned with a Christian production company. The fact that autism was in the news more and more lately, with a general raised awareness about the condition and how it might best be treated. Even Bailey Flanigan, in all her innocence and naiveté, had created quite the buzz in the preproduction stage. People were intrigued by her. Bailey's mother, Jenny Flanigan, would be on the set most of the time, and Keith had talked to Bailey. She had her head on straight. The tabloid incident was behind her now, and Keith wasn't worried about the experience changing her, though he sensed Brandon did have a crush on her.

"I've read about him," Bailey had told Keith when they talked a few days ago. "He's talented, but he's a mess." She told him she was committed to praying for Brandon and that she was sharing every detail with Cody Coleman, the boy she loved. But Bailey was also mindful of the opportunity she had working with Brandon. "Being in this picture could change him." Her voice rang with sincerity. "Imagine what that could do?"

Keith lifted his chin and breathed in deep. He could feel God here, sense His Holy Spirit around him and in him. If Bailey believed the Lord could save Brandon Paul through the making of *Unlocked*, then Keith and Dayne would believe it too. His prayer from the beginning was that God would use them to change the culture, make faith in America a mainstay once more. That could happen through the power of the movie, or it could happen with a changed Brandon Paul. Keith was determined to expect a miracle — one way or another.

He heard footsteps and turned to see Dayne. He wore a long-sleeved thermal, jeans, and a white beanie. "Hi." Keith patted to the place beside him. "It's early."

"I've been up for three hours." Dayne sat down and grinned at Keith. "Couldn't sleep."

"Chase called last night." Keith had talked to his former co-producer a couple times since Dayne had come aboard. Chase thought the two of them made the perfect team.

"Does he wish he was here?" A couple frogs battled it out in the distance. "I know I would, if I were him."

"Actually, he doesn't." Keith was still surprised by his conversation with Chase. "He loves being a youth pastor. Feels like he was born for it." Keith chuckled, remembering the way his friend had sounded. "They're already making plans for next summer's Vacation Bible School. The best ever, Chase says."

Dayne laughed a little. "I bet it will be." He paused, and the two of them listened to the frogs for a minute. "He and Kelly doing well?"

"They are. Better than ever. The whole change has been great for them." Keith still missed Chase, but he was happy for him. "He said he's praying for us."

"We'll need it." Dayne uttered a low-sounding whistle. "An awful lot at stake over the next six weeks."

"Definitely." Again they were silent, and Keith went through a mental checklist of all that needed to be done. "I'm meeting the caterer in half an hour. We should probably get to praying."

"Did you get who you wanted?"

"The caterer?" Keith grinned. "Absolutely. She'll be our secret weapon on the set, no doubt."

He told Dayne a little about how in all of Bloomington the best caterer was Danielle Laatsch, owner of Dessert Oasis. She wasn't more than five feet tall and a hundred pounds, but she made the best meals anywhere in the state. Desserts were her specialty, and Jesus was her passion. If you came through the catering line with a slice of cheesecake, you wouldn't leave without knowing how much Danielle loved God.

"The cast will love her, of course." Keith gazed at the horizon. The first pink streaks of daylight were breaking over the tops of the far off trees. "Danielle's a triathlete. She can speak three languages." Her husband was in the military and, after they had their two kids, Danielle gave up her dream of becoming a spy. She turned instead to catering, where her clandestine and covert operations involved helping people find faith in Christ. Keith could hardly wait to hear the conversations that would play out at the food tent in the coming weeks.

"Glad we have her." Dayne grinned at him. "You ready?"

They bowed their heads, and Keith was overcome by emotion. This was the dream, the place he wasn't sure they'd ever reach. He asked God to give them supernatural wisdom and insight, and an ability to oversee the moviemaking at every level — so every phase of the project would bring Him honor. "Let this movie prove that with you, our powerful God, nothing is impossible. And please let the impact of our work in the coming weeks bring this nation to its knees. In Jesus' name, amen."

As the prayer ended, Keith looked up and saw the sky was completely streaked with brilliant pinks and blues. "Time to meet the caterer."

"We've got an hour before the cast is here."

"I have a feeling about this day," Keith grinned and stuffed his hands in his jean pockets as they walked to the front of the school where the food tent was already set up. "Like it's the beginning of something extraordinary. The sort of day we'll look back on and remember, because we never could've known exactly what sort of unbelievable things were ahead."

They reached the food tent a few minutes later, and the walk through the school grounds reminded Keith that this was yet another detail that had worked out beyond his wildest imagination. Until three weeks ago they faced filming the movie in half a dozen different locations throughout town. But then someone at church mentioned the new school.

"It's not open yet, but it looks finished," the man had told him.

Sure enough, after a five-minute phone call that Monday, they worked out a deal to provide funds for a covering over the football stadium bleachers in exchange for free run of the new wing for the length of the shoot. The site was perfect. The only other location they needed was the house where Holden Harris lived. The house was supposed to be across the street from the school, and on the first day visiting the campus, Dayne had spotted a ranch house nearby with a *For Sale* sign out front.

Again, a quick call to the real estate agent and they had a two-month lease on the place. The rate was high enough that the owners — both retired and desperate to sell the place — could live on the proceeds for half a year.

From twenty yards away they could already see Danielle bustling about in the tented area. Steam curled up and around the edges of the tent, and the smell of eggs and waffles filled the air.

"Smells like heaven." Dayne grinned. "I can't tell you how many food service trucks don't smell like that."

"We wanted the best." Keith chuckled. "With Danielle we got that in spades."

They rounded the corner and Danielle held up both hands. She had a spatula in one and an oven mitt on the other. "Ten minutes till breakfast!" She looked like she'd been awake for two hours preparing the feast. "Belgian waffles are my kids' favorite." She waved her spatula toward the spread, as if it were a magic wand of sorts. "Pastries, fruit, blintzes, and an egg soufflé. That'll give these people a good start to the day."

"Amazing." Keith laughed and patted Danielle on the back. "All that and you've probably been praying for the cast since you woke up."

"Of course." She jabbed the spatula in the air. "What's about to happen here in the next six weeks is nothing short of what the Lord did at the Red Sea. I can feel it."

"You go, Danielle!" Dayne high-fived her.

Keith did the same, and they kept walking, checking on the trailers for each of the stars. A gift basket had been placed inside each of them, welcoming the actors and reminding them to ask if they needed anything during the shoot. That was especially true for their youngest cast member — Annie Sullivan, who was playing Holden's sister in the movie. Her mother would be on hand throughout, but her basket included things to make her feel like this was her home away from home — a doll and some soft stuffed animals and a Bible storybook. Annie and her family were Christians, and Keith wanted this first day to go especially well for the child actress. As they headed for the first trailer — the one belonging to Brandon Paul — Keith thought about what Danielle said. God was about to work a miracle here.

Now it was only a matter of watching it happen.

BRANDON SIPPED A CUP OF COFFEE at Dayne and Katy's kitchen bar. She was his driver — at least for today. He planned to ride around with Bailey Flanigan after they had a chance to reconnect this morning. In the meantime, he'd spent the past half hour getting to know Katy a little better. She was a pretty young mom, patient with little Sophie and very in love with Dayne.

Back when the tabloids could only talk about Dayne and Katy, Brandon had been a junior in high school. He remembered thinking Katy was hot, and that she would certainly move on to another actor — the way most Hollywood girls did. Especially after Dayne's car accident. But clearly Katy wasn't like most Hollywood girls.

"So, you stayed with him, right by his side while he got better?" Brandon planted his elbows on the counter and breathed in the steam from his coffee. "Even after everyone had him matched up with that other girl, whoever she was?"

Katy laughed and pulled a small bowl of oatmeal from the microwave. She stirred it, added milk, and tested it. Then she took it to Sophie, who was a few feet away in her high chair. As she set the bowl down, she looked straight at Brandon, the memories of those days gone by alive again in her eyes. "He loved me. It didn't matter what the tabloids said ... I knew the truth. I would've stayed by him as long as it took for him to walk out of there."

"Impressive." Brandon liked these two. Clearly what held them together was their faith — something Brandon never saw in Hollywood. People thought Dayne had become some sort of recluse, leaving LA, and living on some lake in Indiana. But staying with them here, it was clear Dayne was happy and thriving, living an enviable life here in Bloomington.

"What about your family?" Katy poured him a little more coffee. "What do they think about your fame and the way the NTM series took off?"

Brandon felt the walls in his heart fly up. He didn't talk about his family. Not in interviews and not here. "They're private people." He took a long drink. "Can't say they really approve of acting." He grinned, intending to put an end to the topic. "Some days I can't say I blame them."

They talked for a few minutes about the Christian element of the film. Katy leaned against the counter and looked intently at him again, her eyes warm with kindness. "Dayne tells me you don't really want to be associated with the Christian part of the film. With reporters ... that sort of thing."

"Not so much." He laughed, but it sounded nervous even to him. "I'm not really the choir boy around Hollywood. My beliefs and Dayne's don't line up quite yet."

"You've quieted down though." She grinned at him. "We've been watching."

"Yeah, well ... I had to get into character." He finished the drink, stood, and set his mug in the dishwasher. "Besides, this is a big role. I take it seriously."

"Good." Katy checked the clock on the microwave. "We better get going. But Brandon ..."

He was headed out of the kitchen toward his room. He still needed to get his bag. "Yeah?"

"God has you here for a reason. At least believe that."

"Oh, I do." His grin filled his face. "That's something I definitely believe."

It was true. But not because he was going to turn all Christian or be brought to some enlightened understanding by playing the role of Holden Harris in *Unlocked*. God had him here for another reason altogether.

Her name was Bailey Flanigan.

Sixteen

PAPARAZZI WERE CAMPED ON THE STREET outside Bloomington Christian High School by the time Bailey Flanigan and her mom pulled into the roped off parking lot.

"I can't believe it," her mom peered out the window at the line of SUVs and the photographers hanging out together near their vehicles. "It's seven in the morning. What scandalous picture can they possibly hope to catch at this hour?"

Bailey could only imagine. She remembered Katy Hart Matthews' advice. *Whenever possible, don't stand next to Brandon Paul.* That was the only shot they were looking for. That or something unflattering, like Bailey with crumbs on her face or Bailey blowing her nose. That sort of thing.

She giggled under her breath.

"What's so funny?" Her mom pulled up to a special row of parking spots reserved for the cast.

"I pictured myself in the magazines doing something normal, like tripping or spilling my latte. If that's the shot they want, let them take it. I don't care. The whole gossip magazine thing is dumb anyway."

"That's right, sweetheart." Jenny patted her hand. "Don't forget it."

They headed toward a classroom on the perimeter of the campus, a room that would be the staging area throughout the shoot. Call was seven-fifteen today, and Bailey was glad they were early. She and Cody talked for nearly an hour last night, and before they hung up Cody prayed for her. She had his complete support, and she was trying to understand better about his busy school schedule. Her professors were working out an online solution to her own classes, and the time away from Cody had allowed her the hours she needed to memorize the script. She knew her lines backwards and forwards. If needed, she could recite them half asleep or with her eyes closed. But still, she wanted to be early. If for no other reason than to pray and remember to exhale.

Especially when everything in her wanted to shout out loud because this was really happening! Bailey Flanigan from Bloomington, Indiana, was about to star in a motion picture opposite Brandon Paul! She uttered the slightest squeal as they headed for the classroom.

"You okay?"

"If I start floating, pull me back to earth."

"You might have to ask the director." Her mom laughed. "I'll be in the food tent after the meeting."

"Hmmm. I can't ask him." She teased. "He'll be too busy directing."

They were still laughing as they entered the classroom and already the producers and the director were gathered with several people, holding what looked like a serious meeting.

Mr. Ellison spotted her. "It's okay, Bailey. Come in. Take a seat. We're just working out details on our first few scenes."

A woman from the group of people separated herself and handed Bailey a sheet. "This is the call sheet. You can see what scenes we're working on, and when we'll need you, where to report. That sort of thing. The scenes aren't filmed in sequential order, but by what works best for the director based on sets." She pointed at five spots on the sheet, and introduced herself as the assistant director. "This is when we'll need you today." She hesitated, as if she was remembering that Bailey hadn't taken on a role this significant before. "You'll report to makeup half an hour before you're needed. Then for each scene, we'll do a read through, and block it. When everyone's comfortable, we'll roll camera."

Bailey tried to stay focused. She scanned the sheet and immediately recognized the scenes — all of them pretty brief. Still, the day would be full for sure. Her mom took a seat near the back and pulled out a notebook. She had three magazine articles to write in the next few weeks, so she'd be available on set but busy with her own work. Bailey heard other actors enter the room behind her and she felt herself begin to relax. Her experience might not rival the other actors on set, but God had placed her here for a reason. She didn't need to feel insecure or inferior. God would be with her every moment — and He would give her the words to deal with Brandon Paul. The first time they met, she acted no better than a star-struck fan. This time she was prepared.

She was still studying the call sheet, still standing with her back to the door when she felt someone come up behind her and put his hands on her shoulders. "Hey, beautiful." He brought his face alongside hers, whispering in her ear. "I've been looking forward to this for a month."

Here we go, she thought. He smelled wonderful, and his voice was so smooth it sent chills down her spine. She turned and put her hand on his chest, keeping an intentional distance between them. She lowered her hand and smiled the way she might at her little brothers. "Good morning to you, too."

He gave a slight sideways shake of his head, his eyebrows raised. His expression told her the resistance on Bailey's part surprised him. "What I meant was ..." he did a small Renaissance-style bow, "Congratulations. You deserve the part."

"Thanks." She handed him the call sheet. "Have you seen this?"

He glanced at it and gave it back to her. "Someone will tell me where I need to be. I'm ready." He shrugged, his eyes full of challenge. "You?"

"I think so." The call sheet gave her a place to direct her attention, so she wouldn't be affected by his charisma. "I know my lines, that's for sure."

"No, Bailey." Brandon laughed lightly. "Not that kind of ready."

She gave him a confused look and tried not to notice how handsome he was. "What other sort is there?"

"Ready for this." He put his hand on her shoulder and winked at her. "For me and you."

"Working together?" People were still entering the room, and the seats were filling up. They only had a minute or so before the producers would start the meeting. She smiled and took a slight step back. "Yes, Brandon. I'm ready for that."

"Working together ... or whatever." He put his arm around her shoulders again and led her to a spot in the front row.

"I'm not into whatever." She smiled at him, trying again to get the point across that she wasn't about easy prey. As they sat down Bailey turned her attention entirely to the producers and directors at the front of the room. Getting Brandon to behave was going to be work.

Keith Ellison took the floor, and the room settled to an anticipatory silence. "Welcome," his smile was serious, his eyes bright. "You all know the vision we share for *Unlocked*. You've read the script ... now look around this room." Everyone did as he asked, glancing at the actors and cameramen, the directors and crew gathered around the perimeter. "This is a very special cast and crew. A dream group." He paused, and the energy and passion in his voice filled the place. "Over the next six weeks you will give performances you didn't know you could give ... you will witness chemistry in the dailies that will take your breath away ... and you will understand that only once in a lifetime does a chance like this come along, a chance to be part of a work that will define you."

Bailey felt like he was talking to her alone. She sat straighter and silently prayed everything Mr. Ellison said would actually happen. He went on, talking about the specifics of the scenes on today's call sheet. Then he did something Bailey doubted happened on most film sets.

"My faith and the faith of Dayne Matthews is not a secret, and since this is our shoot, we're going to pray to open things up." His prayer wasn't long or overly preachy. He thanked God for the chance to do something extraordinary, and he asked that everyone involved might be blessed by the experience.

Next to her, she could feel Brandon shifting in his seat, clearly uncomfortable with the concept of prayer. That was okay. Bailey had two months to help him get more comfortable. She could hardly wait to get started. Brandon was in the first scene to be filmed, a scene where Holden Harris was working in his class of disadvantaged kids. A teacher would try to reach him, but he'd be moved by nothing. Later in the morning, Holden and Ella would both film the scene where Holden first glimpses Ella, singing on a stage with a group of theater kids.

"Come on," Brandon motioned to her. "Let's get makeup and wardrobe out of the way. I already scoped out the campus. I know where we have to go."

Bailey told her mom goodbye, and started to leave with Brandon. But when they reached the door she stopped. "Paparazzi," she whispered, before they came into view. "Here." She took three steps back. "You go first."

"Are you serious? He gave her a strange look and he laughed, this time in disbelief. "Who cares if they see us together. We're costarring in a movie."

"I wanna stay out of the tabloids. I like the challenge." She kept her tone upbeat, so he would have no choice but to go along with her game.

"You didn't tell me you were paranoid." He laughed again,

shrugged and headed out onto the campus, toward the classroom where makeup and wardrobe was set up. She waited seven seconds and then followed, careful not to position herself next to anyone. Sure enough, she spotted the paparazzi in the parking lot twenty yards away, their cameras aimed at her. *This is perfect*, she thought. *Thank you, God, that I didn't walk out with him.* The victory made her heart soar, because this was the advice Katy had given her. If she were to stay out of the same shot as Brandon, the tabloids would have nothing to run.

But after makeup, when she reached the classroom at the back of the school where the scene was being shot, she found Brandon quiet and moody. She went to him, brimming with excitement. "It worked! They didn't get the shot they wanted!"

"Tell me you're not going to do this every day for the whole shoot." He flashed frustrated eyes at her. "Some sort of hide and seek with the paparazzi."

"Brandon ..." She let her smile fade. "It bugged me, that story they ran after you were here the last time. Like we're dating or something."

"That bugged you?" His frustration morphed into mild amusement. Like he might remind her how many millions of girls would love to be in her place.

"We're not a couple. It gives the world the wrong impression."

He stared at her for a long time, and his eyes softened. He put his hand on her shoulder and eased his fingers up the back of her neck into her hair. "Yet, Miss Bailey." His face inches from hers, he whispered, "We're not a couple *yet*."

This was probably Brandon's usual way with girls, but something in his expression seemed completely genuine.

"I have a boyfriend." She laughed and gradually moved free of his grasp.

"I thought you were figuring things out." A mock sort of hurt came over him. "Give me time. I'll show you I'm serious."

The rest of the day Brandon was on his best behavior. He turned in tender performances in each of their five scenes, and between takes he brought her water and snacks. As for Bailey, the acting came as easily as laughing or talking. She loved every scene, every take, and she had to remind herself that she wasn't really Ella Reynolds.

Brandon watched her in one scene, and afterward he came up to her, looking over his right shoulder, then his left. "No paparazzi." He gave her a sheepish smile. "Is it okay if I stand here?"

She laughed. "I'm not that bad. I just don't want people thinking I'm your girlfriend."

"I know ... I get it." He nodded with great flourish. But as they stood there, he seemed fascinated by her. He wanted to know about her college classes and her experience on stage. He asked about her brothers, and her father's work as a coach. It was as if he were captivated by her normalcy, and his questions made her feel grateful for her life — though somewhat sorry for him. "So what's it like ... living here in Smalltown, USA? Having all that family around you?"

"Our family really loves each other." Now that he understood her boundaries she was enjoying herself. "We have something special." Bailey waved her hand at the room across the hall, the grips and electricians, the cameras and lights. "But this ... this is my passion. Acting. My real dream is Broadway. Movies make a person too visible." She smiled. "I don't need all that attention."

Her answer seemed to come over him slowly like an idea he'd never fathomed before. They were sitting on a couple of desks in a classroom across from where the set was being dressed. No one else was in the room at the moment, and Brandon touched her cheek. "I've never — not in all my life — met someone like you."

Bailey resisted the compliment. She took his hand from her face and squeezed it in a friendly sort of way. "You need to get out more."

Between takes on the last scene of the day, the two of them went to the food tent for a late lunch. Bailey met Danielle Laatsch, the caterer, and after she filled her plate with sliced turkey and fruit salad, Danielle pulled her aside. "I've been praying for you, Bailey. Dayne tells me you're a Christian."

"Yes, ma'am. Thank you." Bailey nodded in Brandon's direction. "Pray for that one. I think he's curious about God."

"Oh, I am." She grinned at Bailey. "I have a feeling God's going to use you to change that boy. Mark my words."

Bailey felt her eyes soften. "I hope so."

While they ate, Brandon respected her wishes, sitting across from her and down a few spots. But the whole time he grinned at her or winked at her. He even used a Sharpie to write *I miss you* on a napkin and hold it up for her benefit. Later he told her he was careful so the photographers couldn't see the napkin.

Just before the last few takes of the day, Brandon's agent, Brock, approached Bailey and introduced himself. "Whatever you're doing, keep it up. I haven't seen him like this since his first film."

In addition, Dayne told them the team was thrilled with what they were capturing on camera: an even more tender and honest performance from Brandon than what they'd hoped. Bailey wasn't sure what that meant, but she was glad Brandon was on his best behavior. She didn't want to argue with him for six straight weeks, trying to convince him she wasn't interested.

They were back in the classroom across from the set, and this time Bailey had her purse with her. Her mom had left the set to run errands and pick up the boys from practice, and she wanted to make sure she had her phone handy.

Brandon was telling her about his favorite Southern California beaches when Bailey heard her cell phone vibrate one short time in her purse. In case it was her mom, she pulled it out, and as she did Brandon leaned close. "The young coach?"

Bailey grinned, but she turned her back to him — just enough so he couldn't see the message. The text was from Cody. She stared at what he'd written, and her heart soared.

Thinking of you ... constantly. I believe in you, Bailey.

"Bailey, come on ..." he played with her hair. "Is it him?"

"It is." She turned her phone off and slipped it into her purse again. "He misses me." She grinned. "Don't we have a scene to get to?"

He looked at the clock on the wall and made a face like he might actually be worried. "I guess so." He nodded toward her phone. "Tell me this, Miss Bailey ... what is it about that football coach of yours?" He was playing with her, having fun, but she had a feeling he was looking for a serious answer.

Bailey figured it was as good a time as any to give him more than a glimpse of who she really was. Also *whose* she really was. Despite the uncertainty still exploding through her heart, she hoped he could see a peace in her eyes he knew nothing about. "You really want to know?"

"I do." He leaned a little closer and again his charisma was like a force field. "What's he got that I don't have?"

She felt a strength and certainty. "He has Jesus ... and he has me." Whatever was going on with Cody, he still loved her. He thought about her all day long.

Brandon looked at her for a long time, but he didn't say anything. Just nodded slowly, thoughtfully. Before they could talk more, the director called for them. As the day of filming finished, as she went home with her mom to a macaroni and cheese dinner cooked by her dad and brothers, she thought about the look in Brandon's eyes. How her answer had affected him. She thought about it while her brothers asked every detail of her day, and while they laughed around the dinner table about the possibility of the paparazzi catching pictures of Bailey with ketchup on her face. Even as she finally crawled into bed that night and tried to fall asleep, she still thought about Brandon's reaction. It was the first time all day he didn't have a quick response or a flirty comment. And that could only mean one thing. The part about Cody having Jesus was getting to him. Which meant God was working in Brandon Paul already.

Bailey could hardly wait to see what the second day would bring.

Seventeen

CODY HADN'T SEEN BENNY DIRK'S RED Honda again, but he was watching for him. He was always watching. Another week had passed, and he spent Saturday in Indianapolis visiting his mother. But he might as well have stayed. As he drove to dinner that night at the house of his deceased Army buddy, Art Collins, Cody realized he was becoming way too familiar with the road from Bloomington to the city. The whole ride there he worried about what to say and how to act. Art hadn't been a close friend, but he'd been part of Cody's platoon all the same. The only one of their local unit who didn't make it home.

Fitting, he told himself, that Art's mother would want this dinner tonight. Veteran's Day was coming up. And maybe this was the best way to remember the privilege and hardship of serving the United States, surrounded by people who understood the sacrifice in a very real and personal way.

By the time he reached the Collins' house, Cody had convinced himself this was where he needed to be tonight, and that the most difficult thing about the coming hours wouldn't be the awkwardness of Art's empty chair, or the sadness in meeting his fiancée, or the challenge set forth by his mother that the group have fun. The hardest thing would be that Bailey should've been there with him.

But tonight thoughts of her would only chill his heart and rob him of the mission ahead, so he put her out of his mind. Art's mother met him at the door. She was a willowy African American woman with ebony skin and beautiful brown eyes. She introduced herself as Tara, and Cody knew instantly that she was a believer. She hugged Cody and thanked him for coming, then she held onto his arms and searched his face. "Art would've loved this. Yes, sir." She smiled, even as tears gathered in her eyes. "I like to think he's looking down right now wishing he could be here for dinner."

Dave walked up, a soft drink in his hand. "If it tastes as good as it smells, that's exactly what he's wishing." He put his hand on Tara's shoulder. "If you wouldn't mind, I think maybe you should be the chef when we all get up there with Art."

Tara laughed, and the tears that had started in her eyes evaporated in joy. "Thank you, boys. Really. Thank you for being here."

They headed into Tara's living room where ESPN was on a TV that sat over the corner fireplace. Three other guys from their unit were there, some with wives. Working alone in the kitchen was an exotically beautiful girl with long dark hair that swished around her face like something from a shampoo commercial.

Tara led Cody by the hand and showed him the cooler of drinks. "Help yourself. Don't be thirsty on me now." She laughed and, after Cody grabbed a water bottle, Tara led him to the kitchen. "This is Cheyenne." Her laughter faded, but her smile remained. "She was going to marry my Art." Tara kissed the girl on her cheek. "He would've loved this, don't you think, Chey baby?"

"Yes, mama." Cheyenne was stirring a pot of chili. She had brown doe-eyes and a face that must've made people stare wherever she went. She was black like Tara, but her skin was much lighter, like maybe only one of her parents was African American.

"This is Cody. He saved a whole bunch of boys in the war."

Cody felt his cheeks redden. "No, ma'am, it wasn't like that. I was only — "

"Now, Cody!" Tara held up her finger, her eyes teasing, "Don't give me none of your lip. If I say you're a hero, you're a hero." She turned to Cheyenne. "He's a hero. That's that."

Cheyenne giggled and wiped her hands on the towel hanging near the stove. "Nice to meet you, Cody." She held out her hand.

"Nice to meet you, too." Cody took her fingers in his, nodding. He looked to Tara again. "Thanks for including me."

"This was Art's favorite thing, everyone gathered together, sharing a big meal, laughing about old times."

A picture of Art came to mind, the big grin and muscled arms. Art had played college football for two years at Indiana University before being shipped out. "Being here ... meeting you." Cody pursed his lips. "Makes me miss him, ma'am."

"Well, now ... we all miss him." Tara gave Cody a side hug. "But Art woulda wanted us to celebrate today. Even a week late." She nodded hard, clearly struggling with her emotions. "He's in the arms of Jesus, so we got no reason to cry for Art. Not anymore." Again her eyes shone with unshed tears, but her smile never let up. Not through dinner or dessert, and not afterwards when everyone gathered around the table for coffee and happy memories each had shared with Art.

Cody mostly listened, but he looked at Cheyenne often. How must she feel, her plans for marrying Art and having a family shattered? Every now and then Cody caught her looking at him, too. A little later Tara brought out a deck of cards, a Michigan Rummy board, and a bag of jellybeans. "If the good Lord woulda wanted us to gamble with money, he wouldn't have given us mortgages," she laughed and everyone else did, too. She divvied up the jellybeans, and Cody sat next to Cheyenne.

"I don't know how to play," she whispered to him. She was desperately shy, but the warmth of the evening had made them all feel like old friends.

Cody smiled at her, and a strange feeling poked fingers at his heart. "I'll teach you. Follow my lead."

The game was full of noise and celebration, highlighted by the moment when Tara cried out: "A royal flush! I got a royal flush." She looked up toward the heavens. "You hear that, Art? Your mama got a royal flush!"

Not until after midnight did the game end and people start making their way out to their cars. Tara stood at the door, hugging every one of Art's former Army buddies, the way she must've once hugged Art. She didn't cry or allow the moment to become sad. Rather she laughed with each one about something from the night, a funny story or the jellybeans or her royal flush. She patted each of them on the back and remarked again and again that, "Art woulda loved this."

Cheyenne had stayed close by ever since the card game, and now they wound up leaving at the same time, Cheyenne just before Cody. Only then did Tara stop and look long and intently into Cheyenne's face. "Thanks for being here, baby. It meant the world to me."

"Ah, Mama," Cheyenne framed Tara's face with her slender olive-skinned fingers. "I wouldn't have missed it."

"Seeing you . . ." Tara was still smiling, still beaming from the life that had filled her house that night. But now a hurried sob slipped into her voice. "I miss him. My Art."

Cheyenne's eyes pooled with tears for the first time that night. "I miss him too, mama." She hugged Tara for a long time. "I always will."

Cody felt awkward, caught in the private moment between the two. He wished he would've left a few minutes earlier, but instead he could only try to stay back a little, giving the women their space. Cheyenne kissed Tara on her cheek and hurried down the steps. At the bottom, she turned and waited for Cody.

"Ma'am, thank you for a great night." Cody received the same hug the others guys had gotten. "This was right where I needed to be tonight."

"I thought so." She pulled a list from a pocket in her sweater jacket. The list was worn and faded, something she must've carried around for years. She opened it and showed it to Cody. "See this? I have all your names, all the buddies Art went to war with."

Cody stared at the paper and, sure enough, his name was among a list of others — most of whom had filled the house that night. "You ..." he looked up at her, "carry this with you?"

"All the time. Art went to war believing it was a calling. He wrote to me after he landed in the desert, and he told me you boys were his mission." She smiled, and it reached a weary place in Cody's heart. "He prayed for you every day, Cody. After he died ..." she sniffed in, struggling to keep control. A smile spread across her face, "After he went home to Jesus, I took over his work."

"You pray for us?" Cody was stunned. He'd come here thinking he was doing some sort of duty, trying to spread life where there was none. Nothing could've been further from the truth. Here in the Collins' house, life breathed in all its abundance.

"I do." Tara glowed, her smile full and sincere, despite the few tears that slid down her cheeks. "I pray for you every day, Cody. The Lord told me you needed to be here tonight." She nodded at Cheyenne waiting ten feet away. "Now go make sure that young lady gets to her car okay." Tara raised a single eyebrow. "You hear me?"

Cody smiled. "Yes, ma'am." He loved Tara Collins, and he knew without a doubt he'd be back to see her again. Sooner than later. He thanked her again, and bounded down the stairs. Tara watched from the door as Cody approached Cheyenne and walked with her to her car.

"She's a little protective," Cheyenne whispered, stifling a couple giggles. She looked back over her shoulder and waved a few fingers at Tara. Then she turned a sincere smile to Cody. "No one loves me more than she does."

Cody heard the door behind them close, and he looked back

to make sure Tara was no longer watching. Then he faced Cheyenne and angled his head. "I had fun tonight."

"It's impossible not to have fun at Tara's house." Cheyenne made a silly face. "I mean jellybean Michigan Rummy? Everything about that woman's pure fun."

"So you get the game now?" Cody had no idea why he was drawing this moment out. Maybe because he felt sorry for the girl. She didn't seem to have moved on since losing Art two years ago. Or maybe because the two of them had a certain loneliness in common.

"I get it. Thank you." She did a slight curtsy. "You're a good teacher, Cody."

"And you're a good student." He thought about asking her if she wanted to get coffee somewhere, an all-night diner maybe. He could find out more about her and tell her about himself. But the idea left as soon as it came. He took a step back. He wanted to call Bailey on the way home. "Nice meeting you, Cheyenne."

"You too." Her smile was shyer now than it had been before. She climbed into her Volkswagen Beetle, shut the door, and with a final wave she was gone.

He watched her go, and then he walked slowly to his truck. As he did, he heard the front door open and saw Tara step out onto the top porch step. "Cody Coleman," she crossed her arms, her voice stern. "I hope you at least got her number."

"What?" Laughter caught Cody off guard. "No, ma'am, I didn't."

"For heaven's sake." Tara shook her head. "I can see I'll have to keep praying for you."

"Thank you, Tara." He waved at her, still laughing. "Good night." He climbed into his truck and realized this had been part of Tara's plan all along, the reason she'd arranged for Cheyenne to sit next to him for the card game. Tara was trying to set him up with the girl Art had once loved.

A sad sigh came from him as he drove off and headed for the freeway back to Bloomington. Cheyenne was beautiful and sweet, the sort of girl he might've liked to get to know if his life had been different. But as he drove away, only one face filled his heart and mind and soul. And as pretty as she looked, it wasn't the face of Cheyenne. It was the face of Bailey Flanigan. The girl he would love until the day he died. He could only hope if Tara Collins prayed for him every day, somewhere along the way she would pray for the one miracle he needed now.

That Benny Dirk would be arrested.

Eighteen

ANDI PARKED HER CAR IN THE empty Lake Monroe lot and stared at the shimmering water in the distance. The afternoon sun warmed her through the windshield and she settled back against the headrest. The sky was endless and blue from here, but even that didn't stave off her anxiety. No one knew she was here, not even her parents or Bailey. This was the second week of filming, and the whole town was caught up in the excitement. Andi rolled down her window and breathed in the sweet air. The smell here was different than in town, near the university. Here wild lilacs and honeysuckle mixed with the fresh smell of lake water, beckoning her to stay, to let God's beauty fill her senses and clear her head.

She pictured Bailey today, working alongside Brandon Paul like it was the most normal thing in the world. They'd talked about him a few times since Brandon came into town for the screen test, and Bailey wasn't interested. She had eyes only for Cody, and why not? Cody adored her. He had loved Bailey every day she had dated Tim Reed, waiting patiently for his time. No way Bailey would throw away the realness of Cody Coleman for a fast-living Hollywood guy. No way.

But what about her? Who would there be for Andi and the baby boy growing inside her? She stared across the water, and on the far shore she watched a pair of deer creep free of the woods. They crossed the meadow and headed for the water's edge. Who would stand by her when she made her move toward being a single mom? Yes, she had her parents support, but how long could she live with them? Until she was twenty-five? Thirty? And meanwhile watching her only friend live out her dream of acting?

Andi slipped her sunglasses into place, climbed out of her car, and locked it. She needed to walk, needed time to think about what she was doing. Not even three weeks had passed since she'd made up her mind to keep her baby. At first, the decision had brought an indescribable peace. A certainty she'd done the right thing. But since then? She pulled her sweater jacket tight around herself as she set out. What was wrong with her? And why couldn't she hear God's voice the way she needed to hear it? She walked down an empty gravel path until the trail turned, and after another fifty yards she came upon a bench. One she'd seen here before. She sat down and tilted her head up, savoring the sun on her face.

What was this constant, gnawing nervousness in her? The uneasiness that stole her peace and made her wonder if she'd ever feel right and whole and content again? She spread her hands softly over her stomach, over the place where her little boy was safe inside her. He was her son and no one could take him away from her. God had made it clear — the choice was hers to make, and she'd made it based on a very simple bit of knowledge.

The photos of her baby's face.

Looking at him, imagining him as a newborn, and a two-year-old, and a kindergartner, picturing him learning to ride a bike or take his first steps ... she couldn't imagine giving him away. Not now that she knew what he looked like, not when the lines of his face had etched themselves into a forever place in her heart. Andi ached at the thought of someone else — a stranger — going through those experiences with him. The photos still sat on the table beside her bed, and she looked at them every morning, every night. Nothing had changed about how much she loved this little boy, or how much she wanted to watch him grow up.

But no matter what she did or how she prayed, she couldn't get back to that place of perfect peace.

Andi folded her arms in front of her and rested them on the small bump where her waist used to be. She watched the deer again, how they moved with caution across the open field and how while one drank from the edge of the lake, the other would stand watch. That's how it should be. One standing watch. The scene made her think of what happened yesterday as she was leaving her history class. She was walking alone along a busy pathway through campus when, coming from the opposite direction, Taz almost knocked her down. He was with a group of film students, kids Andi recognized.

None of them noticed her, not even Taz, until they nearly brushed shoulders. He started to smile and say, "Excuse me," but then he realized who she was, and his eyes grew instantly dark. He caught a quick look at her extended stomach, and his expression could only be described one way: *disgust.* Like it was her fault she'd slept with him, her fault she'd wound up pregnant. He allowed a quick sadistic-sounding laugh and a shake of his head, as if even her presence turned his stomach. Then he jogged on to catch up with his friends.

Andi stopped right in the middle of the mid-morning foot traffic along the pathway and watched him go. For almost a minute she felt like she might faint or drop to the ground from the sorrow and anger, the fury raging through her. How dare he look at her that way? Like she was yesterday's rotten garbage? When she was finally able to walk again, her entire body shook and she remembered a Scripture she and Rachel had looked at back when they were seniors in high school.

It was the story of Tamar and Amnon from the Old Testament. The thing Andi remembered was that Amnon had a burning desire for Tamar, and so he called her to his room, feigning an illness. Tamar came to help, bringing cakes and homemade food for him, and taking it into his room since he was too sick to get out of bed. But then Amnon pulled Tamar to himself and raped her.

The verse Andi remembered yesterday as she walked away from the scene with Taz was the one where it says that after Amnon slept with Tamar, he despised her with a hatred greater than the lust with which he had once desired her. In other words, Amnon had it bad for a girl, he forced himself on her, and then he despised her. When Andi and Rachel had read the story their senior year, Rachel had been very touched by it.

"If every girl read that story, maybe they'd stay away from bad guys," Rachel had said.

It was a conversation that should've come to Andi when she was first hanging out with Taz. Andi squirmed on the bench, looking for a position that would relieve the ache in her back. But there was none. She lifted her eyes to the blue above, and she thought about the other detail that had come to light yesterday. At home after the ordeal on campus, Andi had gotten on the computer and googled Taz's student film, the one where she allowed him to film her topless. Every muscle in her chest and stomach tightened at what she found. According to Google, the film was becoming something of an underground cult favorite. Kids were downloading it and watching it on their iPods and phones. The information she found praised Taz for being an up and coming director, and for using cutting-edge style and technique — whatever that meant. They also said the nudity was handled tastefully. Two words Andi no longer believed had a right in the same sentence — tasteful and nudity.

Already twice she'd been in the cafeteria or in a class when a couple students started whispering and looking in her direction. Did that mean they'd seen the film? Were they snickering because they'd seen her virtually naked? Or because she was pregnant? Each time she wondered if this was what Mary Magdalene had felt.

How could Taz have talked her into such a thing? And now proof of her poor choices would circulate around Indiana University and so many other college campuses forever. She could never round up all the copies and destroy the evidence of her rebellion. Her innocence was gone, and there was no way to get it back. She'd told her parents about the film, of course, and they had grieved with her and prayed with her, hoping it was a piece of work that would fade into oblivion.

But what if it didn't?

What if her little boy was in middle school some day and his friends found the film? How could she subject him to that sort of ridicule — especially if he found out the filmmaker was his father? Andi leaned over her knees, fighting off the nausea, looking for a position that would help her lungs take in enough air. That was the other thing, of course. If she kept her son, he would want to know about his father. All little boys did. A friend of hers back in high school had been raised by a single mom, and the kid searched and searched until he found his father. Didn't matter that the guy dealt drugs or that he'd been in and out of prison. Never mind that his mom had a respectable job and had poured her whole life into loving the boy. In his junior year he moved in with his father. When Andi asked him why, he said, "Because ... he's my dad."

She straightened and tried to draw a full breath. Could that happen? Her little boy, growing up and finding Taz ... leaving her for *him*? She pursed her lips and blew out, staring once more at the trees across the lake. *God ... I know you don't want me to be afraid. But I'm not sure I can do this...*

Lean not on your own understanding, my precious daughter. Lean on me, and I will make the path straight for you.

The answer spoke to her through the late autumn breeze,

drifting over her soul with a certainty that God was here. He loved her and he loved her son, and He would walk her through the coming months — whatever she chose to do.

For a long time, she sat utterly still, her face turned to the sun. As she did, an answer began to come to her, slowly at first and then with the sort of clarity that comes after the morning fog burns off. She knew her baby because of the pictures, and knowing her baby had caused her to love him. She loved him with all her heart, more than anything in her life — even herself. She could walk away from her dreams of acting, walk away from the possibility of finding a guy like Cody Coleman, and even let go of the hope that her child might have a father.

But she couldn't do any of that unless she was absolutely certain God wanted her to keep this baby. And with a clarity she hadn't known before, she was suddenly and positively certain that her precious baby boy wasn't hers ... he didn't belong to her. He belonged to the adoptive family she'd found in the photolisting book four months ago.

Tears filled her eyes, and though she didn't cry out or weep, they fell in hot silent streams along her cheeks, dropping onto her jeans and leaving tiny wet circles. She would miss her baby, her little boy. And it would take a courage from God Himself for her to hand him over to another family. But this was what God was calling her to do. This new truth took root and filled her heart and soul.

For half an hour she grieved the loss and reckoned with all it would cost her, both now and in the coming years as her little boy grew up without her. She would feel his loss every day for the rest of her life, but she would feel it knowing this was God's plan, and it was the right decision. Her sacrifice would be best for her baby. By the time she stood and headed back down the path to her car, she could feel a different sort of sunshine on her shoulders and emanating across her soul. A warmth and peace that could've only come from God, because here on this beautiful October morning she had listened to His voice, and she knew — without a doubt — she was about to make things right. She would tell her parents tonight, and then there would be just one thing left to do.

Call the adoption agency.

Nineteen

LUKE BAXTER WAS HOME THIS WEEK, since his clients were all in town filming *Unlocked*, which was a wonderful change from the weeks leading up to the shoot. Dayne had asked him to be on-call, but only in case a legal matter arose on the set.

"Spend the week with your family," Dayne told him Sunday when they met for dinner at Ashley and Landon's house. The Baxter house. "Come by the set for fun, but be with them."

Now it was Thursday, and Jeremiah Productions was nearing the end of the second week of filming. Luke and Reagan had enjoyed every minute of their time together, letting the kids stay up late and sleeping in each morning. This morning Luke had promised to make breakfast for the family, so while the rest of them slept he found the Bisquick and poured most of the box in a mixing bowl. He hadn't made pancakes in a while, but he was pretty sure he hadn't forgotten how. *Sort of like riding a bike*, he told himself. *Once you've made a batch, you can pretty much whip up another batch any time.*

Luke docked his iPod into a set of kitchen speakers and found his favorite playlist — the one with Matthew West and Mandisa and several other Christian artists he loved. The first song was the one he most wanted to hear this morning. "When God Made You" by Newsong. He and Reagan had danced to it at their wedding, and ever since then — always at key times in their lives — Luke went back to it.

This was one of those times.

He and Reagan were closer than ever, and their children

Tommy and Malin were healthy and happy, but their family was at a crossroads. Luke had to keep reminding himself that God had given him Reagan and the kids, and that He still had good plans for them. Plans, they prayed, that would include more children. But the sad news from the adoption agency last week had hurt more than either of them had imagined.

"Birthmothers change their minds," their caseworker at the agency had told them. "Don't feel defeated. There's a baby out there for you."

Luke wanted to believe that, and because he was busy with the whirlwind of activity surrounding Dayne and Keith and Jeremiah Productions, he could mentally move on more quickly than Reagan. But when he came home Sunday after another week in Los Angeles, he knew instantly she'd been crying.

"I felt like I knew him. I was already making a place for him in our family," she told him that night when the kids were in bed. "It's like ... like I lost him."

Luke understood, and since he'd been home this week he had come to feel the same way. Why did the birthmother change her mind? Was it something about their family or their profile? Was she making the right decision? Luke had never known her name or circumstance, but he had to wonder if she was acting on impulse or if this was really the best choice for the little boy. Since then, he and Reagan had prayed often for the birthmother and the baby ... and for any other child God might bring into their lives instead. Tommy wanted twins — so maybe that was the reason. Somewhere God had twins for them. But even that idea didn't sit right. He still wanted the baby boy they had planned for — same as Reagan.

He sang along quietly to the song on his iPod. "When God made you ... He must've been thinking about me ..." He looked at the back of the Bisquick box. The words were smeared — someone had gotten butter or syrup on the box and tried to wipe it off. Whatever happened, the recipe was unreadable. He frowned for a few seconds, still trying to make out the words. Then he shrugged and put the box back in the pantry. Water and eggs, milk and oil. Something like that, right? He stared at the mostly full mixing bowl of powdered Bisquick. *Hmmm. A half a cup of water?* Yes, that sounded good.

He pulled the measuring cups from the baking drawer, and then ... just in case, he grabbed the spoons too. What else did he need? He rummaged through the contents of the drawer until he found a wire whisk and a sturdy mixing spoon. *Pancakes coming up.*

"He made the stars, He made the moon ... to harmonize in perfect tune ..." His voice cracked and Luke chuckled. Good thing he was a lawyer. He definitely couldn't make a living singing.

Over the next couple minutes he added half a cup of water, a cup of oil, and six eggs to the mound of powder. For good measure, he poured in a quarter cup of milk too, so they'd be light and moist. But as he tried to work the whisk through the ingredients, the batter felt stiffer than he remembered. *A little more stirring, more muscle*, he told himself. *Or maybe more oil.* He added another cup. Then he switched to the mixing spoon and worked the batter, round and around. The longer he mixed, the more the feel and texture started to look right. Slippery, but familiar.

He found the skillet, buttered the bottom, and brought the batter closer to the stove. His memory told him pancakes needed to be poured into the pan, but his batter wasn't about to pour. It had formed a nice solid ball — smooth and soft-looking. Maybe he was supposed to shape the pancakes in his hands like hamburger patties? Yes, that had to be it.

The song changed and became Matthew West's "The Moment of Truth." Luke loved the words because it reminded him to look at mile-markers along the journey of life — moments of truth that needed to be remembered so that when trouble came he would remember that God was still in control, He still worked miracles, and He loved His people too much to comprehend.

"Go back … go back … to the moment of truth." Luke used the spatula as a microphone. This was another great one to sing along with, as long as the rest of his family didn't wake up. Tommy liked to tease him about his singing, not that Luke minded. Musically speaking, the two of them were strictly a no-talent father-son outfit, whether they sang together or separately. Reagan and Malin would give them pained sorts of smiles and nod along, as if to say, *Please, can you hurry and be done?*

Luke laughed to himself. He formed two pancakes, nice and round, and set them in the sizzling butter. He stared at the two patties and paused for a moment. Something didn't seem right. He turned down the heat. He couldn't cook them on high, otherwise they'd burn on the outside and be raw on the inside. Again he stared at the white round circles. Wasn't he supposed to see little bubbles forming? Maybe the heat was too low now. He turned the flame back up again.

Ten minutes later Tommy burst down the hallway and into the kitchen, a toy fire-truck in his hands, one his Uncle Landon had given him for his fifth birthday. He made shrieking siren sounds as he raced into the kitchen, and his footie pajamas slid, causing him to wipe out against the kitchen cupboards. "Where's the fire, Daddy? I'm ready to put it out, so where is it?"

Luke raised an eyebrow at his son. "There's no fire."

"Ah-huh," he scrambled to his feet and looked around, his eyes big as he tried to peer up at the stove. "I smelt it in my room."

"It's just the butter. Butter smells like smoke sometimes." Luke smiled patiently at his son and flipped the pancakes. Only then did he see maybe he'd been a little overzealous on the heat. The cooked side wasn't black, but it was a very deep shade of brown. He winced and cast a quick side look at Tommy. "These are well-done."

Tommy hurried to the pantry, found a step stool, and placed it next to Luke. As he did, he giggled. "Those are burnt, Daddy. That's why it smelt like smoke."

"No, no." Luke pressed his spatula against the two pancakes in the skillet. "They're well done. There's a difference."

Reagan walked into the kitchen just as Luke was stacking his first two finished pancakes on a plate and starting to shape the next two. She wore a pink silk robe and she looked young and beautiful, her long blonde hair hanging in tousled ringlets. But as she walked into the kitchen, her eyes began to dance with unreleased laughter. "What's burning?"

"The chef gets no respect." He stretched out his arm and gave her a side hug as he settled the next two pancakes onto the skillet. "A little too much butter in the pan. No big deal."

She squinted at the contents of the skillet, and a ripple of laughter came from her. "Luke ... what *are* those?"

"Lemme see, Mommy!" Malin reached her hands up, dancing around the three of them.

Tommy was still on the step stool, and now he looked at Reagan and shook his head, as he'd tried to tell Luke there was a problem. "Daddy says they're pancakes. But they don't look right, and plus I smelt a fire."

"Yes." Reagan pulled the bowl of batter closer. "Honey ... this isn't pancake mix. It's ... it's oily cement." She looked at him, still laughing. "How much oil did you use?"

"Two cups ... two or so." He cleared his throat. "Which is healthy, because it's olive oil."

"Two or so cups?" She was giggling harder.

"That's a lot of oil, Daddy." Tommy nodded, his expression serious. "Just a little oil for pancakes, right, Mommy?"

"Now ..." Luke still wanted to redeem himself. He turned the heat down and picked up the plate of well-done pancakes from his first batch. "These are just how we like 'em. Cooked all the way through, and light and airy."

"Light and ..." Reagan laughed again. She picked up one of the pancakes and made an exaggerated motion as if she could barely hold it. "Honey, this is a paper weight. You could tile the floor with these."

Luke was about to explain how in the olden days people liked their pancakes to have a little substance, when the phone rang. He looked at the time on the microwave and saw it was already after nine in the morning. Hopefully nothing was going wrong on the set. He held up his pointer finger to Reagan and Tommy, indicating for them to wait for the rest of his explanation about the pancakes. Then he answered the phone. "Hello?"

Tommy jumped off the stool, slid a little, and grabbed a dish-towel. "I'll clear away the smoke, Mommy ... I'll do it!"

On the other end, the woman must've heard Tommy because she uttered a quick laugh. "Uh ... is this Luke Baxter?"

"Yes, it is." He gave a shush sign to Tommy, while Reagan took the bowl of batter and began spooning it into the trash.

Malin stayed by her side, her thumb in her mouth, and Tommy waved the towel around the room. "There ..." he was making an effort to talk more quietly, but Tommy was loud even in a whisper. "See, Daddy? Now I'm a fireman like Uncle Landon! A quiet fireman!"

Reagan took one of the first pancakes and hit it hard against the sink. Only a few crumbs chipped off, but otherwise it stayed steadfastly intact.

The woman was saying something, but Luke missed it. The entire scene was suddenly too funny for him to keep his composure. Luke began to laugh, and he had to turn his back on his family to find his composure. "I'm sorry ... I missed that. We're having a wild sort of morning here."

Again the woman's laughter filled the line. "That's okay.

Sounds like fun." She took a breath and tried again. "I'm calling from the adoption agency. I have good news, Mr. Baxter. The
birthmother we told you about?"

Luke pressed the phone closer to his face and covered his
other ear. He closed his eyes, so he could focus on every word.
Something about the birthmother. "Go ahead ..."

"The birthmother has thought about her decision, and she's
changed her mind again. She says God convinced her this week
that the baby doesn't belong to her." Tempered emotion filled the
woman's voice. "He belongs to you. She'd like to start the paperwork as soon as possible."

Luke spun around and looked at Reagan, but she was working what looked like a gallon of milk into a fresh bowl of pancake mix. Tommy was still bounding about in his footie pajamas,
swinging the towel, clearing the kitchen of smoke. And now Malin was following him, giggling and waving her hands in the air
as if the two of them were performing some kind of tribal dance.

Joy surged through Luke, and he thanked the woman for
calling — assuring her he and Reagan would come in as soon as
possible for their part in the process. Then he hung up and, for a
long moment, he took in the scene playing out before him. The
birthmother could change her mind again, of course, but he had a
feeling she wouldn't, that this was the answer they'd been praying
for all week. An answer that had come far sooner than they dared
hope. The little boy would be theirs, and as long as Luke lived —
he had a feeling — he would look back on this morning the way he
looked back on other pivotal times in his life. Moments of truth.
The day he learned he had a son with Reagan. Their reunion after
a year apart. Their wedding day. And the day they brought home
Malin. And now this very special morning of burnt pancakes and
oily cement and children dancing in the kitchen.

The morning they learned God was going to give them a new
baby boy.

Twenty

CODY MOVED ALONG THE SIDELINE of the Clear Creek High football field with the other coaches and half the team. Connor Flanigan had the ball and he was running it, evading one tackler, then another, and heading for the open field. "Run ... keep running!" Cody waved his arm, and the other coaches did the same thing. "Keep running!"

Connor never slowed down, and seconds later he scored with just a minute left to play. The touchdown put the game out of reach and Cody high-fived the other coaches, cheering and celebrating a win in what was their toughest game of the season. As Connor ran off the field, Cody grabbed him and hugged him. "Thata boy, Connor! This is your team!"

Connor thanked him and joined his teammates in a huddle of cheers and congratulations. Cody watched the clock run out, grateful that at least this part of his life was going well. He almost didn't come today, because he wouldn't put this team in danger any more than he'd risk Bailey's life. But police in Columbus had spotted Benny, and they were about to move in for an arrest. At least that's what the detective told him earlier that afternoon.

As the buzzer sounded, and after the players had walked the line with the other team, the guys gathered around Cody and the other coaches. "Who are we?" Coach Taylor bellowed.

"Clear Creek!" The guys answered with a deep guttural sound, more like a battle cry than a response. They had formed a tight group, their arms around each other's shoulders, and now they began jumping, the intensity building.

"Who are we?" Again Coach shouted the question.

"Clear Creek!" From there the guys took over the chant, asking the question and answering it half a dozen times, jumping higher, pounding each other on the shoulder pads and getting fired up for the biggest game of the season.

"Five more games to playoffs, men. Five games." With that Coach Taylor took off his hat. "Let's thank God."

Cody loved this — that Coach Taylor prayed before and after games. The guys wanted him to pray, the parents, too. So he never missed an opportunity. The guys — all of them sweaty and breathing hard — dropped to one knee and prayed with faith and honesty. Cody hung on every word. This was a different team than it had been when he was a player. All because the guys in charge — guys like Connor — were good kids. Kids who lived out their faith.

When the prayer ended, Coach Taylor leaned in close to Cody and patted his back. "We wouldn't be here without you." He had to shout to be heard. "You're a tremendous asset to this team, Coleman."

"Thanks." Cody felt the compliment to the core of his being. Between his weekend visits to the women's prison and his distant relationship with Bailey, nothing seemed to be quite right lately. Nothing except this. "I love it," Cody yelled over the growing noise. "I really love it."

"Well, then ... let's keep this train going!" Coach looked from Cody to the rest of his staff. "On to state, men!"

The team jogged back to the locker room, and Cody gazed up at the still packed stands. Even fans from neighboring areas were starting to take notice of something special happening at Clear Creek. It seemed like every week the stands were a little more full. Bailey was here with her parents and Ricky and BJ, sitting with the extended Baxter family, like always. Cody shaded his eyes and looked up at the section of bleachers where Bailey and her family usually sat. Sure enough, there they were. He needed to tell her about his mother still, and now he needed to tell her about the dinner at Art's house. Tara had apparently given his number to Cheyenne, because over the last week they'd texted a few times. Nothing flirty, but they shared common ground in the way they'd been forever affected by the war. So Cody hadn't minded the few times they'd chatted.

The thing was, options or not, Cody wasn't interested. He still thought about Bailey constantly, wondering how she was doing every day last week while she was on the movie set. They had talked less this week, and the buzz from the Flanigan boys was that Brandon had a crush on Bailey. He looked up at her again, and squinted. A commotion seemed to have broken out around her. Cody shaded his eyes and immediately realized what had happened. Brandon Paul had arrived, and he was sitting next to Bailey. He'd missed the game, but he was here. From the high corners of the stadium, Cody watched a couple cameramen inch their way closer, snapping a constant stream of flash photos. Only then did he realize that in addition to Dayne and Katy, Keith Ellison and his wife were there. And maybe a few other people from the cast and crew. Maybe they'd been there all along.

As Cody watched, Brandon slung his arm over Bailey's shoulders and hugged her. Even from where he stood on the sidelines, Cody could see they were both laughing, both caught up in the moment. Brandon hugged Bailey's mom and dad next, and then he turned and began talking to Dayne Matthews. Cody looked away, colder than he'd been all night. Everything in him wanted to race up the stadium steps and take her hand, lead her to a quiet place outside the football arena and tell her once and for all that he loved her. He would explain about his mother's arrest and the danger of Benny Dirk. And he would assure her that all he wanted was her, the two of them together the way things were over the summer.

But he could hardly do that. He held a clipboard and he flipped a page, checking Connor Flanigan's stats. He needed to get back to the locker room with the rest of the team. The last glimpse he caught was of her and Brandon, their heads turned toward each other, smiling and talking — completely absorbed in each other. A pain cut through Cody's heart as he lowered his gaze to the tunnel ahead. No, they certainly wouldn't be talking tonight. But then, maybe he and Bailey didn't need to talk anyway. Maybe Bailey was moving on without an explanation from him. He certainly didn't need to ask her how things were going with Brandon Paul.

The answer was as clear as the smile on her face.

BAILEY NOTICED EVERY TIME CODY looked her way, but she didn't want him to catch her looking at him. It was no longer enough to hear that he was busy, or to spend an hour each night on the phone. Not since last Monday. Bailey watched Cody jog across the field, toward the locker room, and the memory came back again — the way it had a hundred times since Monday. She'd been about to film a scene with Brandon, when she heard her phone vibrate.

Like always, Brandon was interested. But Bailey kept the phone away from him as she checked the message. A few seconds passed before she realized what she was seeing.

Nice meeting you too, Cheyenne ... I had a great night. I'm sure we'll talk sometime soon.

Bailey had felt the blood leave her face, felt the room begin to spin. Was this the reason Cody couldn't meet with her, the reason she hadn't seen him hanging out at their house? Because he'd met some girl named Cheyenne? She had refused to show what she was feeling inside. Brandon was still staring her down, dodging around her, teasing her, trying to see her phone. She absolutely couldn't let him know what had just happened. He didn't have a right to see into the part of her heart that belonged to Cody Coleman. But since then, she'd barely talked to Cody. Brandon had even teased her that her relationship with Cody was only a figment of her imagination. Seeing Cody tonight, realizing how much he'd kept his distance from her, she was beginning to think Brandon was right. Brandon had told her he might come with Dayne and Katy to the game, and she'd told him to be careful. The paparazzi were camped in town, following both of them pretty closely.

"That's right," he'd teased her as they finished up on the set. "We wouldn't want anyone to get a picture of us. They might think we were making a movie together." He grinned, but it was his new grin — the one he'd taken on since they started working together. Not the over-the-top flirty smile from the audition a month ago, but a grin that made him look like a smitten school boy.

Bailey had laughed the way she'd been doing more often lately — because how crazy was it that Brandon Paul might really have a crush on her? The idea was crazy from a hundred different angles, but mostly because she knew his background. They had nothing in common. Even if Cody had found someone else, Bailey would never be interested in Brandon. For that reason she kept things light, laughing easily, and not taking him too seriously — on the set and here at the game when he showed up just as the contest ended.

From the moment he arrived, Bailey could see the photographers snapping a constant stream of flash photos from a far corner in the stadium. "Don't worry about the paparazzi," he whispered to her. "I told them this was a family football game. I'm just here showing my support."

"Is that right?" She looked amused. "The game is over. That's not very supportive."

He gave her an apologetic goofy smile. "I thought they lasted longer."

"Hey," Brandon still sat beside her, like he was unaware that the coaches and team were no longer on the field, or that the stadium was emptying. "Guess what Katy bought me?"

On the other side of Brandon, Dayne patted his wife's knee. "The perfect gift." He smiled at Brandon. "Isn't that right?"

"It is." Brandon's eyes still sparkled with mischief, but in this moment he wasn't teasing. "She bought me a Bible." He tapped Bailey's waist with his elbow a few times. "Wild, huh? Me getting a Bible?" In a hurry he turned back to Katy. "Not that I don't like it. I do." He nodded at Dayne and then back at Bailey. "It's nice brown leather, and it smells good. The pages are new."

"We're going to read it every morning." Katy raised her eyebrow at him. "Right, Brandon?"

"Right." He made a terrified face at Bailey. "If you weren't praying for me before, you better start now. Me and the Bible haven't been best friends. Not for a long time anyway."

Bailey doubted they'd ever even been mild acquaintances, but she was proud of Katy. This was a start, a piece of the puzzle that had to fall into place if God were going to reach Brandon while he was there. And the change in him since the shoot started was something everyone had noticed. He seemed more like a kid, as if the character of Holden Harris had rubbed off on his soul. Bailey knew it was more than that, of course. It was God softening Brandon's heart, because before he left Bloomington she truly believed he would be a different person.

Brandon was still going on about the Bible. "And," he put his arm around her again, "I have something else." He flashed a grin at Katy. "Not as good as the Bible, mind you, but pretty fun all the same." He pulled what looked like half a dozen tickets from his back pocket. "Third row seats to *Wicked* in New York City tomorrow night."

"What?" Bailey gasped. "You can't be serious?"

She jumped to her feet and looked at Dayne and Katy and then back to Brandon. He took her hand and eased her back to the bench beside him. "Wanna go?" He elbowed her playfully. "Your ex is in the ensemble from what I read." His smile was intended to melt her heart. "Of course, you can't believe everything you read in the tabs."

Brandon explained he'd already arranged for his private jet to pick them up in the morning at Indianapolis Airport. They would fly to La Guardia before noon, get a ride into the city, have dinner at Sardi's in Times Square, and then catch the show at the Gershwin. The plane would bring them back that night, and — though they wouldn't return to Bloomington until almost sunup — they would have all day Sunday to catch up on sleep before Monday's filming.

"Keith and Lisa, Dayne and Katy, you and me ..." his grin was as boyish as Bailey's youngest brother. "Is it a plan?"

Bailey spun halfway around and grabbed her mother's hands. "Please ... it'd be so fun. I'd love to see Tim ..." she released a slight scream and looked back at Katy. "My goodness, I can't believe this is even happening. Seriously." She turned to her mom once more. "What do you think?"

Her mom and dad were sitting together, and they both chuckled at Bailey's exuberance. "It's fine." Her mom touched Bailey's arm and they shared a knowing look. Bailey had told her about the strange text from Cody, and her mother had suggested she allow some distance between her and Cody. God would make everything clear in time, when the movie was finished and school was out for the term. Her mom smiled. "It'll be good for you, honey."

"Go have fun." Her dad leaned closer and put his hand against her cheek. "You deserve it, sweetheart."

And like that they had a plan — the craziest plan Bailey had ever been part of. As they made arrangements for their departure and how the details would come together — and as Bailey texted Tim to tell him they were coming with Brandon Paul — she wondered just for a minute if this was what Cody wanted: for her to move on without him. If it were possible, this would've been the time to feel herself breaking away. But, instead, as everyone headed for the Flanigan house, and as Bailey spent the next hour talking to her parents and to the producers and to Brandon, as they dreamed about their time in New York City, all she could do was ask herself a series of painful, pressing questions. Where was Cody and what was he doing and how come he was texting some other girl? And most of all, the obvious question.

How had she and Cody lost again?

Twenty-One

KEITH HAD TO AGREE WITH BAILEY — the trip to New York was the wildest, craziest idea Brandon had come up with yet. The idea that they might go from begging for financial support during *The Last Letter* to this — flying to New York City in Brandon Paul's private jet was just a little more than he could believe. It helped take the edge off the sadness he and Lisa were feeling about Andi's latest decision — that she would give up her baby, after all. He and Lisa had talked about Andi's choice, and they agreed it was the smartest one, the decision that would best benefit the baby.

But not before the loss would break all their hearts.

Keith sighed, imagining the day a few months from now when he and Lisa would stand by their daughter, watch her give birth to the beautiful baby in the photograph, and then tell their first grandchild goodbye forever. They would pray every day between now and then for the strength they'd need to pull it off.

Laughter came from the rest of the group, and Keith turned and glanced at his wife. She was doing better today, glad for the diversion of the trip to Manhattan. She and Katy were sitting with Bailey on a white leather sofa , drinking fresh lattes brought to them by the flight attendant — a young blonde who clearly knew Brandon by name. Dayne and Brandon were talking about Dayne's accident — and how Dayne could've possibly felt drawn into making movies again after such a terrible ordeal. Keith was hanging on every word.

"At first I only wanted to be out of Hollywood," Dayne was stretched out on another section of leather sofa, across from two leather recliners where Brandon and Keith sat. "I had Katy and I was in love, and I had a family I hadn't known about until recently." He smiled, peace emanating from him. "Why would I need Hollywood?"

"Exactly." Brandon crossed one leg over his knee, intent on Dayne and the story. "Why would you come back?"

"Really?" Dayne slid his feet back to the carpeted floor of the jet and leaned over his knees. "Because God wanted me to step back out. He convinced me that Hollywood in and of itself wasn't evil. Certain movies, yes. The way most actors live and behave, definitely. But the medium of movies is still a very powerful way to reach people."

"In other words, do something good with moviemaking?"

"More than good." Dayne eased back again, sitting straighter against the cushioned seat. "Something life-changing. Where people leave the theaters knowing that their lives are empty and meaningless without a faith in Christ."

Keith wanted to stand up and applaud. This was a much more direct message from Dayne than the way he'd presented his role earlier, back when they'd had their first meetings with Brandon.

"Really ... you think the message of the film is that religious?" Brandon swallowed, clearly more nervous than he'd been a moment earlier.

"Not religious. That's not the right word." Dayne breathed in slowly, taking his time. "Faith should be a relationship with God. You can grow in that relationship a lot of ways. Certainly by going to church and reading your Bible. By praying. But not by being religious. Some of Jesus' least favorite people in His day were the religious leaders. Pious and self-righteous. He's looking more for the broken people ... people who need Him."

Again Keith could've cheered. He could see by the look on Brandon's face that those last two lines would stay with him. *He's looking more for the broken people ... people who need Him.* What a great way to describe Jesus. The whole scene made Keith certain beyond any doubt that he was there for a reason, that flying in a private jet for a night in Times Square really was mission work.

He was proud of Brandon for engaging Dayne in a conversation like this. From the beginning, Brandon had wanted to avoid any discussion of the film's Christian content. But here he was genuinely interested in Dayne's motives, in what could've transformed him from a playboy tabloid favorite to the faith-filled conscientious man he was today.

Whatever it takes, Lord ... speak to Brandon's heart. Don't let him go off on his own or get crazy in the city tonight. Help him really hear what Dayne's telling him.

Keith and Lisa often talked about the fact that a change in Brandon Paul — a public change — could have greater impact than any movie, anywhere.

He thought again about what Andi was doing this weekend, and how she was gearing up for Monday afternoon — when Lisa would take her to the adoption agency office so they could meet the adoptive family for the first time. If Andi resented not being invited to the spur-of-the-moment New York trip, she didn't show it. She only smiled, happy for them. Homework would keep her busy all weekend, she told them. Also she wanted time to pray and prepare herself for Monday, for the meeting and for the goodbye ahead. Which, despite the pace and noise of the city, Keith planned to do, too. But for now he could only marvel at the change in Brandon Paul.

Because if he was reading the young star right, the miracle they'd prayed about was practically at hand.

BAILEY FELT LIKE SHE WAS IN A DREAM. The flight was amazing, Brandon's private jet warm and cozy with plush throws and pillows, the cabin rich with the smell of soft premium leather. Bailey

noticed the flight attendant making eyes at Brandon, and she figured somewhere in the course of travel Brandon had gotten more
than beverage service from the girl. But he didn't seem even the
slightest bit interested today. He introduced her to Bailey and the
others, and then never again seemed to notice her — except to
thank her for a Sprite or the turkey sandwiches she brought out
before they landed.

Every year Bailey and Connor and their mom visited New
York City, staying at the Doubletree Hotel in Times Square and
seeing as many plays as they could in a three or four-day span.
But never had they traveled like this. Once they landed at La
Guardia — near the airport's private access building — they were
met on the tarmac by a shiny black Escalade and taken straight
to the city.

Typically, Bailey had been the one to keep her distance from
Brandon. But on this day he seemed content to let her hang
out with the producers' wives. They had a little extra time before their dinner reservations, so the driver took them to FAO
Schwarz across the street from Central Park. The last time Bailey
had been there she and Tim were dating — so the trip was a little
nostalgic. But even back then she'd known Tim wasn't the guy for
her. It had just taken a while for her head to tell her heart.

Brandon brought a beret and sunglasses, so he wouldn't be
recognized. But Bailey had a pretty good idea that by the end of
the night they'd have a trail of paparazzi following them anyway.
Inside the famous toy store, Brandon led the way up the escala-
tor to the giant floor piano, which stretched out more than thirty
feet.

"I could've played that role in *Big*," he whispered to her as
they rode up. "Watch me. Twinkle toes, for sure."

She laughed and again she appreciated that he didn't stay by
her side. Not that they had anyone tailing them yet, but still ...
she'd made it clear she didn't want people assuming they were

dating, and on this day he was very careful to make sure no one might've thought so.

Upstairs, the five of them watched Brandon dance across the keys. He was true to his word, and Bailey figured he'd been here a number of times. His rendition of "The Entertainer" was both charming and spot on.

"You try it." He waved to Bailey.

By now a few moms and their kids had stopped, and several of them were whispering to each other. One was on her cell phone. *Brandon Paul! Here in FAO Schwarz!*

Bailey couldn't resist joining in. She took off her shoes and joined him. "Okay, stand back. Watch this." She had learned only a few songs from Connor over the years, but she could hold her own on "Mary Had a Little Lamb." She found Middle C and jumped up onto the E key and back down on D and C, then up again along the same notes. But she messed up and hit the C twice, and when she aimed for the E, she was laughing so hard she accidentally hit the D.

"Mmm-hmm, just as I thought." Brandon brushed his knuckles against his shirt. "No one can touch me on the life-size piano."

"Not fair." Bailey was still laughing, trying to catch her breath. She was standing close enough to him that the other people watching couldn't hear what she was saying. "What'd you do, rent the place out and take lessons?"

"Well . . ." he grinned, the grin that was beginning to grow on her. "Actually, yes. They closed early one night and let the cast of my NTM TV show in, and well . . . yeah, they gave us lessons."

"Ah-haaa . . . See? I knew it!" she pointed at him. She tried her song again, but she made a complete mess of it. Again she laughed, this time half bent over. She could barely walk by the time she reached her shoes, and only then did she notice how the crowd around the piano area had grown.

One little boy — maybe 8 years old — stepped up to Brandon with a piece of paper and a pen. "Hey, could I have your autograph?"

"Sure." Brandon smiled graciously. He signed the boy's paper, and before he could get his own shoes on, he was asked five more times. Within a few minutes people were posing with him, snapping photos with their phones and calling out to other shoppers in the store, telling them Brandon Paul was here. *Really ... right here!*

Bailey pulled away with the producers and their wives, and she stood next to Katy. "Crazy, huh?" Katy smiled, amused. "I remember when that was Dayne."

The only reason it wasn't Dayne now was because he was looking down, intent on a puzzle in his hand, as if the pieces contained some pressing information. Katy helped, too, shielding him from the people — all of whom were too distracted by Brandon to think that a second megastar might be here in their midst.

Katy was still standing very close to Bailey. "So ... what do you think about him?"

"Brandon?" She watched him, surrounded now by a growing crowd of fans. "He's nicer than I thought." A quick side glance at Katy allowed her to express with her eyes what could've been missed in the commotion. "I'm not interested, if that's what you mean."

"Cody?" Katy knew her, and now her eyes softened. Clearly she had noticed that Cody hadn't been around on set, and that Bailey hadn't talked to him at yesterday's game.

"We're struggling." Bailey bit her lip. She didn't really want to think about Cody today, in the middle of feeling like Cinderella at her first ball. But there was no way around it when she was talking to Katy. Dayne's wife knew her as well as almost anyone. Katy had lived with them, after all, back at the same time Cody did. Katy was like a sister, and so Bailey appreciated that she'd ask now about Cody. Katy was still watching her, still waiting for the rest of Bailey's answer. "There's no reason really. He started staying away, and then ... Monday he sent me a text intended for some other girl. I don't know ... " She sighed and the sound lingered in her heart. "We need to talk. But at this rate that probably won't happen until we're done with the shoot. I'm not even sure I want it to happen until then. I need to focus on my work."

Katy's smile was kind, proof she truly cared. "I remember how hard those years were, when I was your age and even for years after. Always wondering why love wasn't easier."

"Until you and Dayne." Bailey was happy for Katy, for how things had worked out.

"Dayne?" She whispered his name, but her laugh was straight out loud. "Nothing about Dayne was ever easy." She let her laughter fade, and she looked deep into Bailey's eyes. "When you think about Cody, keep that in mind."

A few yards away, Brandon raised his hand and smiled big at the people still gathering. "Gotta go, folks!" He motioned to Keith, who took the cue and was immediately at his side. "Thanks for saying hi!" Brandon waved, and his eyes were genuine.

Keith put his arm around Brandon and ushered him through the crowd. Lisa stayed on the other side, while Katy and Dayne and Bailey followed. Dayne averted his eyes from the crowd, and in a rush of chaos, they made it through the store and to the waiting car outside.

"To Sardi's," Brandon told the driver. He laughed as he took his seat in the back row with Bailey. "Wow ... people are crazy."

"You're used to it." Bailey was curious. "You handled it really well."

"I guess." He shook his head and brushed his hair off his forehead. "I'm not sure you ever really get used to a scene like that."

"True." Dayne laughed. He sat next to Katy and Lisa in the second row. Keith stayed up front next to the driver, passing on information about where they were headed. "There's always that sense you can't possibly give everyone what they want. And it just takes a few people criticizing you or cussing you out because you didn't sign something for them, and you feel like forgetting the whole thing."

"Which, by the way, I noticed you did quite successfully." Brandon leaned forward and gave Dayne a look of mock frustration. "You coulda helped me out there, buddy."

"No, thanks." Dayne laughed and took Katy's hand in his. "It's your turn, my friend."

They made their way up Fifth Avenue, past the window shoppers and business people pushing ahead in both directions, past the jewelry district and Radio City Music Hall. Sardi's was on West Forty-fourth Street, and after fifteen minutes of serious traffic in Times Square they pulled up out front.

Bailey had eaten at Sardi's before, and the well-known restaurant could always be counted on for quality food and service. But more than that, it was fun seeing the caricatures of celebrities, which lined the walls. "Let me guess," Bailey said to Brandon as they stepped out of the car. "You've already got your own picture in Sardi's."

"He does." Keith put his arm around Lisa as they headed toward the front door. "I asked when I made reservations. I requested that we have a table near his picture."

"You did?" Bailey was amazed. The whole day was like something from an unbelievable dream. "Do they know he's with us?"

"No." He looked at Dayne and the two of them shared a knowing smile. "My guess is they will soon enough."

Again Brandon wore the beret, but this time he kept the sunglasses in the car. He used Dayne's trick — averting his eyes, acting fascinated by a menu at the front desk and the pattern of the carpet as they were seated. But, even so, Bailey watched more than a few heads turn as they were led to their table.

Brandon pulled out her chair for her, but then he took a spot across from her. "In case anyone has a camera," he whispered as he winked at her.

He was teasing, but only partly. The truth was something that touched Bailey. Brandon could've played up the leading man role tonight, acting like her date and giving anyone who saw them a chance to blast the news across tabloid headlines: *Brandon and His Innocent Costar Take New York City by Storm!* Especially since they were with two married couples. But instead Brandon saw to it that Bailey sat between Katy and Lisa, while he sat between the producers.

Over dinner, Bailey found herself being charmed by Brandon. Not in a way that turned her head or made her forget about Cody, but in a way that disarmed her and made her feel like she was spending the night with a group of old friends. Again, by the time they left the restaurant, news had gotten out. They were interrupted on the way out by people asking for a photo or an autograph, and by the time they climbed in the car, a sea of cameramen were waiting outside, bunched up on either side of the door, all of them snapping pictures a mile a minute and yelling Brandon's name and then Dayne's.

"How'd that happen?" Bailey whispered to Katy as they rushed for the waiting Escalade. She was careful to stay between Katy and Lisa as they climbed inside the SUV.

"This is New York City." Katy handled the throng expertly, not looking directly at them, never hesitating as they entered the vehicle. Once they were inside, Katy laughed. "Wow, it's been a while."

"It has." Dayne chuckled too.

"They recognized you," Katy nudged him. "Those pictures will definitely see print."

"I know." He smiled at Keith. "We're okay with that. Some tabloid press is a good thing, as long as they can't do more than report we were here together."

"I still don't get it." Bailey's head was spinning. She belted herself in, but she turned questioning eyes to Brandon. "How did so many get here so fast?"

"Like Katy said, this is Manhattan." Brandon looked calm, unaffected. "The paparazzi live here and in LA, because most celebrities split their time between the two cities. The few cameramen hanging out in Bloomington during the shoot are nothing. I actually feel like I have a normal life again."

"Join the crowd, buddy." Dayne turned around and high-fived Brandon. "Now you see why I love the place."

Bailey let this new knowledge about the paparazzi sink in a moment longer. If the press mainly hung out in New York and LA, then celebrities need only leave those places for a little peace from the constant barrage of tabloid exposure. If they didn't, if they chose to live and eat and work and play in the places where the paparazzi lived in droves, then they could hardly blame anyone but themselves for the attention. It was a comforting detail, one she tucked away for later.

In case this movie was only the beginning.

Twenty-Two

EVERY MINUTE THAT PASSED MOVED THEM closer to the reason they were here, the reason Bailey was so excited about being in New York City: the chance to see Tim perform on a Broadway stage. Bailey settled against the backseat of the Escalade and watched the teeming life moving in every direction through Times Square. The excitement here never grew old — even if this was no longer a place where Bailey wanted to live.

Brandon seemed aware of her thoughts. "Looking forward to seeing Tim?"

"I am." She appreciated her costar's sensitivity. He clearly wasn't threatened by any former boyfriend of Bailey's. He wasn't threatened by her current relationship either — whatever it was. "Thank you. If I haven't told you."

"I'm just glad you could come." He patted her knee. "I love this show."

In the front seat, Keith turned around and smiled at Bailey. "So, what's Tim say? Should we meet him at the stage door?" He glanced at the Gershwin, coming up on their left. "We're about an hour early."

"Definitely." Tim was thrilled they were coming, and he'd arranged for them to spend the time before the show in the cast greenroom. Bailey grinned. "He says there's a lot of Brandon Paul fans in the cast."

They pulled up and Keith climbed out first — to explain at the stage door that their group was there and make sure there was a clear path for the others to get straight from the car to inside the building. Bailey could hardly believe all that had happened since she'd been to New York City last time, auditioning with Tim in August. Only two months ago she'd been unsure what God had for her, since He'd so soundly closed the door on her attempt at getting a part in *West Side Story*.

She and Tim had texted a few times and talked once since he'd moved to New York. He was attending the church at Times Square, and casually seeing one of the other dancers in the show. He told her he missed her, but he never once asked her about Cody. Bailey was just as glad. Tim would never understand her feelings for Cody, so that was one topic that wouldn't be discussed tonight. She was sure.

They signed in and took a freight elevator up one floor to the stage level. There, they found Tim with a few of the other ensemble dancers. When he saw Bailey, his eyes lit up. "I can't believe you're here." He hugged her and swung her around and set her down again, his hands on her shoulders. "You won't believe the show. Every night I have to remind myself I'm really here."

Brandon walked up and cleared his throat just enough for Tim to remember Bailey wasn't the only one in the group. "Sorry." Tim laughed and introduced himself and the other dancers to Brandon and the producers. When he got to Dayne and Katy, he hugged them both, since he'd known the two of them as long as Bailey had. "I miss Bloomington," he told them. "But, man, do I love it here."

Tim showed them around the costume area, navigating the group around the time clock and Glinda's bubble and a dozen other props from the show. As Tim explained what they were seeing and gave the backstage tour, Bailey studied him, analyzing what she was feeling. Here was a guy she'd dated for two years, and yet she didn't miss him at all — not any more than she might miss any other friend she'd known in high school. Again she was grateful she'd broken up with him, and even more so that they weren't enemies. They'd been through too many good times for that.

Halfway through the tour, Tim walked them out on the stage. Since the doors hadn't opened yet, the theater was empty. Bailey walked out onto the slanted wooden floor where the entire play was performed. The group was busy remarking about what a severe angle the stage had been built at and how difficult it must've been to learn how to dance and move on such an angled surface.

But all Bailey could think of was the hundred times she'd taken a stage for the CKT shows or her show run at Indiana University last winter. She loved Broadway, and one day if God allowed, she would be here, too. Performing here or on another stage a few blocks away. There was something so magical about the lore and lure of theater. She and Tim exchanged knowing smiles, and she was sure he could read her mind. This was an arena they had shared for years until now. But at least God was still letting her perform, just on a different sort of stage.

They were still standing there, still taking in the feel of the theater and the sets, when the actress who played Glinda bounced onto the stage and squealed at Brandon Paul. "Someone told me you were here!" She screamed again, very Glinda-like. "I can't believe it!"

Tim introduced the two of them and, after she'd met the rest of the group, she pulled a camera from her bag to have Bailey snap her picture with Brandon. She was friendly with everyone, but there was no question her attention was devoted to Brandon. "What're you doing later? I mean, maybe we can all go to my place. I live in a flat on the Upper West Side."

Brandon looked interested for a minute, and Bailey figured this was how he got in trouble so often before filming *Unlocked*. Too many offers, too few no's. But this time, after only slight hesitation, he explained they'd be back on a plane after the show, headed to Indiana.

"I know, I read about your new movie." She seemed to actually notice Bailey for the first time, and she stopped, her mouth slightly open. "Wait! You must be ... are you Bailey Flanigan? The girl playing Ella?"

"I am." Bailey could hardly believe this. The star of *Wicked* knew who she was? It was the first time Bailey had felt the headiness of the role she was playing, and how the world clearly viewed it.

"So you've done theater, right?"

"I have." They talked for a little while, until someone showed up at the wings and informed them the doors were opening in ten minutes. In a flurry of activity, the *Wicked* star thanked the group for being there, gushed over Dayne, and finally slipped Brandon a piece of paper as they all exited the stage. She leaned close to him and whispered something Bailey couldn't hear.

But she would've bet the paper held the girl's phone number.

Only as they were exiting the stage did Bailey notice another dancer had joined them — the same blonde who had been with Tim when they first got off the elevator. Only now she and Tim were holding hands, and he was gazing into her eyes, laughing about something in a private world all their own.

Brandon came up beside her. "Jealous?"

She looked at Tim, at the way he and the dancer seemed more in love than Tim had ever seemed with her. "Definitely not." Bailey didn't have to work hard for the confident smile that lifted the corners of her lips. "I'm happy for Tim. This is his world now."

"Oh," Brandon gave her an exaggerated look of surprise. "You thought I meant about Tim and the blonde?" He put his arm easily around her shoulders and brought his face close to hers. No one was around to see them back here and, in this moment, no one was paying them any attention. He brought his voice down to a whisper. "I didn't mean about Tim. I meant about me." He pulled the slip of paper from his pocket, held it up, and then returned it again. "Glinda gave me her number. In case you missed that."

"I see," Bailey nodded slowly, playing along. "And you thought I," she pointed to herself, as if she were shocked by the possibility, "might be jealous … of her?"

Brandon's face fell and, though he was teasing, there was something serious in his eyes. "You aren't?"

"No." She laughed and slid her arm around his waist. "Call her if you want. Come out here and date her when you're done in Bloomington." She smiled at him the way she would smile at Connor. "Whatever makes you happy, Brandon."

He stopped and took both her hands in his, facing her. "What if … what if you make me happy?"

Her heart pounded, because she knew from his expression that this time he wasn't teasing at all. Gone was the slick attempt at hitting on her. Instead this was Brandon being genuine and caring, truly interested in her. She didn't know how to handle the glimpse he'd given her into his heart, so she did the only thing she could do. She giggled. "You make me laugh, you know that?"

For a long moment it looked like he might correct her, explain he wasn't kidding and he was truly interested in her. But people were being urged to take their places, and warm-ups were happening all around them. Tim was explaining they should probably take their seats, and he was leading them to a secret passageway that ran below the stage to the theater area. So instead of saying anything that might dampen the mood, Brandon allowed his famous smile to fill his face once more. "Come on …" he released one of her hands but kept the other, running after the group so they could all be seated together. "We've got the best seats in the house."

During the show, she thought at first he was going to have her sit between Katy and Lisa again, but at the last minute he took the spot beside her. "Let 'em talk, that's what I say."

Bailey wasn't too worried. They'd managed to get through their entire day without anyone catching them in the same picture together. And here in the theater there were no flash pictures allowed anyway. The paparazzi would be waiting outside, but not in here.

The show started with a dramatic clash of cymbals and the famous music the entire theater world had come to know. Bailey could hardly breathe, she was so excited, so anxious for Tim and what it must've felt like to be in the wings, about to take the stage for *Wicked* right here in New York City. She silently prayed God would bless his performance and that in the midst of the often ungodly lifestyles that made up theater life, Tim would become a very bright light.

The show opened with the ensemble singing to Glinda, who was above them in her bubble. Bailey watched closely and, sure enough, the first thing the actress did was make eye contact with Brandon, seated beside her. Bailey was sure Brandon noticed her make eye contact with him, so what he did next took her by surprise.

He discreetly reached for her hand and held it — not with his fingers laced between hers the way he certainly would if this were a date, but in a nonthreatening way that told her he wasn't interested in Glinda. Not tonight. This trip to New York was a gift to her. To Bailey. And no matter who tried to interrupt their time together, Brandon wasn't going to let it happen.

Bailey didn't move her hand. She liked this, sitting here watching Tim perform in *Wicked*, holding Brandon Paul's hand the way she'd hold the hand of one of her brothers. She felt like they'd reached a new level in their friendship on this whirlwind trip, and she was grateful. The cast began singing "No One Mourns the Wicked," and as the chorus built, Bailey felt tears in her eyes. How amazing that this was really happening for Tim, and that God had placed her in such a major leading role for her first real acting part. A year ago they'd prayed about the plans

God had for them, but neither of them could've dreamed they'd be here.

Well before intermission, before the house lights came up Brandon released her hand. He leaned close again and whispered. "See, Bailey ... no one will think a thing."

"Good." She smiled at him, careful to keep her tone light. She felt her eyes sparkle in the darkness of the theater seats. "Wouldn't want you to tarnish my reputation."

He laughed, and she was grateful he hadn't taken her too seriously. The last thing she wanted was to hurt him. If he had a crush on her, it would pass. Brandon had plenty of girls to choose from — she'd seen that much back stage before the show. At intermission, Brandon stayed in his seat, his eyes downcast. But, even so, a buzz had begun to spread through the theater, much as it had at FAO Schwarz. *Brandon Paul was here ... in person ... right in the third row!*

A few minutes before the lights went down again, three people lined up to ask him for an autograph or a picture, but the security guards at the front of the theater ordered them back to their seats and apologized to Brandon. Keith must have informed them to keep fans away so they could enjoy the show. "Sorry about that," one of the guys told them. "It won't happen again."

Brandon brushed it off. "No big deal." And it wasn't. Brandon had a way of handling the public adoration so that it didn't make him seem bigger than life. He was approachable — same way he came across on the screen. It was probably one of the reasons he was so wildly popular.

In the second act Brandon held her hand again, and for a few minutes Bailey let the headiness of it all get to her again. This was Brandon Paul, after all. The world's hottest heartthrob, sitting beside her, asking if she was jealous of Glinda. Brandon Paul with his hand wrapped around hers. What would it be like dating him? Allowing herself to fall for a guy like Brandon? But as soon as the thought flitted through her mind, she dismissed it.

The idea didn't resurface until after one in the morning, when they were halfway home on his private jet. By then the cabin was dark and the others were sleeping. Brandon slipped back to the sofa where Bailey was stretched out, and he carefully moved her legs so her feet were on the floor again. He took the spot beside her and put his arm around her again. "This was one of the greatest nights of my life."

Her heart beat harder than it had since they left Bloomington, and she wondered if he was going to try to kiss her. She swallowed hard, inching just a little away from him. "Isn't that supposed to be my line?" She laughed quietly. "I'm the one who feels like Cinderella."

"You could feel like that every day of your life." He put his hand alongside her face and looked deep into her eyes. "I mean it, Bailey. I'm crazy about you."

"Brandon," she uttered a quick urgent prayer for the right words. "Your kindness means the world to me." She put her hand over his and gently removed it from her face. "But I told you ... I'm in love with Cody. If I weren't ... if things were different, maybe ... maybe."

He didn't break eye contact, didn't look away. Something in his expression told her he'd probably never been turned down by anyone other than her. "Can you at least ... can you consider me as an option? For down the road?"

The fact that he was serious almost made her laugh out loud. Their conversation still felt like something scripted, a scene she might watch in a movie, not a real dialogue playing out between her and Brandon. He was waiting, and she didn't want to frustrate him. "I can do that." She nodded, willing herself to be more serious, because in truth it was like her mom had told her a while ago. Brandon was a person like anyone else, and he saw something in Bailey that he wanted.

He grabbed a remote control and clicked a button. A video screen flipped down from the ceiling a few feet away. "Wanna watch *Remember the Titans*?"

This time she did laugh, because he looked so much like a kid, happy to have a friend to watch a movie with.

"Definitely."

He moved his arm from her shoulders and settled for sitting beside her, shoulder-to-shoulder. As the movie started, he caught her eye. "Want to know a secret?"

"What?" She relaxed, and remembered to enjoy herself.

"Growing up, I wanted to be a football player. In the worst way."

"Really?" She couldn't picture it. He was so good at what he did, so not the football player type. As good looking as he was, he wasn't overly tall or muscular. She figured he would probably have been leveled on a football field. But he was being honest with her, so she smiled, understanding. "And I wanted to be on Broadway."

This time his smile warmed his expression, and he settled in beside her. "Look at us now."

"God had different plans." She turned toward the screen. "Better plans."

As they watched the movie, Bailey realized how often through the night she'd thought about Cody, and how much she missed him. Her parents had often said money and fame would never bring them joy. She could hear her dad telling them true joy could only come from having a passion for the work they'd do when they grew up, from living within their means, and — even more — from the people they surrounded themselves with. Bailey felt the familiar ache in her heart.

People like Cody.

She allowed herself to get comfortable on the sofa, and when she mentioned it was a little chilly, Brandon gave her one of the plush throws. "Wrap this around your legs," he told her. But he didn't try to share the blanket or move in too close to her.

Bailey was grateful. By giving her space, she was allowed to think a little more about why God would've placed her here. She wondered how many Christians across America prayed for Brandon Paul to find a stronger faith, and she thought about the Bible Katy had given Brandon yesterday. She could hardly wait for him and Dayne to start reading it together.

That was it, really. That's why Brandon was falling for her now, why he thought he wanted to date her. It wasn't that he wanted her — Bailey Flanigan from Bloomington, Indiana. He wanted Bailey's faith in God. Because more than anything or anyone else, joy came from having faith in God. Bailey believed that with all her heart.

She could hardly wait for Brandon to believe it too.

Twenty-Three

SOMETHING VERY BIG AND VERY DRAMATIC was happening inside Brandon. Like maybe all his days until now had led up to this moment in his life. Against everything he'd told himself leading up to this movie, he was reading the Bible — actually studying Scripture with Dayne and Katy in the early morning before the shoot each day.

And more than that, he was liking it.

For the first time in his life there seemed to be answers for his empty life and meaningless relationships. Almost as if life hadn't made sense until now. But still he didn't want to get crazy. He was a celebrity, after all. Celebrities didn't become public Christians — not hardly. He wanted to keep the whole Bible thing as quiet as possible except around one person:

Bailey Flanigan.

The producers and their wives and Bailey all spoke some sort of language the rest of the world didn't seem to know anything about. Except maybe the caterer, Danielle. She was always telling him, "God bless," and reminding him she was praying for him. And maybe there were others too. There must've been because the mood among the cast and crew was definitely different on this set.

Still, he wasn't ready to go public with the fact that he was reading the Bible in his spare time. He doubted he ever would. Right now it was enough that the Bible study gave him more common ground with Bailey. After the trip to New York, he had fallen for her a little more every day. She wasn't interested, and that was fine. For now. Eventually she would change her mind. So the more he knew about her faith, the better chance they'd have of connecting.

The next two weeks blurred together—one long day of shooting after another. But Brandon never got tired of reporting to the set. Just seeing Bailey made his heart feel light and young and whole again—the way he hadn't felt since before NTM made him famous.

Many times Brandon and Bailey watched the dailies together, and he was amazed at what the director was getting. The story was compelling, no doubt. The book was one of his all time favorites. But the movie *Unlocked* was going to be a piece of work people would talk about for generations—Brandon could see it in the performances they were turning in one day after another.

"This is more than we prayed for," Keith said often. "God is blessing us beyond anything we could've asked or imagined."

Brandon wasn't sure if the performances were God's blessings from above or the chemistry between him and Bailey—or the fact that she was simply an undiscovered talent who was only tapping into her potential. But there was no question Keith was right. The footage was stirring and honest and beautiful. Especially the scenes Brandon and Bailey did together.

Now it was Saturday morning and they were finishing up after meeting for a few hours to catch up on scenes they'd missed during the week. Brandon thought they might work through dinner, but it was a little before noon when Keith called it a wrap. "Danielle's made a great chicken enchilada casserole—so don't miss that," Keith told them as the cast and crew gathered around. "After that, we'll see you at seven Monday morning."

The day was once again unseasonably warm—in the mid-seventies with sunshine and blue skies as far as they could see. Brandon had been careful about spending time with Bailey off the set. He wanted to respect the fact that she had a boyfriend, or at least that she had feelings for the high school coach. But today he couldn't stop himself.

At lunch he sat across from her — careful as always not to give the paparazzi the chance to make more of their friendship than it was. "You know what I haven't seen?"

She smiled, and her eyes lit up. "A textbook?"

He laughed and looked down at his plate for a minute. She was always rubbing it in that she had a full load of college courses to contend with in addition to the shoot. "Actually," he looked up. "I was thinking about Lake Monroe Beach. Everyone says it's a great place, but ... well, I've never been."

"Hmmm." Bailey angled her head. "You're staying with Dayne and Katy right on the lake. The beach looks like that. Like a lake."

This was the comfortable place they'd found together — one marked by laughter and teasing. But this time he gave her a pleading look, the one that employed his best puppy-dog eyes. "Your mom's not here today ... you have a car."

"Yes ..." She took a bite of her lunch and acted mystified, like she hadn't the slightest idea what he was getting at. "I should be home studying, don't you think? Or would you like to write my online English essay?"

"See, that's just it. English essays need inspiration, and the best inspiration for that sort of writing is a trip to the lake."

"Really, Brandon ... I have to get home." She tried a slightly serious tone. "You'll see the beach another day."

But he wouldn't give up and, by the end of lunch, Bailey agreed to a quick walk along the shore. She left alone, and then picked him up at the back of the school — out of sight of the paparazzi. When she was sure no one was following them, she drove to the lake, and Brandon raised his brow, impressed. "Our Southern California lakes look nothing like this. More like craters in a desert."

"Sign me up." She laughed lightly. "Sounds like a great vacation spot."

"Not really." Brandon made an exaggerated look. "People rent houseboats and drink enough beer so they don't notice the surroundings." He peered out at Lake Monroe. "But this ... wow. How cold's the water."

"Great in July. Today ... a little cooler." Her eyes took on a faraway look. "Lots of memories out here."

"I'm sure." Brandon figured she was probably thinking about the young coach, but he didn't want to ask. This day was about the two of them, no one else. "Let's take a walk."

"Okay." Bailey smiled, the faraway look gone. "Come on. I'll take you down near the water. There's a path that's pretty easy."

"What?" He jumped out of the car and held his hands up. "I don't look like I can take on the tougher paths?"

She laughed and shook her head. "Not really." She hesitated and came up alongside him. "Just kidding. You could probably swim across the lake."

He puffed out his chest. "Now that's what I'm talking about." They walked down an earthen path toward the water, and then stayed on a sandy section of shore at the lake's edge. It was less of a walk and more of a meandering, which suited Brandon fine. He trusted Bailey more than any girl he'd ever known. Now that she'd made time for him, he felt old feelings welling up inside him. Frustration and anger from his childhood. He had a feeling Bailey would listen, and right now — for the first time in years — he wanted to talk about it. "Remember I told you it'd been a long time since I'd been in a Sunday school class?"

Bailey angled her head, not rushed. "I figured you were kidding."

"Nope." He stuck his hands in the pockets of his jeans and stared at the far edge of the lake. "I was raised in the church. Until I was fourteen."

Bailey looked at him, surprised. She must've realized this

wasn't a time to tease. Her tone was gentle, sensitive. "After that?" Her attention was completely on whatever he was about to tell her.

"After that I stopped going," his tone was tense, the story painful from here. "No one could make me go."

She let that sink in for a while. Then she turned to him, their pace slower. "So what happened? God suddenly became the bad guy?"

"Not at first. But eventually, yeah. I thought He was." Brandon could see that better now than ever in his life. Another benefit of the Bible study with Dayne and Katy.

Bailey's eyes held no accusation, no judgment. "Maybe start at the beginning."

"Yeah." He breathed in deep. Was he really going to tell her all this? It would be easier to pretend he was shallow, but that wasn't the truth. There was so much more to him, pieces no one else knew about. He exhaled and turned to her, their pace still slower. "The drama club at school ... they were holding auditions. My dad wanted me to go out for football. I was the scrawniest kid out there, and the first day I got knocked flat on my back. Couldn't breathe for half a minute." He could hardly believe he was telling her this.

"Football's rough. I always worry that my brothers will get hurt." Again Bailey was understanding. They reached a fallen log and Bailey sat down. She patted the place beside her. "What happened?"

"I wanted to play. Remember?" He grinned, but his eyes held a pain undimmed by time. "But I couldn't. I didn't have it in me." He told her how the coach had pulled him aside and suggested as kindly as possible that football might not be his thing. "The next day I tried out for the school play. Won a lead role. When my dad heard what happened — that I quit football and got a part in the school play — he sat me down and stared at me, real angry."

"He was mad? Seriously?"

"More than that." He smiled, more so he wouldn't get too emotional. Talking about this took him to a place as foreign as the lake spread out before him. He sucked in a quick breath through his nose, and looked away until he was sure his voice was steady. Then he turned to Bailey again. "He asked me if I was gay." Brandon watched the shock play out on her face. His eyes stung, but he cleared his throat hard, refusing to give in to the tears. "He said theater was for wusses, weak girly guys. He told me God was against people who became actors."

"He did not!" Bailey's voice was barely audible over the breeze off the lake. "Brandon, that's awful."

"Yeah. It was." He looked down at the damp sand at their feet. But suddenly he wasn't on the shore of a beautiful lake with the most amazing girl he'd ever met. He was sitting across from his dad in their family living room, his father's words exploding through him, shredding his heart and destroying him all over again. He could smell the chili cooking in the kitchen and see his mother watching with furtive glances from her place near the stove.

Again Bailey seemed to know what he was thinking. "What about your mom? Was she home?"

He rubbed the back of his neck, hard so he wouldn't get sucked back into that scene a moment longer than he needed to be. "She didn't say anything. Nothing." He looked at Bailey again. "She looked ... embarrassed. Like she couldn't contradict him, couldn't ... couldn't stand up for me."

Bailey put her hand on his shoulder. "I'm sorry. I ... can't imagine."

"Yeah. That's why I gave up on God." His tone was bitter now, acid and unforgiveness. "Then forget it. Forget all of it." His anger was building, clawing its way quickly to the surface. "Better to party every night than judge everyone. Like ... like my dad."

"Brandon ..."

"No." He jerked away from her touch. "Never mind." He didn't want her sympathy, didn't want it from anyone. Why had he told her this anyway? Why had he gone and ruined a perfectly good day, probably a perfectly good friendship? No one could understand this sort of detail about him, and now she'd never see him the same way. He stood and walked hard and fast toward the water. When he reached it he stopped and walked a few feet one way then back again the other direction. If he could have jumped in and swum across the lake, he would've.

At first she waited, letting him have his space. But then she came to him slowly, quietly until she was at his side. He didn't want a spew of kind words and her insistence that everything would be okay, that the accusation was a long time ago and certainly his father hadn't meant it. Didn't want her words about God being good and kind. He didn't want that, and she didn't offer it. Instead she put her arms around his waist and hugged him from the side, leaning her head on his shoulder.

After a while, he put his arms around her too, and they stood that way for a long time. Finally, Brandon led her back to the log and they both sat down again. "Sorry." He was in control again. Embarrassed, but no longer angry. "It's just ... I haven't talked about that before." He looked up just enough to meet her eyes. "Not to anyone."

She didn't ask what happened next, but his story came unbidden, the way Brandon figured it needed to come after so many years, after reading in the Bible about being new and finding redemption. From a God who his father had used against him.

"A week later, after my dad had told me the same thing every day, I ran away."

"Where to?" Bailey's eyes were the kindest he'd ever seen.

"Four blocks away. To my uncle's house." Brandon told her how his Uncle Joe was nothing like his dad. And as he told the story, Brandon was there again, cold and sweaty, pounding on his uncle's door, a bag of clothes in his arms. "Uncle Joe was the roughneck in the family, the guy always getting into scrapes with the law and embarrassing the family. My family ... they were the Christians. And they thought I was gay." His laugh was filled with sorrow, with a pain that still lived in a part of him that would always be that fourteen-year-old boy.

"Did you stay?" Bailey's eyes were damp. "At your Uncle Joe's?"

"I did." Even now Brandon relished the freedom that move had given him. No one would call him gay just because he liked to act. His parents threw a fit, and tried several times to force him to come home. He remembered once hearing his mother's shrill cry from their bedroom over the phone lines. "*You did this, Martin, you drove our son away!*"

But in the light of day, she never said a word on his behalf, never once stood up to Martin Paul. After a few months of bringing him back and Brandon running away again, his parents stopped trying. "They didn't really want me." He filled his lungs, trying to rid himself of the hurt. "If I couldn't play football, if I was going to act in the school play ... then good riddance." He frowned, staring at the wet sand. "Let's just say I never went to church again. I couldn't imagine a whole building full of people like my dad." His voice was angry again. "I still can't."

In time, his parents signed over custody to his Uncle Joe. Living with his uncle's family, Brandon was free to do whatever he pleased. They had no qualms about him being in a play or drinking with his friends — or doing anything else he felt like doing. Eventually, Brandon moved with his uncle's family an hour away. He kept acting and, even after he grew taller and stronger, he never went out for the football team again. "See," he slid his foot close to hers and gave it a slight tap. "Now you know why I wish I could play. The whole *Remember the Titans* thing."

"I was thinking about that." She had a way of listening with her whole body.

The lack of judgment, the acceptance he could feel from her allowed him to finish his story. "I moved to Los Angeles after graduation and got an agent. Sort of like Dayne, things went great from the beginning. NTM cast me in their new series, and the whole success thing was sort of overnight."

"America's heartthrob." She smiled at him, careful that her eyes never left his. "What happened ... with your parents?"

"After I was on the cover of *People* the first time, my dad wrote me a letter. Told me he'd been wrong. He was sorry. Asked for my contact information so we could talk."

Bailey waited, letting him tell the story at his own pace.

"I figured it was easy for him to be genuine when I'd already made it," Brandon still felt disgusted by his dad's effort. "He quoted a bunch of Scripture in the letter, talking about how wrong he'd been." Brandon shrugged. "A few months later I talked to my mom on the phone. She started crying, told me she was sorry too. They'd been wrong ... yada, yada, yada ..." Brandon furrowed his brow, working once more to keep from letting his feelings spill into his eyes. "She told me God wanted His people to forgive."

She'd been listening so intently that at that part she sat up straighter and raised her brow, shock working its way across her expression. "Wow ... like you'd be interested in God after that." She clasped her hands in front of her and stared out at the lake, almost as if she were praying. Or maybe she simply had no idea what else to say.

"That was three years ago." He could feel himself pulling out of the memory, finding his center again, remembering who he was. He was Brandon Paul, Hollywood's favorite movie star, voted best-looking young celebrity by *People*. His parents couldn't hurt him now. He breathed in slowly, working his way back to the moment. "Two things came of that time."

She turned to him, and in her face he didn't see pity, but rather a strength and support. Her smile told him she understood. "You don't go to Sunday school ..."

"That too." He chuckled and stared out at the lake. The sun was high overhead, splashing light across the surface and warming his shoulders. "But, yeah ... I swore I'd never have anything to do with the two things that made up my life back then — Christianity," he turned to her, "and my parents."

Bailey nodded slowly. "Which is why you didn't want to think about *Unlocked* as a Christian film."

"Right." He'd come this far with his heart. No reason to stop now. "I thought about pulling out. Right up until I flew out here for the screen test with you." He smiled, and the heaviness from earlier lifted. "You changed my mind — whether you know it or not."

"Come on." She laughed, waiting, knowing there was more to the story.

"Seriously. Before I came here, I looked you up on Facebook."

"I remember ... you friend-requested me."

He grinned and again the mood between them felt light and magical. "It was more than that." He put his arm around her shoulders, careful once more to make the moment feel like two friends sharing an afternoon, nothing that might threaten her. "I saw something in your eyes, something I was missing." He was confused by his own feelings. "I'm still mad at God ... because how could He make my dad say those things?"

"Brandon ..." Bailey's voice was more gentle than the sound of the lake against the shore. "You don't think that."

"I did." He searched her eyes. "But with you ... I'm beginning to think I was wrong. I don't know." He angled his head so he could memorize her, the deep blue eyes that shone with goodness and truth and a love he had never really believed in. As much as Brandon wanted to hold onto this moment and not inadvertently push her away, he suddenly couldn't stop himself from going further. He brought his free hand up along her cheek and gently kissed her.

At first he thought she might return his kiss, because she didn't pull away or complain or walk off angry. But she carefully removed his arm from her shoulders and took both his hands in hers. Slightly breathless, she searched his eyes. "Brandon ... no." She wasn't mad, but the passion and intensity in her voice took him by surprise. She stared at him, as if she were willing him to understand her the way she'd understood him. "Don't you see?"

"I see that I want you," his voice was deep, thick with desire. He ran his thumbs over the tops of her hands. "Is that wrong?"

She gave a quick shake of her head. "God brought you here because of your soul ... not your senses." She angled her face, never breaking eye contact. "You don't want me ... you want the peace I have. You want my faith."

"Not when I'm this close to you." He hung his head, because if he looked into her eyes another moment he'd kiss her again. "All I know ... all I feel is that I've never met anyone like you, Bailey. God ... if there is a God ... must've brought me here because of you." He allowed himself to look up again.

"There is a God. He brought you here to be around me, yes. But not just me. He has you here with Katy and Dayne, Keith and Lisa ..." she smiled. "Even Danielle, the caterer. All because He's calling you back to Himself." She was talking quieter than before, but she implored him with her tone. "God loves you, Brandon. He gave you the ability to act." She laughed, a quick laugh full of a childlike awe. "And you're a tremendously talented actor." She paused. "Can you imagine how this world would be changed if someone like you really lived for God?" She shook her head, dizzy-like. "There'd be no way to measure the number of people you could touch."

Brandon hadn't thought about that, but the responsibility seemed overwhelming. "That's a lot to ask ... from anyone."

"The responsibility is there whether you want it or not." She still seemed to be practically bursting in her attempt to make him grasp what she was saying. "You influence people one way or another. That's how celebrity works. Especially now."

He still wanted to kiss her, but the impulse of the moment had passed. "If God's really calling me ... if you're right, then can you do me a favor?"

"Of course." She squeezed his hands, her smile shining through her eyes.

"Ask Him to show me, okay? Because right now ... I still don't see it."

Bailey agreed, and they both decided it was time to get back. They walked together to her car and, on the ride to Dayne and Katy's house, they laughed about some of the scenes they'd filmed today. Before she dropped him off, he thanked her. "What I told you out there ... that's just for you, okay?"

"I know." She put her hand on his. "You can trust me."

He smiled and then he jumped out and jogged toward the front door without looking back. Katy and Dayne and Sophie were gone for the evening, which was good. He went out back and sat on the deck, staring at the lake once more. He was grateful he'd seen the beach, grateful for his time with Bailey. But he was still angry about God. If God loved him, why had He allowed his father to be so mean? The man's rejection stayed with him every day, no matter how well he pretended to be over it. And something occurred to him as he sat in the afternoon sunshine thinking about all he'd told Bailey and the truth about his past. If God wanted to reach him, He'd have to do more than reach the famous Brandon Paul.

He'd have to reach the kid inside him, the fourteen-year-old who was still sitting on a sofa being mocked and cut to pieces by a father who thought he was gay.

Twenty-Four

BAILEY TREASURED HER DAY AT THE lake with Brandon, and afterwards she saw him as more than her costar or someone to pray for. He was her friend. Often in the final weeks of the shoot she remembered their time on the shores of Lake Monroe, his painful honesty and the horrible truth about his past. She cared not only for the guy he was now, but for the boy inside him who had never moved past that terrible time.

She tried to imagine a father inflicting that sort of emotional pain on his son, just because he didn't play sports. Her own dad was a professional football coach, but not once had he ever pushed the boys to play. Their dad was no more proud of Connor now than back when he was acting on a CKT stage. It killed her to imagine Connor hearing a comment like the one Brandon's dad had given him. Often when she watched Brandon delivering yet another stunning performance as Holden Harris, she was reminded of his talk with her at the lake that day. She wondered if some of the inspiration for the character of Holden hadn't come from his own days feeling locked in the prison of rejection. Either way, his honesty would stay with her.

And of course she often remembered his kiss.

For a few fleeting seconds, she wanted him to kiss her, wanted to involve herself in the moment as if nothing else mattered in all the world. But the truth shouted at her before she had time to enjoy herself. Thankfully, God had given her the words so he would understand the truth. His involvement in *Unlocked* had nothing to do with her and everything to do with God.

The way God was calling him.

But even so, as the weeks ran by in a blur, and as Brandon kept reading his new Bible with Katy and Dayne, little seemed to come from it. Brandon was kind and funny, and the two of them were rarely apart on set. He had found a close friend in her, and Bailey was certain that much would remain long after the movie wrapped. But he hadn't talked again about God, not since their time at the lake.

On the last day of filming — two days before Thanksgiving — the producers gathered the cast and crew in the same classroom, the one where they'd had that first meeting, which felt like just a few minutes ago. Brandon and Bailey entered the room together, and he gave her a teasing smile. "Can I sit by you?"

"You better." She slipped her arm around his waist, and they walked to the same seats they'd had that first day. "I can't believe it's the last day."

"Don't worry. You can't get rid of me that easily." He whispered close to her as they sat down. "We'll have reshoots and the premiere of *The Last Letter* — here in Bloomington, I believe."

"It is. The day after Christmas." She laughed. "You mean you're coming?"

"Hard to believe, but yes ... I made the list. Like I said ..." his look was intended to melt her heart and it did — though in a different way than he probably meant. "I'm not going anywhere."

Bailey was glad for a reason to see Brandon again. She hadn't fallen in love with him over the last six weeks, but he'd carved out a place in her heart. She had a feeling no one knew him as well as she did, and she realized the privilege came with great responsibility. It was why she still prayed constantly for him.

"Okay," Mr. Ellison looked weary, but he beamed with joy all the same. They'd climbed a mountain together and here, today, they'd reached the top. "Everyone take your seats."

The cast and crew were friends now, but their respect for

Keith Ellison drew the room to an instant silence. People sat down and Bailey and Brandon, along with the others, turned their attention to the front of the room. Rumor had it they'd be treated to something special today, and Bailey could hardly wait. She was exhausted emotionally from all she'd given to the film, and she knew the others felt the same way. Giddy to have made it this far, sad to see the process end, and certain they could be proud of their work here in Bloomington.

Andi's dad wore his usual — jeans and a buttoned down shirt, nothing too flashy. "Six weeks ago I told you about my vision for *Unlocked*. I asked you to look around the room at what I believed was a very special cast and crew." He smiled, and his eyes shone with emotion. "I was right." He paced along the front of the classroom, making eye contact with each cast member, each person on crew. "I told you that over these weeks you would give performances you didn't know you could give, that you would witness chemistry on film that would take your breath away."

Chills ran down Bailey's arms.

Mr. Ellison stopped and faced them. "I was right about that." He grinned at Dayne. "My co-producer and I believed ... we believed with everything inside us, that once in a lifetime does a chance like this come along, a chance to be part of a work that might define you." He nodded and looked at Brandon, pride emanating from his whole face. "I believe we were right about that, too." He stepped to the side and pointed to a cameraman at the back of the room. "Take a look at this."

Someone hit the lights, and a video began to play on a screen at the front of the room. The message read:

Cast and crew of Unlocked ... *here's to you!*

The words faded and the screen came to life with emotional music and a sequential series of highlights from the last six weeks, footage that wasn't exactly a trailer, but some of which was bound to make the cut when the trailer was made.

From the opening scene, where the couple playing Brandon's parents receive the diagnosis of his autism and they realize they'll never again have their toddler the way he once was, the footage was gripping. Bailey leaned over her knees, and she barely noticed as Brandon put his arm around her back. The story jumped from that early diagnosis to Holden Harris's high school years. The director and director of photography had done a brilliant job getting inside the prison that was Holden's mind, helping the audience see how strange and sometimes beautiful it would feel to go through a crowded high school corridor trapped inside the prison of autism.

Scene after scene, the performances were so gripping Bailey had to remember to exhale. The impact brought tears to her eyes. Around the room she could hear people sniffling, and she knew everyone was feeling the same way. Especially during the Holden Harris scenes, the way Brandon had brought his character to life. She put her hand on his knee and squeezed it in a way that told him she was beyond impressed. "Amazing," she whispered.

"You were my inspiration," he whispered near her ear. "How could I miss?"

The compliment warmed her to her core, but she refused to believe it. Brandon's performance was all part of what God was doing here on the set. What He wasn't finished doing.

After five minutes, the piece ended and the lights came back up. Around the room people were drying their eyes, looking at each other in disbelief and rising to their feet. At first a few began to clap and then several more, until the entire room was standing in wild, raucous applause for what they'd just witnessed. Bailey hadn't been part of a movie shoot before, but she couldn't believe this was normal — that at the end of six weeks it was this clear they'd been part of something unforgettable.

From the back of the room someone shouted out, "Incredible work, Brandon!"

Another person shouted his name, and then another, and the applause continued — loud and intense mixed with a cheering that made Brandon wave at the others. Then he gave Bailey a crooked smile and a slight shrug, as if to say he didn't know what all the fuss was about.

Bailey gave him a side hug, holding on longer than usual. If he was capable of a performance like that, then certainly God was working within him. His heart was being changed by the living Word of God. It would only be a matter of time before he admitted it and turned running back into the arms of Jesus.

Mr. Ellison took the front of the room again. "So you see ... when we said people would talk about this movie for generations to come, we meant it." Tears glistened in his eyes, and he laughed to ease the intensity of the moment. His words were now slower, deeply deliberate. "I'm so very, very proud of each of you. No matter who gets talked about and who receives top billing, you're all stars in our eyes."

Dayne came to the front of the room and stood beside Keith. "I've been acting for more than a decade, and that," he pointed at the wall where the video had just been shown, "is more special than anything I've ever seen." He nodded, smiling at each of them and finally giving Mr. Ellison a hearty side hug. "Congratulations!"

The room erupted into hugs and laughter, everyone beyond excited, but sad to see the shoot come to an end. Bailey and Brandon had only a few brief scenes that day, so they spent most of their time working with the assistant director on the list of shots that would need slight additions or even partial reshoots.

That night Danielle, the caterer, made a steak and seafood feast, and after an hour the producers hurried everyone to the school gymnasium. There Bailey could hardly believe her eyes.

As a surprise to the cast, the producers had secretly decorated the place like a high school prom, complete with massive pink and purple streamers and a DJ playing from the stage.

But more than that, the entire room was filled with family and friends of the cast and crew. Some had clearly flown in, and as Bailey walked in, her brothers ran up to her. Brandon had been to the house a few times, so they knew him and they gave him high fives. "Isn't this the best thing ever!" Ricky spun around. "I've never been to a prom!"

Bailey and Brandon swapped a look, and they both laughed out loud. Her parents joined them and the buzz continued through the night, with people reflecting on all they'd accomplished, and the DJ bringing everyone onto the floor for the chicken dance and the twist. Bailey was pretty sure her brother Justin was going to throw out his hip from twisting so hard, but instead he fell to the floor laughing.

She and Brandon danced much of the evening together, but always one or more of Bailey's brothers was with them — keeping the group feel to the night. Around the room the cast danced much the same way, in groups. Some people had no family or friends along, so they joined in with those who did, and the evening took on the feel of a reunion.

Only once, when the DJ played the song "Gravity" by Sara Bareilles did Brandon take her into his arms and insist that they deserved this one slow dance together. As the words began, he sang them to her, his lighthearted laughter in his eyes replaced with something far deeper and more meaningful. "Something always brings me back to you ..." his voice was smooth and on key. "You hold me without touch ... keep me without chains ..."

He knew every line, every lyric and he sang each word straight to her. When the song reached the part where the singer cries out, "Set me free ..." Brandon brought his face close alongside hers and sang, "Don't set me free ..."

She smiled, appreciating his efforts and moved by them. When he finally gave his heart to Jesus, she wondered if her feelings for him would change, if she'd be able to resist him the way she could still resist him now. As charming as he was, as great a time as she'd had these past six weeks, he still didn't share her faith.

And he wasn't Cody Coleman.

At the end of the dance, he looked at her like she was the most precious treasure, and he leaned close and kissed her on the cheek. "I'm not giving up, Miss Bailey."

She hoped her eyes told him how much his kindness meant to her. She would never think about mocking his efforts or disregarding his attempts to make her fall for him. She cared far too much about him for that. "I've had fun, Brandon ... every day. I won't forget it."

He gave her a quick, meaningful hug — nothing that could've been taken by anyone in the room to be more than a show of deep friendship. "It's not over yet." Again he smiled at her. "Now let's get your brothers and your parents out here."

Two hours into the party, the group gathered for a showing of the blooper reel, also put together by the directors. The cast laughed until they cried, and Bailey was grateful at the end when they were each given a gift bag with both the highlight reel and the bloopers, along with a custom coffee mug that read *Unlocked* across it, a T-shirt with the same, and a thank-you card from the producers. Memories of a six-week period in her life Bailey was certain she would remember forever.

But as the night ended and she returned home with her family, it wasn't the movie or Brandon or the cast party that consumed her mind. It was one simple truth — now that the filming was done she and Cody were going to share Thanksgiving. Cody could explain about the Cheyenne girl, whoever she was, and he could tell her why he'd stayed so completely away. And if things went the way she prayed they would go, they might find common ground again, and pick up where they left off.

As if nothing about the strange break between them had ever even happened.

THE POLICE HAD CAPTURED BENNY DIRK. The arrest happened last night, and the detective called Cody within the hour. They had evidence that he was linked to three murders and more drugs than they had imagined. With Cody's mother's testimony and the evidence against him, Benny was going away for a long time. He was no longer a threat to Cody or to Bailey.

Cody stretched out on his bed. He was supposed to be studying for a physics test, but thoughts of Bailey made homework impossible. His heart was still raw over all he'd missed out on ... and all that laid ahead. He had read in the paper that the filming for *Unlocked* was wrapping that day. The cast was probably celebrating somewhere in Bloomington, maybe even there at the school.

I miss her so much, God ... help me get through this ...

His room was quiet, a bunch of empty boxes lining his wall. He'd made his decision. He'd sent his resume to six high schools in Indianapolis over the past few weeks, and the athletic director at one of them — a new Christian school — had offered to make him the head football coach in the coming year. He would have to live there, of course, find an apartment near IU's Indianapolis campus to finish his degree.

There was more to his decision. He wanted to be closer to his mother, and he needed time to think about his life, his future. Bailey was moving on without him — at least it felt that way. The most loving thing he could do was let her go — which meant the move to the city was the right decision from every angle.

He didn't have much to pack, and he couldn't leave until the first week of December, after finals. Clear Creek High had finished sixth in state—far better than any time in the last few years. Coach Taylor had told him after the last game—an away loss to a big Indianapolis school—that the team would never have gone so far without his help.

"Connor is a different kid this year," Coach told him.

Cody was still pretty sure Connor's passion laid in performing —lately he wanted to be a Christian recording artist—but Cody had to agree with Coach Taylor. The work he'd done with Connor had helped him mature into a different, more confident young man. The changes in him were only one of the rewards Cody would take with him from this past season. Jim Flanigan had thanked him too.

"We miss you around the house," he'd told Cody after the last game. "When things settle down, come back around. I'd like to talk sometime."

Cody had agreed, but he didn't let the conversation linger. Leaving the Flanigans was going to hurt in a way that would stay with him all his life. Not just leaving Bailey, but her whole family.

Now that there was no football practice, Cody had put all his focus on his schoolwork. He wanted nothing less than a B, especially since he was transferring. He'd already made the arrangements with the counselors here and at the Indianapolis campus. He set his physics book down and laid on his back, staring at the ceiling. If only he could get through this week, through the conversation he was finally going to have with Bailey.

Jim Flanigan had called and invited him for Thanksgiving, and Cody had accepted. He understood why the invitation hadn't come from Bailey. They weren't talking at all now, not even a few random text messages or brief awkward phone calls. Several weeks back he'd stopped responding to her, and in very little time she gave up altogether. Cody didn't blame her. The break was his fault completely.

But he'd only done it because he loved her more than life. At first, because he wanted to protect her from Benny. But then because he wanted her to enjoy the life God was giving her. He would only slow her down now. If the paparazzi found out about their relationship and Cody's mother … her arrest and Benny Dirk. The news could tarnish Bailey forever.

His leaving was just one more way of protecting her.

He breathed in and felt a little rush of adrenaline at the thought of seeing her. She'd made the cover of the tabloids twice since filming started, once when the group of them flew off to New York City for the day and the headlines shouted: *Cast of* Unlocked *Gets Friendly.* The picture was of Brandon and Bailey leaving the Gershwin Theater together, holding hands. The quality was grainy, and clearly they hadn't known anyone was taking their picture.

But the photo said it all.

The second time a photographer had caught them laughing together on the set of *Unlocked. Good Times Ahead for B&B* the cover announced. Cody had purchased both magazines, so he'd have proof in case he ever needed a reminder about why he was doing what he was doing.

The tabloids were merciless. They knew Tim Reed was in the *Wicked* cast, and they announced that already Tim was seeing one of the other ensemble dancers. If they found out about Cody and his mother, Bailey's reputation would suffer. There was no need for that or for him to drag her down in any other way. Their lives were simply too different.

He thought about Thanksgiving. *Lord, let our time together be special … not strained or awkward. Please … I want her to remember what we shared before. Not how it is now.*

He wanted a proper goodbye, a chance to tell her how much he cared and to convince her he only wanted the best for her. On the bed beside him, his phone vibrated, alerting him of a text message. For half a second he hoped it might be Bailey, but then he knew better. Not tonight, with the cast party undoubtedly in full swing.

A quick look at his phone and he smiled to himself. Cheyenne. *You studying?*

He tapped out his return on his phone. *Trying ... you?*

They'd been texting a little more, gradually finding a friendship. As it turned out, he was moving into an apartment a block away from her. They'd both be taking classes at the Indianapolis campus, and Tara had made it clear she expected them to be at Sunday dinner often. "Art would love this," Tara told him when he stopped by last time he was in town. Cody had picked up a bouquet of flowers at the market, just to tell her he was thinking about her, about Art.

Tara had buried her face in the flowers and breathed in deep, and when Cody told her he was talking with Cheyenne occasionally, Tara's eyes teared up, a smile stretched across her face. "This is good. My Art would've wanted this. That girl's already had a hard life. She's too special to sit home alone for the rest of time."

Cody was still certain the pre-Veteran's Day dinner she'd arranged was intended to introduce Cheyenne to Art's war buddies. Tara was right about her — Cheyenne was special. Cody had learned she was a Christian, and since losing Art she'd done little more than go to school and work each day. No wonder Tara was concerned about her. Another text came in.

Maybe when you move here we can study together. Might pass the time easier.

He thought about that, and he liked the idea. She was right; the time would pass more quickly if they studied together. He texted back, *Sounds fun ... talk to you later ... have a good night.*

He didn't want to talk at length with her, not now when all he could picture was Bailey and whether she was falling for Brandon or how she was feeling now that they had finished filming. The thing about studying together was that this should've been the year when he and Bailey shared that time. Last summer, everything was headed that way, and by now they might've been so in love, so strong in their relationship, nothing could ever come between them.

But it wasn't meant to be. He'd made arrangements to move on, and he was at peace with his decision. He'd accepted the head coaching job at the new Christian school in Indianapolis, and in a few weeks he would be moved out of Bloomington — maybe for good. He'd taken care of his utilities, and his first and last rent at his new apartment in the city, and he'd met with the athletic director at the Christian school to fill out paper work and talk about next year — the off-season and Cody's vision for the program. Now there was only one thing left to do, the thing he'd put off as long as he could.

He had to tell Bailey.

Somewhere down the road, he and Bailey might find a friendship again, but Cody wasn't sure. He could never again see her as only a friend. And she needed to move on, fall in love with someone else, and find her way making movies or landing a role on Broadway. He knew her well enough to know she wouldn't be interested in Brandon Paul — the guy wasn't a Christian, and his personal life would only make Bailey want to pray for him, not date him. But one day she'd meet the right guy, and when that happened, Cody didn't want to be in the way.

His next three years were laid out for him.

Now it was only a matter of trying to survive the heartbreak of living it.

Twenty-Five

BAILEY LOVED EVERYTHING ABOUT THANKSGIVING. She woke up early Thursday morning, showered and dressed in her best black skinny jeans and a pale pink JCrew cashmere turtleneck she'd gotten for her last birthday. She felt more alive and full of hope than she had in a long time, and she realized again how much the shoot had taken out of her.

But more than that, today she'd see Cody again.

She hummed a Jeremy Camp song while she finished curling her long dark hair, and then she hurried down the stairs to the kitchen. Like every Thanksgiving, her parents were already working on the turkey, pulling it from its plastic wrapper so her dad could set it in the roasting pan. Bailey took a seat at the kitchen bar, watching the two of them. "Happy Thanksgiving!"

"Happy Thanksgiving!" They both said it, her dad peering over his shoulder while cool water ran over the raw turkey.

"Have I told you lately how glad I am you don't coach the Lions or the Bears?" Bailey grinned. "You'd never be home for Thanksgiving."

"Makes me grateful for traditions," her dad chuckled. "I'll take a Sunday game any day over missing this."

"Yes, because no one knows turkeys like you, honey," her mom came up behind him and massaged his shoulders. "You're the best turkey-maker this side of the Mississippi."

"That right?" He pulled a bag of gizzards from the inside of the bird and set them on the counter. "Or maybe you're just buttering me up so I'll keep doing this every year."

"Maybe that." Her mom nodded quickly and grinned at Bailey. Then she nuzzled her face against his. "Either way I agree, I'm glad you're home."

Her dad finished his part, cleaning out the turkey and positioning it back in the pan. Then he headed out to the garage to find the family's Christmas lights. Every year they decorated their house the day after Thanksgiving, and since tomorrow afternoon figured to be rainy, he wanted to be ready for an early start.

Once he was gone, it was up to Bailey and her mom to stuff the bird. All six Flanigan kids had stayed up late the night before working on various parts of the dinner. The boys had shredded six loaves of bread, ripping the slices into small pieces and filling an enormous bowl. The bread had been left out overnight and now it was ready to be turned into stuffing.

Ricky and BJ had crushed two bags of pretzels for the crust of their family's famous strawberry and cream cheese gelatin salad, while Bailey and Connor had worked together to make the pineapple lime salad. This time they hadn't spilled a drop when they poured it into the ringed mold and put it in the refrigerator. Bailey thought the lime Jello salad was always the prettiest item on the table. Shawn and Justin had the job of peeling a ten-pound bag of potatoes — which they loved because each year they raced to see who could peel the most before the bag ran out. Like most years, Justin won, but Shawn was a good sport. He promised to make up for it by beating Justin in a game of Around the World on the basketball court sometime this morning.

With all the preparation from last night, Bailey and her mother didn't have much work to get dinner going. Bailey found the celery and onions from the fridge while her mom set the gizzards in a small pan of boiling water. Later they would use a few tablespoons of the water to help season the stuffing.

Her mom talked about the upcoming football banquet Sunday afternoon and how great a job Cody had done. "I'm glad he's joining us today." She gave Bailey a curious look. "Have you talked?"

"No. Not in weeks." She had determined not to let that fact bother her. They needed to talk in person in order to work everything out. She minced the celery into fine pieces, careful to remove the stringy parts. In the background her dad had put on the Macy's Thanksgiving Day Parade. "We'll talk today." She smiled at her mom. Everything was too perfect for that not to happen. She would forgive Cody for being distant, and explain she understood how he might've been feeling out of sorts — what, with her working with Brandon. She would ask about Cheyenne, but she was sure the girl was not the problem. And now that her movie was finished and school was out, the two of them could find what they'd started last summer. She could hardly wait to see him.

The boys came down a few at a time, and each of them stopped to admire the work Bailey and her mom were doing. "I can't wait till it starts cooking." Ricky made an exaggerated sniff at the air, his face upward. "That's the best smell ever!"

Bailey's mom had set out cinnamon rolls and bacon for breakfast — another family tradition for Thanksgiving morning. Bailey's brothers watched them add the chopped celery and onions to the dry bread, and Bailey carefully poured in several cups of chicken broth and a little of the juice from the cooked gizzards. The last ingredient was a cup of melted butter.

"I could eat it just like that," Shawn's eyes were big. He craned his neck over the counter so he could get a whiff of the stuffing. "Cinnamon rolls and stuffing ... the perfect combination."

The other boys laughed, and after they watched Bailey and their mom stuff the turkey — and baste the outside with more melted butter — they ran to get their dad from outside. He and Connor were in charge of the next part.

Bailey stood back and admired the turkey. "Best one yet."

"Definitely." Her dad walked in, washed his hands, and together with Connor they eased the stuffed bird into the baking bag and back into the roasting pan. This time Connor put the turkey in the oven without help.

"Way to go," Bailey linked arms with Shawn and Justin, watching as Connor shut the oven door. "Wow, Connor, you're as strong as dad."

"Come on," Ricky raised his eyebrows. As the youngest Flanigan and a football fanatic, he always saw their dad as bigger than life. "Connor's strong, but no one's as strong as Dad."

The boys followed their dad outside to organize Christmas lights and decorations, and Bailey and her mom washed their hands. Already it was eleven in the morning, and Bailey wasn't sure what time Cody was supposed to be there. "Did Dad tell him a time?" She ran a soapy wet rag over the granite countertop, cleaning the area for the next round of preparations.

"We'll be eating at three, like always." She brought a bowl of whole sweet potatoes to the sink and grabbed two peelers. "I think your dad told him to be here by two. He invited Cody's mom too, but I guess she's busy. That's what Cody said."

As they worked, they talked about the movie and the re-shoots that were scheduled for the week after Christmas. They also dreamed about what they'd wear to the premiere for *The Last Letter*. Bailey wanted to take Cody, and she told her mom as much. Then Brandon could see Cody wasn't only a figment of her imagination.

"Be careful, honey." Her mom's voice was tender, the way it always was when she had wisdom to impart. "What if something's changed with Cody? I mean, the boys said he's different. More distant." She hesitated. "And remember the text he meant to send to that girl."

"It's nothing. I know it's not." She pushed the peeler deeper into a sweet potato, forcing large sections of skin into the sink. "It's just the movie thing. We'll be fine after today."

Her mom didn't press the issue. The answers would play out soon enough, so there was no point in either of them guessing about what Cody was thinking or why he'd been so distant. The hours passed slowly, and Shawn made good on his promise to beat Justin at Around the World. As the boys' game came to a close, Bailey and her mom finished everything they could do in the kitchen, and except for their dad — who was showering — the whole family met up in the living room for a recap of the parade.

Finally ... finally she saw Cody's car pull up the drive, and her brothers celebrated the fact. Bailey padded through the house to her favorite window, the one in her mom's office. From there she could watch him park and head up to the door without him seeing her. She felt her heart skid into a dizzy sort of rhythm. He looked taller, his shoulders broader, and she realized just how much she'd missed him.

Before he reached the front door, she was there to open it. But her brothers arrived at the same time, running and sliding down the hallway in their socks, creating a happy chaotic atmosphere that wasn't exactly what Bailey was hoping for in this, the first time they'd been together in nearly two months.

"Wow, we're like the welcome committee or something," Ricky laughed out loud and rushed to get the door. "Hey ... we're all here!" he shouted as he welcomed Cody inside.

Cody was hugged from either side by Ricky and Shawn, and he got a fist pound from Connor all while Justin and BJ peppered him with questions about why he hadn't been by and how come he didn't come earlier in the day so he could've played Around the World. Before he took even a few steps, he reached one hand in Bailey's direction and squeezed her fingers. Their eyes met, and Bailey felt her knees grow weak. He still cared about her. He *must*. Otherwise, he couldn't speak to her like that, without even saying a word. Bailey stood back, smiling, taking in the way her brothers loved Cody. She would have time with him later, but for now there was satisfaction in knowing he was clearly where he belonged.

Here with her family.

From the time he arrived until dinner was served, the group did everything together. They watched football and spent half an hour on the basketball court outside so Justin could take another try beating Shawn at hoops, and the whole time Bailey forced herself to be patient. The Baxters and the Ellisons were coming for dessert — nearly fifty people by her mom's latest count. So if they didn't find time alone soon the night could get away from them. It could be nearly midnight before they talked.

Dinner came together the way it usually did on Thanksgiving, in a frenzy of teamwork with every Flanigan doing his or her part to make it happen. The table was set with their prettiest creamy satin tablecloth and a deep brown and gold table runner. The china was the same they used every year, a set their parents picked up in London years ago. Even the pine-coned centerpiece was the same, and as Ricky had announced before the meal came together, it wouldn't be Thanksgiving at the Flanigan's if the table looked different. Cody pitched in too, filling the crystal goblets with sparkling cider and letting his eyes linger on Bailey's when their paths crossed.

Finally the meal was spread out on the kitchen counter, the plates stacked at one end, and it was time to walk through the line and fill their plates. After they did, they took their places at the table and Bailey's dad prayed — one of the most beautiful Thanksgiving prayers Bailey could remember. "We are grateful this day, Lord ... because so many in our country will do without this year. Please know we are thankful for our health, our family, our friends, and our faith, and we ask that You continue to bless us not for our glory, but for Yours."

After a round of *amens*, they continued with the other tradition everyone had come to look forward to. Around the room, each of them would say what they were thankful for. As always, the opportunity started with Ricky. "One of the benefits of being the youngest," he grinned at the others, his words barely distinguishable because of the mashed potatoes and gravy filling his mouth.

The answers were similar to other years. The boys were thankful for their family, for football, for their Savior, and — on this night — for the presence of Cody among them. Bailey smiled when her mom said she was thankful Bailey was done filming *Unlocked*. "Every day was a little crazy back then," she gave Bailey a weary smile. "A few times we even had the paparazzi camping out at the end of the driveway."

Bailey, too, was thankful the filming was finished, but she added she was even more thankful for something else. "I'm ready for life to move on." She kept her glance discreet, but she couldn't help looking at Cody. "Everything sort of seemed on hold while we were filming."

Cody was next, though he was seated across from Bailey because Ricky and BJ had called dibs on sitting beside him. "I'm thankful for God's guidance." He gave a slight nod, and he looked at Bailey's parents. "I've felt that pretty strongly lately."

His answer set off the first screeching siren of alarm in Bailey's otherwise quiet heart. God's guidance? Meaning what? That Cody had undergone a transformation or a change of heart in some way recently? She tried not to think about it, while her Dad explained he was thankful for the spiritual growth in the Flanigan kids. Whatever Cody had meant by that, she would ask him later. As soon as they had a moment.

Bailey meant for that time to come as soon as dinner was finished, but they were still clearing the dinner plates when the doorbell rang. Cody must've seen her expression fall a little because he came up alongside her with a stack of dishes. "Don't worry." He set the plates down in the sink and hugged her shoulders. "I'll stay late. We'll talk after everyone goes."

Bailey could barely hear him, barely focus on the words he was saying because this was the first time he'd touched her in far too long. The feel of his arm around her was like home to her, so right it practically hurt when he moved back to the table for another load of dishes. Whatever he wanted to talk to her about, the news couldn't be bad, right? Cody was here and he was loved by everyone in her family. Whatever guidance he'd been getting from God it must've been the sort of thing she'd been picturing — that they would come to an agreement to put the last few months behind them and move on. As if they'd never taken a break at all. Bailey wanted to know this instant what he was thinking and feeling, his intentions toward her.

But members of the Luke Baxter family were already streaming through the front door, bringing pumpkin pies into the kitchen and laughing about the warm weather this year and how the kids had helped carve the turkey. So Bailey resigned herself.

Whatever Cody wanted to tell her, it would have to wait.

Twenty-Six

KEITH WAS GLAD ANDI DECIDED TO JOIN THEM for the trip to the Flanigan's tonight. Thanksgiving had been quiet — just the three of them — and had included a poignant discussion about how Andi was feeling, how the baby would be coming in little more than a month.

Not once since her time down at the lake that first morning of filming had Andi wavered in her decision to give her baby up. She had met with the adoptive mother and her two kids at an arranged meeting at the agency office. The woman's husband was apparently in Los Angeles on business. Eventually Andi wanted her parents to meet the family she'd chosen. But that first time she had decided she wanted to be alone with her baby's new family, so she could watch them interact and imagine her baby growing up a part of them.

The meeting had gone perfectly, according to Andi. That had been a few weeks ago, and Andi had been busy with school since then, but tonight she wanted to get out, wanted to see Bailey, and meet some of the Baxter family. Keith realized, as they parked out front and he and Lisa walked around back to get the deep dish apple pies, that Andi had never met most of the Baxters. She hadn't gone to the Baxter Sunday dinner back when Chase and Keith were here filming *The Last Letter*, and though she'd been on the set, she barely remembered meeting Dayne's wife and a few of the married Baxter girls.

"So many cars," Andi carried the whipped cream. She looked pretty tonight. Her hair was still dark — she'd dyed it again, promising sometime next spring she'd find her way back to blonde once more. She no longer seemed self-conscious about her belly. She hadn't gained much weight, and from the back it was impossible to tell she was pregnant. She wore a long brown cardigan, brown leggings, and a white long-sleeved shirt.

"The Baxters make for a lot of people." Lisa laughed as she walked beside Andi. "I'm proud of you, honey. Coming out tonight. I think you'll be glad you did."

"Me too."

Keith walked a little behind the two women in his life, and he had to agree with Lisa. He was very proud of their daughter, of the way she'd embraced this baby and released it back to God all in the same season of life. But now that they were done shooting the movie, the reality was hitting him a little more every day. His daughter was about to have a baby boy, but it was a baby none of them would ever have the chance to know or love. Maybe tonight the three of them could talk to Luke and Reagan Baxter about the gift of adoption — the way Keith had imagined several months ago. That way they might all be more ready to give up the baby.

As they walked up the steps, Keith and Lisa both carrying the pies, Keith prayed again silently as he'd prayed many times. *Lord, give me peace about Andi's decision. I was ready to love that little guy ... I already had a place in my heart for him ... please, Lord ... just give me peace.*

He barely finished the prayer as Jenny Flanigan opened the door and welcomed them inside. She hugged Andi for a long time and kissed her cheek. "You look beautiful, sweetheart."

"Thank you." Andi's eyes glowed the way they had before her freshman year at Indiana University. "Where's Bailey?"

"Inside with the rest of the gang." Bailey's mother smiled at Lisa. "Mmmm. Apple pies! You can never have too much dessert."

"They're still warm," Lisa walked in. "Lead the way so we know where to put them."

Andi waited, and the three of them walked down the short hallway to the Flanigans' enormous kitchen. But as Bailey's mom kept walking, Andi stopped suddenly and put her hand to her head.

"Honey ... what is it?" Keith and Lisa passed their apple pies off to Jenny and Jim Flanigan and immediately gathered around Andi. Keith's tone must've sounded his concern, because a hush fell over the kitchen. People pouring coffee and setting up the desserts turned to look at them. Keith barely noticed any of it, his attention completely on Andi. Her face was pale and her eyes wide. She was staring straight across the kitchen at...

A gasp sounded from the other side of the room, as Reagan Baxter—Luke's wife—dropped the fork she was holding, her look as shocked as Andi's. "What are ..." her voice faded and she started coming closer. Luke joined her, looking from Andi to Reagan and back again.

"What's going on?" His laugh sounded nervous, like he wanted to make sure everyone was okay before trying to figure out like the rest of them what was going on.

But at that moment Luke's five-year-old son, Tommy, spotted Andi and yelled out loud, "Hey! I know you!" He smiled big and ran right up to Andi, who was still holding the whipped cream in her other hand, the one that wasn't pressed to her forehead. As Tommy reached her, he looked up, his eyes sweet and full of charm. "Can I tell my brother 'hi'?"

Andi touched the child's head, and Keith saw tears fill her eyes. "Yes, Tommy." She handed the whipped cream to her father, as her voice cracked. "You can say hi to him."

Keith's mind raced and he looked at Lisa, who shook her head as if to say she had no idea what was happening. If Tommy knew Andi, and if he knew the baby she was carrying was his little brother ... then ... Keith felt tears well up in his eyes too. It wasn't possible. This ... this was the adoptive family Andi had chosen all on her own? Looking through a photolisting book? Luke and Reagan Baxter?

No one moved. No one seemed even to be breathing. Attention from everyone in the room was fastened on the miracle playing out before them. Tommy didn't seem to notice. He hugged Andi and then put his hands on both sides of her belly. "Hi there, little brother. You can hurry up and be born, okay? Because me and Malin can't wait to see you."

Andi's tears streamed down her face and she looked across the room at Reagan. "Your last name ... is Baxter?"

"Yes." Reagan made her way closer and took Andi in her arms. Tommy was still standing beside her, still rubbing Andi's belly, still talking to his unborn baby brother.

"Okay? And guess what? We have a swing set and I can push you way high, and after that we can play baseball all day long even after dinner. Okay, little brother? After you learn to walk, okay?"

"This is the family?" Keith could barely speak the words. He looked at Andi. "Luke Baxter and his wife?"

"Yes." A sob slipped from Andi's lips and she laughed at the same time. "I had no idea ..."

Tommy took a step back. "I'm glad you came for Thanksgiving." He grinned at Andi again. "I was just thinking about my brother right before we got here." He patted her stomach again. "Hurry up, baby." Then he skipped off to be with his sister Malin.

The reality was just hitting them, and even still no one could believe what they were seeing. Luke joined his wife near Andi and hugged her. "All this time ... I've been praying for the birthmother of our baby ... and I've been praying for you, Keith's daughter. But I didn't know ..." his voice choked up and he hung his head, shielding his eyes with his hand for a moment. "I was praying for the same person. How is it possible?"

Other Baxters were arriving, and as they did they joined

the circle in the kitchen, and the miracle began to spread from one person to another. Luke and Reagan were adopting Andi's unborn baby boy. Most of them were meeting Andi for the first time, but they all knew Keith, and they certainly knew Luke's connection with Jeremiah Productions.

Keith watched his daughter, at the center of the most amazing God moment he'd ever been a part of. He watched her laugh and cry, and he saw how Luke and Reagan embraced her, and suddenly he felt the very presence of God in this place. Moments ago he had wondered how he would handle the loss of this baby, how he could possibly see his daughter give birth, only to watch her give the child away. But now ... God had answered his prayers in a way he never could've dreamed. There was nothing to fear, no reason to be sad for this grandchild he would never know. Everything was going to work out exactly like it was supposed to. They would know where the baby was, and that his life would be the most wonderful life ever. Because he would be in a place where any child would want to grow up.

Here, in the Baxter family.

IT TOOK HOURS FOR THE COMMOTION to die down, for Bailey and everyone else to fully grasp the possibility Andi had gone into a random Christian adoption agency and chosen, from a book of possible families, none other than Luke and Reagan Baxter. The Ellisons announced they planned to move to California early next year, and Andi was going with them. So while she was grateful to know the full identity of the adoptive family — and though she intended to keep somewhat in touch with Luke and Reagan — Andi confided in Bailey that she thought it best she'd be living in another state.

"It's too confusing otherwise," she said as she left that night. "But the way it is ... God worked out every detail." She thought for a minute, her eyes filled with wonder. "The day I decided for sure that I wanted to give this baby up, I felt convinced that God already knew that he was supposed to be with this family." She smiled. "Now I know why."

Bailey was still in awe over those details as the last Baxter family member left that night. Because of the craziness of what happened with Andi and Luke and Reagan, only then did Bailey remember what was yet ahead tonight.

Her talk with Cody.

After dessert, he and the boys had gone to the den where they were playing Wii Olympics. Bailey wandered toward the back of the house until she could hear her brothers' voices, laughing and playfully bragging about who was faster in the sprint event. She reached the doorway and leaned against it, watching them. Cody wasn't actually playing. He was watching from a beanbag in the corner of the room. Rather than his usual way of joining in and becoming one of the kids, he was quiet, a distant look in his eyes.

"Cody?" She stepped into the room, quiet enough that her brothers didn't notice her. "Wanna talk?"

He didn't smile.

Later on, when she would look back on this night, she would remember that detail. After waiting all afternoon and evening to talk to her, when the time finally came for them to be alone, he didn't show even the hint of a smile. He pulled himself up and walked toward her. Taking her hand, he led her from the room and out the nearest door — a second front door at this end of the house.

"You cold?" He stopped just outside and looked at her, ready to go in if she needed anything.

"Not yet." She wondered if he understood the double meaning in her answer. "What is it, Cody? Why do I feel like this isn't the talk I thought it would be?"

He eased her into his arms and held her close for a long time, the warmth of his body promising her everything was going to be okay. It had to be okay. What possible reason could he have for wanting a sad talk with her? She rested her head on his chest and listened to the steady thud of his heart. The faint smell of his cologne made her head swirl, and she lifted her chin just enough so he could hear her. "Don't let go, Cody. Please ... don't ever let go."

No answer came from him, but he tenderly stroked her lower back, in no hurry to release her. After a minute, he pulled away and led her down the long covered porch toward the main front door. Halfway there they sat in their favorite porch swing. Only then did Bailey begin to shiver. He offered to get a blanket, but she didn't want one. The cold she was feeling couldn't be helped by a blanket, but only by the knowledge that no matter how much time had passed, nothing between them had changed.

"Can I ask a question?" Her teeth rattled a little. She wanted to bring this up and get past it.

"Ask me anything." He didn't break eye contact, wouldn't look away from her. Like after so much time he couldn't get enough of her eyes.

She felt the same way, and she had to turn her eyes to the starry sky so she could remember what she wanted to say. "A month ago ... you texted me, but it wasn't for me." She met his eyes. "It was for a girl named Cheyenne." Her heart pounded. "Is that ... is she what this is all about? Why you've stayed away?"

"No." His answer came almost like a cry. "Absolutely not." He was embarrassed by what he'd done, she could see that. "She was going to marry a buddy of mine. He died in Iraq. My friend's mom had a big dinner, and she was there." He sounded like he was rambling, rushing to clear himself. "I'm sorry about the text ... I was probably thinking about you."

She nodded, but she didn't feel any warmer. His answer still left doubts in her mind, but she believed him. Cheyenne wasn't the problem. He still wasn't saying anything, so she took the lead, her mind racing. "If this is about Brandon, there's nothing be-tween us." She brought one leg up onto the swing so she could face him. "Nothing at all."

Cody turned a little so he could see her, too. "This isn't about Brandon." A sigh came out with his words, and Bailey noticed something else — a finality in his eyes. Finality and love and longing all mixed together. Whatever he was about to tell her, clearly his mind was made up. He reached for her hand.

"You've avoided me for the last two months. Every time I called or texted." She tried not to think about how wonderful his fingers felt between hers. "Did I do something to make you mad?" There were tears in her voice, and Bailey struggled to keep her eyes dry. "If I did, maybe you could tell me. Because this … this silence is more than I can — "

"Bailey." He didn't blink, didn't look away. "I'm moving to Indianapolis."

Moving where? Her mind spun, her stomach suddenly sick. She shivered harder and his words come at her in a series of jum-bled letters. It took a few seconds for them to reassemble in her mind so they made even the slightest sense. "What?" She with-drew her hand from his and folded her arms tight at her waist. "Why … why would you do that?"

"I accepted a coaching job at a new Christian high school there." He smiled, but it did nothing to take the edge off the sad-ness in his eyes. "I'll be the head coach."

Bailey wasn't sure what to say or do or how to handle the feel-ings storming her heart. Cody was leaving? Was that what he was telling her? She fought the urge to stop him from talking, forbid him to say another word. Of course he wasn't leaving. They had just found their way back together. He couldn't go. She wanted to run as fast as she could so he couldn't tell her he was serious. "You already have a coaching job. Here. In Bloomington."

"I know." He pursed his lips, as if he were trying to find the right way to make her understand. "Bailey, this can't work — you and me. Not now, anyway. We'll only hold each other back if I stay."

Anger joined the emotions raging inside her. She stood and walked a few fast steps away before whirling around, her eyes blazing. "How could you say that?" She lowered her voice. The last thing she wanted was for someone in her family to hear them. The chill had worked its way down her body and into her legs, and she shook, unable to believe a word of what he'd told her.

He stood and came to her. "Bailey ..."

"No." She took a step back and grabbed hold of the nearest porch pillar for support. "We've been through this, Cody. We have." She waved her hand toward the driveway. "I told you at the lake there's only you. No one else I think about, no one else I want to be with." Tears filled her eyes and she could do nothing to stop them from spilling onto her cheeks. "I bared my heart to you, and this ... this is how you handle it?"

"It's not ..." he held his breath for a few seconds and then let it out in a frustrated rush. Once more he made an attempt to reach for her, but he changed his mind and slipped his hands into the back pockets of his jeans. "It's the same thing, Bailey ... our lives are too different. God showed me that these past few weeks."

"It wasn't God!" She yelled, and once more she forced herself to quiet down. "God would never tell you to leave me, Cody. Not after all we've been through." She shook her head, not caring any longer that she was crying in front of him. "You come back from Iraq and tell me to ..." she tossed her hand in the air, "stay with Tim Reed because he's better for me." She felt her face twist in angry confusion. "That was a *terrible* idea, because the whole time all I thought about was you." She glared at him. "You, Cody ... do you hear me?"

He blinked hard, fighting tears of his own, his chin quivering. "I hear you." He looked from the porch ceiling to the midnight sky that hung over the field out front. Anywhere but into her eyes.

She waited, her chest heaving. The fight was leaving her; she could feel it. In its place a sadness consumed her, and nearly knocked her to her knees, a sorrow she'd never felt before. "Please, Cody," she sounded defeated, and without the porch pillar, she would've fallen to a heap and wept until morning. "For once ... why can't you understand how I feel?"

His chin was still trembling, but finally he looked at her, straight to the place in her heart that would always only belong to him. "Bailey," his voice was a broken whisper. "Can I hold you ... please?"

She wanted to tell him no. If he wanted to hold her he had to promise never to leave, he had to care about her the way she cared about him. But she hurt too much to do anything but take a step toward him. He closed the distance between them, taking her slowly into his embrace, wrapping his arms around her, and clinging to her like the last thing he ever wanted to do was let go. "I'm sorry." His voice was shaky, a mix of heartbreak and desire that reflected how she was feeling.

"Then don't go." She was still crying, sobbing quietly against his chest. "Coach here at C-C-Clear Creek and never leave."

He pressed his face against hers, and she sensed in him a desperation, a certainty that his heart had never agreed to any of this. "I don't want to go." He stepped back just enough to see her, his hands still linked around her waist. "I have to, Bailey. I'm looking out for you. For your future." He released a shaky sigh. "It's complicated."

"Only because you make it complicated." She was still crying, but she couldn't be angry with him. She searched his eyes, pleading with him. "Don't you see?"

"I see all this ..." he released his hold on her and motioned to her grand house, the sweeping drive and manicured grounds.

"You're a princess, Bailey." Tears pooled in his eyes. "You've done everything right." He shook his head, fighting the emotions that seemed to be strangling him. "Now you're in the public eye, and you don't need anything damaging your reputation." The hurt in his voice sounded almost angry. "That's what I would do, Bailey. Tarnish how the world sees you." He paused, composing himself. "I won't do that to you. That's not what you need."

"No!" she broke free from him again, her anger back with a vengeance. "You don't know what I need!"

He tried to take gentle hold of her arm, but she pulled away, and when he came still closer she pushed his chest. "Don't touch me." She felt herself losing control. "Not if you don't know me after all this time, Cody. Stay away."

"Bailey, please ..." he wouldn't back up, wouldn't give in. She flailed against him, trying to break free. But tenderly he caught her in his arms, and before she knew what was happening he had her face in his hands and he was kissing her — kissing her and holding her. And for the sweetest moment, even as she was still crying, there was only her and Cody and this kiss she'd wanted every moment since he'd walked through the front door.

"This is how I feel," she spoke the words between their desperately sad kisses, because even now — when she wanted to stay like this forever — she knew deep within her that he wouldn't stay. This wasn't a beginning, it was an end, and she wondered if she would die from the pain. "Cody," she pulled back, breathless from the intensity of their kisses and the desperate sadness of what was coming.

He looked at her, lost in her eyes once more. His lips were parted and he looked torn between kissing her again and telling what his eyes were already saying. "I can't stay."

"Listen ... " She grabbed hold of his shoulders, fistfuls of his sweater clenched in her fingers. She had to tell him, because if she didn't ... if she let him leave without saying how she felt ... she would regret this moment as long as she lived. She released her hold on him with one hand and wiped her tears, her eyes never leaving his. "I love you." Saying the words felt wonderful, and for the first time since they'd come out onto the porch Bailey felt truly happy. A happiness that couldn't be dimmed no matter how sad the moment. "That's how I feel. I love you." She sniffed, and she smiled despite the fresh tears that filled her eyes. "I've loved you for so long."

Surprise flashed in his eyes and he shook his head, slowly, subtly at first and then with more intensity. "No, Bailey. You can't … there's someone else for you. I'm … I'm all wrong. A girl like you should have a — "

She took hold of his face and this time she kissed him, in a way that rendered him incapable of doing anything but kissing her in return. His arms came up along her back and he kissed her until it was impossible to tell where desire ended and heartbreak began. She didn't want to hear him tell her how wrong he was or that she deserved someone else, and so she kept kissing him, loving the way it felt to be in his arms and to know that here, now he was hers. Completely hers.

But after a minute or so he broke free, his breathing fast and jagged. "We can't … I have to go." He looked almost angry with her, as if her kisses had only served to confuse him. "I'm not coming back, Bailey. I can't." He raked his fingers through his hair as if he was trying to find the strength to continue. "I waited … so I could tell you goodbye."

He was leaving, and she couldn't stop him. She realized that, and as she did she made a decision that he would not walk away from this time together with her yelling at him or sobbing. "Go, then." She lifted her chin, her vision blurred by unshed tears. "But this isn't goodbye." She shook her head, holding her ground, giving him the distance he seemed to need right now. Her eyes shone, and she could see all the way to his soul. "You can't make me stop loving you, Cody Coleman. You can't."

For a few seconds he looked like he might pull her back into his arms and forget he'd ever said a word about moving away. But instead she watched him fight himself, fight the love he felt in his heart — even if he wouldn't admit his feelings to her. The muscles in his jaw flexed, and he gave a single shake of his head. "When ... when I get settled, I'll call you."

"No." She wouldn't look away, wouldn't let him make the rules.

"Bailey." His eyes begged her to make this easier. For the first time there were tears on his face too.

"I won't wait that long. I'll call you and I'll text you and when I can't go another day, I'll find you." She felt tears hit her cheeks once more, but she maintained her smile. "You're wrong about us ... but if you need to leave, then leave." She wiped her face with her fingertips, still lost in his eyes. "But I won't ever let you go."

There was nothing left to say. He swallowed and rubbed the palm of his hand roughly beneath his eyes. Then he hugged her once more, as long as either of them could stand it. Before he pulled away, he kissed the top of her head and quickly walked to his car without looking back. Bailey stayed there, leaning on the porch pillar, watching him go. He was wrong about God, wrong to think the Lord would want him to leave now — when everything was almost perfect. God didn't want them apart. God had brought them together. He was the One who had convinced her long ago that no one would ever love her the way Cody did. She could see the truth in his eyes years ago, same as she could see it tonight.

She watched his car move down the driveway, watched as he turned left and drove out of sight. Her tears seemed to come from an ocean somewhere inside her heart, and she could do nothing to stop them. He could move to Indianapolis, but this wasn't the end. She wouldn't let it be the end. She loved him, and she would keep her word — calling him and texting him, finding him when she couldn't draw another breath without looking into his eyes. If he needed time, she would give him that. But one day she would make him see God wanted them together, and no one could ever be better for her than him. She would pray for him and believe with every passing day that this wasn't the end, until one day he believed it too.

Even if it took a lifetime to convince him.

Twenty-Seven

KEITH WAS GRATEFUL HE'D CHOSEN TO hold the premiere for *The Last Letter* there in Bloomington. Andi's baby was due any time, and the last place he wanted to be the day after Christmas was two thousand miles away from home in LA. Instead, the premiere was taking place in half an hour at Kerasotes ShowPlace East 11 — the nicest theater in town, not far from the university.

Most of the cast from *Unlocked* had flown in today to be here. That way they could make the Indiana premiere and also be on hand for reshoots and any last-minute work on the film. Keith didn't expect a lot of photographers and paparazzi, like with the Los Angeles Film Festival showing of *The Last Letter*. This would be more low key, which was fine with Keith. People in towns like Bloomington were the ones Keith figured would be most touched by the movie.

Andi had chosen to stay home, and Keith and Lisa understood. If one photographer were to take her picture walking into the premiere alone and pregnant, and if the paparazzi were to do even a little research, the story would be all over the tabloids. Keith wasn't afraid of what people would say about his daughter. She'd made a mistake, and now she was handling the consequences as well as she could. It was Andi he was worried about. She didn't want to be the center of a media attack on Keith or Jeremiah Productions — not now or ever.

Besides, Andi was tired and she'd seen the film a number of times. She'd kissed him and Lisa goodbye and assured them she was fine. She was planning to read the rest of *Unlocked*, and turn in early. Keith and Lisa were in the lobby of the theater, making sure tables were set up with commemorative thank-you cards for everyone who attended, and seeing to it that bags of popcorn were lined up, ready for their guests. Keith had given out a hundred tickets, and the rest had been offered to the public. The show had sold out a month ago, and now Keith could hardly wait for the minutes to pass.

"We should go outside." Lisa checked her watch, and then adjusted Keith's suit coat. "You look very handsome, by the way."

"I look okay?" His heart raced, and he wondered what the scene was like at theaters across the country.

"Perfect." She stood on her tiptoes and kissed him. "I'm so proud of you, Keith, of all you've accomplished. Your dreams about a mission field in moviemaking ... they're all coming true."

"Not yet." He gave her a nervous smile. Moviegoers needed to show up this first weekend, or the movie could disappear in financial disaster. But there was no way to know for several days, so Keith forced himself to focus on the moment. "What time is it?"

"We have twenty-five minutes." She took his hand and they walked toward the front doors. The theater had set up a red carpet for their guests, and Keith and Lisa wanted to be outside to greet everyone as they came in. As they stepped outside, Lisa gasped softly. "Look at that!"

A line of people stretched down the chilly sidewalk and around the building, all of them craning their necks, looking to see who was arriving, and hoping they'd be let inside soon. In the parking lot a line of SUVs had pulled up, and two theater attendants were clearly keeping them from stepping outside until Keith and Lisa were there. One of the attendants motioned to Keith to hurry. "Let's do this!"

Keith's heart soared. He hurried to the edge of the red carpet, waving a couple times to the line of people. Was this really happening? Had this many people really turned out to see *The Last*

Letter? Lisa grinned at him as they took their places. The first carload held the Flanigan family. A valet attendant took the car from Jim Flanigan, and the group moved onto the carpet — all of them clearly excited about the experience. They waited for a moment as Keith greeted them and thanked them for coming.

"We wouldn't miss it," Jenny hugged Keith, then Lisa. "The world needs more films like this."

Bailey wore a dress that turned heads; long navy silk draped the length of her body, and the hem of a white cashmere coat swished a few inches above the ground. Her hair hung in dark curls, and her eyes glowed with a beauty that could only come from within. She was poised and at peace, comfortable in this world — because of her deep and abiding faith, no doubt. Keith hugged her, and Lisa whispered, "Before you know it, we'll be at the premiere of your movie!"

Only then did Keith notice half a dozen photographers gathered on either side of the carpet. They snapped hundreds of photos of Bailey and her family, Keith and Lisa, and then a buzz came over the staging area as Brandon Paul stepped out of the next car.

Keith watched him, how he graciously waved to the people in line and then to the photographers before heading straight to Bailey Flanigan. No question the guy was infatuated with her, and Keith was grateful for Bailey's resistance. As much as Brandon had changed for the better since he'd arrived on set to film *Unlocked*, Keith still would've hated to see him date Bailey Flanigan. Between the tabloid frenzy the two of them would create, and Brandon's extensive worldliness, a relationship with him would sorely threaten her innocence. It was something Keith worried about at first — after he saw the intensity of Brandon's pursuit.

But he shouldn't have doubted Bailey. She was strong in her faith, and she had the support of a great family. Instead of caving in to Brandon, she'd held her ground and he'd taken to doing a Bible study. Now, watching Brandon hug Bailey and walk alongside her, he could see again the young actor was smitten. But he could see something else too: a change in Brandon's eyes. They needed to keep praying for him, that much Keith was sure about.

With the cameraman snapping a constant stream of photos, the Flanigans and Brandon headed inside the theater, and a stream of Baxters began making their way down the carpet. Ashley and Landon and their oldest son, Cole; Ryan and Kari and their oldest, Jessie. Keith was glad they'd kept the little ones at home. The movie was appropriate for any age, but it wouldn't keep the attention of a preschooler. Next came Luke and Reagan, Erin and Sam, and Peter and Brooke with a few older kids between them.

Finally when Keith was sure his guests had been seated, they opened the carpet to the waiting public. In ten minutes the theater was packed, and attendants were carefully guarding Brandon and Dayne and Bailey. Already Keith had made an announcement that this was a special premiere for the producers' family and friends. "Please don't use this time to ask for autographs. Tonight let's all just be an audience together."

The people in the seats might've been practically frantic over the idea of watching a movie with Brandon Paul — let alone Dayne Matthews — but they respected Keith's wishes, and there was no mad rush for photos or autographs. Once the theater was seated, Keith thanked everyone for coming, and as the lights dimmed he took his seat between Lisa and Dayne. After a few seconds the movie began. Keith had watched it come to life from the very beginning — through the script phase and while they hired the right actors for every part. He'd been in the editing room as he and Chase Ryan brought the picture to life, and he'd traveled the country through six film festivals while it won a series of awards.

In all, Keith couldn't count how many times he'd seen the film, but none of them had made him feel the way he did right now — seated in a movie theater on the opening night of his first major motion picture. Somewhere in San Jose, Chase was doing the same thing and he wished just this once they could've been together again. Because this was their dream come true.

But it was Dayne's dream, also, and Keith believed with all his heart God had improved the strength of Jeremiah Productions when he brought Dayne aboard. Still, as the movie started, he was filled with nostalgia for all they'd been through, all that had led them to this place, this night. Throughout the film, Keith did what he'd learned to do at previews and festival showings of the movie. He didn't listen to the dialogue on screen so much as he listened to the people around him. His heart swelled with hope when the audience laughed at all the right parts, and when they quietly sniffed and reached for tissues during the many poignant scenes throughout.

The message of the film was clear by the final credits. A college kid thinks life is meant to be lived fast and frenzied, with a high budget and high-end tastes. Until he reads the last letter written to him by his dying father. Only then does he understand that the real meaning of life is faith and family — things money can't buy.

Timing for the film couldn't have been better — debuting the movie the day after Christmas when buyer's remorse was hitting many Americans square in the face. All the shopping and wrapping and gift-giving typically fell a little flat on December 26, when people stepped back and tried to assess what they'd done, and what was accomplished by the money spent. *The Last Letter* held an answer for those people, if they were paying attention. And by the sounds of the people around him, they were.

When the movie was over, the audience rose for a standing ovation, many of them still drying their eyes. Then, just as quickly, they sat back down and began filling out their response cards — which they'd received at the door. Keith's heart pounded inside him. All over America, the first showing of their movie was wrapping up. What reactions must be coming from people even at this minute, and how would the film be received? Most of all, had *The Last Letter* filled the seats? Lisa hugged him and whispered near his ear. "Stop worrying." Her face beamed with joy. "This is your moment. Live in it!"

She was right, and he busied himself around the room, thanking people for coming and accepting one round of praise after another. Strangers came up to him, and in broken words they told him they'd been changed, that they would never look at life the same way. Near the top of the theater, a group of people had formed a circle and they were praying — someone in the middle had her head bowed and she was weeping. A few spots down from where he was standing, a husband and wife held hands lost in an intense conversation intended for just the two of them. Was this what was happening across the nation? Scenes of redemption and healing filling theaters across America? *Thank You, Jesus … I feel You here … this is Your movie, Your moment.* Keith had not expected this, not for a minute. He thought he'd have to wait until the reviews hit — or at least until hours later when they were reading the response cards — before knowing what people thought of the movie, but he was wrong.

The reaction was playing out before his eyes.

BAILEY LOVED EVERYTHING ABOUT THE MOVIE. Her part was small, but she was grateful to be a part of it all the same. She noticed the few times when Andi was in the background as an extra, and she wished things were different, that she hadn't succumbed to Taz's charm and that she could still have her innocence — the way she'd had it in the film. But God had His hand on Andi, and He would make beauty from the ashes of her life — same as He did for all of them.

Including her.

She smiled at Brandon as he winked at her from across the theater. He was talking to his fans, happy to oblige them with autographs now that the movie was over. But it was clear to her and probably everyone in the theater that he only had eyes for her. When they'd first sat down, Brandon had unabashedly taken the seat beside her. "Let 'em talk," he had whispered.

She had laughed, but only because she wasn't worried. She'd kept her distance during the filming, and now the paparazzi had moved on to other targets. No one would think anything of them sitting next to each other here. Before the movie had started, he gave her a lost-in-love look. "You take my breath away, Bailey," his voice was barely audible, but his intent was unmistakable. "See?" He grinned at her. "I'm still here."

"And you still make me laugh." She patted his knee, and her expression softened. "Seriously, Brandon. I missed you. I'm glad you're here."

She meant what she'd said. Brandon was fun and good looking and he brought enough energy into any moment to make her dizzy. But on this night — like every night since Thanksgiving — the ashes in her life came from a loss too great, too personal to talk about with anyone except her parents. The loss of Cody. In the end, she hadn't called him or reached out to him the way she'd planned to. He'd asked for time, and she was giving it to him. But with every passing day she only missed him more. She'd come to believe something was terribly wrong with him, otherwise what possible reason was there for him to move to Indianapolis.

Was it that Cheyenne girl? Bailey didn't think so, and lately she wondered if maybe something were wrong with Cody's mom. He hadn't talked about his mother in their brief contact since that night months ago when he'd left after her mysterious message, and whenever Bailey had brought her up or asked how she was doing, he gave only a brief answer and quickly changed the subject. Even in their talk Thanksgiving night, he hadn't mentioned her.

As the message in the movie had played out, Bailey caught herself wiping away tears, because Christmas was over and she and Cody were apart. If she didn't figure out a way to reach him, maybe they'd never find their way back together again. By the time the film ended, and Bailey and her family had bid goodbye to the producers and Brandon, Bailey had come up with a private plan, a way that might at least shed some light on what had gone wrong with Cody. After the New Year she would go by his mother's house and find out for herself how the woman was doing. Maybe then she could start to find her way back to him, start to find what she was looking for. The same thing Andi wanted ... what all God's people wanted when life didn't go the way it was supposed to go.

Beauty from ashes.

Twenty-Eight

SINCE THE PREMIERE, BRANDON HAD KNOWN SOMETHING was changing inside him. And now, sitting on the back deck of Katy and Dayne's house in the late afternoon of New Year's Eve, Brandon couldn't shake the memory of things he'd said and done last summer. The wild partying and crazy stuff with girls ... the way he'd declared to anyone who would listen that he wasn't a Christian, and he wouldn't become one any time soon.

Katy and Dayne were going to the Baxter's soon, and they'd offered to take him. But Brandon didn't want to go. He could've called for a car or rented one, but he didn't want that either. He wanted peace — perfect peace. Something he hadn't felt since he was fourteen years old. Images from his recent past circled him, laughing at him as the sun set over the lake. So what if he was the most famous movie star in the world? His parents might've handled their fears wrongly, and they might've been the worst possible examples of what Christians should act like ... but the verse his mother had told him three years ago was dead on.

What good was it for a man to gain the whole world and yet forfeit his soul?

He could die in a plane crash on the way home from Bloomington in two days and then what? The fame and money, his looks and charm ... all of it would amount to nothing. And where would he be? A shudder passed over him. People had a way of ruining God for those who really needed Him. But that wasn't God's fault. Maybe the truth was like Bailey had told him that day at the beach.

Maybe the Lord had been calling him all along.

"Brandon?" Dayne stuck his head out and gave him a funny look. "You okay? You've been out here a long time."

"Yeah," he looked over his shoulder, pulling his windbreaker a little more tightly around his chest. "You leaving?"

"Soon." Dayne stepped outside and shrugged. "You sure you don't want to go?"

"No ... I'm just thinking. Good thing to do on the last day of the year."

Dayne nodded, and a smile filled his eyes. "I like that." He paused. "You wanna talk about anything? The Bible verses I showed you earlier?"

"That's okay." He gave himself a light tap on the place just above his heart. "It's in here, man. Can't get away from it if I wanted to."

"Good." A smile filled his face. "That's what Katy and I've been praying for."

An idea hit Brandon, something he hadn't thought about before. "Hey." Brandon stood, leaning against the porch railing, facing Dayne. "Could you do me a favor?"

Dayne hesitated near the sliding door. "Name it."

"Could you take me to Bailey's house?"

A ripple of laughter came from Dayne as he opened the door. "Be ready in five minutes." He hesitated a moment longer. "And make sure she's expecting you. It's New Year's Eve, after all. We probably won't be by to pick you up again until after one in the morning."

"True." Brandon ran his tongue along his lower lip, suddenly nervous at the thought of surprising her. He grabbed his cell phone from his pocket and tapped in her contact information. The phone was ringing seconds later, and Brandon paced the back deck, squinting at the lake through the barren trees, willing her to answer.

"Hello?" She sounded surprised.

Give me the words, God ... I have to see her. Right now ... before this feeling goes away. "Hey, Bailey ... I'm not doing anything tonight, and I wondered if ... if I could come over."

"Now?" She laughed on the other end, but it sounded friendly. "For how long?"

Even the sound of her voice made him feel like a high school kid. "Like till one in the morning."

"Hmmm. We're having an open house ... there'll be people here." She wasn't going to tell him no, he could hear that in her voice and already he could hardly wait to see her. "But you can come, sure. Maybe wear your disguise so you don't cause a stampede or anything."

"If you wear that dress you wore for the premiere ... you're the only one who could cause a stampede. Let's just say that for the record."

They both laughed, but then her tone changed. "No, really. You can come. Of course."

"Thanks." He allowed the seriousness of his afternoon to seep into his voice. "I've been thinking a lot today, Bailey. I really need to talk to you." He realized how that sounded, and he quickly corrected himself. "Not about us ... about me."

For a while she said nothing, and he could almost picture her smiling. "This could be interesting. Maybe God's getting your attention."

"Yeah." He headed for the back door of Dayne and Katy's house. "Maybe that."

Half an hour later, after he'd been dropped off at Bailey's house, and after he'd said hello to her family — all of them getting ready for the party — he asked Bailey if she'd sit with him in the family's backyard.

"It's freezing out there," she gave him an uncertain look. "You sure? Outside?"

Her dad must've overheard him, because he was walking by the family room just then and he pointed out back. "I started a fire in the pit ... figured it's a clear night even if it's cold. Some people might want to sit outside."

Brandon swapped a look with Bailey, his more pleading. "Could we?"

A laugh came over her, as if she couldn't quite tell him no — at least not on this. "I'll get my coat." She started to run off, then stopped and turned back. "And one for you. California boy with the lightweight jacket."

While she was gone, her dad told him about the stack of wood not far from the fire. "Build it up. But not too big, unless you're going to stay out there."

Brandon agreed, and Bailey returned wearing a brown coat with a fur-lined hood. She handed him a black North Face jacket. "This'll keep you warm."

He wanted to say he'd prefer if she kept him warm, but he let the thought go as soon as it hit him. She made him dizzy, no question. He'd never met a girl like her, and he wasn't giving up. The young coach wasn't pursuing her — at least not as far as Brandon could tell — so he'd find a way to make her fall for him someday. He'd have to work harder, but he was ready for the challenge. Already this week she'd agreed to do another Jeremiah Productions picture with him. This time she'd play his girlfriend, so there was hope.

But today wasn't about any of that. He was here because God wouldn't leave him alone, and right now more than fame or money or movies ... even more than Bailey Flanigan, he wanted answers. Answers and certainty that he wouldn't go to hell if he didn't make it home tonight. That he wouldn't start the New Year headed down the same path he'd been headed before filming *Unlocked.*

He and Bailey walked across her back patio, past her covered built-in pool and hot tub, along a path out to the open field behind her house. "Your house should be on that *MTV Cribs* show." He grinned at her, not sure how to get serious about what was on his heart.

"I guess the producers asked my dad once." Bailey made a face. "He said no, because ..." she shrugged, "that's not why we have the house. It's nice and big and all, but my parents taught us to think of it as ... I guess sort of like a church. We use it for Young Life and church youth groups, team parties. Whoever needs it, you know?"

"Yeah." Brandon didn't know at all. He owned a house like this with a staff of help, but the last time he had someone over who didn't work there ... his stomach turned at the memory and he looked down, unable to meet Bailey's eyes. *See, this is how I don't want to feel ... I don't want to be that guy anymore, God ... give me the words. Help me explain myself.*

They reached a five-foot section of fallen tree trunk the Flanigans had placed strategically near the fire pit. There were four other sections like it making a circle, and beyond that there were chairs — enough seating for twenty people easily. "Best fire pit I've ever seen." He lifted his eyes to hers, but only briefly. The memory of the girl at his house still strangling him. "You're right about the cold. Especially out here in the open." Before he sat down, he pulled two large logs from the woodpile and placed them at different angles over the small fire. "There." He dusted the wood chips off his hands. "That'll help."

They sat down on the fallen tree section opposite the direction the smoke was blowing. Brandon intentionally left considerable space between them. He didn't want to be distracted by her nearness. Plus, he wanted to see her face, so he could really understand what he was feeling and her opinion about it. He stared at the fire, organizing his thoughts, looking for a starting point. He breathed in deeply and took in the moment, the starlit sky overhead and the smell of campfire, the love and warmth that filled the Flanigan home. Like at the lake on the last day of filming, the words came before he was sure what to say. "I spent half the day sitting on Dayne and Katy's back deck ... thinking about my life."

Bailey pulled up one knee and hugged it to her chest, her eyes sparkling from the light of the fire. "New Year's Eve does that to me too."

He looked at her briefly, but then he turned to the fire again, still sorting. "I've done a lot of stupid things. An awful lot."

She could've pointed out that she wasn't surprised, given his reputation, or that he didn't need to list his indiscretions because she'd watched them play out on the tabloid covers. But instead she reached out and put her hand on his shoulder. Not for long — only a few seconds — but long enough so he knew she cared. This was why he'd come, right? Because he'd known without question she wouldn't judge or criticize or mock him.

The feel of her hand on his shoulder stayed with him, encouraging him to continue. "I did something I never should've done." He leaned over his knees and wrung his hands together. "I was at a club before we filmed, and some girl ... she knew I was starring in *Unlocked*. She was ... surprised I'd star in a Christian film." He shook his head, disgusted with himself. "I told her not to look for me to become a Christian anytime soon." He angled his head so he could see her. "Because you know, when I was a kid I never really gave my life to Christ. And that night I sort of promised I never would." He sighed, wrestling his emotions. "Those words haunted me all night. But I guess, after a while I forgot about it."

He wasn't sure he could tell her everything, all the awful details of his recent life. The girl at his house, the drugs ... The memories of who he'd allowed himself to become made him sick. Darkness was closing in around them, and Brandon was glad for the fire. The heat cut the chill running through him. "Anyway, those words came back to me today." He sat up straighter and shifted so he could see her. "You told me God brought me here ... because He was calling me back." He nodded, his head moving only the slightest bit. "I didn't think so then, but now ... I think you're right."

"Not only that," her voice was faint and it mixed with the slight breeze swirling around the pit and the sound of the crackling fire. "I think that's why I got the part. Because God wanted you around people who would help you hear His voice a little better." She gave him a partial smile. "You know?"

He smiled, touched by her statement. "You won the part because you deserved it. Plain and simple."

"Maybe." She shrugged one shoulder. "I guess I just see the big picture. I mean, acting's fine, but what's the point, Brandon? You and I in a movie together ... The Bible says all good things are a gift from God." Her simple smile made her look like a much younger girl. "So why would God give me this part ... except to have an influence on you?"

The possibility filled his mind with wonder, because maybe she was right. A book comes along that sweeps the country, and he falls in love with the story same as everyone else. He has a chance to star in the film, and he jumps at it — not realizing the story's bound to be considered a Christian picture. In the end he'd told Bailey the truth — the only reason he'd taken the part was because of her, because of something special about her. Something he couldn't define at first.

Maybe the special part of Bailey was God in her life — the Lord at work in her heart and soul.

"I guess what I'm saying is, I want to change." He felt his expression change, felt himself grow more serious. "I'm sick of the old me." He clenched his teeth, filled with a sudden rush of anger and hurt. "Sick of blaming God for something my dad said ten years ago."

Bailey slid closer to him and put her hand on his shoulder again. "You can change if you want to. You can decide that right here ... tonight."

"That's what I wondered. I mean, I was raised in a Christian home, but in the end ... in the end I walked away not believing any of it." He swallowed, nervous and unsure. "I mean, shouldn't I take a class or read a book or something? I can't just decide, right?"

Her smile did more to warm him than the blazing fire a few feet away. "Of course you can. A life of faith starts with a single decision."

"But then what?" He rubbed the back of his neck, unsure. "I mean, so I decide ... how does that change anything?"

"It's a beginning. You've been reading the Bible, right?"

"Yeah, with Katy and Dayne. On my own too—since I've been back home."

"So that's God's letter to us, God's way of helping us live a life of faith." Bailey explained that making a change involved admitting past mistakes and acknowledging the need for a Savior in Jesus Christ. "And getting baptized. Jesus talks about that too."

"We read that." He had loved that part of his Bible study. "Dying to the old self and coming up out of the water brand new ... ready to live for God instead."

"Exactly." Bailey gave his shoulder a tender squeeze and then folded her arms in front of her. "You understand more than you think. But it's a big decision, Brandon."

"It is."

"Because everyone's watching you." She slid a little closer to the fire and warmed her hands together. "Make a choice like this, and you almost have to be willing to tell the whole world."

He nodded slowly. The idea seemed terrifying, because what

if he made a decision here and couldn't follow through? But it seemed comforting too. Like he would be at peace finally. "That's the other thing you said at the lake ... the purpose of celebrity."

"Right." Her look was tender and kind, more understanding than he could've hoped for. "Your fame ... that's why you have to be sure."

"So ... I turn my life around and then the whole world waits for me to fall?" This was part of the problem, right? The reason he hadn't wanted anyone to think he was a Christian before.

"Maybe you step out of the spotlight for a while." The light from the fire shone on Bailey's face. "Sure ... hang out in bars and clubs and you're bound to be in the tabloids. But stay home on a Friday night and read your Bible, or go to church Sunday morning. Then see who wants to write about you."

Brandon sat up straighter. She had a point. "I could try that."

A slow breath slipped between Bailey's lips and she looked at the flames for a minute. "I guess the bottom line is what's in your heart." Her eyes met his again. "How badly you want to change."

The urgency from earlier returned in a rush. He didn't care what the world thought or what he might have to give up. He didn't want to go to sleep tonight without knowing he was safe. That he and God were right — for the first time since he'd left home. "I want it." He stared at her, unblinking. "I want it more than my next breath."

"Okay," she breathed in sharp through her nose. "So you want to make a decision about living for Jesus? Is that what you're saying?"

"Yes." The smoke was still blowing the opposite direction, and the fresh wood was fully burning, warming the air between them. "I want that right now."

Bailey didn't hesitate. She reached out and took hold of his hands. "I'll lead, okay? And if you agree with what I'm praying, then you pray it after me."

Already Brandon felt the beginning of a release, like every wrong thing he'd done and every regrettable statement he'd uttered were gathering in one dark corner of his heart. He nodded. "Go ahead."

Bailey's prayer was as simple as it was beautiful. She prayed the way she talked, like holding a conversation with God was as natural as sitting by a bonfire on a cold, clear winter's New Year's eve night. She acknowledged she was a sinner, and she could never be good enough to deserve a place in heaven. Brandon reiterated that part of the prayer with emphasis. No question he was a sinner. That's why he hadn't been sleeping at night.

She went on to state that she believed Jesus was God's Son, and that He had died for her. Brandon agreed fully, and he prayed as much. "Finally, Lord, I'd like to ask Jesus to be my Lord and Savior. Please, come into my heart so that I might be dead to myself and alive to you. I want to live for you, God. Only you."

Something happened as Brandon opened his mouth to repeat that part of the prayer. Tears filled his eyes and caught in his voice. Because this was what he'd needed, what he'd wanted. It was the reason he was here, and Bailey was right. It was the reason he'd been drawn to take the role in *Unlocked*. God had planned this moment for him the whole time. And as he asked Jesus to be His Savior, as he asked Him to come into his heart and forgive him for his sins, he felt something he couldn't remember ever feeling before.

Perfect light. The Light of the World was shining across the darkness in his heart, so that there were no hidden parts, nothing to be ashamed of. He was forgiven and whole, once and for always. When the prayer ended, Brandon released Bailey's hands. He ran the back of his hands across his cheeks and sniffed. "I feel like ... like my whole life has led up to this."

"It has." She laughed, and he saw that there were tears on her cheeks too. "You did it! You heard His voice and you ran to

Him." Another ripple of laughter danced on the night air. "Isn't that great?"

Brandon felt new and whole and younger than he had in years. But he wanted something more. "You told me about baptism, about how it's part of giving your life to God."

"It is." She nodded. "You read about it with Katy and Dayne, right?"

"Right." An intense compulsion was building in him, as strong as the one to give his life to the Lord. Only this time he didn't need to talk about what he was feeling. "I want that, Bailey. Right now." He stood and stared across the open field at the covered pool and adjacent covered hot tub. His eyes found hers again. "Your party doesn't start for an hour. So why not now? That's what they did in Acts. They made a decision to follow Jesus, and they got baptized."

Bailey looked like she wanted to argue, but instead she stood and slipped her hands in the back pockets of her jeans. "I don't know ... I mean, the water in the pool is freezing."

"What about the hot tub?"

"Maybe a little warmer. We used it a few days ago, but ..."

"I don't mind cold." He grabbed a stick from the ground and poked at the fire, making sure no big wooden pieces were sticking out of the pit. Then he dropped the stick and took her hand. "Come on! Let's go get your dad. He'll do it."

Brandon was pretty sure he'd always remember the look on Bailey's father's face as they opened the patio slider and Bailey announced that Brandon wanted to get baptized. But as surprised as he might've been, he paused for only a few seconds. Then he was on his feet, rolling up his sleeves.

Ten minutes later, with Bailey and her brothers and mother gathered around, Jim Flanigan and Brandon climbed into the hot tub. It was cold, but Brandon barely noticed. All that mattered was the commitment he was making to his Savior. Jesus had died for him to have this second chance. Now he could climb in ice water if it meant living a life for God. Jim quoted a few Bible verses about baptism and making a public confession of faith.

Then he turned to Brandon and grinned. "I wasn't expecting this tonight." He put his hand on Brandon's shoulder. "But I can't think of any better way to bring in the New Year."

With that he asked Brandon a series of questions. Whether Brandon understood his need for a Savior and if he truly wanted to accept Jesus' gift of salvation. Brandon felt his heart practically bursting inside him. He wanted to pump his fist in the air with each positive answer. But instead he stayed focused, claiming each part of the process as his own.

Finally Jim came alongside him and put one hand on the back of Brandon's head. "Brandon Paul, because of your public declaration of faith in Christ, I baptize you in the name of the Father, the Son, and the Holy Spirit ... buried with Him in baptism," Jim eased Brandon back into the water, until he was covered, and then eased him up out of it. "And raised with Him to new life." He hugged Brandon hard and patted his back. "Congratulations."

This time nothing could stop Brandon. He thrust his fist in the air and grinned at the starry night sky. There were no words necessary, because his soul was shouting for joy and the feeling was beyond anything he had ever felt in all his life. Better than his first big break in Hollywood and better than fame, better than being wanted at every party and for every big role. And suddenly the ache in his heart was gone and he realized something in a reckless abandon sort of a way.

He was free!

His past wrongs and bad choices, his pride and errant ways couldn't touch him now. He hugged Bailey's dad again and then hurried out of the hot tub and hugged her. She had tears in her eyes, and she made a few soft sounds that were more laugh than cry. "What a night!"

He pulled back and searched her face, the light in her eyes. "Best night of my life." Then again he looked up, and in that moment he could practically feel the arms of God around him, hugging him, holding him close. He would live the rest of his days for this love, this certainty, and all because the Lord had brought him to this picture, to this family. He turned to Bailey again. Because He'd brought him to this very special girl.

"I'm not sure," his teeth clattered together a little, "I've ever felt this good." It was true. He wasn't sure he could force the smile from his face.

"We'll remember this New Year's Eve forever," Bailey's dad stepped out of the hot tub, water dripping from his shorts. "Best decision you'll ever make, Brandon."

Her dad patted him on the arm, and beside him Bailey laughed. "As happy as you two look, you're both about to freeze to death." She ran off across the patio. "I'll get the towels."

Brandon watched her go. He had hoped to find love with Bailey Flanigan, and maybe there was time for that somewhere in the future. But that sort of love didn't matter as much now. He had found something so much more. He had found faith and forgiveness and redemption — forever and always, and into eternity. He had been on the brink of death, toes over the edge of a chasm of destruction, without peace, without hope, without meaning. But here ... here he had found much more than love.

He had found life.

Twenty-Nine

FRESH SNOW FELL ACROSS BLOOMINGTON all afternoon on New Year's Day, so Bailey had to wait until after ten o'clock the next morning before roads were clear enough to carry out her mission. That was okay. Bailey didn't mind waiting. The plans she had for this day were all she could think about over the weekend. Even with Brandon's amazing decision.

She had waited long enough to finally figure out what was happening with Cody Coleman. His actions made no sense at all. He was moving to Indianapolis to finish school? To take a coaching position an hour away from the one he already had? Most of all, there were the words he'd left her with Thanksgiving night: He wanted to protect her? He needed to move on?

Time hadn't made his actions or words any clearer, so now she would do what she should've done back then. She'd drive to his mother's house and find out for herself why Cody had — once again — shut her out of his life. She would knock on the door and then ask to come in. And she and Cody's mother would sit face-to-face and talk about what happened. Surely his mother would know why he was leaving, what had caused the change in his heart.

Bailey spent the morning catching up on her reading for advanced literature. She kept the radio on in the background, and when they announced that roads were clear, she quickly got dressed for the day. Now she pulled a dark wool coat over her pale blue turtleneck and grabbed her car keys. She found her mom in the kitchen opening mail. A smile softened her face as Bailey walked up. "You look pretty."

"Thanks." She took a breath and felt her resolve double. "Today's the day."

Her mom didn't have to ask. Bailey had shared last week that today she would probably head over to Cody's mother's house. "Will you call first?"

Bailey had wondered about that. This morning she'd even prayed about it. But she felt a peace about going over unannounced. She didn't want a planned meeting, a prepared response from Mrs. Coleman. She wanted the truth, as honest and uncensored as possible. She smiled at her mom. "Not this time." She shrugged. "Who knows, she might not even be home."

"A snowy Sunday morning? Unless she's at church with Cody, she's home." Her mom stood and kissed her on the forehead. "Maybe after today you'll have the answers you're looking for."

"Maybe." Bailey smiled, but her heart felt heavy. So much time without a word from Cody had only served to make her miss him more. Even when she wanted to be angry at him for leaving.

In the next room, the boys were playing Wii Olympics again, and the cheery sound of their laughter filled the house. Ricky spotted her, and he bounded across the tile floor. "Hey," he wrapped her in a bear hug. "Wanna build a snowman?"

"I'd love to." She messed her fingers through his blond hair. "But not now. I have a meeting to get to."

"Oh." His face fell. He nodded toward his brothers. "Soon as BJ wins the Olympics we're all going out. We're making a snow fort and the tallest snowman ever. A Flanigan family record."

"Hmmm." Bailey could picture her brothers rolling the base of the snowman and struggling to get the midsection up onto it. One year they'd built a snowman ten feet high. He lasted a week after the snow melted. She angled her head, trying to curb Ricky's disappointment. "Maybe build your snow fort first, and then I can help you break the record when I get back home."

"Yeah! Good idea!" Ricky was almost as tall as her now, something she wasn't used to. But at least he was well. With Ricky's heart trouble and his asthma, none of them ever took his health for granted. "That's what we'll do." He gave her another quick hug and ran back to watch BJ win the Olympics.

Their mom smiled over the exchange. "I love those boys."

"Me too." Bailey grabbed her purse and kissed her mom on the cheek. "Pray for me." She blew at a wisp of her bangs as she took a few steps toward the hallway that led to the garage. "I have a feeling I'll need it."

She headed to her car, pulled out of the garage and took the drive across town slowly. The roads were clear, plowed, and passable. But there were still sections of ice and packed snow. Fifteen minutes later she turned into Cody's mother's neighborhood. She'd been here just once before — years ago, when she and her mom had brought a book to Cody's mom after his capture in Iraq.

Now she was using information from her family's address book and her GPS system to navigate her way. Finally she pulled up in front of a small house, old and weathered. The yard was covered in snow, like the other houses on the block, but even from the road Bailey could see the paint was peeling on the porch rail. Bailey glanced at the driveway and saw it was still buried beneath eight or ten inches, and there were no tracks leading down from the single-car garage.

She hadn't gone anywhere, that much was sure. And Cody mustn't be in town. Otherwise certainly he would've been by to help shovel her drive. Bailey parked, turned off her engine, and climbed out. A chilling wind took her breath, and she pulled the collar of her wool coat up around her neck and face. Next door, a man in his thirties was shoveling his driveway while two small children played nearby. He waved at her, and kept working.

Bailey breathed deep the warm air inside her coat. *Please, God, be with me ... this won't be easy.* As she trudged up the sidewalk, she was pierced by an unsettling thought. If Cody had moved to Indianapolis, who looked out for his mother? Throughout the holidays Bailey had been busy with parties and premieres, but what about reaching out to someone like Mrs. Coleman? Or maybe she was planning to move to Indianapolis too? Bailey squinted, against the glare from the snow, at the dark windows of the house. Who knew? Maybe she'd already moved.

Each step was an effort, so Bailey took her time. She wore boots, but still her feet were damp by the time she reached the front door. *Please, Lord ... I know You're here with me. Give me the words ...* She knocked once, and then again louder. She waited, but all she could hear was the pounding of her heart. This time she rang the doorbell, but she didn't hear it make a sound inside the house.

Again she knocked, still louder. She was waiting for a response, about to give up when she heard something behind her. The sound startled her, and she gasped lightly as she turned around. There, a few feet away and out of breath, was the neighbor from next door. He still had his shovel in his hand. "You looking for Cassie Coleman?"

"Yes." Bailey noticed the man's kids had stopped playing, and were now standing motionless, watching their father. "Is ... is she home?"

"No." The man's brown eyes were kind. He bit his lip, clearly uncomfortable with whatever he was about to say. "She ain't here. Been gone awhile now. A few months at least."

What was this? Cody's mom had moved too? That must be why Cody wanted to move to the city. "Indianapolis? Is that where she went?"

"No. Not that sorta move." Again the man looked uneasy. He shifted in the snow and dug his shovel a few times into a nearby drift. "You a friend a' hers?"

"Yes." Bailey felt another wave of guilt at the way she so quickly identified herself as a friend. What had she ever done to help Cody's mother or reach out to her? She swallowed, held out her gloved hand and shook his. "Bailey Flanigan. Nice to meet you."

"Roger Denning. Been her neighbor for three years."

"I'm actually a good friend of her son's. I came to see about him."

"Cody?" The man nodded. "Fine young man. I think his mama just about broke his heart."

Broke his heart? Bailey felt the blood begin to leave her face. "I'm sorry? I guess … I'm not sure I understand. It's … it's been a while since Cody and I have talked."

"Oh." The man's face fell, and he stared at the snow around his boots. Finally he sighed and shook his head, glancing at the house and then back at Bailey. "She got herself back into drugs. Police took her away." In the distance the man's children began playing again, tossing snowballs at each other, and squealing with laughter. "She's serving time in the city." He motioned to his house. "My wife and I went by over the holidays. Paid her a visit. Saddest thing."

Bailey's heart was beating so hard she could barely hear the neighbor, hardly focus on what he was saying. Cody's mother was in prison again? And he hadn't told her? No wonder Cody was moving to Indianapolis. He wasn't leaving his mother to fend for herself, he was following her, making sure he could be there for her. If she was in prison, then that's what Cody meant … leaving so he could protect her reputation. Suddenly everything about his goodbye made sense. She blinked back tears and crossed her arms tightly around her waist. But there was no way to ward off the chill that had come over her. The man was going on, saying something about Cody being an upstanding young man, and how a weekend hadn't gone by when he wasn't there for his mama.

"We seen him when we was up there." A shadow fell over the man's face. "He looks different. Like he's walking around with a broken heart."

The news hit Bailey like the coldest winter wind, one that cut straight through her soul. And suddenly, standing there in the snow, she was absolutely sure this was why Cody had walked out of her life. His mother was back in prison, and he couldn't find a way to tell Bailey, let alone continue his life in Bloomington. Another thought hit her all at once, and the realization nearly dropped her to her knees.

How come she hadn't gone after Cody until now?

The Cody she knew never would've walked out of her life without an explanation. But she'd been so caught up in her own life she hadn't thought to come here, to find out what was wrong with him ... until now.

Fine friend she was.

The man looked back at his kids and freed his shovel from the snow. "I can probably get the address of the prison. It's the only women's prison in the city."

"No ... no, that's okay. I'll find it." She walked carefully down the snowy steps. "Thanks for telling me. I ... wouldn't have known."

"If you see her, tell her we're praying for her."

Again, Bailey felt the impact of her own selfishness. This would've been one of the hardest times in Cody's life, and she hadn't been there. The man waved once and returned to his work, and Bailey pushed back through the snow to her car. The bitter wind left her cheeks raw from the cold, but she barely noticed. She climbed into her car, drove around the corner out of sight, parked again, and hung her head.

The shock was wearing off, and the truth pressed in like

walls closing around her. Cody's mother was in prison again and she hadn't been there to help him go through it. Tears flooded her eyes and she gripped the steering wheel. Never mind that Cody hadn't told her. She couldn't blame him. She'd been making a movie, the subject of paparazzi gossip and photo spreads. Of course he had kept his pain to himself.

Bailey looked up and yanked her gloves off her hands. She grabbed her phone and dialed her mom's cell. Suddenly she wanted to get there before another hour passed. It was Sunday after all. Cody might even be there if she hurried. Her mom answered on the last ring.

"Sorry." She sounded out of breath. "I was helping your dad take down the tree."

"Mom ..." she struggled to speak above the sorrow welling inside her. "Mrs. Coleman is in prison again. She got back into drugs."

Her mom seemed less shocked than Bailey. She sighed, and sadness filled her voice. "I was afraid that might happen. How's Cody?"

"I haven't seen him. Her neighbor told me." Bailey could hardly wait to get on the road again. "I want to see her. Will you come with me, please?"

There was lots to do today at the Flanigan house. Her dad would help take down the tree, then the kids would take a break from the snow and pitch in, boxing up the decorations that filled the house each Christmas. Bailey planned to be a part of it after her talk with Mrs. Coleman. But now .... Her mom barely hesitated. "Come home, honey. I'll be ready."

Bailey let her mom drive. She'd found the women's prison online and put the address into her mom's GPS. She told her mom what the neighbor had said, how Cody seemed deeply hurt by the situation with his mom.

"He should've told us." Her mom kept her eyes on the road,

but her tone was full of empathy for Cody. "We could've helped him. No one should have to go through that alone."

"Exactly." She was right. Cody never should've kept the situation a secret. But the guilt in Bailey's heart was greater than before. She should've known something was wrong. She could've demanded he tell her, or she might've gone to his mother's house sooner.

When they were on the freeway headed to the city, Bailey texted Cody. *Are you there?*

She waited, staring at the snow-covered countryside in the distance. *Text me back, Cody. Come on ... don't do this to me.*

"Anything?" Her mom glanced at her, hopeful.

"No." She was grateful her mom was with her. If anyone understood her feelings for Cody, the impact this news had on her, it was her mom. "I think I'll call him."

She wasn't sure what to say or how to act, but she had to hear his voice. She sent the call and waited. But after four rings his voice mail came on. She didn't want to leave a message. If he wasn't answering his phone, she'd wait and talk to him in person. If they had to drive through the whole city of Indianapolis to find him.

Her mom put a Brit Nicole CD into the changer, and skipped to a song they both loved. "Don't Worry Now." The music filled the car, and Bailey closed her eyes. She couldn't worry about Cody or about how he would react when she saw him — if she would even find him at all. This trip wasn't about Cody. It was about his mother. If nothing else came from the visit, Bailey wanted one thing clear from this point on.

She was sorry for not reaching out sooner.

But now ... now she'd never let so much time go by without caring for the people in her life. And one of those people was Cody Coleman's mother.

They reached the prison half an hour later, and as they pulled into the parking lot, as they studied the gray brick compound and the razor wire surrounding the snowy yard, Bailey was filled with despair. How would it feel to have her mother living here? Serving a sentence for drugs? She couldn't imagine how Cody must feel, or how he could possibly be handling this. It didn't matter that he'd been through this before with his mother.

Bailey sighed as they stepped out of the car. "Cody had so much hope for her."

Her mom slipped her arm around Bailey's shoulders. "God still does." She narrowed her eyes and looked at the prison entrance ahead. "Sometimes it takes time in a place like this before we really hear God."

Her answer soothed Bailey's anxiety. *Lord, give me peace ... use us to encourage Mrs. Coleman today. Please, God.*

They went through a series of rooms and visitor processes, and at one point her mom took her hand and the two of them quietly prayed. Then a uniformed deputy led them down a hall into a waiting room. "You'll have ten minutes. After that you'll return here and wait for someone to get you."

From the waiting room, another deputy led them into a small visiting area. Someone had brought Mrs. Coleman there, and she was sitting at a simple round table. Her hands were shackled, and she wore an orange jumpsuit.

"Cassie," Bailey's mom took the lead. She hugged Mrs. Coleman for a long time, and afterwards Bailey did the same thing. They sat down and immediately Bailey saw something different in the woman's eyes. She was thin and gaunt, the way she'd often looked in the past. But her eyes shone with a new sort of truth and hope.

Bailey's mom led the conversation, but quickly it was apparent Cassie Coleman had found a real and lasting faith since her sentencing.

"I'll be here three years at least, shorter than my sentence since I'll be testifying against … against a very bad guy." She looked down at her bound hands for a long moment. When she looked up, the regret in her eyes was so strong it hurt to look at her. "I let myself down, but worse, I let Cody down." She turned her sad eyes to Bailey. "Have you talked to him?"

"No, ma'am." Her own regret doubled. "Not since … Thanksgiving."

"Don't be mad at him." She spoke in soft tones, tears brimming in her eyes, pleading with Bailey. "He cares so much for you and your family." She looked down again, too embarrassed to maintain eye contact. "I think he was ashamed." She lifted her eyes. "Not about me, but about … about the situation. Like you good people didn't need to be brought down by all this."

Good people? Bailey felt sick at the thought, and a Bible verse from a CRU meeting at the beginning of fall came to mind. The words were from the book of Romans. *There is not one who is good … all have turned away.* She shook her head, her eyes locked on those of Cody's mother. "No one is good, Mrs. Coleman. Only God. The rest of us can only try."

"I'll try the rest of my life. I've never needed God before this." She wrung her hands together, her chin quivering. "Maybe just give Cody another chance, okay?"

Bailey wanted to ask if he'd been by today or if she were expecting him, but she didn't want this visit to be about finding Cody. She wanted only to care, the way she should've cared sooner. The visit was over too quickly, and before they were ushered away Bailey and her mom put their hands on Mrs. Coleman's shoulders and prayed with her. "I'll come back again, okay?" Bailey covered the woman's hand with her own. "And I'll pray for you until then."

Mrs. Coleman didn't say anything, but she looked at Bailey for a long time as if to say everything she couldn't put into words. That she was sorry for letting Cody down, and sorry the situation had come between Bailey and him. Tears spilled onto her cheeks and she nodded. Then in a broken whisper she said, "Thank you, Bailey. I won't forget this."

Bailey hadn't realized she was crying until they were in the sterile hallway being led back to the waiting room. She wiped at her cheeks. "Three years?" She sniffed. "She's the only family Cody has."

"That's not true." Bailey's mom stopped and hugged her close. "He has us." She kissed Bailey's head. "He'll always have us."

CODY WAITED UNTIL BAILEY AND HER MOTHER drove out of sight before leaving his car and heading into the prison. Seeing Bailey again, watching her through the falling snow, had nearly killed him. He loved her more than ever before, more than he loved anyone in all his life. It was the single reason why he had to let her go. He didn't want this for her. She didn't belong in a prison parking lot, not for any reason. The heartache of his mother's drug addiction didn't need to affect her. No, the life he lived now that his mother was back in prison was one he would live alone. Without Bailey or any of the Flanigans. She was better than what he could give her, even if she couldn't see that now.

Dear God ... get her out of my heart ... please, let me forget I ever saw her.

Love never ends, my son ... there is faith, hope, and love ... but the greatest of these is love.

Cody nodded, grateful for the Voice that rang through his soul. The message was true. He wouldn't forget Bailey. He couldn't. He blinked back fresh tears and drew in a full breath, trying to get a grip as he headed across town to his new apartment near the Indianapolis campus of Indiana University. The idea of Bailey's friendship tempted him, but he couldn't allow that either. Yes, their paths might cross again the way they'd done today, but not by his doing. The words that had come over him did so again. *Faith, hope, and love ...* Yes, love was definitely the greatest. It was why he had to set her free, once and for all. Because he loved Bailey Flanigan that much.

The way he would always love her.

Thirty

ANDI WAS FEELING CONTRACTIONS, AND KEITH couldn't stop pacing. He wore a path from the living room — where Lisa and Andi were keeping track of the pains — to the den at the other side of the house and back again. Over and over and over. It wasn't just that his only child was at the beginning of labor, or that the baby set to come into the world was his first grandchild. That would've been enough to put him on edge this Sunday afternoon.

It was another reality that kept him pacing, the fact that in a matter of hours or days they would bid this child goodbye. Keith stopped in the den and ran his fingers through his hair. His feelings were all over the map. It was impossible not to be excited for Andi, for the baby about to be born. But he could practically feel his heart breaking in half over the loss that would follow immediately after.

He walked to the desk and stared at his computer. The screen saver showed Lisa and Andi and him, when Andi was three. Her smile lit up the room, even from a photograph. Innocent eyes shining with hope and possibility. Other grandpas would have that again, experience that moment once more through the eyes of their firstborn grandchild. But not him.

And this baby was a boy.

Keith slowly sat down and gripped the chair arms. He would've taught him how to love baseball and how to catch a spiral pass. They would've joined Scouts together, and he might've taught him how to build a pinewood derby car — the way he'd done when he was a boy. They would have shared a lifetime of adventures together.

But none of them would ever come to be.

"Another one," Lisa shouted from the other room. "They're about ten minutes apart!"

"Okay." He responded loud enough for them to hear. What was he supposed to say? That he wasn't ready? That he wanted a day or a year with this child before Andi could give him away? He hung his head and closed his eyes. These were crazy thoughts, absolutely crazy.

Andi had prayed about her decision, and she was completely at peace. The counselors at the adoption agency had explained that some birthmothers choose not to hold their babies, never wanting to bond with a baby they couldn't raise. Others took their time, knowing the birth experience would be their only chance to hold their children.

After weeks of praying about her options, Andi had chosen the latter. She would hold her baby, take her time saying good-bye. Keith and Lisa would be there with her, and they would have the same opportunity. In fact, when the time came, Andi had asked Keith to hold the baby while he and Lisa took him down the hospital hallway to the waiting area and handed him over to the Baxters.

Something Keith could only do in God's strength.

In time, this season of sadness would pass. They were set to move to Los Angeles in March, in time for Andi to start the spring quarter at Pepperdine University. She wanted a degree in film, something she'd been thinking about for weeks now. She no longer wanted to be in front of the camera, but behind it, where she could work with Keith and Dayne. She wanted to learn her way from the ground up and one day be an equal partner in making movies that could impact the culture. She was passionate about it, and convinced beyond any doubt that giving her baby up for adoption was the right choice.

Keith opened his eyes and breathed in deep. Of course it was the right choice. The baby was going to be a Baxter. A heaviness touched in around Keith's heart. He didn't question the rightness of his daughter's decision. But no matter how right, there would be loss over the next few days. A loss he would carry with him all the days of his life.

He moved the mouse and found his way to AOL. They were nine days into the New Year and Brandon Paul had been the talk of Tinseltown. To that end, Keith could only stand back in awe. The media had caught wind of Brandon's baptism, of his decision to give his life to Christ. They would spend the rest of his career waiting for him to fall, but for now they were simply taken by the story. Brandon being led to a deeper faith because of his costar, the daughter of a famous NFL coach. One tabloid said: *Mainstream America Miracle for Brandon Paul.*

He'd given a few interviews, and now Keith checked again to see the impact Brandon was having on current pop culture. The top Twitter trending topics of the moment were *#BrandonPaul* and *#Christianity*, along with a verse Brandon had mentioned from Romans and *#NIVBible* — the version Brandon had quoted from during his interviews. Millions of people were on Twitter, and this was what they were talking about. Brandon and the Bible.

Chills ran down Keith's arms and he felt his eyes well up. This was the miracle they'd prayed about, and it was playing out before his eyes. And that wasn't the only area in which God was working. Already critics who'd looked at some of the daily footage from the *Unlocked* shoot were saying this might be one of those rare times when the movie lived up to the book. Brandon Paul's defining moment.

He skipped to the Hollywood People website, and a story

about *Unlocked* graced the home page. "This was the must-read book of the past three years, and the movie — based on what we've seen — will be the must-see movie for the next decade. That's a tremendous accomplishment for any production team."

Keith clicked a few links and found what he was looking for. *Brandon Paul* and *NIV Bible* were the two most googled phrases over the past week. Sometimes Keith would hear news like that or read reviews like the one on Hollywood People's website and he'd blink a few times. Just in case he was dreaming. He leaned back in his chair and considered all God had done, all He had brought them through. Chase's role in the beginning and his move home to be with his family. Dayne's involvement, which raised Jeremiah Productions to another level. And of course Brandon's decision to take the lead role in *Unlocked*. There were times along the way when Keith wondered if he was selling out by casting Brandon, times when he thought the whole idea of changing the culture with the power of film was just some futile attempt to bring himself into a position of power and fame.

But in the end God had done what Keith and Dayne could never do. He'd used the faith of a precious college girl to lead the nation's top celebrity into a saving relationship with Jesus Christ. Yes, they would have to pray diligently for Brandon, and along the way he was bound to make mistakes. But churches would be filled at a different level today because of Brandon's decision.

"Another!" Lisa yelled out. "They're getting closer."

"Should we go?" He was already out of his seat.

"No ... not yet. Let's see about the next one."

"Okay." Keith settled back down in his seat. He moved to another website and read a report on the dollars earned and number of seats filled by their first movie, *The Last Letter*. The film was still doing very well in theaters across the country, touching hearts, changing lives, and giving confidence to the entire movie industry that this was a production company to reckon with, one any top actor would want to come alongside.

Amazing, God ... you're absolutely amazing.

The success of *The Last Letter* was another miracle, another piece he couldn't claim as his own. But he knew this much: God had placed a vision in his heart, a driving desire to make films with a message of faith and hope. He had begged God to let him see this desire become a tangible success, and now that's exactly where things were with Jeremiah Productions.

In the mission field that was Hollywood, he and Dayne were merely tools in God's hands. By themselves they couldn't change culture with the power of film. They couldn't bring God back in vogue or fill churches because of a movie. But they could do their part, keep their fire for America and her often hopeless hurting people, and they could stay true to the mission they'd been called to.

God would do the rest. The way He'd done it in the past nine days.

Someone walked into the room, and Keith turned to see Andi and Lisa. His wife had her arm around their daughter's shoulders. They both wore their winter coats, and Lisa held an overnight bag in her free hand. "Daddy," Andi smiled at him, her eyes wide with anticipation and a little fear. "It's time."

And like that, Keith was on his feet, grabbing the car keys and ushering the two women in his life out the garage door and into the car. His daughter was about to have a baby, and he ... he was about to take part in the miracle of life.

For now he couldn't let himself go even a minute beyond that.

THE CONTRACTIONS WERE ONE ON TOP of the other now, and Andi couldn't think about anything but pushing. Her mom stood beside her, squeezing her hand and wiping her forehead with a cool washcloth. Her dad was in and out.

"It's too hard for him to watch you like this." Her mom explained the situation in the minute or so between contractions. "He can't stand seeing you in pain."

But the pain wasn't as bad as Andi had thought. It was nothing to the pain of losing her innocence or the pain of compromising everything she believed in. This pain almost felt good, cathartic because it signaled the end of this journey.

"They're here right," Andi was breathless, her body drenched in sweat. "Luke and Reagan?"

Her mother smiled and gently touched the side of her face. "The whole Baxter family is here, sweetheart. The nurses had to find them their own waiting room."

Joy washed over her, filling her with a peace that this was right. As hard as the next hours might be, it was the most right thing she'd ever done. This baby would have the best family ever — a mom and a dad who would love him and each other, aunts and uncles and cousins all right here in Bloomington. And he'd have wonderful grandparents also.

"How's ... how's Dad?" Andi turned just enough so she could see her mother's eyes. "This is hard for him. I know ... I see it in his face."

"It is." Her mother's voice was warm with compassion. "He knows it's the right decision." Tears welled in her eyes. "But yes, it's difficult. This is our first grandchild."

Andi felt a wave of sorrow rise inside her. She squeezed her mother's hand again and rode out another contraction. This one long and more painful than the others. As it passed she laid motionless, spent for half a minute. Then she looked at her mother. "There will be more grandchildren. God will see to it ... I know He will."

The doctor breezed in and checked on her progress. "I'd say

you're just about ready, Andi ..." he looked at her. "You feel like pushing?"

"Yes. A million times yes." She uttered an exhausted sort of laugh and again her mom pressed the cool cloth to her face. "More than anything in the world."

"Okay, then ... I think on the next contraction you can bring your legs up."

For the last few months she'd been instructed on what to do at this point of the delivery. So when the next contraction began, she pulled up her legs. "Okay ... okay, now?"

"Almost." The doctor was in position at the end of the table, guiding her every move. "All right ... now, Andi! Push now!"

She did so with all her might, with everything she had.

Her mom was still by her side, still holding her hand. "You're doing great honey ... keep pushing."

"I can see the head. He has a lot of hair." The doctor grinned at them. "Keep it up, Andi. You can do it."

The contraction felt like it lasted forever, but finally ... finally it let up and she could breathe again. She felt hot and breathless. Her heart beat so hard she could barely concentrate. She blew out several times, pushing the air from her lungs so she could take a full breath. "How ... was that?"

"Perfect." The doctor was working between her legs. "A couple more pushes and he'll be out."

Andi was starting to feel like she should push again, but the doctor held up his hand. "Wait for the contraction."

She nodded, squeezing her mom's fingers. For a few seconds she looked at her mom, and she saw tears sliding down her cheeks. Happy tears ... tears of awe over the miracle taking place. "I love you, Mom."

"I love you, baby girl. I'm so proud of you."

The words found their way to a forever place in Andi's heart. Her mother was proud of her. Six months ago she was sure she'd never hear those words again, but now ... now God had brought beauty from ashes — just like He promised.

"Here it c—" the contraction didn't give any more warning than that. Andi waited for the doctor's okay, and she pushed again. They'd given her a local anesthetic, so there was no pain, but this time she could actually feel the baby moving out of her body. It was the most unbelievable sensation, and it made her excited for the next time — however many years from now — when she would go through this for a baby she would keep, a baby who would be her very own.

The contraction ended, but she had only a minute or so rest before the next one hit. "Keep pushing, Andi!" The doctor's voice was more intense. "This should do it. Here he comes ... here he is. One more little push."

An emptiness came over her as the baby left her body completely, and after a few seconds her baby's cry filled the room. "It's a boy," the doctor grinned at them as he stood and handed the baby to the nurse. "Just like you thought."

Andi couldn't see him very well, because the nurse was clearing his mouth and wiping his face and body. But from what she could see he was beautiful. Tears filled her eyes and she let out a quiet cry. "Mom ... can you see him? Someone should get Dad."

But at that moment, her dad walked in the room. "I thought I heard a—"

"Dad ... he's here. He was just born."

"Andi did great." Her mom soothed the washcloth over her head again. "She delivered him in three pushes."

"Yes, it was textbook." The doctor was still working on her. "I wish all births were like this."

They cleaned him up, and he stopped crying. As the nurse weighed and measured him, the sound coming from him was a sporadic complaint. Andi giggled a little through her silent repressed sobs. "He's a fighter. I can hear it in his voice."

"Like his mother." Andi's dad stood next to her mother, up against her bed. He stroked his daughter's hair and smiled at her. "I'll never forget you holding court with a dozen Indonesian women, telling them about Jesus at the ripe old age of ten."

"Yes." She wiped at her tears, her smile stretched across her face. "He'll have that from me."

The nurse wrapped a white and blue blanket around the baby and carried him over. "He's tall. Seven pounds, eight ounces and twenty-two inches." She handed him carefully to Andi. "I'd say he looks like his mama."

Andi couldn't stop the tears, but she couldn't stop smiling either. She took her newborn son into her arms and cradled him close to her chest. The feeling was warm and full, and in that moment it completed her. She stared into his deep blue eyes, his full lips and beautiful face. "Hi, little boy," she whispered to him, using her shoulder to catch her tears before they could fall on him.

Only then did she realize her parents were both crying too. They leaned close, looking at him, in awe of him. "He's perfect, Andi. He looks just like ..." a sob made it too hard for her to finish.

Her dad cleared his throat. "He looks like you did ... when you were born."

"You had the same satiny dark hair." Her mom reached out and touched the baby's head. "It didn't turn blonde until you were six months old."

Andi leaned down and kissed the baby's head. "Did you hear what your grandma said?" She breathed the words softly against his face. "You're perfect, little one. So perfect."

Her dad took a few pictures, nothing too invasive. Just a shot of her cradling the infant in her arms and one of her kissing his cheek. He took another from a different angle, so that the baby's face took up the entire picture. The minutes were slipping by, and Andi wanted her mom to have a turn to hold him, so she lifted him gently and passed him over. Only then, as she released him, did she get the first hint of the pain that was to come. He was her baby, her son. Her blood and the blood of her parents ran through him. Suddenly it seemed like the craziest idea, giving him up, and she wondered if she'd regret this decision all her life.

As her thoughts turned on her, she felt a surge of panic, a rush of terrifying adrenaline speeding through her body. What if she was making a mistake? She watched her mother cradle her little boy, watched her nuzzle her cheek against his and then, when she clearly couldn't take another moment, she handed the baby to Andi's dad.

He was more stoic than her mom, but as he held the baby close the connection between them was undeniable. He also didn't take too long for his turn. The unspoken phenomenon happening around them was obvious to Andi: no one wanted to fall in love with a baby they had to let go of minutes from now.

The baby made an attempt at a cry, but then grew calm again.

Andi was hit hard by a truth she hadn't expected, which was that she already knew his voice. Like an indelible stamp on her heart, his sound and tone had already made its mark and she was sure as long as she lived — if she were a hundred years old and this precious boy was eighty — she would know his voice.

More tears flooded her eyes, but she wouldn't cry, wouldn't give in to the emotion of the moment. Instead she received her baby back from her father and held him straight out in front of her. His feet kicked at her stomach, and there was a familiarity to it. An hour ago he had kicked her stomach from the other side. She smiled at him, studying him, willing herself to remember every detail, the way his eyes met hers, the peach fuzz on his soft cheeks, and his sweet, newborn smell.

She held out her finger and touched it to the palm of his tiny hand. Immediately he gripped her finger, and the connection ran all the way to the center of her being. "Sweet baby ..." She lifted him close and kissed his cheek again, and in that instant she could feel it, feel the strength of the bond forming between them. She understood now why some moms pass on this experience. No question, the time with her son would make their impending goodbye more difficult. Unbearable, almost.

But as she held him, as she ran her hand over his dark hair, the panic from earlier faded. She loved this baby, and she always would. But it was a love she would best show by letting him go. She wasn't ready to be a mother, not at all. Luke and Reagan Baxter were. Andi smiled at him. *Don't hate me when you're older, little one. I'm doing the best I can do. It's the right thing.* She would always remember him. But he didn't belong to her. This was a baby she'd almost aborted, and she pictured the faces of the Kunzmann family and Clarence — the mysterious man who had steered her away from having an abortion that long ago morning.

God's plans for this baby involved her giving him life and the Baxters giving him a family. She felt the time pressing in around her, felt the clock screaming at her that she'd held her baby long enough. He needed to meet his mommy and daddy, his brother and sister and the rest of his new family.

"Okay, little boy, I have to let you go." Her tears came harder than before, but her voice held no crying. Instead it was clear and calm and she kept her smile. Because if it were possible for a newborn to remember, she wanted him to remember her smiling. She brought him close one last time and pressed her cheek against his. Her precious firstborn son.

"Mom ... Dad," she looked at them. "Come closer. Let's pray for him."

Her mom was quietly crying, and her dad was still strong. "You want me to pray, honey?"

"That's okay." She looked at her son again. "I'll do it." She sniffed and again wiped her cheeks with the part of her gown that covered her shoulder. "Heavenly Father, you are a miracle worker. You brought this precious little boy into this world and now ... now the plans you have for him will begin. Good plans, to give him a hope and a future and not ... to harm him."

She didn't take her eyes off him as she prayed, her voice gentle and soothing. "I ask that you be with this boy and raise him up to serve you. I pray that his life will be a bright light to the world around him, and that he will lead people to You." She steadied herself, keeping her deep sadness far below the surface. "Be with his new parents, his new family, and when he thinks about me ... help him know the only reason I gave him up was because I loved him too much to keep him. In Jesus' name, amen."

Her mom turned to her dad and the two of them hugged, giving her a final moment to say goodbye. She leaned close to him one last time and pressed her cheek to his. Then, in a whisper so faint only the two of them could hear it, she said simply, "I'll never forget you."

She kissed him again and then handed him to her father. As he left, as the weight of his body moved from her arms to his, she could feel the fibers of her heart being ripped apart. "Go, Dad ... it's okay." She turned so she could see her parents. "Please, go."

The last thing she saw of her son as her parents took him from the room was his small hand, reaching up from the soft blanket, his fingers outstretched. She and her parents were moving on, and God would have much in the months and years ahead that would help fill the hole gaping inside her at this moment. But this was not an open adoption. Her son would not share his time between his adoptive family and her. Yes, she would be there to meet him someday, if he were to choose that. But he might not. And so for all Andi knew, this was goodbye.

Her sobs came then, seizing her, suffocating her. She covered her face with her hands and relived everything about the last ten minutes: the way he felt in her arms, the look in his eyes, the sound of his cry. Time would heal this, and even as she gave way to her grief, Andi was convinced this was the right decision. She hoped she would never again doubt that. Her baby would have the best life ever, she was convinced.

But here and now the pain in her heart was too great to ignore. God's Word said it best, and in her crying she could hear her father reading from Ecclesiastes to the people in Indonesia. *There was a time to laugh and a time to dance. But there was also a time to weep and a time to mourn.* And that was okay.

This was one of those times.

It was the longest walk in Keith's life. The longest and the shortest, all at the same time if that were possible. The hundred steps from Andi's bedside to the room where the Baxters were waiting was all the time he would ever have with this grandson. So he walked slowly, cooing at the baby and savoring each second. But, even still, the walk was over in what felt like a few heartbeats.

A nurse led the way and when she reached the waiting room, before he opened the door, he hesitated. "Can we have a minute, my wife and I with the baby?"

The nurse smiled and nodded. "Of course. When you're ready, the adoptive family is just inside."

He nodded, and when she was gone down the hallway, he smiled at the little boy in his arms. Lisa came up beside him and put her arm around his waist. She leaned in and kissed the baby's forehead. "He looks so much like Andi."

"He does." Keith thought about everything he'd like to tell this child, all the advice he'd give him and the stories about Jesus he'd share with him if he'd had the time. Even as he thought about all he would miss, he felt God giving him the perfect words. "I would love to be your grandpa, little guy. I would love everything about it." For the first time, tears blurred his eyes. "But guess what? Your grandpa is going to be John Baxter. He's a pro, sweet baby. The best grandpa ever. Everything I would ever tell you, everything we'd ever do together … you'll do with him. That's why I can let you go."

He winked at the baby. "See you up in heaven some day, all right?"

With that, before he lost the strength to do so, he opened the door. A quiet round of gasps and light cries came from several of the adult Baxters, and Luke and Reagan stood to meet them.

Keith looked at the love and support that filled the room. This baby would be loved all the days of his life. He would have the greatest support system, the best family Keith had ever had the privilege of knowing. If he could've hand-picked a family to raise this precious grandchild, these would be the people.

The Baxter family.

He turned to Luke and Reagan. "He's beautiful. Seven pounds, eight ounces. Twenty-two inches long." He smiled through his tears. "He looks just like Andi did."

Reagan didn't rush to take the baby. Rather she let her eyes hold Keith's and then Lisa's for a long time. "We can't imagine how hard this is for you and Andi."

Keith nodded and exchanged a look with his wife. "Very hard." He turned to Luke and Reagan again. "But also very right." With that he passed the baby over to Reagan, and Luke put his arm protectively around both of them.

"Thank you." Luke looked back up at Keith. "We've named him Jonathan. It means 'gift of God.'" He looked at his father, John Baxter, who was with his wife in the corner of the room. "And it represents the greatest man I know." The two shared a meaningful look, but it was broken up by Tommy racing across the room to his mother's side.

"The name's Jonathan, but we're calling him John-John." Tommy was six years old and always full of energy. "Can I see him, Mommy, please? Please can I see him? I have a lot to tell him."

Nearby, Malin — Reagan and Luke's daughter — was in her Aunt Ashley's arms, sucking her fingers and looking a little overwhelmed. Reagan held her finger to her lips and smiled. "Shhh." Then she bent low enough for Tommy to see him. "He's very new. You can talk to him a little later."

"Wow!" The boy breathed in deep and tried to whistle. "He's the smallest brother I ever saw. Smaller than a football, I think."

Around the room the other Baxter aunts and uncles giggled, and from around the circle came comments about how perfect he looked, how small. Keith took it all in. They were anxious for the chance to love him, to welcome him into their family, and now it was time he and Lisa gave them their space.

"He's hungry." Keith grinned at Reagan. "The nurse said you have a special formula."

"Yes." She nodded, and tears filled her eyes. "It's all made up."

Dayne and Katy were there — Dayne being the oldest Baxter sibling. For a few minutes, the two of them talked to Keith and Lisa about their plans to leave Bloomington for Los Angeles. They all agreed they'd keep in touch, and of course Dayne and Keith would continue to work together in post-production for *Unlocked*, and on whatever movie God brought to them next. There would be updates about John-John as often as Keith wanted to hear them. But most likely he wouldn't ask.

"Do me a favor," he put his arm tight around Lisa's shoulders and fought to keep his composure as he looked at Luke and Reagan once more. "Let him know how much we love him. How much Andi loves him."

The young couple nodded, and Luke took the baby tenderly from his wife's arms. With the infant close against his chest he swallowed hard. "You have our word."

Keith nodded and looked once more at the little boy, his

grandson. Then he and Lisa waved at the others and left the room. Out in the hallway, he understood fully what Andi must be feeling. The loss was so great it was hard to stand up beneath. But then he and Lisa and Andi were missionaries — all of them. Never mind the mistakes Andi had made, she was back on track and she wanted to change the world for Jesus.

And that came at a price. It came with pain and loss and moments when moving forward was only possible in Christ's strength alone. Moments like this. But when they'd been led from one mission field to another, God had always provided. He'd done so with *The Last Letter*, with *Unlocked*, and even with Brandon Paul. Now he would do so again as He moved them to Los Angeles.

Along the way God had always allowed them their memories, and this would be no different. They would move on, but they would take with them memories of Indonesia, and of filming their two movies. Memories of Northern California and Bloomington, Indiana. And now another very special memory, one they would cherish for the rest of their lives.

The memory of their grandson, Jonathan Baxter.

READER LETTER

Dear Reader Friends,

The feelings I have when I end a series are wildly contrasting. There is a sense of enormous completion and satisfaction, the feeling that God gave me these books, and I did my best to bring them to life. In this case, these stories have stirred in my heart for years, growing and building and coming to life. But with the publication of them, I hand them over. Four books I felt compelled to write, four pieces of my heart that now belong to you.

Now, if you're like me ... you're about to scream because of one aspect of *Take Four*. What in the world is going to happen with Bailey and Cody and Brandon Paul, right? Good! I hope that's how you feel. Their story is absolutely not finished.

But it will be.

Next year I will debut the Bailey Flanigan series. It'll have plenty of interaction with the Baxters, more about the Flanigans, and dozens of triumphant and sometimes tragic adventures that God has already laid upon my heart. I can't wait to write them, and I can't wait for you to read them. There will be four books, and the first will be called *Leaving*. You can find out more on my website — KarenKingsbury.com!

With that in mind, please know the series I've just finished dealt with very emotional, very difficult issues. The idea of a missionary kid heading off to college and going off the deep end is disturbing. Very disturbing. I allowed Andi to get in trouble, because that's what so many Christian kids do when they go away to college. The truth is, Andi's experimenting and compromising were very tame compared to some of the real-life dramas playing out on our college campuses. I know, because so many of you have written to me about the heartache caused by your kids, and the way you're praying for them.

I would say this, I guess. Before you send your kids away to school, make sure they're really ready. There's no shame in junior college near home and then a transfer to a four-year school. And if your student is ready as a freshman for the adventure of college life away from home ... pray for them every day, throughout the day. And keep lines of communication open. They will be around some of the craziest kids, doing the wildest things, and they will be hearing lectures that could shake their foundations — in many cases.

When God gave me the Above the Line series, I knew He wanted me to tackle this subject — the subject of what can happen to a Christian teenager away at college. I hope you've seen not only the pitfalls and temptations, but also the consequences of choosing those temptations — and in turn the redemption that could only come by finding the way back to the Lord.

In addition, of course, these books were about the power of film. I posted a question on my Facebook about whether you, my reader friends, would like to see the Baxters as a TV series. In less than 12 hours I had more than a thousand positive responses. So you understand the power of film, the need for quality programming for our families. But the road to making those sorts of movies and TV shows happen is marked with pitfalls and temptations. In the end when producers have a goal like Keith and Dayne had, it only succeeds by God's grace.

So hopefully this series will remind you to pray for the growing number of Hollywood producers making films with a Christian message. The battle for the hearts and minds of our generation has never been more fierce. And so we must pray.

Now ... guess what my next stand alone book is?

That's right — *Unlocked!*

As I wrote in *Take Three* and *Take Four* about Keith and Dayne making a movie based on *Unlocked* — a national bestseller, a story about autism and bullying and the miracle of friendship — a thought finally occurred to me.

I had to write the book.

Unlocked has pressed in and around my heart for a few years, and it will be one of my strongest ever. God gave me the complete outline on a recent cross-country flight from Dulles Airport to Portland. Twenty-four pages of handwritten notes in a spiral bound notebook. When I was finished, I was quietly crying — the story is that real and rich in my heart. I can see Bailey playing Ella, and Brandon Paul playing Holden Harris. I can see every aspect of the story, and now you can share that with me. *Unlocked* comes out this fall, and I can only thank God, because the story feels like such a gift. And maybe one day a real-life Dayne Matthews will want to turn it into a movie. Only God knows! Look for *Unlocked* and find me on Facebook so you can tell me your thoughts!

As always, I look forward to hearing your feedback on *Take Four* and the entire Above the Line series. Take a minute and visit my website at www.KarenKingsbury.com, where you can find my contact information and my guestbook. And guess what? You can even join the Baxter Family club — where you'll get every book as a Collector Signature edition — and every book comes with a Baxter Family newsletter tucked inside. There's no membership fee, but spots in the club are limited.

I'm also on Facebook every day! I have Latte Time, where I'll take a half hour or so, pour all of you a virtual latte, and take questions. We have a blast together, so if you're not on my Facebook Friend page, please join today. Check under "pages." The group of friends there is very special, indeed.

In addition, feel free to write me a private letter or post a public guestbook entry about how God is using these books in your life. It's all Him, and it always will be. He puts the story in my heart and He has your face in mind. All Him. It's helpful for other readers to see how God is working, so please stop by and leave a comment.

Also on my website you can check out my upcoming events page, so you can see where I'll be speaking at an Extraordinary Women or other event near you. As this book releases, we're even having the first annual Baxter Family Reunion in Bloomington, Indiana! If you're not here with me now, then plan to come next year. Details are — of course — on my website. Also, on my website you can get to know other readers, and become part of a community that agrees there is life-changing power in something as simple as a story. You can post prayer requests on my website or read those already posted and pray for those in need. You can send in a photo of your loved one serving our country, or let us know of a fallen soldier we can honor on our Fallen Heroes page.

My website also tells you about my ongoing contests including Shared a Book, which encourages you to tell me when you've shared one of my books with someone. Each time you email me about this, you're entered for the chance to spend a summer weekend with my family. In addition, everyone signed up for my monthly newsletter is automatically entered into an ongoing once-a-month drawing for a free, signed copy of my latest novel. There are links on my website that will help you with matters that are important to you — faith and family, adoption, and ways to reach out to others. Of course, on my site you can also find out a little more about me and my family, my Facebook, and Twitter and my YouTube channel.

Finally, if you gave your life to God during the reading of this book, or if you found your way back to a faith you'd let grow cold, send me a letter at Office@KarenKingsbury.com and write *New Life* in the subject line. I would encourage you to connect with a Bible-believing church in your area, and get hold of a Bible. But if you can't get hold of one, can't afford one, and don't already have one, write *Bible* in the subject line. Tell me how God used this book to change your life, and then include your address in your email. My wonderful publisher Zondervan has supplied me with free copies of the New Testament, so that if you are unable to find a Bible or afford a Bible any other way, I can send you one. I'll pay for shipping.

One last thing. I've started a program where I will donate a book to any high school or middle school librarian who makes a request. Check my website for details.

Again, thanks for journeying with me through the pages of this book. I can't wait to see you in the fall for *Unlocked* — the story everyone is talking about! Until then, my friends, keep your eyes on the cross, and don't forget … we're all missionaries one way or another, called to make a difference in the place where God has placed us.

In His light and love,
Karen Kingsbury

www.KarenKingsbury.com

READER STUDY GUIDE

1. Whenever I reach the end of a series, I take stock of the lessons learned. What did you learn reading the Above the Line Series? How did God speak to you through the four books?
2. Keith Ellison had a dream to change the culture through the power of film. How did God make that dream a reality? How was the reality different from what Keith might've pictured at the beginning?
3. What movie have you seen that left you closer to God and your family? Talk about what aspect of the movie was most powerful.
4. Another theme throughout this series was the struggle our young people face on college campuses across our nation. What personal experience do you have in these struggles? Share an example.
5. Do you think a series like Above the Line could help educate parents and college kids about the pitfalls of going away to school? Was there anything about the situations depicted in this series that surprised you? Do you think the real atmosphere on college campuses is better or worse than what was depicted?
6. What were Andi's struggles during this series? Why do you think she rebelled so completely from the truth she'd been raised with?
7. Do you personally know of any students who walked away from their faith during their college years? What caused them to rebel? How did their stories end up?
8. Bailey struggled in ways that were different from Andi Elli-

son. What were Bailey's struggles throughout the series, and what caused her to recognize them?

9. What's one thing you can do to help a college student in your life? Do you think a group like Campus Crusade is helpful to kids living at school away from home? How can you support such an effort?

10. Through prayer, Andi decided to give her baby up for adoption. Do you know anyone in your life who has done this? What were their struggles?

11. How did Andi process her decision? Explain how her feelings sometimes changed in regard to giving up her baby.

12. The idea that Andi would choose Luke and Reagan Baxter to parent her child was a miracle in the Baxter family. Adoption is often associated with many different types of miracle stories. Share an adoption story you're familiar with. How has that situation touched your life?

13. James 1:27 says, "Religion that God our Father accepts as pure and faultless is this: to look after orphans and widows in their distress ..." How has this verse personally affected your life?

14. Bailey realized too late that she hadn't made an effort to reach out to Cody or his mother. Instead she was too caught up in her own world to take the time to contact them. Is there someone in your life who maybe needs more of your love and time? What could you do to reach out?

15. Brandon Paul experienced a life-changing transformation in *Take Four*. What led to his decision years earlier to walk away from his faith in God? What are your thoughts on what Brandon's parents said to him back then?

16. Do you know anyone who walked away from God because of something someone said, or because they weren't treated with love? Tell about this person or this time.

17. Like Brandon Paul, it's easy to be angry at God because

of something someone else did to hurt us. Read Romans 8:28 – 39. What is the truth about God's love for us — according to the Bible? What does Romans 8:28 mean to you?

18. What impact would happen in our culture if a highly visible celebrity chose to become a Christian? What good might come as a result? What risk is there in holding up celebrities for everyone to emulate — even when they have a very real faith?

19. Can you think of a highly visible celebrity — in any aspect of life (sports, arts, music, etc.) — who has a genuine and active faith? What good has that person done for our culture? What cautions must we keep in place regarding our heroes of the faith?

20. Explain the victories Keith Ellison realized along the journey of the Above the Line series. Give examples of how he saw God working even in the difficult times. God calls all of us to be missionaries where He has placed us. In what way are you a missionary in your world?

Coming Home

A Story of Unending Love and Eternal Promise

Karen Kingsbury, New York Times Bestselling Author

Coming Home is a novel about tremendous victory and unprecedented loss, a story of faith and a forever kind of love, love that will stay with you long after the last page. This stand-alone novel will serve as either a grand introduction or a beautiful conclusion in the saga of the Baxter Family.

The Baxters make plans to come together for a summer lakeside reunion, a celebration like they haven't had in years. But before the big day, the unthinkable happens. As the Baxter Family rallies together, memories come to light in the grief-stricken hours of waiting and praying, memories that bring healing and hope during a time when otherwise darkness might have the final word.

In a season that changes all of them, the brilliance of family love overshadows even the valley of heartache as the Baxters draw closer to God and each other. Along the way, secrets are revealed and the truth about the Baxter Family history is finally made known. Ultimately, in this portrait of family love, the Baxters cling to each other and to God's promise of forever.

Coming June 21, 2012

ZONDERVAN®
.com

BAILEY FLANIGAN SERIES

Leaving

Karen Kingsbury,
New York Times *Bestselling Author*

The Bailey Flanigan Series begins with Bailey leaving Bloomington for the adventure of a lifetime. She has won an audition for the ensemble of a Broadway musical in New York City. She's determined to take advantage of this once-in-a-lifetime opportunity, but is she really ready to leave family and friends for the loneliness of the city? And what of Cody? His disappearance has her worried about their future and praying that their love can survive.

In order to be closer to his mother in jail, Cody takes a coaching job in a small community outside Indianapolis. New friends, distance, and circumstances expose cracks in his relationship with Bailey Flanigan.

Love, loneliness, big opportunities, and even bigger decisions highlight the first book in the new Bailey Flanigan Series that features members of the popular Baxter family and finally completes the Bailey Flanigan/Cody Coleman story.

Available in stores and online!

Learning

Karen Kingsbury,
New York Times *Bestselling Author*

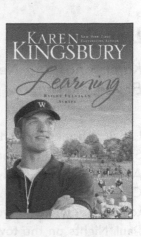

Learning, book two in the Bailey Flanigan Series, picks up where *Leaving* ended. Bailey Flanigan and Cody Coleman are not only separated by physical distance, they are also faced with great emotional distance. While Bailey grows closer to her dream to be an actress and dancer in New York, Cody coaches a small high school football team ... on and off the field. But neither feels complete without the chance to share their dreams with one another.

Can distance truly make the heart grow fonder? Or will Cody learn to turn to others to share in his happiness? And in the face of tragedy, who will be there to provide comfort?

As Cody's past catches up with him, he must learn to reach out for help or risk withdrawing permanently inside himself. Both Bailey and Cody find themselves learning significant life lessons in this poignant love story, featuring members from Karen Kingsbury's popular Baxter family.

Available in stores and online!

BAILEY FLANIGAN SERIES

Longing

Karen Kingsbury, New York Times Bestselling Author

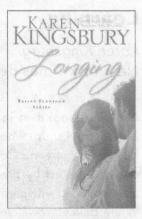

Longing, book three in the Bailey Flanigan Series, picks up where Learning ended. After a long and lonely silence from Cody Coleman, Bailey Flanigan becomes closer to her one-time Hollywood co-star, Brandon Paul. Nights on the town in New York City and long talks on the balcony of Brandon's Malibu Beach home make Bailey dizzy with new feelings and cause her to wonder if her days with Cody are over forever.

Meanwhile, Cody's work coaching a small-town football team has brought him and his players national attention. In the midst of the celebration and success, Cody finds himself much closer to a woman who seems to better understand him and his new life. Even so, never does much time go by without Bailey and Cody experiencing deep feelings of longing for each other, longing both for the past and for answers before they can move forward.

Will an unexpected loss be the turning point for Cody? Will Cody and Bailey find a way back together again for the first time in more than a year? And if they do, will their brief time together be enough to help them remember all they've been longing for?

Available in stores and online!

BAILEY FLANIGAN SERIES

Loving

Karen Kingsbury, New York Times Bestselling Author

The answers Bailey Flanigan once longed and prayed for are finally becoming clear.

In Loving, the fourth and final book in the Bailey Flanigan Series by New York Times bestselling author Karen Kingsbury, Bailey is planning a wedding and making decisions that will shape her future. Bailey enjoys the beginning of her new career and time spent with Brandon while Cody faithfully coaches his team on and off the field. Will she spend her life with Brandon Paul in Los Angeles, or will her heart draw her back to Bloomington, Indiana and Cody Coleman, her first love? Bailey has learned much and grown over the years, but the greatest challenges, the richest joys, and the deepest heartaches are still to come.

Featuring members from Karen Kingsbury's popular Baxter family, Loving completes Bailey and Cody's story — the finale thousands of fans have been waiting for.

Available in stores and online!

Unlocked

A Love Story

Karen Kingsbury,
New York Times *Bestselling Author*

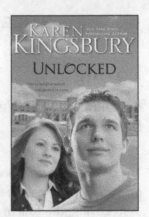

Before You Take a Stand ...
You've Got to Take a Chance.

Holden Harris is an eighteen-year-old locked in a prison of autism. Despite his quiet ways and quirky behaviors, Holden is very happy and socially normal — on the inside, in a private world all his own. In reality, he is bullied at school by kids who only see that he is very different.

Ella Reynolds is part of the "in" crowd. Star of the high school drama production, her life seems perfect. When she catches Holden listening to her rehearse for the school play, she is drawn to him ... the way he is drawn to the music. Then, Ella makes a dramatic discovery — she and Holden were best friends as children.

Frustrated by the way Holden is bullied, and horrified at the indifference of her peers, Ella decides to take a stand against the most privileged and popular kids at school. Including her boyfriend, Jake.

Ella believes miracles can happen in the unlikeliest places, and that just maybe an entire community might celebrate from the sidelines. But will Holden's praying mother and the efforts of Ella and a cast of theater kids be enough to unlock the prison that contains Holden?

This time, friendship, faith, and the power of a song must be strong enough to open the doors to the miracle Holden needs.

Available in stores and online!

Share Your Thoughts

With the Author: Your comments will be forwarded to the author when you send them to *zauthor@zondervan.com*.

With Zondervan: Submit your review of this book by writing to *zreview@zondervan.com*.

Free Online Resources at
www.zondervan.com

Zondervan AuthorTracker: Be notified whenever your favorite authors publish new books, go on tour, or post an update about what's happening in their lives at www.zondervan.com/authortracker.

Daily Bible Verses and Devotions: Enrich your life with daily Bible verses or devotions that help you start every morning focused on God. Visit www.zondervan.com/newsletters.

Free Email Publications: Sign up for newsletters on Christian living, academic resources, church ministry, fiction, children's resources, and more. Visit www.zondervan.com/newsletters.

Zondervan Bible Search: Find and compare Bible passages in a variety of translations at www.zondervanbiblesearch.com.

Other Benefits: Register yourself to receive online benefits like coupons and special offers, or to participate in research.

ZONDERVAN®

ZONDERVAN.com/
AUTHORTRACKER
follow your favorite authors

KAREN KINGSBURY

NEW YORK TIMES BESTSELLING AUTHOR KAREN Kingsbury is
America's favorite inspirational novelist, with nearly 20 million
books in print. Her Life-Changing Fiction™ has produced mul-
tiple bestsellers, including *Unlocked, Leaving, Take One, Between
Sundays, Even Now, One Tuesday Morning, Beyond Tuesday
Morning*, and *Ever After*, which was named the 2007 Christian
Book of the Year. An award-winning author and newly published
songwriter, Karen has several movies optioned for production,
and her novel *Like Dandelion Dust* was made into a major motion picture, now available on DVD. Karen is also a nationally
known speaker with several women's groups including Women
of Faith. She lives in Tennessee with her husband, Don, their
daughter, and five sons, three of whom are adopted from Haiti.